P9-ARP-806

CITIES OF REFUGE

ALSO BY MICHAEL HELM

The Projectionist

In the Place of Last Things

CITIES OF REFUGE

MICHAEL HELM

McCLELLAND & STEWART

Library and Archives Canada Cataloguing in Publication

Helm, Michael
Cities of refuge / Michael Helm.

ISBN 13: 978-0-7710-4039-9

1. Title

PS8565.E4593C48 2010 C813'.54 C2009-905217-2

We acknowledge the financial support of the Government of Canada through the Book Publishing Industry Development Program and that of the Government of Ontario through the Ontario Media Development Corporation's Ontario Book Initiative. We further acknowledge the support of the Canada Council for the Arts and the Ontario Arts Council for our publishing program.

Typeset in Bembo by M&S, Toronto
Printed and bound in Canada

This is a work of fiction. Names, characters, places, and incidents either are the products of the author's imagination or are used fictitiously.

This book was produced using ancient-forest friendly papers.

This book is printed on acid-free paper that is 100% recycled, ancient-forest friendly (100% post-consumer waste).

McClelland & Stewart Ltd.
75 Sherbourne Street
Toronto, Ontario
M5A 2P9
www.mcclelland.com

1 2 3 4 5 14 13 12 11 10

to my friends, the seers through

CITIES OF REFUGE

We watch the foreign girl. She's rendered here silent in greys. An automated teller near her west-end apartment at 8:07 p.m. She wears a sort of party dress though no one in her small circle can think where she may have been going. She carries a little purse on a strap over her shoulder, she is petite, diminutives collect around her. We pick her up on an east-bound subway platform at 8:23. For a moment we glimpse a hair clip in a glint as she turns. She doesn't seem to be waiting for anyone. Apparently returning overground she arrives back in her neighbourhood just before 2:00 and buys a lottery ticket for an elderly neighbour as she does once a week in the all-nite variety store only blocks from her building. The clip is gone, her hair fallen. She has trouble with the clasp on her purse and seems embarrassed and smiles when the clerk says something, though she doesn't make eye contact with him even when she has success and pays and exits the frame with an easy grace we lend her simply because she will never be seen alive again by friends or cameras, by co-workers or anyone in her small circle. She has no family in this country. Then a colour still photo, phone numbers on the screen, a name we can't help but register. The disquiet of this witnessing is there in the pixelated grain.

And we've seen her somewhere and it haunts us. Somewhere in the days we build of marks and remarks, of clocks, hands and faces, or maybe the face we remember is not hers but her double's, a move the big city makes sometimes, echoing forms, gaming with the likenesses of things. In such ways the place remakes itself for us so that at night before sleep we drift through lanes and parks and peer into doorways, spaces we've passed a thousand times without noticing. We look up at a math of windows and there are millions enclosed all around. But we think we've seen her, or know her, or someone we know knows her and we pace back through the week, looking, and what do we find? Women in pairs walking fast in bright downtown streets. A clutch of Arab men speaking at once in a cigar shop on the verges of Chinatown. Some lost son never spoken of propped on a downspout to piss in the streetlight shadows of a house near the Spit. Store clerks. Expectorating neighbours barking on porches. Cabbies' faces staring out above the laminated hack number on the headrest and the face in the rear-view that never looked back, never glanced at us once. A lone rat, quick with a foreknowledge brought miles along the overpass tracks.

And she's nowhere. She was born in the country of a country far off, and she's come all this way to go missing.

In an alley where we walk sometimes the businesses have given over their backsides to graffiti artists and the short passage has a kind of end of rainbow charm. Atop the parabolic spank of colours are five brownhue figures of evolving man, the stoop and brow-ridge receding with the body hair until, at last, like a punchline, the figure of H-Sap as a black kid in jeans, the artist himself, maybe, painting primitive animal shapes on this same wall, the whole thing signed with the mark of a cross inside a circle. The earliest ideogram for the city. It means crossroads within a wall. Something read in a medical waiting room once with dread a faint tang on the tongue.

We wake in the night and the foreign girl's name is with us. A musical name that calls to be spoken. Here beneath a whisper, we consign her to the dark.

PART ONE

I

Before the shift that night she left dinner with her parents and biked south in darkness past her apartment building, along into her usual path. The afternoon storms had broken the heat and departed without trace. The air was drying, late-summer cool. On the side streets near campus were weakly haloed car headlights and shadowed figures waiting to be briefly illuminated. She passed in and out of semi-residential zones, moving now with half-naked teens on in-line skates past the thronging bars and restaurants and the clubs where made-up young women waited outside and men measured them whole in one glance. Down a side street she entered a dark little dead space that emptied back into the traffic and the noisebright streets, on past a long row of trailers and honeywagons, a bored officer on overtime, she stuttered across a dimpled steel ramp over bundled cables, past grips and gaffers with walkie-talkies, and a yellow-lit window full of pretend New York cops. She passed the Vietnamese convenience store always with the same child in diapers in the doorway chewing on a faded cardboard candy ad, past the crowded patio of the ice cream café, across the main arteries of downtown, riding faster, really breathing now, on her way to work.

Three or four minutes ahead of schedule, she slowed for the last few blocks. In a pocket of quiet she rode imagining her morning self in a kind of perpetual approach, cycling home at daybreak beneath traffic helicopters hanging in a pastel smog, then drifted to a stop and locked her bike to the stand outside the all-nite coffee shop, where she always left it with strangers in the window to watch over it, and bought the usual treats for the security crew. Later she would barely recall the others in the café. There were at least two young people working on laptops and a couple of others, maybe, together or not she couldn't say. The freckled girl who served her was named Callie, they had each other's life outlines, and as always she smiled to see Kim and had her order ready.

The rest of the route took her on foot down a cross street, past her father's high-rise condo – he was staying at the house tonight – and she was thinking again of morning. As a girl she'd once spied him through sliding glass doors, weeping at a sunrise over Mexico City. He was standing on a balcony, waiting, and when it finally came he had nodded ever so slightly. Over the years it had developed in her mind that he'd simply been overwhelmed by this oldest of affirmations. Against the tribulations of the moment, there was always that, time ongoing as a sure thing each dawn no matter where you were. Except there was likely more to it, she now realized. Whatever had made Harold cry had been balled up in the new day.

She stopped before a bookstore window display, a gathering of titles without theme. A true-crime celebrity murder, something on Western conservatism, a handbook on Vermeer, an Australian novel, a speed-dating guide. She passed by a short block of closed shops and one bright one, a hair salon with a gospel choir, a church meeting, and going by the open doors she saw twenty or thirty swaying black people, Pentecostals, she supposed, and a tall, angular man leading the singing in front dressed in a dark suit with his hands raised slightly before him as if he were holding a calf up for sacrifice. And no sooner did she pass the door and leave them behind than she knew something had changed, some presence was trailing her in the wake of the music, its last strains and then the memory of it, and the image of the man in the suit, and as she walked on she isolated the feeling. It was the certainty that she was being stared at, with intent.

Or not certainty but a strong intuition. She focused on her walking. She kept a level step, tried to feel the rhythm she missed when cycling, and despite the tray of coffees she moved at a pace she could never sustain on her security rounds. Even for a young woman, she reminded herself, it was still possible to feel safe on foot almost anyplace in this city. And there was some magical deterrence of threat in simply walking like you meant it. She'd been followed once, in London. It was late at night, and she'd spent the day, like all the other days there, making wrong turns, mixing up east and west, and getting lost, so she moved a little uncertainly along the last blocks from the tube station to the hostel off Kensington High Street. He'd come from nowhere. As she crossed the park, thinking of a peacock that had led her out that morning, he had stepped in behind her, at a distance of ten or fifteen feet, and kept pace. To anyone but her he could have been mistaken for just another stroller in the park, but he was fixed on her, she knew it. When she turned and looked, he met her eye with a round, dull face, and held it. There were people nearby, and just as she spotted a group of young women to trail behind, wherever they were going, she was released of the feeling. As suddenly as he'd appeared, he was gone. Though she looked for him, expected him, in her last days there, she never saw him again.

The numbers on female victims indicated that the lone late-night attackers seldom just wanted your money or your life.

She stopped and turned. There was no one she could see. Down the street a young man emerged from a doorway and got into a parked car and when he started it the lights came up and there was no one. The car pulled out and passed by and the man glanced at her, and his car in the dark was maybe grey-silver, and then another car came by the opposite way and its lights revealed nothing, and she suddenly became aware of herself standing with her cardboard tray and paper bag, looking silly, and she walked on.

It was another block before the feeling was back in place. She couldn't hear footsteps exactly, but had the sense rather that under her every footfall, each breath, were other sounds, not hers, the kind of perception you wouldn't normally take note of in a city noisescape, except that this was a side street, admitting silences and distinctions. And then there was the feeling of being gazed upon. Like many women she was semi-used to the gaze, and thought little of it except when it came darkly, as it did now.

The question was whether to trust her intuition and take a longer, busier way to work, heading north and then west, then digressing south, or to stay the course. Or had the question to do with neurosis or sleep deprivation? Was she paranoid? She trusted her reason. And her wits – she should head for the traffic, join the conflux, risk nothing more than a jostle at the pedestrian lights. And yet when she came to the next intersection, she followed habit and turned down the darkest block on the route, most of it unlit next to a vast construction site.

When she entered the covered walkway that had been built over the sidewalk, with its ceiling and the long plywood wall papered in club dates and lost dogs, a shard of a dream returned to her. It was years old and she likely hadn't thought of it since the morning she'd escaped it. She was on the downtown edge of a city that was open on one side to a lake that ran to the horizon, Toronto or Chicago, both and neither. She had her back to a wall, looking at the faces of people looking past her, at something out on the water, and thinking to herself that no matter how unlike one another the faces were, the horror in them looked the same. An old man with sunken cheeks. A fat woman in large tortoiseshell glasses. A tall young couple with dark, narrow, Spanish features. And now she wasn't sure if these were the people of her dream, or the faces of others she'd seen elsewhere.

A few steps from a small break midway in the wall she saw the wire fence and the gate and noticed that it was slightly ajar so that when she heard the last two or three strides with which he closed the ground between them, she knew at once that she'd been stalked, and the gate seemed a trap, a metal device that opened and closed, and then he drove his shoulder into her and together they fell through the opening into the dark site.

She tried to scream but the breath had been knocked from her and now he was behind her, on the ground. She was face down. His legs were wrapped around her knees, his hands in her hair, pulling her back, exposing her neck. He locked her head up in the crook of his elbow and then she heard the tape and felt it pressed under one ear as it was pulled tight, over her mouth and around again and she felt him bend in close to her other ear and bite the roll free with a practised efficiency. A scent she couldn't place. She couldn't see him, his hands were up at his face, she thought, and it wasn't clear what was happening except that she needed more breath through her nose than she was managing and something hot was on her forearm. When he turned her over she saw that he'd been affixing a nylon mask. He sat on top of her with his weight on her hips so that her legs were kicking in space, unable to dislodge him, and the heat was now wetness and it was the coffee, she'd spilled the coffee, a conclusion that mattered somehow so that her failure to smell it came upon a kind of despair at the half-sense of things. His hands were at her shoulders and he lifted her once slightly and slammed her back down, as if trying to hold her still so he could make a point there were no words for.

When she flailed at him, he caught a wrist in each hand, and it was then she felt hopeless, for he was impossibly strong and it seemed as if he would snap her bones. He squeezed until her hands were dead and she was choking on her stopped cries and so gave them up.

He said nothing. He held her still as if to let the fear become conscious of itself. He looked down at her through the mask, through his own featurelessness. She dreaded hearing his voice and, when she didn't, dreaded its absence.

The only movement left to her was to turn her head. The site was huge. There were trailers far across, one of them lit, and parked trucks and tracked machines, cranes with lights along the top, sleeping high overhead with their arms over the dig. Near them were cages of gas tanks, jacks, low stacks of sheeting. Lamps at intervals made little cups of light along the verges with near dark and full dark between them. She thought about the pockets of dark until they seemed to belong to this force on her, until she sensed a kind of breathing like his inside them – the things they knew best, the two of them, they could never tell – and wondered if the lights were gapped on purpose to make a space for lives like his, and if so, then who it was who slivered the light.

She thought, he can't put his mouth on me with the mask on, as if that was what she feared most, and then he leaned closer to her and she thought he would do just that, and still holding her wrists, from a short distance he butted his forehead into her face and for a minute or more she slackened utterly. When she came around there was something in her eyes she knew was blood, and her wrists were taped together. She wasn't kicking but her knees were drawn up and she wondered why he hadn't taped her feet together, and then she tried to stop wondering.

She focused on the lit trailer across the pit, the possibility there was someone inside with a night-shift job like hers. Only when the foreground moved did she realize she was being dragged by her wrists into one of the pockets of dark. She'd brought it on herself by thinking of the dark and then of the lit trailer. This thing on her was reading her mind.

But it didn't know her. It never would. Reduced to her physical being, she sank into her physical history and then it was in her, or she was inside it, her younger self, the high school gymnast trained in taking poundings, in leverage and balance and explosive bursts. She thought, I'm stronger than he thinks. Then she thought, I'm stronger than he is. And she believed it in the moment when she drew up her knees and then shot out her legs and brought them down hard while thrusting her hips and pulling down her hands. When she broke free she knew there was no time to get to her feet so she rolled to the side and as he came down on his knees for her she was moving out of reach, so he half stood and then lunged just as she was turning belly up.

She could do nothing but bring her elbows together, and when she kicked his feet out, the full weight of him came down hard onto her before he could brace himself, and her elbow caught him square in the throat.

He rolled off onto all fours, hacking a short note, then again, with his head swaying oddly, like that of a field animal, and now there was time to get up, though the blood was making it hard to see, and she couldn't guess where the gate to the street was so she ran for the lit trailer. It seemed like a reasoned decision and now she didn't have to think anymore, just to run on the ground she couldn't see well enough to read, towards the light and shadows beneath the cranes and across to the trailer. And the image of the open gate came to her and then the thought that maybe the trailer was empty, that the man who worked there was her attacker, but she kept running, almost forgetting the edge of the dig, and then turning to run along it. She'd nearly made it to the far end when he tackled her. They fell hard, and she rolled free, and then she was falling. Something tore through her thigh as her ribs struck an edge and she spun into a final tumble and landed in a slack somersault at the bottom of the dig.

The pain kept her conscious and then it didn't. She came to once sometime in the night and she couldn't move. She isolated the many sources of pain, her head, her ribs, especially her leg, and realized she wasn't paralyzed, but her thigh was wet and raw and she understood she would bleed to death. When she next gained consciousness it was because she couldn't breathe and she snorted the snot or blood from her air passage. Faint nausea. If she vomited she would choke. The pain was not going away, but if she'd opened a main artery she would be dead by now, so she allowed herself to think she might make it until morning.

Though she didn't remember moving, she was now fetal. She looked up and saw above her a reaching thing, and lights along it, an arm against the heavens held over her. She searched for the name of the thing but could only think "arm." She imagined saying it, imagined her mouth and tongue free and breathing the word, and in her imagined voice the longed-for breath turned the word into "harm," and she tried it again and again it came out wrong, so that what might have been a comfort in its unsayability conferred a curse. The lights along the arm carried her eye to the vague stars. Now and then a jet plane moved through her field of vision and the sound of each one in approach seemed to pronounce time itself.

When the dark finally began to burn off she heard human sounds. A clacking. Voices. Then she heard the name of Jesus and saw a man in a yellow hard hat standing far above, looking down at her. She stayed awake as they came down. One of them kneeled close by and someone said not to touch her and the kneeler said he would cut away the tape and he put a hand on her head lightly and the moment the air hit her mouth she was sobbing. The man cut free her hands and then stood and stepped back. More men had gathered there but even when the ambulance attendants arrived and strapped her on a board, none came closer.

ϕ

There's a sound the earth makes in its transit, a streaming without music or echo, not coloured or pleasing or solemn or one thing so much like another. If god speaks to us in murmurs, she heard them.

There came hours when she thought the violence had involved her only by chance, and others when it seemed that she'd consciously placed herself in its path. As if it had been not a singular event but a kind of sounding within a slow pattern much older than she was. At first she could see no pattern, could not even put the past together in her mind, but she was full of a need to return, and what she returned to were the days before violence found her. The days made no sense at first, then built to sense and beyond it, to a near-unendurable clarity.

What she remembers.

The night of the attack, her visit home. It had been hot and close that afternoon until thunderstorms moved through and tore the smog down into the gutters and knocked out the power for minutes here or there. She'd biked up to the house around noon and she and her mother had cleaned the place together, laughing now and then at things like end tables and hassocks, objects they knew Harold would move to his preferred positions from long ago, and Donald would have to haul back again when he returned the next morning. Harold arrived around four with his usual greeting and gave Kim a hug that as usual was not fully returned. They'd not seen each other since April. He and Marian didn't actually greet one another – they never did anymore. Marian simply asked if he'd remembered the fish and he said of course. He was dressed with his signature note of slight incoherence in dark blue cotton pants, a winter-weight mauve shirt with the sleeves rolled unevenly, and brown sandals. He'd made the effort to put his grey-brown hair into some order but there was a film of grime on his glasses. Everything he came with including the fish was wrapped separately inside a canvas bag he'd picked up at an academic conference long ago with the ghosts of words on the side and the outline of some equatorial country Kim didn't recognize.

Now Marian was lying down in her room, Kim and Harold in the kitchen, their own old family kitchen, slicing peppers and preparing the sea bass for grilling.

There'd been a joke about her night-shift work at the museum. "My pretty, green-eyed daughter," he said, "the security muscle." He glanced at the digital clock on the stove and dropped everything, washed and dried his hands, and began fiddling with the radio. He left behind a jazz station Donald liked and dialed down the FM band, passing blues, hip hop, the news in French, and then on to the end of the lead story on the CBC. That the worst news of the day was a development in a government financial scandal was somehow quaint, even reassuring, given the times.

He resumed his position across the island from her and went back to work on the salsa as she consulted the printed-off recipe and patted dry the fish. The scents were coming up now in the travertine flesh. It was hard not to tell him that buying Chilean sea bass was a way of killing the planet.

"Have you read anything good lately?" His usual point, inserted bluntly. If she wasn't finishing her doctorate, then she was letting her brain go to waste. "Don't tell me. You're too busy with, whatsitcalled – Group?"

"GROUND. The Group for the Undocumented. And okay, I won't tell you."

He cocked an eye at his mango, as if to signal to her that this was just sport for him. They both knew it was more than that.

"You can think and you can write. You have talent. Use it."

"Remember my old rubber bath toy? You'd squeeze it and it sounded the same note every time."

"Beloved duck. What was its name?"

"You named it Lawrence," she said.

"He ended up a dog toy. He lost his toot."

"I loved him more when he lost it."

Harold nodded, or gave the sense of nodding.

"And I guess he didn't seem such an idiot. Sorry, stranger."

They sometimes called each other "stranger." He used the term jokingly, Kim to draw a pinprick of blood, in reference to the day he returned to her life when she was sixteen. Or returned again – he'd disappeared for four months when she was thirteen, and then left Marian for good a year later – but on this second return her parents were promising the establishment of a new order. She had walked home from school with a friend, Alyssa, now long disappeared from her life, who'd confided that she'd just that weekend given a boy what she called "mouth sex," and Kim was still unsettled by the secret as she entered and saw them there in the living room – Marian, Donald, and Harold, who she'd been told was on sabbatical in Mexico for the semester. They stood apart from one another, turning to her as she entered, each wholly occupied with her presence, as if the others weren't there. Donald gave her a thin smile. Marian watched her reaction to seeing Harold with a delicate attention Kim could feel. And Harold stood rigidly, his eyes slightly wide, as if surprised by some change in her appearance, and then there came across his face something familiar to her, his regret at having missed yet another increment of her growing up. The three of them tried to fool her into thinking that Marian had forgiven Harold and they would all be better off if they just tried starting over again, with Donald as the live-in father and Harold as the ongoing presence who wanted to spend as much time with his daughter as she would allow. Kim stood just inside the door. She'd been trained to be physically confident, but now felt a little small, a little thin, and with the others looming there it was as if her size was being used against her. Marian had asked her to sit down but she'd not moved or spoken. Marian had said that they all understood Kim's feelings, and Donald said in a rehearsed but concerned way that they respected her feelings. Kim unslung her knapsack and set it down on the floor. Then Harold said it was important that everyone not settle into "a ruinous estrangement." And then, because he had never had a grasp of his daughter's vocabulary, he defined "estrangement" for her – and Kim walked across the room and hit him in the face with the side of her fist.

It had been a stabbing motion. She hung in the sense memory, the flesh and knuckle of her hand meeting his nose and forehead, thirteen years ago. It must be by chance that she'd tangled up Harold in these small, violent connections before the attack.

Out on the back deck at the grill he was saying that history separates us. They sat drinking wine, looking out at the flower garden and the ivy on the brick of the neighbouring houses. The shaded leaves were still wet from the rain. It had been a very long time since they'd sat there together. Harold's legs were stretched out and resting on another chair, his trimmed toes protruding from his sandals. He told her he'd just been invited to give a paper at a conference in London on recent popular upheavals in Latin America, and the explosion of evangelical Christianity in the region in the void left by anti-Catholic movements in the nineties. He summed up the phenomenon for her with the image of New World peasants somehow swimming the Tiber.

"It's an amazing part of the world, those lands below Mexico. I'd like to do more work on them."

She said he hadn't described it that way when she'd wanted to travel there a few years ago.

"You shouldn't travel alone in some places. And I didn't want you in that army of young, idealistic nortamericanos who go down to pick coffee beans and come back over-pronouncing Nicaragua."

"So I shouldn't be alone but I shouldn't be with others."

"I get waves of students who insist we're all the same under the skin. We are not the same. History separates us. We celebrate skin and the surfaces of things in the well-to-do West. Culture is a difference-maker. And usually it fuels oppression and war. We like to pretend otherwise and pick beans and buy blankets and invite everyone to our house. And hide them in the basement if necessary."

The argument against her volunteer work usually ran that she was in over her head and didn't know it. She did in fact know it, but admitting doubt to him won her nothing. She had to seem sure of herself, not at all who she'd been in university. Long before quitting her Ph.D. there were signs she didn't belong on her father's career path. Her work lacked scholarly rigour. Her undergraduate history papers had admitted quite a lot of speculation. She'd even slipped into the voices of runaway slaves in the mountains of Jamaica and the last thoughts of Jean de Brébeuf, a Jesuit tortured to death by the Iroquois in the seventeenth century. The problem, as one of her profs had said, was that critical understanding didn't interest her as much as empathy. "But you can empathize on your own time, Kim. On mine, you just need to play by the rules." And so she had. She had played pretty well. But her heart was never in it.

Inside the house a band started up and along came Sarah Vaughan. Moments later Marian appeared in their midst with a glass of wine, already half-consumed. She was wearing one of her muumuus, the red one with white orchids. For Marian, this hour in the dead of winter was sober and solitary, often accompanied by Glenn Gould or a Schubert sonata, reading by the front window wrapped up in a Hudson's Bay blanket. In summer the hour was for drinking.

Harold moved his feet for her and she angled the chair away from him and sat. Kim told her she hadn't missed anything. They'd been recycling old arguments.

"Historians do that, don't they?" They were all looking out at the ivy. "It's why I ended up with Donald. Historians argue about religious wars. Mathematicians decode the language of creation."

"You're quoting him," said Harold. "I'd rather be an historian who can cross-multiply than a mathematician who calls himself a 'history buff.' Dressing up for battle recreations. Eating gruel and sleeping on hay. Christ."

Dinner moved along a little too quickly. Marian and Kim sat across from one another, Harold at the head. As always his hands traded the knife and fork repeatedly as he cut and ate, correcting himself when he noticed he was gripping them like gavels. His uncultured use of utensils was the one marker of his origins – poor, rural, and for some months in his boyhood, itinerant – that he'd chosen not to erase. It reminded them all that he'd had to make something of himself.

In the street beyond the dining-room window, a car thumped by in musical assault.

"Never work in a uniform," said Harold. "I should have told you that as a kid."

Marian looked up, paused. "A rare lapse in your fathering."

"Oh, please, the both of you. I'm not an aimless child you need to blame each other for. I don't like being wielded. Let's not do this tired thing again, okay?"

"Yes, indeed," said Harold. "I'm all for defeating cliché."

He'd had more to drink than usual, Kim noted. She hadn't yet worked through how Marian's illness, returned from a long remission, had force in herself, let alone in him.

Harold proposed a toast. "To the war on cliché."

"I've heard that one before," said Marian flatly.

They toasted.

At some point Kim asked about Donald's trip to Quebec City. He'd delivered a paper on the current focus of his interests, Kurt Gödel, that would allow him to use research money to be in town for a re-enactment of the battle on the Plains of Abraham.

"Apparently he wandered into the middle of a battlefield to correct the choreography." Marian was smiling without complication. "But he was a good sport. He joined the French side and mimed a great death. Donald, as you may have noticed, likes to play the fool."

"He's not playing."

"I know the real from the false, Harold. That's news to you, but Donald knows that about me."

Marian lifted her chin slightly. Kim understood it was the moment her mother most wanted to look beautiful. Her father missed it.

"Wandering onto a battlefield," he muttered. "The man believes in observing codes, no matter what's actually going on around him. Did you know that he asked my permission to take you to dinner?"

"When? What are you talking about?"

"Back in the beginning. He came to my office, of all places. Maybe he thought I wouldn't blow up at him there. We were both junior faculty, watching our step in parallel wings of the building. He shows up as if I were your father and asks what I'd think about the idea. I assumed the scene was out of some old foreign novel he'd read. I'm surprised he didn't want us both to drink from a chalice or something."

"I think I'll wait to hear his side of the story."

"What did you say to him?" asked Kim.

"Nothing. I just stared at him until he left. Seems he interpreted this to mean I'd given him the all-clear."

"You were never one for gallantry," said Marian. "Quite the opposite."

He pretended to ignore her. Here was a conversational place he wouldn't be led, at least not in front of Kim. Whether it concerned Donald or some distant episode was not clear. In Marian's exchanges with Harold, Kim saw something of the prize student her mother had once been. She'd practised criminal law at a small firm for three years before Kim was born. Since then she'd mothered and travelled with her husbands. But when drinking around either of her husbands, it was evident that the woman's life had disappointed her. In recent months Kim saw that even the disappointment wasn't real, but rather was a mask for a great dark despair. The mask hadn't worked for some time now.

"At what point do I ask you to let up on the wine, Mom?"

"The wine makes me feel good. The drugs don't. All the best things are contraindicated. But there's something to be said for chalices."

How does the past bear upon us?

Harold had once told Kim that the question mattered less than it might seem to. "The past belongs to itself first, and its value is the same whether an old war still turns heads on the nationalist holidays or it's been completely forgotten." He'd been driving her home from a high school gymnastics meet in which she'd sprained an ankle on the beam. It was the only competition he'd ever attended. She badly wanted to impress him, and when she'd fallen, it took great determination not to cry. She looked at him there in the stands, his mouth open, an "o" of concern she didn't recognize, and waved to him, and he nodded and smiled and assured her afterwards that it was "all a good show," as if he'd been watching a dance number. Beside him in the car with light snow falling on the windshield, Kim began telling him about a new trick she wanted to learn for her best apparatus, the floor, and he interjected that the tumbling had brought to his mind past Olympic Games, and Nadia Comaneci, a name he remembered, and then Romania and tyranny, and the whole destabilized, capitalizing world. Then the lesson about the uniform values of pasts.

The evening had ended with Marian back in bed and Kim and Harold in the living room. He sat in his favourite armchair, his hands palm down on his thighs as he stared out the front window.

"When it came apart for your mother and me, it felt inevitable. It felt right. Sad but right. But you don't think about this state of things up ahead. You don't think about illness. And when it comes, you see things are backwards."

"What do you mean?"

"I mean she has the wrong man looking after her."

It was small of her not to relieve him of the self-punishing thought.

Kim knew the guest room had been prepared but she pretended to go check it. Harold would stay over until mid-morning, when Donald returned. Her three parents could have a late breakfast together, but wouldn't. Sometime after Kim had made the bed that afternoon, she now saw, Marian had come in and placed on the night table Harold's preferred night reading, books on architecture and art.

Just past eleven she changed into her uniform. Before leaving she woke Marian with a kiss on the forehead and told her she'd come around again in two days. For a minute she held her mother's hand, her thumb in Marian's palm as if pressing into it a lucky coin.

She went out and loaded up her saddlebags for the ride to work. The streetlights had taken up in the maple branches. Harold emerged and walked her to the sidewalk and along the block, feigning an interest in her bike. By now he'd have realized he'd said more than he should have inside. It was odd to see him out in open, public space. How could this ever have been his street? He seemed incomplete in it. She recalled, then and now, accidentally meeting him in a bookstore, one of his women friends standing by, waiting to be introduced.

"Is this volunteer work you're doing dangerous? Be honest."

And it was as if he'd struck the final note of a chord, and she felt it as a vibration. Was it then or later that she thought it wasn't just worry in his voice, but a foreknowledge he couldn't expel?

"How could it be dangerous?"

"These people you work with, the rejects, you don't know them. There are reasons they get rejected."

"We don't hide torturers or terrorists. Haven't we been through this?"

"But the truth is, you don't know whether they're dangerous or not. You can hardly take them at their word. It's not enough to say it's the price of living in an open society."

"Sometimes it frightens me to think of you in front of a class."

Down the block the little parkette sat bright and dead. In the playground, far below the lone vapour light, a small green whale smiled on its coiled spring.

"What sorts of people are they? Where do they come from? The ones you hide under your rug."

She said if they had money they'd be immigrants. She said the usual something about the highest immigration rate in the world, three times higher than the U.S. He said pressure on screening mechanisms.

She said, "We screen by sending back the poorest unless they're in danger, so we're bound to make mistakes and send people off to their deaths. We already knowingly hand them over to torturers. It might do you good to get a little more involved in history instead of shuffling its footnotes. I work with real people, not national weaknesses or products of my misplaced idealism."

"It's the real people that worry me."

"Well then come and meet some. I'll call you this week. You can drop by the office and see who shows up. You can't know these people and not want to help them. I'm not inviting you. I'm asking you please to come."

The idea was sound, she must have thought. It had arrived before her as if out of its own integrity.

"Dangerous people are often attractive. Dangerous work is often noble."

"I'm riding off now."

She turned on her light.

"Think about what I've said, Kim."

"I'll call."

She was gliding away from him. In forty-some minutes she'd be gagged, falling.

"Be careful," he said.

Without looking back she waved with one hand and with the other shook the handlebars, tossed out a little wobble for effect, and the weak beam shivered before her, then steadied on its small spot of the world to come.

She drifted, looking for signs. Something she might have read in the flux, the weave of light street to street, face to face. Always she landed on the same hours, from four days before the attack, when she'd felt a foreignness pass into her that now seemed a kind of fate.

Just past sunrise she had left the museum in her blue and grey guard's uniforms and pedalled onto campus, riding crouched across the playing field with her shadow running long before her in the shape of a huge keyhole on the grass, turning north and west along a strip of coffee shops just opening, the bakery smells mixing with the morning's first blasts of exhaust, past a kid bent in a doorway with tattooed forearms and a mop of hair cutting straps from bundled weeklies, the city getting to its feet, these best hours when she felt that she was racing it, dodging delivery vans, a quick stop-and-go at the international newsstand, sweating in her polyester clothes in the fumes. She dipped away from a car door and swerved onto the sidewalk, rebalancing, to coast past produce vendors and people stooped over newspaper boxes, reading the stories above the fold. On into the west-end residential streets, still cool, with the light now tall on red- and burnt-yellow-brick houses, open doors, small pissing dogs, shoulder bags hitched up, wet-haired workers leaving their houses, patting their pockets, pointing remotes at car locks, tossing blind waves behind them, the morning emerging in each yard, until finally she arrived at her three-storey building, to begin the end of her day.

In the hallway she passed fumigation notices that conjured images of men in masks with metal wands in private spaces, uncovering all variety of secretings and abandonments, onward to her numbered door. She went in to find a handwritten message on the entryway stand: "gone out – Sadaf." On the small desk Sadaf's laptop sat open, not yet dormant, with text on the screen, the blinking cursor stopped mid-sentence. She read the half-composed story and felt the little tremor in her core at the descriptions of events in the infamous prison in Tehran. The story was a version of Sadaf's own, altered to give to another refugee claimant in her world of local Iranians. A good story, without the fatal inconsistencies of the original. The other claimant had her own history to tell, but wanted a better one.

The screen went dark.

She stepped into the kitchen and stopped. There was something wrong she couldn't place. She saw the phone reflected enormously in the toaster. Empty dish rack. Artwork fridge magnets, Kahlo, Mondrian. The tray of sunflower seeds on the counter. Someone, Sadaf, had run a finger through, dividing them into continents.

From her bag she took a two-week-old edition of the *Asr-e Azadegan*, what she understood to be a liberal Iranian newspaper, flipped it open, and tried to penetrate a page featuring a photo of someone she guessed was a government official and lines of lettering like slow handstrokes on tickertape. She put it down next to the phone, and there, out of place, was an onyx chess piece, a knight that she'd found on the lawn of the hospital at the time of her mother's first surgery. It belonged on the teak side table. Sadaf must have picked it up and held it absently, while moving to the kitchen. Kim looked at the piece closely. Had she ever really seen it before? The horse's bevelled neck, serrations along the mane.

She sat on the stool. Then she looked up and saw it.

An empty slot in the knife block. It was absent her one good long knife.

And the text had been fresh on the screen.

She stilled herself.

"Sadaf. It's me."

She started down the hallway and she knew now there was someone there. She stopped in the bedroom doorway and said again, "Sadaf, it's just me, Kim." She listened for movement, restrained breathing, and heard only her own. In the mirror mounted on the slightly ajar closet door was her believing face. Either there was someone there behind the cold mirror or there was no one.

Kim pictured her kneeling in the closet, the knife raised and ready. The image was movie-born, exotic, to be dismissed.

But there'd been kneeling and knives in the prison account, not to be dismissed.

Kim stepped forward and opened the door, and this was her closet in her place in her city and so there was nothing until, on delay, a sudden chill and weakness mixed with disappointment in herself. She went back to the kitchen and sat on a stool and wondered at her imaginings.

The referral from GROUND warned that Sadaf might be paranoid. She was convinced that the men who'd come to her apartment the week before weren't removals guys from Immigration but assassins from her government. She'd been out, up in the north of the city, in so-called Tehranto, selling spices in a strip mall, and came home to a neighbour's description of the men, and was now more or less on the run. And it was apparently true that the assassins existed, or had existed over the past decades in Western countries, killing dissidents. It just hadn't happened in Canada yet, as far as anyone knew. But Sadaf was an unlikely target, despite her past. Three hours before collecting her, Kim had received the outlines of her story from the office. Sadaf's history was in the records, some of them in Iran, some filed with Canadian court documents. The verifiable facts were that her religious name was Zahara, her family was Shia, she'd studied Islamic law at the Something-or-other university in Tehran. What couldn't be established for the Review Board's satisfaction was that she had been arrested for writing human rights articles in a student paper and had had to leave the country because she caught the attention of a particular government official, or anything that had happened thereafter.

Even at GROUND Kim had never directly witnessed real fear.

The dimensions were beyond her. She had no idea how to meet it, or even its retreat.

The knife must have just been misplaced. Of course, it would be in the utensil drawer, and she slid it open, and there it was.

And this is what she thought: that it made you suggestible, this business of helping survivors. What she didn't think, only came to realize, is that when you work at the nexus of a thousand bad histories, you breathe something in, some essence of dire luck. Your body knows it before your mind, but the days slowly fill with seeming accidents, nicked fingers, bad timings, a general slippage in the works, as if you've been forgotten in the thoughts of loved ones. The signs are everywhere, you might even be able to mark them, but their meaning will not open until it's too late.

Sadaf appeared at the door, wearing a *rapoosh*, was the word in Persian, unbuttoned for comfort and in the spirit of near emancipation. She'd been drawn out by the sunrise to walk and returned now with a steaming waxed paper cup of tea, and looked at Kim, a severe brow set into a dry, open face, round with thought. Kim felt herself focused upon, and she realized she was still wearing her security uniform. That first night she'd explained that no real authority attached to it, that the museum's nighttime security guards were mostly musicians and artists who wore their uniforms somewhat ironically, but the point had been lost. Now, three days later, there was no way to recover it.

This boarding of illegals was still new to her. Sadaf was only the third woman to stay there. None had remained for more than a week. They'd all eventually found new apartments, new bad jobs, and resumed their newly undramatic, invisible lives.

They ate a breakfast of muffins together, sitting on the stools. Kim explained the concept of fumigation, that they'd have to vacate the apartment tomorrow afternoon. Sadaf nodded, as if at a timeless condition. She'd taken no interest in the newspaper. Out of politeness, to dispel the silence, Kim asked where she'd learned English.

"As a girl. At home."

"Do you speak other languages?"

"I speak Persian, Arabic. French, a little. What are your languages?"

"French and Spanish. I've worked on Russian lately."

"You learned in school?"

"They come from my father, mostly. He's a professor of history. We lived in France and Mexico City when I was young." Kim chose not to add that her stepfather was also a professor. But then Donald had never moved her to new countries, had never meant the world to her, so to speak, as Harold had.

She knew from their other conversations that Sadaf had also travelled with her father when she was young. This fact complicated her view of the woman. She was educated, cosmopolitan, but as a girl during Muharram she'd worn a shroud and marched to the religious monuments.

Kim needed sleep. She felt heavy and floating at once, dream-deprived, as if the dreams might from the sheer need to discharge themselves break through into her waking mind. Two mornings ago she'd skipped a day's sleep, going straight from the museum to take the morning shift at GROUND, and found herself barely able to read. She couldn't make sense of a letter presented to her by a woman named Rahel, who'd been sheltered by an Ethiopian evangelical church. She explained to Rahel that her application on humanitarian and compassionate grounds had been denied. The H&C had not been accompanied by persuasive, objective evidence that she would be in danger upon her return to Ethiopia. Kim had trouble grasping the words "lack of compelling risk material." Because she spoke Spanish, Kim dealt most closely with the Latin Americans, but when explicating the subtleties of judgments or warrants without a common tongue, or when an interpreter's English was incomprehensible, she felt worlds of desperation falling through her.

But Kim couldn't remember whether she'd left a message for Marlene about Rahel. How could a person's fate completely slip her mind? She'd been making mistakes recently, losing details, moments. Losing numbers and names, mixing up words. Checking her burners thrice. It terrified her to think what was riding on her memory. There were worlds kept alive through Post-it notes. She would call Marlene after breakfast.

The phone rang, too loudly. It was Sarah, the one volunteer doctor at GROUND. She had found an Iranian family to take Sadaf in for the indefinite future. Someone would come by around noon. Sadaf received the news without comment. Their few conversations ran with lurching assertions and half-statements. Kim was never entirely certain she'd made herself understood.

"Where is your mother when you are young?" Sadaf asked.

"She was with us. She raised me."

Sadaf wasn't much older than she was, and her voice was young, but age had taken up in her hands and eyes.

"And your father came home with the languages."

"Yes. I wish I knew more of them, though. How do you say 'home' in Persian?"

"And your mother accepts the husband's will?"

"She sort of accommodates him."

Hearing herself, Kim wasn't sure if she meant Harold or Donald.

"And does she accommodate God's will?"

"I don't know what you mean."

"Does your mother see God's will is not the husband's will?"

"I don't think she sees God's will at all, Sadaf. Our family doesn't really have God."

Again she evinced no response. There was a long silence.

"*Khona*," said Sadaf finally. "The word is *khona*. It can mean home, or the house of God. For Sufis, *khona* is the highest state of . . . I don't know the word. In the mind."

"Consciousness."

"Yes." Were there words for what Sadaf had lost, and how she thought about her losses? "And *boshgah* means a place to be, a real place and a place beyond. And a place where travellers stay before carrying on with their journey."

A distance then passed over her and she was closed.

Kim could only hope that she ran a good *boshgah*, here for this soul unexampled to her.

You couldn't read the prison narrative and keep free of certain pictures. What happens to a woman after she has grieved for herself in fear? Lost to trauma, then to exile, is the old self locked away? But then memory wouldn't allow it. And the body would always go cold at the opening of a door. And yet Sadaf had gone out alone simply to buy herself tea.

Kim knew next to nothing in her bones but she trusted her heart. Her heart was willing to imagine itself into the fears of others, but it was not always capable.

The men came at noon. Rather than let them in, Kim went

into the hallway to discuss the arrangements. Sarah's assistant from the clinic, Colin, introduced her to an unsmiling man named Ramin whose family Sadaf would be staying with. He was in his thirties, Kim guessed. He wore an ill-fitting brown suit and had an air of dramatic impenetrability, a serious man on serious business.

Kim left them in the hallway and closed the door.

"Sadaf, my friend Colin has brought the man whose family you'll be living with for a little while. His name is Ramin." She went to the kitchen for a pen and paper. "If you need me, call this number and I'll come right away. Do you understand?"

She held out the number and detected a slight hesitation in Sadaf's decision to take it. She was from a world where the wrong number in your possession could get you killed or tortured, violated in front of your loved ones.

"Yes. Thank you."

Kim opened the door and began the introductions, but Sadaf interrupted her.

"You know these men?" she asked.

"Never mind," said Kim. She grabbed her keys from the table beside the door. "I'm coming with you."

Two hours later she was home again. She closed the blinds against the day and got ready for bed. The ritual involved washing her face and applying a once-weekly brown mud mask that she let dry while clearing a day's worth of phone and email messages. Donald had called to remind her he was leaving town for the weekend and thanked her for arranging dinner with her mother and Harold. Someone hung up. Her old friend Shenny called to make a lunch date, as if they hadn't fallen away from one another.

Someone hung up. The caller's number was unavailable. The members of GROUND and its connected services had been sent two list-serv emails, the first about a proposed change in federal law that would increase the authority of Immigration investigators, the second a "vigilance alert" concerning the need not to volunteer confidential information to the police. Someone had slipped somewhere. Kim hoped it hadn't been her.

Moving Sadaf had been uneventful. When Ramin ushered them into his apartment they were greeted by his sisters and brothers-in-law and their small children. Sadaf accepted their attentions patiently, with grace. Kim tried to read in her an undercurrent of wariness, but didn't know her face well enough, and the inflections of her native language were impossible to construe. A smiling woman whom Kim took to be Ramin's wife invited her to stay for coffee but she declined. At the door Kim took Sadaf's hand in hers and squeezed it, suppressing an urge to hug her, and reminded her to call if she needed anything. Sadaf nodded and turned back into the apartment, and seemed to forget her.

She had squeezed Sadaf's hand but the gesture was not returned. No expression of gratitude – she hadn't wanted one, really, hadn't expected one – but neither of much warmth. She told herself not to read too much into the goodbyes. The woman had some meaning for her that she hadn't yet worked through, and letting go of her hand had touched off this feeling still in her, a small, necessary regret.

She felt what the skin-care tube called "ancient sea mud" beginning to pull at her pores and then because she was still punch-drunk tired the sound of the words "ancient sea" made her think "H&C" and she remembered Rahel and called the office to leave Marlene a message. The impossible complexity of this volunteer work, never knowing enough about histories and languages, religions and laws and social customs, the migrating politics of gender here, of personal space there, of scarification, headdresses, the entering of rooms, exposed skin. Until a claimant was landed, deported, or dead, the only clarity was muddle. Failing to see muddle was failing to see clearly.

She went to the kitchen and prepared chamomile tea. She opened the cupboard and found her Imovane. She shook out a blue oval pill.

With her tongue she lifted the pill inside and swallowed it with tea.

For no good reason she rechecked the phone for the dial tone. Then she unplugged it.

Through the window she heard cicadas buzzing in the trees like electrical wires and again she thought of the prison account. Sadaf had found a way to move past her sufferings, yet Kim felt them inside her now, a heaviness in her legs, call it dread, some chemical reaction to sharp understanding, to knowing you don't know enough.

She set her tea down and went to the bathroom and stripped to her panties and weighed herself and washed her face again and brushed her teeth and didn't floss and peed. She applied moisturizer to her face and arms, and put on a T-shirt and set her alarm clock and got into bed. It was 3:20 p.m.

In four days she'd have dinner at the house with her complicated parents.

These simple moments were the best part of the day. For ten minutes she read *Under the Volcano*, which she'd read before but more or less forgotten. Then she turned out the light and closed her eyes.

Next came the names. It was prayer or it wasn't, she didn't know the word for this offering-up. There was no god to receive the names, she knew, but she needed the old consolation of solemn address. She asserted that she had them in mind, the people she knew were in need. Tonight when she'd thought of Marian and then came to Harold's name, as usual the offering got lost, and so she moved on, name by name, saying Sadaf and her new keepers and Rahel and Sarah and Maureen and everyone at GROUND, pausing with each one to try to truly hold them in mind, towards her own name at the end of the sequence. Sometimes she was asleep before she came to it, and sometimes, like today, she wasn't, wishing now only for a long, untroubled sleep, and then tended to herself further, conjuring lovers, former ones and possible ones. Lately she thought of a lawyer with GROUND named Greg Etterly. He worked for free and was always on call. She'd seen him save lives with arguments and papers. He was long and muscular, though he didn't dress to accentuate his body. He was rumoured to have had several lovers. Long ago, one of them had broken his heart. She thought of Greg and began to touch herself but he wasn't quite there for her so she let it go and then she was floating over the city high enough that she could almost see it whole and there were the people, she could make them out, see their faces though she shouldn't have been able to from this height, and she knew she'd found the secret to it all in a mistake of scale. She looked down with a satellite eye. When she was fourteen, after Harold had left the family, and then returned, he had taken her and Marian west to the Rockies. One night on the prairies he led them out behind a motel and found a place they could sleep under the night sky. He taught her to distinguish the stars from the satellites, and the satellites from the

American B-52s carrying nuclear warheads, heading north to the last allowable mile. It was the summer she'd begun kissing boys. It would be years before she realized that the B-52s were simply Harold's brand of fairy tale.

She'd lost her line of thought.

In another minute the voices in her head fell silent. Then she saw herself two places at once, as the girl under the Western sky, believing, and the city woman in her bed saying prayers to herself, and then both of her, the younger and the older, looking up through the same closed eyes, drifting north to the pole.

2

In late October she moved north to a cottage belonging to Donald's sister. At night, the porch. The moon caught on the screen in the semi-deep woods.

Her leg was well enough to manage the uneven ground along the path to the dock and back. Once in the morning and once before bed, she'd climb down bundled in a flannel coat and sit for a time with the still lake reflecting at its edges deep greens by day and black at night. She had rejected psychologists and group therapies, hadn't looked at the readings Harold had collected for her on trauma and recovery. But she needed time alone and thought it would do her good to be as close as possible to a change of season. Shenny had found three sets of people to sublet her place, Vancouverites and Americans in town to work on movies. Marian and Donald came up on weekends, and once Marian stayed a full week, but mostly it was the quiet.

When the snow finally came in November, a restorative blankness, she seemed to settle with it. She was an urban girl and didn't know the names of things here in summer, the shrubs and trees, the constellations, and the things she did know she now seemed to know less certainly, all of them blunted. But the snow levelled the ground and sky to white and grey, and for a minute or so every morning she resolved into a simpler creature of movement and need.

For weeks after the assault she had drawn against an invisible weight, and she slept and woke feeling no better. But as winter set in she emerged from a dormancy, as if lagging the world, and her body began to come back to her. Her leg had required only one surgery so far. The side of her quadriceps had been impaled on a half-inch steel rebar rod, which had then torn through the outer sheathing as she continued her fall. There was little vascular trauma but undetermined nerve damage. The wound and its repair had left a cartoonish scar and a burning in the leg that might or might not go away over time. Her other injuries had healed, though on the dock or in the porch she often felt an ache in her ribs. Her nose had been slightly displaced. She'd been advised to consider cosmetic rhinoplasty but wouldn't pretend that things could be put back in place. She looked a little different now, as she should.

Citing "personal reasons," she'd quit everything in one-line emails – her job at the museum, her work at GROUND – and now had nothing to do. At first the tasklessness was difficult, and then it wasn't, and then it was time to put her brain to work. She had Marian and Donald bring up CDs and books and when they left again she practised her languages. Listening to herself speaking Russian one day, she thought she detected a slur in her speech in some region of pronunciation she didn't normally occupy. It was possible, but unlikely, that the head blow she'd received or the fall had caused a neurological deficit that would grow over time, but the scans revealed nothing as yet.

"Eto nastoiashaia istoriia."

The story is genuine.

She began to put her time in order. She slept from ten to four a.m. Each morning began in the dark. With fire and tea she prepared herself for the day's rhythm of physical labour and study. Two hours studying languages, then, at first light, building the woodpile she'd need if she stayed into winter. The wood had been hauled before she arrived, unsawed, unchopped boles and thick branches, and so she learned from manuals to use a chainsaw and an axe, and she was terrible at both, these motions she didn't know, and then got stronger and better. In the shed beside the cabin she learned to dress the axe with a foot-pedal grindstone and to cool it in the snow. After two hours she would stop and go inside for bread and cheese, and then again take up her books and audio lessons. After lunch she would nap, and in the afternoon she set out with a shovel to keep the road clear on the steepest grades all the way out to the main highway. If there'd been no new snow she'd hike along one of the routes she'd devised. The only neighbour within walking distance was half a mile away, and the one day she came near the house she peered in the windows – it was shut up tight, lawn furniture stacked in the kitchen. Several times while hiking she saw deer and evidence of other animals, tracks and scat she didn't recognize. There were what had to be wolf prints. Part of her expected an encounter but didn't expect it would kill her. All her fear was occupied. While cooking and eating she listened to the radio. After dinner she resumed her studies. Once a week she started up the car Marian had now more or less given her and drove to a town thirty minutes away for supplies.

Every three or four weeks she went to the city for medical appointments, hers or Marian's. Her mother's test numbers were good, though no one was talking remission. She stayed for two or three days at a time, in her old room at the house, spending the mornings with Marian. The city was in its chill phase. It was comforting to sit in a café window and watch it go by, remembering student apartments past, a harpsichord on FM as she read for her classes or fell in love with a poem. She found she wasn't more afraid in the city, but it was winter, and she hadn't yet been out at night alone. And anyway, the fear didn't reside in the place.

Its power owed partly to her reluctance and then inability to find words for it. She hadn't returned voluntarily to the attack – she didn't have to, it was still immediate, in her physical pain and a disjuncture between her past and present selves – but in the first weeks at the cottage it was as if her imagination had been dulled so she might have time to distance herself from the event. One night not long after she'd moved up she'd heard something outside, a heavy presence, and then came the crash onto branches and a few hard breaths. Whatever it was scrambled up and away. She told herself it was likely a deer, a moose or bear. But for an hour or two she sat cold, waiting, armed with a poker from the fireplace. There was no one to help her. She'd stayed awake through the night.

She'd been told to expect the nightmares, and to think of them as a kind of purging, though they were not. Because her dreams were never literal she assumed they wouldn't be of the attack itself, and the first ones that came had a familiar symbolic slant. She would be dreaming untroubled and then suddenly, thin black veins in the sky or along the walls that no one else could see, and when she looked again, they were gone. A drop of inky poison, absorbed. But then she met the real thing. Consecutive nights of vivid fragments of the event itself, with no illogic or distortion. It was here that she realized his nylon mask had small eyeholes that sat slightly askew. That at some point the eyes came up in the holes and he was looking down and his eyelashes were long, almost girlish. That lying in the dig she'd seen a concrete block near her face and thought how once the dumb square thing was set down the rest of the building would follow prefigured, without further invention.

In her dreams she kept passing by books in a window and the open door of a brightly lit improvised church.

And so she came to learn that she had only been managing the lesser symptoms of the fear. By day, the real fear was a kind of waking in the blood. Or a visitation to her conscious mind from her unconscious. It came upon ordinary moments. A December Thursday, late afternoon. She was making lentil soup, listening to news on CBC Radio, where the stories always began with a sound. This one, a documentary about AIDS education conducted by Canadian missionaries in Kenya, began with a choir. The hymn (the word like "him"), the mind's picture of a singing congregation, and the next thing she knew, she was rigid and shaking. After a minute or so she reached over and killed the radio and in the silence the dread was stark. It remained for hours. She understood then that the fear was going to have her long after her attacker had.

Her attacker. Whom she did not contemplate. There were no suspects, only her vague description for the police. They could barely make a sketch from it. He had said nothing, his smell was particular but she couldn't describe it except to say that he smelled like a closed room after long sex and she couldn't, wouldn't say that. The nylon mask made a false complexion, and she felt for no reason that he was dark white or light brown, not black or South Asian, but she couldn't explain why she felt this.

The smell might have been in the mask. He was not tall, of medium build.

The police investigator, a short, square woman with sharp arching eyebrows named Cosintino, whom Kim liked, had said it was unlikely she'd been followed from the coffee shop or the church when she first sensed a presence – he was more likely waiting for her on the dark block, with the gate open, knowing exactly how the attack would go down. He waited for a woman, not even necessarily a particular kind of woman, and along came Kim. It might have been significant that he found his victim on a downtown street rather than a park, or some jogging path in the valley. Maybe he liked the idea of raping her – Cosintino thought that was the idea – beneath all the high-rise windows, all the people who could be looking down. Knowing such a compulsion had not yet helped the investigation.

But if it were true that he'd waited for her, then how to account for her sense of being followed? Was the feeling not intuition but premonition? The other question was why she had turned down the dark street when she'd thought to trust her instinct and go north.

Some of the fears she had to manage belonged to friends and family. At first her three parents had all objected to the idea of her staying at the cottage. The most complicated moment had Marian asking, "Why would you want to be nowhere?" and then breaking down. She'd been the solid one until then. The assault had given her someone to be strong for. Even after Kim left, the reports from Donald were that Marian was already into her sober season, and it was holding. She didn't drink at all on the weekends at the cottage. When Kim went home for four days at Christmas, the parents were on their best behaviour.

Untaken baits, uncharacteristic silences. Harold and Marian didn't know what to do with her, or with themselves around her. Then she went back to the woods.

One weekend in late January, Donald told Marian that he and Kim were going to drive to a hiking trail. They curved around the edge of the lake with Donald telling her he knew what she was made of. She said that at the moment she was made of confusion, that even the things she thought she knew, not just about the attack but about herself, were now in doubt. When they got out, he took from the trunk a rifle and some shells and began to talk about indeterminacy.

"In math we know that certain things are consistent only if they contain inconsistencies. Some things are built to be undecidable, Kim. You remember the liar's paradox – 'This sentence is false' – which can't be true even though it can't be false."

"The world is an Escher sketch."

"Some parts of it are."

"Those are the parts I'm in right now. And in the world I used to know, you wouldn't be carrying a gun."

They walked over the frozen lake to an island. She let him teach her how to load the rifle and fire it. He told her everything – the name of the gun, a Remington Model Seven SS, its primary use, the names of the parts, their material compositions, then the way to store it, to hold and carry it. To load, aim, and fire it. He said, "Imagine that dead birch down there as your target" – was she supposed to picture her attacker? could she see his face, his eyes in the knots, the light and dark reversed on the peeling parchment bark? – and she shot at it nine times and hit it twice. She had thought rifles kicked upon firing and sort of wished this one had. He said the tree was "at" sixty yards. She allowed him to remind her twice that this lesson was their secret. Because Kim wasn't outwardly in ruin, Marian worried about her mental health. She told Kim it was important *not* to be strong for the sake of others. She had to confront the event head-on, when she was ready. Her mother apparently wanted her in tears.

When the lesson was over and they were driving back, Kim said she wouldn't be keeping the rifle.

"It's not how I want to deal with this, Donald." His familiar baffled, hurt expression. Squinting behind rimless glasses, now fogging in the car. "I liked learning about the gun. I like knowing how it feels to shoot one."

"I just thought you might feel safer."

"No. And I can't shoot what happened."

The gun would call up shadows. A sitting gun, imagining its own completion. It would be different if she didn't know that made-things incline to their use, but she did know it. And she was vulnerable, to images and songs and who knew what else. Already she had to remind herself to take the fireplace poker from under her bed before the others arrived each weekend.

February was mild, sunless. She read novels and listened to Górecki and went skiing with uneven strides on the lake. The thought of the city in spring, the noise and press of it. She would have to prepare for her return.

One afternoon she closed a book in mid-sentence and admitted she was scared. Not just of the city but of this cottage, the lake. The vast forest invited the loss of body and mind. She was scared of the night sky. She lived at a pitch of fear just below awareness. Now and then it welled up, then sank again, but it was always close to the surface. It was a matter of time before she would begin seeing demons. She had removed herself to this place so she'd have no one to be brave for, but she'd been brave for herself from the first moment. The truth was, she didn't know how to get past this. The authority of fear. She was being forced to make a project of herself.

He had calluses, she'd told the detective. She thought she could recognize his touch. She worried about touches, about how she'd respond to a man. She told herself what no one else would, that in some ways she'd been lucky. She hadn't been killed. Or raped. Yet she could not accept the thought that had things gone differently she would feel even more violated. And that was it: *violation*. The expected word. Amid the many others, words like *closure* or *recovery*, it was hard to remember that there were brute facts, and words attached to them, and they were the right ones. Upon this revelation it seemed possible she might collect enough words to describe her fear even if she couldn't describe her attacker. In a photocopied article with the heel of Harold's palm at the base of every page she read about the neurophysiology of trauma. The fear, in material terms, was cerebral. The assault would have released a neurotransmitter in the amygdala that would have set off a calcium reaction that resulted in proteins gluing themselves to those parts of her brain that were active before, during, and after the attack, when her adrenalin was high. A fragment of gospel music, the sight of a construction crane, the smell of coffee, and she was cast back into the event.

And Harold. It was just bad luck that he'd been on her mind in those minutes before it happened.

The man with the calluses had changed her brain and she needed to change it back.

Harold called her twice a week, sent her oddly rambling emails about his work and things he'd read, but he visited just once. He arrived late in the afternoon on a bright Saturday in March when the snow had crystallized and the sap was running, darkening the maples. She'd guided him on his cellphone until he lost the signal, and he made it the rest of the way consulting Marian's written directions along the last kilometres of half-frozen, forking gravel roads. He pulled in at the cottage, somehow appearing out of place even before he emerged from his car.

She came out in her winter boots, in long johns and a sweater, and he looked at her, and there it was. Since the attack she'd detected a stutter in his perception whenever he met her slightly altered face.

She helped him unload the supplies she'd requested. In the spirit of a game they'd devised long ago, he made his complaints in Spanish.

"No me gustan las cabañas."

"Ni siquiera has entrado todavía."

"Imagino que las moscas negras no molestan tanto en esta época. Pero el lugar estará replete de musarañas."

"What?"

"I said I hate cottages and I expect the place is infested with . . . shrews or something."

They ate dinner with him scoffing at the knick-knacks on the walls, the lacquered wood clock in the shape of a fish, the inexpert oil painting of the lake, surmising the low-middle-brow set of Donald's clan.

"These are likely treasured heirlooms I'm ridiculing."

"Didn't E.P. Thompson say something about saving the dead from the condescension of the living?"

He smiled. "So you know your Marxist historians. I'm happy to be forgetting them."

Silences made him uncomfortable. He described a Belgian movie he'd read about, then Warhol films and Tarkovsky and what he called "the dignity of boredom," and how "mind-numbingly dignified" he felt during long, static movie shots. He quoted a study on the growing illiteracy of new university students ("they call them 'incoming,' like shellfire"). He admitted to being "a revanchist" about his lost territories in the department and complained about younger colleagues protesting police patrols on campus.

At one point he looked down and seemed mystified by the food on his plate.

"You think he had a dark complexion."

"Where did you hear that?"

"It's in the police report."

"I didn't say dark. I said dark white. I didn't see his face. I don't know where I came up with that. Maybe his hands."

"Mediterranean? North African?"

"Dark white is meaningless. Even if I'd seen it."

They were never together in strange spaces like this. At the moment they were trapped in this one. Like the fear itself, her aversion to talking of the assault with her father, of all people, was physical.

"You think you were followed."

"It's just a feeling I had."

"I know these are hard moments to relive, but have you considered the possibility that he might have followed you all the way from your apartment?"

It was as if he'd never spoken about it until now.

"No. I came from Mom's house that night. Remember?"

"But you rode by your building. He might have been there, or anywhere along the route. It was the same route you always took. The lock on the gate was already broken. As if he knew you were coming and he planned for it."

"It wasn't broken, it was open. No one cut it. And if he'd followed me I would have noticed him."

"Maybe he was a stranger. Or maybe he knew you."

Here it was, then.

"Or maybe he was a stranger who knew me. Is that your theory?"

"I'm sure it's occurred to you. That maybe he was one of the rejects." He raised his hands in apology. "Sorry. I don't know what to call them."

He wasn't sorry. It was what he'd needed to say. And there was more. As if to slow himself for emphasis, he started back into his dinner, and then resumed.

"What if it was someone you turned down? Some guy you turned down at GROUND because he was dangerous, which is why he was rejected by the Review Board. And he targeted you."

"The police don't think so. I don't think so. Only you do. There's no reason to think the man who attacked me isn't fourth-generation Canadian. I wish you'd see that there are other mysteries to solve here."

He finished his glass of wine and held it out to her. She filled it and put down the bottle within his reach. He shifted to the matter of her recovery. Any experience that marked itself, he said, lapsed immediately, distorted, degraded, into memory, language, story. The process was true of everything in history.

"I'm sure the attack is still close to you. It will stay vivid and immediate unless you consciously process it. It unfolds in real time in memory, in dreams. It confronts you in absolute detail. You have to cast out the details, as it were, by describing them. Find the words and describe them. If you wait too long it'll be too late."

You couldn't always tell with Harold when he was speaking from his researches and when from his experience. For a moment she thought she'd ask him, but he would close down, and wherever they'd arrived now would be lost to them.

"But I can't describe them," she said. "I don't have the words. And so trying just compounds my sense of helplessness. If I say he seemed sure of himself, like he'd done it before, then I sort of believe that's a fact. But then, you know, his mask wasn't on straight, and I got away from him, so how slick was he? And so I doubt myself as a witness. And I feel powerless all over again."

"So keep trying. Maybe take it from angles. Find the smaller composite truths within the larger one. You need to make it something to share. It's the hopeful idea of two or more people seeing the same thing. Disarm it with scrutiny, as if it happened long ago, to someone else."

"Who's my audience? I wouldn't want anyone I know so-called sharing this with me."

"Tell it to yourself. Your older self. She looks in an old journal some day far off and finds the examined details. And they seem very real and very distant all at once."

Did he keep a journal? she wondered. This was not a précis of some article he'd read or the usual hectoring about resuming her studies. He was telling her something he'd discovered.

"Have you told your mother what happened?"

"Not all of it."

"You can, you know. You can tell either of us, if you need to."

"So now we're sharing our worst moments?"

He pretended to look directly at her but his eyes took in only her forehead and then dropped back down to the food, his shoulders now set slightly forward.

"You're very aware of my worst moments, whatever you imagine them to be. I think you've let them shape you."

"Really. What do I imagine them to be?"

"Well. The marriage had its worst moments. You were there for those. Or in nearby rooms, and the aftermath. And you're angry with me, for her sake and your own, and –"

"Yeah, I know. So I sabotage my could-be career to disappoint you. Isn't psychology simple."

There had been not a sabotage but an awakening. Her first two terms in New York had gone well enough. She had a title for her proposed thesis – "Homeless Truths: Pluralism in Postwar North America" – and a lengthy reading list, but in her second year she began wondering what wasn't in the studies, theories, and source documents. To Harold's distress, her inspiration had always been those historians whose work admitted speculation – Donald's interest in the Battle of Quebec began when she'd given him Simon Schama's essay-fiction about Wolfe and Montcalm. As her second winter there began, and she realized that New York had covered her in a mood of broken promise, she returned in her reading to fiction-inflected histories. She became dreamy, stopped attending classes, and wrote nothing but vignettes, scenes that came to her unbidden, written all in one sitting. She was adrift, on other people's money. And so she dropped out and went home.

They'd entered the brief pause before finishing their meals. Kim noticed how they mirrored each other, each with the left hand on the table, holding the stem of a wineglass, and the right resting on the edge. Harold pressed his palm against the table, spreading his thumb and fingers as if measuring the span of a thought.

"There's no use denying the force of large events," he said. "If we're awake at all, we spend our early adulthood discovering that the world is more complex than we thought, and the rest of it discovering the main human themes have been the same for thousands of years. You can name each one in a word or two."

"You know, you're right that I was in nearby rooms. And I remember what I heard you two say to one another."

"That was just dumb emoting. Mostly meaningless."

"Well then maybe that explains my directionless life, because I thought I caught some spit wisdoms."

"I can't imagine which ones."

"That some people live their lives inside a single ambiguity. You said that. All the yelling stopped and there it was. I don't remember the context, I likely wouldn't have understood it. But I've come to think of the statement as hard-won truth, maybe a confession. And I've always wondered what it was, your single ambiguity."

"I don't recall saying that. And I can't imagine what I meant."

"So then it's left to me to imagine. And you're right, after all. I guess what I imagine has shaped me."

They had never talked at such length about anything that mattered, not that he'd opened up newly for her. He was still the sly interlocutor, defending not just his positions (his colleagues found him suspiciously apolitical, at best; she knew some of them were handy with polite recriminations) but something in himself, something she had never been able even to glimpse whole. And there it was again, the particular mystery of him. She could almost touch it.

The next morning he was gone. The day was clear, the light through the pines lined the cottage. Now that she was alone again the place felt not empty but pristine.

What she'd been waiting for was a line of address, and in the wake of Harold's leaving it finally appeared. She needed to discover what she already knew.

She began with a blank computer screen, facing the windows and lake. The first pages covered the day of the attack. She found a space above the story from which to tell it, neutrally, in the first person but a little outside herself. She tried not to invent or speculate, and ignored moments that only seemed true and ironies she couldn't have known at the time. She wrote of her ride to work that night. As she drew it out, as if to delay the occurrence, the moments began to build more acutely with each line, and she found that if she stayed in them long enough, there were returns. The rust on the panel above the rear wheel of a parked car she'd locked her bike beside, the way the door to the café stuck a little, the smell of the spilled mint tea she'd stepped in near the entranceway, and the wet tread prints from her shoes on the sidewalk as she looked back to see if she'd dropped a napkin from the tray. A man walking ahead of her in jeans and a fitted blue shirt. He entered a house and was gone.

Then, the moment when she'd passed by the door of the brightly lit improvised church and a chill fell upon her. She was seeing herself on the page from a ground-level distance. She was seeing herself from the cold.

Every day she wrote to this point and no further.

One crisp morning when the fire wouldn't catch, as she lined up the same moments the same way, a breakthrough. She'd made a mistake. There were tread prints, yes, but not hers. It was the night before the attack that she'd stepped in the tea. And this small error admitted the possibility of others. It showed up the deficiency of her method. On the night of the attack she would have looked back and seen the prints and known they were someone else's and been reminded of her own on the previous night. She might even have felt an echo of the disjointed time she'd experienced minutes earlier when she'd pictured herself riding in the morning, going home in the opposite direction. And wouldn't she then have felt an eeriness? If not consciously, then in some part of her? And mightn't this feeling, and the footprints behind her, have prepared her for the sense that she was being followed?

She began over now, allowing for her interiors. The writing ran deeper, and though the account was sliding to speculation, she felt herself returning in the prose. If a misremembrance could lead her to a fact she'd overlooked, then maybe so could other variations from the narrow-seeming truth. And so she half remembered, half invented the night.

One morning she wrote,

I left dinner with my parents and rode south through the dark towards work.

She stopped. The words that made distances were wrong. She realized that the "I" itself was wrong, for whoever she was now was not who she had been, and one letter could not be them both.

Then she wrote,

Before the shift that night she left dinner with her parents and biked south in darkness past her apartment building, along into her usual path. The afternoon storms had broken the heat and departed without trace. The air was drying, late-summer cool. On the side streets near campus were weakly haloed car headlights and shadowed figures waiting to be briefly illuminated.

She wrote for almost three hours without stopping, finally deep into something true, without any sense of present time and place. Then she turned off her computer. Some minutes later she found herself outside, at the woodpile. She split six pieces of elm and lay them in the handled canvas. She smelled the wood and a sugary scent that she followed around the back of the cottage. On one of the maples a bucket had been knocked off a tap that had begun to drip sap. There were bear tracks all around. She stepped away, seeing everything.

Back inside, she sat by the fire, stared out at the lake. The animals were waking from their dens. Seeing the prints had brought forth the smallest things. The faintest yellow in the grey of the dormant beech buds. The weather seemed no different but it was already spring in the ancient systems.

All moved forward from here. It was time to go home.

Her thoughts returned to the half-written story. She was still standing outside the church and she couldn't go further without confronting what she couldn't. Fear had stopped her, but also an incapability. How to think of him? He was faceless, without even a name to hold the substance of him in place. She wanted him known, not named, not by her. Any name might skew her sense of him one way or another. And so instead she designated him with only a letter, and for reasons she didn't speculate upon, the letter that seemed right was *R*. A letter rolled on some tongues, though she didn't roll it now. A letter that sounds like *are*. Her attacker, a plural state of being.

A verb in English, she thought, at which point her intuition that he didn't speak English was useful to her. The man had language, but not hers. The detail opened up more of the globe than it closed in her conception of him. And it isolated him within the city, which made sense, she decided. And thinking of him without English, in fact, meant she could attribute to him any life she wanted.

She expected he would come to her like this, that one day she'd call up her narrative, and begin writing, and there he'd be, fully present and named.

3

It had been six steady weeks on the new job and it paid the best of any work he'd ever had. Rodrigo worked for a man about his age named Kevin, who bid on contracts from insurance adjusters and then phoned Luis, who called him, and they had to be on-site within an hour because of sitting water that would ruin everything left to ruin if it wasn't pumped out and the carpets and walls stripped away. The work was hard and dirty, and sometimes Rodrigo came across burned-up things he wished he hadn't seen. Last night it had been a child's doll lying in a hard black pool of its melted head and back. One time it had been a dog that the firemen hadn't found. The heat had curled its legs in front of it stiffly, as if it had died in an instant, running, though it had not died that way.

He didn't say much at work. Kevin got them going and then spent a long time on the phone. He brought all the tools and wanted them put back as soon as they were used. Rodrigo and Luis were not to talk to anyone but Kevin or Matt, the other crew member, who took more turns than Luis with the worst of the work.

Most fires were at night. The hours they worked were backwards to the lives of other people. He showered before bed and slept until mid-afternoon. His one daily event was the walk to the internet lounge where he'd check for news from his cousin Uriel in Cartagena but there was never news. Uriel had written only once, after Rodrigo's first message to him, to say that there had been no reprisals yet against the family. Then silence for over a year. Nearly every day Rodrigo sent a small note into the silence.

He felt a great need to lie a little about his days, to make the stories better than they were. He wanted to write that he had a job selling TVs or coaching football, they called it soccer, that he was in school learning business, that a woman he loved was in love with him, or even that their love was impossible, that she was married to a rich man who treated her cruelly. In one version of his life he played a Mexican on a TV show. He imagined these stories at work and at night before bed. But so far he had never written them to Uriel. To write them would be to feel the full difference between his life as he imagined it and his life as it was.

He tried to describe his two thick work shirts. A shirt here could be described in terms of shirts from home, but not the need for them against an October morning in Toronto. In winter he wrote about the snow, but he knew Uriel could never imagine it, and he couldn't write it into imagining. Instead he just wrote, "The days are very cold and there's snow and ice. I have good boots," knowing Uriel wouldn't picture the right kind of boots.

He put down his thoughts as they came to him. He could never allow himself to be questioned by police. He'd met his girlfriends at a language school before he stopped going. It was important not to get hurt on the job and once when a stairway collapsed he'd fallen on his hand and hurt it badly but he didn't tell anyone and now there was a ridge between his knuckles and wrist and it still hurt him and was useless by the end of the day. The first girl was named Halia, she was from somewhere in Africa and he couldn't even kiss her because of what had happened to her in her country. The other girl was a woman, a teacher at the school, named Julie. She wouldn't go out with him while he was in her class and so he had quit and they went dancing. When she had broken up with him, it was only because they could never be married. He was illegal and could be sent back at any time. He didn't tell Uriel that this was the first time he realized that his future here was small.

Now it was Rosemary who helped him with his English. Whenever they ate together she had him read out loud to her from the newspaper and then asked him questions about what he'd read. The stories she chose for him were about deportations and cruel governments and black boys shot dead in the clubs. The news was full of warnings and he felt it made his English more serious than his Spanish. She asked him once which language he thought in and when he couldn't answer her, she asked if he was mostly full of feelings and pictures. His only problem was expression, she said. Maybe she felt she'd insulted him, that she'd made him feel stupid. She said only that he should use English in his thoughts, and it should sound like his voice when he lowered his head at dinner to recite English grace.

Only once had she asked him to tell her his story from beginning to end. He'd been downstairs when she'd come home and he called up hello but she hadn't answered, and then he heard her crying in the kitchen. He let her be. Soon she came down and explained that she'd just found out that a woman she was helping had been detained and deported last week, and the woman would be persecuted in her home country. She said when this happened she suddenly wanted to believe that the people she helped were all lying, that they would be safe when they returned. But she knew, she had proof, that some had been killed, and she grieved for them and there was no place to put the grief, no funerals or graves, except her prayers, but the grief never ended that way.

And so when she asked him to tell his story again, he thought she was asking him to lie to her in case he was ever returned. But he couldn't lie. He wasn't good at it. And anyway his new life owed to the true story, and he couldn't give it up.

And when he began to tell it, he saw that he'd been wrong, that it was the true story she wanted. She nodded at what was familiar to her from the version he'd presented to the tribunal, and she seemed to hang on the details he just remembered then in the course of this new telling.

When he was done he said he understood that he couldn't stay with her for much longer but that she was for him the person who brought together his life past with the life yet to be. He couldn't guess where he'd be if she hadn't helped him. They had never before spoken so well with one another, and never since.

His cellphone rang. Luis said they had a job and he'd come by in twenty minutes. It was past ten. Rodrigo collected his clean work clothes from the laundry room and got into them and went upstairs and packed a little lunch. He didn't put on his workboots yet and wouldn't unless they got the job. They had been someone else's boots once.

Hours later he and Luis were standing in a dining room, looking at a chandelier somehow left undamaged by the fire and water. It had hung just below the smoke in a room that had been saved. But it was a hazard to them and they'd have to take it down anyway and when they put it on the floor, a little cut-glass ball separated and rolled to his feet. When Luis turned away, Rodrigo picked it up and put it into his pocket.

Luis dropped him off at Rosemary's house at five in the morning, and they were to be back on-site by one. He went in quietly. He took his boots off and shed his dirty work clothes in the entranceway and carried them downstairs. On the table beside his bed he found one of the envelopes of money Rosemary sometimes left for him. Before he moved into the house, the envelopes had come to him through Luis. He understood that she didn't hand these to him directly out of respect for his dignity and because she wanted him to feel that it was from the church and not from her alone.

A hundred and twenty dollars. Seeing the cash always made him feel a little worse. After one more paycheque he would tell her to give the money to another.

He set his alarm for noon. As he began to nod off he pictured the clothes he'd dumped in the laundry room and remembered that he had no clean ones ready for the afternoon. He got up and put the clothes in the wash and looked out his window at the early sun drawing along the neighbour's brick and the grey plastic garbage bins and he felt a weakness in his hands from work. He then sat watching the muted TV until the clothes were done. The second time he went to bed, it was to the sound of the dryer, and the fresh images from the local morning show of traffic and weather and yesterday's news from some Arab land in ruin. No one understood the world, he thought. Not even the quietest, smallest part of it.

Harold turned off the lights in the condo and stood at the south-facing window, looking out at the city from twenty-one storeys. The place was in one of its prosperous phases that tended to come in decades of bland Western architecture. As in Buenos Aires, San Diego, Kingston. Marian used to find the mornings in Vancouver deflating. It was a line of theirs, "Blame it on the architects," whenever things got tough and they'd grown tired of blaming each other. Some resentment or small cruelty conducted along a maze of pathways, of past arguments, betrayals, hoping for some surprising new light on things. They'd been lost for so long, they couldn't even find the door they'd come in through.

Commanding views made him feel ridiculous. He removed his reading glasses. He was thinking about culling his books. He'd done it badly for the move, tied up in sentimental attachments to histories and festschrifts that marked out his life. But if he counted the ones he'd actually look at again, there were fewer than fifty. The other three hundred or so along the walls were merely sound baffles. He'd read and forgotten most of them. The others, he either didn't believe or didn't care about. They seemed not so much unreal to him as beside the point. He couldn't articulate the point, but it existed in some dimension where everything he thought of could be beside it.

Depressed by architecture. They'd had no idea.

He studied himself briefly, his image, light upon the window. The glasses in his hand made him look satisfied or contemplative, or something. He looked all wrong, in any case. But then everything looked wrong these days. Down the block a floodlight from a crane died on the beginnings of the new high-rise condos. The site. Ground zero. Had he been here that night and looked down, what could he have seen? He would never stop asking the question. The site was still badly lit, and from this height he could see nothing in the recesses. Not the side street, not the dark spot next to the wall where the attack occurred, not much of the ground across which she'd run, and not the pit into which she'd fallen, which had since been filled. He could see the trailer, though. Even lit up, it looked empty. If Kim had taken his advice she'd have sued the company for not securing their space.

He took a long last gaze at the dark spot. He would have to move again.

Upstate New York on the flat black horizon of the lake. Water, command, guiding points. His mind was shifting to a navigational fancy. Conquest. He thought of Connie, though she was out of the picture. He shouldn't email her, he knew. It wasn't just that she'd turn him down. He'd detect that familiar note of sadness for him, her willing failure to suppress it. When they'd first spent time together, eleven years ago, she was the diligent grad student, his grad student. She was gone and married before they'd had their affair, two Januaries back. A happy-hour drink in a downtown hotel lounge. At some point the lights dimmed in a blunt promotion of intimacy. They ended up in his car, kissing like teenagers. It had come out of nowhere, it seemed, for what else would you call a shared interest in colonial Mexican history. Only later did he see the other mutual factors, marriages failed or failing, their moribund careers. She'd found nothing on the academic job market and now worked as an editor of children's books. At least he'd gained a position before his career had stalled. Now they often stalled right off the line. It was through some sort of conditioning, something in the student–mentor dynamic, that even years later she'd come to him for advice and consolation. In time she understood that his need surpassed hers.

Or maybe, though he didn't like to think of it, she just couldn't be naked anymore with a man twenty-some years her senior.

He'd had this place for ten months when he'd finally persuaded her to come over. He'd wanted her to see it, to see he was free and clear, if not happy. Since then, without even acknowledging the invitations, she'd turned them down. Every few weeks she'd write, the letters weren't even newsy. Mostly she asked about his classes. "Some days when you got going you could change the whole room. All that dead history got up and walked around in front of us. You were the great necromancer. You need to find those days again, Harold." She had always been his champion among students and other faculty, his defender. He had precious few of them, and so forgave her for pretty much anything, even for calling him a necromancer.

She used to check her mail almost hourly. He turned on the desk lamp and tapped out a note – "Come here for a drink. The city's beautiful from my couch. You remember it, don't you?" – and sent it.

If he'd been honest he'd have told her there were ghosts here tonight. All over the papers and the TV was a forensic artist's reconstruction of the face of last week's murder victim, the "dumpster girl," as one paper had settled on calling her. She was the consummate image of the woman who'd inspired his first infidelity. Celina Shey. That had lasted no more than a month, though Marian wouldn't learn of it for years, but it foretold all that was to come.

The silence of his hours here, distracting himself with reading, television, the internet, the phone, cooking – all that was missing was an exercise wheel. He'd bought this place as much for the soundproofing as the view, but it had been a mistake –

he longed for footsteps, music, traffic, any stray notes of ongoingness. Without them he simply lined up tasks and performed them. You could build another day upon the half-awareness of your moving hand.

He opened a bottle of Amarone and started into it in the spirit of wasting a good thing in self-pity. It was now well into what used to be the reading hours. Against his will he turned on the television and flipped back and forth through the channels, finding nothing but the usual bilking operations and fictions to feed a mass idiocy. It was true that the American network news was a sly way of selling cars and bad government, not that he ascribed to conspiracy theories. It infuriated Kim that he so readily accepted her calling him a snob. He liked "snob." The word didn't break down as easily as "elitist."

He kept flipping. Two men fencing with baguettes, a pop star with a navel ring talking about her so-called art. Gene Hackman was on two channels, in different stages of his career. The whole point of the device was to feel a part of the audience, but there was nothing he could stomach.

He checked for email. No messages.

Then the local cable news, and there she was again, the double. How does this work, he wondered, that for two or three days we all walk around with the same picture in our minds, the same bleak facts? The police insist that the unclaimed girl must have had a circle of friends and appeal for someone to come forward.

Did Celina ever think of him? He barely remembered himself from back then, a budding Latin Americanist with some ideas about the Wars of Independence. They'd met in Montreal. He was living with Marian and going to McGill. At a street festival he'd stopped to watch a blind boy playing Italian folk songs on guitar and then there she was, across the crowd. It was a powerful moment of recognition, though he couldn't say who she reminded him of, if anyone. Her features, dark and slightly dramatic against her olive skin, fit perfectly into some still image from his experience. He followed her down the block and managed to come up beside her as she bought gelato. As they ate their treats together there in the street she told him she wrote magazine articles on home furnishings, and he said he was a graduate student, new to the city. She gave him her number unprompted. He told her about Marian and she said it was an old story to her. Years later he tried to explain to Marian this first encounter. In following Celina, chatting, taking the number he'd betrayed her, yes, but he was doing it all against his instincts, even against his desire. What he really wanted to do upon seeing the woman was to turn and go the other way. The recognition, whatever it was, disturbed him, and only a conscious act of will allowed him to confront the disturbance. None of this made sense to Marian – how could it? – who thought he was just revising the past and parsing it in his defence. The short-lived affair was not without pleasure, but the pleasure was always fraught. As he got to know Celina, as she became to him more herself and less the mystery he thought he'd recognized, their passion died.

And yet now, another recognition. Had Celina had a daughter? He imagined the girl growing up, moving to Toronto, dying here on his television.

He'd had two brief affairs during his marriage. Since the divorce, several dates but only two lovers, and only for a few months each. Though Marian and Kim thought of him as a womanizer, he was not, by the modern standard. He was always meeting women who thrilled him, but his attempts to move beyond the talking stage were full of misreadings, misplays, embarrassments. After a while, the attempts came to seem self-punishing.

By the time Connie called he had finished off the Amarone. Early into the conversation she'd begun to cry and he was worried he'd missed something in his drunkenness. It turned out that she and her husband had had to put their dog down the previous afternoon.

"Fourteen years," she said. "Bob's been part of my life longer than you have." It was a second before he surmised that Bob was the dog.

"I'm very sorry, Connie."

"Dog grief is a weird thing."

"Yes. It must be."

Why, in her grief, had she called him? He wondered if this didn't affirm a deep connection between them.

"You can't write me messages like that."

"Like what?"

"You asked if I remembered your loveseat. Meaning what we did on it."

"I don't remember asking that." He tried to recall what he'd written. He thought he'd alluded to other nights looking at the city from rooftop bars. She'd misinterpreted things before. Maybe she wouldn't have been a good academic after all.

"Oh, come on, Harold. You don't have to remind me what happened."

How could he tell her that she would have to remind him? They'd made love there on the couch, and in bed, and in the car once. But he couldn't recall the details of these hours. They'd both been happy, he remembered. He would only remember her body if he saw it again.

"I take it you're not coming for a visit, then."

"You're drunk, aren't you?"

"Yes. I wasn't when I asked you over, though."

"You might not realize that it hurts me to get these messages, but it does. I'm telling you now. So unless you don't mind hurting me, stop them. I don't want to hear from you again. I wish you well, Harold."

She didn't leave him time to respond before she hung up. He was aware that if he'd been sober he'd be in more pain, that the pain he felt was bogus and he couldn't trust it. He'd somehow robbed himself of what would have been a moment of sharp loss, real but manageable. It was more bad luck that he'd missed it.

Unsteadily now he walked to the small couch and pushed it up to the window. He climbed over the arm to take his next position, his head resting on a cushion as he looked out at the city. An airliner hung over the skyline in low gliding profile.

If I was king of the world, he thought. A game he used to play with Kim. If I was king of the world I'd make it go to sleep. I'd utter it into dormancy. I'd shut the place down by fiat. Or maybe I'd say nothing and just pull the plug, casting us into darkness and thought, turning to face our terrors and getting to know them by name, undistracted by noise and duty. All souls but one. One to walk among us as we looked at the sky each night, one to mark who could sleep and who couldn't.

You walk at night, drift through streets. He was down there right now, tucked into the shadow by the steps. Waiting. A few faces and names are with him too, many of them women, lost or deranged or betrayed, one his daughter. For cold seconds it seems she's been mixed up with the lost and it's too late to save her, to separate her from them, and then suddenly it's he himself among them. The fear is absolute. All of the dead must die knowing it.

This time, returning, without the snow, with the wet earth on the air and the city up ahead, she thought: He's still here. I know it. This time she felt the difference between the man she'd imagined and the real thing. The real thing, a mystery she would scream at, and run from or strike if she could. She needed to think about this, this raw force still inside her, but instead she just felt it, in non-thought, and let herself be funnelled into the northern downtown, and she kept driving, hearing herself breathing deeply now, in the quick mud and vapour of memory.

The sublet tenants had left the place intact. Marian had asked her to move home – they missed each other and admitted that even the old mother–daughter tensions would feel reassuring – and so she gave her notice and set about collecting boxes from the stores along Bloor Street, as she'd done before. Counting every chair, she was in possession of eleven pieces of furniture, and three could be returned to the curb, where she'd found them a year ago. The rest would end up in her mother's storage garage until it became too much to live at home again, or until she decided what to do with her life.

Eight days before her phone was to be disconnected she made enquiries about yoga classes, which it turned out she couldn't afford. She dug out notes she'd once compiled for a documentary she wanted to make about a local group home for Liberians who'd had their hands hacked off, and then she put them away again. The Liberians had long ago dispersed.

On her daily transits she made a point of stopping to touch leaves and flowers. She looked a little mad, she supposed, stooping to rub and smell in every second wild garden.

She watched TV and changed channels, forgot what she was watching and then discovered it again, a heist movie, a documentary on mountain apes, and allowed herself to be reabsorbed for two minutes and forget what she'd seen up the dial along some other invisible band in the air. Her sleep patterns began to grow random again. She nodded off mostly in a fetal slouch in an armchair with the quipping bad guys and the apes. She saw the same smoking rubble on three channels, the same victims in the same hospital beds. In a few hours would be the same funeral processions.

At one point it occurred to her that vast uncertainty was a form of knowing. It was a thought she could not get past.

She could go back to the forest and lake, the long thoughts and sure rhythms, or she could hang on and see what became of her.

Having already packed her clocks, she lay in unmeasured quiet every night amid her boxes and the scent of dead candles. In the mornings she sat on her mattress, writing the old way, by hand.

One day she landed in the pissy little food court of the Starr Inn, a hotel that doubled as a way station for deportees, a two-storey cube on Airport Road, facing an Air Canada hangar. It was the last building that jets passed over before touching down on one of the north runways. There she was, watching very young security officers in grey, distinctively ugly sweaters with epaulettes eat doughnuts and pizza slices. At another table a woman and three children – they looked maybe Thai – were bent over the chore of wrapping a package. They would be here to give something to a detainee, for the detainee's use, or maybe for family back home. The woman had given each child a specific task, holding folds, pulling tape, applying it, and Kim wondered if she was worried what to do with them when the package was finally sealed. When the woman saw her looking, Kim smiled at her, and the woman studied her briefly as if she should know her, and then went back to the package.

She'd driven up with Greg. She'd sent a note that she was back and an hour later he'd written from his wireless, "how about a run up? i'll be by in 10 to see if youre there." She used to accompany him for no reason, it was just an excuse to be together in the days when it seemed there were possibilities for them. They'd be shooting along the expressway and someone's life might be at stake and yet for minutes at a time her thoughts ran only between herself and Greg, plying back and forth between exhaustion and desire. Today there was neither, only his kindness at having asked and her sitting there in a small pocket of difference. He had emailed once after the attack to say he was thinking of her, but now didn't even ask how she was. They just sort of skipped the dumb-question phase.

Greg was inside with Robert Plaia. Robert inspired complicated feelings. He volunteered in a program helping victims of torture, but Greg suspected him of abusing the woman he lived with. A few hours ago he'd been detained for reasons unknown. Robert's sponsor had called Greg. "If his sponsor had been at the mall I might never have known. It's happened that people get deported before their lawyer knows they've been detained." It had happened that the lawyer knew and didn't show, that he fell asleep during the hearing, that he confused one client with another and defended himself by complaining about the names. Kim had heard all the stories. She wondered how many of the lawyers had once been like Greg and then been broken by frustration until they simply pulled their emotional investments.

There was a weight to Greg. She felt the pull exerted on her by his mass and solemn conviction. He was not without wit, but any little joke never rose beyond its rightful place, never fully inhabited him. Whatever the opposite of a belly laugher would be, she thought, that was Greg. And yet he enjoyed being social. One winter night the GROUND volunteers had been invited to one of the home screenings in his condo. Kim told herself not to arrive early, but did anyway, and found herself reading book titles while he prepared finger foods in the kitchen and asked about her abandoned studies and basically where she was going in life. In the twenty or so minutes before the others arrived, she managed to make no real impression at all.

The movie that night had been French. Catherine Deneuve as a philosophy professor who gets caught up in a criminal underworld. Some of the criminals were French, some North African or Arab, and there was an ugly, snivelling little boy of the kind never admitted into American films. In one scene a suicidal young woman ate glass. At the end of it, with the credits rolling, Greg had left the room, had seemed to need to leave the room. She took her empty wine goblet to the kitchen and found him looking out a window. She said nothing. He turned. Then they said nothing together – it wasn't like he was weeping or anything, he just needed to be alone, she guessed – and she left him there. But she made a note to herself right then to remember that moment, that fact, that a solid man who spent his days mucking around in real human misery and the occasional triumph could still be flattened by French cinema.

When Greg appeared, when they were back in his Protégé and moving, she learned that Robert would get a hearing.

"Good," she said.

"If we were in his country, he'd be the enemy."

"We don't get to pick and choose. That's the government's job."

"Of course we pick and choose. But just because a man's an asshole we can't stand by and let him be shipped off to his death."

"We can if he's a war criminal or terrorist. Each case on –"

"Its merits, yes. But sometimes there are no merits. And sometimes you can only make them out if you peer into the dark and kind of use your imagination."

They were only ever together in the service of this higher thing, tossed together by global forces, if you thought about it, which allowed them to share confidences, though not personal ones. Before the attack there had been something sexual in their connection – she hadn't imagined it – but she couldn't read him well enough because he was on an established course professionally, and he was older than any man she'd gone dreamy about, in his early forties, she thought, and what did she really know about such men. And now there was the problem of what had happened, and who she was these days. But then he seemed to know (how had he conveyed this?) who she was now, or that she wasn't.

She wasn't dreamy anymore.

He tapped his cellphone and handed it to her. In the little blue window, up came a photo of a photo of a country scene. Four teen girls in white dresses and plaited straw bracelets in the back of a very old pickup truck on a dirt road with furrowed fields in all directions.

"It's hanging in a gallery on Queen West this very minute. We should see it together sometime. I don't know when 'cause my life's sideways at the moment."

"And mine's upside down."

An accidentally suggestive pause. She wondered if he was picturing them sideways and upside down, and she went a little cold. She looked at the faces of the girls in the picture, four captured infinities, so beautiful she thought she might cry.

When they were on her street – he'd driven her home before but had never been inside – he pulled over and she realized that everything about them was between categories. She almost reached over to squeeze his arm before she got out, but didn't, and then just leaned back in and smiled but didn't say thank you and closed the door. When she made it into the entranceway he was still sitting there, looking straight ahead.

By evening she still hadn't settled into her space. Her thoughts were skipping again, from the home-theatre seats in Greg's condo to the planetarium chairs she used to love as a girl and the radio sound of voices at her shoulder at the museum to the cellphone in the car, the picture disappearing into streaming blue words with the time at the tail. Then she thought of Greg and felt, briefly, what she felt. Her desires now all died in the hand.

The beginning was still out there, somewhere earlier in time. Of course it was. She imagined it all began centuries ago, continents away, during the religious wars or a plague or in a sandstone cave lit by torches, with an ibex painted on a rock wall. All beginnings were arbitrary, yet she believed in something like a knowable first cause, one that began in her, or that she'd witnessed, was some part of.

There was no hope of finding the cause in the replayed hours and days, but she did still find herself looking for mistakes, misperceptions, an inattentiveness with which she could accuse herself. The mistakes were there – she hadn't looked after herself, hadn't slept enough, hadn't obeyed her intuition to avoid the dark street – but the self-blame was thin. And so she began retracing the long arc of her life, and the lives of others, and things like chance and the city itself, the zones where lives collided. And then there she was, on the long-ago June weekend. She was thirteen years old. Though she didn't yet know it, Harold was conducting her along what would be the last of their Saturday-morning walks.

As a tradition the Saturday walk had begun three summers earlier, and each year they made it farther from home, sometimes walking back, sometimes taking the subway and then trekking uphill to their neighbourhood. The conversations ran as did the morning itself, inevitable, full of pattern and variation. Typically they argued over whether to plan the route. Harold liked to have it set out – it was a matter of time management, he didn't want to lose the day's work – but Kim preferred the possibility of improvisation. At some point she'd strike upon some inefficiency, a new street or a schoolyard to cut across in the wrong direction, and she would get her way. Both directions along the route they made stops, to buy ice cream or find a park bench to rest on as the heat built and the day entered its swerve.

In this last summer they were accompanied by family tensions and the half-formed theories that Kim would have evolved over the week, gathering what she could from each fight between her parents, each chill silence. In her theories, Harold was the culprit. Kim's anger towards him had only recently started to surface. She had interrupted an argument ostensibly about, of all things, whether Marian had parked the car too far from the curb. Kim walked through the middle of the debate and looked out the front window at the car hunched in more or less its usual spot. She then turned and, in the lull brought on by her presence, asked Harold why he was being so stupid. He told her not to get involved. The next day she told him she didn't want to go on any more walks. That it was her mother who asked her to continue them did nothing to promote Harold's standing.

The last walk followed upon a week in which Kim had heard too much. Outwardly the fight this time had been about a vacation. Harold was spending an upcoming week in Guatemala, chairing a panel. As had been their habit in the past, Marian wanted him to take her and Kim along. Harold had said it was too dangerous, they'd spend the whole time in the hotel. At some point, with Kim in her room, hearing it all, Harold said, "Some countries are just off-limits," and Marian responded, "At least you could tell me her name." That was the end of the discussion. Harold left the house and didn't return until after Kim had gone to bed.

The walk now admitted none of this. Kim had little to say. Harold commented on the late-summer gardens. Eventually they ended up a little farther west than usual, and Harold suggested they take a break at Christie Pits, a park with playing fields, twentysome blocks cut out of the city before the First World War. They sat in the shade of a maple, atop the eastern slope, looking down at the mix of roil and formal play, the baseball diamond in the northeast corner, with boys about her age, in their early teens, going through their motions in turn, peering for signs, following long-established codes she knew nor cared nothing about. Beyond the outfield fence and below them was an improvised soccer field, with men young and old, half with their shirts off, shouting to one another in Portuguese. Far across the park, the huge, teeming swimming pool – they had never been swimming together, she and her father, not even on beaches. And to the south, wanderers, dogs, cyclists, and more young men in groups, some with their shirts off.

"There was a race riot here once. Do you know about it?"

She did not.

"In 1933. On the one side, down there" – he pointed below them – "were working-class Jews and Italians, and on the other" – on the north end – "were Anglo-Protestants waving swastikas. It got nasty, of course."

Kim had trouble picturing the riot against the spectacle of the city playing out below them.

"The riot tells us one thing about Toronto, and so does the fact that sixty years later there's still not a plaque to commemorate it."

"But it's pretty today."

"Yes. Yes, it is."

A few young Latino men appeared on the sidelines of the soccer game, waiting to join in. One of them saw her. Then they all did.

"Those boys, slouching, dressing like clowns. Playing fools. Never play dumb, Kim. It's too easy. It makes us blind in the end. The whole world plays dumb and it's in trouble."

She thought he was about to dispense another lesson but he said nothing more, presumably lost in thought about the whole world in trouble.

One of the young men separated himself from the others and started up the slope. He wore a short-sleeved, checkered shirt with a collar and baggy jeans. It was hard to see how he'd play soccer in them. He came up to them and stood a few steps down the hill, at the level of their folded knees, and addressed Kim as if Harold weren't there.

"You want to come play?"

"No, thanks." She smiled. There was something tattooed on his forearm.

"We're not very good."

— I'd be worse, she said.

— Hah! You speak Spanish –

"She's not interested."

The boy laughed but kept his eyes on Kim.

— Does he speak Spanish?

— I speak it better than you do, Harold said. Now clear off.

There was a moment when Kim wasn't sure what the boy would do, when the boy himself didn't seem sure, and then he laughed again.

"You come back alone and play sometime."

He made an exaggerated swing of his leg and pivoted and took one long stride downward, then trotted back to his friends.

"You didn't have to be rude."

She turned. There was something wrong with her father. He was sitting as before, hugging his knees, looking at the grass falling away in front of him. But there was now an unblinking, unresponsive stillness, and the shade on his face had turned a kind of grey-green that didn't look right. He was far away again. Then very suddenly, he wasn't.

"You never come back here, do you understand?"

She had missed something.

"Come on, Dad. Let's go."

"Listen to me. Promise me you won't come back. You stay away from those boys."

"Why?"

"Because I said so, first of all. And because those boys, that tattoo he had is a gang marking. He's Salvadoran. We're getting some dark characters washing up here because of the mess in mid-hemisphere. And they might look like others of us, but they're not."

She looked down at them. They were smoking, watching the game, waiting their turns to play.

"Yes, let's go."

They crossed the street to a variety store and got provisions for the walk home. Harold bought a coffee, Kim an ice cream bar, her second of the morning. She insisted she buy her own snack from her weekly allowance, and when she left the store, he was waiting for her outside in what was now the high sun. He looked at her directly, a rare occurrence, then looked away. When they were in stride he said, "Your mother and I have something to tell you," and it was as if he thought her mother was there with them, and Kim knew then what it was. For a moment it seemed possible to save them if she could only keep free of the news, from the saying of it.

They had drawn even with a pedestrian alley and as they passed it someone spoke to them.

"My friend."

It was the Salvadoran boy. He was just standing there behind the convenience store, with nothing in his hands, not even a cigarette, facing them, as if he'd come a long way to do so.

"Keep walking," Harold told her.

"You scared of me, man?"

Kim looked at Harold and he took her arm and began away.

"You hold her like she's your fuck. Is she your young fuck?"

Kim no longer wanted to look at the boy, no longer thought of him as a boy, as anything but whatever her father called him. But Harold had stopped walking and she didn't know where to look, so she looked down.

The boy laughed and in its odd melody she was struck to know the character of her father, the physical fact of him. His presence was voice, not movement. Despite which, she thought he would run, go after the boy, but not catch him, or, if the boy didn't run, maybe step close and shout – he'd been stern already. And so when Harold took her arm again, and led her back into motion, she understood in that flash of the unexpected, that in the guise of knowing best, of steering her clear, he was actually steering himself clear. And it worked for both of them. Other than offering a last, trailing laugh, the boy was no further trouble.

Later that afternoon Marian had summoned her and she walked right through the living room – there was Harold, knotted into his favourite chair, looking at her as if to his executioner – and out of the house, ruining their scene. She left in injury, to injure, and walked, crying on and off, all the way to the lake and back, so that by the time she returned and Marian embraced her, she had missed her father's actual leaving.

He'd left a handwritten page for her, tucked into the book Marian had given her, *The Golden Notebook*, face down on her night table. He mustn't have wanted Marian to know about the letter. She didn't even pick the book up for two days – it wouldn't have occurred to him that she'd be too upset to read – but then from under the covers she reached for it and the folded page dislodged itself and a corner nodded out. She plucked it free. Upon seeing the script, a mix of writing and printing, she realized that he'd never before written to her, that she'd seen his handwriting but had never felt the address of it. The letter kept halting her with words and phrases she didn't know, and their effect was only to remind her that her father had never really known how to talk to her, or who she was. He wrote of the need "to absent" himself and of "the perplex of life" and "at least not having had to suffer the politesse of a carefully maintained lie. But it has not been a sham marriage, Kim. I love your mother, no matter how she feels about me. I love her more than anyone (except you)."

The parentheses braced an afterthought. She knew it at once. Not that he didn't love her – he did – but that he couldn't long hold his love for her in mind. Somehow, having thought to write to her, he then forgot her in the act. And yet for weeks the letter was all she had. There was no contact. Not even Marian could tell her where he was. It had been Kim's first experience of grief, the first time someone had been lost to her, made all the more senseless because he'd chosen it. So that even if he were to return, it could only be as a fetch of himself. He would never again make sense to her and even the sense that had been, even what she thought she knew of him – that he got in the way of his heart, that though he was a womanizer or ladykiller (Kim had guessed at the facts and could find only the cheap words), Marian understood something about him that led her to forgive him and go on loving him – even that past Harold no longer seemed true. Upon leaving he took with him not only what might have been, but what had been. Even her body didn't feel her own. She marvelled that any of them, in all ways lost, could stand upright and walk, and for weekends at a time she barely did so, staying in her room, mostly in bed, reading.

Finally, Marian proposed that Kim attend a gymnastics camp in Ottawa the week before school resumed. She said the camp would get Kim's "focus" back, and allow them both a vacation. Marian herself was thinking about a few days in New York. After some argument, Kim agreed to go – she would quit the sport that year – billeting with the family of a local gymnast, a four-and-a-half-foot-tall tumbler whose single topic of conversation was her beam routine. And Marian decided against New York, travelling instead to Guatemala to look for her husband. She didn't find him. He hadn't attended the conference, despite appearing on the program. When she and Kim were both back home, Marian spoke of Guatemala, of fabrics and music, and Kim felt an odd connection to the country for her mother's experiences there, and for its being another place where Harold had failed to appear.

Marian told her of a hike up a volcano on which she'd almost been trapped by hot lava and had been led to safety by mongrel dogs.

"Those dogs got me out of some big trouble," she said, and Kim, to the surprise of them both, announced that she hated her father. Even as she said it, calmly, she knew that "hate" was the wrong word for the resentment she felt at being awash with a spoiled love for him, but all she could manage was the one inexact syllable. Marian put her hand on the back of Kim's neck and said maybe she should have brought the mongrels back with her.

Harold had met Father André Rowe three winters ago during a badly attended lecture series called Religion and the New Theocratic Age at which they'd both delivered papers. Of the priest's address – the first in the series – he recalled only its violent imagery of a "disarticulated church," and the holy word itself ripped limb from limb by the forces of cynical liberalism and reactionary conservatism. Listening to him, Harold had thought the man had no real command of anything, and was barely in control of his passions. But over the weeks, as the group members got to know one another during the informal discussion sessions, all of them lining up at the coffee urn and then angling their chairs into a sort of parliament, he came to think of Father André as the most valuable participant, the one among them who coaxed them from their turfs, translated the terms now and then, and kept things peaceable even as he challenged arguments and core beliefs. By the end of the semester, Harold had had to admit to himself his own academic hubris.

One night they'd walked together out of the college and across the campus with the city lights holding above them in low winter clouds. They'd been trading views of the evening's lecture, a sociologist's work-in-progress on the local adaptations of conservative Islam in European cities. Harold wanted them to get past the subject so that the conversation might move at random. The impulse was familiar to him from his relations with certain especially smart women, a need to be close to the power and authority of a truly other mind. On most days he believed that over his life of observation and thought he'd come to know how to see things. Yet every now and then, it seemed he'd collected nothing but prejudices and a few disguises for them. As they moved single file in the snow onto the packed path that cut across the field, the priest had kept finding new implications in the sociologist's work, kept asking Harold for an historian's assessment and then using it to open other levels of inquiry. Finally Harold stepped into a pause and asked him how a man who spent his day with the unfortunate had the energy or even the inclination to spend his evenings with people whose devotions must seem so removed from the front lines. "I like most academics," said Father André. "They commit to their enthusiasms, as we all should, with mind, body, and spirit." Harold said he wasn't sure that described many of his colleagues, or himself. "It describes you. I know it when I see it." The comment surprised Harold into speechlessness. He had come to value it out of proportion.

They'd had little contact in the past two years. Before he'd called him yesterday to arrange a meeting, Harold had hunted up the online course calendar and found Father André there on Tuesday nights teaching Time and Ritual in Christian Doctrine. The posted reading list would look pretty daunting to an undergraduate, Harold knew, but he'd have better students because of it. They arranged to meet at noon in a café near campus. The view from their table was of southbound streetcars emerging from the underground, and northbound ones disappearing into the station.

"I read your book on Central American Protestantism." The man's faded white short-sleeved shirt was tucked in too far in the back. It gave the impression he was straining at the collar.

"So there's two of us."

"I'm not in a position to evaluate the scholarship, but it has an authority. It seems rigorous and well argued."

"Thank you. But I'm guessing you don't think it addresses the whole picture."

Father André smiled. His boyish yellow hair clashed with the thick parchment on his arms and face. He looked worn and hardened.

"Your book reads like a smart market analysis. Event X leads to event Y. I don't see why the force of living faith has to be put aside in such studies, or discussed exclusively in terms of material needs and politics and American business models used to sell Pentecostalism to the poor."

"Well. There's the whole chapter on the migration of the spirit, conversion as the movements of people from the country to the city."

"Yes, but that's only a metaphor. There should be room for testaments. It isn't that I don't acknowledge the power of need and politics to shape history. It's that I do, I know it very well, and so I know how people endure their hungers and sufferings and despair."

"You're talking about a kind of social history, or simply documentary history, that I don't do. It's not my particular thing."

"I think it should be part of the practice."

"Well, take it up with the ancients, I guess."

"Oh, I do." He laughed. "I debate daily with the Ancient of Days."

They talked about their courses and students, and the vague sense of the world at large bearing down on them. Father André asked about Marian – she'd been first diagnosed the winter of the lecture series – and Harold gave him the short answer.

"If you'd like to talk about that, I'm certainly your man, Harold."

"Thank you. Thanks. No, actually, I wanted to get together with you because of my daughter, Kim."

Harold hadn't realized he could say anything at all to another about Kim. He wasn't sure, starting into it, that he could tell it fully, but he just kept talking and let the story run where it would.

Kim emerged in the telling as a serious woman full of unrestrained heart, or love, he supposed, and anger, maybe a few notes of spite. She was not always aware of her own motives. You couldn't really know her without watching her carefully, but even then there was something elusive. She had ascetic tendencies that seemed to distance her from her generation. New technologies didn't interest her. She had few amusements. Few friends. She was purposeful but directionless, or at least without professional ambitions. It was not just his fatherly imagination, he stressed, that she was possessed of an enormous power that had no apparent means of expression or becoming, and he was worried this power, an intelligence, a talent, if contained much longer would grow sinister and begin to ruin her.

Then he told the priest about the attack. He had never told anyone about it – either people had heard or they hadn't – and he was surprised at how hard it was. He wanted to leave out the details but found himself describing them. At some point he became aware of himself trying to get the story right, and he thought of how much harder the telling must be for Kim, and his voice began to constrict and he had to leave off.

Father André was sitting back. He'd received it all with an expression of pained but warm understanding. Harold knew the look would stay in his mind and do good there.

"To think of what's loose out here." He shook his head. "I'm sorry, Harold. How can I help?"

Harold had an image of himself, a rodent poking his nose out into the light of the calamitous world. The priest was at home in it. Harold hadn't been for most of his adult life. It was obvious to both of them. But the man respected him. Around Father André Rowe, Harold almost respected himself.

"She used to work with rejected refugee claimants. As you do, or your church does. She volunteered for an organization called GROUND."

"I know it. They do important work."

"But the work made her vulnerable. I'm not saying she was naive, but she told her mother once about never knowing enough at GROUND, never being able to see all the things in play at a given time. The faces, the body language. And in that kind of world, even an ounce of ignorance and you pay the consequences."

"You said the attacker wasn't caught."

"She might have been followed. Which means she was chosen in some way."

"Chosen at random?"

"It might be she was followed from her apartment building. That the attacker waited for her there. That he knew where she lived, and knew her. And the attacker didn't speak English. Neither did most of her clients. And he was dark-skinned, but not black. She works with a lot of Central and South Americans because of her Spanish."

"Is this the police theory?"

"Not exactly."

"Is it her theory?"

"She doesn't want to examine these questions."

The priest met his eye. Harold supposed he was wondering about him as a figure in his daughter's life. Would he ask for the salient facts, for direct admissions? He was sure the man inferred it all at some level anyway.

"Not knowing her myself, Harold, I can say only that her soul must be in a state of turbulence. Next up, I'm afraid, is torment. And as creatures, our signature means of dealing with torment aren't so good. Many are lost to it. Some become habituated, and are lost to that. What your daughter needs is what we all do. She needs peace. And we can only find that in the goodness and strength of others, the people we're closest to."

"A simple enough equation."

"Peace is real. It has force. It spreads."

"Like democracy."

"Don't fail it like that." His tone was calm but dead stern. "Don't try to debase it, or disarm it with irony or politics."

"It's all politics at some level, Father."

"There are things that stand outside of politics. We're made of solitude and endure it through the social. We can draw on others for peace. Not abstractly. Our essential networks are very small. A few people. Mutually supportive. People who value others for their goodness, not their sophistication or wit. People who don't pretend there aren't differences between us, and yet know what it is we share."

"All right. And so you've diagnosed her troubles by seeing mine. I don't strike you as at peace."

"Almost no one does."

Harold tried on a rueful smile. "There's no quick fix for us, is there?"

"You don't feel God is watching over you?"

"Not watching over, no. Just watching."

"At least you feel Him."

"I don't know who I feel."

He was not used to talking like this. It was astonishing, what came out of his mouth.

"Years ago, Harold, when I left the seminary, I confessed to an older priest that I wasn't sure what my job was, going out into the world. He said it was to get people to look beyond whatever it was they most wanted in life, and what they most feared in it. But I think maybe that's all it is. People get into trouble because they can't answer those questions of what they want and what they fear."

"And those, also, are more complicated matters than they might seem."

"They might be. Or they might not. Can you answer them?"

"I don't know."

"You don't know, or you aren't prepared to?"

"Maybe that's what I mean by complicated."

He walked Father André into the subway station and when they shook hands he sensed the man's restraint. Surely he wanted to accuse Harold of a fall from reason. It was comforting to imagine someone with reserves of strength and wisdom.

They would be in touch, they agreed.

"I'd like to meet Kim sometime. Marian, too. And I think we should talk more about all of this."

"Put in a word for me with the Ancient of Days."

"I will." He laughed. "I will if one occurs to me."

The word would be xenophobe, Harold thought, or maybe even racist. Unhinged. Lost. As he made his way back out into the light, he felt exposed, naked as the questions of want and fear. From somewhere long ago, the image of an apartment building entryway – he could smell rot in the damp air – until the here and now, the traffic of people and cars overran the memory. Like the familiar faces and routines of his work, the streets had a way of turning back the tide. A city was like primary text to him, alive in itself and in the ways it returned him to his past readings of it. You could hide inside the play of chance, every block another intersection of raw noise, language and fashion, music and work, cicadas and birds and the wind in the trees, small pockets of local remembered time. Now and then upon some stray reverie he'd discover he wasn't here at all, that one city had reminded him of another.

The best memories were of Marian and Kim in one of their travel summers, as they accompanied him in his researches. Walking with his girls, all over the Americas. The days tended to be too hot, spent indoors, but the evenings were at times like scenes from Toronto in July, if with older buildings and palms and a different spoken music in the air.

He drifted along Bloor and passed by a fruit stand, the prices handwritten on cardboard. The vendor was a small woman. He saw that her hands were scabbed at the knuckles, and he thought of Kim when he'd first seen her in the hospital, bandaged and unspeaking, but holding his hand, and like that his state was upon him again. There was no shelter anywhere. He could no longer be the historian who cleaved to the present tense.

Kim evolved a fantasy and somehow it came true. As with any fantasy she left the edges fuzzy and just lived it one moment to the next, or more like she skipped along just the high moments and kept going without even thinking she was acting unlike herself, because who was she anyway, so that turning on the cell and making the call seemed to happen even as she packed her laptop and a small suitcase and left her bared apartment, catching a train and a streetcar with her bag like a runaway and getting off and waiting across the street in the window of the café, exactly where she told him she'd be, so that all she had to do was wait for him to collect the message and he'd have to come for her, come along in his car, or come down from the apartment, just as he did, and out the glassy brass doors and across to her, and come in and not even say anything, just lean to give her a hug and then collect her bag and take her by the arm and so on, saying nothing until they were inside, when he sat her down and told her he was going to make tea.

It was all through her still, she told him, whatever you call it, the mix of emotions.

What she needed was his presence. The physical fact of him, standing, walking, handing her things, resolving sameness and difference into one named being.

She stayed with him for four days.

Greg came and went. She leafed through his books. Biographies of French film directors. A North American road novel. Popular guides to classical philosophy and quantum mechanics. Every one was jammed up with marginal notes in a shorthand border between the page and the world.

His couch was longer than her bed. There was no awkwardness about who'd sleep where. She'd consider it a mark of her recovery when the awkwardness hit her.

At night she heard things in the walls but in the morning he convinced her she hadn't in variations of the same conversation.

"Concrete walls and floors. Triple the code standard."

She tried to imagine the sound. She described it to him as more creaturely than not. She tried to imagine imagining it.

"This high, you don't have rats," she said.

"No rats or mice or roaches."

"Then it's something otherworldly."

"Too high for rats, too new for ghosts."

Sometimes they spent an hour or more in the same room without talking, then he was gone somewhere. The third afternoon he brought her lunch and stayed for a while making notes at the kitchen table with his briefcase at his feet. The picture of him there inspired her to want to hand-write her journal entry for the day and she hunted around for paper and a pen. In a desk drawer she found dozens of rolls of exposed film.

"So this is none of my business," she said.

She held two in her palm for him to see.

"They're mostly from travels. Over the years."

"Why haven't you developed them?"

She saw him take the thought and put it away.

"I do digital now," he said, as if answering.

She wondered where men like him kept their lives. Some vast white space in the mind.

Every night she badly pretended to help make dinners. He was talented and knew where the pans were. It was the dance that mattered, the brushings past, the leanings across. At one point he moved behind her to get by and put his hands on her hips lightly and paused for a moment and she felt him against her and then they continued their business of cooking and eating, neither embarrassed nor especially distracted, as if his pausing had just been a way of putting things.

At home he liked to wear twill pants or jeans.

They spoke every day about GROUND, their past lives, of his clients. He said they were just regular people with jobs and families. "A little more resourceful than us. And who are we, for that matter? Look at us, the so-called support community. We're mostly white. Educated, middle-class origins. We have names like Greg and Kim. You think we know each other?"

She asked him about the notes in the margins of his books. He said he recorded most interviews on paper and had evolved his own shorthand.

He said, "The only way to get through it all is with short, controlled bursts." It was a while before she realized he was prescribing a way of thinking.

Sometimes he saw codes where they didn't yet exist. GROUND was built as an acronym to fit into some abstruse interchange of short forms. Government agencies, insurgent armies, political regions, student movements, aid organizations, all were known by tags. Even distant sentences that had been reduced by a word or two could be brought back whole with an ease that surprised him, for he wasn't in the habit of recall. He privately thought of "proper identity documents" as PRIDS. The "port-of-entry" was PEN. The "corroboration of identity" was CORROID. "Without the PRIDS the claimant needs CORROID that supports the PEN notes," he said by way of example.

His home theatre had been upgraded since the night of the French movie. It now involved a large plasma screen and a floor with four risers and real moviehouse chairs called red rockers that were bolted in place and leaned back and shot forward so you could scull through the film scene to scene. They sat with a seat between them, watching a Palestinian feature about suicide bombers. Near-documentary-realism. No music. The men spend their last nights with their families, not telling them anything. In the morning they get strapped with explosives that can't be removed. They are driven to a woods –

Greg turned it off.

"Sorry. I can't tonight. Bad choice. You go ahead."

He got up to leave and she reached out and took his hand and they stopped in that position like figures on a silkscreen. He seemed to search for something to say but she tugged and he tugged back, and she let him pull her up out of the red rocker and then they were face to face.

She reached up, leaned in and kissed him. Nothing felt movieish anymore. Then he stepped back.

"Kim, even if you had any idea what you were getting into with me, you aren't in good shape to go through it."

She almost laughed. It had been days. But she knew there'd be lines like this. She thought she'd prepared for them but, standing there, so close, just in the hesitation, she realized he was right.

That night on the couch she imagined what might have been, how she might have traced the length of him through his pants and then turned and taken three steps away and stood waiting with her back to him. And of course he would come to her, and she'd lift her arms up high and let him run his hands over her, along the ribs and hips, and then around. He'd reach under her clothes and hold her breasts, kiss her neck, and one hand would move over her belly and on down. She'd sweep her arms low and behind her now and take hold of the backs of his thighs and pull herself against him as he reached down between her legs, the familiar astonishment, and then he'd be unbuttoning her jeans and on his knees helping her out of them and she'd stand facing him now in blue socks and grey T-shirt.

He'd look up at her, his head slightly tilted to the side like that of a confused hound, waiting for a command.

Hey, you, she'd say . . .

The next day, her last at Greg's place, she sits at his desk, writing. Now and then she looks up at a framed photo of African women hanging clothes on branches in a wind, the white sheets mainsailed on their echoing figures, and something echoes in her, though she doesn't at first know what.

Greg is at work and she is at his desk, and she is on the computer page, standing outside a bright church. Something is about to happen.

Then she has it. It's the sails and the desk, having come together. Above her desk in New York was a print Donald had given her when she left Toronto for her doctoral studies. It looked psychedelic but was mathematical, a so-called burning-ship fractal, with the nested repetitions of nearly the same forms in a kind of endless regression of hulls, masts, and sails. He'd called it "God's thumbprint" and said that it was all the god any rationalist should need.

She's closed the loop in her thoughts. She moves forward.

This time she steps inside the church. Everyone is standing and singing and a man at the front wearing a suit is raising his hands in the air. Kim is the only white person in the room. A young woman about her age near the door sees her and smiles, still singing, and gestures to an empty seat and Kim comes in and stands beside her and the woman takes Kim's hand in hers and raises it up and there's nothing but love in here, she knows, her attacker isn't present, and then suddenly neither is she, and she looks away and then back at the page.

She writes, "He wasn't in the church."

This is pure intuition, not fact, but she's sure of it nevertheless.

She isn't in the church anymore, but past it, and she feels the gaze, and though she's not ready yet to imagine the attack, he is already there. She stops writing but he's in her thoughts and growing, and so to get distance from him she begins a new page. She sees herself walking on a summer evening on a calm residential street, somewhere west of downtown, and as she begins to write the scene, she feels it, the motion of walking, and then suddenly she is someone else – these moments of release into her blood are growing into a dependency – walking without intention for more than an hour and happening by a community centre where a girl he'd known in language school used to work as a cleaner. Her name was Maribel. *R* hadn't seen her in months but they'd been in the same small group of friends who sometimes studied together and went out, though she had a boyfriend back where she came from, some country in Asia he couldn't remember, and had no interest in the clubs. She wasn't pretty when you met her but seemed more so every day. As far as they could communicate she seemed a little smart, a little funny. She had her resident status.

The community centre was an old school. When he went in, the place seemed empty, but he found a class of some sort going on in one room. The man leading it asked if he could help and *R* said no and passed by. Finally down a hallway he found a janitor, a fat man who was maybe Italian, and asked him about Maribel, but the man said he didn't know any Maribel and he knew everyone who worked there. The man was lying to him but there was nothing he could do.

He went out back of the centre and watched men his age and older playing soccer in a park. One side spoke Spanish. The others were mostly Brazilian, he thought. They lived some kind of organized lives, these men, that in the evenings they could be in uniforms playing games. The sides were not especially talented.

Most of the players were no better or worse than he was. They called to one another but otherwise it was quiet. He was the only one watching.

He returned every night to the park and watched. The teams were always different. Once or twice he retrieved a ball but otherwise he remained on the margins. Then one night after the game was over and he had stood to leave, one of the players came nearby and spoke to him in Spanish. He said the league was full but new players could join to replace the injured and he gave him a number to call. He said the new players paid only half price. *R* nodded and took the number and started away, and the man added, "If you can't pay, you just tell the man that Carlos gave you the number." *R* thanked him and left. He knew he'd never return there now and already he missed it.

Kim looks up and sees the women hanging their laundry in the picture, the sheets as sails, and thinks of Africans on ships. If she were to turn her head and look around the apartment or out the window at the city below, she'd see all the things of the world stealing glances at one another. Everything connected. Her attacker has given her this way of seeing, and she hates him for the giving, for the beauty of the gift. It's been forced on her and she will never be free of it. She can't separate the gift from the giver.

He is inside her.

The restaurant was Peruvian. Because it was good, and near the university, Harold had come here a few times for lunches with his graduate students, who'd always felt compelled to order in

Spanish. All except one, Davey Voith, a kid from some small town in New Brunswick. Out of high school he'd travelled to Mexico with what sounded like a Christian cult, though a socially useful one that built houses for the poor. When he came home, he quit the cult for the study of Mexican history. He was sharp, if a bit too trusting, a professional naïf, and without an ounce of pretension. He'd married young, a nursing student. Now he taught in Miami. Harold saw him every March at the annual conference. Davey always had new photos of his kids stored on his laptop, and called them up in bars or lobbies. Little William and Leena, another year older. Their father was still happy, producing good work, and somehow still himself. Except when he was in Davey's company, Harold tended to imagine the young man's life was a brilliantly performed lie.

He'd taken the last empty table in the lattice shade of the patio, and had just ordered wine from a blond waitress whom he recognized when another, a mestizo whom he didn't, came and asked if he was waiting for a woman named Rosemary. A moment later she was leading him back inside the restaurant and up the stairs to the second floor. It was empty. He was led to a window table. There was no sign of Rosemary Yates. She must have called ahead to reserve the spot. It was she who'd suggested the restaurant. Now that he'd been moved to her table, the place seemed more hers than his.

Father André had called last night with the arrangements and a kind of warning. "We work together, of course, but I don't always know what she's up to. I've learned not to ask, actually." He'd described her as "plugged in" to the underground world of illegals. He must have thought this woman could give him some perspective, or counsel him to face his emotions more directly instead of producing a misleading analysis of the events. The subtext was all wrong.

Harold had wondered why Rosemary hadn't called him herself. Now it seemed likely that she'd wanted to prepare an entrance, to appear in voice and body all at once. What a lot of calculation had gone into meeting a stranger. She was probably troubled, untrustworthy, of no use to him. Because she was Anglican, he supposed she was dour.

He ate a piece of bread and allowed himself half the glass of Shiraz. By now she was late, and he was hungry, but if he ate more, he'd drink more, and that was out of the question. He'd forgotten to bring something to read. The new *Times Literary Supplement* was on his desk at home. He'd been keeping up with it ever since they'd given him a generally favourable review for the last book. The reviewer had been a rising cross-disciplinary star from Boston, about Kim's age, whom Harold had never met. The kid had called him on a few points, speculations that the documents didn't quite support. It was a small caveat, but Harold had been unable to dismiss it, and he still periodically sent forth a wish for the reviewer's comeuppance upon some blunder in his own work.

Low Spanish voices up the stairs. He briefly suppressed the urge to turn, but when she was in approach, with the mestizo waitress behind her, he looked up, nodded, and stood to shake her hand.

"Harold Lystrander."

"Hello, Harold."

She didn't bother to say her name as she took his hand with great surety. She looked a bit Irish. Dark hair and dark blue eyes. A full, solid body. A medium-tall woman in her forties, in loose-fitting, flared blue pants and a white blouse.

When he turned to sit back down, he noticed the napkin that had been on his lap was now on the floor. He got to it before the waitress did. She took it from him without speaking and went off to get a fresh one. Rosemary was seated now, waiting for him, somehow taller in her chair than she'd seemed standing, as if propped on all her small advantages.

"I hope this place is fine."

"Yes, I come here myself."

"I thought you might. Father André told me your field is Latin America."

"That's right. Mexico specifically. Or that's where I began my career. As a subject, I mean." He sounded like a fool but couldn't stop himself. "But by now I've written around the lower continent."

"Sounds like sailing," she said. The waitress returned with his new napkin and a sparkling water for Rosemary. "I've already ordered. Go ahead if you're ready. Thanks, Carolina."

The young woman smiled at her. There was some confederacy here that extended beyond waitress and customer.

— What do you recommend today? he asked, in his best South American Spanish.

— The specials are all very good. They're on the board. Someone just thanked me for suggesting the mariscos al quesillo.

There were Castilian notes in her speech.

—You're not from Peru, I think. Is it Colombia? The Paisa region?

The question, which he thought had been innocent, seemed to trouble her.

"What would you like?" she finally asked.

He ordered the sea scallops, in English, and she left in double time.

"Sorry," he said. "I was trying to place her accent."

"Better not to ask where they come from."

"I guess you know her."

She looked at his wineglass. Another calculation, maybe.

"I hear you wrote a book about Protestants."

"Well, Protestantism."

"Right. Of course." Academics and their *isms*, she'd be thinking. She was no doubt gauging his response to the shift in topics.

"It examined so-called evangelical Protestantism in late-twentieth-century Spanish America."

"I must have missed it."

"There wasn't a tour."

Somehow she received the humour without actually smiling. There was no end to her ability to hang him up in speculation. She was very quick, this woman, and self-assured. Yet she'd done no more than enter a room, sit down, and offer some opening pleasantries. Harold decided she must be going through life on guard, owing to some past emotional disaster. She presented, to him at least, as a woman once betrayed.

"Father André told me about your daughter. I'm very sorry."

"Do you know her?"

"We haven't met, no."

"That surprises me. I would think it's a pretty small army."

"I don't have much contact with GROUND."

She looked off across the room for a moment. Carolina was behind the small bar discussing something with a man in a cook's apron. He too looked Latin American. He glanced at Harold and disappeared down the alcove.

"Is it true you take on the hardest cases, the people whom even GROUND turns away?"

"I'm not a judge. I take who I can. It comes down to resources."

"But how do you know they're not dangerous? If GROUND doesn't take them, then by definition they're likely somewhere in the range between dishonest and dangerous."

"GROUND has its mandate. I have mine."

"And what's yours?"

"It's a living mandate. It can't be explained out of context."

A shrill note from out on the street below. They both turned to watch a cyclist flying by blowing warnings with a whistle. People watched. A young Chinese man on the sidewalk looked up at him.

"I work mostly with what are called exclusion cases. People who meet the refugee criteria but aren't admitted for other reasons."

"They must be pretty serious reasons."

"At least one person thinks so. That's all it takes. And we're not so far removed from the days when the prime minister's wife's hairdresser was appointed to be one of these people."

"But I've even gotten Kim to admit that the board gets most of their decisions right."

"But who are they to decide?"

"And who are you to decide?" The sharpness was drawn from old professional debates. He hadn't accessed it in years. "Sorry. I didn't mean to sound accusing."

A tilt of the head made her face more intent.

"I'm accused of something every day. Harbouring criminals, undermining the country, the justice system, the social safety net, the underground helper networks, the church. Almost no one approves of what I do. Even Father André has begun to doubt. So don't bother trying to be delicate with me."

"Okay."

His usual company of academics was full of enthusiasm or cynicism, sometimes both. He wasn't used to those with conviction. It was one reason Kim made so little sense to him.

He said, "I guess I have a theory that I can't dismiss. The attacker wasn't white –"

"There are four or five million people within a short car ride of where your daughter was attacked. The majority of them are not Caucasian."

"But investigations move along profiles. They exclude all the millions but a handful. Maybe a foreigner. Maybe doesn't speak much English, that's what Kim thinks, so a newcomer, and Kim worked with a lot of Latin Americans. And dangerous. Suddenly the pool is very small."

"It doesn't sound to me like you're willing to dismiss your theory."

"I just find no reason to."

Carolina and the man in the apron brought the salads. It wasn't a two-person job. The man took a good look at him this time before they both receded again.

Rosemary said that the people she helped weren't any trouble to anyone. She told him about two who had made something of themselves here, and now helped with her work. He barely nodded.

"Your daughter has suffered, and you too. I'd help you if I could, but I can't."

Harold thought of how Father André had represented her in the warning. Even her friends were wary of her. André had called her "a force of righteousness." Harold felt he'd somehow already given himself away. She had learned something about him, likely even more than he could guess.

"I know perfectly well," Harold said, "that if you were to suspect someone, you'd want proof. You could hardly risk your whole operation without it. And so if there's anyone, you can tell me, and I'll arrange things with the police so that you and your people will be protected."

"I'm not running a resistance movement. There isn't a 'whole operation.' I know it's very hard to accept the randomness of violence. We'd rather that the world made sense somehow, and that's what you're trying to come up with. Sense. Meaning. Sometimes, Harold, there is no meaning."

"I disagree. I think we just have to look harder and smarter, and that's what I'm trying to do. And I think you can help me."

"You aren't taking me at my word."

"And you won't tell me why you harbour murderers and rapists."

Her eyes widened on him. He'd set something in motion now. She recognized a certainty as blind as her own. Until this moment Harold wasn't sure he believed his theory, that the attacker might have come from Rosemary's particular circle of the underground, where she perhaps had met him, or knew others who had. Even if he was wrong, there was no reason she shouldn't ask around.

"You don't know my work. And you have a lurid imagination."

When had he ever posed a real threat to anyone? The power, his demonstration of it in blunt speech, her response to it, made him a little high, and then a little nauseated.

Lunch was difficult but they stayed with it. She told him about her job in the public library system; he described a couple of courses he liked to teach. They said goodbye without much warmth.

On the long walk home, he stopped to sit on a park bench and watch dogs run and wrestle around their dutiful owners, who seemed transfixed by them. Animals move us to wonder, Harold thought, because their seeming and their being are the same, while we live in falseness, from our fashionable shoetops to our mimicking tongues. The best we can hope for is that some brilliant artifice busts us back to the real, and not a bullet or bad luck. He considered taking in the new Matisse exhibit at the AGO. He normally made an outing of his gallery visits but today thought he might just follow his impulse. As if anyone paid attention to the routines of a man like him.

He sat there. A cloud shaped like Ecuador was stalled over the sun. Kim had been harmed. He was getting old and labile.

Not Matisse. Pissarro. The one with a little less mystery, the one with the conquistador's name.

A small mutt in chase of a tennis ball came to a skidding stop in front of him as the ball rolled under the bench. The dog thought Harold was part of the game, apparently. It looked at him with its dumb, cocked head, and when the moment was held, it spoke an aggrieved yelp. Do you long to be understood? Harold thought.

He picked up the ball and tossed it feebly back in the direction of the group. The dog took off running and caught it on the first bounce.

One of the owners waved to him.

The surgeon examined his work and told her she was healing well. She thanked him, as if for a compliment. He was quick, senior. He would die on his feet. The news that she'd not been sleeping well lately seemed to disappoint him but he said nothing. She said she would ask her GP for another round of sleeping pills.

"Are you taking painkillers?"

"Not anymore. But it hurts sometimes. It's one of the things that keeps me awake."

"Think of the pain as a sign of healing."

"But it's not in this case, is it? It's just my leg telling me it's torn to shit."

"I see torn to shit a lot and this isn't it."

He had her walk across the room in her underwear and medi-gown. It didn't occur to him apparently that the problems this presented might not be physical. She walked the way she walked, not limping but with slightly foreshortened steps. She did a slow-motion runway turn and walked back.

He said her step was slightly foreshortened, and told her she'd be better off without the sleeping pills for a while, as if the one gave him a read on the other.

That evening she allowed herself to be summoned to a hotel rooftop bar to see her lapsed friend Shenny. They'd met as undergrads and moved to New York at the same time, sharing a dark apartment at 90th and Broadway for two years while Shenny went to film school and Kim mostly failed to attend graduate classes. After the attack Kim refused visits, but because Shenny had found the sublets for her apartment, whether or not they were friends anymore, Kim owed her the get-together.

Kim arrived first and sat looking down at the museum where she used to work, thinking about her move home. It had seemed a good idea at first but now that it was upon her she had doubts, afraid to be so full of need while living with her mother, so needy herself. They'd each put on their best selves, and little by little, it would wear them out. A flecked thought, invisible when still.

Shenny emerged from the door into the slanted light, tall, Nordic, though she wasn't, talking on her phone, out of cadence with whatever it was supposed to mean, this reunion. Kim stood, they hugged. Soon they had fifteen-dollar glasses of wine before them and Shenny was telling Kim to order something, dinner was on her, and she didn't stop talking, about boyfriends, about work, their undergrad days together, as if staving off any mention of the obvious, any expression of concern, until the food arrived and she looked down at her salmon salad and pronounced it ugly.

"Ugliness is the mother of deception. Ask me how so?"

"How are you, Shenny?"

"I produced a nature show all last year and I've retained nothing but the bluegill sunfish. During mating, the less attractive of the male sunfish hang around the breeding site pretending to be females. They're very good at this, the ugly ones. They fool both sexes, and then, when a real female dumps her eggs in a nest, the ugly sunfish moves in fast to shoot off all the ugly little gametes he can."

"Imposture is a pattern in nature," said Kim. "It's probably worth paying attention to."

"I'll pay attention to fish when they're smart enough to be using me as an analogy. We made the scale of sentience. What have they ever made that I rate so low on?"

Over the next twenty minutes Shenny's phone would not stop ringing. She answered it every time. Kim gathered that the callers wanted something from her, work in fact, and the air was full of false notes. Above the city, a few small ink-bordered clouds diffused the late-evening light. Something in the line of the distant rooftops spoke to a peregrine heart. It was getting late. Kim couldn't go home in the dark.

Finally Shenny made a show of turning off her phone.

"These people calling. They all want this job I'm hereby offering you. I'm working on a history show. We need someone to write commentary for the footage."

It had never been clear to either of them how they became friends. Shenny had always embraced conventional ideas of success. She'd had several boyfriends of the kind that would have been lured by her money or early ascendance, and Shenny herself admitted as much. She'd once described her composition of features as "slightly unpretty." Kim used to remember the comment a little too readily at times.

"The writing comes after the footage?"

"It's the footage people want. Someone edits the images, keeps it balanced – for every tracer bullet there's a naked thigh belonging to a Rockette or a fruit festival queen. We balance bullets and thighs. It's practically mathematical. You're given a cut of the images and a text explaining them. You write the voice-over. The tones are grave to chirpy."

"Why doesn't the person who writes the notes just write the voice-over?"

"Because she's a post-literate, put-upon producer. Who can't help alliterating. Who's only good for captions. You work at home. We deliver the material, you courier it back. It won't take long, maybe two days a week. And you negotiate the salary with me. It's not much but it's more than you used to get in your little guard's uniform, I bet."

"Thanks, but I don't know."

She extracted a DVD from her purse and gave it to Kim.

"This is perfect for you. This pays you to be who you are, a writer who knows history. Take a look and see what you think. Then tell me how much you want. We can agree to boost your credit and salary in a few weeks. You're off at least three days out of five. So you can go back to helping the illiterate foreigners or whatever you have in mind."

Kim searched her friend's face, as if they might once have known one another. If one of them didn't leave soon, their faces would fall apart.

"I don't know how to talk to you about what happened, Kim. I don't have a clue what to say."

On the way to her apartment she caught a streetcar and sat by the open window. She'd stayed out too late. The lights were coming up all around. People on café patios, an old man talking to a vendor of, what, something, wearing an apron. There was music from a window, going by. It sounded Cuban but the lyrics were French. Likely West African, she thought, and simply placing the sound seemed to open her to the next, the *pock* of old men playing bocce in a park. The streetcar passed the length of a wrought-iron fence that separated the grass from an upsloping alley that ran between rows of small garages. There were kids with hockey sticks and a tennis ball that seemed to dance along the halberds.

Somewhere she experienced that moment of delayed awareness that felt familiar but unspecific. Because it was there all at once, the city, she couldn't say exactly when it came to her that she was being followed. She told herself her mind wasn't strong enough to trust, but it was as if the time with Shenny, to whom silence was a threat, had awoken a peril. The feeling didn't attach to any one person, or rather it did, at times, on the walk, on the streetcar, but not to the same person. It was like in a movie when the tail is handed from one follower to the next. The woman in dark glasses to the man with the tight black beard. Now there was a beautiful young man in the back of the streetcar who looked Indian or Pakistani. She'd like to have known whom they thought they were following. She'd like to ask them what they knew, what they saw.

When she turned and pretended to look out the back window, the young man looked right at her and she was stricken. She looked down at her hands, she was shaking. The car stopped for a group of teenagers trying to get on two by two. She could get off now, if only she could stand, but if she moved she'd scream out and so she held on. She looked out at the street and tried to focus on a scene. From inside the building she was staring at, a man appeared with a corn broom, which he dipped in a bucket of soapy water. He began scrubbing the door and then stopped suddenly and went back inside, so that the performance seemed less sanitizing than superstitious, a propitiating ritual. Every doorway has a life with observable rhythms, and now they were moving again, into rank winds, past small, contended spaces and sad, darkening corners and there were no more little thoughts to hold her.

She tried to muster awareness and measure threat.

One stop before hers, the young man got off. He wore a white T-shirt and blue jeans. He lit a cigarette as he walked and didn't look back at her and the streetcar started up again and passed him and she should have felt free but her body and mind were lagging. She looked back at him, into the gloom. The distance between them was growing, but elastic, as if he might suddenly be here with her again, meaning harm, and she wanted the elastic to break, and finally when he turned down a street and was no longer visible, it broke, she could almost hear it, somewhere inside her.

She'd been eating off the same plate for a week.

The message light flashed on the phone in her kitchen. The caller had hung up. Number unavailable.

She closed the blinds and got ready for bed. She inserted the DVD, opened it. The last century appeared before her in five segments. There were notes from Shenny that explained the usual method for writing scripts. The images would be tagged, there would be facts. Kim's job was simply to make sentences that ran in time with the pictures. She would write the sentences and then speak a mock voice-over to see that they fit the clips. This was the method.

She was feeling punchy, a little stupid with fatigue. Surely she should sleep before facing the inconsequence and banality of the words she was expected to find, but she hoped a few minutes in the given sequencing of world events would suppress her imagination somewhat and make for softer dreams.

File number one, "The Modern Age, 1896-1932."

Some clips are silent, some retain their original voice-overs and music. She's seen these images before somewhere. Early flight. Jolson. Mary Pickford – America's first sweetheart was a Canadian from Toronto. Chaplin, the tramp caught in the works.

She begins to speak. She's making this up as she goes, being fed the lines from her own long-ago wasted hours, as if by some unseen host of the popular century. Against the footage her voice is continuous. She wants to say something new but nothing comes.

And then she falls quiet before another familiar image. A man hesitates before going up over the ridge of the trench. He knows he will die, surely, but something sends him over. The camera sends him over. He launches up and without gaining level ground slouches back down into the trench, dead. The shot that killed him is invisible. The bullet must be inferred.

A meeting of leaders –

She reverses the clip to the dead soldier. There is more to say.

"What you're not shown here is a clashing of centuries. The armies had cavalries, they wore breastplates, they communicated on the field by hand signals and flags. And they killed each other with artillery shells, automatic weapons, gas."

She will never fit her words over these images so she runs them over Lloyd George and the factories.

"There were 475 miles of trenches. The scale of death is unimaginable. In one place, at the endless Battle of the Somme, 1,200,000 men died. In 1918 there were 630,000 war widows in France alone."

She's doing this by heart. Donald liked to recite the numbers over dinner and by now they'd nested in her.

"For many, even those who lived on, this was the end of the world," she says. She wants to say that after the war more and more of the world was claimed by illusion, sustained with ever more words and pictures, that no one was up to naked silence, but it's just a feeling she has and she doesn't know how to say it.

The reductiveness is compelling, she is a part of it now, or a greater part of it. This insidious softening of the public record.

"The truth is," she says, "these images, this voice, they don't actually record a thing other than our need to keep our distance. We pretend to know where we are by pretending to know what we've separated ourselves from."

This is not making sense. Here's another line of work she is clearly not cut out for.

She tries again, "There are primary processes in play that we'd all rather not think about."

She skips ahead to the second-last segment and tries to put the "boiled housewife" of the air-conditioning ad into context. The images and slogans stream from the point where mass production meets mass media as lives change moment to moment. She blames climate control on the decline of porches.

She says the name Bikini Atoll and stills on an image of two unidentical grass huts on the beach with the hydrogen pillar offshore ruining the scale. She remembers seeing this film when she was little and asking her mother if the cloud was a trick. It's like a picture left out of her grandmother's illustrated Bible. The New Testament was all sheep and miracles, but in the Old Testament, the skies were different. Even then she'd had the feeling there were things she wasn't old enough to know. And what since then? During her years in New York she'd met a Missouri boy in an East Village club who said his great-uncle had flown on the Enola Gay. This came up in their only conversation. He'd been trying to buy her a drink.

She hates the lack of nuance, the dumb blunt killing impression that the whole century has been staged. Rocket Richard is suspended so that we may have hockey riots in Montreal.

Martin Luther King goes to Washington so that he may be shot in Memphis. There's good footage in the U.S. civil rights years, crowds of screaming crackers, police dogs let loose. A young man thrown up against a black-and-white as Kim anticipates his hand positions on the roof and finds them true. She says nothing. How do we form an expectation about the fall of a hand? It seems every frame predicts the one to follow in the illusion of history's logical sequence. This is only a feeling she gets from the imperfectly preserved footage, but it's also the apparent point.

One thing she notices, despite all the people there are practically no eyes. She finds herself looking for a clear glance into the camera, a moment of contact across the fourth dimension.

De Gaulle gets carried away.

The '68 has an American bias. She says so. "We should ask, where is Prague and the tanks? Where is Paris or Lyon? There should be students and workers in the street." In '69 she says, "The moon shot, you might as well close your eyes."

She closes her eyes until she thinks she hears the phone and goes into the kitchen near the end of the FLQ crisis but the phone is silent and the War Measures Act is invoked. She makes tea and tries not to worry that she won't be able to sleep. She feels herself lapsing into fear and fights it. History is running on in her living room, she's afraid to go back in. It's like she's seen a rat along the baseboard.

She waits for a human shadow to appear in her window but it doesn't show.

She eats a tea biscuit. Wets a rag and cleans the counter. Catches a view of herself in the toaster and goes to the bathroom and washes her face. On her right deltoid, the running dog tattoo that she'd gotten last year, the day after an outing with a guy named Liam from the Falls Road part of Belfast. He'd left her mid-date for another woman he was meeting at midnight. The tattoo was a tribute to her mother and the Guatemalan dogs who'd saved her years ago.

When she finally re-enters there are men capping wells after the first Gulf War. They're covered in oil, their Jolsoned faces making a kind of loop of the recorded century and the past half-hour of her life. The camera, overhead now, dropping into a lush rainforest. She turns off the DVD player and the green turns to snow.

My name is Kim Lystrander. I'm twenty-eight years old. I live in Toronto, where I mostly grew up. My hair is dark brown. I'm a skinny five-foot-four. How much do you need to know? My right breast is a little larger than my left. I like curries and slightly muscular men with a social conscience, though not the strident kind. I tend to be sentimental about animals but I think everyone should be. What else? Do you feel you sort of know me? I read more than most in my generation. I read social histories for pleasure and novels that I don't always understand on every level. Maybe I'm a type, maybe you know the kind. I love my parents. I think it's self-evident that our species is fucked-up and on the whole just innately destructive and cruel. What else? I take comfort in pretending a lot of people will hear this and find it interesting, but knowing that no one actually will. My mother is currently dying. My father is faithful to nothing and no one and so he's alone in the world. I was taught as a girl to collect strange dead words for their anciency but don't anymore. My father is at heart a good man. There's an ugly irregular scar on my left thigh. I speak three languages badly, one about this well. Do you get the picture? Are you waiting for something obscene or incriminating? A summation? Can I round this off somehow? . . . My name is Kim Lystrander.

She's practically crying now. Waiting for the idiot tears, from fear and fatigue. It's dark but the walls are teeming in the screen-light.

"I'm forgetting something," she says. "There's something I know I'm forgetting."

4

The fire had been contained in the kitchen but the water had run through the floor and ruined a basement apartment so small that there was barely room for the three of them to work. The basement required full guttage. The carpets, ceilings, and walls had to be taken out, new drywall put up and painted. The insulation in the outer walls was soaked through and would freeze in the winter and lose its R-value and so had to be replaced. All objects in the kitchen would have to be hand-cleaned of soot, all surfaces on both floors sprayed with fungicide.

The insurance adjuster and Kevin came through and then went upstairs. As long as an inspector or adjuster was on-site the work crew wasn't to talk to one another except about the work, and so they were left with their thoughts, and like the others, he supposed, Rodrigo thought about the end of the job and the next two days off. Though he was too young to do so, he thought often about sleep. And always he thought about women and what they wanted. A few nights ago he'd sat in a booth at a club with some Cuban girls and the one next to him had put her hand on his leg under the table and then slid it up and squeezed him until the thump in the music seemed to come from his ribs while the whole time she and her friends traded stories about men who gave gifts and had money. It was a few minutes before they discovered he had nothing and stopped talking to him, even the one who'd been stroking him. What he wanted was a woman, sexy but not made up, who already had money and wanted to talk, not about herself too much, and not about him, but about the world between them, the city and its seasons or its low forgiving streets that felt narrow and open at once. And this world was right next to the possible world. And they would know not to sleep together right away, because it was different with them, and then in time they would have one another and it would all come at once, the sex and the love, so that they wouldn't want to be apart. They'd take a trip to Niagara Falls where he'd still never been and have a stranger take their picture, and all around would be young people on honeymoons, but he'd make no comment about them, he'd just let her see and think, and then maybe in another few weeks, one afternoon, just after they'd had sex, he'd tell her he loved her and say nothing more, so that she'd ask about their future, and he'd tell her what he hoped for as if it had not come to him in the moment they'd met.

Kevin had now gone off to another site with the adjuster so Luis and Rodrigo went outside for a break. Over the sound of the negative-air machine Matt called out that he'd take his break later. Luis gave Rodrigo a cigarette. They stood in a small backyard. Matt had told them the neighbourhood was Italian and Portuguese, "Wops and Porkchops," he'd said. Of these peoples Rodrigo knew only that because of soccer rivalries if he needed a favour from a Portuguese, he should say he was Brazilian but grew up in Colombia. If he needed something from an Italian he should make it clear he wasn't Brazilian. In this city, understanding the national grudges was like learning another strange tongue.

—These little places, said Luis. He looked out over the yards marked with wire fences. A few lattice trellises with grapes grown over, small gardens with herbs, tomatoes, red climbing roses. Luis pointed at a long, hanging fruit and said the English word for it. "Zucchini." Rodrigo repeated it out of habit.

—We don't want much, do we? Luis asked. A shitty house. With an ugly plant in the garden.

—You'll buy one someday.

—And I'll rent you the basement, huh? And you keep it down with the girls. He smiled. Luis had something to say, Rodrigo could tell, but he hadn't found a way into it yet. Usually you looked at Luis and thought he saw only what was before him, nothing more, nothing less, but now and then he seemed to be seeing something other, as if lost in a thought or the near understanding of a bitter thing he'd always wondered at.

On the drive home that night Luis was silent. He liked to tell Rodrigo he was a brother to him, but he wasn't really. Luis made a little too much of a show of his actions. What he really wanted, Rodrigo thought, was to clear his debt as fast as he could. Rosemary had helped him get his status and now he was paying her back.

They pulled into the parking lot of a mall and drove to the far north side. Matt was there in his truck, talking on a cellphone. Then they all stood at the back of Matt's truck and sorted through the stolen things. Luis got out a blanket and laid it on the tailgate and put a few things on it and wrapped them up and put them behind the seat. A glass bowl. A level. A pair of lock-cutters. Kevin might have known that they took things from the houses now and then, nothing expensive, or that would be missed, but things that might have been lost to fire or water. He didn't yet know that Matt and Luis were stealing from him.

Into downtown now, Luis drove south along Yonge through all the lights of the stores and the people crossing without warning from side to side, the way they did in Cartagena, but this was not Cartagena, not without the horses and tanks, the stone and sky, the deadly troubles. They turned down a smaller street and ran west for a few blocks and pulled over to the curb. Luis reached under his seat and pulled out an open bottle of rum. He took a drink and passed it over and Rodrigo took a drink.

Luis said he wanted to tell Rodrigo something and made him promise not to repeat it. He said that the woman Rodrigo knew as Maria was not his wife but his wife's sister. Her name was Teresa. She was here illegally, but soon she would have a place of her own because Maria would come to live with him. No one knew this except Rosemary, who was arranging things for him.

The story was no surprise to Rodrigo, really, but he wondered what story Teresa had told Rosemary. Maybe she said she'd killed someone, maybe her husband in self-defence. Maybe she'd smuggled drugs to pay for an operation. Rodrigo wished Rosemary wouldn't believe every made-up story because it cheapened his own true one. And yet Maria, or rather Teresa, had always been good to him, and he wanted it all to work out for her too.

Luis talked then about what it was like to live with his wife's sister. Rodrigo had wondered why she let him go out to the clubs and be with other women. There was never any trouble from her, it seemed. Luis said that when he didn't come home at night he used the same excuse that Rodrigo did with Rosemary, that he'd had work, but Teresa knew it wasn't always true, and he felt bad for her and for Maria. But he was a man and what was he to do?

He took another drink.

— Do you know the English word "standing"? It means *posicion* and *prestigio*. All things claim their place by standing there. And here we are, in this huge, empty country. What right does anyone have to move a man off the place he stands on the earth? He shook his head. These fucking Canadians. Fuck them. I used to know a pipefitter from the Amazon named Gerry. When it was a bad day at work, or someone was treated unfairly, Gerry used to do this with his hands.

Luis propped the bottle between his legs and held his hands before him, palm up.

— He'd say, "We live right here. We take something in hand, and fit it one thing to another in the way that makes sense."

He let his hands drop. He passed Rodrigo the bottle and then waited until he had it back before continuing.

— Matt's going to get caught. Kevin might fire all of us, or he might call the police. I can't get arrested any more than you can. They won't find the tools but they could charge me with helping you. You can't work with him anymore, Rodrigo. You need a new job. I'll tell Rosemary when I drop you off.

They said nothing the rest of the drive, and when he got to the house, Rodrigo went straight downstairs and took a shower while Luis and Rosemary talked. When he came out, she came down and said she'd find him another job soon and he nodded and she left him alone.

There was a dirt path through high grasses he used to walk along at home. When he was sixteen his girl would come to meet him and they'd go into the grass and make love. He carried a cheap pistol in his belt for protection because the land was between the territories of three gangs who worked for three drug rivals, though most of the time they just shot at one another from a distance and then sometimes, not often, some boys would be dead.

The grass was high. They could hear people walking out on the road. Her name was Taliana and she asked him to be slow with her. They never talked when they were in the grass. They were in danger and talking could give you away.

It's morning. It's late afternoon. The early light is growing in the room. The room is dark. A young couple in white sheets sleeps in their bed on the floor of the gallery, in high-contrast resolution. The camera there must look down from the ceiling, from where the image here is projected. The room is in Tehran. The gallery is in Toronto. The film is ninety minutes long.

From 2001. It's called *Sleepers*.

Kim could hear the Persian traffic picking up outside their window. The couple hadn't quite moved yet.

Sadaf's friend, a woman named Namjeh, had left her here. She'd greeted her by saying, "Sadaf says you're very Canadian," and Kim had to wonder how she'd been represented. She wondered if Namjeh was one of those to whom Sadaf had lent her story for the Immigration and Refugee Board.

When Kim stepped out of the curtained space into the main gallery, Sadaf was waiting for her and thanked her for agreeing to come. She was all casual elegance. A narrow-waisted shirt jacket and grey pants. Close-toed sandals. The single clip in her hair. All her flourishes were Western. Western or secular or maybe just smart looking, at a good price.

She came forward and kissed Kim on both cheeks, seeming very unlike the woman she'd been. While they walked out and along the street, she even managed small talk, chatting about the neighbourhoods they passed through, a consignment shop, a convenience store advertising dry cleaning and a fax machine, laughing at the remains of a bad parking job, breezing past cops on foot patrol, trying to make sense of a belt of heavy black letters misspelling a title on a rep cinema's marquee, into the roil of Chinatown, where she stopped at every stand in fascination. Kim read into the simple courtesy of these exchanges evidence of conferred mercy. The Sadaf she'd known months ago, the intense, possibly paranoid woman on the run in an open foreign city, this creature had finally been given some rest. As reinventions went, the new Sadaf made less sense for her breezy ordinariness. She was not an ordinary woman. But the transformation was hopeful, and Kim felt a powerful need to be with it, whatever it meant.

The walk was full of invitations to sense. They passed a naked mannequin in a window, a tailor's tape coiled on the sidewalk. They headed to the apartment of a friend of Sadaf's, the open third floor of a huge house on a street fronted by a narrow boulevard. The absent friend was never named. The walls presented an incoherent mix of old snapshots of Namjeh with others in foreign settings, intricate Persian designs without figures, David Milne and Emily Carr posters, and framed texts in three or four languages. The only one in English was untitled. Kim couldn't tell whether it was a stanza or complete in itself:

Now, what shall we call this new sort of gazing-house
that has opened in our town where people sit
quietly and pour out their glancing
like light, like answering?

They sat on a back deck overlooking a long yard – every house had one, as did the houses on the next street. Taken together, the mostly unfenced yards made you think you were miles away. Old maples, sculpted gardens, grape trellises, juncos and house sparrows. They looked over the quiet scene, drinking herbal tea.

She learned that Namjeh owned the gallery and carried most of the rent in the downtown apartment the two women shared. Was it friendship or economic need that brought them together? Sexual orientation? Why weren't they sharing tea at the women's apartment? She tried to remember what she knew about lesbianism and Islamic cultures. Nothing came to mind.

She asked about the poem. Sadaf smiled.

"My friend put up this poem for English visitors. The Sufi mystic Rumi, from the thirteen century. The English know Rumi from Madonna. She knows about the whole world." Sadaf laughed at Madonna. Kim had never seen her laugh.

And her English ran truer, Kim thought. Even her physical bearing had changed to something looser, more articulate. Kim had tried to rehearse her main questions but didn't know how to begin into them. How do you think about . . . ? What have you lost? Have you always carried . . . ? When if ever did you stop feeling isolated by memory? Do you allow yourself to form such questions? Do you think a woman loses something even in asking them?

Sadaf asked Kim if she was still working at GROUND and the museum. She said only no and fell silent. Sadaf looked at her directly, briefly, and then continued speaking about her own life over the past months, the places she'd lived, the jobs she'd had, her friendship with Namjeh, the politics at home, the streak of conservatism in secular Iran, a kind woman who'd given her skirts of her own making.

"You're not in hiding anymore. Do you still feel you're in danger?"

"Hiding and danger go together. I disappear from the trouble when I have my real life. When I walk around. When I have the work at the gallery. No one looks for me in the gallery. No one pays attention."

Yes they do, Kim thought. Sadaf was someone you noticed, no matter what clothes she wore or which room she was in. But she looked worldly, not illegal. Her cosmopolitanism was now her disguise. And yet it might also be a difficulty. Most men and women would find her attractive, but the smart ones would be wary. The very fact of her being here meant she knew more about their world than they did about hers. Knowing half the story was enough to keep them away. It was a problem that Kim had thought about in recent months.

"Kim. We come here now so we can talk before tonight, if you want. Me and you. Marlene has said you suffered some event. She did not say the event but I thought you maybe want to talk with me about it."

And so it was out there. She had been configured as the victim now, not Sadaf. And what happened then, in the face of this compassion, had never happened to her before. She decided to say that she had no need to speak about it. That she appreciated

Sadaf's concern, and that she had thought about talking to her, but it was clear now that she was getting past the incident. And she began to say this, and it came out as something else.

She said, "I want my body back."

Sadaf sat still and nodded. The air was intricate. They were part of a repeated design they would never see whole. It had nothing to do with migrations and the new century. It was timeless, re-proved anywhere, on any markable surface.

"I know a woman in Tehran. Many women there, the husbands are drug . . . attic?"

"Addicts."

"Yes." And eye to eye unwavering, shoulders squared to her in a posture of direct address, Sadaf then related the story of this woman. Kim had trouble following it, as if the sheer importance of the lesson to one or both of them interfered with its transmission. The husband was lost to some opiate. The wife fell in love with a woman, apparently without sexual expression. The husband found out. He spread lies about her and had her arrested for adultery and she was imprisoned. Is imprisoned still.

"This story is the same many times. But I know this woman. She says she makes no mistake. If only she could live free. She means a place like here."

Was the point, then, that in time Kim would have her body back because she lived here? Had Sadaf misunderstood her? Was the idea that in the global scheme of enduring losses, hers simply didn't rate?

In purple Persian metaphors Sadaf began to say something about journeys and stars but she couldn't find the English and so let it die away. Just as well, Kim thought.

For the next while they took comfort in solving little problems – where to meet the others, what to bring, how to get through downtown to the lake, which ferry to take to which island. Before long they were crossing the water in an open, quiet light, and Kim stood looking over the rail and feeling herself in the parted surface. The group of them, twelve in all, gathered at Hanlan's Point, grilling wieners and veggie burgers, the downtown imposed across the water. With every docking ferry Kim expected to see Greg. There were rumours of his coming and not until a full hour after they'd assembled did she accept that her ship would not come in. To the extent that she could, she let herself feel relief and disappointment in roughly equal measures. Since her stay at his place they'd exchanged a few short, newsy emails. She wasn't ready for whatever would come next between them, but she wanted to know what it would be, the next thing.

In the group, spread out on the grass inside a rectangle of wildflowers, Kim knew only Sadaf, Namjeh, and Marlene from GROUND. The others were of varying ages and connections. Maybe four were Canadian-born. Kim sat by the portable grill, watching three of them play Frisbee. Two men and a woman in their thirties, all could have been Iranian, terrible players who delighted in their terribleness even as they tried to get it right. Soon they were joined by a young law student who played easily, at half speed without seeming so. He received the disc and threw it all in one motion, with no visible effort. He was thin and strong, the body of a rock climber. Watching him was so far the best part of her day.

The others were managing simultaneous conversations. Namjeh was talking to a pale woman in a floral skirt who said she'd grown up in Manitoba. Namjeh then spoke of her own home province on the Caspian Sea, born into Persian and Turkish, the dialects of Azari and Gilaki. Kim tried to picture a map with the Caspian Sea but it was blank.

To all appearances Marlene was smiling at the lake. Kim could not bring herself to be angry at her for having told Sadaf whatever she had. As always, she had hugged Kim in greeting and said "Dear," nothing more. A motherly hug, not appreciably different than usual. Kim caught her staring once but otherwise Marlene had just given her space, which is how she would have put it. She advised her staff about giving clients space, especially when the news was bad. Kim couldn't escape the sense that Marlene felt she had now crossed to the other side and so made them all vulnerable. There was a degree of magical thinking involved in helping those in trouble, as if it staved off troubles of your own. The fact of her must have shaken the woman.

The downtown sat still, boats tacking by.

"They figure about fifty million unknown species in the oceans," someone said. "Think about it."

At dark now people began to trail away in ones and twos, people she would likely never see again. Marlene squeezed her arm in farewell and said GROUND would always have a place for her. As the others began to leave, Sadaf and Namjeh asked Kim to join them for a walk to the south side of the island. They passed cottages and small homes with their prized reverse angles on the downtown, old factories across the water to the east, the lights along the Spit, and took a path through thick, untended growth that came out on a small beach. They stood in the sand looking west at the lights at the far end of the lake. When Sadaf began speaking in Persian, Kim assumed it was to Namjeh, but on delay Namjeh started up in English, translating, and the two languages together, one coming forth in the lull of the other, though directed at Kim, seemed sprung from some third language more ancient even than the lake lapping at the shore.

"I can't tell you how to live. But no one can live without hope. If you don't know this hope, Kim, you must still believe in it. For me, when I was in prison, every day I would choose a point far ahead. In the distance I imagined. I still do this. The point might be a light, like those across the water, and I can find it anywhere in my thoughts, by day or night, with an instrument of my own making, like an instrument for sailors – she means a sextant – a sextant in the mind. It guides me. It corrects my fears and the deceptions of nonsense and beautiful appearances. What is the instrument in us? You know it already. It is the body, yes. You say you want your body back, it is this point far ahead that you need to find. I must always imagine my way into the next day, the new day. I must never just find myself there. So choose the point and begin towards it. And know that you too are a point on the horizon for your past selves. You are not escaping them but leading them. Soon you are all in a new world."

The women stopped talking, one and then the other. It was Kim's turn to step into the silence but she said nothing. Her faith at the moment was in Sadaf sounding so unlike herself in her own language – on the other side of sufferings and fears, she went on forever, this woman – and the thought that, however foreign-sounding was the sense she'd expressed, there was no simpler, no other way of saying it.

Namjeh had walked off down the shore in the dark.

"What was your point of hope, Sadaf?"

Sadaf hugged herself and turned to Kim.

"It was a person, of course. The most precious one."

The morning light filtered grainy and diffused through the early haze and the Japanese rice-paper screens that Harold used on the west-side windows in lieu of blinds. He went across the room and adjusted them to admit a view of the opposing high-rise. Across from him was the woman he'd named the Lady of Instruments. She sat as always working at a drafting table with a TV on behind her. He had watched her a few times and once had even identified the channel and had gone across the room and turned on the television to the same program so they could each have their backs to the same surface of reassurances resting deep in the defiles of the morning time slots. She liked educational programming, this Lady. And cooking shows, cosmetics. One morning a talk-show guest said, "Women want personal relevance," and she got up from her table and turned it off. That was when she'd noticed him. Walking back from the TV, she'd stopped short, as if having found an intruder, which of course she had. She didn't look long before dropping the blinds. He supposed he wasn't visible to her now, standing farther inside. Every so often the dark hair fell to her left shoulder and she absently replaced it behind her ear to keep the shadows from her paper.

He was not himself so adept at technologies, and had arranged to spend two hours that afternoon with a kid named Drew, learning the digital arts as part of his course prep. He pictured himself sitting there, being tutored by a pimply undergrad, feeling like a Dalmatian staring at a gramophone. He'd collected images from his books and research, postcards bought in Mexico City markets, racist cartoons from old newspapers, stylized maps with mountain peaks and schools of fish drawn into the rivers, church propaganda, anonymous lampoons. The best sequence wasn't necessarily chronological, he decided. Better to counter the headlong linearity of the history with a frame story, and then a few short thematic digressions balanced at intervals in the lecture. Could the new breeds understand temporal frames? Unless a screen lit up somewhere in the lecture hall, they barely knew where to look. The world they were inheriting wasn't his, it was theirs. But they were making it up as they went along. He hoped they'd get lucky, but chances were that in time they'd be trembling at the thunder, and the great fires would take them, like the rest.

The thirty-five-minute walk to his office lately was full of self-rebuke. By his count, along the route were six posters of the dumpster girl, colour photocopies of the approximated face that stabbed him at each passing. The skin was orange, which meant light brown. The features were wide, which meant unpronounced. Police-sketch faces of the missing so often looked the same, like someone dug up from a peat bog, half-familiar, not exactly seen but glimpsed. Yet all the bad art only made this one more itself somehow. Just the picture and the end of her story. No one had yet stepped up to say the name.

The nose was without distinction, meant not to throw anyone off. They would have to be guessing, of course – the girl's face had been torn – but the sketched nose turned out to be exactly that of Celina Shey. How well he remembered her face, one he hadn't seen in thirty-some years. It had found him at a vulnerable moment, full of reflection and regret. The onset of the late period.

At lunch he sat on the patio of the Faculty Club and picked up his cell messages. Marian called with the opinion that Kim was doing well. "Last night we even jousted a little. Whenever you came up in conversation, we took turns defending you.

The defender always lost, of course." Then Kim called to cancel their plans to see a Spanish film that night at the Cinematheque. She gave no reason, but no doubt the reason was her reluctance to be out in the city at night. Or maybe it was the film. Or she wasn't up to fending off more of his questions and theories. They were overtaking him. He knew it but couldn't stop his thoughts. Father André had described a soul in a state of turbulence and then despair, and seeing it – having the knowledge, the privileged perspective – should have saved him. But it wouldn't. He could feel that it wouldn't.

He'd once tried to compliment Kim with the word "undaughterly," but she'd taken it as a criticism. Now she was scared of the dark, and very much his little girl.

On his third glass of a very good Alsatian Pinot Gris he called 411 and got Rosemary's number.

"It's Harold Lystrander. I wonder if you might like to meet again."

The briefest pause.

"I don't know, Harold. I don't have anything more to tell you."

Her voice echoed coldly, as if he'd caught her in the church.

"I just don't want to leave things as we left them. I'd be civil. We could think of it as a social get-together."

"Social."

"It was interesting, our conversation at lunch."

"You mean you don't understand me and it bothers you."

"Let's say I don't understand and I'd like to."

"Well. Honestly."

"Think about it, if you like. Call me back."

She had faith, which meant she had imagination. Both would work in his favour.

"I'll tell you now. I don't think it's a good idea. So I'm sorry but I'll have to say no."

The ambiguity in the invitation should have precluded an outright rejection.

"I guess I shouldn't have called it social."

"Good luck, Harold."

Before him a thin young man in a grey summer suit sprang from his table and to the delight of his colleagues began to dance. He failed again and again to step on a whirling newspaper page in a mulefoot jig with the vortex, a moment of inspired theatre, until the page blew away and Harold saw it drift by and glimpsed the day's tabloid Sunshine Girl in her yellow bikini and like that found himself up against an early memory of bikini girls, from a time of wakeful silences in rooms with his father, of dirty magazines curled into hollow bedposts. He'd been, what, eight years old, making his dad not forty, a widower with his boy in rented rooms across the West. The summer when Harold was old enough to run fast they boosted themselves into boxcars or onto flatbeds to ride hidden in the wide open, each time a great thrill that died fast. His father's one talent was concealment. He could find a dozen places to hide cash in a phone booth, saw every room as a scheme of little hide-aways. He always showed Harold where to find the clip of bills. In case of emergency. In case of drunken accident or absence. His boyhood subsistence was now a mystery. It seemed they'd lived on jerky sticks and the obscurity of their intentions.

Riding in a boxcar like true itinerants or thieves with the door cracked open for light to read a book about a kid with a dog. They hopped off when the train paused for switching on the outskirts of a rail yard and walked into downtown wherever, Leduc, Prince George, from the tracks side of town.

Concealment and deception were skills, even talents. His father hid his poverty from others, Harold hid his shame from his father. Later he hid his origins from girlfriends and professors. But deception was in him, there was no sweating it out through any amount of climbing through classes or ranks.

He had it in him, and he had an eye for it in others. She hadn't simply rejected him. Rosemary was hiding something.

Drew turned out to be a young woman, chirpy and eager to help, and converting and training Luddites was her "lately full-time job." He woke up his computer and got out the images he wanted to use. The idea was to spring this on the students after he'd discussed church and state powers, the *politique* tradition, and the definitions of orthodoxies and heresies. What they always looked forward to – he'd offered this course in alternating years for a decade – was the lecture on physical coercion. They wanted to know about torture, most of them, the Canadian-born ones, and he used their interest to digress into a talk on popular understandings of the Inquisition, then and now. The idea was to make them feel a part of a centuries-old fascination that drove not only the conflicts between natives and Europeans, Catholic and Protestant regimes, and the major faiths of the old world, but popular art from the thirteenth century to Monty Python.

Connie had TA'd this course for him once. After graduating she came to a few lectures, and afterwards they'd meet for a tour of the galleries, arguing over every painting, photo, light box, and film. Those afternoons had been all about desire. It sounded trite, but lovers were like artists, he thought. Desire itself was fundamentally mimetic. It called for an answer. As an act of seeing done by hand, a painting required a virtuosity that he wouldn't claim for himself as a lover, but he did know something of the ways in which the sexual act used to sharpen his perceptions and allow him to forget about the male body in its decades-long deceleration. So it was to be expected, then, that a sexual loneliness, such as he'd fallen into, was attended by a blurring in his apprehension of things, and without the corrective of intimate companionship and the meditative afterstate, he experienced a growing hunger, not only for sex but for something new. He missed his time with Connie at the galleries, standing before some empty scene or still life, some mundane subject. But now, more and more by the hour, he wanted something dramatic, lurid, sensational, whatever it was that the massive fact of the ordinary was held against.

Drew scanned for him three maps of the Americas, made with the early arts of projection, capturing something of the European view of the Americas and their natives. She worked with him on cropping the images to fit them together. She provided a stapled yellow information sheet for him to follow as she stroked and cursored through the commands with her precise fingers. In another time she'd have been a musician, he thought. Maybe she was in this time. High on her left wrist, peeking out from the sleeves of her red brocade tunic, was the lower border of what looked to be a riotous green and black tattoo that extended around her arm. Whenever he saw these things he worried again that Kim might show up one day with Che Guevara gazing up from her neck or bicep. Who knew what she had on her rear end? But there was an incoherence in the surfaces of these young people that he'd given up trying to understand. They were full of confidence and ink. Given the tattoos and her skill at manipulating his images, he wondered if Drew was only a kind of stage name.

She wasn't much of an instructor, it turned out. She moved too quickly, used terms he had no hope of knowing, made no concessions for his stated inability to follow her from window to window, and anticipated the wrong questions. Before long he realized he would just have to let her set it all up, and then make sure he understood how to start the engine and put it in gear. But when they moved from maps to documents to the first drawings of torture wheels and dismemberments, she evinced a sudden distress, and began to fumble with the keys, even though she was looking down at them now more than at the screen, making mistakes and correcting them without comment. He told her that at this point in the lecture he wanted to establish the thematic elements of images of suffering in Western art, from the crucifixion, to Goya, to the World War I sketching of Otto Dix. Central to his lecture was Titian's *The Flaying of Maryssa* in that it allowed him to talk about the attempt to resolve Thinking, Feeling, and Will in a contemplation of suffering.

"That's okay," she said. "I don't need to get it."

"But it's upset you. It's easier to accept if we understand it conceptually."

"Then it's probably better not to know much about it. Whoever painted this –"

"Titian."

"Whatever. He probably didn't do it just to get us all talking." She scanned the image and saved it for him.

It came up onscreen, and he looked at it as she had, as if for the first time. He could think of nothing to say, and then he began to weep.

In his office, with the door closed, he wondered at himself.

There was something powerfully distilled in static images, even when they lied, as if in meeting them we remember something, though the photo is of strangers in a strange place, or the painting is from centuries ago. But then memory is made of stop time. Likeness isn't time-bound.

Everything that mattered, mattered personally. If we were troubled by the pain, everywhere and through time, we'd all be on the floor, fetal, dying of empathy. The perfect world we might aspire to, he decided, would be locked in perfect memory and agony. Only the worst would survive it.

He would not. But then no one was in danger of finding themselves in a perfect world. No doubt he would be done in, as so many were, by the unpursued questions in his life. The particular agony at his end might turn out to be of regret, or self-loathing. If he got lucky, maybe he'd just die suddenly, an old man full of some small satisfaction at the events of his morning, struck down by his heart or a bakery van. He pictured himself lying in a street. It's winter, but a sunny day, not too cold. The police come and perform their duties around the space. He lies in a little heap, then is turned over, confirmed dead. For a second, before he's covered, before the ambulance comes, he is face up, eyes half-open to the sky, and then rising up out of him, not his soul but the questions he's carried the longest, scattered into the world to find other matter, leaving him hollow, light, and alone.

He emailed Drew. He made no mention of his breakdown, but thanked her for her help. "And I think you're right that Titian didn't want to get us all talking about what he'd made, though he did want each of us, alone, to think about it. I'm very sorry that the images disturbed you. It's a good sign for you, at least, that you're capable of being shocked. Hang on to that. Good luck, Drew." Then he sent a note to her superiors at Technical Services, putting in a good word for her, even for her instructional abilities. He lied on her behalf. She had inspired the lie, the good words, and he had no trouble finding them.

Through his window, the world was no fuller or subtler, just a few dead colours and hesitant shades, a little pool of sky on the pavement, the usual distant textured planes.

Before leaving his office he called Kim's detective and left her a message. He heard himself telling her about Rosemary and her dangerous illegals. He heard himself giving up the name, and then the phone number, and he felt a little dirty, a little sick, true to himself.

Then he invented another lie. He said he'd been hearing a rumour. "Some women have gone missing unaccountably, leaving everything they have. No names yet, but I keep hearing about an Eritrean, a Kurd, and a Russian. Then there's the dead girl found in the dumpster, who might be mestizo, it seems from the composite sketch. I'm not saying Kim is necessarily connected, but you can see a pattern. If it can be established that these missing women and the dead girl came through GROUND, then Kim is enfigured into this pattern." It was a strange way to put it – he wished another had come to him. This wasn't a composition problem. "So there might be reason to put more resources into this case."

He sounded strange, even to himself, and he hung up without saying goodbye.

Of course there was a pattern. Men who did what her attacker had done did it again and again. It was all of the violent rhythm of history. There had always been those who would dance to it. Some of them made money from movies and books, exploiting pain they pretended to imagine. Harold thanked god that Kim's name wasn't out there for others to use. If anyone ever hurt her again, he didn't have it in himself not to hurt them back. Of course he didn't. It was no failing. Only pacifist fools thought there were no uses for direct measures. When people identified with groups and formed hatreds for other groups, then yes, violence only led to more thoughtless violence. But on the scale of one and one, a violent act could be expressed and contained. The sins of her father had been visited upon her, and it fell on him to set things right. He imagined coming upon Kim's attacker in a quiet, empty side street, and shooting him once in the belly, standing over him and explaining who he was and what he was redressing, and when he was satisfied that the man understood, administering the coup de grace. The great thinkers and artists would have you believe there'd be consequences to your soul for such an act. But who among them had had their daughter nearly raped and murdered? Who could even truly imagine it? His soul would not be imperilled. His soul would be just fine.

He'd forgotten to tell the detective that there were likely more victims among the illegals, that the killer was preying on women who, if they survived, couldn't go to the police. As would be the case if Kim's attacker was linked to the rejects. It seemed ever more obvious that she might have been targeted through the office itself.

Where to put his thoughts? He looked out at the common, students crossing in all directions. Transit from the Latin *transitus*. To go across or pass over. His scores were lowering lately in these little word-recall tests. The day he failed one, he'd have to quit his job, he supposed, or at least stop drinking. Or see a specialist. Maybe the memory deficits had nothing to do with age. He wasn't hypochondriacal in the least but there was the possibility that a sinister cause might be masked by a benign false one. For a few lethal months, the doctors had thought Marian was suffering from an incipient hernia. Then she wasn't.

Epiphanies were just momentary failures in the seeming of things.

In the evenings, after Donald cleared the dinner dishes and went to his study, she and Marian would stay at the table and talk. They drank and Marian told of her lawyering days as an associate and the succession of unlikely characters she'd helped to defend. In her mother's laughter Kim heard something of the formidable woman she'd been. These were years she'd never talked about with Donald, the early Harold years, full of travels and parties, telepathic witnesses and one-eyed defendants with one-eyed dogs. In the courtroom or out of it, Marian had always been able to argue down charges with style. She could still perform, her dramatic instincts intact, and she came alive now as if in defiance of the cancer and the feeling she would soon disappear. One night she told Kim, "You're the only audience I care about," and Kim didn't know what to say. Seven hours later she found Marian sitting in the dark living room in her emerald nightgown. She switched on the table lamp and her mother turned and looked through her without recognition. Kim said nothing, helped her to her feet and back to bed.

Some days were blind and she didn't want to write. Then the best she could do was read novels and feel herself manipulated for her own pleasure. Nothing predictable. She needed to get lost and feel the author's presence, some gravity bending the light in her, letting him lead her through. Sometimes she cried at the endings like a sap, not always for the characters but because her trust had been rewarded.

And then, strengthened, she sat down again at the small desk in her bedroom and returned to work. She alternated between the two stories, writing her own, then *R*'s, knowing their vectors would meet somewhere up ahead. The writing couldn't yet move her past fear, but added to it a hopefulness or faith that came in the act of braving her interiors page to page. She was putting herself back together. Time alone would not be enough to heal her.

One afternoon storms moved in and lightning was all around. She stopped writing and for just a moment had the urge to go outside and climb into the tall elm and let happen whatever would happen. The thought was not idle, not a girl's fanciful urge, but when she opened the door, and only then, she remembered Marian. She found her looking out the front-room window. In the rain and thunder Kim entered unheard and Marian stood, still thinking she was alone, with her arms crossed, her palms on her elbows, and the heels of her floral slippers slightly off the ground, as if she, too, had the need to lift up into the whirl.

Kim said, "The sky's gone green" just as another bolt sounded over them.

Marian hadn't heard her and hadn't flinched at the booming, but stood as before, so like a ghost that Kim suddenly didn't want to be seen and she turned and everything in the house was wrong, out of time. She went back to her room and closed the door. Even when the storm finally passed, the wrongness held in the appearance of things, every surface slightly miscoloured, as if the portending green had fallen with the sky and suffused all that was with all that would be.

Rosemary was at her old manual typewriter, composing her third letter of the evening, this one to her sister in despair. Her sister was always in despair. Sammy had come to depend on it as the tenor of their mutual lives, both sprung from the same chaos. Last year Rosemary had told her that there was one path to freedom ("and it's not to 'get religion,' as you put it, but to know God"), and that although Sammy had shown strength in accepting professional help, she must surely see by now that doctors and drugs weren't really restorative. "Psychiatrists seem to hold out the illusion that they can unknot us like string," she wrote. "But we're not knotted like string. We're knotted like trees." Sammy had rejected all such characterizations of her distress, because part of her distress involved a fear of diagnosis, figurative or medical. She simply didn't want to know her afflictions, or anyone's. She talked about her life as a "mess" and her "head" as "scrambled," and she lived in a world of dire omens. She was always leaving movies and putting down novels the moment a character developed a cough or suffered a dizzy spell. Her last letter contained the hopeful aside that she was enjoying *Howards*

End and had pushed on through the rough patches ("Mrs. Wilcox does get sick and die, but in Forster's tasteful old-fashioned way, he doesn't specify the illness and doesn't really address it at all and she's dead within pages").

The letter was not coming together. They were never easy, or newsy. Rosemary was not a writer of newsy letters. She wanted things to matter, to have meaning and force. And Sammy, who had no meaning in her life, who had not been granted peace or physical beauty, who had none of the certitude that Rosemary had found in God's dictate, expected as much from her. And so she wrote slowly, composing a structure of words, a consoling architecture built line by line, each one struck once, hard and clean. Sammy always played the tough case, dismissive of her sister's God, and Rosemary had learned not to mention Him anymore. And so it was important that she write prayerfully.

But tonight she was self-conscious. Sometimes her own need for Sammy, her doubt that her sister would ever be free of her dread, made her write with too much intention. She insisted on the reality of saving wonders. She wrote of using pain for wisdom, and the selfless goodness of others for hope; of gaining purchase on her days, and gathering strength to climb out of what Father André called "the morass of pointless anxiety" – but her own language was flat. There was nothing real in it, and certainly nothing of God. You couldn't sit around and wait for inspiration any more than the world could. You had to summon it. Some nights, though, it turned out you hadn't prepared yourself, and the words weren't granted. Those were the nights for the Guinness and Bach.

There wasn't anything in the letter about fire and risk or any of the battle metaphors she herself lived by. Rosemary was a soldier.

She knew the enemy. She wanted to tell Sammy about sly King David, a killer and poet. The great faiths were founded upon blood sacrifice, but she certainly couldn't tell her sister that.

She tried to say something about prayer and doubt. In one of his sermons last winter – there had been ten or eleven people that night, most who'd come in from the cold, some of them drunk, but a better than average turnout – Father André had pointed out that the word "precarious" comes from the same root as "prayer." She'd made a note at the time to save this connection for Sammy. Now she wrote, "Anyone who's really awake (many aren't) lives in doubt. But if they're asked the right way of the right power, prayers are often answered. I know this is true. Please imagine what it means to me to know this."

The conditions were not best for prayer lately. Her A key was sticking. She got her repairs and supplies from an old man who barely had space left for himself in an apartment crammed with wheels and hammers, platens and screws, lettered keys. The place smelled of fresh inky ribbons and grease. His name was Mr. Stubbs. She couldn't see him in there without carrying around the picture of the place for the whole day, this man trying to make repairs in the world he'd made of his mind. When she'd invited him to come to the church, he'd said nothing. He only ever talked about typewriters.

And lately the television made its assaults from the basement all evening. Rodrigo watched with his finger on the mute button, trying to anticipate every shout and siren, but it was hopeless. It seemed that whenever Rosemary passed by the screen with a basket of laundry there was brain matter on a wall or a bullet hole in a dead woman's naked chest. She assumed these were the American shows that were messing up the jury pools down there. Rodrigo just called them "murder shows." He'd seen his first one at sixteen. It might not have seemed to him like make-believe.

Tonight he was in the living room, standing at the front window, looking for Luis like a boy for an older brother. He could simply stare for twenty or thirty minutes at a time, with no book or phone in hand. "The patience of peasants," as an idiot former colleague had called it. A patience often mistaken for blankness. But it was hardly empty. Not in Rodrigo's case. She'd seen this sort of near-violent calm before. Rosemary had been there the day of his Review Board hearing, on one of the tips she got from lawyers sympathetic with her goals. Rodrigo had looked on neutrally as the evidence was presented until, through a translator, his lawyer explained that the details of the drug soldiers' activities, which Rodrigo had acknowledged were accurate, had been put forward not in defence of his claim, but rather against it. The horrors that had sent him running north in the first place now revisited him in the accusation that he was an actor in these atrocities, and he began to fall apart. His face didn't change, it abandoned him. He had had to be wrestled from the hearing room.

"I'm having a drink," she announced. "Would you like one?"

"No, thank you." He turned and looked at her briefly with his thin, hollowed gaze, then turned back and said suddenly, "There is someone watching us."

He moved away from the window. She walked into the room and stood still.

"A man, in the park. I thought there was a man in the shadow and then when I looked again I saw him moving to the tree."

She went forward to the window.

"To the right of the bench. Behind the tree, to the right."

She saw nothing. Either the man had concealed himself or he was gone. Or he'd been imagined. There was a point at which sensible paranoia crossed into illness – she looked for it constantly in herself and her boarders – and this may have been an early warning, she supposed. Whomever Rodrigo had been before he came to Canada, it was Canada that had forced him to imagine himself as a killer. He didn't have to imagine that he was a hunted one.

He retreated to the basement.

There was a movement beyond the tree. A man walking away? The tree obscured him almost perfectly. He was meaningless, this stranger, or else something was wrong and there was nothing she could do about it. And then, suddenly, there he was, just a man lost in thought, waiting patiently for his terrier to piss.

She sipped her stout and contemplated her slight dread of Luis's arrival. He always made a show of arriving. A sustained "hellooo" and a broad smile, a prepared comment on the beauty of her home or the food she'd dropped off. His forced manner saddened her each time. She could hear any number of horror stories and witness killing judgments and actual family-splitting removals, she could feel whole lost lives, but it was the way a new Canadian came through a door that got to her. Just once she'd like him to arrive as a solemn presence, or as whomever he was in the lonely dark.

He knocked his four knocks – tat-tat, tat-tat – and she opened the door. He was wearing a dark red windbreaker over jeans, and cheap canvas runners, as if he'd just been sailing. His looks were often out of place. He'd once appeared in cheap cowboy boots and a western shirt. And tonight he had a prop. He handed her a batch of mondongo, corn soup with tripe. He held out a plastic bowl and she took it.

"Thank Teresa for me."

"You should hide it from Rodrigo." There was the smile.

He stood in the entranceway. If she invited him to come in or sit down, he'd make his excuse – he and Rodrigo were expected somewhere, they were already late – and so she didn't invite him, but turned and walked into the kitchen and put the bowl in the fridge. Then she called down to Rodrigo.

He came up and she told him the man had been no one, walking his dog.

"He thought he saw a man in the park," Rosemary explained to Luis. "He did see one. But it was okay."

Luis hadn't moved. As if his shoes were muddy.

"Maybe the man out there, he's in love with you, Rosemary. He comes with his dog to sing at your window."

He put his hand on his heart and looked up at the ceiling with a face in sweet pain and sang "Oh, my love, Rosemaryyy" and then laughed at himself. Or at her. She wasn't sure.

Rodrigo appeared and went straight to the door. He and Luis never greeted one another. It lent to the impression they were up to something on these nights. Hiding things from her. On the nights they dressed like this, presumably they weren't heading for work but trying to find Rodrigo a woman. There was a dance club the Colombians favoured. She didn't want to know the details.

"Should we leave in the back?" Rodrigo asked. It was only a courtesy to her, to show he was cautious.

"No. It's fine."

"The man hides in the park until we leave," said Luis. "Then he comes to your door with a dog and flowers. He steals them from the park maybe."

"Okay, enough," she said. "You two keep out of trouble. If you get arrested, Rodrigo, no one can help you."

He was busy tying his shoes.

"Did you hear Rosemary?" Luis asked.

"Yes." He stood. "Yes. No troubles."

She had explained the rules when he moved in. He must always have his false ID. He could never be in trouble. He could never be standing nearby it. He could not defend a friend. He could never drive a car. He must always have cash for a subway or taxi. If he was sick or injured, he was to go to this hospital and not that one. He must always know his false name and his story and her address and number. No friends or lovers could ever know his real story, not even Luis, though he likely already did. If he was in trouble, he was to go to the church, not to anyone's home.

Luis left first. Rodrigo paused as he was about to leave, and then turned and approached her. To her astonishment, he embraced her. She hugged him uncertainly, on delay, her head laid against his chest. They had never touched, not once, and now he held her like a grown son. He said nothing and didn't meet her eyes, then left. She went to the window and watched the men walk away.

When her Guinness was gone, Rosemary returned to her letter and found herself writing with new fluency. She told Sammy that despair only proved a depth of heart and a willingness to be open to loss, and that sorrow and loss were not to be feared but accepted, "and then we should put them up on our bedroom shelves like those hippos you used to collect – remember Mr. Boy? – and look at them now and then. But Sammy, you need to celebrate all your feelings, and when you do, you'll find so much to be happy about, there'll be victories, new ones and old ones rediscovered. You can't celebrate triumphs without also accepting loss, or put away your losses without the courage to shout out at your triumphs. And when you least expect it, between the wins and losses, in the calm, you'll see that everything, all of it, is truly amazing."

She didn't want to end there but suddenly she remembered herself, the one who'd received the embrace. She so seldom had reason to think of her physical self. There was little joy to be taken in it, not anymore. Her response hadn't been warm and pure, but complicated and willed. And yet a young man had put his arms around her and either she dismissed the moment and tried to forget it or she took her own advice.

She tried to feel what had been exchanged, but she was not allowed, and so was left with the wish, unsentimental, that she could have felt more. She wished Sammy could feel differently, and she could feel more.

She pictured her sister's troubles lined up on the shelf. Beside them, on the wall, the long-ago school photo of their dead little brother. The sisters lived a thousand miles apart but slept in the same room each night.

When the letter was finished she sealed it and affixed the stamp, and gathered it with the others and left the house. The mailbox was four blocks away. Along the residential streets, people were out walking, or talking and laughing porch to porch. The streetlights spilling on the cars, and teens heading downtown inside the kind of summer night that inspires music and myths and life-altering mistakes.

She opened the box and dropped them away and the door closed with a hollow, metal-muffle sound and, for a moment, she didn't know where she was.

When she got home there was a phone message from a policewoman. She had a few questions and could they meet. Jesus, said Rosemary. She said it again, the name of the Lord, and again, the curse and prayer of it together that received and held her.

Donald and Marian were in bed. Kim wrote them a note and left the house. She took her mother's car, not really sure what she was doing, where she was going, and she drove the tree-lined avenues of her girlhood. She tried to remember who she'd been at fourteen. A girl with three talking parents, living in a pocket of white. She'd loved being in her body, she remembered, a dancer with sore ankles who floated when she walked, a gymnast with bloody chalked palms who could still bend herself expressively and visualize a tumbling run and feel the rhythm of moves and transitions. She missed that. To imagine a thing and then enact it and make it actual and true. It was hard now to know what was true, what to imagine, or how to enact anything. Now she tumbled against her will, out of control. Even a ride through quiet streets shocked her to the bones.

It was her first night out alone since the attack. Undisturbed darkness in her lap. She turned on the radio news and turned it off before three words had formed and she was heading downtown.

Harold had come by in the afternoon and they'd driven to the Beach neighbourhood and strolled on the boardwalk. The scene was busy and dull with occupation. Volleyball, Frisbees, children and dogs at the water line. There were sailboats pressed into the dead blue sky. Harold said the police used to bring people to

Cherry Beach at night to beat them up. He said he wished he had more confidence in cops. "Your cop, do you still think she's any good?" Kim said she liked Cosintino but had no illusions about the investigation. He said, "It's nothing but illusions, Kim," and then, as if regretting the comment, bought her an ice cream cone. Throughout the afternoon, for seconds at a time, he fell silent and a pandemonium played in his eyes. On the way home he was distracted and almost hit a cyclist and then pedestrians getting off a streetcar. He didn't argue when Kim insisted she drive and she took him to his condo and walked home.

Alone now she passed the former dessert place where a girl had been shot dead in a robbery years ago, when this city could be defined by such returns, a time not long past when you could almost remember every unlikely death, murders and subway accidents, the places where famous lawyers and lost kids were last seen, or the buildings and floors and maybe balconies from which toddlers or party guests had fallen, because the place wasn't then yet so violent that the bad news didn't register, that thinking of local sudden deaths was like staring at the rain.

She parked five or six blocks from the attack site, on a safely lit neighbourhood street. The motionlessness was a problem. For long seconds she kept one hand on the ignition before she turned it off, and left the hand there seconds more. She relocked the doors. There was no way she was getting out of the car, but she had done something to come down here and she would sit with it a little longer. She checked her rear- and side-view mirrors and then again, and then realized she wasn't really looking so she looked. Nothing certain, maybe a little movement down the block. She could have parked in the noise and traffic of Bloor but there'd be nothing achieved. So what was she achieving now? The movement became someone on the sidewalk, obscured by parked cars, coming her way. She almost started the car but then waited and it became a couple, a young couple, and they passed by, and before they could get away she got out of the car and followed them.

Weeks ago her old co-workers had emailed a note inviting her to come by one night and "stroll the old joint" with them, and so here she was, now entering the eye of the security camera looking along the south walkway of the Royal Ontario Museum, where Lansford would be able to see her so she waved, and by the time she'd made the door he was already buzzing her in.

He came out of the control room, completely abandoning his post, and didn't think twice about putting his arm around her, and then he was calling Nick on the radio and invited her into the room, a clear violation of protocol, and they talked about this midnight world they always talked about, and about her replacements, who had both gone back to daytime so they were short-staffed again this week, while behind him on the bank of monitors she glimpsed skinny Nick, a songwriter, loping from screen to screen to come say hello, and then there he was and he hug-lifted her right off the ground, and she laughed, and he said he had something to show her.

Lansford fitted her with her old radio and flashlight and then Nick led her in and she felt that moment of release into the building's vast interiors. It was something most people would never know, the great measures in repose, free of life, of school kids and couples, those driven in by heat or cold or loneliness, moving along, knowing what would be there around every corner, the reassurances of same old same old, each foreign treasure in its out-of-place place. Motion detectors caught the passing of anything sentient and reduced to near nothing the possibility of chance encounter. Her being here tonight constituted "a perfect retreat," to use for her own purposes an expression that Donald sometimes deployed.

Nick was describing the ten-foot skeleton of a prehistoric giant sloth. That it was the most impressive item in the museum, that it had been in storage for years and was now in the old rotunda, that he'd seen it long ago, as a student, and in his memory it stood in the exact posture of a 1960s wrestler in one of those publicity shots you could still see through the windows of old barbershops near the Gardens or on the walls of retro diners downtown, slightly crouched, bent arms held forward to suggest full-nelson strike capability.

The real thing, when they came to it, was something else.

"Okay, you don't see Our Lord, you thought He'd be taller, but most of the stuff in here is humanformed. This thing, this gives pause. You feel something like reverence."

Kim was unprepared, how could anyone be prepared? The bones carried ancient time, the dream of an extinct god. Something of a lost creation was foretold in the bare cage and panicle.

"You agree this is truly ball-hiking. Even if you lack that response."

She couldn't look away.

Lansford radioed with a reminder that Nick had under four minutes to get to his next station.

"Fucking Devouring Time," said Nick.

When he was gone she went forward and touched the long femur, if that's what they called it, and ran her hand along, feeling the grade of phosphorus and epoxy. She had the urge to step inside the creature, stand up inside its ribs, become the guts, the life of it. To give herself over and away to a long-lost being like one of the devout.

"You break that thing, you bought it, Kim." Lansford had her on camera. She stepped away and then turned and felt the emptiness in the vaults of her own frame, and started off along her old route. She walked strangely bereft, thinking of her life. She wanted to live freely, not fearlessly but unflinchingly, and yet it seemed likely now that she simply couldn't. Whenever something had to give, it gave in her. She had learned that much, if little else. At some point you had to admit you were alone in the wilds.

Before long she was standing at a Romano-Egyptian display case, trying to focus on the grotesques. Testing herself not to flinch. Seven small human heads, twisted, prognathic, male and female. Two rooms over they showed up as symbols for averting evil, and in the Greeks and Etruscans gallery they appeared as depictions of comic actors and the masks of characters playing the slaves who carried the plot. Then she thought of Harold. His eyes today had looked as if he were seeing grotesques. These were the faces that came to him before sleep.

In the Members' Lounge she reclined on her favourite sofa. To mark their rounds the overnight guards walked to a series of appointed stations and used a key at each one to punch the clocks they carried on their belts. As long as the keys were inserted in the right sequence and in the right time window they were doing their jobs, so the practice was to trot from station to station and manually move the clock hands forward before using the key. In this manner, a two-hour round could be killed in under thirty minutes, and they could nod off now and then with time itself reposited on their hips.

The couch faced a window. In the reflection of headlights streaming both ways along the glass she could sometimes find a state approaching sleep, but more often entered semi-conscious fugues. Her first few nights here she'd used a combination of caffeine pills and oranges to stay awake, but they induced esophagitis and just generally messed her up worse. Nick had told her that years ago, before the planetarium closed, he'd start up a night sky sequence, dial up the southern heavens and take a seat. He liked to imagine himself an ancient mariner. He'd fall asleep tilted back under the nacreous screen. When she was trying to get to sleep, here or at home, she sometimes imagined watching the heavens show. But for planes and satellites, in human terms the sky was now as it had always been. That and the ocean, and a few sublime vistas. Everything else had been humanized, every perceivable thing.

Her dreams now were of textured surfaces, the grey of birchbark or wasp nests, and the moment she understood them to be parchments they bloomed language, characters she didn't know that somehow formed words she did. The parchment began to move until it was water and the words were gone and she was standing in a northern lake, hearing the cry of a loon.

Nick buzzed in.

"Are you ready for this? I've negotiated Paris and I'm standing at Nildate's desk, over."

In the months after his wife had died, an entomologist named Robert Nildate had cleared his office floor and begun the plaster and balsa constructions of miniature replicas of the cores of the great cities of the world. He relied on vacation shots he'd taken with his wife and satellite photographs downloaded from the Net to measure with great accuracy the forkings in Manhattan and the slight meniscus in the fall line of classical pillars in Athens.

"'The two methods for killing' – I'm quoting notes here – 'are cyanide under plaster of paris or ethyl acetate over sawdust, over.'"

"Don't, Nick. Stop."

"He says, 'I prefer cyanide. It's a question of knowing where you stand. With cyanide, if a jar breaks and cuts you, you die. But ethyl acetate kills you through residue on the skin. It can take years.' Unquote. I'm thinking this guy is dangerous, over."

It was the language of torture scenarios. She'd read it almost daily in the literature at GROUND. The lines were declarative shading to clinical. It was the surest sign that Nildate had lost his purchase on reality. She'd once seen Nildate's floor and had never returned. London had the harbour that once belonged to Rio. The Chrysler Building overlooked the Parthenon, and why not? she thought. Cities aren't buildings, they're traffic. They're selected eye contact and the compassing alarms at night and what they set off, the scurrying, the looping guesses at haunchweights. The city is held together by hundreds of thousands of tacit agreements, many forgotten but still in place. The sheer size of things is not to be acknowledged, for instance. The cold terror in the sea depths of personal histories, the millions upon millions of seas. People in their fleeting moments of clarity had full contact with the place, it was that simple, and no one would stand still for what they'd seen if only they could remember it.

The sloth, the grotesques, they'd done a number on her.

Nick radioed Lansford that he was going out for a smoke. They had their own protocol about breaking the rules. Kim got off the couch and pilfered an apple danish from the fridge.

A minute later she was standing over a drinking fountain, eating the danish. She swallowed and listened to her blood sugar. It had a kind of junkie talk of hits and spikes. When the thing was consumed she cleaned up every crumb and washed them down the fountain. She let the spout run thirty seconds longer as if that was enough to bleed out the water that had been sitting in the ancient pipes with their toxic crud, and then she drank and stood again, staring out into the dark guarded spaces.

She still had to get home.

People allowed their creations to bend them out of shape. It turned out that she still believed, in some part of her, that sooner or later you had to trip all the systems you could.

At first he just watched her window, like a lonely creep in the night. The park bench was directly across the street from her door, as if it had been placed there for him. He made no effort to conceal himself. He wouldn't have known how, didn't even own a hat. It was early dark, the lights had just come up along the street and inside now, one by one in the small shuttered windows beside the porch and in the basement. The picture-window curtains were open but the room was dark. At some point he saw someone moving, a dim disturbance, but for the rest of his watching, there was no other motion.

The next evening, though he had promised himself he wouldn't return, he was there again. In the clear evening light the colours of the houses lining this side of the park looked richer, oxygenated, and little by little they darkened. A vague smell of dog piss around the bench added to the sense that he was outside his territory. It felt good to be outside it. Outside his memory, if not his experience. Watching, the risk of being exposed as a watcher, was something he knew.

Now and then you were reminded of your *nature*. That enduring word. It wasn't human nature that troubled him – there was something consoling in common folly – so much as *Harold* nature. There were people, we all knew them, unwitting fools who resisted their foolishness and so made things worse for themselves. And there were others who were just unlucky. He was both foolish and unlucky. His signature instinct upon each revelation of his nature was to make things worse, and to make them worse without much flare as if in the hope he and whoever else was caught up in his mistakes might come to overlook his part in the ruin. There had once been better days, delusional, he now thought, when he had actually believed in something like the incorruptible upper heavens of his soul. He hadn't been able to reach those heavens but now and then on a clear night all the little human worlds, the maddening knowledge of contexts, had left him and he'd found a rare part of himself in art or music, the sprung wonder of laughter. But with age, the little human worlds had multiplied until there was no escaping them and the upper heavens became thin to the eye, no more than a mockery. He was in his post-primitive phase. All he'd brought with him were fears and lusts.

There it was again, the movement, and now coming up in the picture window was a man, looking out, looking at him. He was young and narrow, with dark features, a general impression of concern in his face. There was nothing more to read out of the semi-dark. Harold calculated that some of the lighting elsewhere in the house must have been reflecting in the window, and given that he himself was unlit, the man would have seen him even less distinctly. Then he drew the curtains, the lights came on, and over the next few minutes the man's shadow came and went.

In time, drama was born. A woman's form passed by. Rosemary in her keep. So who was the man? An illegal, in hiding? A young lover? Both? He could have been a son, Harold supposed, but the story there didn't interest him. What interested him was the view of himself as an actor, the idea that he could just leave the audience to be part of the events. He was about to stand, cross a threshold, no longer the shuffler of footnotes, as Kim had called him.

But not tonight.

Two kids passed on bikes, a girl and a boy with the same open face.

He stood, a bit dizzy, and took the path deeper into the park.

She's past the church but leaves herself standing in the moment just after she thought to turn north but then didn't. She's tired of going over the same ground, something she's done not obsessively, but dutifully. There was nothing more to be secured from the night of the assault. The exercise of recall had emptied.

Instead she opens the computer file called "R. doc." It's now twenty-four single-spaced pages, mostly fragments. There are short scenes and half-scenes, descriptions of the city from *R*'s point of view. He lives in a basement somewhere east of the valley. His jobs come and go. He spends much of his time walking but not prowling. Every time she returns to these fragments, *R* seems fuller, realer. She can almost believe he exists.

She's been waiting for a history to reveal itself. His past has been trailing in her blind spot, where he comes from and how he's ended up here, things until now he's suppressed in his thoughts. Even to himself he is half-closed, living hour to hour. But now it comes to her.

He is Colombian.

She's not sure how she knows this, but trusts she'll learn how.

She leaves the house to gather research and returns before dinner with reports from human rights groups, copied pages from three histories of the country, a journalist's memoir, a novel in Spanish, a book of photos. Then she tries to half forget them well enough to reinhabit her character's story, and when she thinks she's ready, she returns to her keyboard and sets about finding him again in her imaginings. It turns out he emerges not as a boy in Colombia but as the man she knows, *R*, who lives in a fictional version of here, a couple of miles away. He is in his basement apartment, watching television. On one channel is a show about wolves in Northern Ontario, on another, a beauty pageant in Italy, and nothing he sees there has anything to do with him, and when he turns the TV off, his mind is full of the whole history of his witnessing, what he's seen first-hand, what he's seen on TV. She feels a great weight for him that his life doesn't register in the world, but he himself seems undisturbed, as if he's had no expectation of being represented to anyone. And of course, she realizes, he wishes never to be noticed, never questioned, except by the woman he hopes is in his future.

When she stops writing it's out of exhaustion. She goes through the house, tidying. She says good night to Marian and Donald. She stands in the kitchen, looks down to find she's holding a glass of pomegranate juice that she can't recall having poured.

Then she goes back to *R*.

It's late. A dark side street. A low creature stiffens its back in the dark.

And here he comes, running.

The next job came through Luis. There were no names or numbers, just an address and a time, and he didn't know the work until he got there. With a sledge and shovel he broke up insulation around furnaces in old downtown houses and then cleaned out the rooms. The boss was Portuguese. The other workers changed every few days. They were mostly white Canadians just out of prison. Rodrigo never got to know them. Everyone wore masks with charcoal filters, so there was no talking. Each worker had only two masks a day, so you sucked as hard as you could as long as possible until finally the filter was blocked. They were supposed to wear two layers of coverall suits but no one bothered and when they were breaking up the fibre walls the air was thick and by the time they went outside they looked like they'd been formed out of dust and ash like the long-dead rat he'd seen fall with the mess from the palm of his short-handled spade.

One day Rosemary asked him to describe the work and then she made him quit. He hated the job but hated quitting it more, each lost job another weight against his chances, and though he felt a great debt to Rosemary, he didn't like having to do what she said, or having to listen to her patient explanation about why the job would kill him. The poison English word she made him say. Her same old reassurance that he'd soon get something more.

For three or four days he hardly came up from the basement. He felt weak but not sick, tired in ways he didn't understand.

He called Luis. They met in a booth in a pool hall where a friend once had bought them some games. Luis didn't ask how he was but started into his own story of how he'd lost the job with Kevin and now worked cleaning building exteriors with a Costa Rican crew who took only ten dollars an hour off the books while he himself made double that, though they'd been on the job for more than a year. He told stories about the Costa Ricans, how they would do anything. They hung from frayed wires in torn harnesses. Many got badly hurt but kept working.

— And then it happened to me, he said.

He took his time describing the work of blasting oxidation off the facing of a warehouse. He set the scene and tried to shape with his hands in the air the instruments and assemblies of this new trade and explain their workings so Rodrigo could see where the dangers lay.

"Thirty-five hundred psi's," Luis said in English, and then explained what it meant.

Then he told the story of the mistake he'd made, triggering the jet of water that tore into his leg and took the skin off from his knee to his ankle. He leaned back and swung his foot onto the table and pulled up the leg of his jeans. It was wrapped in white gauze.

Two of the Costa Ricans had gotten him to the hospital.

— I missed only two days of work. Now I just change the bandages at lunch and when I get home. And now the Costa Ricans tell stories about me.

He had lied to no purpose and not well. He couldn't have hurt the leg so badly and gone back to work so soon.

Luis smiled and looked around, then slid his leg off the table. He wanted a bigger audience, Rodrigo thought. The room was mostly quiet but for two young men playing pool with a girl who didn't seem to have any feeling for them. She was maybe high, Rodrigo thought. She looked at the pool balls and then at Rodrigo and Luis as if they were all of the same problem of angles.

—What happened to your girlfriend, Luis?

He bent over and rolled his pant leg back down.

— She's gone. He emitted a familiar half cough. In Luis, it was a kind of laughter. Back home maybe. What do you care?

— I think I might need to go somewhere else.

— I don't know about anyplace else. Some say things are better in other cities but I don't know. So don't be stupid. Here you have friends.

The manager had been eyeing them from behind the bar, a short balding man with badly scratched lenses in his glasses. Now he came by and asked them to order something. Luis said they were waiting for a friend. The manager said either they ordered something or they'd have to go.

Luis told him to say it again.

"What's that?"

"Tell me again that I have to go."

Luis straightened up against the seatback.

"If you boys want to make trouble, make it somewhere else."

The others were watching now. The girl's companions put their cues down on the table. One of them, with a huge round shaven head, put his hands in his back pockets.

He said to Luis, "You better clear out of here, Tito."

The other man, who had a thin beard along his jawline, looked around the room as if for witnesses.

Luis got up from the booth and Rodrigo stood beside him.

— Let's be quiet and go, he said, but Luis was looking at the owner. Then he dropped his head a little and smiled and began to nod just as he threw his hand out and snatched the man's glasses from his face and the room spilled open and Rodrigo saw the bearded man run for the door and Rodrigo knew he had to beat him to it and he ran and was out and down the stairwell when he heard the door above him close and the bolt thrown to.

He ran across the street in traffic and turned down a darker street of houses, running still, unpursued but unable to stop or to get clear, he could not get clear, and finally he stopped and squatted down, and then sat on a lawn with the trees swirling above him and what came to him was a moment from his arrival so many months ago, the airport baggage claim and an enormous toy bear abandoned belly up on the carousel.

Being here meant he had to behave like a coward. He didn't care whether or not Luis would forgive him. Luis made his own trouble.

A woman walking a large short-haired dog came along the street and crossed over, away from him, and then stopped and asked if he was all right. He found he was reluctant to speak but he nodded to her and said he would be fine. The dog stared at him and its tail rose slightly. The woman gave the animal a little tug and continued down the street.

He walked a long time towards home. He was spoken to only once, by a shirtless young native man asking for change. He was sitting against the suicide hotline phone at the entrance to the bridge. Rodrigo just shook his head and kept walking. The native wished him good luck and then laughed and called out something he didn't understand and then laughed and called out again and again until Rodrigo could no longer make it out in the sounds of traffic on the parkway below.

Father André's church was east of downtown, a few blocks from a housing project that was now being dismantled. Passing by the low buildings, Harold was reminded that he knew the city's neighbourhoods mainly through inexpert media representations. He recalled a magazine story on the unsolved murder of a teen prostitute in a wading pool somewhere here. The white writer described the white residents directly and the blacks in terms of which American movie actors they put him in mind of. In such ways the article invalidated itself. It left the impression that the families had nothing in common except the writer in their midst, a false witness, another trader in stock pictures.

Along the stone streetside wall of St. Eustace by the Lake were illegible words of spray-painted graffiti. Lower than the rest, as if a child had drawn them, a few of what he thought were called tags, vaguely familiar from the backs of subway seats and alley garage doors.

According to the posted list, the next service was evensong, hours away. It occurred to him to wonder what exactly Rosemary's function was in this place that she should be here in mid-afternoon.

She had called the meeting. She said they had things to clear up. No doubt she'd accuse him of ratting her out to Cosintino. He intended to confess, and then ask her to do the same, whatever her deception.

The closing of the door shut out the street sounds and left him in emptiness. The interior was dimmer than he'd expected, a quality of light he associated with a grander scale, the oldest cathedrals of Europe in the rain. He moved along, past an empty wall rack with the sign "Pamphlets $1. Please Take One." Up the side aisle he stopped before a small altar of the Virgin and a few votive candles. The light coloured rose and yellow in a lone window.

Her voice echoed from across the nave.

"A rare visitor."

Was she already implying something? Had she seen him watching her house? He could hardly believe it himself, at least not by day. He was becoming two people.

She wore corduroy pants and a tattered Montreal Canadiens hockey sweater.

"Numbers aren't what they used to be, I take it."

She started down the centre aisle and he reversed his way towards the back.

"We serve the community, whether they attend service or not. But we owe about twenty per cent of our income each year to the diocese, and we can't pay it. And the church is selling off properties to pay lawsuits and debts."

"The story tends in one direction."

"Yes, it does," she said.

"So how much longer?"

"We don't know."

They were outside now. She seemed to have wanted him out of there, he thought. She probably had someone stuffed in the vestry. To the west, the downtown towers were softening in the haze. She was walking ahead of him.

"Let's talk while I run my errands."

She led him to an old dark green Volvo wagon. Harold opened the door and sat in the passenger seat without comment. Very likely it would be useful to him later to assert some advantage now, to claim some small agency in these first minutes, but his positions weren't favourable yet again, and so he allowed Rosemary to think she could lead them.

They headed west. She drove very well, full of surety, knowing the side-street routes. When she leaned forward to watch the progress of a woman in a wheelchair at an intersection, he saw the number 10 on her jersey. Some player from the seventies, he thought, but he couldn't remember the name.

She headed into the university campus and pulled up half on a sidewalk and parked.

"Hold on."

She got out and headed into a college carrying a plastic bag. Her movements lacked fluency but suggested strength. A determined, slightly overstriding march. She was back within seconds.

"I had to drop off some copying for Father André. He lectures here. Tonight it's iconography. You might want to come."

"He's a truly thoughtful man."

"He's worthy of the subject." She eased the car off the sidewalk and stopped to wait out a squirrel's indecision in the road.

"He walked me through icons once, I recall. The Incarnation, how God penetrates matter so humans can contemplate the *invisibilia*."

"Icons and scripture. God's energies are everywhere, but we have to be open to them."

She started forward again. Apparently the church was more to her than a community service body.

They toured back through the east downtown. Rosemary ran a commentary through the passing scenes. It was very much her neighbourhood and it extended for blocks in all directions. The failing history of a soup kitchen, a park forbidden by bylaw to the homeless, the window of a room where a Children's Aid worker had been attacked by the parents of a beaten child. North into Cabbagetown she pointed out the gay club raided twice by rogue cops and told a story of a bashing they didn't respond to that she ended with a blatantly cinematic image of men on their knees in the reddening snow. She was performing for Harold, as if her particular high ground commanded a view that could be known only through her descriptions.

And then finally it came, bluntly, and he was prepared.

"Why did you give the police my name?"

"I wasn't accusing you of anything. Except maybe of not seeing clearly who you're involved with, these people."

"And yet I see them every day, and you've never met them, so how is it you see them so well?"

There was no getting out in front of her, this woman who seemed to live a few seconds into the future. He wanted to tell her that the idea of presenting his theory to the investigator and dropping Rosemary's name, it had all come to him at once, and that he was pleased to find himself acting in ways he couldn't predict, a momentary stranger to himself.

"Ever been to St. James Town?"

"No."

"Well, then you'll experience something today."

St. James Town, the most densely populated area in the country. Twenty square blocks of high-rise apartments built in the fifties for singles and couples without children. A court ruling had struck down the restrictions and opened the place up to anyone. The landlords had been accused by tenants organizations of letting the place run down. The grounds were now thought to be the territory of thugs.

They swung in off Wellesley and turned into a system of lanes that connected the dozen or so towers. Ahead was an attempted piazza of shadowed concrete and blowing garbage. Rosemary found a parking spot with a view of a line of dumpsters – dumpsters were now a motif of Harold's attentions. Between two of them several teenage boys were involved in some transaction. They turned and regarded Rosemary's car and, as if on cue, dispersed without a word.

It was a show, Harold thought. The stylized way they broke, it gave them away as kids, performing.

"How many races did we scare off?" she asked.

"Race is a social construct. My colleagues tell me so."

"How many, really? I see a couple of South Asians, a black kid, two whites."

"It's the national experiment. We've been blowing New York and London out of the water for years. The world gathers at our dumpsters."

Rosemary removed some documents from under her seat, and then a plastic bag of something from the trunk. She walked, Harold followed. They passed an old man in an Afghani hat with a display of knock-off Persian carpets on the sidewalk that looked as if they'd been pulled from front stoops.

"Do you know how many people live here?" she asked.

"I'm guessing no one knows exactly."

"That's right. Even if we could settle on a definition of what constitutes living, there'd still be no fixed number."

"Between birth and death, pretty much everything's provisional."

"You might believe that, but I'm just saying there are a lot of people here unofficially."

"They're here but they're not here. They're here in front of us but they're not in the country."

"Yes. Many of them."

"And right now we're going to visit some of these people who aren't here."

"Off the record," she said. "Okay?"

In the world but not on the record. Globally, it was the largest category.

In a dim lobby they waited along with a young Indian or Pakistani couple for one of the three elevators to arrive. A full two minutes passed.

On the eighth floor Harold noticed that the corridors, though a little stale, looked well enough maintained. The smell of curry. The building was much like the city itself. The mix of races, histories, living side by side, affording incompatible myths. A crime-ridden, unpoliceable mistake of urban planning. Or a self-maintaining, multi-ethnic community, an asylum from any number of worlds gone wrong.

Small pools of light in each doorway. He thought of library carrels.

Rosemary knocked on two doors. At the first there was no answer. She slipped an envelope underneath. At the second she passed the plastic bag with unknown contents to the man who answered, introduced as Luis. In his thirties, likely, a little soft in the face. Luis affected a great delight at the bag and at meeting Harold. He told Rosemary she looked beautiful and asked

Harold if he didn't agree. He couldn't tell whether Luis was truly insincere or only seemed so in translation, but the man didn't inspire Harold to say anything in Spanish.

They walked down two floors and made a last call. When Rosemary knocked and announced herself, they heard low voices and what Harold imagined to be urgent movements inside. A young African man opened the door. Deep in the room, two women at a table were looking at Harold with grave expressions.

"Jonathan, this is Harold. He's helping me today."

Jonathan was taking Harold's presence very seriously.

"Hello, Harold."

"Hello."

Jonathan backed out of the doorway and Rosemary led them into the apartment.

It wasn't well furnished, there was no television even, but a long window provided a clear view of the downtown and the lake and the islands. The floor was parquet.

Rosemary said hello to the women. They nodded at her. One woman was a little younger and she smiled at Harold. The older woman didn't acknowledge him. They were sitting there with nothing between them, no newspaper or coffee. Harold couldn't imagine what they'd been doing a minute ago.

Among the papers for Jonathan was a small envelope. He opened this before examining the documents, and turned his back to the two of them for a moment to look inside. Then he faced them again and nodded slowly to Rosemary.

"Thank you," he said.

"Do you have those names for me?" she asked.

Jonathan went down the hallway. Harold thought he heard voices, and the older woman at the table began to speak as if to cover them. She addressed Rosemary in rapid accented English mixed with some other language, and Rosemary asked the young woman to clarify. There was some back and forth before Jonathan returned. Harold understood that nothing had been conveyed.

Jonathan glanced at Harold as he handed Rosemary a paper with handwriting, which she folded and put away.

"Why do you bring this man?" It was the older woman. Her English was thick but confident.

"He needs to know what I do," she explained. "Don't worry, you're safe."

"Thank you," said Jonathan.

The older woman got up from the table to watch them leave.

In the car again, Harold was still working over what he'd witnessed. There was no use asking. She would tell him or she wouldn't.

"I don't suppose you'll let me in on that smile," he said.

"It was the look on your face. You were trying to be a good sport and make sense of what was happening there, but your expression was of disapproval – I don't know what's happening here but I object to it."

"At least it amused you. I'm not quite so naive as you imagine, you know."

"And I'm not quite so humourless. You think of crusaders as humourless. What else?"

All right, then, he thought, let's get personal.

"Likely in the aftermath of some trauma of your own."

"Let's say a nasty divorce."

"Will we say that?"

"Yes, actually. But it's distant now. And I have my humour intact."

With a crooked smile she seemed to acknowledge a degree of construction in her outward self. In a serious world, she was a serious person, but with a sense of irony, even play. He didn't buy it.

"You haven't reassured me that you don't harbour criminals."

"Reassuring you wasn't my intention."

Without naming countries, she explained that the couple living with Jonathan and his wife were out of options. They'd applied for refugee status and been denied. They'd applied for help from certain organizations and been denied. They had no place to turn. The man sometimes got construction work but most crews wouldn't hire him. And his English was bad.

"He was a member of the military. He wants refuge because he witnessed tortures and executions and he couldn't stomach it and he went AWOL, and so now the military wants to torture him."

"But nobody believes the story."

"There's not much evidence one way or another, but the Refugee Board and GROUND are of the opinion he likely participated in killings."

"So why do you believe him if they don't?"

"What if his story is true?"

"What if it isn't? Suppose they got this one right."

"Okay, let's say they did. Are we then relieved of our obligations?"

Here was the resistance he'd been waiting for. Rosemary had people to protect and he wasn't going to be allowed to threaten them. He would have it out with her, more directly than they'd squared off over lunch that day, but just now he wanted to keep things civil. There was more to be won with civility. And anyway, he wanted more of her company.

"Do you drink? Do you have time for a drink?"

"So you can work up the courage to accuse me of something again?"

"Maybe."

They headed south to King Street and found a faux British pub with Guinness on tap and cricket paddles on the wall, a place of the kind that survived on brokers at the market close and tourists after shows. They took seats at the bar, angling towards one another, and the moment their drinks came Rosemary excused herself.

Maybe she wanted him a little loose before they continued. How calculating was she? For some reason he thought it important to establish whether or not she had children. He had theories about how motherhood changed women by revealing to them the incapacities of men for intuitive empathy and selfless love. It was one of the beliefs he held privately, never to be stated. But he'd leave the question unasked or else they were going to knock themselves out trying to open angles on one another.

When his pint was only half gone he noticed a lassitude in his movements, a strain of fatigue that paid off in a keenness in the senses. The teak wainscotting behind the bottles along the bar. Most days you'd look but never see it. The relative weights of sounds in the distance. If you didn't know steel on steel, would a streetcar seem metal or wind? The twenty-ton pitch of a breeze.

"Sorry."

She briefly laid her hand on his shoulder as she passed by, a warm, surprise gesture, and took her position on the stool.

"In that apartment. The man in the back room. If he is a

killer, why do you feel an obligation to him? Do you think the country should open itself to every monster who can afford a plane ticket?"

"He's not a monster. But maybe he was forced to take part in killing. The Lord commanded there be cities of refuge for the manslayer."

"You're not serious."

"Among the Levitical cities, six were designated as cities of refuge."

"Where the murderers lived."

"Only those who killed without enmity and were subject to the laws of blood vengeance. They didn't deserve to die, so they needed a place where they would be safe."

"You don't think there's enmity between a soldier and the person he tortures and kills?"

"If there was, he wouldn't be able to tell the story the way he does."

"The Review Board didn't find his storytelling so convincing. Maybe you're just . . ."

"A bleeding heart? As I've told you, the board and I aren't judging the same thing."

The Lord commanded. Harold couldn't trust anyone who'd begin a sentence this way. If he'd tried to picture such a person, she wouldn't have been wearing a hockey sweater.

"There's a rumour," he said. "Women have gone missing recently. Women in this sphere of yours. An Eritrean, a Kurd, and a Russian."

"Sounds like the start of a joke."

"Maybe they came through GROUND. Maybe the attacker met them where he met Kim."

"Where did you hear this?"

"It's out there."

She closed her hands into half fists and pushed her nearly full pint glass slightly forward like so many stacks of poker chips.

"This is the world we've made. Lurid stories are self-generating. They form out of dozens of other stories, some of them true, some not. The pieces break off and recombine."

"Well this one grew legs. It stood up and made the rounds."

The lights dimmed.

"These women don't exist, Harold."

"They don't? You know this?"

"They do, but not those three. The story's true in general but not in particular. The rumour would have you believe they're being murdered. But if it's true, then it only happens after we send them back where they came from."

All of Rosemary's stakes were in invisible things, her god, the *invisibilia*, her foreigners who didn't officially exist. Apparently her devotions had made her a great reader of others, and the more you looked at her, the more she saw in you. Yet he couldn't help but look at her. Her face, her mouth. He wanted to reach out and touch her neck, to feel her hair on the back of his hand, a gesture from his past he'd made once or twice to make himself understood, though it had conveyed only his need, not his meaning.

"Take a thousand people in dire circumstances," she said. "We take them in, a kind of miracle to them, and support them only enough until they begin to see that they can't really escape their past here, and many can't ever have a future. And so they begin to rot. Or we reject them and send them running, with no hope even of basic security. Even if by some sheer luck they get ahead, they get work and make money and have families, even when they find one hospital that will take care of them, and will bill them but won't collect, and they find a school for their kids, even then they're still not safe. There's every chance that they might be caught and sent back, and so lose even more than they did when they came in the first place. Now they're in the position of losing their families." Loud laughter burst from another table. She waited it out, then continued. "And all their hope lies in the possibility of a change in the laws. But nothing happens unless someone tells a single compelling story, usually involving some rare case, between categories, and it hits the news, and pressures form around it, and a minister finds himself under siege, and then maybe a bill or some amendment gets put forward, and it passes or not. But either way, the thousands who aren't between categories still suffer, hopeless in a new place. They simply exist. Do you understand when I say they exist?"

Her eyes had been steadfast on him the whole time. It was part of the schooling.

"I guess I do."

"And so rumours of killers, women murdered, they're not just lurid, giving the citizens what they want. Violent stories. They're a way of pretending to look without seeing. They allow people to think they've recognized a problem, without doing anything about it. They make things worse. They're loathsome. They're wicked."

Her voice was level.

"But people do disappear," he said.

"Yes. They get detained and deported, they leave on a bus for Montreal, they move to a new neighbourhood, change their friends."

"My concern, Rosemary, is that you aren't open to certain thoughts, certain signs. That you've got too much invested in your faith in these people. And now even when you're presented with my reasonable concerns, you aren't hearing them."

"I understand them. But on this matter of dangerous foreign-born predators, we each think the other is dead wrong. You should know that I've already been through these questions."

She told him that not so many years ago she'd become close to a young Guatemalan woman, a successful refugee claimant who used to come to the church. She smiled a lot and learned English in daily sessions of Bible study that Rosemary led. One day the study group read of the translation of Elijah, who ascended on a whirlwind to heaven without dying. The young woman – her name was Mariela Cendes – had stated her belief that her own father, who had disappeared in the time of the death squads, had also gained heaven without dying. Then one mid-June day she herself went missing. Her clothes, all her possessions, were still in her room. There was no reason to think she had chosen to go elsewhere.

"And she never turned up?"

"We went to the police, they did their thing. Nothing. She's still on the books."

"I'm sorry she disappeared. But the police probably don't have forensics for heavenly whirlwinds. Religions and their free-pass categories. In Islam, suicide bombers think they're skipping thousands of years in the grave and going straight to their reward."

"You have to understand that I believe in Elijah's translation, just as I believe in the resurrection."

Like that, she was a stranger again.

"Not literally, you don't. Something like the resurrection only makes sense as metaphor. That's its value. Why it's powerful, historically."

"It's powerful because it's the truth. Let us not mock God with metaphor."

"Is that from one of Father André's sermons?"

"It's from a poem."

"And here I thought poetry was metaphor."

"Not this poem. I'll send it to you."

He sat there, dumbfounded that such an intelligence had been carried off by fairy tales. There was a great darkness in her past through which she'd lost her way. He wondered what had happened to her, but more so he wondered at her certainties. In the years ahead for him, his last couple of decades, he would need such certainty, if only he could arrive there. As delusions went, it was the right one for a man his age. Later life was best endured with family and friends – he was not well stocked – a good drug plan, and a hopeful delusion. He saw himself walking out into a summer storm to be taken up by the winds.

On the drive back to his car she told more stories about her missing Guatemalan girl with the musical name, a name made for prayer, and he tried to understand how biblical characters could be as real to her as this person who'd existed for her in flesh and blood. He asked her to spell it out for him as plainly as she could. She said she believed in the resurrection, she believed in the translation of Elijah, and she *could as easily believe* in the translation of Mariela Cendes.

Maybe this Mariela was an invention, a ploy of some sort, he thought. But then no, that wasn't it.

She pulled up by his car. They got out and he stood and watched her wave goodbye and walk away and disappear into the church.

By now she had to remind herself that *R* wasn't real. He was there in her world but he wasn't real. He had being but he didn't exist. They were made for each other as surely as they were missing from one another. It was partly the absence that drew her, and that made his life personal for her. They could never reach one another, never inhabit the same plane outside of her imagination, though they felt loss in similar ways, and if she could write it well enough, they'd feel it in the same way. She would grant him the full apprehension of his loss.

She wanted to tell someone about him, tell Marian here on their late-morning walk, the ritual they'd formed to talk about things. The walk had become shorter every few days. They wouldn't make the end of the block this morning. There were small moments of shock that she came to expect, though expecting them didn't console her. What consoled her was the thought of *R*.

The front yards began to widen as the street grew older in this direction, the houses Victorian, brick. Every morning, in one way or another, Kim asked her mother how she was doing. Usually Marian dismissed the question lightly, but today she said that she was trying to hit a moving target, to get used to a condition that kept changing. The only way to mark it, and her adjustments, was against the constants in her life, Kim and Donald. There might come a time, she said, when she'd ask Kim to give her a read on herself. "It matters that you tell me the truth," she said. "I trust your eye. It consoles me to know there's a good witness to my exit."

"I'll try. But one truth is that I don't think I'm much of a witness."

And so Marian asked her what she felt now, at this distance, when she thought of the attack.

She felt she'd been upside down.

"What do you mean?"

"I was working a night shift, which was half-normal to me by then, but upside down to everyone else. Everything was backwards."

"Sounds like it's still close if you allow it to be."

There was something else, something new. She had tried to remember the sound of her footsteps that night, and the indistinct measure of another's step beneath them, but she simply couldn't hear it. Then yesterday, writing a fresh scene with *R*, she thought of him walking again, this time from a work site to a subway station, and she realized he wasn't alone, that someone was with him, and she heard the steps, syncopated and a little uneven, and then she suddenly closed her laptop and dropped her head and hugged herself.

"I think he had a leg injury."

"Before you kicked him?"

"I can hear his last few steps before he tackles me, and they don't fall quite evenly. And then when I kick his leg, his left ankle, he cries out like I've broken it, but there's no chance, and so maybe it was hurt already."

"All right. And his skin tone. His eyelashes you said."

"Yes. And his hands. He works with them."

"And you told the detective about the leg injury?"

"I called her this morning. But it doesn't matter. I got her to admit that the trail's cold. There never was a trail." Marian reached for her hand and squeezed it lightly. "It's okay, Mom. I already knew they wouldn't find him."

They never would. Not unless he did this again and her description matched another, and then the pieces started to lead places. The pieces always led her to the same place. To get there, she is upside down. She carries a tray of coffees, a bag of treats. She stops at a bookstore window, she passes by a makeshift church. He's there behind her but she can't see him. She thinks to turn north but stays west instead. She sees the chain hanging loose on the clasp. She hears the uneven footsteps, feels the shoulder in her back. The coffee scalds her leg but she doesn't know it yet.

"So I'm dealing with it, as they say. Though I guess I'm distracting myself a little from . . . the state of things with you."

"Is that why you're in your room tapping all day?"

"Sorry."

"Don't be. I love having you around but I don't want you underfoot. I think we're both holding up just fine. It's your father who's crumbling. Last week Donald found him in the garage, going through boxes. Drunk."

"What boxes?"

"Presumably his boxes. He stores his life in there."

She'd felt something like this coming.

"I can't picture the scene."

"Harold lurching around. Donald standing there with a phone and a can of wasp killer. Each calling the other an intruder."

They stopped and looked around at the day, then started again. As a child this had been the limit of her world. Now it was the limit of her mother's.

"Why are you only telling me this now?"

"I don't know. I didn't think I was going to tell you at all."

"Why not?"

"I don't like your father in his pathetic mode. I must be reminding him of his mortality."

"Did you ask him what he was looking for?"

Marian laughed. "God, no." She was smiling but her tone meant she wouldn't say more.

They had made it to the corner but could they make it back? There was no place to sit but a little wooden retaining wall, about eighteen inches high, fronting a neighbour's garden. Kim had marked it on their first trip, when they'd started this routine. Some day soon they would need it, but again today they passed it by, as if floating a little on the thought of how well they were addressing things, so much better than the men, with the simple down-and-back, the same to-and-fro of their slow lines every morning.

"You could ask him." So Marian would say more. Kim had to remind herself that her mother, too, had reason to act out of character. "He's never been able to correct himself. He just crashes and then walks from the wreckage and goes off to another pursuit."

It was the sort of thing Marian would say of Harold, but her tone had none of the usual bitterness. However slowly they were moving, the way seemed to be parting for them as it never had. The air was full of admission.

"Do you still love him?"

"You don't need to ask that, Kim. The man has so much more worth than he knows. Little tragedies knock him over. He won't survive the big ones on his own."

"Have you told him that?"

"I can't help him. He wouldn't recognize the help, or if he did he wouldn't allow it." They stopped walking. They stood side by side, glancing at one another. "And focusing on him would be good for you too. You've always been a helper. Here you are helping me."

"I've been my own project these last months."

"Of course you have. But you might do a lot for yourself by lending him a little spine. You're the only one who could get that close to him."

"You make it sound like an assassination."

Marian laughed. "Well, every love has its own best expression."

That evening after the office was closed, Kim parked her mother's car across from GROUND and stared up at the second-floor window until she was sure that Marlene had gone home. She let herself in with the key she'd never returned and made her way upstairs and through a second door.

It had come to her that this was it, the point of origin. Harold was convinced she'd met her attacker through GROUND. She couldn't bring herself to concede as much, but this office was a locus. How had she come to be attacked in one of the safest big cities in the world? She'd brought it upon herself by working here, as an open host, constantly aware of her privilege, and she had felt guilty. She would not have thought that the guilt determined her actions, certainly not her life choices. But just maybe, one night, the work she did in this place had made her take a risk. Maybe it had taken her down a dark, quiet street when she'd thought to head towards a busy one. There was no other explanation. Either the guilt of privilege had sent her into trouble or nothing had. She chose to think it was guilt.

The phone rang through to the answering machine and there was a voice from one of the many territories of broken English. Someone named Irina was calling on behalf of her brother, whom she didn't name. She invited Marlene to a citizenship party where she promised to serve vodka.

The key to the three standing files was kept in a locked desk drawer. The key to the drawer was under the green plastic pot on the corner of the desk holding the cactus one of the clients had given Marlene as a gift. The cactus was dead but the spines endured as part of Marlene's idea of a security system, as if anything more elaborate would be in bad faith. Besides, the deadbolted office and building doors kept out junkies and thieves, and whoever else might have wanted to peek in the files tended to respect locks and follow rules where they were discernible. Marlene was supposed to be the only person with access. Though it had made things awkward at times, the standing files had been off-limits to Kim and the other volunteers, a fact for which Marlene had apologized. "If anyone has to get in trouble over what's in there, it'll be me." Kim had assumed Marlene was worried about violating confidentiality, or maintaining for the volunteers some plausible degree of deniability, or maybe the trouble in the records ran deeper. If Kim's attacker was in the files, she'd find him on her own, and keep GROUND out of it if she could.

The file drawers were unlabelled. The key to the first stack opened all four drawers. The top one contained old copies of the long-ago-aborted newsletter and a few letters addressed to Marlene and tucked back into their envelopes. The client files, arranged by case number, began in the second drawer. The numbers corresponded to computer files that contained the clients' names, but Kim didn't know the password – Marlene changed it monthly – and she didn't need the name anyway, didn't want it really. What she wanted was a suspect whose story she'd recognize.

She went through files from the months before the attack, looking for anything that seemed familiar, that triggered a face, maybe a tense moment with someone they'd turned down. Every file contained a fact sheet with the claimant's name, blacked out once the electronic file was created, age, country of origin, family information, port of entry, entry date. There was a box to check for "evidence of torture." There were copies of the documents submitted in the claim, copies of the board's decision. Most files listed local addresses and phone or contact numbers. Some had Polaroid headshots that lawyers had clipped to the referral letters.

For a moment she saw herself in mid break-and-enter. Far from enacting this scene, the old Kim wouldn't even have imagined it.

After forty minutes, her attention and hope fading, she came across a translated narrative she barely remembered, from late winter, five months before the attack. Even as she read the header she recalled Marlene telling her the story of a young Colombian man. She said if you spent five minutes with him you could tell he had a sweet nature, and that he couldn't be blamed for whatever violent world he'd been carried into as a boy. And yet he'd been rejected by the Immigration Review Board.

Name removed. Age 22. Colombia. No family in Canada. Pearson, Oct. 18, 2008. No photo. No home address. The contact was to be through his lawyer.

Kim had once met the referring lawyer, Belinda Paul, another smart engagé. She had wild black hair and tended to narrow her eyes as she spoke. Marlene thought that Belinda didn't approve of their work but now and then she'd send clients to GROUND who'd suffered especially unjust decisions. "If Belinda sent them, they'll break your heart," she once said.

Kim photocopied the file of the heartbreaker, then returned it, put the office back together, and walked out to the car.

If the file led somewhere, if it furthered investigations, then bringing it into the house, her bedroom, had implications that she decided to accept. She sat in her desk chair with one arm folded across her chest, her hand clamped under the opposite elbow, and started to read.

1. My name is [removed]. I was born in Yopal, Colombia, in 1986 and am presently a citizen of Colombia and no other country.

2. In 2003 my family sent me to live with my cousin's family in Bogota. My cousin is two years older than me. A few weeks before I arrived he had been recruited by three men to sell kitchen utensils from a cart on the street. He went to the men and got me the same job, working one street away.

3. After only a week or so my cousin Uriel complained to the men about our salaries and we were told we'd be paid more if we took a plantation job to the south.

4. The next day my cousin and I left for work without telling his family about our new jobs. We rode on the back of a truck for several hours. We had not brought anything from home except for the clothes we were wearing.

5. We were dropped off at a training camp for soldiers. When we asked about the plantation work, we were given 10,000 pesos each and told we would collect 500,000 by the end of the month. Our leader, named Volmer, gave us food and a bed and blankets. The next day we were given guns and told how to use them. We practised with them for one day. No one at the camp wore uniforms or arm bands, and we didn't know who we were working for.

6. We were told our work was to protect workers at an agricultural production plant. We were moved to this facility and the same man, Volmer, led us around the area we were supposed to guard. There were about twenty men in all guarding buildings that were behind a wire fence.

7. For several days we did our work with no incident. We slept in one of the buildings inside the compound and met the workers. Some said they were there against their will. Some said they had been kidnapped. Others said they were there by choice. All of them had been paid. There was no agreement about which group we were working for.

8. One morning in the second week Uriel and I and ten or twelve others were loaded again onto a truck and taken to Villanueva, Casanare. We were posted at the side of a road –

She stopped. Whatever was about to happen on the road, whatever would send the heartbreaker running, he'd run clear to Canada, into her life. She skipped to the end. The signature was blacked out. The translator's name was absent. Then she read the rest of the narrative.

She knew why the board had rejected the story. It was of a type with others she'd read, that they all had read, from the war zones. An innocent is caught up in some atrocity and tries to stop it but fails, but somehow survives, escaping reprisals by leaving the country. In this version, the heartbreaker's family had fled too. Or that was the claim. No one had been able to contact the family in Cartagena. Either they hadn't received the petition or had chosen not to give themselves away. Or they didn't exist.

In the evidence was a statement from a man convicted in the killings who named the heartbreaker as one among many drug thugs who shot and then buried a group of seven farmers who had happened upon the armed men and gotten into an argument over the use of a road. It was possible both versions, those of the convicted witness and the heartbreaker, were lies.

The young man would likely have ended up an exclusion case, to be deported, but the file hadn't been updated. Maybe he hadn't come back to GROUND.

Yes, the office held origins. She'd built her fictional man, *R*, out of this real one's history. She was an accidental thief, only slightly disturbed to learn of her crime. She went to her bedroom window and looked out. The farthest line of rooftops down the block, bitten off against a blue field of sky. The neighbour's rectangular backyard fence dissected by a clothesline into triangles of air. She had been drawn all along by something she knew.

The theft had served her well, seeding a life of its own. The fictional story was more alive for her than the featureless, documented one – the one with life-and-death consequences – because her imagination held her fear, and the fear was as real as the scar on her leg. Whoever her attacker was, he'd been displaced. He was not alive in her understanding. In her peopled imagination, it was *R* alone who was fully there.

She felt a sudden thrill in her blood that she remembered as joy. She was returned through some physical memory to her younger self, to the small delights she had felt in the past, at open moments in the house, in the wake of her mother's voice, and outside in the daylight city, listening to buskers, smiling at the shared laughter of workers stacking bitter melons in the jammed Chinese markets where no one spoke English. Yet there was no reason to feel these last bloomings of a young girl's wonderment. Her mother was dying, her father was a mess and getting worse, she herself still couldn't walk even short distances alone in the city at night. And so where did the joy spring from? There was nothing to account for it. Not time, not forgetting.

And then it was gone and the pain returned, sharper. She left the window and sat on the bed, and she understood. The pain itself produced joy only to open her heart and flood it again with its thick liquid truths. And so her suffering had fooled her. But by whatever power they were wielded, the joys were truths too. She thought she just might survive if she kept her eye steady. The pain was just one kind of finite creature, not a condition. She resolved to cede to it only its share of her.

5

At ten in the morning the college's librarian had found Harold drunk and weeping in the Divinity stacks. The librarian called the History chair, who'd called her old Academic Council pal Donald, who was of the opinion that Harold would become unwieldy at the sight of him. And so Donald called Kim.

"Where is he now?"

"In the library office, slouched on the floor. Hannah's with him." Hannah, the chair, was trying to keep Harold out of sight until someone could spirit him home.

Kim took Marian's car to campus. By the time she met Donald on the stone steps of the college, someone from Medical Services had been called in. The librarian was named Danny, a Chinese-Canadian with a look of grave disapproval. He received them wordlessly and led the way behind the information desk to the administrative precincts, an echoing space lit by old windows. They passed a thin, greying woman in a window bay, on a cell-phone, who beckoned to Donald. He veered off, and Kim continued to follow Danny to the door of a small office. Through the glass slit Kim peeked at Harold sitting across the table from a young woman with a blunt haircut. She was leaning towards him, a pamphlet on STDs in the back pocket of her green pants. Harold looked glassy, drunk, yes, and fearful, as if he'd been arrested.

Danny left her as Donald arrived, taking an angle that concealed him from the door window.

"Hannah will protect him. He won't face discipline. Though he could use some."

"What did you say to them?"

For a moment they stood in deeper silence.

"I said sometimes he drinks too much – we've all had our weekends – but he hasn't until now been a morning drunk. I don't even know if that's true."

The subject of Harold had been generally off-limits at home, at least when Donald was around, as it had been periodically since he first moved in, when Kim was eighteen. She left for university and he more or less passed her in the doorway. At home on the weekends she tried to make sense of the new arrangement, and the idea that her parents weren't ever going to mend things. The following spring Marian and Donald married in the garden surrounded by a few old family friends and Donald's Math Department colleagues, whom Kim didn't know and hadn't seen since. Now that she'd moved back, Kim felt old patterns that belonged to her mother and her returning to the house, cleaning rituals, the stacking of shelves and fetching of newspapers, some extending back as far as the Harold years. Whether or not he understood it, Donald must have felt that his claim hadn't taken. The house had never been his.

"You must be Kim. I'm Hannah Posetta."

Her bearing was one of extreme competence. She shook hands warmly, though without smiling, as Donald was, idiotically.

"I'll take him now," said Kim. "Thanks for helping."

"Marilynne's almost done with him. It's just routine."

"I don't see the point of talking to him if he's drunk," said Donald.

Hannah looked at him. He didn't take her meaning.

"Would you excuse us, Donald?"

He nodded, though looking baffled, and walked back towards the outer offices.

"Is this some kind of psych assessment?"

"They're just talking. He knows her, Kim." For a second she considered the absurd possibility that Harold and the counsellor were lovers. "Just take him home when they're done in there. The department will take care of the fine."

"What fine?"

"I thought Donald would have explained. He defaced one of the books."

What did it mean that Kim could believe her father was drunk and melting in a library, but not that he'd defaced a book? She would have thought that the progress of his troubles could be stayed by books. The printed word was his refuge.

Hannah reached over and squeezed her shoulder, then nodded in farewell and left. Kim spotted Danny on the far side of the room and cornered him. She asked to see the damage. He led her to his desk, picked up an oversized, almond-coloured book, and opened it to lambent reproductions, with text, of the St. Francis cycle by Giotto. Harold had torn out the page, now set loosely back inside, containing the fresco *Confession of a Woman Raised from the Dead*. The page had been folded.

"He had it in his pocket," said Danny, a sympathy forming around his eyes. "We can repair it better than you might suppose. I think he's done."

It was a moment before she realized he was telling her that Harold had appeared. She turned and found him staring at her from across the office, as if he couldn't make sense of her presence. The smart thing was to play it cool. She didn't want him falling apart again, if that was in the cards.

"I'll give you a lift home," she said.

He smiled – there was no evident embarrassment or shame, but then he was still drunk – and from their separate places in the room, they started away.

He had returned to her on a warm November day. She was alone. Marian had gone out – where? by now she'd forgotten – and Kim had come home from school to an empty house that had changed on her. The first snow had fallen the week before, but now the city had entered a little false summer, so through open windows the light slanted at winter angles, casting shadows that should never have belonged to the scented air. She took this in all at once, even as she passed through the living room on the way to her bedroom, shedding a bookbag onto an armchair and turning into the kitchen to find him standing there with a cup of coffee in his hand. At the sight of him – in her mind, he was Harold; in her blood, an intruder – she almost screamed, and instead, in the moment it took her to recognize him, a moment not long enough for her sudden fear to abate, she reached to the counter and grabbed the cordless phone and threw it at him. It had felt good to hurl something, to see it hit him in the shoulder, to see him flinch and spill the coffee. He put down the mug and approached warily, hands held palm up before him, as if to shrug, in confusion, or as if in supplication, or to calm her, or embrace her – he was unreadable – but she didn't let him get near. She went to her room. He gave her a few minutes and then came to her door. He spoke her name. Then again. After a long interval, he said it once more. When she didn't respond, he said, "I'll be in touch. Soon. I miss you, darling." His presence outside the door as she stared at her wall poster of Nelson Mandela was very much like his palpable absence had been for almost four months. And now he'd just shown up. At some point, she looked to the door and knew he was gone, though she hadn't heard him leave the house. It had been thoughtless, not to have warned her. He hadn't even parked in the driveway. Later, she'd learn that Marian hadn't known he was coming, that he must have waited until she was gone. He must have been staking out the house.

On the way home from the library Harold had mumbled at the traffic and dozed, but upon arrival he'd sprung from the car and made it up and into his bed without weaving, and Kim had wondered if he wasn't more sober than he pretended. But she found two empty bottles of wine and a near-empty glass on the floor next to the loveseat. Assuming he hadn't had a drink in at least three hours, it would be that long again before he was lucid – what on earth had the counsellor been expecting from their session? – so she set about putting the kitchen in order and then stood at the window, looking down at the city and at the building that had quite suddenly, it seemed, lifted from the ground at the attack scene.

When he'd visited her in the hospital he had spoken of moving from here, and yet he'd stayed, each day with this prospect of the incident being entombed. Would he allow himself to acknowledge that it could have been much worse? Maybe he had. Maybe he was getting past it, and the drinking had other sources. What did she know of him, other than that he had never learned to properly iron his clothes and had no colour sense?

She knew that he often seemed on the verge of a surrender that had never come. That he possessed a capacity for love that he didn't know how to express. That he was at times a liar. Not so long ago, he'd been good at his work. His conversational ploys were transparent. He was guilty, pretended to be guileless. He lived at the limits of his strong intelligence in a state of higher bafflement.

And looking into the long sweep of him, imagining backwards from the man he was to the man he must have been, in stories, in photos, a narrowing. When he was her age, younger, his entirely intellectual interest in history had begun to reward him, and his outward character, a persona he himself was aware of, must have emerged in the trade. He would have left something of himself behind with each success. The post-doctoral fellowship, the first book, the first tenure-track job. There was a sadness inside sure ascendance.

She left him a note and drove to Little Italy for panini, and as she brought them back and parked the car, still thinking about Harold, the way she'd let her attention to him waver so easily over the years, an uneasiness came over her.

When she came through the door he was already up, standing in the kitchen in his underwear drinking coffee. He hadn't seen the note. When he was dressed they took their sandwiches to the dining-room table. The sleep had partially restored him.

"Don't expect me to explain myself. Not even when I'm sober."

"You knew the counsellor. She's had to see you before?"

"I send students to her."

"Hannah suggested that you've seen her too."

He was holding his sandwich before him with two hands, staring into it.

"It's none of your business, or Hannah's, but yes, a few times after what happened to you."

"Why does Hannah know about it?"

"Because I missed some classes."

"So she knows what happened."

"I said it was a family matter. She let it go at that. And you can too."

"And that's what this was about today, then? Me?"

"I know it looks bad, Kim, but don't worry too much. The drinking was just a sort of recreational accident. We're different people to ourselves on the other side of a drunk."

He wouldn't recognize himself passing by.

"Mom says you showed up drunk at the house."

"Well. I happened to be drunkenly in the neighbourhood."

"And my detective says you called her when you'd been drinking. Where's this coming from?"

"Burgundy, mostly."

He had no idea what he was doing to her.

"She also said, Cosintino, that you'd heard rumours and had theories and seemed to be investigating things on your own."

"I sound like a real wreck. I just asked her a few questions."

He was a fleer of rooms. As she had been, as a girl.

She asked about the torn page. For a moment he seemed to consider pretending not to know what she was referring to.

"I think I wanted it for a gift."

"A gift for who?"

"I've met an Anglican woman. She's solid and strong and certainly deluded."

"You're seeing this woman?"

"She'd rather not have anything to do with me."

"Hmm . . ."

"Then she isn't so deluded, I know."

They'd reached the end of what he'd tell her. It was a cold place. They each retreated into their thoughts. Yesterday she'd looked up from her life and found herself on a subway car, rolling into St. George Station. Faces shot past, she caught a few and watched them fly, and then the train stopped and she was out and climbing to ground level and entering the street in the smell of hot dogs and there was the vendor. She began the walk home, along the route she used to take as a student. Street by street, she was reclaiming each old path by walking it.

She wanted to tell him that it was working, this reclaiming, but it might seem she was asking for something he couldn't give her, the sum of his absences.

He stood and took the remains of their lunch to the sink, then began hunting through his bottles of vitamins on the counter.

"What happened to me isn't your fault. Is that what you've been thinking?" she asked.

"Oh, I don't know. We all stand accused of our lives."

"Maybe you should stop showing up drunk for it."

For a second there was no indication that he'd heard her.

"As bad coping goes, it is kind of a cliché," he said finally.

"And we have sworn off clichés."

He opened a bottle and shook out a pill.

"B complex. A good complex for drunks and nervous wrecks. Have one?"

"I'm getting past what happened but you work pretty hard lately at staying wrecked. Why is that?"

"It's just entertainment, pointless sport. But the real always has its revenge, always has the last word. It's the same in every language."

"Meaning what?"

"Meaning we all end up in the same place. And it's not heaven, and it lacks the colour of hell." He smiled for her. "You sure you don't want some vitamins?"

In the mornings now he came upstairs after Rosemary had left for the day and made a small breakfast of bread and cheese and poured a coffee and went out and sat on the front steps. Often he saw faces he recognized from the neighbourhood. One of them was an old woman who spoke no better English than he did. She would pass by and look at him and he would nod. She never spoke or smiled or acknowledged him at all beyond the look and she'd continue to a house two doors away where she'd stop on the sidewalk and talk to someone unseen, a woman in a window behind a curtain. The same exchange each day, about the weather, the garden, someone named David. One morning, finally, he heard the woman say, "He there, same again," and then later, "He sit in front." Thereafter he took his coffee inside.

The early afternoons were spent up on St. Clair Avenue in a little Latin bar that was mostly empty until the evening and would then run all night so loud sometimes that the police would come, which is why Rodrigo never went at night. He went in the day because Teresa worked there. They would sit together and she'd talk about news from home – he never had any, he had stopped sending and checking for emails – and rumours about people she knew here, affairs, business successes, a young girl from the spring who would come in with a man she called her "baby father" and they'd dance all night and then the man had left her and she had ended up in jail and her child taken by the authorities. They spoke not at all about Luis. Teresa told the stories without delight or reproof as if she just wanted them added to the pictures of this place and the place they came from. She always moved them in their talks towards whole things. It was a joke between them that she would say his full name and he would say hers. Teresa Viviana Gallego. It put more truth between them but a secret too because the others still called her Maria. It wasn't clear to Rodrigo if they thought that she was her sister or were simply agreeing to maintain the untruth.

One night as the streetlights came up, he emerged from the subway directly into a police scene and saw a woman officer pulling a line of tape off the pavement next to the chalk figure of a small human body. People stood staring at the marked-off space. There seemed no actual witnesses. The policewoman's partner was sitting alone in the cruiser. The passing cars slowed and drifted on. Someone said "a cyclist, not a kid on a bike," and Rodrigo knew the victim was a woman.

Owing to the accident, the walk south and then west along the café strip was not itself, despite the smell of coffee in the air, young men with instrument cases dressed raggedly, women on patios laughing or bending close, in summer dresses. His love for this street had been failing recently because he knew now he would not be admitted into the possibilities it held. The knowledge had the odd effect of settling his attentions – he saw people as they were, happy, unseeing, hungry for the summer nights while they lasted. They moved differently depending on their decade of life. Some of the older ones, in their forties or fifties, they didn't even look up from their books when the sexy young people walked by.

He sat at a bench on a corner with a view of cafés and card shops, a small movie theatre, a butcher's with sausages the size of his leg hung in the window. When he'd first come to the city he would walk himself lost into parts he didn't know, a new subway stop, choosing a bus at random, getting off, turning corners. He came to know the place by its smells and shapes, its local shops and corner stores and intersections where the sky was crossed with transit lines, where the window signs changed from an alphabet he knew to one of broken characters. In this neighbourhood he'd seen his first winter thunderstorm, near midnight and the grey overcast lit up like a gun muzzle in the rain.

He was falling in love with Teresa and it was too bad for them. Of course they would fall in love. No one else would have them, they weren't people to build a future upon. He wondered if she knew what was happening to them and would she let it happen. She had come here to marry a Canadian and enjoy a Canadian life. She would want children, born here, with at least one parent who could not be sent away.

A block to the south was the church where the Italians ended their Easter procession. He'd seen the Christ in torn robes, a foil crown of thorns, and running shoes, and the Romans in plastic breastplates pretending to whip him. An old woman in black had wailed in the streets at the illusion. He had wondered at her sorrow. Only months ago. Now he thought back, and pictured himself watching them, and wondered at himself, unable as always to make sense of what he saw. When he was a boy his mother often told the story of Jesus at the empty tomb appearing to Mary Magdalene as a gardener. She said the story proved Jesus loved working people above all others. But Rodrigo now thought the story proved something else. Mary did not recognize him as a plain man. If a plain man is unthought of, unseen for what he is, even when he's a prophet or the son of god, then what hope does a simple man have to be marked as good, as a worthy citizen or husband? His watching the procession, the slow, unreal cruelty, meant nothing in his favour because he'd been ruined by what he'd seen elsewhere, and in this new place, judged a killer.

His poor mother, her husband and one son dead, the other gone forever. She went to church twice daily, the new one without priests, full of singing, and believed that God spoke through her in a language no one understood.

He hated the course of his self-sorry thoughts. It was hot and he thought of Teresa, and then he put her out of his mind and thought of other women. He still fell in a boy's kind of love twenty times a day. Men were made more simply than women, with their secret desires. Tonight he would go by the Latin dance club and sit on the patio, watching the women moving inside. If he was lucky, two in a group of three would be claimed by other men, and the third, left alone, might allow him to come by her table. Maybe tonight he would finally lie about himself – it was what some of them wanted – and she would take him home. If he could be foolish enough to live inside his hours and not look ahead, he could have a fool's happiness until sleep, and sleep a fool's sleep until morning.

She wakes and goes straight to her desk, carrying the dream with her in fragments. A street at night lined with maples on fire.

A dog or cat burned up in a yard. Some certainty up ahead of her that she tries to follow. She stops on a sidewalk mid-block and sees a mark drawn in chalk on a tree lit up by the blazes.

The mark won't come back to her. She's seen it before on the periphery of her attention, like something glimpsed in passing. Only now does she realize it had been *R* in the dream, the certainty up ahead had been *R*, he'd led her to the mark on the tree. And sitting here, she thinks it's very close now, this convergence of their lives, this impossible intersection. It's all she can do not to run through the house to the front window and look for him.

And then as she imagines doing so, and begins to write of herself here in the room, getting up from her desk and heading for the window, she realizes the street she dreamt was her street, and she knows somehow where he was going.

She opened the garage. The heat trapped there moved against her and out the door. She stepped inside, let her eyes adjust. She took off her cotton sweater and hung it from the seat of her bike, then walked along the aisle formed by the stacks of Harold's boxes, and already her back was itching from the dust drifting into her T-shirt.

Upon seeing it again, she remembered the pictograph she'd seen in the dream. It was markered on the side of one of Harold's boxes. A cross inside a circle. She'd seen this box before, when she and Donald had carried in her few pieces of furniture, and every time she came in to get her bike or put it back. She must have registered the symbol without realizing it, and it had floated into her dream. A cross inside a circle, or a circled X. A kiss and a hug. Not, she decided, crosshairs in a gunsight.

As she lifted the box to the floor, exposing another behind, she saw the mark again. When she untucked the flaps, she found written in full on top of each box one of his old addresses, for a house in the city's Riverdale neighbourhood. He'd been on sabbatical that year, living in Mexico City, and must have shipped them back home. The symbol was simply a circled letter T, meaning Toronto.

She had learned in the hardest of ways to trust her intuition.

The boxes' contents had been shuffled over the years – the descriptive notations scribbled on the file folders no longer meant anything. She found old typewritten lectures on agrarian reform mixed with letters to Harold from his aunt inside an envelope marked "Grade Sheets, Term Assigns 82-86." Course syllabi, exam papers, flight documents, illegible handwritten notes, phone numbers without names, bus transfers, a ruined pair of black leather shoes. In a folder with pay stubs from the years after he was gone for good, a picture of an unsmiling, dark young woman in shorts and a halter top, standing on an empty beach somewhere, with nothing written on the back.

When she came to it, about ten minutes later, she knew it at once. The script was typewritten, copied in blue, on mildewed pages cranked out with chemicals through some old deadly process. The file they were in was marked "Unreturned Work." The folder's name was "Job Ads." There were three copies of his CV. She would have passed them by but for the thought that he was more or less her current age when he composed them. Years of achievement reduced to tight script. And she would have missed the discrepancies but for the way one line hung out to the edge of the unjustified right margin. The line had been removed for the subsequent CVs. It was under the subheading

Scholarships and Awards. "Hannity Travel Scholarship. Santiago, Chile. June-September, 1973." The other line missing from the later versions was under the subheading Languages. He'd studied Spanish at a school down there.

Why had he never mentioned he was in Chile during the dark days of the coup?

He'd saved the CV, like most of the junk, by chance, and wouldn't even know it was here. But she'd found a line to lead her, evidence to follow. Her training, intuition, even common sense told her so. Here was a detail within the larger mystery of his deep past. He liked to tell stories from his life, often of his travels, and often self-ridiculing, but always from the Montreal and Toronto years – at the cottage last winter he'd remembered a day trip he'd made with a boatload of historians up the Demerara into the Amazon, and when the motor died, their combined education left them unable to make fire and so they sat around in the dark all night imagining snakes in the trees. He never told stories from the time before he met Marian in '74. Only from Marian had she learned that Harold's mother had died when he was two, and his father had been itinerant, an alcoholic war veteran, quite likely a petty criminal. When she was old enough to be curious about his youth, and had asked him about it, he'd waved his hand and said, "I don't live there. I never really did," and that was understood to be the end of it.

It wasn't just that he'd remade himself, or repudiated his origins. She'd always had the sense that part of his remaking involved forgetting his past. Now she had evidence that he'd actually erased a part of it, and a part that must have been at the very least vividly interesting to a budding historian of Latin America, and likely fraught with experience.

His life had two stories. Had she found the time and place where the first one ended?

She repacked and restacked the two boxes, took the CV, went into the house quietly through the back and found Marian still asleep, as she'd left her on last inspection. She sat at the kitchen table. It occurred to her to wonder whether she should bring Marian into the question of Harold's time in Chile. Had she known? And if not, was there any point in altering her mother's sense of the past, the early days with him, with the news that he'd been withholding something even then? Or maybe the missing line was, in fact, explicable, insignificant.

She would leave Marian's past undisturbed. She took the CV to her room and tucked it into her computer case where she'd put the Colombian heartbreaker's story.

When she returned to the kitchen she remembered her sweater and went back outside. The door to the garage was wide open. She'd closed it, she was certain. She'd even registered the click of the bolt as she'd pulled it to. The sense memory was strong, precise. For a second she just stood there, twenty feet from the building. Donald was at work, Marian asleep. Had Harold returned?

She approached the garage, looked inside. Something was wrong but she couldn't say what, a feeling she'd had before but couldn't place. There was no one inside, unless they were crouching behind boxes. The boxes stood in their orderly, nearly true lines. The yard tools hung on the wall as always. Her bike in its profile.

And then it came to her. The sweater was missing.

Once she was inside the house again, and past the confusion of the moment, she decided the missing sweater meant next to nothing. In this neighbourhood, kids cut through backyards. Things sometimes went missing. Often bikes, it was true – kids steal bikes, not sweaters – but she must have interrupted the theft when she opened the sliding-glass door. It made a sound in its tracks, and it had taken a few extra seconds to do it quietly so as not to wake Marian, and in stepping through it she turned a little sideways and so wasn't directly facing the garage. And of course a kid would be quick enough to take off running and be gone before she noticed. Or in fact he might have slipped inside to hide behind the boxes, or concealed himself between the garage and the fence and waited for her to come and go before making a break for it. He probably made his escape while she was back inside, deciding what it all meant.

It was a mark of her recovery that she hadn't run to the phone and called her detective. Cosintino had said that in a small percentage of cases, attackers contacted their victims after the assault. Sometimes directly, often not. But even knowing this, she was going to keep her wits and not let a pilfered sweater get the best of her.

And because she was now practised at securing details, she let the doubts be doubts. As in why, having gotten close enough to take the sweater from the seat, the thief had not had time to actually take hold of the bike. She'd known in one glance that it hadn't been touched. She always balanced it with the front wheel turned slightly to keep pressure off the handbrake, and set the pedals at two and eight o'clock so she could mount it and glide off in one motion. Everything had been in position.

And so, to be honest with herself, it wasn't that she felt no fear but that she knew its causes and dimensions, and thereby had been able to isolate it. And this was a triumph. She felt triumphant. She had not relapsed. And she would not, upon having her mind occupied with questions of Harold, let him come to be associated yet again by chance with the attack. She would spare him that.

Even in bed that night, having told no one about the CV or the missing sweater, she allowed into her thoughts whatever would come, and in not fighting the thoughts, disarmed all but two vivid images. The bike standing there with the pedals at two and eight. And her blue cotton sweater, like the flag of another's triumph, hanging on a bedpost in some dim basement room.

In his office on campus, at just past eight in the morning, Harold gathered himself to read. It had been a bad night. He was just another cowardly insomniac, but things were worsening. The insomniacs he knew tended to be men like himself – he imagined women had a better take on life and death – men who'd remembered the terrors in their little-boy hearts. Around four in the morning he decided to address the problem directly and went online to find the latest research. There was nothing helpful, studies on pills and unlikely therapies, poems about the night bringing its "special way of being afraid," Goya's *The Sleep of Reason Produces Monsters*. In time he managed to nod off on his couch until the sun woke him, not so oddly, from a dream of growing light, to a memory of a morning somewhere long ago when he'd wept with relief at the daybreak.

The disturbances were still with him, laid over his reading, but what was work for if not to dispel fear? He'd been asked to act as a peer reviewer of yet another article on monastic orders in the New World. He recognized the unattributed paper before him as that of Myles DeGroot, who'd authored a book two years ago on *conversos* in Mexico and started a debate about the role of illiterate women as the unreliable repositories of Jewish faith. Myles produced these things despite a crushing teaching load at some sham university in the Carolinas. They'd gone out drinking one night in Cartagena with six or seven other conference-goers, and Myles had put back the rum until he was on all fours on the dance floor, singing into the veneer. There was a similar intemperance in his work.

When he looked up he caught sight, as if for the first time, of the hundreds of spines lining his shelves. He pictured his own two monographs shelved and forgotten in a few such offices around the Americas. The books, so many walled cities in the kingdom of academia. He didn't contribute much to the kingdom anymore. His productivity had fallen off, likely for good. The sheer physical drain of hunting through archives in the tropics, fending off rats and mosquitoes, receiving daily a hantavirus mask from the librarian with elephantiasis – he always had the best archive stories at any dinner party – it took too much out of him now. And the centuries-old documents he'd learned to photograph were an ordeal to work through, dim script in a distant Spanish that he used to read effortlessly. He busied himself these days with smaller projects and a little devoted mentoring. Neither of which kept him quite busy enough to help him through the night.

He missed the old case of Marian's books from the house. The shelves had offered a place to put his thoughts, even on the day she kicked him out for good. The first sign that something was wrong – he knew it as it was upon him – was the cello suite he heard on coming home, music that she listened to, she'd once told him, only when she was "mad enough to stab someone." He closed the door quietly. Everything was in its place but for her keys, which should have been in the hollow-backed ceramic cow on the table in the entryway, but when he went to the kitchen, there they sat on the counter where he'd had breakfast that morning. There had been nothing unusual at breakfast that he recalled except the sight of her opening the fridge door and going still for a few seconds as if transfixed by the leftovers, a moment he now thought it was odd that he'd noticed. He walked in, under the music, and surveyed the living area. Something had changed. The bookshelf, or rather, the books on it, the spines, to be precise. Over time, from his usual corner of the couch, he'd more or less memorized the colour and shape pattern. It was where he looked whenever she needed to accuse or hurt him. He'd find the brightest title – the black, yellow, and red *Barcelona* – and move left or right, up or down, trying to remember what he'd ever known about terracotta, the French Baroque period, eco-activism, all her past aborted passions after she'd quit law. Novels. Travel guides. Bad books expanded out of better magazine articles. A few primers on religions and ideas. Yes, something was different here – the categories were mostly in place, but the order was all wrong. For one, *Barcelona* was now on the far left side of the bottom shelf, next to a study of Voudon. When had this happened? Only hours earlier, he learned when she walked into the room a moment later, her face unmade, bone white. She'd been looking for his first book, to rip out the dedication page. She didn't know what she'd intended to do with the page – *to Marian.* What she did know was that a woman named Marla had left a message for him.

He couldn't now remember Marla distinctly. Celina had been almost two decades into the past, he and Marian and Kim were clipping along, and then one night at a faculty party, the host's sister kept catching his eye and holding it, unambiguously. Her dark hair was cut very short, like a pelt, and she was tall and toothy. Before they spoke, before he learned that she was visiting from Rochester, as she did every second weekend, what surfaced in him, other than desire, was a profound self-awareness. He understood that he was false. His life, its stability, were false. He and Marian hadn't made love in months, going on years. And he had been false to himself and so to everyone. Saying hello to Marla, knowing what it would bring, felt like the truest thing he'd ever done. By the time he realized his error, he was indulging in a disaster, and she had his number.

He'd been the first to arrive in the department this morning, and even now the secretaries were his only company, so upon hearing the bike being wheeled along the hallway, he assumed it must be a grad student who'd been stuck with a summer tutorial class.

When Kim rolled the bike into his office and stood before him, he experienced a moment of disjuncture, the feeling of her being here made sense but only in an earlier life. She said nothing for a moment.

"They have hitching posts out there. Hello."

She was studying him.

Her gaze lifted and fixed on something over his head. Then it was back on him. He invited her to sit down but she ignored him. Her presence made him feel slightly ashamed of his space, his shelves of books, his mounted prints of sixteenth-century maps, the *New Yorker* cartoons taped to his door. She saw through it all so easily; none of it made the least impression on her.

"I found some stuff in the garage. You never mentioned you were in Chile when you were young."

He felt something far in the distance change its course and turn towards him.

"I was down there, yes."

"During the coup."

"Yes. As it turned out."

"I noticed you took the travel scholarship off your CV."

There she was, his talented daughter, finding what wasn't even on the record.

"Well, there I outsmarted myself." He composed his voice. "I put it on in applying for grad school but expunged it as I was going into the job market. I couldn't guess the political makeup of any given hiring committee, so I played it safe. After I got hired I kept it off because, frankly, I was embarrassed by the omission. And if it suddenly showed up during my tenure review, for instance, it would look professionally suspect."

"That explains the CV. But I wasn't hiring you. Why not tell me?"

Where to look? The enduring simplicity of the chain and sprocket, spoke and rim.

"There likely hasn't been occasion to, and I haven't gone out of my way to bring it up. Maybe there is a bit of an old fracture there that I'd just rather not reinjure."

"What kind of fracture?"

He needed to be careful not to speak too long. She would catch any misplay.

"Well. Nothing awful happened to me. But awfulness was

going around. There were moments of real fear, but I don't dwell on them. They passed and I let them go. I guess to some extent this was a forced forgetting. I didn't want to think about what it must have been like for others. I don't blame myself for suppressing those thoughts long enough to save my mental health." Maybe it was good she had asked him, he thought. He was finally voicing the matter something like he'd imagined he might someday. Maybe there would be better prospects for them, sure and fully shared attentions on the far side of this conversation. "I guess I've thought this through by now. You and I both distrust simple explanations, but there is something in all people that makes them want to find a root cause for their behaviour – what's behind my failings as a husband and father and so on? – but for most of us, it's not so simple. Do you understand?"

"You were worried for your mental health but you tell me nothing happened."

What she couldn't admit, he thought, was that a part of her wanted to learn that something terrible had befallen him in Chile, something that could account for his misjudgments and troubles over the years.

"It's easy to make too much of it, Kim. It was frightening to be there under that kind of rule. The day after the coup I hid with others, people I didn't know, in my teacher's apartment, and later I got out of the country while they couldn't. I wasn't brutalized. It's the dead and ruined who deserve our thoughts, not those of us who escaped. So I've never done them the disservice of dining out on my time there."

Her face had an openness, each feature set off by another, and you could see her world in it, her eyes, her brow, little tremors in her forehead, all the disturbed surface tensions, the wind on clear water.

"What about the people you knew there?"

"I only ever knew a few. I shared an apartment with other foreign students. A German and two Americans. I think they all got out okay."

"You don't know for sure? Weren't they your friends?"

"I thought so. One of them, a guy named Carl Oakes, I don't think he was who he seemed to be. He was hard to read. Politically. Anyway, yes, we survived."

It was built into the cosmic trackings that the old would forget who they had been and replace themselves in memory with regrets and wistfulness, an innocence that never existed, even in the face of what does exist in youth, a fleeting, unheeding wisdom. Kim saw into him, she always had. But he saw things, too. Invisible things – not just the sly intents that people carried in their smiles, but darting fiends in shadows. There were safe ways to speak of them, these fiends, but Kim was the kind to call them up directly, as if to do battle. He wanted to warn her but didn't know how.

"There's a report on the dead and missing," she said. "The Rettig Report. I just read it."

And like that, it was all going wrong. It was in her now, Santiago. She knew her history, and had too strong an imagination.

"Did you. I guess it's not exactly a romp."

"When I worked at GROUND I read truth commission findings from all over. The stories are hard. I always ended up sort of drained and hopeful at the same time."

"I see. I don't think my feelings would be so complicated."

Someone was coming along the hallway, then stopped and receded. The moment, as they waited it out, was obscurely freighted.

"You don't think truth commissions serve a purpose."

"What I think is, it's good to get the record straight. And it might help victims, survivors, temporarily, to seem to be expelling their trauma. But there are no talking cures. And often the justice is too little or too late. The killers take asylum in their own cities and stay safe as long as they don't leave and get arrested by an international court. Santiago. Guatemala City. These places are full of monsters, many of them now in suits."

She let his words fall, then glanced around the office as if unable to look at him. Postcards she had given him were propped here and there. Picasso's *Brick Factory at Tortosa*. Klee's *Angelus Novus*, with the angel of history blown forward through time, looking back at the piling wreckage at his feet. Until now he had stopped seeing them. They were just cards she'd picked up in galleries and museums. There was nothing written on them.

"It's not been easy," she said, "going back to that night. Writing about it. I actually found a bit of courage in the thought that it was your idea, something you'd insisted on for my sake."

"I was right to insist."

"I guess it gave me the illusion I was expelling trauma. Is that how you put it?" She watched him. Her neck was flushed, her face lunar. "You know why I quit grad school? Because I didn't want to be a professor. All I've ever wanted to be is a truth commission." When she smiled, so did he, and she trapped him there by changing her face and letting the smile go.

"A lot of junk in that garage," he said. "It might be time to take all those boxes to the dump."

Her forearm pronounced little cords of muscle as she gripped the black foam seat. She waited a moment longer, then lifted the bike and turned it to face the doorway and started off and down the hallway and would have left without another word but he called to her. She walked backwards for a few steps, like a figure on a film in reverse, and stood with her bike in profile. Following any other conversation it would seem stylish, comic, a little Buster Keaton, but now it was just strange, and made her a stranger for a moment, long enough that he saw her face newly, the woman who existed for the rest of the world beyond the narrow idiom of father-daughter.

"We haven't talked about you," he said.

"Yes we have."

She was working something through, one emotion to the next, each routed through her intelligence. Her heart, her brain. His chances weren't great with either of them. But then what did he really know of her heart? Maybe they'd come out of this just fine.

"I can tell when you're lying," she said. "Don't you know that?"

"What do you mean?"

"Lying, evading. You've been at it since I walked in."

"I don't lie to you, Kim."

"There. You've just done it again."

And then she was gone. A minute later she appeared beneath his window, balancing on a pedal, then mounting the bike on the fly. She rode between the buildings, and out towards the common, through the pedestrian traffic of students, all heedless of her, and then moved out of view.

In mid-story, mid-sentence, Kim stops writing. Instantly she knows she's been preparing this desertion for days.

She's going to walk out on *R*.

His life will continue unauthored from this day forward. Now and then she'll think of him, and wonder if he's come to mind because she has come to his. In farewell, she grants him an independent being, a kind of will. When he wants to, this made-up man, he can wonder whatever became of his absconded creator.

She doesn't save the afternoon's work. When she closes the file, she knows it will be for the last time. Then she deletes it. She shuts down the computer. The screen winks and goes dark. Along the base of the machine, four beads of light die rapidly one by one like the windows of a distant train disappearing into a tunnel and she feels stricken.

Then she does the thing she does sometimes, and loosens her jeans and reaches her left hand down and along her thigh, to feel the scar, to press her fingers against it. Pain and numbness. There and not. No one but the doctors have seen it. When she needs to bring herself back to earth, she does this thing.

The room is quiet. Through the open window, no reports from the city. A dog has ceased barking.

Here in this room she had once been a girl. All that was left of the girl was this staring at the back of the door, not wanting to open it, wanting it to open.

She wants to tell *R* that the desertion holds promise, for it falls to a neat equation, in that the man she's abandoned him for once abandoned her. She wonders now if he ever came back, was ever really there in the first place.

When he'd visited her at the cottage, he had argued for disarming the past with scrutiny. He had called it hopeful, the act of writing about the attack, the idea that two people might see the same complexity in the same way. Her hope now is to know her father as no one knows him. He is entirely undiscovered, even to himself. Her new chosen mode will be history, her subject revealed through his own method. She still believes in history. She'll be the true historian's historian, the very daughter he has always thought he wanted.

R has brought her back to the plural, present world.

When she was young she'd known there was bitterness beyond the door, but there was love too. Without much self-pity she can admit now that the love was not as she'd imagined, that it was smaller, and from now on, maybe it's not to be given to her, if given at all, without compromise. When Marian dies, the uncompromised love will end. It would be better not to know as much, but there is no getting free of the knowledge. She has had her life's one lucky escape.

PART TWO

6

One night he heard the walls speak his name until he stabbed the plasterboard with his fishing knife. In the morning he saw the pattern of holes and joined them with a marker to discover the secret constellation that described his pain. That had wanted describing, that was what had called to him all along, wanting its shape to be made. The shape had a centre but was uncertain of itself in the far reaches like it could have been a slow galaxy or spiny poisonous fish. He tacked a sheet on the wall to cover it but the spiny voice came again another night and he took his keys and went out to lose it in the warp.

He took a bright downtown bus and coming the other way they passed the 96 he used to ride two hours a day just to get told in a class that he wasn't trying. He had unspooled and was sent for assessment. He lived by the lake back then and when he quit the class he took the transit everywhere, spending the afternoons in church kitchens and libraries so that he put the city together and held it in mind as a picture of foreign clusters. The Dufferin–St. Clair branch was Italian. College-Shaw, Italian and Portuguese. Jones past the little Chinatown across the Don. He wrote them on his folding map. He wanted the big design, to see what it meant. Forest Hill was Jewish. Gladstone, Hungarian. Danforth-Coxwell was Greek and Indian and some branches were crawling with yowlers. There were pockets of Eritrean, Salvadoran, German, West Indian, Guyanese, he wrote out the names of the languages and looked up the strange ones. He used to be good at geography but he didn't like the peoples if they didn't hold still, didn't stay in their places, or else why have the countries at all. He had said this many times and no one listened. He had said it to separate himself from the impression he made with his skin. His line had been tainted somewhere and he'd caught the dark more than anyone.

He stole books and poster ads. The city was full of things just there for the taking.

One poster was for a picnic, where he'd first seen her, making name tags for the yowlers. They crowded around her, laughing, she couldn't spell the names or the ones who didn't know it, whose sponsors always spelled it for them. In their small corner of the park with the wind up in the treetops like rushing water. He was there alone. He knew no one, and he sat on a picnic table with his feet on the seat and watched the white girl. They crowded around her and the African blacks were the worst, whose names began Nb or Nj or some such senseless thing, taunting their bodily hosts. The tags were on paper you stuck to your shirt and hoped it didn't rain. When the table cleared he would say hello and watch her spell out what he said. The music began, the same dumb guitars and pan flutes he heard everywhere west of Yonge with the same players playing what seemed the same song standing in a half-bent row on the verges of the crowd.

He walked over and said hello. Her face was bright, she didn't know him. He thought of a name and told her Mason, the name of a dog he'd killed once, and when she looked down to write it he saw that she'd put both of hers on her tag. He could find her whenever he wanted.

Long ago a doctor had predicted her in his life and here she was. He wondered if he'd have met her if the doctor hadn't said so and then knew she'd been there from the start, his whole life on this vector, and the doctor had just called the line.

She was not someone he'd pictured. He knew he would know her when the time came.

"There you go, Mason."

He smiled. He wanted her to say his real name, to know it. He felt the sky unlocking and only later would know why.

She told him to have a free burger.

At first, following, it was like he just wanted to find a way of telling her something. Because of her work she kept to a pattern and he reduced his study to the last few blocks. In a black between-space he waited three nights in one week, two the next before he saw what would happen. The site was unsecured. The guard cheated and went home by eleven and left the lock open for the morning shift workers.

He bore no control of his physical self. Things he felt on his skin brought him mercy. What he wanted to say was that in some hours he understood that he was wrongly fitted to this world. There was another world where it would come up right, where the all of him worked as it should, but he was lost to it. It was light years away and he had no means of flying there.

Downtown was a different place. Every few blocks there were internet rooms with curtains around every station.

How to say, it used to be the windows would memorize me but now I can pass without judgment. The virtual world had made him invisible. The place you cross over has no opening, no beginning. You have always been crossing until you do.

Mason, he would say again. He killed a dog once with a grappling hook. In his heart he was wrongly fitted.

"I just heard the music," he said. Then the next ones in line started laughing. She waved him goodbye with a smile and he only wanted to show her himself open the same way. He wanted them both open at the same time. He walked off towards the grill and kept walking, saying her name, letting it carry him clear. In the night she would do the numbers, thinking back, not knowing what had happened, that he was more numbers than the rest. She might think "Mason" and he could almost think it with her.

The thing that happened came out wrong. He still wanted to explain, all day every day for months now. In his fantasy she wins the struggle, and beats him, and before she throws him into the pit, she holds him for the one moment he had been sent here for, the one he could stay inside forever.

One evening, at the table with her mother after dinner, Donald in his study, Kim recalled for Marian a conversation they'd had years ago about intuition. Marian had said that when women spoke of intuition, they were just in some suggestible, wishing state in which they pretended to see signs. Kim had said her intuitions were sometimes colder than that. It wasn't just that she knew things before they happened – what someone would say, however strange, just before they said it – but she felt she knew what they were thinking. She knew their silences.

Especially Harold's. And she knew something very dark was going on in those silences. Marian had said only that she didn't doubt it – it wasn't clear whether she meant the intuition or the darkness – and that had been the end of the conversation.

"You remember all of that?" Marian asked.

"For some reason you were full of silences yourself that night."

"I don't remember. But don't get carried away about intuition, Kim. Women can make no more sense of men than they can of dogs or mooses. They're hurt, they love us, a doubt is buzzing around, bothering them, they don't know their own hearts. It's all us, projecting. Which is why they think we're trouble." Marian had energy tonight. It had combined with the wine to make her voluble. "They think we're full of enigmatic forces. The sins of Eve."

"That's not what I'm talking about."

"And we scheme. Here we are scheming. It must be a man who set this off."

"Now there's *your* intuition at work. He's someone who came to mind today from long ago. Second-year undergrad. A Chilean guy. He told me his father was killed before he was born. During the coup in '73."

Kim measured the pause. She'd wondered if mention of Chile would expose Marian to something she'd rather not talk about. In trying to be considerate of her mother's feelings, Kim was becoming sly – they had never before had slyness between them – but it turned out she couldn't read Marian's reaction. Her face had been slowly departing over the weeks. It had lost its set. Often there was a translucence, something resinous on the surface.

"Who was this man from Chile? And why think of him now?"

She said his name was Eduardo something and explained that she'd met him at an International Students Union party, an older guy she was half interested in.

"He worked at a music store. I used to go by with my friends." Kim kept to herself the memory of Eduardo joining them in a soundproof booth. They went in with gorgeous instruments and wailed away terribly, with the exuberance of ignorant youth. As if sax and guitar and a little squeezebox could ever come together no matter how much they wanted it. She and her friends only ever wanted anything for ten minutes tops. Then she met someone else and forgot him.

They could just hear Donald's voice from the study. He was on the phone.

"What does this Chilean man have to do with intuition?"

"I don't know yet."

Marian reached over to Donald's half-full wineglass and placed it in front of her daughter, who now had two. The family always finished each other's wine, and never poured glass to glass for fear of spilling, and so depending when each had had enough, or how the conversation was running, the glasses moved around like gaming pieces.

The tablecloth tonight was yellow with a blue-lined border. Marian had bought it in Cuba years ago. She had fabrics and pottery from every trip she'd taken with Harold, small quetzal bird paintings and decorative lizards and jointed snakes. Most were in storage but she kept them in rotation, as if to insist the experiences they commemorated were hers, uncompromised by what was to come between them. She'd travelled with Donald, too, to Montreal, Chicago, London, Kim couldn't recall where else, but she'd not collected so much by that time in her life. Or maybe she had but the objects were not for display. It had been years since Kim had seen this bright cloth. Last week there had appeared ceramic coasters with painted Cuban scenes, little wedges against the narrowing of Marian's days. She had always claimed to love Havana above all cities.

"What do you think Harold was looking for in the garage that day?" Kim asked.

"This intuition of yours. Maybe you got it from your father. Except in him it's more like superstition. He would never admit it – it runs counter to his self-image as a rationalist – but he's prone to some pretty loopy thoughts."

"Especially when drunk, I guess."

"All his bad luck," said Marian. "Harold thinks he brings it on himself. And because it's usually true that he does, he sees it all linking back through the years to a kind of original sin. And we've all paid for it."

"Has he said that?"

From the study, the sound of Donald braying delightedly into the phone, as if hearing news of some enemy undone.

"What if he's right, Kim? What if the years of trouble begin in some distant mistake and how he came to regard it? A mistake with real consequences, one to the next. Of course you wouldn't be free of them. Neither of us would."

"You can't let what happened to me get you thinking like this."

"It's my life that gets me thinking. My life and yours. I can't blame him for all our troubles, but I can for a lot of them."

She'd had too much to drink. Tomorrow she'd repudiate it all. Kim had learned to pay attention to anything that might come to be disavowed.

"I found a few of his old CVs."

Marian looked down at her napkin and straightened it. "So you were digging around in there too." In her next breath she seemed to draw them both to a single point of focus. "You know, the things that are precious to us, that we keep to ourselves, they're not all consoling." She was using her bitter-wisdom tone. "But still they're ours and no one else's."

"Why does it sound like you're protecting him?"

"Because you shouldn't snoop."

"Historians snoop. He does it."

"You don't snoop, Kim. You snoop and worlds fall."

She only covered for Harold when he wasn't around, but even then she seemed to allude to the broken marriage.

"He was in Chile during the coup. I think it's odd he's never mentioned that to me."

The words took hold and Marian looked out at her from some endless space.

"Chile. I didn't know that," she said. "I guess I knew he'd been somewhere."

"He was at a language school and –"

"I don't want the details."

The statement seemed addressed to herself. How many times had she uttered it?

"There was a list of names," Marian said. "Spanish names. He had it when I first met him. I found it tucked into a book I'd just taken down from a shelf, and I asked him about it. He came up and plucked it from my hand and walked off. After that it would turn up now and then, hidden away somewhere around one apartment or another."

"What happened to it?"

"It stopped turning up. After a while, it just disappeared."

Kim finished the night alone, on the porch.

She had snooped, yes. She'd done it at GROUND and in the garage. And she had found things. Marian must have decided long ago never to dig around in Harold's pockets. And yet mysterious lists and women's names had come to her anyway, by chance. It would have been better to have known, and known early. Learning another's heart too late ends up knocking your own out of true.

But her intuition was still at work. She could feel it, the slight lifting in her thoughts. She looked out into the night. In the yard across the street a family of raccoons walked along a shed roof and dropped one by one over the back, and it came to her. It was her attacker who'd taken the sweater from the garage. At the time she'd talked herself out of the possibility. But it was him. His communication had now reached her, three days later.

She went back inside the house. Before bed she called Cosintino and left a message. She found herself arguing against what she knew, sounding calm. She made the case for the thief being a kid. And regardless there would be no evidence, no fingerprints – she'd been in and out of the garage for her bike several times since then, and anyway he wouldn't have been so careless.

"I'm telling you just so you know," she said. "Just for the sake of the record. But please, if my father calls you again, don't mention it."

The sources were ever harder to trace. Increasingly Father André found himself cribbing his new sermons from his old ones. This morning, rather than reread Athanasius, he'd employed the lines he knew by heart. Man bears the Likeness of Him Who Is, and if he preserves that Likeness through constant contemplation, then his nature is deprived of its power and he remains incorrupt. But this man doubted that even constant contemplation would be enough. It was ever harder these days to find contemplative space, and when he did find it – walking, in his study with scripture, in the lull after service – he often felt no longer equal to it. Most of the things that were once true to him were still true, but he'd worn through his ways of thinking about them. When repeated endlessly in the same forms, revelations emptied, little by little. This was aging.

Athanasius. Doubts about him had crept into the histories. Could a church father have used violence and murder for political ends, a man who wrote of the need for the "active, arduous peace of poise and balance in a disordered world"? The words were thinning but true.

Outside the door to the parish hall, the homeless were gathering for the Thursday meal. There were maybe twenty today. He knew most by their first names. As he approached them, Leonard the Dubious waved to him with a dirty palm. Leonard, who was more or less his own age, had once expressed his life philosophy, which he clung to though it had not served him well: "Take what you want and then chow the fuck down." The man was a compendium of useless aphorisms, many of them vaguely sexual, if one followed the mangled metaphors. The idea seemed to be that Leonard was fuller than André of experience in the world. It was no small ministerial project to lead him to the realization that, mostly, he was just full of shit. Someday Leonard would understand, because he would need to, that the project had been mounted for him.

"Hey, Father. Looks like we all come running to the same dinner bell."

"We do, Leonard."

"A man needs what he needs." He tossed up a canted grin. The others were watching their exchange. A young man named Jules looked at André sympathetically.

"And he needs to know what he needs to know," said André. "Beginning with who he is, and who he serves."

"Well, if you just open these doors, I'll serve myself, thanks."

"Let me see if it's ready."

He nodded to the others and passed inside. As usual Maggie and Molly, the Keegan sisters, were present, and David Asodi, an old Trinidadian who wore sweater vests year-round. None of them had been at the morning service.

Maggie tossed him an apple, which he almost caught.

"You had that look on your face," she said. "Lost in space again."

"We can't have that." He picked up the bruised apple and set it in one of the fruit bowls. "How are you all?"

However they were warranted no complaint. Molly said they'd been discussing summer movies.

"Not your kind of thing, Father."

"Not mine either," said David. He had a wife who'd never come to the church.

"We used to show old black-and-whites in the basement," André said. "They didn't draw flies." The table was ready. It was time to open the doors. "What holds more meaning, do you suppose? A year's worth of movies, or this bowl of fruit?"

David laughed gently and nodded. André regarded the bowl and thought of the works, vividly representational, of the neighbourhood's graffiti artists, the best of whom seemed limited only by their available colours. If he himself could paint, he'd depict this bowl of fruit, bruises and all. Most of the things he valued had a memorial aspect.

Molly opened the doors. In they came. André excused himself and went to his office. As was her habit, Rosemary was on his computer. She seemed to resent her time with it, and so didn't have one in her home, but there were things she couldn't call up during her work in the library. She said hello without looking away from the screen.

"Lunch is served," he said.

"Soup and conversation."

"Sorry?"

"You remember Mariela Cendes."

"Of course."

She looked at him now with that familiar fixed gaze of slight accusation, as if he'd misled her somewhere long ago. It had been seven years since she first showed up in his night class, six since she began coming to the church, and almost that long since she'd made herself central to its mission. Only in those first months was she capable of expressing joy at having been granted a certainty of direction so anomalous in her life. Eventually, working in the community, the joy left her. He used to be able to talk her back into her own capacities for calm devotion. But his words no longer reached her.

"I told your friend Harold about Mariela," she said. "Then it came to me later that his obsession with what happened to his daughter, generating theories, getting tangled up in lives, lives like mine, it's completely the right response. Anything else is a lie. I think I felt something like his freefall back when Mariela disappeared. And I wonder what happened to me that now I seem able to eat soup and make conversation."

"I see. What are you looking at there?"

She glanced at the screen.

"Obscenities. We live in an age when obscenity is the given."

The best he could do now was to alter her course slightly, enough to bring her, in time, to a service that wasn't haunted at the edges with the worst human actions, the heaviest mourning, suffering as a kind of lodestone she couldn't help but turn to upon every waking.

"We do. But we don't have to look."

"Everyone looks, Father. If only to see what the others are looking at. The internet brings us beheadings, war deaths, celebrity autopsy reports. Traffic accidents, and sexual acts so bizarre they seem the result of traffic accidents. This isn't a new democracy. This isn't freedom. We've poisoned ourselves. How can we survive this?"

"Humour helps." He forgave himself the comment, and only wished something funny had come to mind. She was once capable of easy laughter; now it was work all around. "And so do our disciplines. I have my daily orders. The internet is just another of our enemy's weapons. It must be stunting to witness so much meaningless spectacle." Was it truth or self-pity or pride that allowed him to see himself as belonging to a dying breed, the Retainers of Long Knowledge? "We need to bring people news from the un-uploadable worlds. The historical, the private, the spiritual."

"In case you haven't noticed, they aren't buying." She was right. They'd lost the battle for the common man. Microelectronics could do anything with a standard-issue forty-watt brain. But then the brain was full of wonderful atavisms. As was the present. The Anglican Communion was fracturing and its leader was writing books on Dostoyevsky.

"Things take time. It's partly because the Book of Psalms was six centuries in the making that one day everyone will be reading it again."

"And one day the sun will explode. Right now I'm worried about us."

Here was his opening. He stepped through it without much hope, and offered up a small, silent prayer.

"I am too. I've been thinking we could use you in some of the other social outreach programs. Lately –"

"I don't have time, Father."

"It's a matter of balancing your efforts."

A man's laughter rose up from the hall. It sounded like Willy, the young AWOL American soldier. He'd never really come back from Iraq. Every second face in the city spooked him and he laughed at scenes in his head. He seemed to be laughing through the walls at André's proposition, another Distant Audience.

"You want me to give up my work. You don't trust it, or me for that matter." Her voice always softened as her accusations sharpened. "You've come to see me as a zealot, blinded by – what's that word you like? Hubris?"

"You know I value your work, Rosemary. And I value you. But we all must attend to our humility."

"I'm too big for my britches."

"Not all our social justice work is done in battle gear. Maybe you need to allow yourself a break. Maybe to feel some reward, and a bit more hope."

"Why are you saying all this?"

"Because week by week you're becoming harder, more indignant. I don't blame you, I'm just trying not to lose you. And you're in danger of losing yourself."

She pushed herself away from the desk.

"And what about those I help? What's to become of them if I take your recommended R and R?"

"They're resourceful. That's how they ended up here."

And then it was Rosemary laughing. It was low and brief, but derisive. She'd never sounded this note before with him. She got up from the chair.

"I've never asked you to sanction my work. You or the church. I raise most of the money on my own anyway. Actually most of it's mine. So what do I need you for?"

"You know the answer."

"Yes. I do. But you seem to have forgotten it." She wouldn't soften again. She walked past him, saying, "I'm off to feed mouths," and left him alone. In her simplest statements he sometimes heard the compressed rhythms of biblical Hebrew. On meeting her, against his good sense, he'd felt a force of need in her that he supposed had a personal aspect. In fact, the need was for the knowledge he could impart, first of theology, and then of faith and its practices. He'd wondered if there wasn't something for them both to learn of the lessons of the heart. Now she was able to leave his presence without apparent loss, not the smallest pang of parting. He'd brought her out of one world into a larger, more fraught one, and it had worn her down. He'd animated her sense of the holy without knowing how to guide it, and so she'd wandered into the fray with a half-formed spiritual intelligence. It could be that her heart was stronger than his. In any case, it was about to exile itself. He would lose her, if he hadn't already.

The Old Testament God sometimes played his adversary. There was a lesson in the arrangement that he had never understood.

Stranger,

In the weeks before you left us, we used to make jokes, the three of us, about the famous last words of historical figures. Do you remember? Henry VIII, Napoleon. Minnesota Fats, calling a kiss off the tombstone. Mother had all the best lines. And then one night there was a tension in the air that I didn't understand and I wanted us all to play, and you said you were tired of the game. You said, "Nobody really dies quipping."

It wasn't one of your usual evasive remarks. This one sounded earned. I thought so even then.

More and more of your lines have come back to me lately. They seem to want to be put together.

When I worked with the clients at GROUND, I often felt the force of plot design, some hand at work, rounding the periods in their lives into legible wholes. Their testimonies were full of high drama, veered off in unlikely directions. And now in my own life I've experienced such a turn and it's had the effect of clarifying for me which things matter and which don't. It's important to me that my life doesn't become a banal story, a lesson in pity or self-deception, an example of courage or staring down misfortune or whatever. I want instead to be accepting of ambiguity, even contradiction, and hard truths. And to be without illusion, and yet still hopeful.

I don't expect to make sense of senseless events, but hope to find a way of accepting a world that contains them. Things can change, all in a day, a given hour. That hour can run in us forever. Some people hold it too close even to speak of it. Others go over it compulsively, telling the same story for years (maybe they get the story wrong, it doesn't matter unless a tribunal is judging). The one wrong thing is to turn from it.

We recognize one another, those who've lived through that hour.

There's much you haven't told me. But your ways of not telling aren't strategic, I now realize. They're part of you. Which means, I think, that there's much you haven't told yourself.

You don't believe in talking cures. I do believe in telling ones. The hard part is to begin. But begin at the beginning.

Who were you?

k

He nodded.

"Hello, Rosemary."

She was just outside his door. He made room and she stepped past him and walked to the window, as he'd imagined she would. He closed the door and looked at her fully from behind. She'd made a slight effort to dress attractively, a long skirt and low-cut top mottled in yellows and browns. She carried a woven red bag.

"Does everyone comment on the view?"

"Invariably."

She turned and surveyed the place. It looked orderly enough, he thought, in the late-afternoon light.

"My friends in St. James Town love their views," she said. "People mistake altitude for perspective. There's a little Roma boy who has the sense to be scared of living in the sky, but I told him the angels were up there with him. He asked if that meant he'd see his dead brother."

She wouldn't make this easy for them.

"That's quite an opener. Can I get you something?"

Maybe she doubted her decision to come. He'd asked her over the phone. He said he was in trouble and wanted her help. He'd never said anything like it before.

They took their drinks at either end of the couch, looking down at the city. He pointed out the better new buildings among the older ones, with their squared-away expressions of nearly the same thought. Often the lowering light caught some wonder in the downtown architecture that was never there on the local cable channel with the traffic cameras marking the main arteries and crawl lines parsing troubles from the streets.

"I used to think all the urban confusions could be resolved in a good prospect."

"I'm not impressed by views." She seemed as composed as usual, but there was a new stillness, as if to contain herself. She held the glass with both hands and balanced it in her lap. "No one learns anything without their feet on the ground. I wish we'd stay in our element."

"Our nature is bigger than our element, it seems."

Having said so, he could now confess to her, carefully, that he'd been watching her house. He would apologize and explain that he didn't understand the compulsion, that he'd never done this before, that most hours of the day he was fine, and in those hours he thought of his spying on her (though it wasn't as if he'd ever followed her or crept up and peered in her windows), or surveilling of a sort, as something other than erotic, even though here and now he'd admit to being attracted to her in otherwise acceptable and healthier ways. That in fact his watching involved a kind of overwhelming need to observe and to understand her and her life, even as this observation also seemed to him a kind of surrender to certain truths about his own life, certain failures, that he seemed incapable of addressing directly.

She said the idea of being outside our element reminded her of a photo Father André had once called up for her on his computer, a spaceship picture of a monster storm on the south pole of Saturn. She began to describe it, and Harold couldn't get back from Saturn to the first words of his admission.

"I think I know it," he said. Kim had sent him a link a few years ago. She was always sending him links in those days. Never the funny kind. Now she sent notes boring into him.

"It's five thousand miles across, forty-five miles high," she was describing the alien storm. "You look into the eye of that thing and it sees you. But it's not meant to, not in God's scheme."

"It looks like the eye of a dread sea creature," he said. Did Rosemary understand that that wasn't God out there, in the places where no one was looking? "It's best not to contemplate."

The couch wasn't working. Somehow the city was different with her here, not at all what he'd try to describe. Their little perch wasn't intimate so much as remote. Far off, dazed sun on the water, the wind on the lake spinning up white flags. Out along the expressway, a strange signal reached him.

"What is that?" he asked "Two fingers left of the wind turbine." He held his arm straight and invited her to sight along it. Instead she looked from her side of the couch.

"It's the news." Of course. How hadn't he noticed it before? It was one of the electronic billboards playing its package of ads and headlines. Now that he knew what it was, some impression in the lines and colours reassembled in the eye the entire image. All he saw were dark green lines, dead straight, but somehow it meant that another Canadian soldier had been returned home in a coffin. You glimpse from a distance or drive past and picture the rest by yourself. The dead kid's haircut and uniform, the very frame of the headshot there over the news anchor's shoulder (the anchor's haircut and suit). The military spokesman (his haircut, his uniform . . .). And back to the flag-draped coffin and the young family standing strong. He tried to explain the phenomenon to Rosemary and then found himself describing how the brain makes things up, reassuring us with a false sense of stability.

"Neurocircuitry corrects for curvatures in receding lines. Realist painters know all about it and take countermeasures. Art correcting for nature."

"So we're back to nature again," she said. "Will we be going in circles some more?"

"Maybe we'll stick to art. I forgot to thank you for the poem."

"I'm glad you got it. Though that doesn't mean it reached you necessarily." "Seven Stanzas at Easter," by John Updike. She'd typed it out and mailed it to him care of the department. The old, slow technologies were likely intended as a message of sorts in themselves. "*Let us not mock God with metaphor.*"

"That's certainly a handy line to have in your pocket."

"But you won't be keeping it in yours, I guess."

"I have no real memory for poetry."

He recalled a line or so from the last stanza. *Let us not seek to make it less monstrous* . . . something, something . . . *lest, awakened in one unthinkable hour, we are embarrassed by the miracle, and crushed by remonstrance.* Did she presume he'd never known remonstrance? Things had been proven to him. Certain lessons of history had been directed at him personally.

She said a trailing-away thing he couldn't make out.

"Sorry?"

She'd looked at him once since they sat down. Now she held to the view that didn't impress her.

"You said you were in trouble. But sitting here with your drink you seem pretty well adjusted to it."

She moved a hand to her leg as if to smooth her skirt but then returned it to the glass, no doubt afraid to invite his eye to a certain movement.

"All right. I wanted to talk about you."

"How am I part of your trouble?"

He smiled. "If you're in my life, you're part of my trouble. But honestly, it's that you confound me. And I won't be able to understand you unless I can spend time with you, which you know I like doing. Though I won't complicate things if you'll allow me to –"

"Observe? I sound like an interesting bug."

"I know it sounds ridiculous. It's not hard to make me sound ridiculous. Not for you."

"What's your question, Harold?"

"I don't know exactly. It has something to do with recognizing the enormousness of things. Have you always sensed it, even before your . . . religious turn?"

"I don't think you understand what you're asking. But if it helps you, I'd say yes. I've always known. And the turn, as you put it, wasn't something I was aware I was looking for."

"So it wasn't that you were an agent of your own change but that change just happened to you. One self supervening another."

"I guess so. It didn't have anything to do with feeling blue, or being mixed up. It still doesn't."

They entered a silence. He was instantly at swim. He could think of nothing to say, and watching her seemed to hold him still somehow. Her eyes were fixed on something far off. A half minute passed. As if to find what she was focused on he looked out again at the city. She was out there somewhere – he believed that she'd forgotten him, or maybe she was trying to lead him into her prayerful quiet.

His actions of finishing his drink, rising, and preparing another didn't penetrate her attention. Maybe she needed to know if she could be alone with him, outside the chatter. Could he be quiet with her? Who was he without talk and ideas?

When he returned to the couch, she took a sip, then put her drink on the floor and went off to the bathroom without even asking directions. He marvelled at her underplayed theatrics. The manipulation of him, body and mind. The timing, the way the talking prepared for his question – she'd been waiting for it – the question for the silence, the floating in strange empty space. He felt he'd been led into a trap, bent inward. The silence now was liquid. The past had been returning in waves. All these dead little worlds exerted a drag. You don't see your life as a shape, don't really believe it has wholeness, until a certain age, a certain break of luck, good or bad, that allows you to see a kind of ending. The ending can come at any stage, and after it, you just float for years towards your death like so much space junk destined for burning re-entry.

Circling thought. The spacecraft carried him back to the hurricane's eye on Saturn, and because it had been Kim who'd sent him there, he'd seen the thing, unnamed, unnameable, looking out at him. Kim must have seen it too, and known whom it was watching. And now it seemed that Rosemary's turbulences had something in common with his own. Different fears stirred by the same shapes. Maybe she feared her convictions, or feared for them. He feared for himself in having none. The two fears this close together could kick up a real storm.

"I should be going, Harold." She stood behind him.

"Please. At least finish your drink."

He turned and gestured to the couch rather than the drink. She sat beside him again, and now he was helpless. In one of her last emails, Connie had quoted Thoreau on the "awful ferity" of virtuous people and lovers. He hadn't understood it at the time but now it seemed to describe Rosemary and him. Though he was not her lover. He was the man watching at her windows, wondering at shadows.

Astonishing, all he'd squandered over the years.

She began to tell him about her conversion and what seemed to be going on in her when she first met Father André Rowe. She stressed that her spirit was prepared, and if it hadn't been Father André it would have been another, though at the time she didn't see this. As she spoke, her voice caught Harold, convinced him, though he knew he'd not stay convinced. He thought of it, her voice, as what it was, a physical thing born upon the metaphysical, the resonant workings of breath and belief. And if she stopped her voice now, it would be her body that would have him. If she would have him. He'd been the same fool all his life.

She believed in the resurrection, she said, not only because the Bible told her so but because the world was old enough to contain it.

"To have needed the resurrection, and still need it, and to contain it. When we think about the resurrection, really think about it, we can feel just how old things are, all creation." She straightened her legs and crossed her ankles. Harold took in her calves and feet and thought of depictions of the Prophet on the cross. "The resurrection is eternal."

"I'm familiar with the idea."

"And so is the moment before the resurrection, when everything was at stake. That's eternal, too. Everything's always at stake, Harold."

She made creation sound consoling, as if it weren't a bad job from the outset. He pictured a long-abandoned, listing farmhouse on some unknown bald prairie, he and his father looking out from the bed of a passing train. Anything might have gone on inside the house, anything still could, but one more hard winter or one bitter wind, and that would be the end of it. Never more to contain a thing.

He wanted the words to stop now. Simple contact. His emotions were boyish, most of them.

When he reached out for her she stood and picked up her bag, and when he stood she made for the door. He caught her there, and turned her towards him. He kissed her, and she received it, but there was no desire returned, only mercy. She tilted her forehead into his neck. She might have tried to change him, to remake him into something more. She'd been tempted to come his way – that's what he wanted to think – but then had seen he was too far out. And he was too old to have seduced her. The wrong face, wrong body, wrong words.

"Such a good soldier," he said, pulling her close. She put her palms on his chest and slowly, easily pushed him away. The end.

"The young man who lives with you," he found himself saying, "Who is he?"

There was a moment of surprise in her expression and then a distance he knew he would never close.

"Stay away from me, Harold."

And then she turned to the door, and the door made light, and she left.

Marian had gone to bed. Kim was eating coffee yoghurt in the kitchen, sitting on a stool at the island, looking at *The Guardian*. From Donald's study, through the half-closed door, the CBC show *Ideas* had just finished up a three-part series on some thick-accented theories about global consciousness, the breakfast topic for the past two mornings. It was his habit to turn the radio off at the end of the show – she'd always liked that Donald wanted to sit with things, even when they were the wrong things – so when the weather and then the news came on, she assumed he'd fallen asleep in his desk chair, another of his habits.

Even before the newsreader got to the story, something in his voice – or was it the way it was coming to her, half-heard in her distraction? – promised a small completion. She lifted her head for a moment, then looked down and began reading again about war, and to her awareness under the newsprint came the radio story in fragments. The reader said a break in an unsolved murder and the words unknown victim and steel waste container. More than three weeks ago, he said, and on the weekend in Vancouver a man arrested in connection and she turned now and listened, catching up, as the reporter in Vancouver, a woman, took the story from there.

The name of the accused was Dwight Myron Lane. He had stolen four cans of pears from a supermarket and the security people had called the police, who searched him and found a folded-up poster of the police sketch of the dead girl, and the Toronto phone number of what turned out to be a recently shut-down massage parlour. Within the hour, Toronto police were questioning the former owner, who claimed not to have known of the murder or the sketch but admitted it looked like a girl he'd employed. Her name was Anna Huard. Her adoptive parents in Saskatoon hadn't heard from her in months, which was not unusual, they said. Forensics had determined that the unknown woman was of mixed race. Anna was part native Canadian.

Dwight Myron Lane, she knew, somehow, had nothing to do with her. Whoever he was, he'd never touched her.

She called Harold, she wanted to tell him, but it rang through to the machine and she hung up. She went into the study and there was Donald asleep in his chair with his hands folded on his small belly. He might have been praying. He opened his eyes when she turned off the radio but he was still swimming towards consciousness and for two or three seconds he looked terrified.

"I came in to turn off the radio. Sorry."

He looked out the window into the dark. "What's it doing out there?"

"Nothing much. There were storms to the north but they missed us."

He barely nodded. "A small story on page seven today," he said. "More evidence that we're past the tipping point with climate change. Apocalypse is assured."

"They run that news once a week."

"It's just the first phase, they say. From here on it's hell all over." He ran a hand through his hair and then fell still.

"You want some tea?" Kim asked.

"We can't travel like we used to. And the best places have all changed for the worse. We'd be better off under a single potentate who'd turn us all back into peasant farmers."

"Jesus, Donald, what's gotten into you?" She had the odd feeling that he was addressing someone other than her. There were ghosts with him. She thought it best to assert the Kim he knew. "The only hope now is, we'll all go to war and wipe each other out without much nuclear or biological ravaging."

"But then the next malign thing would heave over the horizon."

"I wish we shared happier perspectives."

He looked at her and she saw that the terror had not entirely subsided.

"We'd think we were rid of us," he said. "But then we'd appear again."

His eyes welled up. She'd never seen him cry, and she thought she should come forward but he turned his back to her in his chair and waved her away.

She went out to the porch. So she would get through Marian's last months better than Donald. She'd never really thought about what would become of him, and he must have felt the disregard. She wondered what could be done for the man.

Empty street, without breezes, a sky without cloud or stars, washed in the city lights. She conjured the deep country, an unpaved road under constellations. She tried to hold the place pure, but then the interference set in, Donald in his study asleep in his chair like Greg in one of his rockers. She hadn't thought of Greg in a while, not even alone in bed. He'd kept in touch through one-line emails – the last one informed her that the number of refugees abroad who'd applied to come to Canada was now 700,000 – and one long, newsy phone call, after which she felt she knew him better for having been undistracted by his physical presence. Rather than give away anything of himself he'd told tales about secretly detained terrorist suspects, Russian mobsters who made charity donations, Sudanese refugees starving in a far-off desert, visa disputes at the U.S. border, the wiretaps on his office phone, a whole construction site worth of Portuguese men deported, a program to help undocumented street people, a pro-choice song thrown in at a fundraiser to the bafflement of Catholic new Canadians. The stories weren't elided. He wasn't manic. And he modulated precisely between irony, ardency, humour. But it came to her that he was, in fact, a mess.

You had to love a man in the right kind of trouble.

By the time she went back in, Donald had gone to bed. He'd made the tea himself and had left a cup out for her, sitting atop a note that read, "Sorry. Bad dreams."

She folded the clothes heaped in the laundry basket. She set the coffee maker for the morning and laid out Marian's next pills, closed the curtains in the living room and turned off the lights, and made her way to her bedroom.

For a long time before sleep came she lay awake in the dark and thought of her father, and then said a sort of prayer for Anna Huard.

7

He'd slept sober. Since the morning Kim had sprung Santiago on him and then called him a liar, he'd entered an odd state, swinging between dread and a calm so deep that it bordered on elation. He couldn't decide which mood was warranted, and which the emotional figment of a mind made unknown to itself from a life of dedicated self-distraction. If dissociation were a paying talent he'd own half the city. Whatever was happening to him, he wanted to give it time. It was important that he not get ahead of himself, as he had with Rosemary, and not let Kim push him into places he wasn't ready to go. He hadn't replied to her last email. Yesterday someone called up from the lobby but he hadn't answered in case it was her. Now she'd left a message saying she'd come by this afternoon to see if he was in. Within minutes of picking it up he had packed a lunch and was heading for the country.

An hour later he was in the woods of a conservation area, watching his footing as he descended into a gorge beneath a pounding waterfall. The world changed from old oaks, maples, and beech trees with their wrinkled grey elephant skins, to pines and huge boulders, erratics, he thought they were called, happy with the word. It felt good to be alone in an otherwise wordless, alien place. Kim had brought him here once, knowing that the loud falls and rapids would prevent him from entering into some palaver about history or education, or some other misconceived fathering strategy. That afternoon with her had been happy, but was now a little indistinct, as if the actual fraught waters had joined their own and carried them off, and there was no one moment of regret or shame that might have lodged in his cortex. The memory of their hike came and went, and he might have been left in the present moment, but instead he was vaulted further back, to the British Columbia landscapes of his boyhood with his father. There were plenty of jagged memories from his transient days, but at least he had once been comfortable in the so-called natural world. He was someone very different now.

He walked on, stopping to look at deer tracks, the light on the ridge above him. He found the tiny, perfect skull of what might have been a squirrel, lying on pine straw, its lower mandible still attached. The half-exposed root system of a black locust on a slope so steep that the tree seemed suspended by its very age. Such isolation, empty of people or event. Anything could happen to a person down here and no one would find you. He followed the river for another half-hour until it calmed and then he took lunch, a peameal bacon sandwich, sitting on the small log of a tree counterpoised by the taller one whose fall had broken it off and crashed to rest extending over the water to the other side. Nothing had ever been cleaned up here. It wasn't clear how anyone would go about it.

In her message she'd said the dumpster girl had been identified. Her name was Anna and the police had caught her killer. He was not Kim's attacker, she said. What she hadn't said, though he understood, was that it was her letter, not the attacker, that she wanted to discuss. His worst hour, not her own. She was certain he'd had such an hour. He didn't know what had given it away.

He saw something approaching through the woods, at speed. As he dismounted the log the shape emerged as a large dog, what looked like a Lab-shepherd cross, more black than tan. It stopped at about ten feet and its ears shot up, alert. After a second or two it began to bark at him. Harold squatted down, holding the remains of his sandwich, saying, "Here you go," and the dog quieted and came forward, wagging but cautious. Despite itself, it couldn't close the last few feet.

The dog's name turned out to be Josef, with an *f*, Harold guessed, given that the owners who finally appeared had Czech accents. They were in their forties, he thought, dressed almost identically in what must have been the latest in outdoor gear, narrow brown shorts with a slight synthetic sheen. There were reflective tabs on their expensive-looking boots.

The woman said Josef's name and he came immediately. When he arrived before her she batted him sharply on the nose and he dropped to his belly.

"Sorry," said the man.

As a boy Harold had once made the mistake of laughing, though briefly, quietly, at the sight of a fat woman attempting to board a passenger train. His father, sitting beside him on the platform, had wheeled and struck him with an open hand hard across the face. It had happened just once. Once was enough. Harold had always reminded himself that he'd been hit in a time and place when such occurrences were accepted. Though no one now would think so, in the context of its time, the blow was not out of place. He had deserved it.

"Nothing to apologize for," said Harold. It wasn't true, he thought. "At least not to me."

The woman said, "I instruct him in a way that he understands."

"You instruct him on the snout," he said mildly.

"It's for his own good," said the man. He seemed sympathetic to all sides.

The couple moved on without further acknowledging him. Josef looked back once, presumably in regret, until the woman whistled and he straightened up, face forward, and kept to her heel as they disappeared around a bend. Harold had borrowed the disapproval from Kim, and had voiced it on her behalf. On a downtown street he'd once seen her reprimand a smartly dressed young man wearing the rectangular glasses of a Belgian film critic. He'd pinched the ear of his husky and set off an argument about dog training. Kim told him people ought to have to pass tests before owning a dog. The man doubted she could teach a dog to sit. He said he knew the type and he was serious, how would she do it? "You want the answer?" she asked. "You get down on your back and play with the animal until you're both exhausted." The man laughed. "What kind of answer is that?" "The answer is screw the question." In Kim's life, the answer had often been screw the question.

The ridge now cast a shadow over the gorge. It was time to go home.

The ascent left him breathless and a little high. Back in the car, it was as if he was back in time, stuporous in the worst days of the estrangements. When he'd returned to Marian and Kim after four months of silence in '95, he walked around afraid to show himself, feeling their judgment and his own.

He must have seemed, must still seem, to be harbouring something. They were right about that, his family. But his secret was love. He was paralyzed with love, speechless with love. He cowered under the magnitude of his love. His love was the one sure thing in his life, though it was beyond him, beyond his expression, and anyway, he had grown superstitious, knowing there was still a chance it might be returned to him if only he didn't say something to extinguish the possibility.

He wanted to remind Kim that people are more than the sum of their experiences. He reminded himself that, given the attack, it was natural that she'd have these bouts of distrust. He didn't know how to help her, other than to be patient, and let her call him a liar if that's what she needed.

The light through the windshield was streaming with inclemencies, he couldn't stay with his thoughts a breath further, but then did so.

I'm alone, he thought.

Then said, "We're alone."

He'd stood her up without so much as a note and she'd gone to the research library and lost herself in study. At home now she found her old running bra and sweatshirt and sweatpants and expensive ridiculous cross-trainers and they still fit her, and as had been her habit, she made a point of avoiding mirrors on her way out of the house, into stride.

This was part of her resolve, a half-hour of open fleeing. She liked to imagine she was sweating away some poison and today the poison she settled on was her mother's pain. This morning

Marian hadn't come out of her room when Kim made breakfast, on the cusp of another bad day, and had finished her lunch and was sleeping again when Kim returned. A few blocks on she concentrated on letting go of other disturbances. A bird dead under a window, dismal events picked up in passing. Like this she would detox her system and then swear off the daily news for a week or two, running, melting away the verb-mangling sportscasts, rooftop weathermen, vapid celebrity junkies, maybe even the murders and wars. For a week she'd carried around the high school yearbook shots of the lead local terror suspects who wanted to blow up buildings and behead parliamentarians. They were late teens, mostly, and not prepossessing in appearance. She'd been troubled by one in particular who was just plain downright ugly, and she wondered if his ugliness had worked upon him, and of course it had. All young men were stupid and impressionable, their imaginations full of cartoons and dirty pictures, and nothing was real to them like it was to everyone else, except the physical facts, like if they were thought attractive or ugly by whatever the dominant standard. That much they could figure out.

Not all young men, maybe, but most of the ones in the news.

As her body began to feel tested she lapsed into a thought of something blue and stolen and she lengthened her stride and upon the new rhythm escaped it.

Nothing sweated out, of course.

Harold was avoiding her. That her inability to reach him might open an old wound in her hadn't occurred to him. He was reenacting his absence.

Terrorists. Political kidnappings, murder. Last week she passed by the TV Donald was watching. The old man superimposed on his younger self was James Cross, the one from the FLQ crisis who didn't get killed. He said, "I think of it as a storm. You might say my life since then has been a calm after the storm. The storm didn't take my life. But it has made it less my own." There was Trudeau, Laporte. Months ago, inside one of their debates, Harold had told her Canadians once knew who they were and who they weren't, and that was the beauty of them. "But there isn't a 'we' anymore, Kim. There's only who we used to be."

The running felt bad until it felt good. Even the old wrestling with her quitting mechanism made her feel like a kid again, absorbing self-discipline in furtherance of some abstract quality of character. Years ago her gymnastics coach had told her that training would make her a fighter. The short, unsmiling woman made mantras of goal-result thought and broke things down into lists of three. Balance, line, explosion. Practice, technique, focus. "Training makes the fighter." "Fight means focus." Anything that mattered, meant for memory, fell to clipped phrases, in the limited English of a transplanted Romanian instead of the Scots-Irish old blood she was. But maybe she'd been right, Coach McKinnon. Kim had fought gymnastically. She'd been trained into focus as if being prepared all along for that moment years away of thrust and escape.

She walked for a minute before the turn home, another minute after, then began again. A little flush, like the kind she felt before vomiting, but she pushed through it and tried to hold her pace. She was strong for her size but her lungs had never been very good. As always she blamed her former smoking father – the flush had always led to blame – and then she pushed through that too. Her scar was itching. She was sweating real sweat now. It had been too long.

She pictured Pinochet and Thatcher in an old news photo. He'd ordered men to be mutilated, dropped from helicopters, throatslit. He'd ordered women burned alive.

It wasn't just poetry, the news that stayed news.

With the house in sight she let off and trotted to a walk. Short of a brain disease she would never again be newsless, wordless, but soon she'd be naked in a glass stall, staring at a bar of green soap with its carved name washed away and keeping her thoughts there with her, in the steamy present, where the flesh lived.

It happened one afternoon that he came later than usual, near the time she was going home, and so he waited and accompanied her onto the streetcar and down to the subway platforms and the silver train and then onto a southbound bus. When he'd first met Luis and Teresa he'd hoped that their common pasts and language would inspire in him things to say, but he was not a talker, not to anyone, and now on this route home with her when he felt most in need of words between them he felt only his deficiency. When he looked around at the city he saw cars and people, buildings and trees, not anything more particular, and many of the things, he didn't know the names of because they existed only in English. There were blocks of store windows to the south full of metal things he wanted, knives, watches, lighters, studded belts and boots, and he used to imagine that if he had one or two of these things they would remove the mocking absence of the names of other things, but because he had no money he stopped walking by those windows and thought less and less often about them until now he didn't feel their pull at all, and didn't believe now that the metals had any power to help him anyway.

He walked her past towers, to her tower building. He looked at her in wonder, the black hair, her head level as she walked. She at least was all in the particular – the skin, the flat bones of her face, her hands turned in slightly – of a kind anyone who really looked at her could know.

In the lobby she stopped at her mailbox and collected a package from her sister, and she guessed it would contain crayon drawings from their nieces and one or two books. In the elevator she told him about her brother's daughters and then he asked about the books. She laughed a little, and opened the package and showed him. There were two romantic novels, each with a picture of a man and a woman on the cover. One of the nieces had drawn a picture of the very tower they were now inside, with a stick-figure Teresa waving from a window.

— Maria is more a mother to them than our brother's wife, she said.

She mentioned her sister more and more, it seemed, and he hoped it was to remind him that she only played Luis's wife, but he wondered why she would. There was no shame in her secret, he wanted to tell her, but the truth was that there was shame in it, and they both knew it. Luis knew it but didn't care because it wasn't his shame.

Inside the door she called out for Luis and then pretended to discover that he wasn't home. She said the job he had now often kept him out past midnight.

Rodrigo sat at the table off the kitchen. He looked out at the view of the other towers, with the city between them running north as far as he could see.

What he most wanted was to see what Teresa saw when she looked at him, to think about himself however she did. What he wanted to talk about, and there was shame in this too, was himself. He had been falling away from his own thoughts for days. The only time he felt he belonged to his life, all of it, was when he was with her, and he didn't even know her very well. But when he was with her he thought he knew a few things, that she should stop living with Luis, that he should leave Rosemary's basement and get free of her charity and find work somewhere lucky, with the right man to teach him a trade and a way of being in this country so that he had money and friends and could build a life, even if it had to be in the shadows. He didn't mind the shadows, and thinking about them filled him with the only anticipation he felt, other than when he was with a woman.

She took two cans of beer from the fridge and sat opposite him.

— When will you get your own apartment, Rodrigo?

— I need a good job. Rosemary's looking.

— I think maybe she wants you to stay with her. Teresa smiled. I think maybe she's in love with you, her hot young Latin man.

He looked to his beer. He didn't think it was love but there was something. More and more Rosemary came to talk to him, and more often now about her life than his. What bothered him was that she knew he couldn't always follow her, the words she used, how fast she talked, and yet she spoke on without bothering to ask *claro*, as she once used to do. He was serving some function in her life, the listener who only half understood and wouldn't question her or enter his own thoughts into matters. She was full of stories, usually the events of her days, but sometimes she seemed to pause before one and then not tell it. Maybe she'd fallen in love with someone. The closer she got to this story, the more silences in her speech. He had no sense of what it might be but it was only when the silences began that he felt close to her.

When he finished his beer Teresa went to the fridge and got him another, and this time she came around to his side of the table to put it before him. She was there, close at his side, and when he didn't turn to her, she put a hand beneath his chin and pulled him to her belly and the smell of her skin in her shirt. He opened his mouth against her. She stood him up and kissed him and it all happened like they had been blind until now. The need for talk was gone. She had brought him forth by touch.

He wanted to have her where they were, high up over the city, looking down on it, but she took his hand and led him to her bedroom. Then she placed him at arm's length and just looked him in the eye and so they stood for several seconds, saying nothing. She was wearing blue jeans and a denim shirt with clouds or flowers, Rodrigo couldn't tell, stitched in white into the front, swirling around each breast. A thin braided silver chain lay against her neck.

She held her hands out again and he took them and she pulled him onto the bed on top of her. He knew he was too hungry for her but couldn't slow himself. She let him continue kissing, biting her mouth, as she rolled him to the side and unbuttoned her shirt. When he tried to help he got in the way so he went to work on his own clothes. His shirt was off now and he reached behind her and unhooked her bra and at first she didn't let it fall. He got to his feet and removed his shoes and pants and stood in his underwear, hard before her. Then she let the bra fall and he saw that her breasts weren't full, as if she'd had a child somewhere in her past, he didn't know, and she seemed shy about them, and he found himself kissing her nipples as they both got her out of her jeans and panties. He wanted inside her and she said it was safe and then he was there and she was someone different again and she told him to come inside her but he pulled out and came on her belly. With her hand she wiped the come on her breasts and in her pubic hair. He got up and cleaned himself and put on his pants and she asked him to come back to bed. Then he sat with her and they talked about food.

That evening they walked in the city for hours. Later, alone in his bed, the day returned to him half-crazy. He replayed the sex and the streets, what they'd said, what they'd seen, and the moments fell out of sequence. A young boy asleep on a hammock in a yard. Hard-rolling kids in a skateboard park. Her face beneath him. Store clerks and the way she stood next to him at the table and pulled him in. The blue in the necks of the black birds that resettled on the lawn after they'd passed by. How she held him with the printed flats of her fingertips and brushed him with her nails. All of it summoned out of the basement ceiling and looming all night in the unlit room.

In one of the seminars I took at Columbia (yes, I did attend some classes) the prof began the year by asking us what we thought it meant to practise history. "I mean, why do it?" she asked. Instantly, nine bodies tensed, ready to answer. Only I sat calmly, with nothing on my tongue, and so of course she asked me. The room waited me out. Finally I said something along the lines that it's the historian's responsibility to help those whom history has abused to bear it forward. She responded by asking the guy next to me what he thought, and around the table it went, all of them positing and expanding, quoting Hegel or Le Goff or Hayden White or Spivak, who'd taught some of them. They were parrots in a pet store, the acolytes, but the prof seemed to like them. Mine was not the answer she was looking for. At least she never called on me again.

Why write history? Haven't all the points of view, all the expert opinions, drained authority from one another? Is there one answer that stands above the rest?

You're not replying to my emails or calls. You're not in when I come by, or at least you're not answering when I buzz you. The department secretary says you haven't been by your office for days as far as she knows. Should I file a missing persons report? Or have you yet again gone dark, as they say in the spy movies?

When you depart from your life as I know it, I can't imagine where you are. Your failure to appear in body or word feels directed at me but it becomes a condition of all things.

Do you understand?

Unless you reply, this will be my last note to you. I'll see you whenever, with mother at the house, and nothing that matters will pass between us.

The differences: her body and face had changed; she lived by need, isolated, but against her need, lonely. Every day she took shelter in her room to write or read or simply to lie on her bed, exhausted at having had to maintain an outward self, and yet more alone, more separate than a year ago she could have come anywhere near with all her volunteer witnessing and empathy.

She slightly despised mystery. Particular absences, gaps in the sequences, holes in the known were intolerable to her. She thought less. She simply felt and needed.

One afternoon she announced to Marian an intention to go gallery hopping, alone, and off she went, taking in a few small spaces on Ossington and then Queen. Nothing much caught her interest. She headed north on Spadina, then along Dundas to the Art Gallery of Ontario. In the museum's pre-Gehry era she and Harold would take in riotous Rauschenberg and Picasso and all the artists whose names she could never remember. The place was different now, the interiors, the vistas, the collection itself with its new orders and none of the old disappointments and tantalisms. She ended up in a small room, staring at a painting, *Helga Matura*, a murdered prostitute, according to the explanatory text. There was something about the fuzzy realism, like a slightly unfocused photograph that made it falsely romantic and yet more present, like a memory. Another male artist sly with violence. When she was a girl Kim had imagined the beautiful woman she hoped to become, with fine, dark brows set high over brown eyes, a full mouth like her mother's, and shoulder-length black hair. It turned out she'd been imagining a dead woman.

Through the windows the city kept coming up newly. She stood for several minutes in one of the back winding stairwells, ascending through a blue incandescent cube, with its medium-level view of mid-downtown, the lake winking between columns to the south, construction cranes everywhere, ponderously knitting themselves skyward. The city in its remaking. She considered taking in a few Old Masters, but instead she simply left. Outside were Japanese and American tour groups, couples, single men and women on cellphones, giving directions, arranging rendezvous. She became one of them, calling Marian to tell her she'd bring home Indian takeout.

"Was there anything good?" her mother asked.

"Mostly the same things. But the best of them get better."

At the back of the gallery, in the park, the half-closed sky produced notes against the wall of blue cladding. She walked south and picked up the dinner, and was out on the street again when a rain caught her and she took to a bar patio and sat under an awning.

Near the end of her half-pint the long light of the afternoon began to return. After the rain a passing car made silverblack salmonskin tracks in the wet pavement and the sun caught the side-view mirror and burned on her retina and she looked into the recesses of the bar now dancing in red and took in the unlikely collection at the tables, locals and tourists, a homeless old man standing neither here nor there, slightly apart from the bar, a mother and preteen son, all of them like her gathered out of the weather. When the waiter came she asked if she could buy a round for the old man, anonymously. He said, "One," and she ordered for herself another glass of beer to stay inside this feeling, this need of her father's to be lit with drink.

What was it he yielded to?

Whatever it was, she wanted the full account. He knew as she did that certain events are not time-bound, that they're never really past. She imagined the shape of the account, of what might be revealed. She'd glimpsed it somewhere. As she turns a corner, it's ahead of her, then disappears in mid-air. The shape is not of an animal but something harder, time-encrusted, a dusty, runnelled curving surface, the length of a life held miles distant, hanging before you until the wind comes and it turns and thins to seeming nothing.

This was what she was after, this dusty surface. Whatever its substance, the surface would be hard, rough. Otherwise Harold would already have offered the full account. He must have thought that she would judge him, which meant he couldn't accept that she believed him to be, at heart, though starkly flawed, a good man. Unless he allowed her closer, she had no way of proving to him that *despite all, despite whatever,* she loved him.

The takeout was cold. She thought about having another drink. The alcohol wasn't courage, it was faith. The faith felt good, warm, but then all in a few seconds some cold, clawed certainty began moving under the warmth and she hurried to put cash under her glass. When she left the bar she looked back to see the old man sitting at a table now, talking with the waiter. They both looked up and the old man smiled for her and slightly lifted his hand from the drink in farewell.

He had to be careful how often he watched and where he called it up, the cops tracked these hits and saw patterns, but today in his booth he couldn't help but click on the re-enactment, re-amazed how they got it all wrong. For one it had been too dark to see, not lit for cameras. From the back his actor looked Chinese or something, you couldn't tell. He always felt like asking the stranger at the next station if they thought he looked Chinese. And she didn't look like herself either, not like anyone he'd have chosen. Her hair was too flat and her face overfed. She didn't even walk the same, too slow and showy. And the actor attacker sort of hustled her through the cage gate instead of how it was, how he'd slammed into her shoulder, how he heard her breath shoot out so it hung a second in mid-air with the coffee and sweets, and how he landed on her so she was stunned all over again when they fell into the deeper darkness and she knew his weight and belief.

Whoever made these films for the cops, they had no real standards or talent. He wished they'd done more to get it right. He didn't like being misrepresented to the world.

He surfed around the local news and cop sites. Break-ins, assaults, a car-jacking. The newest missing girl, caught by cameras in the subway, in a store. He couldn't understand a killer's way of thinking. They were busted, stupid people, not the twisted geniuses in movies. Or they probably had sexual problems. There were cross-Canada warrants for this guy and that. He shared no element with sexual assailants, only a definition. He could prove against statistics he was humanly complicated beyond others in his category. When it started he broke into homes like a lot of rapists, it was true, but only when he knew they were empty. He'd choose the women, get to know them from a distance by name and appearance, and plan how and when to break in. It happened seventeen times before he was caught coming out a window with panties stuffed down his jeans. He always took the underwear but he loved just to be in their spaces, the places they thought of as theirs. And he wasn't as violent as people saw him. He'd killed the dog in self-defence in a shipping bay in cold Saskatoon when he'd lived three weeks at the Y without incident, a block from the bus station. Animals did not seem to take to him. And he'd tackled his one victim Kim in a classic so-called blitz approach only because he couldn't deceive her, couldn't even really speak to her in the circumstance. It was not easy for him to be physical. He'd hurt his knee as a child that had never healed to all-better.

He knew numbers but didn't trust them. The numbers said about half of serial attackers feel remorse for their crimes, but how could you believe them? The numbers said between eight and thirteen per cent communicate afterwards with their victim, but how do they communicate, what could they really say, and is it understood?

He entered her name and hunted around. It linked to some old campus job with someplace that helped foreign students. She'd listed two phone numbers. One of them hit in a reverse directory and he had an address. Her last name turned up a father and mother, and the mother lived at the same place. He fed it into a map site and then zoomed a satellite picture. He tried to feel her presence there but couldn't say for sure.

The numbers said he was in a low percentage that he'd not attacked anyone since and he wanted to believe it. It was something he wished she could know about him, though he knew she never would. In his fantasies she passes by in a crowded city street and sees him, smiles, not knowing, because he seems harmless, just another downtown character. And then he says her name, and she turns. What happens next is grey.

Things of no worth in themselves can mean something when they're gathered.

He put Yonge Street on the satellite and scrolled to the place where he was. He zoomed inside a hundred feet. There was a perfect viewing distance for every place that was. The picture seemed just about right. It was summer then and now. He had a long time left on his two dollars so he angelled over the city, flying over and back, up and down, like he was already past his sad ending and could visit the past and replay it. He tried to find a billboard with the date and time but the readouts would not come up clear. Whatever this day he was hovering over, the whole of it was his. He could drop down to the physical buildings and then swoop in his mind through the windows, into any one of the millions of lives.

He did not mind not belonging. He had never known his own street addresses, the climbing falling numbers did not apply to him. People pretended to know themselves by finding their lives on the grids. There were things he knew that they didn't, outside of numbers and names. Nothing repeats the same way twice. Nothing stays. Pictures hold still for us but we don't for them.

In the future was someone to show his thoughts to. It was hours later, in his room, when the angelling finally failed him and he felt himself floating in the deeps. They gave ships women's names. The ship out there was one he'd known. When she was close enough to see him, it would be too late for her.

Marian's getaway was an organic farm about an hour west of the city owned by her oldest friend, a tall strawberry blonde now going grey poet named Lana Keyes-Little, and her husband, Daniel. She had spent days there in every season for years, sometimes helping with the farm work, often preparing large dinners for the seasonal workers, who tended to be environmentally savvy students, and Lana and Daniel's writer friends, who drove great distances for the dinner conversation, and for those who stayed over, the wonder of being there in the morning for breakfast and a walk through the barn or the fields. Daniel was an African-Canadian from Manitoba who wrote possibly brilliant plays about obscure historical figures, mostly scientists, that tended to close before completing their planned run. There'd once been a rumour that Robert Lepage was going to revive Daniel's drama about Kepler, but nothing had come of it. Kim had always liked him – he'd always taken an interest in her, and she was old enough now to understand that he was living the life he wanted to, without expectation or disappointment. But Lana was unpredictable, prone to making a bloodsport of conversation, and Kim had more than once had occasion around her to feel embarrassed for her mother, whose early life with Lana, in their student days, had been wilder than her own. The stories were told not for her but for Donald, whom Lana liked to shock, maybe because, as Kim read it, her husband was more interested in Donald's views on math and science than in hers on art.

They arrived just after two in the afternoon. Kim hadn't been there since the year she left for New York but it was as she remembered, the vegetable fields all around, the open barn, the brown, weathered side buildings, the gated pasture falling off to the north, and the huge old oak shading the nineteenth-century red-brick Italianate house. Inside, the thick planked softwood floors and, everywhere, kittens.

Marian had slept in the car and had a forty-minute window of energy as they all took seats in the front room, with a view of the long gravel driveway, the road, a neighbour's corn rows. Lana and Daniel did well not to react to Marian's appearance – Kim was watching for it, she'd told Lana on the phone to expect to be a little shocked – but earlier than usual she broke out the dope and the writers and Marian passed a joint between them as Donald and Kim sipped their tea. Kim watched the cigarette pass from Daniel's thick fingers to his wife's long ones to her mother's small hand and then followed it up to her mouth and watched her purse and inhale so that her face took on a new appearance, because she was not a smoker, as if whatever they all shared there in the room could be drawn in only through a self-estranging act, and it was all a little strange, out of time and place, and it felt good.

Marian asked Daniel about his writing and, with some prompting from Lana, he fell into a story about negotiations with an Unnamed Great Director who had been workshopping his new play on Marshall McLuhan.

"His genius is counterintuitive, but so are his faults. He wants complete control of the text. At best I'd be a collaborator in the defiling of my own creation." He laughed at his absurd predicament. Lana called The Director "a no-talent blustery asshole" and laughed a little more meanly. Donald then steered everyone into a discussion of something he'd read about methylation and the genetic inheritance of emotional trauma, but at some point seemed to find himself having forgotten his company, and simply trailed off in the middle of a point about stress responses in rats.

When Marian got tired, Lana set her up in the guest room and then invited Kim for a hike around the farm as Donald and Daniel took up on the back porch. Lana introduced her to two sturdy young women working in the barn with the horses in their rented stalls. They did the work in exchange for wages and food and riding, they said, and because they liked their employers. "That's more or less how I taught them to say it," said Lana.

Everywhere in the yard were small chickens. Lana led Kim out into the pasture, where a few horses were grazing and looked up at them for a moment, and on into stands of old trees, telling stories of deer and raccoons, wild turkeys, grinning possums in the woodpile, and coyotes scared off with shotguns. Eventually they came back, approaching the house from the side, and sat down on wooden lawn chairs by a little blue concrete swimming pool with a waterline that sat several inches too low.

"She's worse than I pictured," said Lana.

"Yes."

"And how are you doing? Be honest."

"I don't know."

"Marian says you're spending a lot of time managing Donald and Harold."

"Donald's been on his own. I wouldn't know how to manage him. And Harold's kind of disappeared."

"If only he'd done that years ago."

"He did. But then he came back."

When they left that night, after the duck and the wine and the conversation about how all things are unlike one another and Daniel quoted Augustine on prayer being a journey to "the land or region of unlikeness" and Kim said she could stare at horses for hours and Lana spoke of her sense of the wild and Donald had trouble keeping up with the metaphors and wondered if they were all about burritos and Marian laughed quite a lot and said it was always one ongoing party out here, always was and always would be, Kim found herself craving the silence of her room. Once they got home and Marian was put to bed with a kiss on the forehead, Kim fell hard into her own bed and allowed herself to feel the fullness of the day, though within it, a coldness coming in on the night tide of sleep that she knew would still be there the next day. Old and unresolved, brought forward by what Lana had said just before they left their poolside chairs and went in to make dinner.

She'd said to hell with Harold. He'll stand before you at point-blank range, look you in the face, and lie. The lies will be well appointed. He will hand you over to his lies and let them lead you around like a pull toy. You underestimate him if you think he just fibs now and then, or that he lies only to protect others, or himself, out of cowardice. He lies wholeheartedly. He lies to others and to himself, yes, but also to rocks and trees and heaps of scrap metal and coffee stains on his shirt. I have never known a more thoroughgoing liar, and I have known a great many. Your mother came here once, this was the dead of summer, and she sat out by this pool in a sundress and big sunglasses. I watched her through the window, and she went over and picked free a bit of blue paint that was flaking off the side and she took it back to her chair and studied it as if it were ancient parchment. She turned it over and over again, then let it fall to her lap. And then, from behind those big glasses the tears began to stream. She barely moved, but here came the tears. And I went out to her and made her tell me what was wrong. She said the pool had made her think of a motel pool that the three of you had once played in on a road trip across the country – she couldn't remember where it was – but there you all were, and she had stood at the end of a slide and caught you as you hit the water, and your father had sat on the deck, fully clothed but fixed on the scene with great surety and love, she said, but that isn't what she was crying at. It was that the motel had made her think of a call she'd received from the police, this was a few years after the road trip, a few years before she was there by my pool, telling the story. Some girl had been killed in one of those lakeshore motels, a hooker, they said, and they'd gone through the desk registry and taken the licence plates of all the cars there that day, and one of them was Harold's, and so they were calling to see if he was in. They said all this at once, as if not imagining what they might be setting off, though of course they didn't care. The fact that they were calling and not at her door meant they knew who they were looking for, and only wanted the liar as a witness, if he'd seen the guy there, but none of this mattered, really. What mattered was that the night of the afternoon in question Harold had come home and told a long story of his day. There'd been a trip to St. Lawrence Market that had reminded him of the day you, at the age of five, had gone missing there when each of them thought the other was watching you, and he'd dropped to his hands and knees to see you across the way, staring up at some fish on ice. Of course Marian remembered that day. And then, he said, he'd gone to some talk by a visiting French historian who wore a black turtleneck under a safari jacket and a bunch of them went out afterwards to a Spanish restaurant with flamenco dancers and they all had too much to drink and one of his colleagues who nobody liked had bought the castanets off the fingers of one of the dancers. It's all vivid, isn't it? That's why I remember it. It's vivid almost to the degree that it's fantasy. Because there'd been no market trip, no visitor in black. He'd spent the day in a motel room, with some woman. I know you know about his escapades – your mother always regretted that you knew – still maybe I shouldn't have said all this to you. I've done it to set things straight, or straighter.

And because I'm telling the truth here, I might as well add that I've always wanted to run him through with a burning sword.

PART THREE

8

Kim,

Once when you were about fourteen I showed you photos of yourself as a six-year-old. Do you remember? A former neighbour in Mexico City found them and mailed them to me at the university. We were in our courtyard (or was it theirs?). In one of them, you were in the act of battering me with a plastic baton of some kind. I'm sitting in a chair, rearing back, afraid that you'll hurt me. My expression would be familiar to you, I suppose. I remember showing you the pictures when you came home from school. You claimed not to remember Mexico City at all.

I can tell you that in some ways you haven't changed much. You were born a batterer of authorities. I've always admired and feared that in you. And feared for you because of it.

Because it's not clear to me yet whether I'll ever send you this letter, I just might see it through. I'll take your place as the reader while I write. I remember you also accusing me once of not sounding like myself in the letters I sent you in New York. I was someone else when I wrote, you said. A little smarter, and less prone to complaint, and less passionate. It's odd that you find me at all passionate in person, or once did. It seems a risky word, somewhat accusatory, as if it was my appetites only that had hurt us all. And anyway you and your mother have always been more truly passionate. Even your intellects had all of you down to your toes. The two of you running out in "the sudden rain of a deep conversation just to smell the air." Did I get that right? Do you know whom I'm quoting? I remember things you've said all your life, and how you said them. I don't have a brain for metaphors – I'm not even all that strong on analogy – but I have a memory for yours.

Do you recall defending me in that bleak driveway scene when I'd dropped you off and there were Marian and Donald out front, waiting by their car to take you somewhere else? He made as if to compliment me on my new book and then added that he hoped to get a contract for a book of his own (we're still waiting) on Gödel, with "crossover appeal," that a non-academic publisher might be interested in. Beware dumbing down, I said (or just plain dumb, I didn't). He said my own book would have been strengthened had it been written in "a less mandarin prose." And I likely said that simplified language is a tool of tyrants and so on, and then Marian stopped us. We are such a couple of brats together, he and I.

And they got into the car, and then you gave me a hug and told me (I wish they could have heard you) that you weren't an expert but you liked my book and wanted to talk with me about it sometime. We never did have that talk, but you should know how much that moment means to me.

People like me are always marvelling at people like you, those who connect directly, effortlessly, who passionately batter and compassionately embrace. I don't want you ever to lose that passion. But there are signs, I think, that you're following it blindly, letting it undermine you. It was a mistake for you to drop out of school. And, yes, I think you dropped out to hurt me. You've always assumed I've withheld myself from you – and I have, parts of my past, and my very presence for those months when I was more or less lost to myself, having left you both. But it was never my intention to withhold love. In fact, it was love for you and your mother that kept me closed.

And so, what to say? Where to begin?

Think of yourself in New York. Then imagine me the same age. In 1973 I won a travel scholarship to fund sixteen weeks of language instruction in a country of my choice. From this distance, I'm inclined to see myself as more naive than I was, but everywhere then students were politically aware, campuses were engaged, and I'd just completed my master's degree that spring, and so I knew about Chile – the world's first freely elected Marxist leader, the American attempts at "destabilization," the bribes, the funding of armed opposition, the kidnappings intended to spark revolts. It was the place to be, a place I could never afford to visit otherwise, and I knew even then that my doctoral work would be in Latin American history. Whatever was happening in Chile was going to change that history. I don't even recall there being a decision about where I should go. It was self-evident.

The Santiago of mid-June that year turned out to be full of young Allendistas from the Americas and Europe. Though it was quite clear from my first days there that you weren't to make assumptions about the political allegiances of anyone who didn't declare them, it seemed that everyone at the school was either actively in support of the government as Marxists themselves or, like myself I suppose, as fellow travellers of the cause.

I lived with a German named Armin and two Americans, Will and Carl, three of us attending the same school, though different classes. We had rooms in a small house in a once prosperous neighbourhood by then fallen to a barrio. It was off Moneda Street, at the far end of which was the presidential palace. Many houses were now apartments, in disrepair, with bright balconies and clover gardens. The jacaranda in the austral spring. The looming Andes. The city's sheer beauty, I thought, must surely hold a promise of peace. There's nothing like sharing joy and hope with so many in such a place.

My first couple of weeks were spent working on my Spanish and talking with my housemates about important matters such as women and politics. We cursed the Alliance for Progress, the CIA, ITT. Armin wrote out Kissinger quotes and taped them to the door of his room ("I don't see why we need to stand by and watch a country go Communist due to the irresponsibility of its own people"). Will and Carl were harder on their government than we were. Will, a short, muscular hippie from some university town in New York, I think, was prone to broad statements. He liked to say that he hoped revolution would spread north "clear to Canada." Carl Michael Oakes was from Berkeley. An epicene kid, he looked younger than the rest of us but was in fact already two years into doctoral work, and his Spanish was far the best. He'd do running translations of TV and radio broadcasts, somehow finding places to add his own commentary.

Carl took to me because we were both budding academics, I think, and maybe I appreciated his layered, nuanced readings of even the brutal events. I was on the street with him on the day I got my first harbinger of things to come in the form of a tank brigade moving past on its way, it turned out, to the Moneda.

In its stupid manner, an ultra-rightist cell was trying to spark an uprising. While I didn't know what was going on, Carl made sense of the whole thing as it was happening. He said we could expect more trouble, that the Americans and the business sector weren't going to let things rest. Because of his Spanish, I assumed he was picking up better signals than some of us, but it occurred to me in time that he had connections with the government, and when I asked him directly, he said he knew one person who worked in a ministry and told him things. If this person was a lover, a man or woman, I never learned.

Carl was our interpreter, and time has proved out his talent for finding causal order in the daily chaos with an accuracy that historians of the period have needed years of research to match. It was Carl who brought home the papers to compare editorials in *La Nacion* and *Última Hora* with those in *La Tribuna* and *El Mercurio*. He explained the inevitable repercussions of the agrarian reforms. He told us who had U.S. funding – the rightist papers, the truckers' association, and militia groups. Someone was cutting phone lines, planting bombs, using snipers. It was Carl who understood first that it was the fascist group, Fatherland and Liberty, busily building a youth militia. All of this was going on around me, and yet I wasn't quite a part of it. There were two- or three-day stretches in which all I did was study, eat, chat with young women about exotic Canada with its forests and bears (I had never seen a bear but my stories were full of them). And yet the very ground was convulsing.

In late July, *El Mercurio* published a call for uprising written by one of the Christian Democratic senators. That night, under the pretense of a celebration of the anniversary of the Cuban

Revolution, thousands of leftists went into the streets and gathered in an arena. I expect you know the night I'm talking about – you will if you've read the histories. Trade unionists, students, communists, militant MIRistas. I was among them, with my housemates, and it was Carl who told us that the rally might get ugly. The lines were split between those who wanted armed response to the rightist militias and those who thought violence would tip the country into civil war. As groups tried to out-chant one another, skirmishes broke out and things devolved into denouements and schisms. The illusion of unity – it was my illusion too by then – was lost.

That night one of Allende's aides was assassinated.

And it was Carl who told us that same night, before we'd even heard of the assassination, that it was all coming apart. We didn't want to hear it, and Will got angry enough with him that he'd have thrown a punch, I think, if Carl hadn't been so uninviting of violence, so physically delicate, and devoted to clarity.

Or so he seemed to me then. I wonder how he seems to you. There's the Carl I knew, the one presented here, and the one you imagine. At some level, they're all inventions. Of course I believe we can recover a lot from the past, and we need to do so (and our world is ever less interested in doing so), but we'll never know anything comprehensively. The boundaries around our certainties about people and historical moments are sometimes hard to find – any retelling asks us to admit conjecture – but when we come to those borders, we must respect them.

I could as easily have described Carl as an unattractive young man, proud of his learning, who took private pleasure in deflating ideals, unravelling slogans. More quietly serious than the rest of us. Unsmiling. I could have mentioned my feeling that his lack of physical presence, a small body folded in on itself, seemed to have fiercened his intelligence. His brain was what he could extend into the world.

And I might have mentioned that one day I saw him by chance on a street bordering the better neighbourhood of Providencia, climbing out of a car with diplomatic plates. And that I heard an American voice and glimpsed a face inside the car that would become familiar to me later, long after I'd left, that of an American "advisor" who showed up again in the margins of a photo I came across in my researches into the horrors in El Salvador eight years later. I've never known this man's name, but even in that first instant I knew all I needed to. What he said to Carl, I thought in that moment as I walked past, was "good work."

Two English words set into my Spanish afternoon. As I turned them over, it came to me for the first time, I think, just how language betrays us. It can obscure our seeming understanding, and it can reveal us to others through meanings hidden perhaps even to ourselves. When I think of good work, I can think of you, full of goodness and duty, or I can think of Carl. But I no longer assume that common speech has absolute and precise values.

I kept walking, and Carl must have walked the other way. I didn't tell him I'd seen him. It was as if I failed to process the image, that I thought I might have been mistaken, though there was no mistaking Carl for anyone.

I've left out of this account so far the people at the language school. Students came and went. They were from Britain, Brazil, North America, North Africa, the English and French Caribbean.

Some of the teachers were university students, others were older professionals, working the late days or evenings. My instructor was Jaime Prieto, a full-faced man of about thirty, with thick glasses that magnified the delight in his eyes. He designed lessons based on his many enthusiasms. The preterite tense and American jazz, stem-changing verbs and Camus. I think he'd grown up in Santiago. Whatever his origins, he was, like the city itself, full of kinetic revelations, one of those people you can't imagine in blank spaces, without the concentration of random energies in a metropolis. And neither can I imagine him in a calmer time. In the classroom, we never discussed Allende or what was happening, because we never had to. A politics of hope imbued everything. Everyone was awake and dreaming.

Because he was a constant presence in my days (and I, his longest-serving student in those weeks, in his) I spoke of him to my housemates in slightly reverential tones, I think. They've always been so important, these questions of how I spoke of him, what I said exactly, and to whom I said it. It's not an exaggeration, Kim, to say that the questions did, long ago, send me to my knees in the dark. If you ever could imagine such madness, try to examine every action you take in a day, from morning habits to phone calls, to your words, your decision to cancel a date or eat Chinese. You'll see that you cannot work back to a cause, a true one, for most of them, even though you know it exists, and beguiling false ones are all around you. How much harder, then, to understand an experience in memory, through memory, struck into you by confusion and fear? How do we measure? What weight do we give conjecture? How do we keep later knowledge from contaminating our judgment? How can we base an attempt to understand on a recreation of ignorance? On trying to decontextualize? Do you see that, for me, everything I think to be true about those days in Santiago is in question? It all seems based on wrongly invested beliefs, on lies, conscious or otherwise, then and now. On the distortions caused by the sheer need to make sense. On the misinterpretations of the moment, and of the oh so fallible self.

You can't remember Mexico City, but you were there, bashing me. Of course, you'll say, but that was a few months in childhood and you remember very well the main events in your adult life, and remember too well the main trauma. I'm telling you that you're wrong to think this. We don't purely remember anything, other than maybe a searing moment here and there, and these along with the rest are strung into as much narrative order as we can give them, if we need to, when there may well have been no coherent narrative in the experience. I'm leaving out the defence mechanisms of memory and forgetting, of rationalizing, of dream, all these fully human factors. I'm speaking only of the higher deceptions that work into our efforts at reconstruction – the very moment we think we've finally put a few things in order, we're most likely to miss the little fictions we've imposed. Did I really see Carl or was it another? I turned in the other direction and walked away so as not to be seen. Did the man in the car say "good work" or "good word," as if they'd been discussing euphemisms or Spanish? Did I describe my teacher to Carl as "accepting" of an Algerian student's anti-Americanism, or as "tolerant" of it, or "encouraging"?

Doubts can take their toll but I value them, even the ones I'd give anything to resolve. Pinochet and his bloody friends were of a type, the type that dismisses doubt, that never qualifies a statement (this is exactly why I write as I do, in the prose Donald so despises). They believe a world can be made of blunt utterances. Killers think they're gods.

You already know where this story is going. I'll try to deliver you in good faith to the ending. The worse things got towards September, the more confusing. Even Carl, who must have known where it was all headed, gave up his commentaries. Will went home at the end of August; Armin moved in with a local girl. New boarders arrived but kept to different hours and I never got to know them. I spent more and more time on my own. One evening Jaime and his wife, Emma, had me over to their apartment, where I met a few of their friends. The discussion then was all politics.

I saw them there in the apartment, with a few others, once more. September 12, 1973. A Wednesday. I arrived in early afternoon. Many of those I'd met at the dinner were staying there, in hiding. As was I. The coup had happened. Allende had made his speech on radio. Then he'd committed suicide (as it seems we know now – for years we thought he'd been murdered). Thousands were being rounded up, including foreigners. Including students at the school, it was rumoured. I tried to make for the embassy but there was no safe route. I was a leftist foreigner. I called the embassy but couldn't get through. And so I took shelter with the only people I knew.

There were only brief introductions – no one wanted personal stories. I accepted a bottle of beer and sat on the living-room floor with the others. The radio played congratulations for Pinochet from the doctors' association, the lawyers' guild, all the business elite of the country, it seemed. And then came the names of the wanted. I waited to hear my own. Two of those sitting with me heard theirs, I think. I'd already forgotten some of the names of those I'd been thrown together with, but a young, pregnant woman began to cry and some of the others tried to console her and her boyfriend. The boyfriend announced that they would leave and the others insisted they mustn't. The argument was losing steam when the door flew open.

I won't describe the soldiers. Everyone in the room was told to produce identification. The ones who didn't were taken. The ones who did were checked against a list and taken. All except me. I had my passport. It was clear that the passport meant nothing, only the name. It was also clear that my name was on another list. The first list was long, many pages, typed. The physical fact of it, all these pages, was hard to account for. It had to have been compiled over time, and this was only the day after the coup.

The second list, the one I was on, was one hand-printed page.

I was told to leave. The others were lined up in the hallway. I walked past them, and in some the terror in their faces gave way to looks of betrayal, contempt. I understood that two things counted against me, from their point of view. That I'd arrived only minutes before the soldiers, so it might have seemed that I'd led them there. And that my name was on the second list (even from their perspective they might have seen that these two pieces of evidence were unlikely to both be true, but there was no time to offer a defence). I stopped in front of Jaime and asked for his lawyer's name. I said I'd get help to them. But it was as if he didn't hear me. I said it in English and Spanish. He wouldn't look at me. His wife did look. I can't describe it.

You remember as a teenager overhearing me say that some people exist inside a single ambiguity, and I pretended at the cabin not to know what I meant. Now you see I do know. I walked to the embassy, fully expecting to be detained by troops without the saving list at hand. I saw a man carrying a child of three or four, walking the opposite way. His face was bleeding badly and the child was crying. By this point I couldn't stand to be seen. He slowed and I felt him looking, maybe in warning, or pain, and I couldn't meet his eyes and so I walked on and he said nothing. Around us, soldiers in trucks, and the usual traffic, the hackled city continuing amid the incontrovertible facts of bullets and (real) batons and bodies. In those first hours, with the horror going down right before me, I found it impossible to make sense of these facts, even to connect them to the coup. The unfolding history of it made no impression on me against the fear and blood. The past, mine and the country's, had fallen away, and we were physically trapped in an unending moment of hell.

A car pulled over and the driver waved me inside. It was a few seconds before I registered that it was a cab. I got in. He asked where I needed to go and I told him – an exchange from another world. He said I didn't look like I should be in the streets. He dropped me off half a block from the embassy, and refused payment. He asked that I remember to pray for his country.

The embassy was in chaos, all of them were in those first days and weeks. I lived inside for seventeen days as reports came in about the murder campaign, the horrors at the National Stadium. These still stand as the worst days of my life. I could do nothing to help, and nothing to escape them. And after I finally did escape – our embassy got me out through another, to Argentina and eventually home – I more or less covered up and did nothing then either. In January a single Canadian Forces plane was allowed to leave with embassy staff and refugees, 128 people in all, some of whom I knew well, and I used the news of their arrival as the first real block to shore myself against what had happened.

As far as I've been able to determine, Carl Michael Oakes of Berkeley, California, never existed. And yet he's close by me every day. The ones I've been able to keep from my mind until recently, strangely, have been my friend Jaime, and the others. It's possible to skew a profound memory so that you recall the clover and the mountains, the traffic, even the texture of discontinuous moments, but not the faces and names. Over the years, the decades, I found a place to put them away.

Did someone in that apartment other than me survive? How many? Why aren't they among the dead? Was it the couple who'd heard their names on the radio? Or their unborn child, and did the child ever learn the story?

I imagine scenarios in which this child grows up and moves to Toronto and comes across my name and confronts me, and explains what he thinks he knows, how I betrayed them all, and how he's come to be here, and I then tell him my side of things, uncoloured, leaving the gaps I can't fill, presenting myself as I was, as well as I can. As if I could.

But that wouldn't happen. If I'm ever so accosted, the words exchanged won't be slow or shaded. I'll be asked to answer accusations, not allowed to put things in the order that seems truest to me, who claims not to trust fully in remembered narratives.

And anyway, my story isn't for the disappeared or their children, whomever they are. It's for you. And there'll be no account but this.

Having opened with her own name she could not now sign another, and so she dropped her hands from the keyboard and sat there feeling like some lesser angel's heart had just shot into her body.

She went out to the front porch and at that moment a breeze stopped dead so that it seemed the day met her with a halted expression. On the step in the high afternoon she felt the sun on her bare arms and closed her eyes and tilted her face skyward and here came the breeze again. Someone upwind was cooking cumin seeds.

She'd stayed in control for as long as it took to start into the story and look back halfway through – there was Carl Oakes emerging from the car with diplomatic plates – and seeing the places where the rage that she'd brought back from Lana's farm, and woken with, had blunted the telling, and so rewriting them and then moving forward again and finishing it all in a trance. All for a story no one else would ever read.

The Santiago of decades past, scattered all around her room in books in two languages, in printouts and journals, this city had grown in her, it turned out, and organized itself into one fixed perspective. And now she felt in some way that she was inside it, still there, sheltered, the bitterness gone, in the very place he had known. In recent days her thoughts of him had become obscured. She hadn't been able to call him up in mind with any certainty. The idea of him. The image of him, his face, doubtful, failing to resolve. But now, even out here in the resuming day, he was with her.

She'd described the world as he saw it, an evil world guided by an evil god, but in doing so found a way to penetrate confusion, guilt, anger, even evil itself. And yes, she held to this word, *penetrate*, to mean what she wanted it to mean – she had put herself lovingly inside another. And writing in his voice, she understood that Harold was someone else from the inside. In the time it took to truly imagine her father, to inhabit him, language and thought, the anger gave way to something like forgiveness, something she didn't, finally, have words for. A place to rest, to stay, so that a soul might find itself.

A car driven by a young black woman passed by and from inside came two notes of a ring tone and the street sat down differently. The light was soft but brimming, as if the invisible world vibrated to a sound she couldn't hear.

The house was quiet. Donald and Marian had gone to receive the new blood test results. She went back to her room and lay on her bed.

The ring tone notes were still with her, the familiar first notes of an ice cream truck's overplayed, fuzzy, demagnetizing jingle. She was still high from the writing, overoxygenated, she could see all the way to Peru.

That she'd found this place in herself, there was hope in that. She wished she could grant her father the same reprieve and take him up into this amazing air, this sunblasted air, and in those few moments when she believed she really could take him there, that this reprieve was available to him in the very words she had found, she returned to her desk and sent him the letter.

Harold stood on a slight rise in the lawn, with a prospect of the Humanities faculty and graduate students. He sipped his wine and scented rain.

The Dean's Reception marked the start of the fall term. For years he'd met the event with calm forbearance, and then the year arrived when he no longer had to feign that he'd been put out by company, that it was a strain simply to say hello to acquaintances in other departments. This year, today, he was somewhere else again. It seemed likely that at some point in the next thirty minutes he would be addressed and be unable to respond. With their little exchanges, their show of good enterprise, they were all only re-enacting a ritual diversion from things as they really were. They affected to disarm these things, terrible things, by talking at angles to them. In years past, he himself partook of the show. One minute he'd be comparing the patriarchal leadership of Pentecostal churches and *caudillismo* on the haciendas, and the next he was complaining about the new hours at the library, or listening to someone hold forth on a dead Frenchman's theory about forced relocations in the early soviet. But he saw through it all now. The only true thing that remained was that the wine was never very good, and there was never enough of it.

Now it was his own name on the wind. In approach were the graduate chair of History, Richard Trevorian, and a woman in a floral summer dress. Brown hair, with bold blond streaks. Her face was sharp and intent, but amiable. Harold allowed himself to notice that her arms and calves were those of an athlete. Not long ago, he would have desired her.

"This is the Harold of lore. Harold, this is Carrie Hughes. Our new Americanist. She's from New York by way of the original Cambridge. You two have overlapping interests, I think. And she knows your work."

"Hello, Carrie Hughes."

"It's all true, what Richard says. He's thought through my

connection to everyone quite brilliantly." She briefly put a hand on Trevorian's arm. He was clearly delighted. Harold suppressed an urge to shake him by the shoulders as if to make him see. "I could have used you before the interview."

"You nailed the interview. That committee made for a complicated landscape but you moved over it like . . ."

"Like a lithe beast of the plain? Can I have been that?"

"Clearly you still are," said Trevorian.

"You know," she addressed Harold now, "we just missed meeting each other in Tarrytown, at the Rockefeller archives last summer. I was there the week after you left."

"You were going through the log books."

"The archivist, James, told me. He knew we had common pursuits." A lithe beast in pursuit, thought Harold. The fool he once was would deceive himself to think he'd just been sighted. "And this was before I got the job here."

"Yes, old James." He could see she didn't know what to make of his response. He wanted to help her out, but couldn't. Trevorian was looking at him oddly, on the verge of concern, but then dismissed himself and went off to find Carrie a glass of wine. She stood with her arms at her sides, and felt no need to do anything with her hands, a posture that most people couldn't carry off. The woman must have been near thirty-five but she stood unselfconsciously, like a girl. Why had he been in New York? He would recall if he could muster the words. "I was researching suspect sources of missionary funding in the eighties. But then I abandoned it. I've abandoned every idea over the last few years. It turns out I've been right to do so."

She looked him in the eye, searched his face briefly. She could see he wasn't kidding.

"Well. I have to choose a faculty mentor. Forgive me if you're not on the list."

"Get tenure and then save yourself. That's what I've learned."

"I have to say, this is a strange party. I just met someone who claimed to be from Cultural Studies. She's one of those among us who's built a career on hostility. She's found a way to commodify her rage."

"We all have to do something with it."

"I confessed to her that I didn't know what Cultural Studies was if it wasn't what all of us were doing. But it must be something else because she didn't seem to know about history, literature, or languages. Apparently she writes on popular subjects for one of the newspapers. A scholar of American celebrities."

They began to walk along the edge of the party. The expected thing would be to ask about her work, but he didn't want any expected thing between them. On the lawn beyond the group a couple of young men were playing catch with a baseball, and for several seconds it seemed to him that the parabola of the ball's flight was the most beautiful thing he'd ever seen.

"Not that I don't enjoy a slant on things." She was talking about the scholar of celebrities. "I have a feminist friend who reviews movies for journals read by six people."

She seemed to be hoping for returned wit, or at least a smile from him. He was a disappointment. At least the impression he was making was true. Trevorian spotted them and brought the wine. Now that they all had a glass, they toasted Carrie's arrival. Then they all agreed it was important for her to meet as many of the faculty as she could. As Trevorian led her away, she turned back to Harold and fluttered her fingers and arched her brow comically.

And then something struck him, a kind of knowledge. Within it, a seed of the familiar, and so the promise that it could be forgotten, for it had come to him as a revelation. He must have known it once and lost it. In the past he would have escaped the knowledge by involving himself in a strong distraction. Back when the distractions still charmed him there was hope, though his preferred distractions tended to damage, and the damage replicated. He told himself to leave the party, but that would trap him alone.

He stood at the edge of things, hoping not to be approached. When next he saw Carrie Hughes she was standing, unchaperoned, in a group who weren't from the department. No one could see, as he could, that she was by herself in the world. He drifted near.

A young man was saying that the college had just been cleared because of a bomb threat. Everyone stole quick, dumb glances at the stone building before them. A campus security guard was in the doorway but none of the bomb police or dogs had arrived yet.

"Another student lunatic trying to reschedule an exam." The speaker had a shaved head and wire glasses. He was trying to look like Foucault.

"No exams this time of year," said the young man. He worked in the building, apparently, but Harold didn't recognize him. "I hear the caller had . . . altogether, an Arab accent."

"Bomb threats are a tradition of the institution," said someone.

"In winter term we're always evacuating into the snow," said the Foucault. "I never invigilate without my parka. It's all part of the dialectic of external influence and local adaptation."

"Did you say that you shit in the snow?" Carrie asked.

Harold smiled, at last. She was reckless where she could be. The bald man gave her a curt glance. She took a few steps towards Harold.

"I thought you Canadians had a famous sense of humour."

A cool breeze came out of nowhere. The sky was massing over them. He wished he hadn't left his jacket in his office so he could offer it to her. He wanted to tell her that he knew of her loneliness, but that for her, this was a good place. A good university in a global near capital, a place to be. Maybe, in human terms, and if you were lucky, the best. In the history of the species, to be here, now, was to have won the lottery of all creation, to have been swept by the waters of time and chance up onto the shores of a greenness, full of spectacle and quiet, wonder and certainty, possibility. A place that would provide. As long as she hadn't brought with her some corruption.

The wind stiffened and took up in the white tablecloths of the catering station, and the staff scrambled to save the wineglasses from disaster. Everyone made for the unthreatened buildings. Harold was slow to follow. He began for the nearest entryway, from which Carrie Hughes now watched him, tucked into the old stone. It was a movie rain when it came. The sky falling. When the lightning and thunder arrived he maintained his pace. She stepped aside for him and they stood together a moment and then went into the building and watched the storm become everything. The darkening stone. Then it really came down.

"Do you suppose this is what that phone warning was about?" Carrie asked.

He turned and saw that she was soaked. A little shyly, he thought, she looked at his chest, and her face seemed to change in the dim light through the rain running down the old lead windows.

Even now, he felt no physical desire. Was it that he'd finally come to inhabit his own heart, or had he been relieved of it?

They watched for another minute or two and finally it began to let up. Carrie said she was going to make a run for her car. She asked if he needed a lift somewhere.

"No, thank you. I've got to get back to my office. Now that the bomb's gone off."

"All right. I'll think about your advice."

"The department," he said. "There are bores and lechers, and a couple of crazies I should have told you about."

"I'll avoid them."

"Don't do that." She wouldn't understand. "They'll attach to you, I know. But be kind to them. We lose so much to choose differently."

She paused for a moment. She nodded and he knew her. She gave his hand a little tug and then she left. He watched her fade.

By the time the building was clear and he got back to his office he was almost dry. He locked the door and took off his pants, shirt, and socks and hung them on the coat rack where they'd catch the breeze from the window. From his filing cabinet he took his bottle of single malt and a glass and set them up on the desk. He sat in his underwear and jacket, only a little chilled, his feet wrapped in a throw rug, and tried not to picture himself as he called up his email, and opened a message from Kim that began

Kim,

Once when you were about fourteen

Teresa was asleep on his chest as he replayed the sex and the stories she had told after it, the way she opened up and led him into her disappointments and pride at having overcome many of them, that no matter how tired she was, she arrived at the café each day upon a kind of illusion that as she moved from table to table, overhearing, entering conversations and leaving them, she somehow held together all these bastards of luck – what her father used to call them, the exiles – and he told her she was right, that it meant something to them to see her move between them, the way they were aware of her without always watching, or watching without knowing why. Her boss had told her she inspired the better men to keep the worse ones in line and so it was a good bar, by day. Her happiness about her work surprised Rodrigo and led them into a round silence, and the silence back into their desire and they began again, in the spirit of surprise happiness, maybe, this time making love for what seemed like hours until the light through the window had tilted away from them and the walls had died a little, and she was still asleep in his arm when he heard the apartment door open.

He didn't move. The sound of the television woke Teresa and he looked down at her and found a stranger there, though one he'd seen before in other women stricken with fear. He himself was not afraid. There was nothing Luis could say against them.

She crawled across him naked and hurried to close the bedroom door. Only when she locked it did he see that it had been fixed with a small brass bolt, mounted crookedly.

— Don't worry, he said, and she held a finger to her lips to quiet him.

Her face had hardened by the time she'd dressed. She gathered Rodrigo's clothes in her arms and presented them to him and he got out of bed and tried to kiss her, just to calm her, but she pushed him away.

— I'll talk to him, he said.

The channels were changing every few seconds, then stopped on an ad for an exercise machine people bought for their homes. The voice in English said "see the difference in just four weeks." A minute or so passed before he and Teresa both jumped at the sound of something thrown hard against the other side of the door, and then falling and rolling, empty beer can, and crushed underfoot.

— Who's in there? Luis was at the door.

Teresa stood back, near the window. Rodrigo still didn't have his shirt on. He unlocked and opened the door.

When Luis saw Rodrigo he seemed not able to make sense of him. Rodrigo nodded slightly in greeting but Luis did not acknowledge it. He wore black jeans and a frayed blue shirt Rodrigo had seen dozens of times. His feet were bare, and this made Rodrigo aware of his half-nakedness, so he pulled his T-shirt on, and in the second it took to duck his head and look up again, he saw that Luis had settled on a meaner expression.

— I let you into my life, he said. I help you out. And this is what happens.

— This has nothing to do with you.

— You drink my beer and you fuck my wife.

— Don't talk like that.

It was too late, Rodrigo knew, but in that moment he understood that the three of them were different because of the ways they were mistaken. Every day Teresa in her fantasies was beautifully mistaken. He himself was mistaken to believe he was too young and ignorant and out of place to fully trust his knowledge. And Luis was mistaken to believe his life could be different if he took it in hand and bent it to the shapes he saw in his dark thoughts.

—Teresa only pretends she's your wife.

—Yes. And she pretends to do the cooking and cleaning. And she pretends to fuck me when I want her to. She pretends very well.

Then it was Teresa flying up at him and Rodrigo holding her back with one arm, finally turning to push her onto the bed, with Luis laughing at them. He turned back then and hit Luis even before forming a proper fist, a clumsy punch in the face, without much force, but enough to satisfy Luis that he'd led them where he intended. They crashed to the floor and up again and wrestled without clear advantage until again they fell and Luis was on top and throwing elbows into his face. The blood and pain didn't scare him. What scared him was that close by were new arrangements, like a sudden light that broke through to dreams and woke you into some strange, closed place. He had seen men die, boys too, no one he had known, but like him just the same.

Luis lowered his form and head-butted him on the brow. When Rodrigo found his senses, Luis was standing over him, telling him to get up, and Teresa was somewhere crying.

He got to his knees and then his feet and stood before Luis, seeing him with one clear eye.

—What do you do? Hit me? Luis laughed at him. I'll call the police and they'll send you back to your jungle. Get out of here.

Rodrigo turned to search for Teresa. She was framed in the bedroom doorway. She seemed to have blood on her too, on her hand and across her shirt, and he knew it was his blood. He started towards her but she shook her head. She disappeared into the bedroom and then came and gave him a wet towel and he mopped his face. Then she took it from him and went to the kitchen. She found scissors and cut a strip from it and tied it around his forehead. Luis had gone to the window and turned his back on them.

He reached out for Teresa but she backed away.

— Come with me.

— No. You have to leave.

She walked to the door and he followed, and she opened it and took hold of his belted waistband and tugged him past her. He stood in the hall. She kissed her bloody hand and touched it to his cheek, and closed the door.

It would be an early bedtime. Marian got into her nightgown and sat with Kim on the sofa. They were both slightly drunk. They'd gone with Donald to a Shakespeare in the Park production of *A Midsummer Night's Dream*, and then on the way home, with the car windows open and in clear violation of the law, passed around a bottle of Pinot Grigio and took in the noise and nighttime improvisational spirit of Bloor Street West.

"Who knew dying could be so much fun?"

"Jesus, Mom."

Marian hadn't expected to make it to the end of the play but surprised herself.

"I think I'm through the hardest part. And I can't stand moroseness. Is that a word? Morosity."

"Morosery."

"Gloomism. Blueyness."

Kim smiled. Marian brought her feet up onto the couch and rested them in Kim's lap.

"Maybe I'm mostly faking it at this point, but the faking feels real. It's a way of waiting. I want to make the best of each day. And not say too many banal things."

Donald entered and announced that the news on the internet described Russians rattling their sabres again up at the Arctic border.

"You see," said Marian, "it's not a bad time to be leaving," at which point Donald seemed to flinch. He turned and left the room.

"I guess that's a border I can't cross with him."

Kim was the last one up. She sat alone, wondering how the play's comic energy had so easily influenced her mother's mood. It was possible that, as her days ran out, Marian was more often cheery than she had been before her illness. Absurdity counted for more at the end.

On her way to bed she heard Donald's radio in the study. She went in and caught a few seconds of the CBC overnight service, another Radio Netherlands documentary about the international sex trade. When she turned it off, the new quiet held her, and she thought of Harold. She hadn't heard from him since sending the Santiago letter. It struck her that she might have made a mistake.

In her room she found an envelope on her pillow. Inside was a yellowed page in Harold's hand – fifteen names, most Spanish, some partial – and a note in Marian's: "The list I mentioned. I stole it years ago to free him of it, but I couldn't throw it away, with all its mystery and weight. I produce it now inspired by the

Bard, like a prop in a play. You can give it back to him, your choice – I'm letting go of these things. But you've inherited this territory, wherever it is."

Before she dropped away minutes later she tried to think about what it meant, the list, Harold's silence, but instead it was the radio documentary that carried her to sleep. She felt her heart freely given into capture and then she was flying, falling into some impoverished hill country where parents sell their children into labour or prostitution and she sees it all, sees the kids sold away, sees maps of their journeys with arcing lines like cinnamon routes or advancing campaigns and the rest of the world lays indurate, watching, as their hearts and hers travel by.

Rosemary's door opened before he reached it. She must have seen him coming across the park. She stood behind the screen door.

"Why are you here?" She turned on the foyer light. She looked a little rough, as if she'd not slept. "I can't invite you in."

He tested the door. It opened. She stepped back as he stepped in. Then she went to an armchair and sat. He closed the inside door and looked around. The small front room was dominated by a tall, old standing stereo cabinet with wicker speaker covers. Set along the top were a white china fish and a propped image, a golden detail from some iconographic painting. The only other art was a small colour photo of a horse grazing in a field at sunset. The poor taste of the thing jarred him. The horse didn't belong with the woman as he thought he knew her, but it fit the room.

"I've come to apologize to you."

"Then you should have called."

"I'm doing what I can face to face. All of it."

"All of what?"

From outside, the electronic chime from an open car door warning of keys in the ignition. He recalled the bell of the knife grinder going down the street he used to live on with his young family, his two girls.

"I want to meet him. This man you shelter."

She looked off towards a table lamp as if reading something on the stained shade. Her face looked malarial. There were things this fearless woman didn't really want to confront.

"He's none of your concern, Harold."

"Maybe you think of us the same way." His voice was rising. "Do you see me like one of your charges? Am I in need of saving, is that it? He and I and all your undocumented semi-literate bloodstained young monsters."

She looked at him in a kind of horror, her mouth open and wordless. There were times when he would fall into himself, down a long darkness, tumbling beyond language or control. He would come to rest for only a moment in a state of unendurable clarity, and then the words would find him and like that he was back on the surface, in the falseness of things. Kim's letter had stranded him far from the surface. But the deep order was all around him if only he'd be granted light to see it. There were, at least, one or two answers he could bring to his possession by force.

As if he'd conjured him by will, he heard the young man begin up the basement stairs on the far side of the kitchen. He appeared, paused momentarily to look at him, and then came straight across. Rosemary stood as if to come between them.

"It's all right, Rodrigo."

He stopped and stood under the archway to the front room. From the park this Rodrigo had appeared handsome in a boyish way. Smooth and young. No doubt Rosemary would see the divine in his beauty. Showing the so-called path, being the way, she would think the way was shown back. But up close he was something else, his features harder, older. And today he had a fresh shiner and a cut on his brow.

"Go back downstairs. Everything's fine here."

—Where did you get those wounds?

"What are you asking him? Speak English."

—A man hit me. A friend. A man I work with.

—Which answer should I accept?

Rodrigo looked briefly to Rosemary, the warning in her expression.

—We're good people.

"What's he asking you?" she demanded.

— Have you ever gone to an organization called GROUND?

"Don't answer, Rodrigo."

"No need to," said Harold. "I'm calling the police."

"To tell them what?" The tone was measured, her eyes level on him. She was used to drama. Voices raised, hands flying up. "That I rejected your advances and now you want my tenant arrested?"

She was saying he didn't know what he was doing. She wasn't seeing the long view. Whatever he did or might do made sense from a distance. Kim had tried to find the distance, to look back at him. Whomever she'd seen, not him exactly, but someone he seemed to know, she'd seen with a clarity that changed everything.

"There are criminals among us. Here. I've found one."

"This is how you apologize?"

He was sorry for having kissed her but not for wanting to. The attraction was unknowable to him. Through a window he saw a small group of racing cyclists glide by in their glossy forms. He thought of a night river sheen. An image of himself standing with his father in the wilderness dark on a shore somewhere. It may have been a memory.

"Conviction," he said to Rosemary. "Loaded word, isn't it?"

"What does he ask?"

— I'm asking for your story, whatever it is. Convince me.

"Don't listen to him. Go back downstairs."

— I'm no harm to you. I'm no danger. I don't make trouble for this country.

— You can barely speak English. I doubt you can even read your own language.

Rodrigo leaned slightly against the archway without somehow relenting his readiness to advance. Something in the line of him suggested an ease with his space. This was his home, after all.

— I can read. I can work honest work.

— You sound Colombian. So you were with one of the paramilitaries, no doubt. What have you been trained to do in a circumstance like this?

— How do you know me? You don't know me.

— I know your kind.

Fuck them both, Harold thought. Exactly that. He wanted to fuck them over, fuck up the kid's pretty face, fuck Rosemary's brains out. Fuck them bloody.

"I won't have this."

"You don't get to call every shot, Rosemary. I'm here. I want his bogus story. I want you to watch me hear it and judge it. If I like it, maybe I won't turn him in."

His breathing was short. He'd never been aware of it before. This was all a charade, their little drama with its presumed stakes, the imagined echoes of distant conflicts, his very breaths. He was caught up in a mockery of the real world, with its events of scale, its oceans of misery. He'd made actors of the three of them. All he could do was bring them to the end, or if the end wouldn't come, to somehow *make* them real. He'd walked out into the day still trailing Kim's letter, in a spell brought on by the persuasions of fiction, its magic dust. But the spell broke upon anything of substance. The only dust that mattered was the pulverized earth of history. He recognized it by kind wherever he went. He collected it now and then in his travels, kept it in his pockets, the names of the killers, the numbers of the dead, the manners of deaths, and spilled it from his fingers to season the air on pleasant, forgetful days.

"Your issue with me has nothing to do with him," said Rosemary. "Or with your daughter. You've been rejected and you're behaving like a child."

"And what about you? What are the sources of your passion right now? Are you playing mother to him? Or is it something else? Or both? What good work you do, making murderers into motherfuckers."

They both came towards him and at first it wasn't clear who was intercepting whom. Then it was Rosemary stepping between them. Rodrigo put his hand on her arm to move her aside and Harold took his wrist in hand and wrenched it away to free her.

— Do you like hurting women? Is that it?

And then before he could make further calculations he was hit and down on the floor and the kid was kicking him in the ribs. The pain was astonishing, he knew instantly he'd never before felt its kind. He covered up with his arms and his elbows were driven into him and so he rolled a little to and fro and the blows were general. They hit him as proofs in his favour. He looked up once to see Rosemary tugging on Rodrigo and screaming to no effect. There was no wind in him to stir the least of events and it seemed there never again would be. The intensity was focused and unfiltered and it made nothing of the crying and chaos so that the sounds seemed not entirely human as if the thing upon him had never known him, had nothing to do with him. The three of them connected only through his breaking body. He felt what he felt and he thought he detected some good in it and then all-that-was cracked into his skull and the darkness came up and he was gone and he said so to himself and kept saying it until he knew he was not gone at all but instead present in a new way.

It was Rodrigo who was gone. Rosemary had put something under Harold's head. She was kneeling over him, with a hand on his face.

"He thought you were threatening me. He misunderstood. I'm calling an ambulance. You can say you were in the park. You were in the park and you were beaten. Do you understand, Harold?"

Did he understand Harold? He had never much understood him, no. Except he was a talker and you could never trust a talker. It was an early affliction that had never left him. His father in a hospital bed, waking and finding him there sitting by, and his first words were, "Don't you say a thing," to bend him from his nature. And sure enough when the old man died Harold talked his way through school and on into higher learning, higher culture. And he had never stopped talking. He could never be the still point in a room of people. Only when he forgot himself was he quiet. He had never just shut up.

He told Rosemary to call him a cab. He said if he felt any worse he'd get to a hospital himself. She took no convincing. The pain was almost unmanageable through the cab ride, the arrival at the condo. He went straight to the bathroom and stripped with the short, deliberate movements of the old man he would soon become. He stood before the full-length mirror. There were cuts on his forehead, on the bridge of his nose, and at the top of one ear, and the makings of a shiner of his own, but his bad body looked mostly like itself. To the eye, the damage was less than he'd supposed. The bruises would look worse tomorrow but he was hardly a specimen of abuse.

How had this day begun? Yesterday had never ended. Deep in the night the phone had sounded once. Sleep had finally come as the window reported first light. Then the clock radio had woken him with the morning's humidex reading and a prediction of heavy smog. He missed the old mornings of the knife grinder. They'd rented the bottom floor of a house. Kim had just been born and nobody slept and he'd walk the west-end streets in the pre-dawn with Kim in his arms and old men leaning on wrought-iron porch railings and Italians with scarred workboots and dented grey lunchpails squatting at corners awaiting their rides, smoking and looking meditatively before themselves in attitudes of faint recall. In the early hours the place was a village, people nodded to one another, and him with his baby girl, strangers stopping to talk to him, acknowledging a value in the easy transaction. He imagined some corrective measure in the mind's design that the best part of the day should follow so close upon the worst part of the night.

He'd spent much of the morning composing a letter to Kim. It was time they talked, but not until he'd said in print precisely what he wanted to. There was no room for misunderstandings. He needed to be exact and direct. There was a responsibility to the record, and to the real people on it or affected by it. They both knew the record took you only so far, but only one of them respected its limits. He pictured them walking across an open plain, coming to the outer edge of the last mapped, marked territory, standing side by side at the end of solid ground. Beyond them, air or water or the dark unknown, some element that generated only illusions. She stepped forward. He turned back.

He ran a bath with Epsom salts, walked naked into the kitchen and poured a tumbler of Scotch, returned to the tub with his drink and set about soaking the dull chords and sharp notes of injury. The phone rang and he let it go, but when a minute later it rang again he got out and walked dripping onto the floor and missed it anyway. Standing there, naked and sopping, he checked his messages. An automated voice named Lisa tried to pitch him a financial service until he deleted her. Then a hang-up from Marian's house.

He returned to the water. The pain was now in his ribs and on his phone. In future he would be able to retrieve the pain in his body just by thinking of Kim's refusal to leave a message. A word or two from her seemed to go a long way.

From so little, she had imagined his days in Santiago so well. She'd conjured them from his posture, the set of his face, things he was unaware of. Her letter was a cruelty. She must have been in great pain to have written it. Of the pain he was certain.

Today he had felt certainty. Upon a certainty, he had lost his bearings, and would still be without them if Rodrigo hadn't beaten them back into him. It was in the balance of things that the beating would have consequences. He was a simple kid, Rosemary's Rodrigo. He might never understand what was about to happen to him.

The online profile revealed that Eduardo Jofre worked in a northern suburb for a self-proclaimed "socially progressive" investment company called Rahv Ashbaugh. He'd come to Canada from Santiago. He held a degree in Social and Political Thought. He spoke three languages. He researched and wrote reports, translated documents, advised the people who designed the portfolios. He knew a lot about factory farms and leather dyes and the economic ravages of global warming. He was available for presentations. There was an email address and a phone extension.

There was also a photo. It was the man she'd known years ago in university. He didn't look much older. He was smiling. His eyes were a shade too dark, maybe, and his features a little softened, but he was the same halfway handsome she'd always preferred.

Another site, in Spanish, said that he worked from abroad in the Chilean reparations movement.

The traffic would be murder so she didn't take the car. His office was ninety minutes distant by transit. A last subway stop, two buses, a long walk across a hot parking lot, medium office towers in every direction portioning out the lower sky. Suburban business park nowhere. You looked and saw nothing, stunned wordless. She walked past a copy shop, dry cleaners. A massage parlour with a Thai girl reading a magazine at the desk. Kim knew no one who lived or worked up here, not even among the clients at GROUND. These lives were unimaginable. That seemed to be the point of the place.

On the eleventh floor the view from the reception area was a little deadening, expressway traffic clouding off to the west. The receptionist took Kim's name and gestured to the empty seating area. The decor's only concession to the outer world was a framed photo she knew from somewhere of workers in an open-pit mine in Brazil. They climbed ladders. They were covered in mud. Guards stood over them like centurions. It was like a photo of hell from the fourteenth century.

She looked up and there he was. He didn't seem to recognize her. Standard greeting, practised handshake, and then her face, though altered, came to him, and he smiled a killer smile.

They took lunch in a so-called bistro at the foot of a neighbouring office complex. By the time they arrived she'd told him all she could remember about their three or four meetings. He remembered her visits to the music store. They didn't account for her being here. When they were seated, the sun on an opposite tower was in her eyes so he adjusted the blinds and sat across from her in louvred light. He seemed to understand that she didn't know how to explain her presence, so he spoke for a while about the company, as if she were a potential investor.

"When Rahv Ashbaugh started up, it was a struggle. There was more money to be made off of people with no conscience. That's not the case now, necessarily, but we wouldn't have entered into this business unless we meant it. We try not to deal with those companies who borrow against the future. Or those who ignore the past."

"Do good-guy companies exist?"

"They do. Often in unlikely settings, countries trying to get clear of some dark period. And we find some business with good labour practices, that monitors health and safety and wages and vendor compliance, and that can't be blamed for the tanks in the streets."

She wanted to believe that capital could have heart, or at least a clear conscience. And beyond that, she wanted to believe him. He seemed a slightly shy man of substance. No matter which of them was speaking, he looked Kim in the eye, but seemed to be receiving her in some way. He thanked the waitress for everything she brought to the table, and he looked at her too, and she was pretty, but didn't glance at her when she walked away. He was present.

"How well do your clients know the histories? They must rely on you to know it for them."

"It's my view," he said, "that Canada has won itself a great naivety. This is the most naive country in the world. Which is why it's the most compassionate."

"Well, that puts us in our place."

"It's my place too. Coups and revolutions don't happen to nations, they happen to people, one by one."

"One of them happened to you. Your September eleventh."

"Yes. Five months before I was born." He explained that the troubles became his about '77, when he was old enough to attribute the absence he sensed to a cause. "I grew up into a kind of obsession about the events in the months after I was conceived, and about my father's murder. When I began university I had every intention of continuing my life at home. It wasn't as if we were all in shadow all the time. But one day I was out with a girl and her friend – these are young people, students, in most respects idealistic, I thought – and it came to light that they wanted to know nothing more about that period. They had chosen to avoid the subject, to let it go by. It was a small moment, but right then I knew I had to decide, either to stay and devote myself to sharpening this national memory or to leave the country and choose a different life."

"That's a lot to let go of."

"Less than you might suppose. I ended up choosing both. The country's still with me."

She sensed he'd keep going if she prompted him. He'd release the obsession like this, in tellings, again and again, as he needed. This expert in progressive investments.

"You told me when we first met that you were in the resistance movement."

"Did I? That's embarrassing. I would have been trying to impress you."

"No. I was peppering you with questions. You finally just mentioned it. But because you did, you've come to mind, now that I'm researching the coup."

He looked at her somewhat searchingly, then smiled. "I guess this isn't a school project."

"I have a list of names. I've typed them out." She produced the list and slid it across to him. "Fifteen names. Seven are in the Rettig Report. I have a kind of picture of what happened to them, how they might be connected. Of the other eight, I know about these two – they're Americans – and this German, but not these five. I don't know where to look to find their stories." She was trying not to sound too intent.

"I know where to look. But it might involve disturbing people's memories, and that's no small thing, especially if it goes beyond what's already on the record. Why do you want to know all this?"

How to answer? Because she'd entered a city. Because she was afraid for her father, as if it was all still happening, he was still there, and her actions could get him out, or trap him. And because in her new world everything seemed to ride on her willingness not to back down from her fears.

She told Eduardo it was about her father. She said his name. She said he was down there in '73 and she wanted to know what happened to him.

"How old was he?"

"About twenty-three."

"Is he Canadian? Was he then?"

"Yes. He was a student."

"But he won't tell you what happened."

"A little. Not much. The seven in the report were arrested from the same address. Two were murdered and accounted for. The rest were all disappeared. The last line on them is the same in every instance. They're 'presumed to have died as a result –'"

"'Of the violence prevailing in the country at the time.'"

"Yes." This man's country was haunted. It must have ghosts on every street. Harold had been there for only a few months and he was still haunted. It was only human to feel responsible for your bad luck.

She watched Eduardo fold the list and put it in his shirt pocket.

"There's a story somewhere for every name, but not all the stories get told. I'll see what I can find out. As long as you're willing to hear what I learn."

She nodded. She was very close now to the hard fact of who she had become.

The topic then shifted to the one person they had in common, Renner, whom they'd both lost track of, and it wasn't her father or Eduardo she thought of now on the way home, but Renner, as she and Eduardo remembered him. Renner had had a crush on her and trailed around doing impressions of everyone they met. The diminuendo of the shy girl serving them beer in a pitcher, the professor's stentorian address, the stutters and pauses of the campus radio news reader. He did them everywhere, the impressions – do him, do her, they were always saying – before class, on the phone, at parties, and Renner would always add an incongruity, a misfit word or two in the wrong diction, and make them nearly fall over laughing. Cathectic, adamantine, educe. She'd been inspired to write down the best-sounding words and look them up later. He would never say where he got them from or if he knew what they meant. It was the only mystery that attached to him, and she almost fell for it.

Assuasive, unregenerate, inexpiable, effeir.

They'd hang out in the music store, and who was she then, so full of words and music? And the store had led her to the rest of her life because of Eduardo's co-worker, what's his name, the Mozambican, Armando. He was the one who'd first told her about GROUND, which she'd remember a few years later. GROUND had gathered the evidence to prove that a rich family in Maputo had tried to kill him. That was the what but she couldn't remember the why. No doubt he'd asked the wrong whats and whys.

And upon this thought, Harold came back to mind.

He had spent the mid-afternoon at a farmer's market for the purpose of later being where he now found himself, chopping herbs for his soup in a rich, transporting haze. The hour of preparation was better even than that of the dinner itself. The ritual and pleasure had the authority of goodness. One of the ways of discerning goodness, as Richard Hooker had it, was through "the observation of those signs and tokens, which being annexed always unto goodness, argue that where they are found, there also goodness is." Hooker hadn't been thinking of garlic and fennel, but André added him to the air anyway and found the mix agreeable.

As he turned down the flame, the phone rang. He considered ignoring it, but the soup had to simmer for twenty minutes and no longer needed his attention, a quality of the finishing stage that on some days recommended it.

The call display was lit up with Harold's name. Now there was something else in the air. Not, he hoped, an undertone of spoilage. He summoned his voice and said hello. The pleasantries lasted ten seconds.

"Will you hear a confession over the phone?" Harold forced a laugh.

"I'm not that variety of priest, but of course we can talk."

"One day I believe in talking cures, the next I don't. I've voiced both opinions to my daughter."

By the time he'd turned the soup off to cool he'd heard the story of Harold's trials with Rosemary, of his mishandling her romantic refusals, and of last night's events; how, along with some bruises, Rosemary's Rodrigo had given Harold the power to determine the young man's fate.

"I behaved like an ass, but nothing warranted his assault on me. Frankly I feel vindicated."

Harold seemed not to know there were always more things in the balance than anyone could guess at.

"What did you want to confess, Harold?"

"Well, to begin, I wanted to tell you that I know what kind of man I am. I'm a pretty sorry creature. You must have known this about me since we met. I've known it always. But it's a very real condition, full of inalterable facts. And so in being a sorry creature, I've learned a truth. It's that people like you – the devout – you live in illusion. You do your work in the world upon an illusory belief, and I fail to measure up upon the sure knowledge that your kind are mistaken. Of course you know some things that I don't, other truths, but you never wade into them without your mantle of illusion. I confess that I judge you, Father. It's a long, harsh judgment. I'll spare you the exact wording."

His voice was full. This wasn't a confession or judgment, but a proclamation, as if to unleash the power of his word upon whatever was troubling the borders of his life. But he didn't know what it was out there, or even where the borders were. The man had been wandering lost for a long time.

"You've not called me in the hope I'll bring you to a different light."

"That light of yours isn't available to me. It's just not fucking available."

The dull profanity might have betrayed more passion than it did.

"Have you ever expressed these beliefs to your family?"

"That's not our mode. We're trapped in this sort of loop. Each in our own orbit around some fixed point we've never named. We're thousands of miles apart and there is no closing that distance. Some physics of shame and regret won't allow it."

"I see."

"This is where you tell me I'm wrong, and cite your experience with families in trouble. But I'm not talking about them."

"You could have had this conversation by yourself."

"Maybe. But I never have. Not all of it at once."

The sorry creature made the point that he didn't feel sorry for himself. "At least I know to struggle against grand illusions." Then he stressed that though he judged people like André and Rosemary, he admired them "at some level" for their good works.

"The hope of salvation is incredibly durable," Harold said, "for being such a thin tissue, so thin anyone could see through it if they held it to the right light."

"The light of reason."

"I know I'm drawing the same old lines, but yes."

The image came to André of a man who lived with a ticking inside him. He'd dreamt it once. He's standing behind this man whose face he never sees. The man asks him to remove the ticking. He feels the knife in his hand, lifts it, and cuts at the base of the neck. The pain is accepted, the man only wants to know what's there. And what's there is a shell of some sort, like a pecan shell. He takes it out and pries open the top half, and there inside is a red insect, the size of his thumbnail, kicking its hind legs against the shell wall. Tick. Tick. What is it? the man wants to know, afraid to turn and look. And André knows the answer but can't find the word. He can't utter a syllable. And when the dream ended and he woke, he still didn't know the word.

"It isn't that you don't believe in salvation, Harold, it's that you don't want it. To find out why, you might have to trust some other grand illusions. If not talking cures, then therapies. If not therapies, then maybe a useful mantra or two. Or go further into the one you do trust – learning. You certainly won't find salvation in any of those, but you might find what you're looking for. A temporary reprieve. I can't give you that."

"It might surprise you to learn that I do have convictions. And I have no choice but to follow them, as you must follow yours."

"And where does following them take you?"

"The easy thing would be to let it go, the assault. But that's not the right course of action. This kid is violent. I don't know his story, but those who've heard it know he's violent too. He must have done a lot worse than beat up a fool to have had it follow him all the way here. And men like him don't get cured of violence."

"That's not always true."

"Well it's true in this case, Father. If you want to see them, I have the wounds to prove it."

"I know Rodrigo. He came with Rosemary to the church a few times. Do you think he's the one who attacked your daughter, is that it?"

"If I thought that, if I was sure of it, I wouldn't be talking to you. What I do think is that he attacked me."

"Yet you haven't called the police."

"I want him never to hurt anyone again. Or at least not anyone here. In my country."

"So you've called me. And you're giving me a choice."

"I'm doing the right thing, aren't I? Even for him?"

Harold was involving him so that what was ahead would look better to Rosemary, as if it wasn't vengeance.

"I'm sorry you're in this position," said Harold. "But you need to see that I have thought it through."

"Reasoning gets us only partway to goodness."

"I'll let it take me as far as it goes. All I'm hoping for is a good night's sleep."

When he turned off the phone Harold felt the heavy silence. For some reason he was sitting naked in his entranceway, with his back to a wall. The silence and nakedness together conducted him along some avenue of thought to Marian. For all their shouting at the end, what the marriage had really suffered from had begun in silences, a poverty of admissions.

It was dark now. He'd kept the blinds drawn all day. It was time to open them but first he'd get dressed. He didn't care anymore about keeping up appearances, but there was something to be said for common decency.

Teresa answered. Rodrigo hadn't appeared there, no. Was there some trouble?

"Just call me if he arrives, okay?"

And she did call, twice that night, wanting Rosemary to explain something, or needing to explain something herself that she wouldn't say. It would have to do with Rodrigo's cuts and bruises. She could almost put it together on her own. There'd been trouble in both their places, it seemed. Teresa knew of no others Rodrigo would run to.

The next day Rosemary asked around. His circles were very small – past employers, the coordinator at the language school (who couldn't remember him), people he'd met once or twice at the church – but no one had seen him. She hoped faintly that in the part of his life she knew nothing about there was someone to take him in or give him money to catch a bus. There was a chance that he'd sought her out at St. Eustace and missed her. The church itself would offer no sanctuary. If the police became involved, investigating an assault charge, all the tacit agreements were off. Father André was reluctant to offer a living space to any of Rosemary's cases to begin with. The truth was, he didn't want to know about them.

She thought he might need to come back to the house but was ashamed or afraid, so she stayed out but left a note in simple English on the counter telling him to leave a time and place to meet. She said she wasn't angry but they had to arrange some things for him. These were the things she'd conjured for him over the weeks, an apartment, a better job, nothing more. They were still possible and he needed to know, as she needed. Whenever she thought of her life before what Harold had called her conversion, it returned to her badly preserved, because she didn't remember what things like hope had meant to her then. Hope and love and service to others. Had she thought of them at all? This woman carrying around not a metaphysical bone in her body? Had she imagined they existed inside herself, or that they were independent of her, as forces in the world, like goodness and duty, powerful running waters that humans could wade into. This woman, the woman she'd once been, must have had some notions worth her existence, but as she recalled her, the younger Rosemary came up a little flat, a movie character, someone who made sense too neatly. Rosemary didn't really believe in her. And the person she did believe in was a mystery, until now, when she recalled all at once that she had survived for a long time by holding a small hope that she could never acknowledge to herself, a hope that her life might still open up into meaning.

And it had been granted her, conferred, as grace was conferred. And now it turned out that though she had been a worthy keeper of hope, she was unworthy of the meaning because she was full of righteous pride. There was no one outside of her sister and her small network that wasn't subject to it. Father André had often felt her pride, and Harold, and city politicians and clergy from the diocese, those who assumed that she was at heart sentimental – how else could she be doing this work? – and that the sentimental were a little stupid. She'd often found leverage in playing dumb, leading them into their condescension and then trapping them. The Lord was less retributive these days than in His Old Testament youth, but she was quite willing to take up the slack. What was the difference between doing God's work and playing God? Between saving, and sorting the living from the dead? Wasn't God full of surprises and correctives? Wasn't He capable of deception?

It was noon when the call came. She'd spent the morning tracking late items from the audio library, sitting at her terminal, and then she was standing in a pizza joint staring at a display of slices, trying to decide, the Margherita or the Très Spicy, and felt a heat in her face that she thought was the oven but then it wasn't, it was a flush of dread, dizzying dread, and she had to leave and take a seat on a parkette bench. And that's when Father André called her cell. He said, "You need to go home right away. Rodrigo's been detained. I'll meet you at the house." A cyclist on the sidewalk sent street-tough pigeons flutterflopping and she knew the whole bleak ending, awaiting her.

Father André was there with the removals men, two of them. One stood near the front door, an overweight, smiling man who looked a little embarrassed or apologetic. Father André was sitting next to Rodrigo on the couch. Across from them was a smaller man with a buzz cut and a rat-tail who looked once at Rosemary as she came in and didn't so much as nod to her. The interview was well over. Out of deference to Father André the officers had delayed their arrest until she arrived.

Rodrigo hadn't looked at her. Did he think she'd turned him in?

"Don't be afraid," she told him. He kept his eyes down. She addressed the rat-tailed man. "What's your name, your first name?"

"Damon."

"Well, Damon, you can glare at him all you want but he knows not to fear you. And you shouldn't fear him."

"I don't."

"But you should fear God. Otherwise you have to fear men and their natures, right, André? And your fears will never hold still for you."

"I got him wrapped up pretty good right now," said Damon. His expression was of amusement and contempt.

Father André stood. "May I talk to you in the kitchen, Rosemary?"

"The proper place for fear is theological. That's what you said. This is all about things in their proper place. And mine isn't in the kitchen. And Rodrigo's isn't in the hands of killers. And yours wasn't to call these guys." Now she looked to the fat man. "Have you been watching my house all day?"

André put a hand on her shoulder. She couldn't recall him ever touching her before.

"You're in a tricky legal position here. You don't want to aggravate them. These men were good enough to let me call you."

She paused in the idea that any of them were good enough.

"All right. The kitchen it is, then. Damon, will you join us?"

Damon looked to Father André as if to say he'd had enough. "Humour me. Please."

"You don't seem like the humouring type," he said, but he went along. When they'd assembled, Father André laid it out for her. Either Rodrigo would be charged with assault and very likely do jail time, and then get deported, or he could be sent back directly, now. Father André stressed that Harold would prefer not to press charges.

"How big of him."

Rosemary turned to Damon. "If you send him back, he'll be killed."

"I'm not the judge."

"But you are the judge. You have all the power now. If he dies, it's on your hands."

"Yeah, I know. It's my fault what happens to them if they go, and my fault if they stay here and shoot someone."

"I know this boy" – *boy*, what was she saying? – "and he's no harm to anyone."

"Tell that to Harold," said Father André. It must have pained him to speak so sharply, but he'd done it anyway.

"That wasn't Rodrigo. He wasn't himself. He thought he was defending me."

"But who is he, Rosemary? That was some beating, by the sounds of it."

Whoever Rodrigo was when he'd arrived in the country had been distorted by the judgment and compassion of others, expressed in the wrong language. She was not absolved.

"I do empathize," said Father André. "To be in the country but not of the nation. It's a tough spot. But it's not a defence."

"Bingo," said Damon.

They each knew the other's position, as if it came down to positions.

"I've always known you to be a fair man," she said to Father André. "You've helped a lot of people. You've helped me. You're full of knowledge. But you can go to hell."

She strode back into the living room trailed by the others and started into the fat man.

"This young man is innocent and you're going to endanger him."

"He had his shot here, lady. We're just executing a warrant."

"We're gone. Let's load him up, Ken."

She went to Rodrigo and he stood. When she moved in to embrace him he held her away.

"I tell you something," he said. "You think I'm some good man. But I'm not a good man. I'm not a bad man and I'm not a good man."

"I know who you are."

Then he leaned in and kissed her on the cheek and whispered into her ear a thing said for her sake, though it wasn't true, and she wanted to let him know that she understood why he'd said it, that it was for her, his way of saying he forgave her for her love. And even as he said it, "My story is a lie," and she'd responded, "It's not true," she saw how her words could be misinterpreted to mean that she accepted his statement when she meant to say she did not, and so when he nodded to her it wasn't clear what he was affirming. She let the uncertainty stand.

As they took him she wanted to say that she'd get him a lawyer but she couldn't speak without breaking down now, and she was determined not to break down. She watched as they led him out. Father André stood next to her. Rodrigo's hands were cuffed. She thought he might run. The men were on each side. Everyone must have known he would run except Rodrigo. The car door closed. He looked straight ahead. The fat man got in on the passenger's side.

When they were gone Father André said he'd stay with her for a while.

She said, "Leave my house."

Then she was alone. She did an odd thing. Though the day was warm, as if to preserve the air she closed the windows and blinds and carried her floor fan down to the foot of the stairs to bring up the cool from the basement. She began to go through his things. She would have to pack all of it into his one suitcase. He would be gone in days, maybe hours. She gathered his clean clothes, folded in neat piles on the floor – an unopened box of condoms hidden there – and took his dirty clothes from the hamper, and put them all except his work gloves into the wash. His underwear was semen stained. There was blood on a shirt.

This part of the basement had been off-limits to her. She'd entered it only when leaving the cash envelopes. The suitcase was under his bed, an old brown hardshell with a frayed rope handle. A name had once been markered on the side but was now scribbled out in a neat black rectangle. Inside was a collection of random things, mostly junk. A picture book for tourists to Nova Scotia. A cut-glass ball that could only belong to a chandelier. A small brass rocking horse, still soot-stained. A fridge magnet of Van Gogh's *Sunflowers*. There were things, she didn't know what they were, clamps, and a forking, hooked device that could have come from a musical instrument or game or machine.

Loose cassette tapes of singers she hadn't heard of. A pen with a flattened picture of the waterfront skyline. A broken mobile with animal shapes that once must have turned for a child. Were they stolen from the living or the dead? They had no value unless as mementoes. What could he have been hoping to remember in thieving such little things?

She walked to the clothes pile and chose the gloves and a long-sleeved T-shirt he sometimes wore on cool evenings and set them aside for herself. She gathered his few bathroom items into his toiletries kit. His personal papers were in a plastic portfolio case she'd given him. She looked through them in hopes of finding a picture of him and came up only with a bad photocopy of a headshot on one of his court documents. It might as well have been a thumbprint. She put it back.

Upstairs again she sat in the dark living room and it came to her that she'd forgotten Sammy's birthday last week. Where had her mind been? She would call later and Sammy would tease her about a failing brain and growing old. Rosemary knew that her sister would outlive her – she'd told her so and it was true and Sammy hadn't even pretended to joke about the ways we sometimes know things. She'd said, "It better not happen until we're ancient or I won't recover from that," and now she thought not about her death but about Sammy's recovery, and then Rodrigo's junk stolen from burnt ruins, and how she was in the salvage business herself. The whole city was. Her first weeks of work, on call for the sick anywhere in the library system. Her marriage had broken up and she helped students from around the world researching their papers and measured them for grades of need and relative privilege. High school and university papers on sports heroes, Victorian table talk, the devices of espionage, minor

Canadian historical figures, and trilobites. They were good kids and they broke her heart. She had felt the city reshaping her. This place that spoke two hundred languages. There was a collection of books for every migration.

She would visit Canterbury someday. Jerusalem Celestial, as André Rowe referred to it. A place of pilgrimage for troubled souls and tourists. She wondered which kind of pilgrim she would be.

It was hot now in the house. She was suddenly very tired. It had been a mistake to stop moving.

Dear Father, what do you ask of me?

The breeze from the basement was dying on the stairs.

9

He closed his office door and looked out the window at the campus. It was the end of the first day of classes, hundreds of students in every direction, walking alone or in groups, gambolling on the grass, with shouting here, little moving pockets of silence and promise there. He sensed their beauty in the autumn light.

He sat down and revised his reply to Kim, then sent it. He found a message from her in his inbox:

How does one person's worst hour, long ago and far away, close around another's here and now? What I sent you, that imagined thing, brought you close to me. Let's know that redress is ongoing. I'm putting my time in, and so are others, everywhere.

Below she'd attached a link. It was too early for a drink but he poured one anyway and sat looking at the tumbler. Then he clicked on the link and up came a video. Funa al principe asesino de Victor Jara. 16:00 hours. The James Bond movie theme playing over random street shots. We see signposts, we're in Santiago, it's three years ago. People in ones and twos, carrying wax cups of coffee, going about their days. A few glance at the lens and look away too late. Then a cameraman, a second one, preparing. 16:30. A line of drummers in the street, beating and chanting for justice, the idea is surprise public spectacle. People gather, most look under thirty. A banner rises – "El Sueño Se Hace a Mano y Sin Permiso FUNA" – and the march begins. We cut to a small group, ahead, four or five people, with cameras, walking fast in the sound of a daytime street, then back to the chanting, marching crowd, cameras and phones and phone cameras, now with photos of the dead man held high. A young face from thirty-some years ago, the shot seems captured yesterday.

The guerrillas, the advance group, moving faster now. We pan up an ugly tower. Veering into the building, part of a sign says Prevision Social, and now they're in the lobby of a government office, getting on an elevator, and the doors close. The number notches higher, up to floor 14. Down on the street the marchers take up position and unfurl a new banner. "Edwin Dimter Bianchi Asesino del Estadio Chile."

The guerrillas move calmly through the corridors, looking for an office. Workers at their desks look up and no one knows the intruders and all must know what this is about. They breach the door to the killer's office. He's wearing a dress shirt and tie. There's a moment when he thinks he can turn them back, then he tries to hide from the cameras. Now he's on his desk in some kind of contorted distress, kicking at them. Shouting and cameras. The guerrillas are reading from flyers, reading the judgment against him, and now the killer is back on his feet. He grabs from one of them a placard with the victim's face on it and masks his own. He's doing everything wrong. Then finally he drops the placard, exposed again, and tries on a reasonable bearing. He smiles and gestures, now drops the smile. When the group finally begins to recede the killer reaches for one of them from behind and brushes his hand along the side of his face, lovingly, and the man who's been touched recoils and moves out the door and the clip ends.

Half an hour later he was still at his desk. He poured his untouched whisky back into the bottle and went out to the hallway and rinsed the glass in the drinking fountain, then came back and put away the glass and bottle. At the bottom of the drawer was an old file folder of stories he'd cut from newspapers and magazines, a habit he'd fallen out of. He followed a compulsion to leaf through them and chose a few pages and put them into his briefcase. Before he left he thought to fold closed his office laptop, then stood over it, still not quite satisfied. To turn it off would be a way of pretending. From his supply drawer he took out a roll of masking tape and covered over the little pulsing bead of light. It would bother him to imagine it out there in the city, boring all night into the empty dark. When the job was done he looked over his shelves briefly, not really seeing the books and journals, simply to acknowledge yet again the many worlds at once present and closed, this glancing habit always there in the final checks he made before going home.

One night he walked along her street in defiance of how people thought of him. According to true-crime reality shows most perpetrators did not physically return to their victims in this way, and the ones who did, the returner perps, intended particular harm. On these two scores he did not belong to the common profile. The first time he had come along the street he had stopped there in the open, in front of her house, and he felt himself seeing angles, running numbers in his blood, thinking of what had been given him here and what might be. The door wagging open. The light falling into the mouth of the garage. On his second pass the door was closed. When he took the sweater he brushed his hand along the bike seat and then saw where things had taken him and he ran.

For days he had talked himself out of going back but then did. In the driveway beside the house across the street from hers was an aluminum garden shed so it was this house he checked first, walking clear around to the next street and coming down between two places, over a fence into one backyard, then another, and on up beside the shed. He waited no more than a minute before he stepped out and checked the doors, and they slid open, so he had it. Now he was back before sun-up and took the same route to the shed across from her house, and slipped inside, brought the doors to within an inch of closed, and squatted. When the light was up a little blade of sun came through and he could see a plastic crate that he used for a stool. Everything about where he was said widowed or retired. There was no evidence of dog. If someone came out here he could likely hide, but even if he couldn't he'd be gone before they squawked or he'd break them in the face.

He gave himself this, this one day of watching without food, water, or pissing. The boredom and discomfort were part of the deal of being who he was. The street woke up in human sounds that he mostly couldn't see. In the opening the light seemed to stab right through her house and all of what had happened between them had come down to this long finger of seeing. If he shifted left or right he could make a bigger picture that was still not the whole of where she lived but at no time would he open the doors any wider. At some point she would come out. He wondered if she'd know what was different, the doors on the little tin shed, the one watching her inside it. He knew from the event between them that she sensed things, and she must wonder at her feelings now and wonder should she doubt them. Did she know the life of watching he had known? His life bled out of hospital windows, seeing the garbage tossed from the doorway to the steel bin, the alley light shot suddenly into ratscramble amazement, the sparks from the incinerator fire catching in the field, and water jets from hoses making cotton of the flames. Bled out of bus windows, correct change only. Bled into television shows for people that he wasn't, thinking they said something about people like he was. Did she know the brain fooled you in the same way that it solved, how one thing hid inside another of the same general shape. Sometimes he heard echoes that weren't really there.

First to appear was the man of the house, leaving for the day. He wore dull brown clothes as if he didn't mean them. Then an older lady came out onto the porch, collecting the paper in a wild-red robe. They seemed like a lazy place. It was hot in the shed in a way he had not accounted for. Then at 10:47 the door opened and she came out for him. Her caramel pants stopped at the knee. Her T-shirt was loose, sagging a little senseless. She carried a cup of maybe coffee and the paper and sat on the step right opposite him, taking in the sun, and read in the posture of someone in a waiting room. For a long time he could not get beyond her wrists. He could feel them in the memory in his hands. He held his hands up now and pretended to be squeezing. He'd tried to crush her wrists and yet there they were, still themselves. There were kinds of defeat he accepted with love.

He could feel her inside him now, the familiar things she did to him. What he wanted was for her to know that he could be this close and her inside him and still she would be safe. That she would never know this, that was what he struggled with. It would be enough if she would look up at him but he waited for minutes in vain. He told himself to make no noise. When he stood he felt her tight in him. Then she looked up, not his way exactly, and not seeing whatever she looked at, a little lost, and she stood too and turned and went inside. In some life or other, he had come to her.

By early afternoon he was soaked through and wondered if the heat and lack of water would make him pass out. As he understood his body he decided to remain. The day became kids on bikes and women jogging with strollers, cars and a few lone passersby. And birds shooting through his vision. Two cardinals, crows in mostly threes, and little ones he couldn't see the names of. He tried to guess their motives, not in pattern but in cause, but what went on in their heads was not available to his view, so that after a time their motions seemed a taunt from the forces of chaos that knew him by name. Still he wouldn't fall. She was in no danger. He honoured her with safety. But he felt a bend coming on and told himself it was not about her but the door, and so he opened the crack two more inches, breaking his vow, and shifted himself to the left. His view now admitted more sky and trees, more air. The air helped him accept that he waited for a signal that would tell him what to do. He could not stay until the night dragged in its carcass but he would wait for her one more appearance.

When it came it came like a gift and he almost teared up and cried. She had a computer and a book this time, and she sat in a chair on the porch. She had changed into blue jeans. Her feet were bare. She sat typing, copying from the book, and he started seeing copies now, foot to foot, bird to bird, the times of his watching her, then and now, the second things drawn from the firsts. There were beats in his head that he couldn't escape. She closed the book and stopped typing, then touched what she touched and sat reading her screen what seemed a long time. When she looked up, it was almost right at him. Her face was different somehow, he had to remind himself to breathe. He had been here all day but her few minutes of sitting quiet made her seem like some kind of animal in the woods. As the time ran on he didn't notice at first the mail-lady come into view. She came along the walk on the edge of the frame and above her the sky was bruising to black, though the front of the house outside the porch was still in sunshine, and went up the steps and stopped for a second to say something that she didn't really respond to, and handed her the mail. She watched her leave, then went into the house and came out with a phone.

She dialled and then gave him another gift. He could barely hear her voice, could only hear the notes like bird notes like whimpers and so in this way too she returned to him. The world so full of pain, it sings a little. She put the phone down and sat for a minute, then touched the machine and began reading.

When she got up there was something wrong with her body, like it wasn't really hers or had shrunk a size since she last used it. She stood hunched a bit or something and looked like she was about to step wrong. Her head was cocked out and her face was tilted down like she was about to fall forward but she stood that way for a while, then went inside the house and she had missed the sky, didn't know it was gathering, didn't know he'd been with her today. In the sky was the last thing they shared, he saw it now, the way the dark strip he looked out of, that she had looked at, was like the vertical tear in the storm clouds behind her, with the blue beneath like gasoline flared on a wet shop floor.

In minutes there was a motion out beside the house and he opened the door a little more to see her flying away on a bike.

He waited for her return but in time it didn't come and instead there came the rain.

He made himself leave. He walked out into it. It came down hard, fell like wedding rice and jittered on the street and the car roofs. It was still raining when he caught a bus and took a seat with others smiling at his sopping condition. There was nothing to see through the pouring windows but he had a compass the size of a watch face and when the bus took a curve he watched it turn and stay true. The woman she was was still out there, in Kim or in someone else. This Kim or someone else was open. She would know him right off as lost and unsponsored. Any day now, she would turn her face to him, and he would say her name.

Kim,

Back in the '90s an anthropologist colleague of mine named Zazic was working on the genocide in the Ixil region of Guatemala. He collected first-hand accounts from the villagers and farmers about the atrocities they'd suffered as the army terrorized them in the belief they were aiding the guerrillas. Rapes, tortures, massacres by the dozens. Entire villages wiped out, thousands murdered. I'm sure you know the history.

One survivor told the story of soldiers rounding up all the men and boys in his village. About half were taken into a church and beaten and made to lie in a heap, then covered with leaves and dirt. Those on the bottom suffocated, but if anyone moved they were shot. Then the other men were led in and told to climb onto the heap and jump up and down on their children, fathers, friends, and neighbours. They too were shot if they didn't comply. At some point the soldiers collected all those still alive and marched them out to the cemetery. They designated the ones who'd been buried as "hell" and the ones who'd climbed on them as "heaven." The men in heaven were then ordered to find their sons in hell and claim them. Once they'd done so, they were told to choose which of their sons they would save. For every one saved, another would die. When the condemned had been designated they were made to stand at the edge of a mass grave and they were shot. Then the rest of the men in hell were pushed into the grave and shot. Many died slowly.

The man who told the story told it neutrally, as I've tried to do here. When Zazic asked what had happened to him personally, the man said nothing. Only then did Zazic realize this man had never told the story from his own viewpoint. After a long pause he thanked him for his time but the man took hold of his arm, asking him to stay. It was a minute or two, the man looking away, gathering himself, before he lifted his head and said, "My beautiful son died by my hand." He held out the palm of his right hand. It was covered in ugly ropes of scar tissue. Someone, perhaps he himself, had sliced it repeatedly.

Zazic never learned the story of how the son died, nor of the sliced palm. And so they have never been entered into the record. But in seeing the man's hand, he says, he felt closer to the horror than at any other time in his researches. What happened was truly unspeakable.

We can guess at what happened with the man and his son, but we shouldn't.

We know only ourselves, and ourselves thinly. What happened to the ruined and the dead? Inside acts of evil, what is witnessed is never what happened. What happened belongs only and always to the victims. If we acknowledge this solemnly, we won't live in ignorance, and we won't make the mistake of thinking we can pretend our way into knowing.

The story of the hand, such as it was told to me, and I tell it to you, is not to be mistaken for the hand itself. And even if we were to meet the survivor, that scarred hand held before us is one thing to us, another to him.

I would never presume to know, Kim, what you thought or felt on the night of the attack. Neither do I presume to know what it was like for any of those who suffered more than I did in Santiago.

Your imagination has led you into folly. Maybe you suppose that because you had no audience other than me, who at least knows your intentions were loving, your little fiction about my days in Santiago isn't irresponsible. In fact it is much worse than that. You have committed an abomination, all the more vile – I'm sorry, but that's the word – for its believability. Good aesthetics don't promote good ethics. They often nurture evasion. Or worse. Powerful myths drive history. Ideologies, religions with their playbooks, messianics of all stripes blindly trusting in the inerrancy of ancient, made-up stories.

You've used the name of someone real – Carl Oakes – someone I knew, and ascribed it to a character you've invented. The real Carl was not at all as you've imagined. Neither were the other housemates. Neither was I. You did get something of the city then, the events, of course. But there's a dramatic arc in your story that wasn't an arc in reality. I probably wasn't paying attention enough to have felt a building drama.

I'd forgotten the jacaranda.

You do intend good, I know, but what does your imagining add to the world? What you've added to our lives here, yours and mine, is presumption and self-pride. You've not characterized me well. I don't think you've got my writing voice down (I would never write "We are such a couple of brats together"). Moreover, you haven't guessed well at my thoughts, or the degree to which I know them ("everything I think to be true about those days in Santiago is in question" – well, it isn't, I know what I know). I am not haunted by guilt. I am not caught inside an ambiguity.

I hope you've found it therapeutic to write your own story, and that you've begun to put the attack behind you. But if you hope to inspire me to answer with mine, I can only say that I'm not in need of therapy. I was hardly a victim, barely a witness. It has always seemed self-dramatizing to tell it. People can get a better sense of it by reading the histories, as you have. You should have left it at that.

If only to settle your imagination, I'll tell you what I remember. It's not long, and not much colour. Your version is much more alive. On the day of the coup I stayed in my rented room. The next day I ventured out, as I've already told you, to my teacher Orlando's apartment. There were a few people there, most I didn't know, some coming and going. Orlando told me to get to my embassy. I asked him if he wanted me to help him and his wife get asylum, and he said he did not, that their place was there, whatever happened. I left in the early afternoon and was a few blocks along when I was stopped by a soldier, a commander of some sort, with a machine gun, I guess it was. He questioned me. I said I was a

Canadian studying at a language school. He said I was a communist. He said my leader was a communist, too – I remember he alluded to Trudeau – and then he asked for the name of my school and my teacher. If he really cared about these he would already have had the names. The question was just to humiliate me. And though I knew that, I told him that I wouldn't betray my friend. He laughed and said I was a good student, and then, as if I no longer amused him, he let me go. I phoned Orlando right away but the call wouldn't connect. There was no way to warn him, and anyway, the soldier had been inventing his threat as he went along.

That's it, the hardest moment. I eventually flew out of there and went on with my studies. But then I learned a lesson about experiencing a near miss – the truth of it, how close I might have come to harm, arrived on delay, as more stories of what happened that day began to be told. The next year, at school in Montreal, this was about February of '74, I borrowed a classmate's car to visit a professor in Sherbrooke who'd offered to introduce me to his visiting academic friends from Mexico City. I set out alone at just before noon, and in about forty minutes lost my presence of mind, you might say, and came to consciousness bouncing to a halt in a snowy farmer's field, with a view of ice floes in the St. Lawrence, and a pain in my thigh where it had bashed against the steering wheel. The constable who questioned me decided I'd fallen asleep. I didn't argue. There were no charges, but I was made to agree that I might have killed someone.

I had not fallen asleep. The feeling, when it came on me, had been quite the opposite, a waking sense of awakening. Because it was the past I'd waken into, I lost the present moment, for however long it took to slow down and drift off the highway. I would learn week by week that I was in trouble – that I was possessed by trouble, there in my imagination of what *might have* happened, and couldn't expel it. I prepared myself for a life of sudden dislocation. And, in fact, I came to experience other such moments over the months ahead.

And then, within another year or two, it was gone. The event was truly passed.

In the weeks after I arrived back in Canada I wrote two letters to my teacher, care of the school, and heard nothing back. I do feel guilty that I didn't try harder to learn his fate and admit I failed to do so out of fear of what I might discover. I learned to live upon an unanswered question (all right, there's an ambiguity). And when the truth commission report was published, I didn't have the heart to read it.

But I now teach the Chilean coup with no more passion than I do the dirty wars in Argentina and Uruguay, the Tlatelolco massacre in Mexico City, the genocides in Guatemala and El Salvador, and, sadly, so on. There was one conference in Santiago I might have attended if I hadn't been needed here for a thesis defence. I know a few scholars in Chile. They know my friend Zazic.

Gather the facts as they're available, Kim, and then leave them be. You have failed that time and place. Fiction, no matter its scope, will always fail history. Beautiful artifice, there's nothing true in it. Real stories have no endings, except the one that includes us all. I do believe in that story. I respect it. But it has no teller.

There was something happening in the light. When she looked up from the screen, the last lines stayed before her like a burning afterimage, as if printed over the opposing houses and yards. He could only have written this to her, she told herself, if he'd forgotten her again in the writing, as he had in his letter to her years ago, when he'd left them. But he hadn't forgotten. The letter had been aimed.

It wasn't intentional or an oversight that he hadn't typed his name. It was just how he saw things. She knew there was something eternal in a person's owning up to their authorings, and her knowing separated them. Something else was eternal in her father.

A uniformed figure was approaching from another plane.

"Here you go, hon."

The woman handed her the bundle and turned and went back down the porch steps, back into the sun. The mail was held together with a blue elastic band, fully in its own possession, yet she held it as if it were hers. She drew out a single sheet, a real-estate flyer with small dim pictures of homes like those around her, and wondered at it. Across the street the light deepened the brick of the houses, the early-fall gardens and trees. A breeze stirred the paper in her hands, made a crepitated sound and moved on, only a lungful, really. She tried to imagine herself a year hence and sensed that the light would be different.

She clicked on the truth commission bookmark and scrolled through the day in question, down to the teacher named Orlando.

> On September 12, 1973, Orlando Ropert SARMIENTO, 29, a university student and teacher, and his wife Maria Alicia SARMIENTO, 30, a homemaker, were arrested with others at their apartment by government agents. According to testimony given to the Commission, the couple was detained in the apartment after the others were led away. They were found dead that afternoon in the entranceway to their

> building. The death certificates list "bullet wounds" as the cause of Orlando Ropert Sarmiento's death, and "blunt head trauma" as the cause of Maria Alicia Sarmiento's death. Given these circumstances, the Commission concludes that Orlando and Maria Alicia Sarmiento were executed and suffered a grave violation of human rights at the hands of government forces.

She retrieved the phone from the house and called Eduardo Jofre's cell number. She was leaving a message when he picked up. She asked if he had anything for her.

"Yes, I've prepared something, but I'm in Chicago. I intended to give it to you in person but I can send it if you want."

"Please do. As soon as you can."

"I'll send it now. Call me again if you want to talk about it."

Her thoughts stood outside her, converging in the slow burning street. Somewhere a woodpecker was tapping at a tree trunk at a speed that made a texture of the beats. She recalled a distant scene from the music store. Eduardo had told her that every day he would tune two guitars and hang them back on the wall ten minutes before a father and son would come in, saying nothing, and take them down and play. She saw them once. They were short, dark, maybe Roma, and when their music began it was the surest creature in the room. Immaculate folk jazz in black canvas shoes. When they stopped, the new absence had whole lost gods in it.

The air suggested rain. The day was lapsing, and implicit in the now deadening light was something very hard.

She clicked on the inbox.

Hello Kim,

My contact has had some back and forths with witnesses. I've attached a letter (in Spanish) from her with the details but, to summarize, 3 names on your father's list were unknown to anyone, the German and the 2 Americans. Of the remaining 12, my friend has identified all 5 on the list not in the Rettig Report through their connection to the 7 who were. 1 died in 1981 of illness. The other 4 are still alive, 3 still live in Santiago. These 3 were asked if they recalled a young Canadian student named Harold Lystrander. None knew the name. 2 knew of a Canadian only after their arrest, from the 3rd. The 3rd, Bastio Eyzaguirre, though not recognizing the name, had met or been in the presence of, on at least one occasion, a Canadian student of Orlando Sarmiento, in whose apartment he and the others were hiding on September 12, and believed that, as he and the others were being led outside and into a military bus, he saw the Canadian across the street, standing with army officers, unrestrained.

Eyzaguirre is quoted as saying that he thought he recognized the young man but didn't place him until later. It is possible, he says, that now or then he confused the Canadian with some other foreign student, but at the time, he was sure it was the Canadian. He is quoted as saying that it was his impression that the soldiers' attitude toward the young man suggested a complicity. The young man and the soldier next to him were both smoking cigarettes, "como si ellos contemplaran el enfoque de una tormenta," as if watching the approach of a storm.

Eyzaguirre sat near the back of the bus. As he looked out the back window, he saw the 2 people whose apartment he'd been hiding in led out of the building and stopped in front of it. The young Canadian, if that's who he was, was led across the street toward them by a soldier. There were soldiers on all sides and some confusion and, he admits, the view from the bus wasn't perfect. But Eyzaguirre says the young man stood before Orlando and Maria Alicia and there was a moment of talk. Then the bus, though it wasn't yet full, began to pull away, and Eyzaguirre remembers thinking first that his friends would be spared arrest, and then that it was bad for them to still be on the street. The last thing he saw was Maria Alicia stepping forward and slapping the face of the Canadian.

I relayed the question, Was the Canadian there in the apartment at any time on September 12?

He was not present when Eyzaguirre was there. Eyzaguirre was in the apartment for about two hours before the soldiers arrived.

I relayed the question, Does the section in the Rettig Report addressing the deaths of the Sarmientos seem in any way lacking? Eyzaguirre points out that he and the others had been led away but were still present, in the bus, at the time the Sarmientos were led out of the building. None of the survivors in the bus testified as witnesses to the deaths – they didn't see the killings – but the full story should include the fact that the couple was in the street before they ended up dead back inside the entryway, and that there was a confrontation between Maria Alicia and the young foreigner.

All of these exchanges were electronic. I then called my friend and asked her opinion of Eyzaguirre. She said that she's known him all his life, and that though Eyzaguirre isn't the smartest of her friends, and in fact in his youth he talked a lot of shit, he had grown into a reliable man.

Kim, I can't judge the accuracy of Eyzaguirre's story or whether it should be admissible to the record. You might be surprised how many such stories, however well intended, however much their teller believes them, turn out to be full of error. So before you believe too readily, let me write Eyzaguirre myself. Do you have a photo of your father from that time? We could scan it and send it to him and see if he thinks it's the man he saw that day.

There is a great responsibility in gathering these stories and trying to make them fit. But they don't always fit. We mustn't speculate without sound proof. Whether or not we have that here is a question I'll leave to you.

Eduardo

She got onto her bike and she rode. Down through the upscale neighbourhoods, then south under the train tracks and into her favourite streets, emptying onto Bloor and up onto the sidewalk, then out and along in the heavy, honking traffic to the museum and then south. She rode into Queen's Park and there was the homeless woman named Fran who'd once told her about seeing wolves bring down a deer in the snow. She was asleep under an oak tree and a torn wool coat. The last morning she left work at the museum, without waking her, Kim had opened her saddlebag and brought out the danish she'd been saving and wrote a hello on a paper napkin – "From Kim, who works at the ROM" – and placed the note and the treat wrapped in wax paper by her side, and as she left, two mangy squirrels hopped near Fran's head and froze, staring at the pastry. But now she rode past Fran and nearer the legislative buildings and past the statue of Edward VII and the balls of his horse painted another lurid colour in prank and vaguely directed protest, out into traffic, along the curb, where ahead a border collie tied to a signpost greeted her like an old friend and then she rode hard, feeling herself working, thinking of the dog's instinct to cower and wag all at once, into the residential streets east of campus, and saw a woman on a porch spank a child with two measured smacks and a tossed towel falling from an attic window, unfurling the word "Resort" into a garden.

And she rode through the rain that came suddenly and hard like pebbles, rode half-blindly past the cars with their wipers crazed and useless, and kept riding until the rain passed and the sun returned and the gutterflooded streets began to dry on the crests, and she was soaked through, and she looped around and near the bookstore came into the route she'd taken that night, so many nights, so many times in her writing of it, and swung her leg over, gliding on one pedal, then stepping into stride.

Something about the window had changed, not just the books, of course, now graphic novels, political lampoons, idiot's guides to Islam and jazz, but the display itself, the size and frame of it, lit in her memory like a diorama, now seeming too small, without enough depth to have made an impression. Down the next block the hair salon that had served as a church was now a costume rental store. There were deals to be had on monsters and elves, it was not a season for getups, and everything about the shop seemed out of time. A single moment of overlaid worlds, the daily interchange of the downtown streets, extended through months. The shop that had been a church in a salon was only itself. What she'd returned for. Majorettes and alien faces, dummy cowboys with orange faux-hawk wigs. They made sense just for being.

From the costume shop window, wheeling her bike she walked at the pace she'd walked that night, as she'd walked in her stories replaying it. But it was afternoon now. She felt the sun hot on her and smelled the pavement's fading carbon sheen. The night wasn't coming back like she'd thought it would. A part of her wanted it back if only to attach it to this hour and this light because there was the night in her imagining, even in her blood, but now was another kind of revisiting, the literal kind, and she wanted it to mean all it could. The thing she couldn't get inside, that had nothing to do with this street, was the feeling of being followed and the moment when she'd decided to do one thing and had done another. Here and there were not the same. She could come back but she couldn't return.

The dying animal knows something we don't, homeless Fran had said. And the wolves eat it up, the bones and the knowing and all.

The site was of course now a building, thirty-some storeys high. The Bonifice. New Urban Living. Available for Occupancy Soon. The former open darkness had been named and numbered. She could press a palm to it if she wanted.

She locked up her bike and went through the doors and a smiling redheaded woman sitting at what would soon be a security desk greeted her and asked if she'd like to see the show suite on the twenty-first floor, where the view was quite something.

"No."

Kim turned. It was right here, she realized. It had all gone down around here. On this carpet and floor, through the lobby, under the chandelier, through the marble back wall, down along the banks of elevators.

"Is everything all right?"

She lived in a place ever fuller of matter and her father was lost to her and these were the facts.

"Someone once tried to murder me here."

She walked deeper into the lobby and did as she'd imagined, putting her hand on the marble wall, trying to let it work on her, this reassertion of substance and solid design. The only place left from that night was within her. She'd worked long and hard at it, remaking the space as she could. And she thought she'd nearly done it, engineering a new physical being – the bones, the knowing and all – though even now a heat was rising in her shoulders as if her body had only just discovered where she'd arrived, and it was time to leave these two places she was.

When the rain let off, Harold got out of the car. Through the little window of the garage he saw that Kim's bike was gone. He found the spare house key in the place he'd devised long ago, on top of the lamp by the door.

He took the white chair. Marian lay on the bedspread under a green and red blanket he'd never seen before with her body barely there among the folds. Her mouth was slightly open. Floral slippers by the side of the bed. Afternoon windowlight through lace curtains. He didn't remember it, this light. The room was a new place, as if it had never been his.

He knew the moment she was awake before she did, before her eyes had even opened.

"Hello, Marian."

She opened them. His presence made no more sense to her than wherever she'd emerged from.

"It's just me."

"God, what's happened?"

"It's me."

"Are you drunk?"

With much effort she sat up against the headboard. Her face was still far away.

He shook his head.

"Then what is it? Tell me."

"I'm not here with news."

"What time is it? Where's Donald? What are you here with, then? This is pretty creepy, Harold."

He was calm. He said it had been raining hard.

"It didn't wake you."

"No. You woke me."

"Do the drugs make you sleep?"

"You've come to enquire after my well-being?"

She brought her arms above the blanket and let her hands rest on her stomach, the sleeves of her thin, blue gown hanging as if empty. Even when they were young she kept her arms covered in summer. He remembered the shock when she bared them at night before bed. Arms known only in lamplight for months at a time. One by one, such memories lifted up and then fell away forever. He wouldn't again think of her arms.

"We used to fly a kite. Kim and I. Whatever happened to that kite?"

"I don't know what you're talking about. You and Kim never flew kites. You never even took her swimming."

"Once, we did. Where were you? I saw some kids flying kites in a schoolyard and so I had the idea. I went out and bought it that afternoon. She must have been about eight or nine. And we went up to that big park below St. Clair. I got it in the air for her. I had to run down a little slope to get any serviceable breeze, but then it took off and she screamed, she was so excited. I gave her the line and she flew it. All of about twenty minutes. A big kite up there with a cartoon face on it, a bear or something, peering down at us."

"You've made all this up."

"No, I haven't. I don't know where you were."

"It's another of your stories. This one with a bear on a kite. Am I supposed to think you had your moments as a father?"

The kite story had sounded made up but it wasn't. He was almost certain.

"Do you remember Celina Shey?" She did not, and then, he saw, she did. The first affair. "I spoke to her, said hello, because she looked like my accuser."

"What are you talking about?"

"I had an accuser. She looked like Celina Shey. Who looked like the dead girl, the dumpster girl from the news, named Anna Huard, it turns out. Or the sketch of her."

"Stop. What's wrong with you?"

He'd thought there was more to say about the resemblances. How they'd linked Kim to certain times past. Marian's and his together, and his alone. But now he realized the connections meant less than he'd assumed. They might not have meant anything at all.

"I'm feeling fine just now, actually. I'm feeling good. It's good to talk to you. I'm sorry I missed Kim."

There followed some subtending moments when he thought she would right him. She drew up her knees. The blanket made voluted shapes of her feet.

"So this is about Kim. You're worried about what she's digging up on you. You should be told, I guess, that I gave her your list. I've had it for years, your mysterious list. I've begun divesting myself of things. And I don't want you to put new things in their place. You come in here like a terrier with a rat. Dropping some old girlfriend at my feet."

The light in the room changed. The last clouds had cleared off. The day was full of openings. The sky would hold for a while, with its imaginary gods for those who believed, and for those who didn't, with the names of the colours of blue. And still, under the gods or whatever, an alien intelligence, it was possible to say one or two things that were true, and to marry them to one or two things that were half-true, and so to approximate a universe, partly understood, playing itself out.

"We'll let things be, then," he said. "We better just let them be."

He stood. He thought about coming forward but didn't. He imagined holding her. She was all bones.

"I'm sorry," he said. "Tell Kim I was by."

As he walked past the foot of the bed he squeezed her toes lightly through the blanket. She looked at him and breathed a small sigh.

He left the room and stood in the hallway for a time. He wondered if he heard her crying. He stood not knowing for certain what he'd ever said or done to her, what she'd done to him. Not knowing what to do. They'd almost made it to the end, he and Marian, without an opening up. But things caught up, the way they did out there. If only they'd caught him and not their daughter. He still didn't know what to call it, what happened to Kim. An inevitable return, or just bad luck. Maybe it was the century that had happened. The century, the city. You couldn't escape them. And yet now that they'd been caught, they would survive, he saw. When she calmed down, he thought, Marian would see it too.

By her sudden arrangement she met Greg for dinner in a murmuring lounge that served tapas. He wore a light blue dress shirt with the sleeves rolled. Somehow the muscles in his forearms were taken up in his jawline and the mastoids of his neck and it all was present for her. He started into another account of his work in the asylum trade and she stopped him this time. She saw he understood what it was about, what she hoped for. The food inspired them each to tell stories of travelling in Spain, conjuring for one another the small towns of Estramadura, the Alhambra, quail dishes, the bridges of Rhonda, and minarets, fields of sunflowers. Whenever the conversation veered off she brought it back to the sensual. Buñuel. Greg said he'd once studied flamenco guitar for a month in Seville. He'd fallen for a girl there who led him along but wouldn't sleep with him, and he needed a project to keep him sane. He was full of passion but no technical ability.

"Your whole life seems unlikely," she said.

"Everyone's unlikely."

And so between them now was something from his distant past. He'd never let her this close before. She wanted to smell his skin. She would tell him this if she had to, if he started to doubt what she wanted, or doubt he should agree to it, though yes, he would agree, and she wanted to tell him anyway. And so when he said, "It's early, but would you like to go to my place for more drinks?" she didn't answer or even nod to uphold the pretense. She just got up and waited for him, and she left her bike locked up outside, and they walked to his building. They said almost nothing, and what they'd just talked of, the wonders of Spain, his boyhood in the true west, drifted off in the slanted air. They brushed arms twice, once on the street, once in the hallway to his door, and she wanted the weight of him. The mystery was that she knew he understood this. He understood. So when they were finally inside his door and he kissed her, and she found herself crying, she knew he understood that it didn't matter, that the crying was part of the desire, and then the tears let off and she could feel him and he touched her and undid her jeans and they were gone and he was on his knees. She slid down to the floor. She seemed to be lying in shoes. His thumb was on her, and then his fingers were in her and he moved down further to kiss her until she shuddered. Then he picked her up and carried her to his bed. It was hot and he threw the covers and sheets to the floor. Then they were both naked. She turned onto her belly and he covered her.

In time, afterwards, he started talking again. He couldn't seem to help himself. There were human smugglers on the Detroit River. There were politicians buying votes with temporary permits, Indian surgeons accidentally deported, Tamils extorting their kind. There were claimants stuck in a Buffalo refugee shelter and a new government snitch line. A DNA test that reunited a family, children detained in front of their elementary school classmates. For a while she wasn't really listening, and then something passed and she caught it.

"What did you say? The Colombian?"

"Turned in by an Anglican priest."

She drew her knees up and hugged them.

"What's his name?"

". . . Cantero. Rodrigo Cantero."

It wasn't admission, after all. There was only the world going on.

"What is it?" he asked.

Rodrigo Cantero. She hadn't known his name. She'd failed to give him one.

"I don't know. A coincidence maybe."

She asked him to tell her about Rodrigo Cantero. He was suspected of having been in a Colombian paramilitary group that had kidnapped and killed local farmers in a documented incident. He'd been here for a couple of years. He'd gotten into some legal trouble or other and a warrant had been issued for his arrest and removal.

"What does he look like?"

"He's thin. Boyish. He's quiet. Maybe a bit acquiescent. So you know him?"

The bed, the walls, the building, all the made things that held her. The imagination had force, she wanted to tell her father. It was real, its movement changed governments and traffic and air currents in the room. In the right mind, it could do good work. Her own imagination was supposedly healing her. And at some point the fully imagined world could touch on the world that was. She ran her finger over the idea that through *R* she had written Rodrigo into existence. *R* or someone very like him was out there in the city right now.

"Can I meet him?" Already she felt what would pass between them, the recognition.

"No."

"Why not?"

"They flew him out this morning."

They spoke through glass. Teresa had brought her lawyer, named Greg. The man wasn't old. He gave the impression of having once looked stronger. He told Rodrigo there was nothing to be done and no money to do it. Then he wished him luck and left. He looked like he spent his days walking out of the same room.

Teresa then sat before him and looked at him hard. She wiped away tears without blinking. She was trying to memorize his face. He would try not to remember her crying. She said she had written him a letter and given it to Rosemary. She wanted him to read it before he left, to know he was not alone, that he was in her thoughts and would be all the way out and thereafter. She said she had already left Luis and was living with a girlfriend from the café, but the space was too small so they were looking for another.

It was a minute or two before she understood he had nothing to say.

There was nothing to say.

He dropped his head and waited for her goodbye but she stayed and stayed, saying his name, and then finally left without another word. If she had said goodbye he would have said it too.

He had lunch in the cafeteria. The uniformed guards looked about his age. None of them white. It was hard to see what they were guarding against. Seven prisoners eating in seven places. They seemed not to want to look at one another and Rodrigo stared a little longer only at an African woman who looked too thin to have deceived anyone, and an old, maybe Arab man who was crying at his table. He had no food or drink and so Rodrigo brought a tea and set it before him. The man looked up, surprised, as if he'd thought he was alone in this place. He nodded to him and Rodrigo nodded back. They sat together sipping for a few minutes, not even trying to communicate. If they had had a common language he would have asked the man respectfully if he could tell him something, and he'd have advised him to keep his thoughts gathered tightly together, watching for strays, like a cowboy in a movie, moving them along to wherever they needed to be. Many times in his life a man so old must have needed to master his thoughts. It was disturbing that he couldn't keep them in order.

After some time Rodrigo moved a distance away and ate. He thought about what lay ahead. It would be stupid to go to his family or old friends, he would only endanger himself and them. His uncle had paid someone to get him out of the country. The man gave him a ticket and a false passport and American dollars, and told him to tear up the passport in the washroom of the plane and to say the English word "refugee" when he landed. The uncle and Uriel were now in Cartagena. Maybe he could find them. Unless he was unlucky, he would live long enough to get away again, if he could find the money.

The last meeting was with Rosemary. She didn't look like herself. She wore a white shirt with long sleeves and a collar. He'd seen it once before. It looked wrong on her. She always looked wrong when she dressed up, even for church. He didn't like it that she thought she needed to dress up to see him in this place, as if she were showing it respect.

She said that he had done nothing wrong, that she was the one who had made mistakes and brought the trouble to their door.

She didn't say what he knew to be true, that she had kept him too long, that with his first paycheques he should have found an apartment and disappeared into the city, that his chances would have been better if he'd made his own attachments, people connected through him, to whom he himself was a way further into the city and so of value equal to that of any new friend. She gave him strategies for returning and asked about namesakes and documents, and the cost of false passports. He was to write her with an address once he had one.

He nodded now and then. It was as if they were again in her basement. He didn't tell her about the interview with the officer named Luke. He'd told Luke that he'd met good people here at a church but they were too open, too ready to accept foreigners, and that he agreed with Luke that it wasn't right to accept the bad with the good. Luke told him he could use the phone as often as he liked, but there was no one to call.

He still hadn't spoken. She was going to ask him if his story was true. She was going to make him lie to her again, for her own sake, not thinking of him. He couldn't tell her that he'd already begun to return home even now, before leaving, or that he in fact did have some hope that he'd be safe upon his return, that maybe those who would wish him harm had forgotten him, that they had more recent scores to settle, or had turned on one another, or were long gone, in prison, or dead.

She said she'd brought his bag and his things. She'd put a letter inside from Teresa that he was to read on the plane.

"Where will you go first?"

"There's a town where my aunt lives, where I went as a child."

"Tell me something about it. I want to be able to picture you there."

Very little came to him.

"It's a stone town. No grass or trees. No sidewalks. At night the power goes out and it's quiet, it's full of peace. Just the dogs barking."

"You'll be safe there."

"Yes."

"Will you have friends?"

"Maybe my aunt knows a man with work for me."

"Write to me. I can send money."

He focused on the markings scratched onto the glass. They were all on her side.

"I'm sorry, Rodrigo. I just want to help."

"Yes."

She was out of things to say. Soon she would say anything to keep talking. She had no idea who he was.

"Remember the Lord loves you."

"Yes."

"Remember you are loved."

"Yes."

"You are loved here."

He got up and nodded his last goodbye.

In his room he opened the suitcase. The clothes were not folded carefully, as she would have folded them – someone had gone through it. On the bottom was a large envelope with his name in huge letters, as if he wouldn't see it otherwise. He took out the letter, only two small pages, handwritten. They began with his name and before reading further he tore them in half and then again, and then balled up each piece and put them all in the toilet and flushed them away.

There was knocking in the pipes. From a nearby room came the sound of someone beating on a wall in a slow rhythm. He lay in the dark on the narrow bed and waited for the rhythm to end and remembered the sound of Rosemary's typewriter above him at night when he'd lay thinking of her fingers, the quarter inch of keystrokes no more than moved a trigger. He shut his eyes and above him came the faces he hadn't seen in months, the ones close behind him again. The way one man's face pinched when he fired his gun, and another's folded when he was shot. Someone down the hall knocked on a door and opened it and the rhythm stopped, and minutes later Rodrigo lay thinking of the town where his aunt lived, and the dogs in the dark and after the rain the water dripping on the stones. In the morning he would wake to singing and electric music on loudspeakers cast over the town from the evangelical church where the same people were saved every morning and lost again by night. His aunt believed it was the night itself that tried to take them. The light and the dark fought for them every day until one or the other took them fully and they walked in the world in service of a master that wasn't of this place or any, a master they couldn't name, though they would choose a name, and that couldn't hear them when they sang or asked questions or cursed, couldn't know their thoughts, wondering at the flaws in the fabric of things or the meaning of their dreams, of ancient footprints baked into a plain, or the faint stars pretending to be of the day. There is no hope but in people, she would say, and only some people. You know them by their faces when they think no one can see them.

If she was right about souls, then his was still unclaimed. He would never be saved once and for all, but maybe luck and forgetting were such that he could be won piece by piece, hour to hour. It helped, he supposed, that there were those who would keep him in their thoughts.

In the night, a knock came on his door.

He opened his eyes in the dark, still dreaming.

In mid-afternoon Harold left his condo, steeled for the twenty-minute walk to his first class of the year. It was all beginning again, another season of slotted times, as if anyone knew what would happen next. He rode to the ground floor. The doors opened – there was the bank of elevators opposite, the hallway with mailboxes, angling off – but for some reason he didn't move. When the doors closed he pressed G1 and then there he was in the garage, where he'd paid as much to buy a parking space as his father had for his first house. He threw his portfolio case onto the back seat of the old Saab and took it out into the bright, calamitous streets. Minutes later he was heading west out of the city on the Queen Elizabeth Way, a little ahead of the rush-hour traffic.

He cruised through forty miles of sprawl particularized only by the exit signs. The highway forked near Aldershot, named after the English town where his father had marched on parade grounds during the war. He'd always wanted to go back there, his dad, but hadn't managed it. Harold had never been able to picture the old man in a uniform, in lockstep with anyone. A part of him had always suspected the war stories were a lie, but in his father's papers after he died was an old newsy letter from a woman in Bristol. It gave nothing away but of course there was a story there, now lost.

The story to be revived was his own. Early in his boyhood, earlier than he should have had to, he had followed time out of grace, or whatever the phrase was. But if you only hung on, and if you were lucky, and then maybe lucky again, you could even on the earthly plane follow time back into grace. That no one seemed to acknowledge this return suggested how rare it was. The luck had simply been conferred upon him, just as years ago, through no volition of his own, he had been given freedom long enough to build a life. Now he had been forced into memory, but it had delivered him somewhere unexpected, somewhere he sensed would provide for him. And there was the luck, finding him largely by chance, as of course was its nature. He had never felt so full of understanding.

At St. Catharines he turned off and jotted up to Niagara-on-the-Lake, teeming with white and Japanese tourists buying marmalade and carriage rides, books about George Bernard Shaw, and then he joined the procession at 60 km/h along the semi-famed wine route. By the fourth stop, he was pretty sloshed on the samples of bad Chardonnays, bottom note of bile, but had finally found one to his liking. He took two bottles to the counter. The young woman at the till had acne and rings on her fingers and thumbs that clinked on the bottles as she scanned them. "I'm celebrating," said Harold, "and have no one to drink with me. Will you raise a plastic sample glass with me?" The woman looked at him for the first time. "They don't let us drink on shift," she said. "We might lose confidence in the product." She winked at him and snuck into his bag a shiny new titanium cantilevered corkscrew. He paid up, winked back, and walked to his car, marvelling at the gift she'd given him. Apart from its function the corkscrew was beautiful, and unlike those overproduced contraptions, when put to use the design conveyed power efficiently. The titanium cantilevered corkscrew belonged on the short list of perfect objects. Rowboats, bows and arrows, books. Too bad it had so many syllables.

The stripping out of syllables was the only worthwhile thing he could remember ever having imparted to Kim, and it had been returned to him in the trophies of an elegant prose. Details from her little fiction had returned in hypnagogic flashes, charging his dreams, and the dreams had bled into his day. He wasn't usually knocked over by words, but then he'd never before been granted characterhood, an alternative story with all the charms of false immediacy. There were ironies they could now observe together, he and Kim. And they could admit that events had changed them both, but their inspired turns had been prepared for by ordinary life and death.

Yes, that. Marian's illness was working on all of them. At any point in the day he could look back over his thoughts and find he'd circled the same blunt fact without directly approaching it. A musing on insomnia would lead to another on how men fear death, but somehow he'd not then think of Marian. And so he circled while the illness progressed, simply not facing the facts. She might well have gone into remission and outlived him, but it wasn't going that way for her, it seemed. They were looking at the end. It had struck him fully upon seeing her in their old bedroom. Kim and Donald must have known it for a while. When he'd phoned the house last week Donald answered, called up from sleep or a bit drunk – normally he would have checked the call display and let it ring through to the message – and for a minute or two they pretended to talk about Marian like serious men. Finally they ran out of words, a silence of a few seconds, and Donald said, "She doesn't look like herself, you know. She's wasting." He got the poor sap to agree that she was still herself, however she looked, but then came Donald's last line before hanging up. "Gödel was sixty-five pounds when he died."

One of the cars up ahead drifted to the narrow shoulder and stopped, and then cars all around, in both directions, were pulling over, so that the road was barely a lane. He was too drunk to guide himself past them so he stopped too. In the cars ahead people were looking back his way. Everywhere windows were lowering, so he lowered his. He looked across at an SUV. A large young man was smiling at him. "Don't get out of the car," he said. Harold nodded though he didn't understand. Finally he looked into the field beside him and there, not ten feet from his car, stood a large dog, staring at him without interest, like a zoo animal. He heard the guy in the truck calling to people up and down the lines not to get out of their cars and he heard him say "coyote." The animal walked up to the road and in front of Harold's bumper and crossed into a fallow field. The guy in the truck backed up a little so Harold could see. The coyote paid none of them any attention. And then a beautiful thing happened. It stood in profile and began to lower its head, elongating its body into the ancient lines of a rock painting, a glyph of single-mindedness. It stepped a perfect step. And then it was over, the mole in its jaws. It flipped it into the grass and watched it, then flipped it again, playing with its prey until the prey stopped moving. A minute or two later, the other cars had left. Harold stayed watching awhile, perfectly disregarded. By chance he'd found what he wanted. The disregard comforted him.

Yesterday he'd found in his department mailbox a typed letter from Rosemary. She said she'd try for the rest of her life to forgive him for having called Father André, and she expected to fail. The last page was taken up with several short paragraphs about her Rodrigo. She listed the jobs he'd worked here. She called them "shit jobs." The letter explained that when he was twenty he'd tried to stop the shooting of farmers by the narcotics thugs who employed him, and had pointed his automatic rifle at them. These men knew his name, where he was from, and they thought of him now not just as someone who'd threatened them but as a potential witness against them. They'd shot the farmers anyway and he took off running. The killers had contacts all over the country. It had been "a miracle" that the kid had escaped. His family had had to move to Venezuela. And now he'd been sent back, without money or friends, because, she believed, Harold had been jealous of his youth and resentful of her care for him. She said that Harold's pain over the attack on Kim excused nothing, not his suspicions, and certainly not his actions.

He had reason not to believe Rodrigo's story but even so he had tried to square it with the young man's face as he recalled it and found he could not. He didn't believe it, he couldn't say why. Maybe because the story so easily invited pity. A heart like Rosemary's, nothing warped it like pity, and she was full of it for everyone but him, it seemed. Sentimental pity was one of her evident failings. She would call it a virtue, but it was delusion. He had always had a sharp eye for the difference.

On past Queenston, where Laura Secord had saved Upper Canada from the Americans two hundred years ago, and into Niagara Falls. The actual place was never as dreadful as he imagined. The tourist cafés and museums were avoidable, the walk from the parking lot along the ever-awakening river was already sublime, and nicely managed by the stone and iron fencing, and the Falls themselves never got old. Thunder rimmed with lime. He'd been here first with Marian and Kim, when she was just four or five – a winter scene, he could still picture her blue mittens gripping the iron railing – and had been back a few times since with women, on outings, most recently with Connie. They'd eaten in the restaurant at the Falls and that's where he was headed now. He needed food and a table to read at. Better not to read drunk in a car.

When he got to the real commotion the crowd was four deep. Their faces suggested that they were not disappointed at what they were seeing, or rather they seemed surprised not to be disappointed. He expected to have to wait for his table but instead got one right off, overlooking the something-or-otherth wonder of the world. He had another glass of wine, French this time, and a chicken club sandwich held together with toothpicks. From nowhere he was overcome by a wave of dizziness, elations, he supposed, and it almost took him but he steadied himself by getting out the page and starting into it. On the backside of a news story among the clippings he'd taken from his office – the old news stories, all his lost ideas and intentions – he'd found a photo of a bridge. The story was from 2004. He'd read it with horror, unable to stop himself. It concerned the death of a woman trying to smuggle herself over the border. She'd jumped off a freight train and fallen under its wheels on the upper level of the Whirlpool Bridge, hereabouts. Her leg had been severed and she'd bled to death. The mystery was that none of the border patrol cameras on either side that night could determine which train she'd been on, or even which direction she'd been travelling. Two trains had used the bridge within minutes, heading opposite ways. Her body had been found near the midpoint, her leg "about eighty feet into the Canadian side," but whether the body or the leg or both had been dragged, and by which train, or both, wasn't clear. The woman had no ID. It was unusual for such a person to be travelling alone. And no one had identified the body. "Because most of her remains had come to rest in Canada," she'd been "buried at Canadian expense in a potters field adjacent to the Riverview Cemetery." She mustn't have known, this woman, that she could have crossed by foot into Canada. It was just her practice, no doubt, to cross borders in boxcars, as she'd have done all up the continent.

He studied the approximate map in the story, then looked out at the people looking out at the Falls. They stepped into openings to get closer. They gave their cameras to strangers and struck poses. They pointed at rainbows and threw bread to the gulls. It had all been going on every day for decades, the same movements, the same public rituals for the disarming of awe. No one wanted to be still with it, certainly not alone with it.

He paid up and left.

Despite its name, the cemetery did not, in fact, command a river view. It was eight or ten blocks from the river, the usual mix of maples, elms, evergreens, and chestnuts. The stones nearest the main road all had fresh flowers, keeping up with one another and the politics of tending the dead. The sections were lettered, though there seemed to be no X, Q, or Z, and then double-lettered. When he'd driven a couple of interlocking loops, he stopped in at the little administration building. In the small foyer a young man in a white dress shirt was talking to a woman in coveralls. The man offered Harold a practised, sympathetic smile and came forward to shake his hand. He introduced himself as Kyle. The woman watched Kyle perform for a few seconds and then drifted down a hallway and disappeared.

"What can we do for you, Harold?"

"Back in 2004. A woman died on the bridge. She's here somewhere. I'd like to see her."

"I'm sorry, I don't know who –"

"There's no name. She lost her leg. A train took her leg."

Kyle dropped his eyes to Harold's left hand, the one he hadn't extended in greeting, in which for some reason he was holding the cork he'd extracted from the second Chardonnay before putting the car into gear. Something in Kyle's earnest face changed. It's called twigging, Harold thought, and wondered why. Kyle looked briefly beyond Harold as if for a handler. His focus never entirely came back. He seemed to be dialing up training scenarios.

"Harold, have you been drinking?"

"It's pretty obvious, isn't it?"

He reached to extract the news story from his pocket but it wasn't there. He must have left it on the table at the restaurant.

"Is that your car out there? Is there someone who'll come and get you?"

Harold laughed. "You're a responsible kid. That's great. Now can you give me a map to her grave. I'll walk there."

Kyle excused himself and retreated into an office with an ascending bird designed into the blasted-glass window. Harold hoped he wasn't calling the police. He heard himself mumble something but didn't catch it, and only then realized just how tanked he was. Now he recalled the open bottle between his legs on the way over. The truth, the innocent truth, was that he'd had to drink it down a ways to keep it from sloshing onto his pants. If they came for him, he'd explain that his public drunkenness, the danger he posed, was all because the cupholder in his car could not accommodate a wine bottle. Neither he nor his defence could stand up well to questioning.

Kyle re-emerged with a folded piece of paper.

"I think I've found out who you mean, the woman. And here's the map. I'll trade you for your car keys."

This was a good kid. There were a lot of them out there. Then, for the first time, he thought of the class he'd failed to meet. Filled with this affection, this spirit, he could have done wonders for them. He found the keys and handed them over. Kyle gave him the map.

"All right, I'm off. And when I come back in a few minutes I'd like to buy a plot."

"But you're drunk."

"I'm inspired to buy a plot. Next to the woman, or as close as you can get. I want that spot, and a piece of paper, a deed or whatever, that I can put with my papers to be discovered by my family when I drop dead. You can see I've thought it through. I couldn't have thought it through drunk."

"You'll have to come back when you're sober."

"Jesus, Kyle." Harold opened the map. On the top border Kyle had circled what looked to be a pretty large area. "Can you at least X the spot for me?"

"Well."

"Well, what?"

"The sort of remains you're talking about, there's no actual grave." He was saying the record was wrong. "Cases like that, it's cheaper to cremate. We just handle the ashes."

"What does that mean?"

"They're sort of in storage. We don't use up space on the grounds. But there's plans for a modern mausoleum. That's what I circled there, where it's going up. In four or five years." He turned to the wall nearest them and pointed out an artist's sketch of the building, a concrete gazebo relieved with ivy features that looked like legumes. "Then we'll move the remains in storage to their final resting place. But you're still welcome to come back and buy the plot."

There was nothing for him so he devised a new course of action. In the time it took to retrieve the second bottle from the car and walk to the river and along the avenue of pretty houses there he contemplated what it was in him that defeated his every inspiration. He was not good at inspiration. In fact he could say without self-pity that he was not good at very many things beyond the practice and teaching of history. The scene from Kim's story that most often returned was of Carl Oakes, or her version of him, getting out of the car with the diplomatic plates, and someone inside saying "Good work." He could see it all, though he hadn't. He could hear the voice. If only he'd stepped forward then. If only she'd written him as someone who would step forward. But she knew him, and had found a way to tell him what she knew.

What she couldn't know was that he knew the man in the car, the man on the edge of the photo from El Salvador. He had known him for years. The dark angel of human event. The man, the angel, would turn up all the time in his researches, in dreams. In the documents he was the unnamed agent of evil never entered into the record. Dream to dream he spoke with different accents, in different languages. Smiling at him from the edge of a dull party, or in the car beside his, turning to look. The stranger in the crowd, viewed from a panellist's chair on some stage, who looks up from his listening posture and finds him. Always this recognition. In a recurring dream Harold is walking with a small group at night, people he knows, and then a new voice enters the exchange with a word or two that won't be recalled upon waking, and now it's Harold who turns to find him, the most vivid of his company, there and then gone, and none of the others saw or heard him.

In his second season on the job market, just as his thesis was published, he'd landed on four short lists – along with Toronto were San Marcos, the Colegio de México, and the American University in Washington. The San Marcos position fell through but he was offered the others all in the same week. He'd chosen Toronto not because it was in his homeland but because it was safe, he thought, barely registering the troubles of successive global moments. He'd chosen it in retreat. But there was no hiding. The angel was there at each cardinal point, and now, having grown ever nearer over the past year, he'd found Harold out. The man in the car with diplomatic plates was very close now, but Harold no longer feared him. That he should have shown up in Kim's imagination did not mean that Harold had drawn him to her. That he might have appeared one night in the flesh to tear into her body and mind was just so much self-punishing, self-indulgent fantasy.

Across from the Whirlpool Bridge was another, apparently closed off. The only trouble posed by the access was to keep from spilling the wine as he scrambled up a steep embankment through shrubs with the earth sliding away beneath each step. When he reached level ground he looked to the bottle and found it was still with him, about half-full. He felt sick and bent over as if to wretch but managed not to as he caught his breath. Nearby, a circle of stones, charred wood, broken beer bottles. He walked on.

This had been a train bridge too. He walked next to the dead tracks, over the last road and out onto the span above the river. The way was blocked there with a low steel wall. A warning sign. He turned to look across at the Whirlpool Bridge and found it a consummate thing. The trains ran on top, he saw. He marked where the woman would have fallen only two or three feet to her death, and he looked down to the waters, two hundred feet below. She'd messed it up, he thought. Better to die in the waters than on the tracks. Even he could see the poetry of the long fall.

In time, on some delay, he found himself motionless, listening. He drifted towards a sound, barely audible, and looked up now as he'd looked up then, and at first he couldn't see it. Then there it was, high above. Watching him, no doubt. It was because he'd been looking up that he hadn't noticed that a group of six soldiers was approaching. Unable to stop thinking of Carl Oakes, who was, in fact, something like Kim had written him, an insider, fluent, though older and thicker of body, he'd begun to feel unsafe in his room, and so he'd taken his passport and money and walked out in the direction of the embassy. At some point a fighter jet flew overhead and he looked up, for only seconds, and then looked down and there were the soldiers. They wore helmets and five carried machine guns. One, with a white arm band above his elbow and a pistol in his hand, walked straight up to him and asked who he was. A Canadian, he said, and the guard said – You're a communist. Your leader Trudeau is a communist too. Harold said, No, and the guard laughed at him. Harold said, It's complicated, and the guard mimicked his voice, what he'd said, in Spanish, and the way he'd said it, and then told him to explain himself. – Explain in perfect Spanish and I will let you go. The other soldiers stood in a line behind him. Their faces were distorted by the helmet straps but they were very young. Harold said Canada had supported the U.S. embargo, that it had done its part to destabilize the government. He knew as he spoke that he was being understood, but that he'd made errors. For one, he'd used the noun form *desestabilización* instead of the verb *desestabilizar*, and though he hadn't believed the guard would have let him go for his Spanish, he couldn't be sure, and knew only that he'd failed the test. The guard asked if he himself supported the embargo, and Harold said nothing. The man's pants were tucked into his boots. — Give me the name of your school and your teacher. Even as he replied, Harold reasoned that the soldiers would already have the names, that they wanted him to say the names just to implicate him, and Orlando would already have been arrested or be in hiding. Harold said the name of the school, then of his teacher. He said it and spelled it. The guard holstered his pistol and made a show of writing it down.

— Is this correct? He showed Harold what he'd just printed out. There were a couple of dozen typed and hand-printed names with addresses after many of them. Harold said it was the name. He tried to think of something more to say but his fear got in the way. The place was upside down. It was time to get out of the fucking country. The soldier asked him for the address of his teacher. Harold said he didn't know it. The soldier nodded. —You go back to Canada now. I will kiss your teacher goodbye for you. And his wife – he has a wife? – I will kiss her twice.

Harold turned and walked away then, and when the man said stop he might have kept walking and might have been let go but instead he stopped and turned again, for years he sees himself turning, and the soldier explained that he'd had an idea. Harold would accompany them to every building on the list. He said no more and Harold couldn't bring himself to ask what would happen then. He imagined the soldiers leading people out and past him as they were taken away. He might have been asked to humiliate himself or the others. Whatever the soldier had in mind, the idea seemed to be that Harold would be released of this duty only when they found his teacher's apartment, and they would find it anyway, and Orlando would surely be elsewhere by now. This is what he told himself. He gave the soldier the street and intersection. He allowed himself to be ushered into a military truck. He would show them the actual building.

When they arrived, the two of them stood across the street as the others with guns went inside. — They talk about their dream, said the soldier. They sing songs about it. You must know the songs. Sing one for me now. Harold said he didn't know the songs and the man smiled. — You knew them yesterday but already they're forgotten. He lit a cigarette and gave it to Harold. He said he didn't smoke but the soldier made him take it. Then he lit one for himself. A minute or so later those who'd been hiding in the apartment were led out of the building and into a bus parked a short way down the block. No one looked his way until, just as the last of them were loaded into the bus, one man turned and saw him standing there across the street. Harold recognized him, had met him somewhere on campus. His name was Eyzaguirre. Harold had no doubt that he'd been discovered. Over time he came to assume that Eyzaguirre, all of them, were dead.

Then the last two were brought out of the building. Orlando, a thin poet and teacher, and Maria Alicia, who taught at the Technical University, where Harold had met them at rallies on nights that had ended with drinks and song. She was classically beautiful, with large dark eyes that caught him that day before her husband's did. The soldier took Harold across the street to them. The couple was made to stand against the wall of the building squarely before him. The soldier asked Orlando — Do you have a last lesson to teach your Canadian? — I don't know him, said Orlando. — But he knows you. He's given me your names and brought us here. He says you're a very good teacher. Orlando looked down. Maria Alicia then stepped forward and slapped Harold in the face, to the obvious pleasure of the soldier, who began to say something when she then turned and punched him in the throat. Only then did Harold think of the soldier as anything like him, a breathing, feeling man, for he was down on his knees taking loud, sucking breaths as Orlando, being restrained now, began to plead and two soldiers ran up to hold Maria Alicia. She offered no resistance then as the man she'd struck got to his feet, took a machine gun from one of the soldiers, raised the weapon, and brought the butt of it down hard into her face. She had turned her head and received the blow along the cheek and jaw. She fell to the ground and he hit her once more, squarely in the face, as Orlando cried out for his wife, and when the meaning of the cry reached the soldier, he swung around and shot Orlando in the chest. Harold saw his teacher slump and fall, quite dead. Then he and the soldiers looked back at Maria Alicia. At the sight of her, one of the soldiers emitted a sharp breath and the leader, the killer, as if only just seeing what he'd made, recoiled and stepped back. He then told two of them to drag the bodies back inside the building. They left the dead couple there, then left Harold – he didn't see them go exactly – standing in the now orderly street.

When her face returned to him, as it had for years and more often now in the resemblances, it was composed as the face that had looked into his. It was this face that shocked him in memory now and then, and not the final, brutalized one, the one for which there were no likenesses. This never returned. It had never left him. What he didn't know, what he couldn't be sure of, was whether or not, before dying, Orlando had seen what had happened to his wife upon the second blow. He had chosen over the years to think that Orlando had not seen her but he had had to keep choosing. Now he was inclined to think that all of them had seen it, and once he accepted this, it was hard to doubt it.

He finished the wine, then made his way in full trespass to the railing. At the foot of the opposite bridge there was, in fact, a whirlpool. It had fallen on him again, the monster eye of that alien storm, and he knew all at once whose eye it was. As if to blind the thing he hurled the bottle as far as he could and leaned over to watch it fall until its entry into the river was lost in the disturbances.

He was walking fast then, back the way he'd come, along the tracks and over the edge of the bank, sliding down to the street, landing hard on his hands and knees. He got to his feet and started into a half run, two short blocks to the approach to the second bridge, an open incline, and out to the working tracks. He was drunk and the drunkenness at least was familiar, something to hold on to. In one direction the tracks ran atop the bridge to the U.S., and he thought he saw men far across them. They would be wearing uniforms and they'd be warning the men here of him, and so he started back the other way, towards the station and the freight train sitting there. He must have imagined the uniformed men, he thought, but it didn't matter. The helicopter was louder now, it had zeroed in on him, he was quite sure, and so he ran as he could, to the end of his breath, and approached the train on the blind side, away from the station.

There was no escaping the gazing eye out here. He understood that it was what had killed the woman on the bridge, that she knew she'd been seen, and so jumped. When he could run no farther he stepped up to the door of the boxcar beside him and slid it open, a boy with his father again, and hauled himself in awkwardly, kicking the air, then shut the door.

He lay in the new utter dark. Silence. The helicopter had been extinguished. In the reeling drunken space he turned and turned, losing his position on the floor, until he came to rest, and lay still a long time. He closed his eyes to find scenes from he didn't know where. The poor part of a town on a lake, boarded-up buildings and wet winds, the bobbing hip-hop figures of two black kids in long parkas, hoods over caps tilted roadward, in otherwise peopleless snowblown streets. An old man in a white undershirt sitting on his bed in a hospital or retirement home, staring at the floor inside some memory, a secret love that kills you, with strains from other times reaching him from the common room. A blond woman alone in a restaurant, turning her face, removing her glasses, a Slavic flatness in her forehead and orbitals, her eyes flickering to a wineglass and a look of resignation surfacing in her expression. They were looking down, all of them, in passing thoughts yet to come. Soul-lost harbingers, he could do nothing for them. He stared into whirl, unmoving but in motion, eyes open but blind, buried alive but still spinning, as if the vortex was upon him and he was the prophet falling into the sky like the missing girl whose name was always with him translated to heaven, and the missing like the failed like the dead. The darkness swam with semblances. He called out, "Who's there?" and it was with him. He was not alone. The winged presence had found him out. Through the blackness it watched.

When the door rolled back (had he opened it?) it was the night hurtling by and he was presented an escape that he understood to be false. He moved to the doorway and felt the stiff air. Here he found at last a time of gathering, and all was resolved. The voice behind him said something that was lost on the wind.

The merciless streaming unseen world. It had always been his.

He steadied himself, and awaited his moment to step forward.

PART FOUR

10

The deepest questions we pursue are themselves in pursuit of us. It was the first line from his lecture on evil, a kind of warning to the students, as if fair warning absolved him for taking them where he would. They were into the second week of it now, halfway through evil, on their way to sin, and eventually redemption, a thorny matter, as he liked to say, and André was, for the first time after years of teaching this class or something like it, beginning to understand what it meant to be pursued by the deep questions. The measure of pointless suffering and death had grown recently, and grown closer. And Rosemary had absented herself from the church and from him. He hadn't returned to her house, and wouldn't, but there was no trace of her on the usual routes, nothing except the bookmarks she'd left on his computer. Pages on William Temple, weather forecasts, discount stores, Thomas Merton, a badly mic'd woman at a lectern talking about coal-fired plants, a bank. He chose a newslink she'd marked and up came footage of a missing woman from the late summer. He watched it all the way through. He imagined that as Rosemary watched it, she would have been thinking about Mariela Cendes. Here was a new woman, a different name, but year by year, city by city, Mariela just kept disappearing.

Today he was to book his trip to Canterbury. It was his last chance to follow through on his decision to invite Rosemary. When his call rang to her machine he left the message that he hoped she'd accompany him. He said the church could help pay for her ticket. He said this would be the case wherever she wanted to go, and that if she wanted to fly south instead of east, he would be happy to accompany her there, too. If she wanted to go alone, the offer stood nevertheless. He said that though he made no apologies for his actions, he understood and respected her need to practise her beliefs by occupying them. Upon some passage of lateral thought he then told her in some words or other that he'd not later recall, except a few phrases that he knew from lectures and sermons, that he was reading *The Brothers Karamazov* and wondered if she had, he would love to talk with her about it, and how he loved vast, cold, northern literatures, that he had grown with age into his appreciation of the Russian greats and couldn't help but feel they offered just the counter to this world of noise and ever-replicating surfaces and – the message cut out and he called back – he spoke of pages here and there, a bowl of soup or a river, the day before us, we look up from these things and where do we find ourselves? As if we might uncover and reassemble the bones of the first ones, the creatures closest to God – we run ourselves down to the last ounce of hope and begin to shed our own faiths, thinking in our weakness that there is no order beyond nature and loss upon loss, no truths that don't melt into pools of illusion, and so we become vulnerable to a dark mindlessness always making raids at our borders, enlisting despair, infirmity, corrupted instincts, even chance in our undoing, and all evidence of God is withheld, every new day appears drawn to light by no command, only our turning in space.

And then we find a shard. By night, above us, the lights of heaven, or by day, some mercy extended, some selflessness full of meaning, and upon witnessing such a soul, we feel the very substance of – the message ended, he called back – We have our proof in those rare others. We have our shard, Rosemary. We take possession of it, carry it in our pocket, rub it with a thumb. In time, yes, it wears away, people fail us, people we most trust, and whatever it was we once held disappears, becomes a memory, and so we examine our memory, we wonder at its nature, and see that it deceives us, at times, and so we're lost again, wondering if we truly ever held this knowledge, this shard of the original ongoing moment, of the godhead. We promise ourselves that, should we find another, we'll mark ourselves with it, we'll cut its shape into our skin. And so by longing we're blinded to our true condition, that we are already marked, marks we not only fail to read but fail to see. Unless, perhaps, something should remind us, should truly *re*mind us, that there is meaning outside of our making, that the details of the real world deserve our full attention, that we're witness to daily miracles – however cheapened the language of saying so (how ingeniously the corruption spreads in language, rotting the very form by which we lone, trapped souls reach out to one another, and sapping the beauty from unsayability itself). And that, though the weight we bear is the weight of all, and though we cannot truly know the pain we witness, any pain greater than our own, we can nevertheless know love, a greater love, this is its advantage, and we can aspire to it. If compassion is what Bergson calls "aspiration downwards," if it requires our imagination, then love for those outside our given circle of loving requires it too.

Here I am with my orders and my Holy Bible, reading again to the end, growing old. Every day is a reclaiming against the world outside my window, in chaos even in those places it desperately strives not to be. Maybe these events could not be Authored. But remember, dear Rosemary, that even the end of this unsigned world has the Maker's mark on every page.

ϕ

The state had no name.

She had a memory she couldn't place from her girlhood of the moment when she understood herself to be separate from her parents, them in the front seat, her in the back, and the sure thing they'd been, the three of them, lost on a frozen prairie road she could still see curving into river hills. Long ago she'd lost history and god. She kept losing god without once getting god back.

It began with a scene on the lawn, their own front lawn. Donald had come outside and everything about him said that her mother was dead and so she was already there in the knowledge of one parent's death when he had to bring her out far enough to tell her it was Harold, not Marian. His name sent her wandering out of the yard at an angle to nowhere, and Donald trailed her into the street, thinking he was explaining, when she fell. She fell all the way to the country, to Lana's, where the doctors still made house calls. For some days Donald was the only one not medicated. The doctor was very tall and thin, an old man with huge hands. Kim asked for more drugs and said she didn't want to know their names, and he wrote out the dosages and handed the instructions to Donald, and then sent her half out of being.

A nameless state, cottoned, neither waking nor sleeping. When she felt the rising to time-place, she tricked herself to drop away again by following little things to their ends. Something like an ice cube, call it an ice cube, runnelling from a crested summer street to a gutter and sliding to a grate, dropping through, from dim to dark passageways running on, losing its very self, then suddenly shooting out into light again for some brief dying moment, into the thing it was, water falling inside water with no border between them.

Following voices, near or trailing, administering, but not letting them form into sense upon sense. Beneath the voices, a streaming she'd known once before, without music or echo, not coloured or pleasing or solemn or one thing so much like another.

Her hand in air became a bird of prey tracing sky, and in time she was her hand, waiting for seeing to become hunger, for wanting to become desire, and then a movement in the grasses below wrenched her into another form that cast her down full of all-things-in-the-balance and the ground rushed up.

She came down enough to see that someone had bought pyjamas for her. The sleeve across her pillow, striped light blue and a sort of meringue, a sky-and-clouds colour that sent her following the light tracking across a country yard, coming and going, and rain, water again, and then returning in evening to fire in the trees, setting them alight with markings until they all read as one equation that held true forward and backward: she had ended him, he had ended her. She had only to remove the variable she was to render this truth beyond mattering.

There was yet no stability, they said, just lapsing in and out, and upon one of these lapses she had the last vision, cold and clear. A bluntness is watching a dark street in summer. The city is weakly playing at sense. The selected one approaches along the draw. For moments at a time in the watching the bluntness is bent away from itself to some undernature and it feels its deep wilderness mind, moving, intent, fully itself, crossing through bush, over saplings, crossing road into encampment, wilderness mind, two thousand miles to the west. And then at once it's back, in the alien space of this same dark street, somewhere nearby, in the folds of the sheet, waiting for her. And she is going to it.

She will come to think that she remembers what happens next but she won't for a very long time. Until one day, when she's old, she'll forget what happens next in the vision, though what happens next is everything and always. What happens next is what is.

All of this, by some counts, passed in eleven days.

Donald arranged the service. Kim sat with her mother, absent, among strangers in a small chapel. She had to be told when to walk out.

In the days following, back home, there came hours with the television. Vertical desserts, clever cartoons, strong men pulling truck rigs, soldiers real and fake, sterilization in Puerto Rico, space-saving tips for the closet. Her body, she'd worked at it for so long, had closed back down. Words failed to be recalled. It was all happening again and she had to stand, get up off the couch and literally stand, or fall. For a week she ate almost nothing and had never been so heavy.

It would have to begin, the next recovery, as a kind of show.

For Marian, for Donald. For herself, given that they'd all know it wasn't real, the dark humour, the sure movements around the house, the half-lively voice she used on the phone. It would begin as a show and at some point become real, or seem so, which would be enough.

She would examine her actions and find them loving or cruel, she didn't know which. Confronting him, conducting her researches. Sending him the letter she'd written to herself, beguiled by a moment of hope. And then, as if knowing her Santiago story had presumed too much, had stolen from him, she'd sent the video link, casting after her presumption an act of redress that, in the end, redressed nothing. Whatever she would find, looking back, she'd impose a reading that would keep her free of ruin. She had a secret she would never tell. She was culpable or she wasn't. It was true, he had lived inside an ambiguity, whatever it was, and had died inside another, and bequeathed it to her. Only now, facing facts, were the contradictions of her heart apparent to her. At one moment it seemed she'd acted only for his sake, and at the next to prove that he had lied to her so that he might admit all of his past, including that which had shaped her. She'd loved him and she wanted to hurt him. She saw it all, and saw how she deceived herself to think that her actions were passionate and principled, driven by moral instinct, rather than calculated upon her old pains. And then it seemed she was granting the old pains too much of herself, and that there might have been a way through for both of them.

At some point she just said fuck it. She turned off the TV and began reading. Then she went through nineteen days of uncollected email. Five people had sent sympathetic e-cards, two of the cards were the same.

Eduardo said Eyzaguirre had offered to look at a photo. She knew where to find one from '74, but declined their further help.

In time, by turns, Greg and Shenny came through as they could. The idea was to resocialize her. Greg visited once, then took her out with a friend named Winston and the three of them went to an oyster bar that in the twenties had been a garment district sweatshop, the original machine layout marked with dozens of vestigial floorbolts that sent ever more customers stumbling as the night wore on. Winston was a short, round man, with narrow designer glasses that seemed to frame more than his eyes, his whole literate, avid bearing. He seemed like someone Kim should have known a long time but she suspected she'd never see him again. That Greg had people like Winston in his life opened her idea of him. Shenny took her to a spa with a woman named Parmja, a film reviewer with a gender politics slant who made a kind of sport out of over-informed commentary. On both occasions Kim ended up describing an article she imperfectly recalled on evolutionary biology and religious belief. The feeling of an ordering mystery beyond us could be explained by the human mechanisms for agent detection, causal reasoning, social cognition, and god formed there in the spandrels. She said, "God's just a place in the physical brain." The heretical sense of it should have played well, but her friends and acquaintances, godless all, said almost nothing, as if she was presenting them her crisis of faith.

Which she was, she supposed.

One evening she was downtown walking west into a sun bowing down and came upon a movie lineup wrapping around a corner for a block and a half as hundreds spilled out from the early show, some of them mulling under the marquee, forcing others into the traffic, and the cars patiently waiting, and from her vantage across the street she saw the teeming shape, the massing and the long tail, and in the high murmuring heard her name called from somewhere. Even from a slight distance she couldn't see far past the edges, over the heads. She turned, turned away really, and looked through the open windows of a restaurant where her attention was caught by a young woman alone at a table, not ten feet from the street but seemingly miles from the throng, flat-boned, Russian-looking, staring at her glass of wine, lost there, and Kim saw her, this woman she didn't know, as someone's daughter. Then her name, called again, and she almost walked away, a part of her wanted away, but instead she drifted across the street and into the crowd and again her name on the air – it was Harold calling her and she thought she would cry but she didn't – and then she stopped hearing it and the moment it hit her that he was gone a hand fell on her shoulder and she turned to see a man she knew, she knew him well, though the how and who escaped her, and he said he'd been thinking about her because something had opened up and he wondered if she needed work.

And like that it all came back, his name, the day of the week, the place she was, what she needed. And she thought that she'd been wrong, that she'd just missed it when it happened this way, that a divinity or whatever came to her upon seeming accidents like this, in the play of chance on a noisy city street in the fall. Maybe it was less than god, but it was more than luck. It was certainly mystery, a small, conferred radiance. Because the city gives you this, too. One day it tries to kill you and another it finds you and hauls you clear and gives you something not entirely rational to believe in. Like that healing mysteries didn't fall on you but rose up, drawn forth simply by your paying attention to the lives of others. That you had anything to do with it, this feeling, these mysteries, was one of those illusions that worked, that served, so necessary that it had force, and so became real.

The man – his name was Ryland something, Ryland Coombs – he knew a woman in Central America who was looking for someone like Kim, a writer and speaker of languages, to help with the work she'd be starting in January. It was a chance to be a part of an international team. He said, "Think about it." And so at home that night she thought of the mountains and cities to the far south, and when she began whispering in her thoughts the names of those in need, she was the nine-year-old converted for the winter by the maid in Mexico City – yes, she remembered it now, that city, a lost place that had been returned to her – the maid who'd told her of miracles, and now as then she brought her hands together, palm to palm, as if still holding what had already escaped her grasp.

On what Marian felt would be her last good day, a dark young woman appeared at the door, holding a crimson and yellow shoulder bag. She was about to be canvassed or solicited, and she waited for the girl to see that she was in no shape for petitioning.

"Hello. I'm Teresa."

"No, thank you, dear."

"You're Marian, yes?"

She'd forgotten the arrangement. She had no head for arrangements lately. Even when she had had one, she'd learned to reject the whole idea of them.

She and Teresa took tea on the back deck, waiting for Kim to show. The sky was clear but not deep. The blue that greeted the eye was not the blue of years past, but the dimming was not hers, she felt. It was cool so they shifted their chairs into the sun and without being asked to or making a fuss about it, Teresa tucked the blanket behind Marian to cover the small of her back. The girl talked easily but not too much. Upon only two questions she explained that she'd met Kim through a mutual friend, her former lawyer (this would be Kim's Greg, though that was already "half-ended," Kim had said). She said openly that she was in the country illegally and hoped to stay here and "make a life." The arrangement, as Marian now recalled, had Teresa here on weekday afternoons, while Kim worked her part-time job, proofing copy at the CBC. In cash terms there'd be no net gain to the household, but Kim needed the time away from her, though she wouldn't say so. And this Teresa needed the money.

The girl wore a thin tunic that looked as if it were stitched out of decorative tea towels. There was a name for it Marian might once have known.

"What has Kim told you about me?" The young woman hesitated. "I know she's told you I'm sick, but do you know exactly what the work will involve?"

"I know, yes."

"Have you done this before?"

"Yes. I looked after my mother."

"Was she dying?"

"Yes."

"Well. So you know what's ahead of us."

When the phone rang Teresa asked if she could answer. The question confused Marian and she didn't respond and Teresa went inside and took the call. It was just that it was backwards, the guest answering the phone. Marian had to remind herself that she wasn't a host.

Teresa brought her the phone. Kim said she was sorry, that she'd be late. She was still waiting to see Harold's estate lawyer.

"Why is he always running late?"

"I'm spending my life in this waiting room, just me and the expired magazines. I can tell you a lot about burrowing owls. Do you like Teresa? Say 'Tuesday' if you do."

"I Tuesday very much."

"Good. I think she's wonderful."

When she ended the call Marian looked at the phone receiver. She ran her finger lightly over the number pad, as if her touch could hold there and surprise her daughter some day in the future when Kim was ordering Thai or phoning a plumber. Kim called again half an hour later to say she had to go straight to work, and Marian and Teresa moved to the living room and began to tidy, though this was not part of the arrangement. Teresa said it was all the same work, and she liked doing it, and so they went over the method for dealing with Donald's papers. Marian lay on the couch and explained that they were never to be stacked together. The ones on the coffee table were to be moved to his desk in the study, all others to the shelf inside the hutch. When Teresa took the pages from the mantel a stray condolence card fell to the floor. Marian asked for it. It was from Rosa and Tom, the Lams, old acquaintances from Montreal whom they hadn't seen since Kim was six. They'd heard the news and were very sorry for her loss. Of course they'd heard the news. It travelled even among far-off strangers. Professor Found Dead in Ditch had become Professor Likely Struck by

Train had become Fallen from Train had become High Alcohol Levels in Professor Found Dead by Tracks. Professor's Death Ruled Drunken Mishap.

She handed Teresa the card and said garbage.

"My first husband was a sad fool."

She'd known it always, but knew it differently now. The circumstances of his death were ludicrous, clownish, a little slapstick, a man falling on his head at fifty miles an hour, but it was the fact of the death that cast a colder light on Harold, on all of them. All these years he'd worked like hell at the wrong things to keep his purchase and then Kim had been hurt and he started into the long slide. Or maybe it wasn't so simple. Maybe he'd have lost purchase anyway.

It was not a mishap. His car had been left in a cemetery.

Teresa looked at her and then went into the kitchen, as if evading a question. It made her seem a part of the fractured family rather than a complete outsider. Maybe Teresa had heard how things had ended for Harold but so what. She'd never had to suffer him. Her connection was Kim. They were all connected through Kim. It should have made them lucky.

When she woke, Teresa was sitting across the room, reading a book.

"How long was I asleep?"

"Not long. What can I do?"

"What are you reading?"

The girl put it back in her bag, smiling. "A silly book. My sister sends some from home."

"Can I see?"

She withdrew the book and handed it to Marian. A ratty paperback with an illustrated scene of jungle mountains. On a dirt path crossing the foreground stood a young girl, looking off to the peaks. *El Viaje de Mariela*. The girl on the cover wore a necklace of a kind Marian had once bought somewhere in Central America or the Caribbean. She could picture herself leaving a courtyard with the necklace in hand. A first morning in a new city in the rain and when she left the market the sky had cleared and looming there was the volcano. Had the air been Spanish or Caribbean French? The necklace was jade.

They found it in a jewellery box in a basement dresser drawer. A black leather thong tied around a jade disk with a large round hole. She told Teresa to take it as a gift.

"To celebrate today, the day we met."

The girl's protests were sincere. She was going to feel bad about it, but Marian didn't care.

"There's no one else I'd rather give it to. Kim doesn't wear jewellery and I don't want it forgotten in a box. It's to bring good fortune. Not luck but money. That design with the hole is from ancient coins. All the way back to China, I think."

"I understand."

"Now let's see if I can get up these stairs."

Though it took long enough coming up that she knew she wouldn't go down again, she decided that rather than get into bed she'd just keep moving, out to the front porch. Teresa got the blanket and tucked her in and then let her be to sit alone there, looking off to the end of the street where Kim would appear in time. She traced back from the necklace to the memory of buying it. She didn't like them, stray memories. They didn't belong in her now. The dying animal turns from memory towards one short tapered thought. At the end of the thought is a shape that grows more certain as the animal closes. Marian knew it was before her but couldn't see it yet. She didn't exactly fear it but now and then worried it would be something absurd. It would look to her like a half-dressed opera villain or a drunken town crier, or a shingled outhouse, something in wooden shoes. Harold's death had been absurd. There was no way to think about it, account for it. Even the timing was comically bad, with everyone focused on her last weeks. Something had passed between Kim and Harold, she felt, but Kim hadn't said what. His death was not a mishap, but neither could it have been chosen. He didn't have to drive an hour to catch a train if he wanted to kill himself. And what he was doing on a freight train defied understanding. He was not the kind to go mad when he drank, so the madness of it must have already been in him. There was a thought – Harold had had an absurd ending in him from the outset, even before she'd met him all these years ago. Not that it was fated to claim him, but it lay dormant, and only by chance had something brought it to life.

She could only sit so long but she stayed. She wanted it to be Kim but Donald might be home first. He'd insist that she go inside and lie down, as if it mattered, because he was powerless and so needed to have things to insist upon. And she would have to put up a small resistance and then do as he asked. Their pretend negotiations. Back when, she'd learned to make love to him the same way.

This neighbourhood of porches. The jack-o'-lanterns were not far off. Then their crumpled November faces. She'd rather not have to see them. Strange kids appeared at the door each year. She'd lost track of the turnover on this street. In most of the houses were new families or the grown children of old ones. From the day they moved here there remained only the old man named Betts, who'd outlived his wife and two children and went for a walk each warm day in his dressing gown, looking for anyone to hear his views on the royals or black people. And the family with the delinquent girl who had shouted the worst imaginable profanities at her parents all through her teens and now worked at a daycare. Across the street and a couple of yards over, a woman Marian had never spoken to was raking an early shedding of maple leaves in her front garden. She wore a wide-brimmed straw hat and every so often it would tilt up at passing cars or dogwalkers. Then a robin caught the woman's attention, flying by, and she followed its path over to Marian's yard and then saw her there and for the briefest moment paused, looking at her, then tilted the hat down again and went back to work. What had occupied her in that moment of apprehension? What thoughts or half thoughts? What doubts? Maybe she hadn't known she was being watched. And now, what did she suppose Marian saw? What picture was she a part of? Could she imagine her way into the wasting woman on the porch? If the sky was closer in these last days, the made world, the human things, went on forever. Marian was aware. It was all composed before her, every facet, every line, ongoing, without frame, until it touched upon the other made world, creation, and there the wind moving in the tall trees, and the day being day, and the light on her own house, and the stranger inside it.

In Zona 1 of the murderous city comes the warning not to go out after dark or you will surely die and so there is nothing the first night but a ceiling fan and the sounds of someone retching down the hall. The next afternoon, moving along Avenida Roosevelt in a veering spangled bus past shops and schools you see beside the eight smog-clotted lanes a goatherd with a bullwhip driving his animals in profile along the narrow sidewalk against the stucco and corrugated metal walls until they stop at a pay phone in blunt tableau. Vendors climb on selling coloured feathers, ice cream candies, fried bananas, moving down the aisle and then appearing somehow through the window on the neighbouring bus, though the traffic has never stilled. Radio music, a machete under the driver's seat. Negotiated stops and a dozen near collisions every block, and so it continues until the city is gone.

In the square of the colonial town that she had loved are firecrackers, white couples with dark bought babies, kids selling tickets to the volcano. In a cool dawn you ride up and find yourself on the same path she once climbed, through the green terraced hillsides and pastures, with tourists and stray dogs and a young running guide. In an hour you're on the lava field of shifting rocks, some white and red hot, stepping over melted water bottles and sunglasses onto the smooth dark hollow back of a whale, hearing the very blood of the earth burning inside it. The dogs show the way, like the dogs that had rescued her in the story she used to tell, when her guide had moved ahead and she found herself in a spot of hell, far from the others, farther from anyone she knew, and the home where she'd been abandoned by her husband. You stop and let the others, your others, move on, searching for the moment when she'd felt saved, but of course it's unavailable, lost to the years and geology, to the distance between the pain or knowing or received grace of another, and the story of it. You walk on to the end and the open vein burns on your eye.

On the phone your lone contact describes the place you'll be arriving. This is where it all happened, she says. The whole team's assembled. The forensics people, the psychologist for the families has been here a week. You'll be with us by dinnertime. We're digging up graves in the morning.

The woman is American, famed among justice seekers, is said to be older than she looks. She warns you not to take pictures en route. They'll think you're a spy or a kidnapper. And no pictures at the graves. These are crime scenes.

Don't state your business to anyone. No one can know why you're here.

As if you knew why you were here. You tell yourself that tomorrow's unearthed dead are not yours, but that your dead can't be served except through them. This is not quite true. You do not feel elected to this duty. It's that there's no one left for you now. No one and nothing except the solid earth and what it might hold.

The woman's voice is with you saying mercy all along the last leg, winding up into the mountains, into hard towns of unfinished buildings, with plastic roofs, rebar spikes, the illusion of perpetual improvement, and exactly on the median of the highway is the deadest dog in the world, legs splayed out from what looks like squashed watermelons, every torn moment dressed with newness. Then down into the town, past fruit and fabric stands, toddlers in the streets, signs reading microcredit, the open doorway to a room of kids at typewriters, and a row of trees painted with election graffiti for a party run by killers, the woman's voice saying love and god's blessings, words once no more than a flutter in a cage now seeming all-resolving. You arrive here with only her name.

You promised to arrive in one piece.

She promised to be waiting for you.

ACKNOWLEDGEMENTS

Thank you to Ron Poulton,Victoria Sanford, Holly Dranginis, Carmen Aguirre, Susan McKeown, Stephen Streeter, Nasrin Rahimieh, Stuart McCook, Alicia Viloria-Petit, Nelofer Pazira, Sandra Helm, Tracy McDonald, Thomas Lahusen, and Ellen Levine. For valued readings, Ken Babstock, Richard Helm, Alayna Munce, and Michael Redhill. For being a part of this novel, and the others, I am deeply grateful to Juanita DeBarros. Thank you to Lara Hinchberger for keen editorial suggestions and, especially, to Ellen Seligman for lending this book her unfailing heart and great talents. And to Alexandra Rockingham, for her artistic wisdom, bravery, and the ever-present mindfulness that guides all who know her.

I'm happy to acknowledge the support ofThe Canada Council for the Arts and the Ontario Arts Council.

The novel owes a debt to several text, on-line, and film sources, especially Virginia Garrard-Burnett's *Protestantism in Guatemala: Living in the New Jerusalem*, Marc Cooper's *Pinochet and Me*, Brian Loveman's *Chile: The Legacy of Hispanic Capitalism*, Samuel Chavkin's *Storm Over Chile*, and Joanna Bourke's *Fear: A Cultural History*. The story told on pages 337-339 is partly invented, and partly drawn from the events of the Acul massacre of April 21, 1981, recounted in Victoria Sanford's *Buried Secrets*.

Brazil

Brazil, Guarujá
Outubro 1991

To Dr. Martin who with an admirable Latin spirit has faced a 40°C tropical heat and the intensive agenda of the "II Congresso Paulista de Cirurgia Pediatrica", the expression of our gratitude and hope of an early return to our country.

José Bueno Martins
Luiz Carlos Monteiro
Edson Khodor Cury
Napolitano Neto
Bruno Herzowitz

Brazil

Jürg Müller Armin Bollinger
Gilberto Cavalcanti Rudolf Moser
Photos: Peter Frey

All colour plates by Peter Frey, Pernes-les-Fontaines/France, with the exception of Nos 105 and 106 (Rudolf Moser, Zurich).
The photographer and the editor wish to thank Brazilian carrier VARIG for its generous support.

Translation from the German: Urs-Peter Haller, Muri.

Agência Siciliano de Livros, Jornais e Revistas Ltda.
Alameda Dino Bueno, 492 - CEP 01217 - São Paulo - Brazil.
*Printed in Switzerland - Edições Siciliano 1987 - ISBN 85-267-**0154**-1*

Brazil – the Other Half

With regard to surface area and population, Brazil is as big as all the other South American states put together. But this does not mean that it makes up only half of South America, on the contrary, Brazil is the other, different half.
The mere fact that Brazil, fifth largest state in the world, takes up such an enormous space is the result of a history which has run its course differently from that of other South American countries. In contrast to the Spanish empire which on independence fragmented into countless and sometimes arbitrary states, Brazil managed, despite all separatist pressures, to maintain the same frontiers as the former colony. Brazil is already a different, other half by virtue of the fact that Portuguese is spoken here. A portuguese language which in brazilian form, to be true, has taken liberties in grammar and intonation, and extended its vocabulary with Indian and African expressions. Even today there is still a tendency to equate South America with Hispanic America, as if besides Spanish America there were not also the other, Portuguese or Lusitanian Latin America.
This difference is not merely a matter of language, but also of historical and cultural patterns, and not least, of mentality. The Hispanic loves the radical gesture of "death and blood", whereas the Lusitanian would under many circumstances stand aside with irony: conviviality rather than confrontation, the "convivência" of "we are all Brazilians together" which includes "jeito" the everyday tricks and skills of modern survival.
This totally different development began with what in European terminology is called the discovery of South America, a process which if one thinks about it, continues till today, with the opening up of the Amazon, and the sad extermination of whole Indian tribes.
To a large extent the Spaniards came upon highly-developed cultures, but their interest was centred less on the cultures than on the gold to be found there. Initially Brazil had little to offer in the way of precious metals, and significantly the name Brazil comes from a rare wood, the Pau brasil.
At first Brazil became an agricultural colony, with sugar cane being planted in its northeastern and northern regions. A society based on sugar resulted, and this was visibly evident even in the settlements, where slave huts and the manor house were grouped around the church and the sugar refinery. Even today one can still come across such settlements in the northeast, and then as now one finds feudal and semi-feudal conditions.
Economically speaking, the northeast has for many years been dethroned, not least because sugar cane has been more profitably grown in the south of the country. Recurring droughts have made the northeast a crisis area where fanatic holy men and social rebels of every shade can prosper. A region which has inspired ballad singers, as well as the Cinema novo, and which has brought forth first rate authors and sociologists.
This sugar-based civilisation as a first colonial enterprise could only function thanks to the import of labour from Africa. Brazil became the biggest importer in South America of black slaves, who were also introduced into the Spanish colonies.
But as regards the scale and consequences of black slavery, Brazil has no equal on the South American continent. To find any parallel situations one would have to go to the Antilles. With its present proportion of Blacks and Mulattos in the population, Brazil once again proves to be the other half. It is totally different from its mainly European stock neighbours Argentina and Uruguay, as well as from

the mestizo nation Paraguay, and the Indio countries like Peru and Bolivia.

This ethnic composition has made its mark on Brazil. It is not mere co-incidence that the first major sculpturer and first autonomous writer were Mulattos. The African inheritance in religion is stronger than the Roman Catholic Church may like. It is an inheritance that lives on in the cuisine, the language, and above all in music. The Black past continues to add spirit to Brazilian phantasy, be it erotic or artistic.

But with the passing of the years, Brazil has become "whiter", on the one hand because the import of slaves was stopped, even though the institution lasted almost till the end of the last century, and on the other, because the 1822 independence was followed not only by an economic opening, but by an influx of Europeans. The Portuguese were followed by Spanish, Italian, German, and Swiss settlers. They mainly emigrated to the temperate zones of the South. So today a whiter south confronts a darker north.

The gaining of independence, which preceded this European migration, was a process for Brazil which again was totally different from the experience of other countries on the continent. The Spanish colonies rose up in arms against the colonial power, Spain. "Liberators" are the heroes of Hispanic-American nations. But the same is hardly true of Brazil, even if the loosening of ties to Portugal was not as unbloody as the school books suggest. But ultimately it was the case that a Portuguese monarch proclaimed Brazil's independence. Brazil achieved its freedom not through a war, but through a declaration of independence. While the Spanish colonies turned into republics, Brazil became an empire, a status it retained for nearly all of the 19th century. The discovery of Brazil was as much a matter of chance as the rest of Latin America. But initially the Portuguese kings were not very curious about their possessions in the New World. They were more interested in the spice trade, and therefore the routes to India and the Far East. Only after Portugal had lost its pre-eminent position in Asia to the Dutch and the British did its attention turn to its American colony. This happened just at a time when Brazil was producing a new attraction: gold.

One consequence of finding gold was the transfer of the capital from Bahia (actually Salvador da Bahia de Todo os Santos, known today officially as Salvador) to Rio de Janeiro, in order to be closer to the mines. Brazil had acquired a golden province which to this day is still called Minas Gerais or "general mines". A reminder of these times are the magnificent Baroque churches and secular buildings in Minas Gerais, which together with those of Bahia, Recife, and Olinda amount to an impressive cultural heritage. Because at first Lisbon only concerned itself half-heartedly with Brazil, there was all the more scope for individual initiative. In comparison, the Spanish monarchs from the very beginning sought to get their possessions under control, not least by forestalling the "Conquistadores" and their clans. In Brazil there was hardly anything like the "Conquistadores", but the country did have another kind of conqueror, known as the Bandeirantes. This term was given to those who rallied round an ensign or flag (bandeira) and pressed on as a small troop into the interior of the land, in rather the same manner as the North American pioneers.

The Bandeirantes started a movement which is still in motion today – the urge to get away from the coast to the interior of the country. All the main towns had been built on the coast, and possession of the vast hinterland became an economic challenge. But the catchphrase "away from the coast" also had a psychological significance: a beach or the Praia is the epitome of paradise for a Brazilian. Brasília, the present capital, was built not only to demonstrate Brazilian prowess in town planning and architecture, but also to underline the necessity to move the focal point away from the coast to the interior of the country. The building of the new capital naturally called for the development of an infrastructure which for the first time established a terrestrial link with distant parts of the country.

As the purpose-built capital, Brasília now has a whole ring of unplanned satellite towns around it. Reality has caught up with planning. Every urban settlement represents a great attraction for a rural population which can hardly make ends meet, and lives away from schools and medical care, even if in the final analysis it is merely exchanging the rigours of a rural existence with life in big city slums.

This internal migration is a phenomenon which Brazilian cities share with all others in South America. But on the other hand again, Brazilian cities are different. Neighbouring states like Argentina und Uruguay are composed of one large capital city encompassing virtually one third of the national population, plus the remaining hinterland. Besides such vast capitals, other cities hardly have any significance. The same is true for Peru, with Lima, or for Venezuela with Caracas. Brazil however has a whole row of more or less equally important cities: in the north, Fortaleza with its one million population, Recife, the gateway to the northeast. Rio de Janeiro together with Belo Horizonte and São Paulo forms an industrial triangle, and to complete the list one should mention Bahia and Pôrto Alegre. Amongst all these cities, São Paulo occupies a special place as business capital. This city symbolises Brazil's economic development with all its achievements and contradictions. São Paulo began its career as capital of coffee, and it included a hinterland of coffee plantations, and a port in the shape of Santos. But São Paulo also stands for the development of industry which helped on the path away from monoculture, and its concomitant dependance on world markets.

São Paulo is not only the largest industrial centre of Brazil, but of all South America. From it, it once again becomes clear how different a path Brazil took from the rest of the continent. There is hardly a Latin American country which has such huge economic and social discrepancies within its own frontiers as Brazil: contrasts such as the industrial conglomerate of São Paulo and the underdeveloped territories of the northeast, or the geographical variety ranging from a tropical to a temperate climate which is repeated in the social scale that runs from development to underdevelopment.

Whether one looks at present-day Brazil or its history, one will in different ways ascertain that this Brazil is a very different half of South America. Bearing this in mind serves as a prerequisite to replace projections or phantasies with hard and fast realities. This will permit a more balanced view not only of Brazil but of South America as a whole, because it takes into account the special factors that have influenced the region.

Hugo Loetscher

1 *Map of Brazil*

2 ▷ *The Iguaçu waterfalls in the south Brazilian federal state of Paraná lie in flat countryside near the frontier with Argentina. The Brazilian shore is on the left side of the picture, the Argentinian on the right. The waters tumble down over a prominent step of basalt rocks from the Mesozoic period, which are part of a basalt layer covering much of south Brazil. The waterfall has a drop of 70 m. The brown colour of the water is due to the large quantities of suspended matter in the river, mainly grains of sand and clay which only settle to the bottom after the water has been still for many hours. The forest around the Iguaçu Falls is protected. The Rio Iguaçu is one of the large tributaries to the east of the Rio Paraná. The confluence of the two rivers is some 25 km downstream at the point where Argentina, Brazil and Paraguay meet.*

Caribbean Sea

VENEZUELA
COLOMBIA
ECUADOR
PERÚ
BRASIL
BOLIVIA
PARAGUAY
URUGUAY
ARGENTINA
CHILE
GUYANA
SURINAM
Guyane Française
PANAMÁ
COSTA RICA
NICARAGUA
HONDURAS
EL SALVADOR
JAMAICA
REP. DOMINICANA
TRINIDAD AND TOBAGO

Tropic of Capricorn

1 : 28 000 000

0 250 500 750 1000 km

Recife	Ort mit über Ville de plus de Locality of more than	1 000 000 Einwohner 1 000 000 habitants 1 000 000 inhabitants
Manaus	Ort von Ville de Locality of	500 000–1 000 000 Einwohner 500 000–1 000 000 habitants 500 000–1 000 000 inhabitants
Santos	Ort von Ville de Locality of	100 000– 500 000 Einwohner 100 000– 500 000 habitants 100 000– 500 000 inhabitants
Belmonte	Ort unter Ville de moins de Locality of less than	100 000 Einwohner 100 000 habitants 100 000 inhabitants

Hauptdurchgangsstraße, Fernstraße
Route à grande circulation
Principal through highway

Hauptbahn
Chemin de fer principal
Main railway

Staatsgrenze
Frontière national
International boundary

Printed in Switzerland © Kümmerly + Frey, Bern

3 *The Sunday outing of many Cariocas (the name given to the people of Rio de Janeiro) is a visit to a football match in the Maracanã stadium, which can accommodate a crowd of 180,000–200,000. Such a match almost inevitably turn into a public festival, at least for the supporters of the winning team. In this picture the spectators are sitting on the broad steps in the afternoon sun and expectantly awaiting the kick-off. The drinks and ice-cream salesmen, recognisable by their white clothing and the containers on their backs, are being kept busy.*

4 ▷ *A tributary of the Rio Purus. This narrow, meandering stream is typical of tens of thousands in the whole Amazon basin. The Rio Purus is a tributary of the Solimões, which it joins from a southwesterly direction. The tropical rain forest seen here is in its most untouched form, with many trees of varying height. As there is no change of seasons in the interior of the tropics, and at most differing levels of rainfall through the months, the trees are in leaf all the year round. But most do lose a few leaves at each season, and others grow anew. There are also trees on which at one and the same time some branches are in blossom, while others are carrying fruit. Yet other species lose all their leaves in a matter of days, immediately grow new leaves again, blossom, and later bear fruit. Because of the verdant roof formed by the trees, little light ever reaches the forest floor, which is in permanent twilight. Humidity is as high as 90–100%, with the result that the trees often drip with water even if it has not rained for days.*

5 ▷▷ *Palm trees on the Anhangabaú in São Paulo. Tropical nature and technical civilisation – together or in opposition?*

Geography and Economy

Observation of the nature and the socio-economic relationships to be found in Brazil highlights the tremendous range of conditions met in this vast country, characterised by three major poles.
On the one hand there is the drought-stricken northeast, with its land and property structures rooted in colonial times (Latifúndio and Minifúndio), resulting in problems such as widespread unemployment, or under-employment, migration of the rural population to the cities, combined with the establishment of slum areas on the periphery of the urban centres.
Northeastern Brazil is by far the poorest region of the country, marked by low per-capita income of a broad spectrum of the population, an extremely high illiteracy level, poor medical services, and sometimes insufficient nutrition in terms of quantity and quality, added to a deficient infrastructure.
Things are different in the southeast, south, and mid west of Brazil, which so to speak form the second major pole. Here too the aforementioned difficulties can also be found, but not to the same acute extent, because counter-developments have played a role: increasing industrialisation combined with remarkable expansion of the infrastructure, not least in areas which by Latin American standards have already reached a high standard in agriculture. However, it was precisely this unreasonably rapid industrialisation which led to the creation of the big cities which in turn are confronted with countless new problems.
The third major pole is the Amazon basin, which till recently was almost undeveloped, and which today is going through a transition. The Brazilian administration as well as private entrepreneurs are engaged in the integration of the Amazon into the economic life of Brazil: tropical forests are being cleared, roads constructed, mineral resources exploited, and agriculture pushed forward. That this development also entails dangers to the ecological system of the tropical forests which should not be underestimated is only now becoming clear to Brazil and the world.

The Land and its People

Brazil is a tropical country. Its 8.5 million km^2 are for the major part situated north of the Tropic of Capricorn, which runs between the two cities of Rio de Janeiro and São Paulo. The tropical siting manifests itself most in the climate and vegetation, and therefore also has consequences for land use, as well as influencing in no small extent the way of life and the character of the Brazilian people. For this reason, comparisons with temperate zone countries, above all those in Europe, are always incomplete and consequently difficult to make.
Politically and administratively, Brazil comprises five major regions, 23 federal states, 3 territories, as well as the capital Brasília, which forms a federal district. While the five major regions are only of significance for statistical and administrative reasons, the federal states are political units with a certain level of autonomy, and their own governments and parliaments. The territories on the other hand, which were founded for strategic reasons, are areas which could hardly survive as federal states, and which come under the aegis of the federal government in Brasília until such time as they achieve a measure of economic and political self-sufficiency.

Area and Population of Federal States and Territories 1989

1989 population figures estimated last census 1980

Major Regions and Federal States/Territories	Area (km²)	Population in 1 000 s
Brazil	8 511 965	150 052
North	3 581 180	9 923
Rondônia	243 044	1 001
Acre	152 589	411
Amazonas	1 564 445	2 141
Disputed area Amazonas–Pará	2 680	
Roraima	230 104	130
Pará	1 248 042	4 996
Amapá	140 276	258
Tocantins	277 321	966
Northeast	1 548 672	42 561
Maranhão	328 663	5 131
Piauí	250 934	2 657
Disputed area Piauí–Ceará	2 614	
Ceará	148 016	6 401
Rio Grande do Norte	53 015	2 336
Paraiba	56 372	3 281
Pernambuco	98 281	7 302*
Alagoas	27 731	2 409
Fernando de Noronha	26	
Sergipe	21 994	1 429
Bahia	561 026	11 625
Southeast	924 935	65 124
Minas Gerais	587 172	16 062
Espírito Santo	45 597	2 499
Rio de Janeiro	44 268	13 879
São Paulo	247 898	32 684
South	577 723	22 833
Paraná	199 554	9 167
Santa Catarina	95 985	4 402
Rio Grande do Sul	282 184	9 264
Mid-West	1 879 455	9 590
Mato Grosso do Sul	350 548	1 775
Mato Grosso	881 001	1 930
Goiás	642 092	4 082
Federal District	5 814	1 803

*inc. Fernando de Noronha

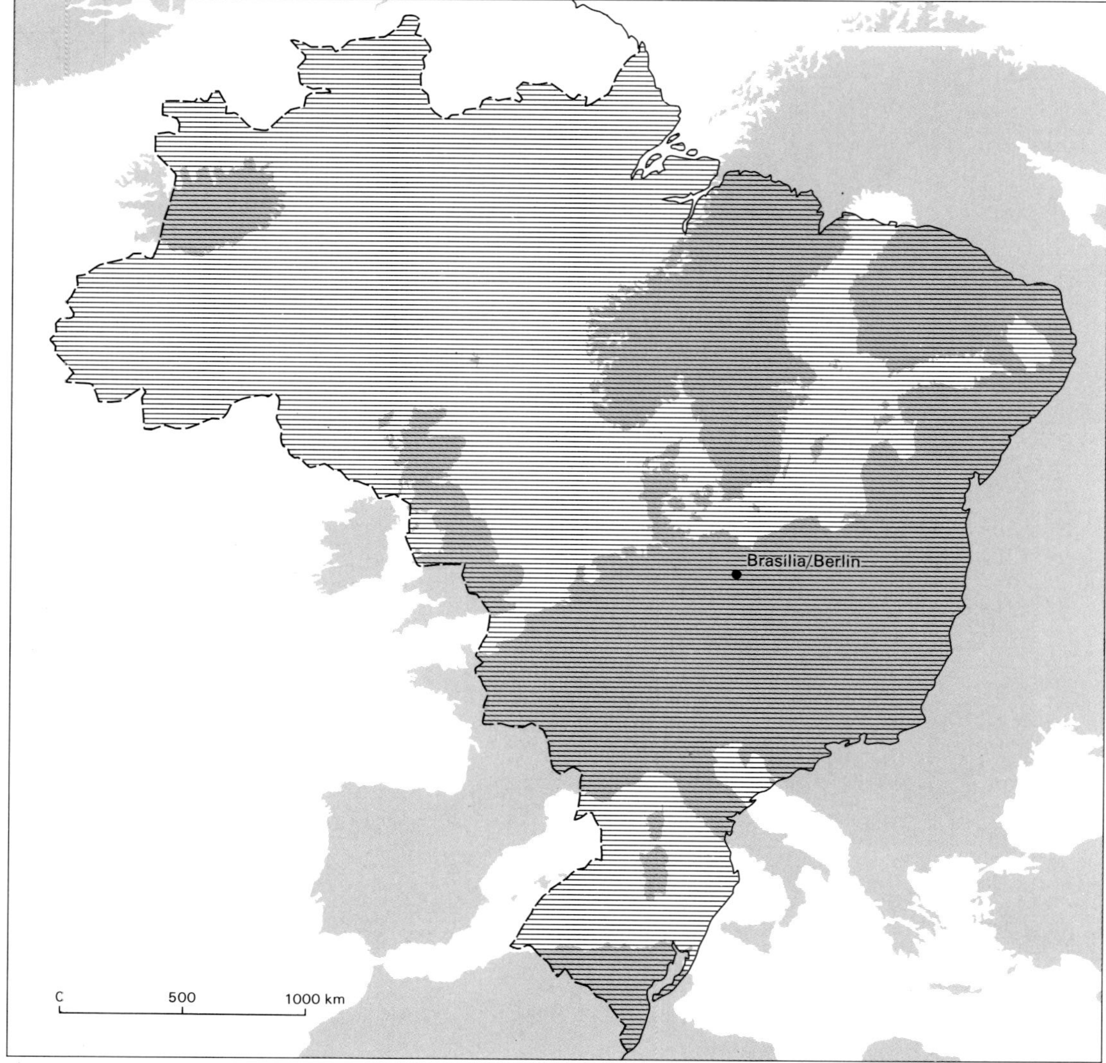

Comparative areas Europe – Brazil

Population Density of Federal States and Territories

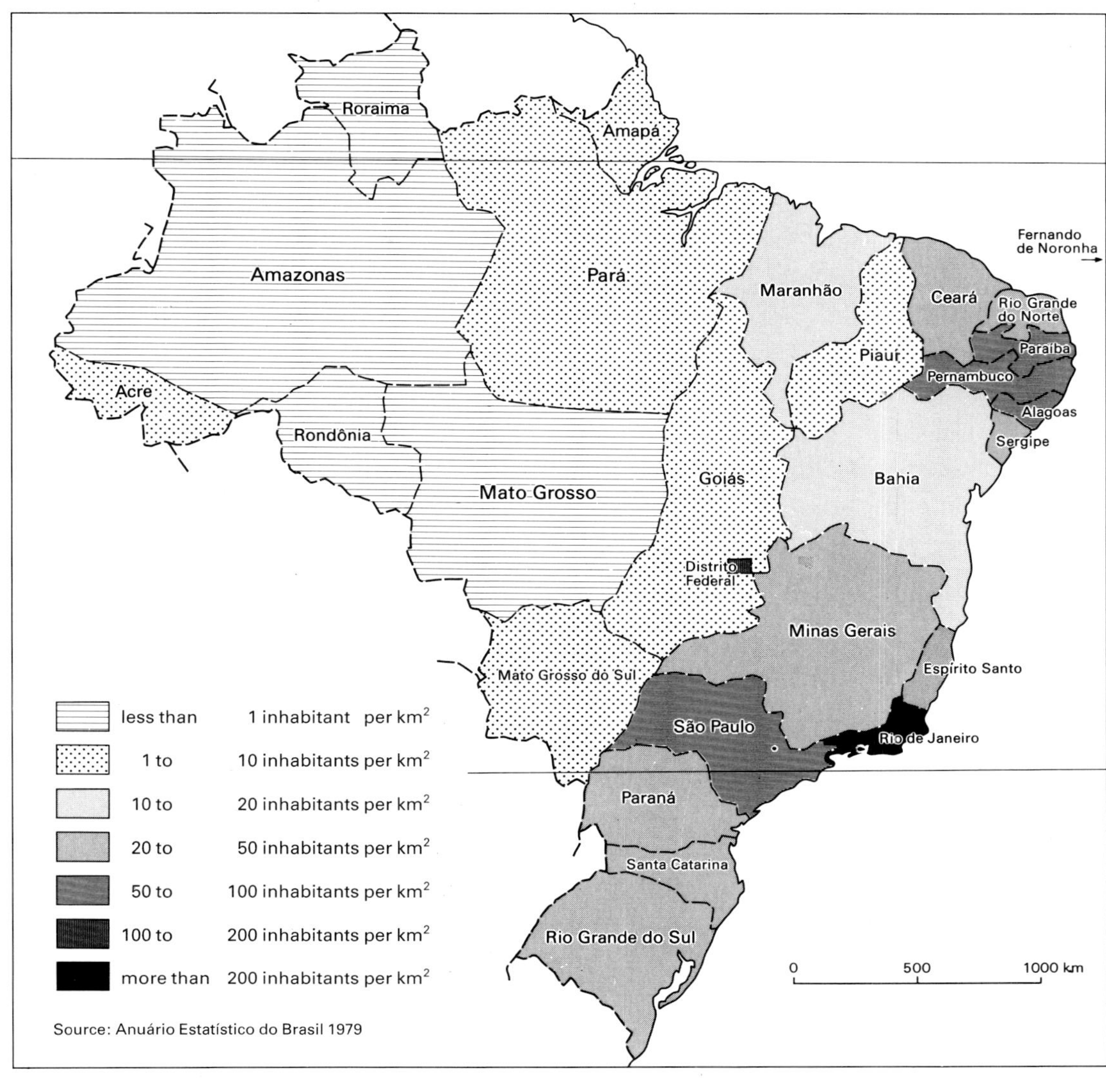

The Brazilian population is a diverse mixture of different skin colours, made up, according to the official statistics of 1976, of 56% whites, 31% half-castes of all shades, plus some 8% of blacks. Only a very small part of the remaining percent is made up of Indians (American Indians, to be correct), whose numbers are estimated to be anything from 50,000 to 200,000. A much larger group are the Japanese who make up between 1% and 2% of the population, as well as all those whose skin colour was not clearly declared. Although Brazil does not have any real race problems, the upper classes are largely white, while the lower social strata are drawn from the half-castes and blacks. The population distribution is one-sided, with the large majority of the 130 million total population living in the relatively narrow coastal corridor, which only widens somewhat south of Minas Gerais. Even today, the whole interior of the country is either lightly populated or still uninhabited. However few years, additional development areas have sprung up alongside new highways, but all in all, the development of the interior remains a problem closely tied to this one-sided distribution of population.

Statistically, 92% of Brazilians are Roman Catholics, which nevertheless does not hinder many of them from being members of the prevalent Afrobrazilian cults whose basic tenets came from Africa in historical times with the black slaves. Also intermingled with African and sometimes Indian elements is Brazil's national language, Portuguese, although usually it is only a question of incorporating single words from the foreign language.

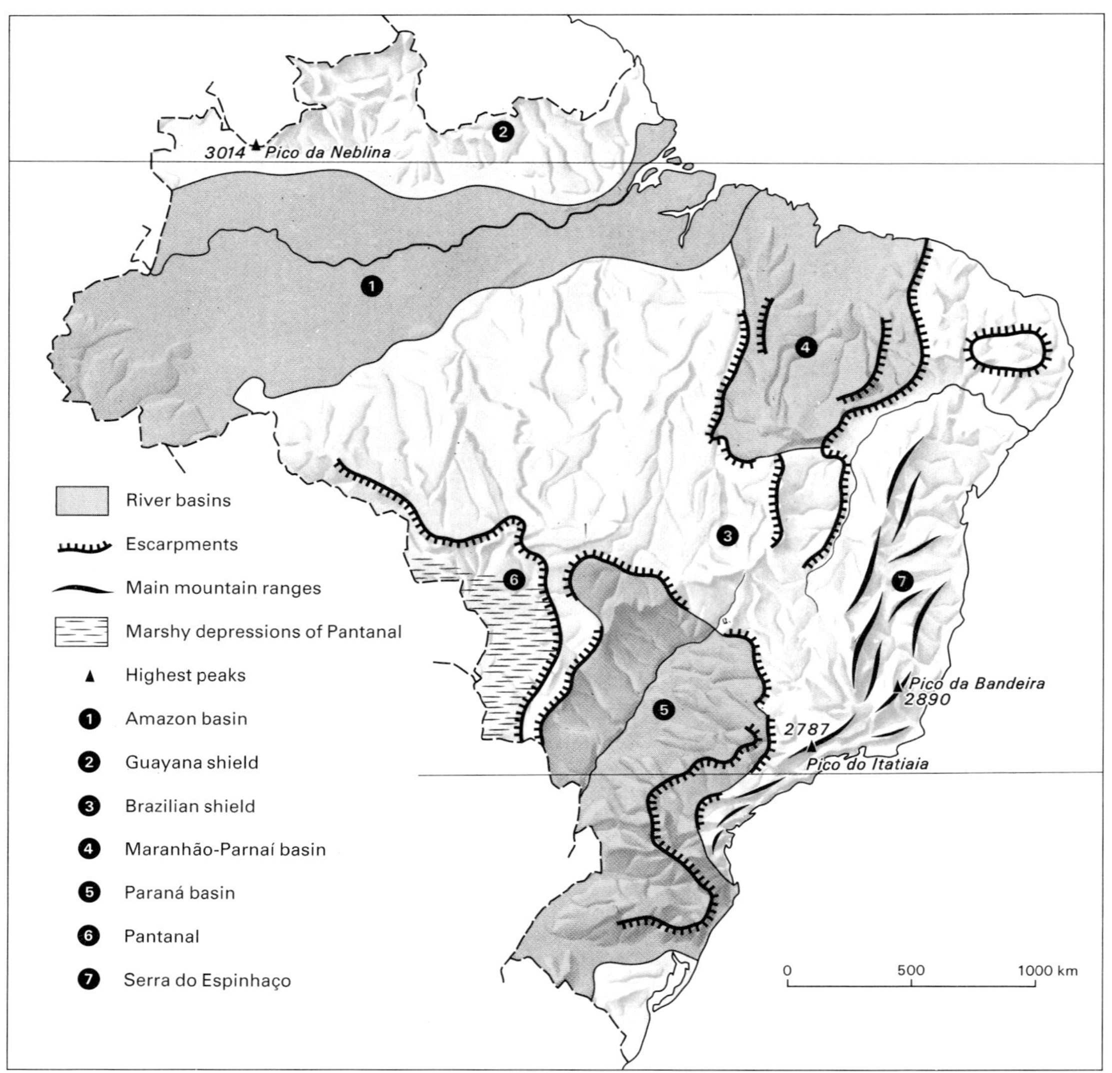

Relief

Geologically and tectonically, South America can be divided into three main parts:

1. In the east, on the Atlantic side are the oldest strata of the continent, forming the basement of the Brazilian and the Guiana shields, separated by the Amazon rift running west to east. Both once formed part of the ancient southern continent of Gondwanaland.

2. In the west lies the pacific fringe of the continent with the Andes range, that is younger rock strata of about the same age as the Alps, subjected to much upheaval in geologically recent times, as well as volcanic activity coupled with earthquakes until the present day.

3. Between these two main elements lies the Andean fore-deep, so to speak the connecting link between the old shields and the young mountains. The Andean fore-deep is composed of geologically very young deposits which today form the plains from the North Argentinian Pampas, over the Chaco and Beni lowlands up to the Amazon basin and onto the Llanos of Colombia, and the Orenoco in Venezuela.

Brazil is composed largely of the old basement of the Brazilian highlands, and parts of the Guiana highlands, the Amazon trench, and the eastern areas of the Andes trough. In particular, three river basin landscapes determine the relief, separated by flat ledges, and characterised by more or less horizontally lying sedimentary layers of Palaeozoic, Mesozoic and Tertiary rock, with marked escarpments on the edges. The three basins are the Paraná, the Maranhão-Parnaíba, as well as the eastern part of the Amazon basin, or valley.

The higher regions of the old Brazilian complex are only partly covered with sedimentary rock. Till the end of the Jurassic period, geological development was relatively quiet, but became much more active from the cretaceous period onwards, with the opening of the Atlantic, and in the tertiary period in connection with the formation of the Andes. Through this activity, the whole Brazilian block was tilted to the west, so that its greatest height is in the vicinity of the coast in the east. Combined with this tilt was the appearance of numerous faults and eruptions of volcanic rocks, such as the extensive basalt deposits in Paraná. The final shape of the relief did not come about till the end of the tertiary or the coming of the quarternary period. This description makes plain why practically no large river, with the exception of the Rio São Francisco, flows directly into the Atlantic, and why they all flow from the watershed near the coast, towards the interior, and the Rio Paraná, or in the northwest, even towards the Amazon basin.

A distinguishing feature of the Brazilian relief is the absence of any geologically uniform mountain chains or folded ranges. But there are nevertheless remarkably long mountain ranges such as the coastal Serra do Mar, which extends from Rio Grande do Sul state to Rio de Janeiro state, or the Serra da Mantiqueira which from São Paulo at first runs parallel to the coast, and continues as the Serra do Espinhaço into Bahia state. Apart from the already mentioned river basin landscapes, the Brazilian relief is dominated mainly by plateaus such as Minas Gerais (800–1100 m) or the Borborema plateau in the northeast (over 1000 m).

Climate

The climate of tropical Brazil is largely determined during the year by successive air masses of differing origins (by air mass we mean a large volume of air of uniform physical properties, especially with regard to humidity and temperature). The air masses and the pressure centres for their part are determined by the path of the sun, above all by its zenith at midday. In March and September the sun's highest point is over the Equator, in December it is overhead the Tropic of Capricorn. In January the interior of the South American continent is beset by a hot low pressure zone. The south Atlantic high withdraws over the ocean. The equatorial trough of low pressure is broken up and over large parts of Brazil there is an equatorial airstream of continental origin which has entered from the north. This air is moderately humid, but very unstable. Because of the prevailing air pressure this air is forced to rise, and forms thunderclouds. With the exception of the

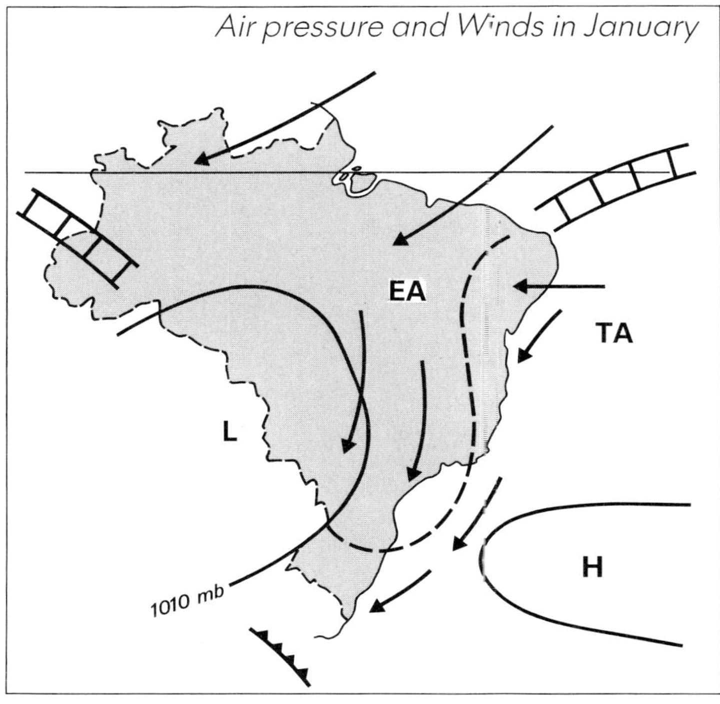

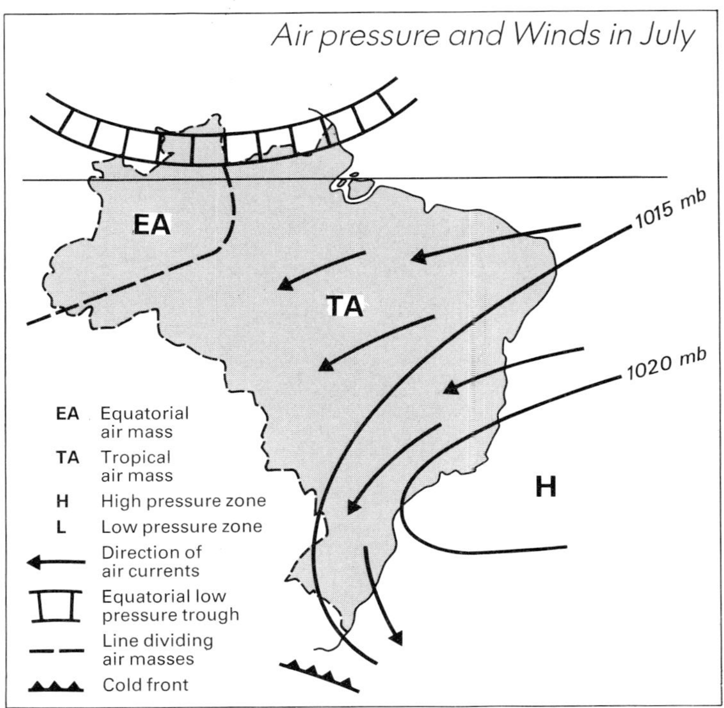

northeast coast and the very south of the country, it is now the rainy season in Brazil. Cold fronts travelling from the southern part of the east coast can at most reach São Paulo and Rio de Janeiro and provide some additional rain and cooling effect to the coastal zone.
In July the equatorial low pressure trough is north of the Amazon, practically over Brazil's northern frontier. The unstable mass of continental air with its thunderclouds, which in summer brings rainfall to nearly all of Brazil now only covers the northwestern tip of the country. The weather in the rest of Brazil is determined by the extensive south Atlantic high

Santarém

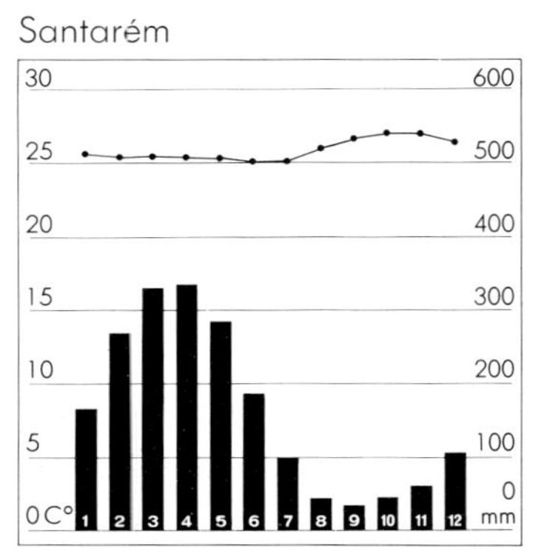

Rio de Janeiro

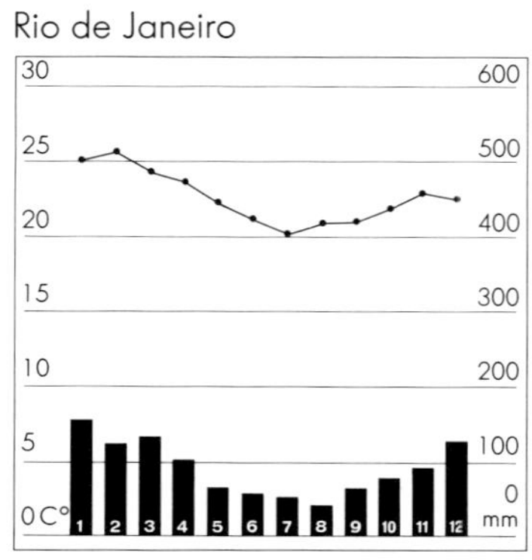

Recife

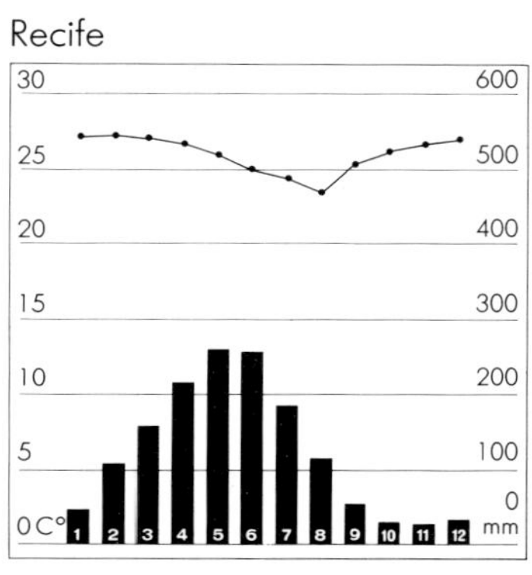

Três Lagoas

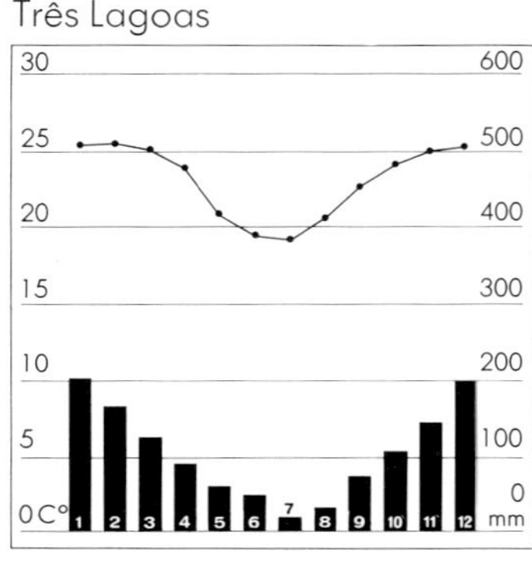

Remanso

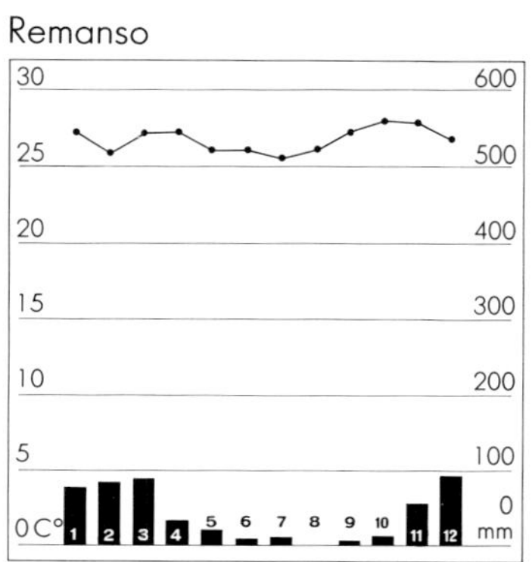

Porto Alegre

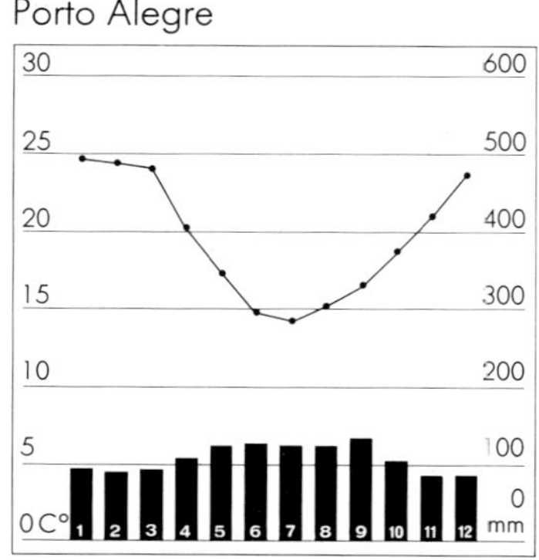

which brings easterly or northeasterly winds to nearly all areas. As these air currents tend to warm up rather than cool over the continent there is hardly any rain, with the exception of coastal regions where convection rainfall can occur. In nearly all of Brazil and particularly in the interior, it is the dry season. Disturbances from the southern Polar fronts can reach up to the north coast, which is why these areas have the highest annual precipitation in July.
The six climatic diagrams from selected areas of Brazil complete the weather picture.

Vegetation and Fauna

The natural *vegetation* of Brazil has remained to a very large extent in its original state despite the depredations of man. It is largely determined by the climate and also by the soil.
In 1975 arable land usage was put at 3.24 million km^2. Included in this figure are all cultivated land, bush and tree plantations as well as the usually intensively used pastures. All in all they account for 38% of the total land area. In other words, 62% of Brazil is still covered by natural vegetation. Even taking account of the fact that some of this area was productively used in times past, although not today, there still remains at least 50% of Brazil in its natural state. It is not evenly distributed in the various regions, but even in the most developed areas of the southeast one continually comes across stretches of untouched nature with their original flora and fauna. In line with the size of the country, and its enormous expanse from north to south, there is wide diversity in its vegetation, ranging from forest, bush and shrub to grassland.
Almost the whole Amazon Basin is dominated by the tropical-equatorial forest. It fits in to the permanent climate of high humidity (over 80%) and ample rainfall, together with an evenly high average temperature (24–28 °C). Its area is put at just under 3 million km^2, and in it can be found countless tree and bush varieties, of all sizes, in addition to thick undergrowth, creepers and ferns. The tropical forest contains thousands of sorts of wood, with over 2000 coming in the shape of tall-growing trees. In this jungle there is a permanent struggle for light which in many places hardly reaches to the ground. Experts distinguish between three to five storeys in the

tropical rain forest, depending on various criteria. The top storey is formed by the tips of the highest trees, overlooking the interlaced foliage, and reaching a height of 50–60 m. The trunks of these trees, like those of most others in rain forests, are very tall but not particularly thick, and they have few branches. In order to find a better footing in the flat forest floor, some of these trees have buttressed roots. They are further anchored by lianas and creepers which like netting, link neighbouring trees together. Free-standing trees would hardly stand a chance in thunderstorm gusts. The lower storeys of the rain forest are formed by the medium sized trees whose closed and interleaved foliage make up the jungle roof, by individual smaller examples which do not grow so high, such as tree ferns, and finally by the thick, almost impenetrable undergrowth. At the very bottom, even though rarely, can be found a covering of grass or moss.

In the Amazon, three types of tropical forest are distinguished, depending on their site with regard to the rivers. On the banks one can very frequently see trees in the water: this is the Igapó forest, which includes many palm species. In the wide flood plain can be seen the Várzea forest. This is the most fertile soil, because the regular flooding by the river deposits sludge that fosters growth, and thirdly there is the forest on "terra firme".

According to the newest research all this luxuriant vegetation grows only on a very thin and vulnerable layer of humus. If this is destroyed, for example when clearing the forest, it becomes virtually impossible to re-afforest successfully. This is above all true of large areas, because smaller clearings stand a better chance of regeneration. There are two different reasons for this. For one thing, the roots of the tropical forest are, by volume, three-quarters embedded in a shallow layer that only extends some 50 cm downwards, and this in turn means that most of the organic material of the forest in the plants is situated at or above ground level. If the forest is cut down, a large part of this organic material is lost, and with it many valuable nutrients are quickly washed away by the tropical rainfall. The thin humus layer is destroyed, and the infertile soil falls prey to further erosion. The second reason is that forest clearance interferes with the water cycle. In the Amazon a large part of the precipitation is formed of water that has evaporated from the leaves of the tropical forest. If these trees are lacking in great numbers, then there is no water for rain. The sea only accounts for a small proportion of the necessary humidity (estimates put it at between 15–30%. If one day, through too much forestry clearance, only sea-sourced rain is available, it will be absolutely impossible to re-plant new forests. In the long term one would have to reckon in terms of a prairie or a desert.

Just as varied as the tropical rain forests is the *animal world* of Brazil. Because the landscape is made up largely of thick forests and waterways, large animals would be at a disadvantage were they not also able, as indeed most are, to climb and swim in an emergency. Rather better off are the aquatic animals in the river and the birds in the treetops. In fact though, all the other denizens of the rain forest are adapted, sometimes in interesting ways, to their environment.

Among the birds, the toucans (Rhamphastidae), parrots (Psittacidae) and humming-birds (Trochilidae) are probably the best known South American tropical forest representatives. Parrots and toucans have short, broad wings, and are therefore not good flyers – but that is no disadvantage in thick jungle. The humming-birds on the other hand are a constant source of renewed amazement, when with their whirring insect-like flight they suck the nectar out of blossoms with their long, thin beaks. In Portuguese they carry the pretty name "beija-flor" which means "kiss the blossom".

Like the birds, the monkeys also hardly ever touch the ground in the Amazon forest. Many of them have a prehensile tail which serves as a fifth hand when sitting in the branches, or jumping from tree to tree.

The New World apes of South America are somewhat smaller than the Old World monkeys. The smallest is surely the pigmy marmoset *(Callithrix pygmaea)* which weighs only 100 g and without the tail, only reaches a height of 15 cm. The three-toed sloth *(Bradypus tridactylus)* spends his life hanging upside down from the branches of trees, using his hooked-claw extremities. He moves in slow-motion to fool his enemies, can turn his neck through almost

180°, and the parting on his fur is on his belly, the uppermost side of this animal.
The tall trees of the tropical forest are the habitat of a remarkably large number of bats *(Microchiroptera)*. Among these bats is the common vampire *(Desmodus rotundus)* which with its sharp teeth is a much-feared bloodsucker. The tapir *(Tapirus terrestris)* lives in the undergrowth of the rain forest as well as on the banks of the rivers and also the sandbanks and low-lying islands. The tapir is a solitary hoofed animal about a metre high, and twice as long. It is a distant relative of the rhinoceros, as well as of the capybara *(Hydrochoerus hydrochaeris)* which with its 130 cm long body makes it the largest rodent. Also to be found in these regions are reptiles, such as snakes, alligators, and tortoises, or the armadillo (Dasypodidae), a relative of the sloth, not to mention the New World members of the marsupial family, including the cat-sized opossum *(Didelphis)*.
In every storey of the forest, from the floor to the treetops can be found insects, ranging from huge and colourful butterflies, as well as articulated animals such as spiders, scorpions, centipedes, and others. Predatory members of the cat family such as the jaguar *(Panthera onca)*, the ocelot *(Leopardus pardalis)*, the similar but smaller margay cat *(Leopardus wiedi)* as well as the tiger cat *(Leopardus tigrinus)* are at home in the tropical forest, although they are more often to be met on the fringes of the forest, where the puma also lives *(Puma concolor)*.
In the rivers, the ecological niches have also been occupied. Of particular interest, and typical of the Amazon basin is the South American lungfish *(Lepidosiren paradoxa)* and the electric eel *(Electrophorus electricus)* which can deal out electric shocks with its special organs, as well as the predatory arapaima *(Arapaima gigas)* which can grow to 2.5 m in length and weigh 130 kg making it among the largest freshwater fishes in the world. Countless horror stories have been told about the small, up to 30 cm long piranha *(Serrasalmus)*. Some of these species, which have sharp teeth, when attacking in shoals can endanger even large animals such as pigs and cows, not forgetting humans too.
Also worthy of mention are finally the Amazon dol-

6 *The Caracol waterfall at Canela in Rio Grande do Sul. This is a favourite Brazilian holiday area north of Pôrto Alegre, where the Brazilian wine comes from. As along the whole coastal strip, even in the southern states, the mountains are covered in luxuriant vegetation due to the relatively high rainfall throughout the year. This in turn is caused by sea breezes and weather fronts coming up the coast from the south. One of this zone's characteristic trees is the Araucaria pine, of which there are two species in South America:* Araucaria araucana, *found mainly in the Andes of Argentina and Chile, and the* Araucaria angustifolia, *which is endemic to Brazil. It is found in the zone between 20 and 30 degrees latitude South, and mainly at moderately high altitudes. This pine thrives in a moderately humid, but not too warm climate, which is why it is seen only at altitudes of above 400 m above sea level in Rio Grande do Sul, above 600 m in Paraná, and only above 800–1000 m in São Paulo and Minas Gerais. It is easily recognisable even at a distance, its straight trunk standing 25 to 30 m high, and above it umbrella-like, the tufts of broad pine needles. The Araucaria pines are relics of trees found all over the world in earlier times, i.e. in the Mesozoic era. This has been proved by fossil finds in Europe, and even in Greenland. In the picture they can be seen at the top edge, with a few examples just above the waterfall on the left side.*

7

8

7 Torres beach, in Rio Grande do Sul, just south of the border with Santa Catarina. The individual basalt promontories and bays are typical of the whole Rio Grande do Sul coast. Torres itself is a small seaside resort with a few hotels and pensions. It is a popular weekend destination for city dwellers, in particular from Pôrto Alegre. In summer, and sometimes on sunny winter days, the weather is usually inviting enough for a swim in the South Atlantic – if the breakers aren't too high.

8 The Feradura valley near Canela is typical of the low mountain landscape north of Pôrto Alegre in Rio Grande do Sul. Geologically, this is a canyon formed by more or less horizontal layers of harder and softer rock. Terraces have resulted in the places where the rock is soft, and they are now partially under cultivation.

9 At Florianópolis, the capital of Santa Catarina, the beach is composed of crystalline rocks. The rounded shapes of the granite and gneiss are typical of the weathering that occurs in a subtropical climate.

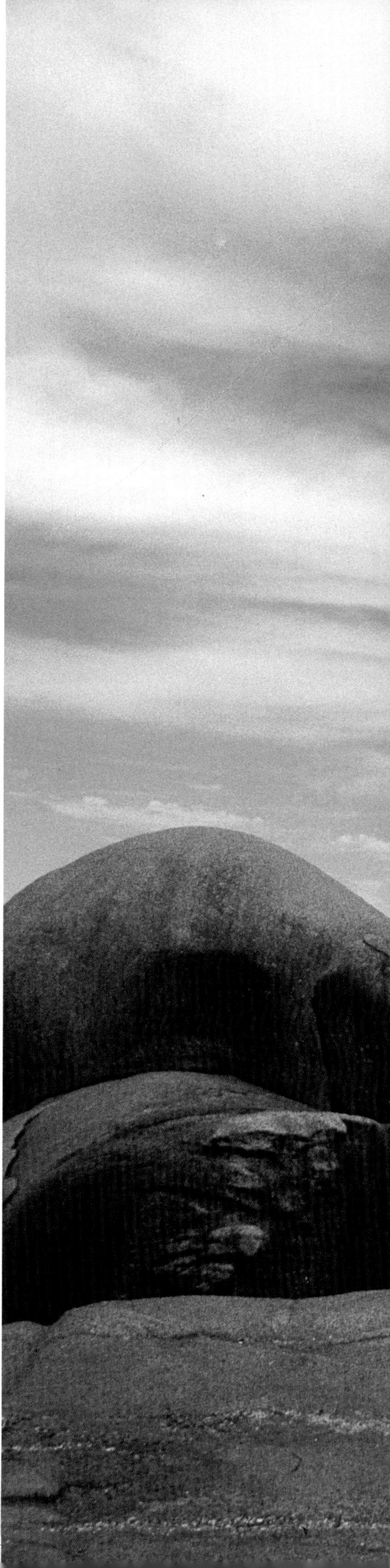
9

10 ◁ *Vila Velha is, after the Iguaçu Falls, the second sight of geographical interest in Paraná. It is the remains of a Mesozoic sandstone layer that has been weathered by water and wind. Its strange shape rises up above the low undulations to a height of some 10 m. Vila Velha (old town in English) is situated near Ponta Grossa, some 100 km west of Curitiba on the Paraná highlands, and it is an excursion site visited by countless people from far and near who think they can make out all kinds of shapes among these rocks.*

11 *The organ pipe cactus or "mandacaru" in the Sertão of Northeast Brazil (photo taken in Pernambuco) is typical of the dry thorny woodland to be found in the region, and known as Caatinga. There are different kinds of cactus in the Caatinga, but they all share the ability to store large water reserves in their trunks or branches. The frequently found spikes are leaves, which have been transformed, leading to a reduction in the surface area, and consequently less water loss by evaporation, an important factor in a dry season lasting eight to ten months of the year. The functions of the leaves (photosynthesis, respiration) are taken over by the green trunk. The Caatinga is often a veritable thicket of small trees and bushes, or on the other hand, in certain areas because of a lack of undergrowth it becomes quite sparse. This photograph was taken after one of the few rainy periods, at a time when the Caatinga for once becomes green in colour. Normally it is a mixture of yellow to brown shades, with hardly a green blade of grass or leaf to be seen over large distances.*

12 *The mouth of the Amazon is one vast, flat, primeval landscape, made up of meandering tributaries, sandbanks, and countless large and small tree-covered islands, the largest of which is Marajó, with an area a little larger than Switzerland. Its population is engaged in a primitive form of farming and livestock breeding, as far as this is permitted by the differences in river level and tides. Large tracts of Marajó, especially in the West, are covered in tropical forest which is periodically or permanently inundated, i.e. the tree trunks are in the water always or some of the time. This form of vegetation is called "Mata de Várzea" (Várzea is periodically flooded land), or "Mata de Igapó" (permanently submerged land) in Brazil. These two types of land should not be confused with the mangrove belt found in the east of Marajó, which is already in brackish water.*

phin *(Inia geoffrensis geoffrensis)*, a river dolphin species, and the manatee *(Trichecus inunguis)*. These were both originally sea mammals who later adapted to life in a large freshwater area. Countless plant and animal species of Brazil are still not known or not researched by man. This is above all true of insects. Some animal species are threatened by extinction, for instance the giant armadillo *(Priodontes giganteus)*, various turtle species which are hunted, and the manatee which is regarded as a valuable catch. Nowadays however, the value of the manatee has been appreciated because it keeps the waterways free of obstructing underwater growths.

Two other forms of tropical forest, only differing slightly from the equatorial forest of the Amazon, can be found in Brazil. They are situated further south and southeast in the alternating humidity of the tropics where it is humid enough again for forest vegetation to succeed. One is the tropical coastal forest which forms a narrow strip from Rio Grande do Norte to Santa Catarina in the south, and everywhere covers the slopes of the coastal range. Here the convection currents from the sea lead to rain and frequent fog. Of note is the reduced number of tree species in comparison with the equatorial forest, as well as the shorter trees (25–30 m), although with correspondingly thicker trunks for the most part. The same is true for the tropical forest in the interior of the southeast in the states of Espírito Santo, Minas Gerais, and São Paulo. This forest can survive short droughts successfully, and is remarkable for, among other things, the widespread tree ferns. This is a form of vegetation which more than any other in Brazil has been subjected to decimation, being prevalent near the large cities where large surfaces have been turned into arable land, and where most of the wood has been cut down for heating or building purposes.

Besides the forests there is another widespread form of vegetation in Brazil, a form of savanna known as Cerrado, which extends from the Mato Grosso do Sul through central Brazil right down to Minas Gerais and Maranhão in the south. In the interior of northeastern Brazil grows the even drier Caatinga woodland.

Cerrado is mostly a low, dry woodland with trees

usually 4–7 m high, often with short, gnarled branches. The ground is covered with grass, 30–50 cm in height. In many places the earth is bare. During the dry season the grass withers completely and feeds the not infrequent bush fires. As well as trees, many species of bush and scrub grow in the Cerrado, and in contrast to the trees with their deep roots, the bushes lose their leaves in the dry season, as protection against drying out and all too great water loss through evaporation, because they no longer reach the water table. Large stretches of grassland are inexistent or rare, which is why the Cerrado cannot properly be described as savanna. Depending on the region, the winter dry season lasts from 2 to 6 months. In addition, because of varying conditions, the Cerrado looks different in every region. As well as mammals there are many birds, reptiles, and insects there. The termites *(Isoptera)* whose high, hard heaps are destroyed by that very old species of South American mammal, the giant anteater *(Mymecophaga tridactyla)*, are typical inhabitants of the central Brazilian Cerrado. Close relations of the giant anteater are the various armadillo species who are at home not only in the rain forest but also in the Cerrado and the Pampas. Snakes, scorpions, and bird spiders have their habitat in the Cerrado too, and in the southwest lives the nandu *(Rhea americana)*, a bird related to the African ostrich. Also to be found in the Cerrado are rodents, foxes, and dog-like animals such as the maned wolf *(Chrysocyon brachyurus)* as well as hares. In the rivers, the same species are to be found as in the Amazon. Finally, the jaguar as well as the puma can be seen here, although the water-loving jaguar stays away from pronounced drought zones. The jaguar is one of the most dangerous animals in the region, preying as he does on fish, and rodents, right up to cattle and horses. After the tiger and lion of the Old World, the jaguar is the third-largest of the cats' family *(Felidae)*. With his weight of up to 80 kg and his length of 185 cm he appears to be much more massive and heavy than the leopard, whom he otherwise resembles very closely. Among the hoofed animals can be seen various species of American deer – the marsh deer, the pampas deer, and the red brocket – and again the lowland tapir, and the peccaris *(Tayassu)* including the species collared peccari and white-lipped peccari. Although similar in appearence to wild boar, the peccaris are anatomically closer to the ruminants.

In the Sertão in the hinterland of the Brazilian northeast the Caatinga is the dominating feature of the landscape. It is a thorny scrub woodland well adapted to the extreme climatic conditions (6–10 months dry season). The Caatinga is usually a copse of little trees and bushes, in other places, lack of undergrowth can turn it into almost a thornbush desert. Characteristic of this form of vegetation are the stunted, gnarled trees which all cast off their leaves in the dry season, and which additionally often have special organs to store water. The majority only produce small leaves, or in their place just thorns. It is only thanks to this multiplicity of adaptive measures that they can survive such long periods of drought. Once rain starts to fall again, even the Caatinga becomes green again for a short while and comes into bloom. Naturally the fauna here is poorer than in the Cerrado, but also more specialised. The Caatinga is largely inhabited by insects and other articulated animals as well as reptiles (snakes and lizards) and various bird species.

In the east, the Caatinga is bordered by a narrow strip of forest – a dry forest similar to the Caatinga – but with rather higher-growing trees, which can be explained by the proximity of the sea, which results in more rainfall. But even this forest loses all its foliage in the dry season.

In the actual subtropical south of Brazil, from São Paulo to Rio Grande do Sul, there is subtropical forest, already described above, as well as partly extensive stands of araucaria or Paraná pine, and also grasslands (Campos) which go over into the Pampas of Uruguay and Argentina, still further south. The creation of these Campos, to be found mainly on the plateaus of Paraná, and the lowland plains of Rio Grande do Sul, is the subject of research, but so far without any hard and fast answers, so that it remains an open question if in fact the Campos are the result of human hand. A distinction is made between the so-called Campos limpos, the pure grasslands, and the Campos sujos (literally the "sullied grasslands", that is grass interspersed with scrub and small trees). In the extreme southwest of Brazil are the marshlands of the Rio Paraguay, the Pantanal. This is flood plain that comes under water every year, and is well known for its varied animal life, similar in many respects to that of the Amazon, with highly interesting bird and reptile species and rare fishes and mammals.

The Northeast

The Brazilian northeast, made up of the federal states Maranhão, Piauí, Ceará, Rio Grande do Norte, Paraíba, Pernambuco, Alagoas, Sergipe, and Bahia, with a surface area of 1.5 million km^2, and 36 million inhabitants (1980) is the real problem area of the country, and is often referred to as the poorhouse of Brazil. A large part of the population lives in extremely marginal circumstances, despite the fact that the economic underdevelopment has been combatted for years by every possible means. One of the two main problems is without a doubt still the drought, which at irregular intervals returns above all to the interior of the country, destroying the crops, killing the cattle, and forcing the local population to emigrate. Thus from time to time, and at odd intervals, whole waves of emigrants reach the coast as well as the southeast of Brazil, and above all the major cities of Rio de Janeiro and São Paulo. This of course does not solve the problem, it merely transfers it. Half of the surface area of the northeast belongs to the semi-arid zone of the Sertão, where rainfall is erratic and sparse. Yet 35% of the total population of the nine states lives there.

Drought and Landscape Structure As already mentioned, drought is a phenomenon which recurs with a certain regularity, but which can hardly be predicted because it depends not only on the global air circulation in the southern hemisphere, but also on

Vegetation

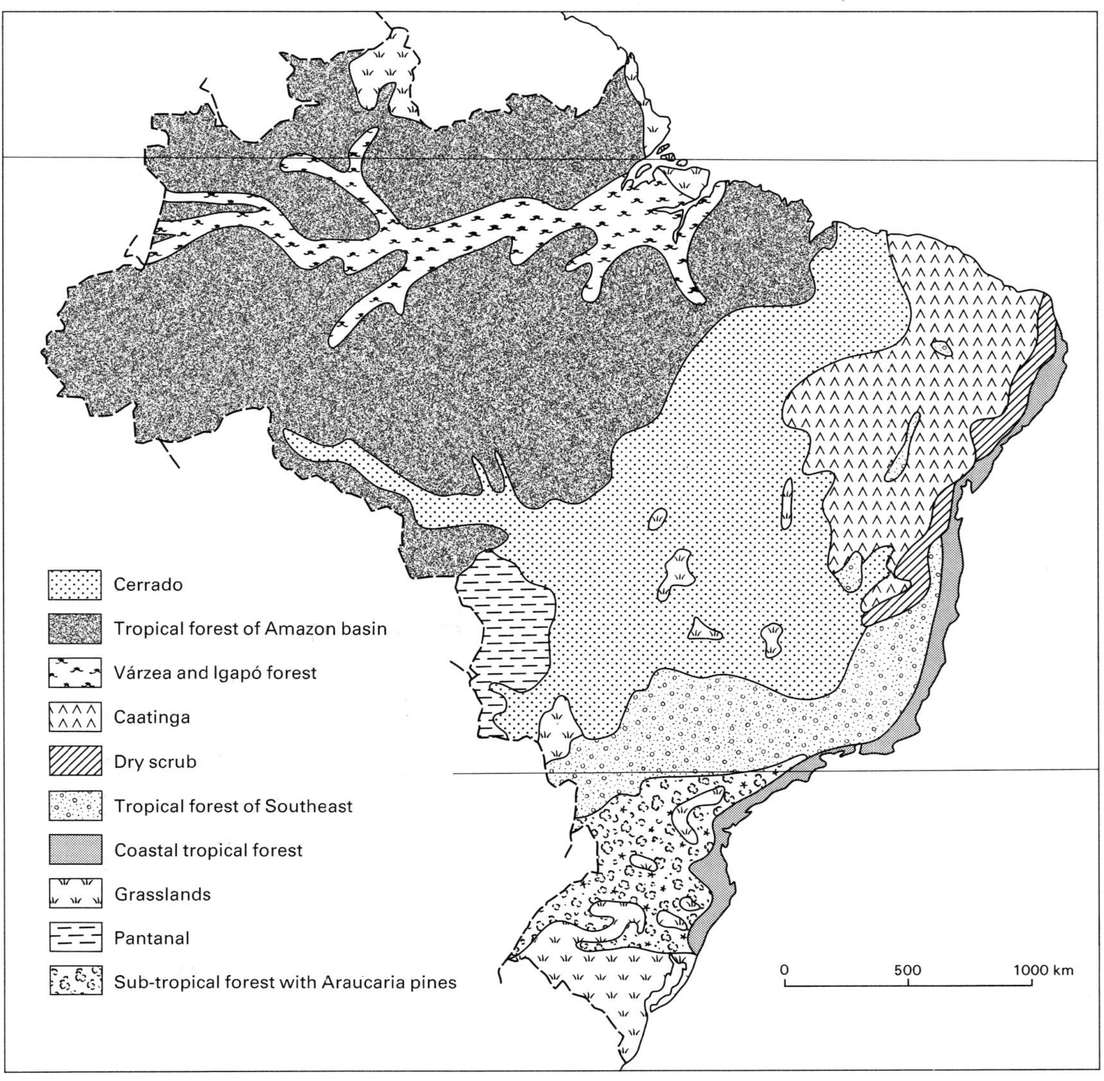

Comparison of Vegetation in Northeast			
	Sertão	*Agreste*	*Zona da Mata*
Precipitation	300–1000 mm	1000–1500 mm	1500–2000 mm
Natural vegetation	Caatinga	Caatinga/ jungle	tropical coastal forest
Agriculture	extensive cattle rearing cultivation just for own use	cotton, maize, black beans, tobacco, coffee, cattle, sugar cane	sugar cane, cocoa in South Bahia, rubber, coconut palms
Industry	little	little	sugar refineries, textiles, processing of agricultural products
Population density	low	high	high, big towns

weather developments right up to the North Atlantic. There have been more than enough efforts in the past to predict droughts, but as yet no reliable methods have been found. Even if such a means could one day be found, it would not change all that much as concerns a drought or its consequences. It is known that, in principle, a drought comes to pass in that the whole of norhteastern Brazil lies for most of the year in an airstream which flows from the almost stationary high pressure zone of the South Atlantic in the form of a southeasterly trade wind, which because it increases in warmth all the time, takes up little humidity in its lower layers. It arrives at the South American continent as an only moderately humid mass. The lowest and most humid layers cause rapid precipitation over only the relatively narrow coastal strip, while the upper, dry levels reach the interior, with only mountain areas receiving minor precipitation. The rest of the land remains dry. In summer, and in the southern hemisphere that means January and February, the situation changes normally in that the equatorial low pressure zone, which moves south when the sun is highest over the equator, reaches the interior of the northeast and brings rain. This applies from the north down to about Pernambuco or north Bahia. But this southern flow is dependent on the global air circulation and differs in size from year to year. If the air mass does not shift sufficiently southwards, this means drought for the interior of the northeast.

Such climatic conditions have resulted in a natural structuring of the landscapes in the northeast. Their differences are largely due to climate and vegetation, but also in part to the relief. The zone along the coast, which enjoys profuse rainfall is called the Zona da Mata. Further inland there is a parallel running strip, some 50–100 km wide, the Agreste, which forms the transition to the semi-arid Sertão in the interior. In the north, however, the Sertão reaches to the coast.

The Zona da Mata stretches from Rio Grande del Norte till Bahia, it has yearly rainfall between 150 and 200 cm, and was previously an area of tropical rain forest. In colonial times the forest was largely cleared to make room for sugar cane plantations. On huge Latifundia blacks planted sugar cane which was afterwards refined in simple factories. The sugar was exported mainly to Europe. At the same time the Sertão developed into a cattle-breeding country, and supplied the coastal strip with meat and leather.

The transitional zone, the Agreste, has remained a transit route and then as now produces food crops such as maize, cassava and black beans. The picture that the northeast presents today has only partially changed since colonial times, and it still carries many of its original structure.

On the Rio São Francisco The longest and most abundant river of northeastern Brazil, the Rio São Francisco, rises in the highlands of Minas Gerais near Belo Horizonte. From there it flows to the north, through the states of Minas Gerais and Bahia, and after a sweeping bend to the East on the border between Alagoas and Sergipe, it runs its course into the Atlantic ocean. The rise of the automobile has meant that the river has largely lost its original role as an important waterway between the northeast and the south. Its title as "Rio da Integração Nacional" is also no longer as apposite as in the first half of this century. Nevertheless the river is now more than ever in the limelight, above all because of its abundant hydroelectric potential. This has been under development since the 1950s. A major role is played by the Paulo Afonso power station near the spot where the three states Alagoas, Per-

Northeast Brazil: Vegetation and Drought Frequency

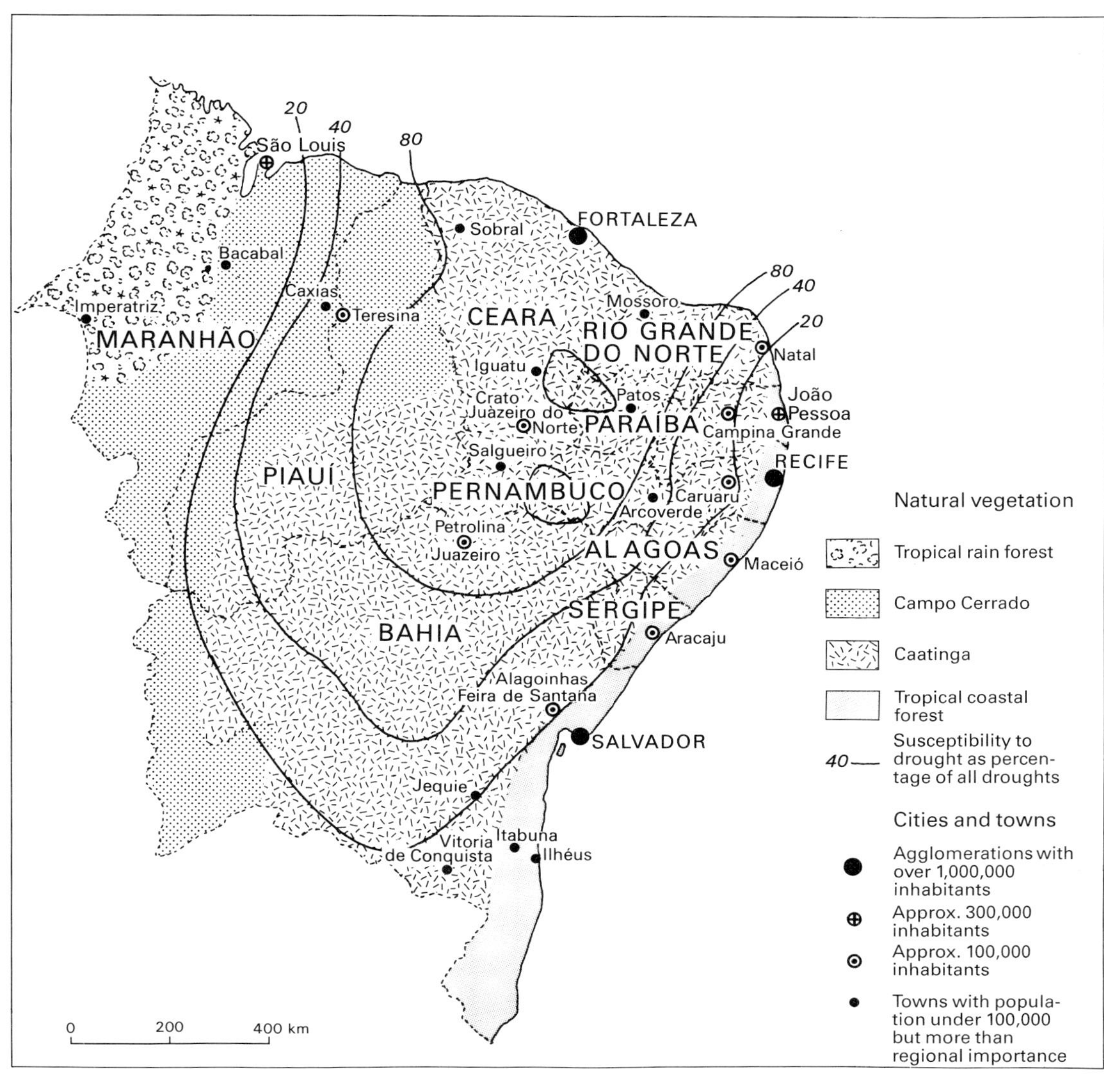

nambuco, and Bahia meet. Here the river drops 100 m into a narrow gorge, and efforts to harness this energy with more and more power stations have never ceased till the present day. Another highly important environmental change which occurred in the latter half of the 1970s was the construction of the Sobradinho dam, upriver from the twin cities of Juazeiro/Petrolina.

The 13 km wide earth dam was built principally to act as a water regulator for the Paulo Afonso power station in order to ensure an optimum head of water for the turbines, but it will also be used to generate electricity itself. Above Sobradinho, a lake has been created with an area of 4,200 km^2, 350 km long, and for which 100,000 inhabitants had to make way. The electricity company apportioned replacement plots of land, and built new settlements. But this solution did not satisfy everyone, as no real replacement for lost homes could be found. The Três Marias power station lies on the upper reaches of the Rio São Francisco, about half way between Belo Horizonte and Brasília.

The dry banks of the river São Francisco are part of a wide landscape, which despite the blue sky and its white cumulus clouds is monotonous. The flat brown countryside, overgrown with Caatinga, usually reaches down to the river. The distant horizon is commanded by individual mountain ridges with steep escarpments. The riverbanks are sparsely populated, villages and towns few and far between. The few small farmers in the area primitively subsist by growing maize, cassava and sweet potatoes, and perhaps by a little cattle husbandry or fishing. It is very rare for a larger plot of land to be irrigated by river water. Most planters lack the money for a motor pump.

The population lives in small, thatched mud huts, and are hardly ever owners of the land they cultivate. The few central settlements such as Xique-Xique, Ibotirama, or Januária have little to offer, and consist merely of a dozen or two houses, a church, a few shops with not much to sell and a number of bars. These places are all "at the end of the world", and can mostly only be reached by boat, or at best by bad roads which become impassable in the rainy season.

Ships are by far the cheapest means of transport, and so people will wait for hours on the banks of a river, until one of the old-fashioned Gaiolas (which means birdcage) comes along and picks them up. These ships are called Gaiolas because these are veteran sternwheelers of the kind that used to ply the Mississippi. Three of them can still be seen on the Rio São Francisco where they connect the Sobradinho dam in Bahia and Pirapora. Downstream, that is to the north, the 1,300 km run takes six days, upstream ten or eleven days. The timetable merely notes the day and hour of departure, afterwards timekeeping depends on factors such as the river level, the number of wayside stops, and how much cargo has to be laden. A not to be underestimated factor is how often the boat runs aground on sandbanks, and how much time has to be spent getting it afloat again. At regular intervals, firewood has to be taken onboard. This has resulted in the fifty years of shipping on the São Francisco river in a major denuding of the forests. The problematical aspects of this plundering of nature have been brought to people's awareness, without however anything being undertaken against further misuse of resources.

Year for year, thousands of youngsters migrate from the São Francisco area, as indeed from all of the Sertão, to the big cities on the northeast coast, or to the southeast, to Rio de Janeiro and São Paulo. Lacking education, they rarely find work, and end up in the Favelas, or slums, having failed to measure up to the requirements of big city life.

Agricultural Structure The main feature of the agricultural structure of the northeast is the unsymmetrical distribution of land ownership, which must be seen as a result of earlier colonial conditions. Thus in the Zona da Mata extensively cultivated large farms, where sugar cane, but also cotton and other products are grown, dominate the picture. In the Agreste on the other hand, there is dense agricultural population, but almost exclusively the smallest possible smallholdings. In the Sertão, both variants are represented, although the small subsistence farmers tend to live in the somewhat more humid vicinity of the river plains. Both forms of landholding, Latifúndio and Minifúndio are the main obstacles to successful agricultural development. The large farms of the Brazilian northeast are characterised by their absentee landlords who often live in the cities, and merely cash in the takings, which are usually ample enough to discourage any thought of making structural improvements to farms or plantations. This implies very extensive use of land. Where even the best quality soils are often not properly used, there is also no incentive to reward the efforts of the badly-paid farm workers. In addition the soil is rapidly exhausted by monocultural planting, and it is rare for anything to be done about this.

But there are also problems inherent in the Minifúndio, or smallholdings, even though the self-interest of the owner or tenant is very much in evidence. For one thing, the Minifundiários, or owners of smallholdings suffer from a chronic shortage of funds. The majority of the agricultural population in the northeast earns less than the government set minimum income. This means that no one can save, and in fact this is all the more difficult due to the high inflation rate in the past. Investment in smallholdings is therefore out of the question. This is one reason why revenue is poor and the economy is stagnating. There are no funds available for any technical improvements, and even the construction of irrigation canals or the purchase of better seeds is often too expensive. In many places the soils are exhausted, most smallholders cannot afford fertiliser, and classical means such as dung and sewage are not available because hardly any cattle are kept on these small farms. Additional deleterious factors are the rudimentary farming methods, with little sign of rationalisation or division of labour, and the lack of knowledge regarding efficient production.

During the colonial era practically only Latifúndio or large farms existed. Since then, the number of

Minifúndio or smallholdings has constantly increased, a trend which is apparent to the present day. Even more rapid has been the growth in numbers of those employed or partially employed on these farms – a reflection of the high birth-rate that is characteristic for the northeast.
No agrarian reform has been carried out yet in Brazil. It has always failed because of the influence of the large landowners, worried by the thought of losing their property. Many agricultural experts (not large landowners!) see the real solution for the above described problems more in the amalgamation of the smallest plots of land into co-operatives or similar structures, to be led by trained workers, rather than in the breaking up of the Latifúndio into unworkably small farm settlements.
About one third of the surface area of the northeast is used agriculturally. 27% is tilled, 53% is pasture, and 20% for crops such as oil palms. Two thirds of the agricultural produce from the northeast is made up of field crops, a quarter from cattle breeding, and the rest from collective crops and forestry. Some 34% of all farms in the northeast have an area of less than 2 ha, a further 44% are between 2 and 20 ha in size, but all these properties only account for 10% of the agricultural land. In the light of such a property distribution it is hardly surprising that a very large section of the population of the northeast lives in abject poverty, not only on the urban fringes, but also in the Minifúndio area. According to a study carried out by the University of Pernambuco between 1972 and 1974 in Ribeirão community in the state of Pernambuco, the average daily calory intake per capita was only 1,350, whereas the minimum requirement in this climate would be 2,300 calories. There was a similar situation with regard to protein: daily requirement 60 g, actual intake 17.5 g. This chronic undernourishment leads to increased susceptibility to illness, deficiency diseases, reduced physical and mental capacity, increased child mortality and other disadvantages.
The Sudene In order to tackle the enormous problems of underdevelopment, the Brazilian government in 1959 set up the Sudene (Superintendência do Desenvolvimento do Nordeste). Reporting directly to the Federal government in Brasilia, it is the state planning body for the development of the northeast, that means the nine northeastern states, plus part of the northeastern part of Minas Gerais. Its founding by President Kubitschek (the famous constructor of Brasília) was a signal for more attention being paid to the interior of the country and the northeast. The Director of Sudene de facto had the rank of Minister, and had corresponding powers. At the beginning – and this is basically still the case today – planning strategy foresaw emphasis on the development of agriculture and industry, as well as the creation of the necessary infrastructure. In agriculture, the aim was to increase productivity in the humid coastal zones by means of improved agricultural methods, and in the hinterland large agro-industrial enterprises were principally designed to replace the primitive subsistence economy. The already existing or newly-created redundant farmworkers were to be used to cultivate virgin territory in the neighbouring states of Maranhão and Goiás. New employment was also to be created in industry, mainly in sectors catering for local needs, so that dependency on imports from the southeast could be reduced. Foreseen above all were steel, cement, and fertiliser works.
However, from the very start, Sudene was confronted by what later turned out to be an apparently insoluble dilemma: on the one hand far-reaching and irrevocable reforms were necessary to reorganise the region, while at the same time there still existed an institutional framework which prevented such reforms, for example the already mentioned property distribution (Latifúndio–Minifúndio), the concentration of power in the hands of the big landowners, the low educational level of the large mass of the poor, including a high proportion of illiterates. This unpropitious set of circumstances was certainly recognised by the proper authorities, but could not be changed overnight. In addition, the Sudene staff, often clever, progressive young academics, especially in the beginning tried to move too fast and offended the influential, and still often feudalistically-minded big landowners. Under these circumstances Sudene soon transferred its energies to politically uncontroversial, or less disputed projects. These were to be found in reorganisation of the infrastructure and in the mining of natural resources. In second place came efforts to industrialise, while

re-structuring agriculture by for instance founding co-operatives, or building irrigation schemes came as last priority.
After the military seized power in 1964, the powers of Sudene were continually curtailed, until it ultimately was degraded into becoming the mere executor of Brasília's plans for the northeast. Sudene's funds were also cut piecemeal, because the available finances were needed for other ambitious projects – from the late sixties onwards principally for the Transamazônica.
But the Sudene still plays a major role in the development of the northeast. Its headquarters are in a large building on the outskirts of Recife. Some 2,000 people, a third of them graduates, work there on development plans for the northeast. Much has already been achieved since the founding of the body, much of it probably only possible thanks to Sudene's efforts. The first task was to carry out basic research into the natural conditions and surroundings of the northeast, till then little or nothing was known about the vast region. In co-operation with the national universities the region was carefully mapped, and meteorological, climatological and geological data collected. This was followed by studies of the vegetation, the water table, and many other facets. Finally, the development of the infrastructure was taken in hand, roads were planned, built, and surfaced, ports enlarged, and the telecommunications system improved. Of note is the expansion of hydro-electric power, mainly on the Rio São Francisco, where the Paulo Afonso power station started generating in 1955, and since then has repeatedly been extended so that output rose from 0.6 million kW in 1971 to 4 million kW in 1980. Further hydroelectric works are under construction on the Rio São Francisco, and another large power station has been in operation since the 70s at Boa Esperança on the Rio Parnaíba. This supplies mainly Maranhão and Piauí states. The transregional electricity grid, with a length of several tens of thousands of kilometres was also largely planned and built by Sudene.
The difficulty of industrial development in the northeast is best illustrated by the example of Aratu, a planned industrial town on the periphery of Salvador (Bahia). This case is a model of its kind. Preparation of the 400 km^2 site began already in 1966. The state supplied the necessary infrastructure for the future industrial estate, that is roads, port facilities, telephone system, electricity and water supply, as well as waste-water clearance and so on. By offering tax incentives the state tried to induce private enterprises to invest in Aratu under these best possible terms. Success was at hand: up to the present, 100 industrial firms have settled in Aratu. They in turn have invested no less than eight thousand million Cruzeiros, and what is even more important for the northeast, created employment for 27,000 people.
The tax incentives for investment activity are in detail rather complicated, but essentially it means that an enterprise which is already domiciled in Brazil can opt to withhold a certain percentage of the tax payable on profits, and invest this in a subsidiary in the northeast, for example in Aratu. This basically amounts to a state subsidy to build new industries. Such a subsidiary company in Aratu would not have to pay taxes on its profits for the first few years, and there are also massive reductions on the tariffs normally payable on imported goods. This has awoken the interest of many companies in the south, and it is understandable that their desire to invest in the northeast is motivated less by the development of the northeast than by the self-interest of the company. Due to widespread entrepreneurial scepticism with regard to the long-term economic prospects of the northeast, investment has been confined mainly to those industrial sectors where there is a quick return, that is in a matter of a few years. Few have made long-term plans, so that it has been left to the Brazilian state to fill this gap. This applies above all to the refinery and petrochemical sector, where local resources, that is crude oil and natural gas from Bahia and Sergipe are processed (a large petrochemical complex is under construction in Camaçari, not far from Aratu). The iron and steel industry is also being developed with state aid. Apart from the financial incentives, firms setting up in Aratu also profit from the large cheap labour force, which however is untrained and unskilled. This means that one either trains people on site before starting production, or one has to import skilled workers and above all, the chief engineers and

13 Heliconia *blossoms, which belong to the Musaceae species, whose best known representatives are the banana, originally from Southeast Asia,* Musa textilis, *from which manila hemp is produced, and also the colourful bird-of-paradise flower,* Strelitzia.

14 ▷ *Fruit of the annatto tree* (Bixa orellana). *The Urucum seeds from this plant are used by the Indians to make the red paint with which they paint their bodies, on the one hand for decorative effect, but also to keep insects at bay.*

15

16

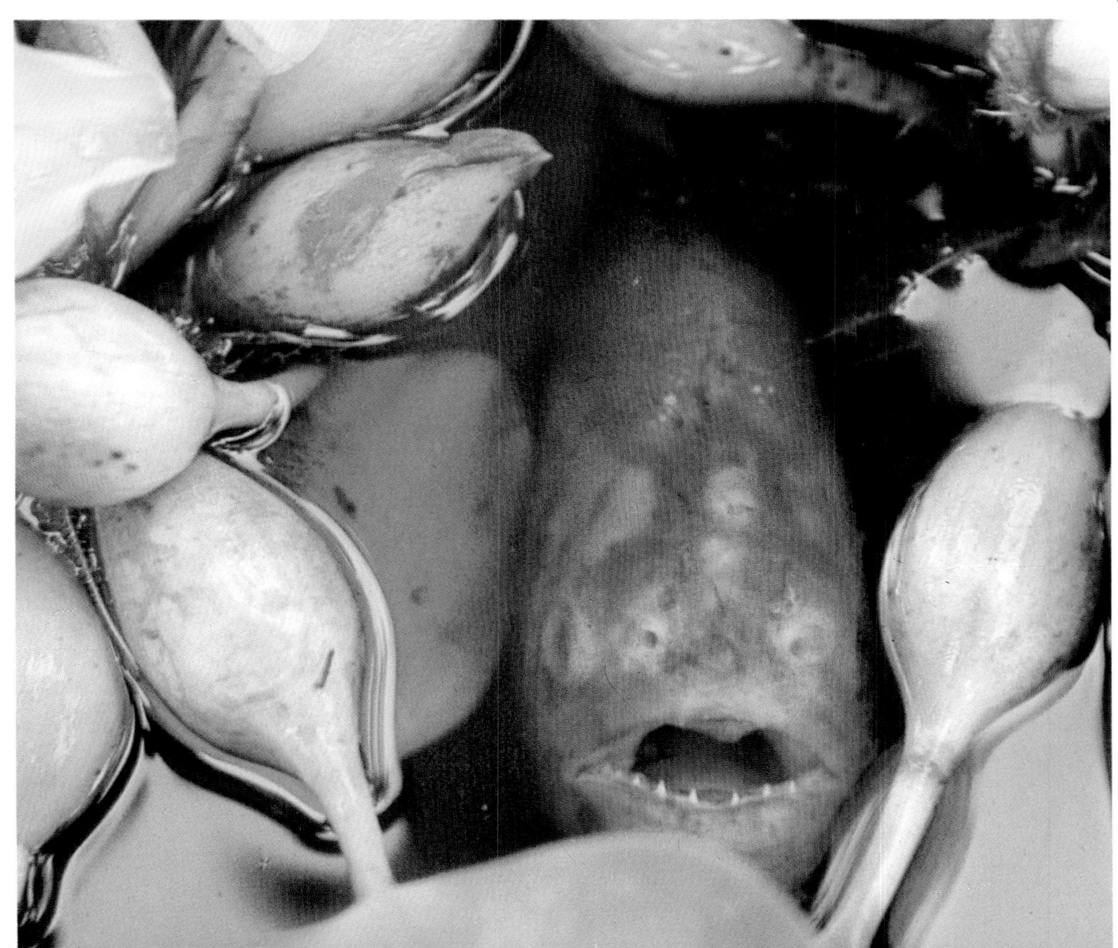

15 *A tree, typical of many tall species growing in tropical rain forests, with buttressed roots, which increase their stability. This is not only necessary because of their great height, but also because of their shallow roots, as the nutrients are only to be found in a thin layer near the surface. These giant trees are additionally anchored by lianas and creepers linking them to other trees.*

16 *Black caimans are mostly to be found in the rivers and swamps of the Amazon, and in the Pantanal of the Mato Grosso do Sul.*

17 *There are various kinds of piranha fish – from just a few centimetres in length right up to 30 cm – they are found in the Amazon and are notorious for their razor-sharp teeth.*

18

18 *The sloth (two-toed sloth in picture), belongs together with the ant-eater and the armadillo to the family of edentates. It spends its life, seemingly motionless, clinging to the branches of trees, and moving very slowly if at all. It thus remains virtually unnoticed by its enemies. Its fur falls "in reverse", i.e. from the belly to the middle of its back, so that raindrops can drain off evenly when it is hanging in typical pose on a branch.*

19 *The lowland tapir, belonging to the odd-toed ungulates and thus related to the horse and rhinoceros, is a peaceful vegetarian whose habitat is usually in or near water, to which he always retreats in case of danger. With a weight of 200 kg, and a shoulder height of approximately 1 m, the tapir is one of the largest mammals to be found in South America.*

20 *Most of the Amazon birds live in the leafy roofs of the trees, but some species like the great white egret wade around in the shallow waters of the rivers, snapping at fish near the surface with their sharp bills.*

19

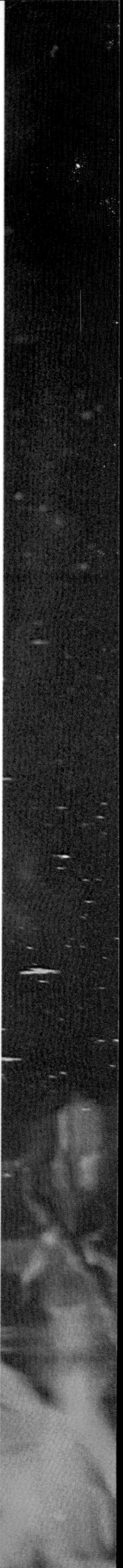

20

21 Parrots are often regarded as typical examples of South American bird-life, even though they occur on nearly all the other continents. Among the species to be seen in the Amazon forests (e.g. the blunt-tailed parrots) are the aras, which are remarkable for their size (a scarlet macaw in the photo). They are clumsy fliers, which does not really matter in the dense forests, because they are all the stronger climbers, using their characteristic curved beak as a sort of "third leg" with which to hold on to branches. In addition they use their beaks to crack the hardest of nuts, whose shells they have previously filed down.

technicians from the southeast of Brazil. This latter procedure is not desired, because the main aim is to find employment for the local population. Another unintentional development has been that many Nordestinos, or northeasterners, once they have been trained in a factory in Aratu are subsequently attracted by the higher wages and more comfortable life in the southeast and migrate there, either directly, or after being hired by a company from the area. This despite the fact that they have better conditions in the Aratu housing estates than in the middle-class quarters, or even the Favelas of Rio de Janeiro or São Paulo, the main centres of attraction.

Many of the new plants in Aratu are to a high degree automated, in order to be competitive with the South or on export markets. This means that little new employment is created, and what there is, is only open to specialists. Other firms make use of the development incentives merely to move certain simple production processes from the southeast to Salvador, and profiting from tax relief and cheap labour, carrying out labour-intensive procedures, only to assemble the final product in the southeast. This was hardly the aim of the founders of Aratu, and contributes little to a successful industrial structure.

Taken as a whole, Aratu's role in the development of the northeast has not been very big. This is particularly true when one considers that many of the already existing industries in the northeast, often obsolete, but still functioning, ran into difficulties through competition from Aratu, and were forced to make workers redundant. Unemployment remains high in the northeast and the attraction of Aratu has been relatively small. Many entrepreneurs take the view that increased development of agriculture is the only way to raise the standard of living in the whole northeast of Brazil. Aratu is only one example, and industrialisation is making progress in other parts of the northeast. Not in such major industrial complexes, but everywhere on the periphery of the larger cities, usually the state capitals. Besides Salvador, this is the case above all in Recife and Fortaleza, which however have the disadvantage of being situated even further away from the industrial centres of the southeast. The problems are pretty well the same everywhere.

Sudene's greatest difficulties no doubt concerned the development of agriculture. As already mentioned, a major change in land ownership was impossible for political reasons, and so efforts were concentrated on simple technical aid. Together with the FAO, Sudene launched a pioneering programme in the 1960s in Bebedouro, not far from Petrolina in Pernambuco state. Today one can see on the north bank of the Rio São Francisco an agricultural co-operative producing fruit and vegetables on irrigated soil. It can serve as a model for further such projects. Today it is an ordinary, financially largely autonomous co-operative receiving moderate support from the Organisation for the Development of the São Francisco River Valley (Companhia de Desenvolvimento do Vale do Rio São Francisco CODEVASF). Originally it was founded by Sudene. About 100 families cultivate the 850 ha of land, and when one speaks to the planters, one gets the impression they are happy with their lot. To be sure they have to work hard, but the living they earn is in proportion to their input. The co-operative's management buys in the seeds, fertiliser, pesticide, tools, and so on, for all the members. Every farmer is free to plant whichever crops he wishes, as long as this is technically possible, and by and large in conformity with market conditions. After harvesting, it is again the co-operative management which takes over the produce – mainly melons, grapes, bananas, tomatoes, maize, beans, onions, and peppers, and brings them to market, even as far afield as Rio and São Paulo. After costs have been deducted, every farmer receives the profits from his own production.

Those seeking membership of the co-operative, which is not being further expanded, had to show evidence of certain basic knowledge of irrigation farming, and had to participate in a three-month course encompassing theory and practice. Having passed the test, the farmer was accepted into the co-operative, and apportioned 8–12 ha of land, plus a small house in one of the settlements. All the land belongs to the co-operative, and is only lent to the members. Should the farmer leave the co-operative, he receives no recompense. Planters who neglect their fields can be expelled from the co-operative, but this hardly ever happens. The irrigation water is pumped out of the nearby river into the concrete-lined main distribution channels, and gravity takes it through smaller ducts into the fields, whose green colour is in agreeable contrast to the perennial brown-yellow of the Caatinga.

Along the whole of the Rio São Francisco there are some one dozen irrigation systems in various stages of planning or construction. This does not include several giant projects in the vicinity of the lake formed by the Três Marias dam, and Sobradinho where large areas have been made fertile for sugar cane. Unfortunately such development projects, and in particular those serving small farmers which are the most useful, are far less spectacular and therefore less urgent for the government than prestige schemes to open up the Amazon basin, such as the building of the Transamazônica.

Besides a few projects of this kind, Sudene from the very beginning supported the improvement of agricultural infrastructure – by building wells, or by raising the educational and training level of the simple countrypeople. It also carried out many social reforms, and in the public health field it did much to fight diseases such as malaria, typhus, and yellow fever.

The question whether Sudene has achieved its original objectives cannot simply be answered by a yes or no. It all depends on the standpoint of the observer. Undoubtedly much was done which without this body would never have been tackled. On the other hand, critics often say that Sudene's activities were just a drop in the ocean, and that only a tiny minority of the people have benefited from its work. Accusations have been made regarding water supplies, and sewage disposal, above all in the cities, where conditions are still poor. Child mortality, at 120 per 1000 is still too high, and then as now, large sections of the population suffer from hunger and malnutrition. Furthermore there are still too many unemployed and short-time workers, despite the increasing gross national product. The irrigation schemes, it is said, are over a too small area, and the average income of much of the population is too low. The list could be continued.

The northeast is confronted by enormous problems which cannot be solved in a matter of years, and not even within 20 years. Whether the political course taken is the correct one will always be open to doubts, especially when one sees that every drought brings the same recurring problems. Food for thought is also present in the fact that not even the beginnings of a moderate land reform are in sight, and that Brazil's population policy is hardly designed to solve any difficulties, a situation which can only be reversed if an attempt is made to stem the high birth rate.

The Southeast, South, and Middle West

The southeast, the south, and to a lesser extent, the middle west of Brazil are more developed than the regions further north.

The Southeast Region This includes in an area of 924,000 km^2 the federal states of Espírito Santo, Minas Gerais, Rio de Janeiro, and São Paulo. Over 40% of the country's population lives here, and 60% of the national income is generated here. But even though the region forms the economic and cultural centre of Brazil, there are still vast differences between highly-developed industrial zones and backward areas similar to the states of the northeast. On the one hand there are the prosperous big city regions of São Paulo and Rio de Janeiro, as well as the rapidly growing industrial city of Belo Horizonte. And at the other end of the scale we find practically all of the state of Espírito Santo, several remote areas of Minas Gerais, and the sugar cane region of Campos, northeast of Rio.

Minas Gerais – already the name of the state (it means "general mines" or more freely "mines of all kinds") indicates the richness of the resources in its soil. The whole history of this mountainous landlocked state is linked with mining. Settlement started at the beginning of the 18th century with the discovery of gold in the extended hinterland of Rio de Janeiro. Originally the gold was panned out of the gravel and sand of the rivers. When this became uneconomic underground mining of gold-bearing strata was commenced. The first settlements, Villa Rica (today Ouro Preto) and Sabará resulted from mining activity. Diamantina was built after diamonds were discovered. Precious and gemstones as well as silver were already mined from an early date, whereas the iron ore, manganese, and bauxite deposits were ignored for a long time. Today Minas Gerais supplies almost 100% of the iron ore quarried in Brazil (no mean quantity at 100 million tons per annum), a quarter of the manganese, and over 90% of the chrome mined in the country, to give just a few examples from the mining industry.

The state is also a considerable source of lead, nickel, and zinc ore. Raw materials for the building industry, above all limestone for cement production come from this state too. A large part of the iron ore mines are to be found in the so-called "Quadrilátero ferrífero – in the "iron rectangle", a more or less square-shaped area in the environs of Belo Horizonte. Although now in smaller quantities, gold, silver, and diamonds are still mined to the present day. Morro Velho, the largest Brazilian gold mine is in Nova Lima not far from Belo Horizonte. Its shafts reach down to a depth of 2500 m, and it produces some 400 kg of gold each month. Now and again one can meet prospectors panning for gold or diamonds on the river banks, giving the impression of being throwbacks to a past age, and one which surely will only be the source of tales soon.

Today the mountainous region of Minas Gerais is the third largest industrial area of Brazil, and at the same time its great past and historic relicts make it a source of attraction for countless tourists from Brazil and abroad. Ouro Preto is mentioned in every guidebook, and visited by every tourist group. This former state capital founded in the early 18th century is a treasure trove, not only for the art historian interested in colonial baroque, but for everyone wishing to get a picture of a historical Lusobrazilian town. The whole site, going back to the last, and partly the 18th century, has been preserved, with its countless churches and chapels, ancient fountains, steep and narrow alleys, as well as the Governor's palace which today houses a well-known mining faculty and an outstanding mineralogical museum. By the end of the 18th century, gold fever was already waning in Minas Gerais, and the sumptuous mining town became impoverished. For several decades there was little activity in the resource-rich mountains. It is only in the present century that new towns have been built, again on the basis of mining, but this time of iron ore, manganese, and bauxite, and with the beginnings of industrialisation to be seen, largely factories processing the raw materials from the mines. At the beginning these consisted of small foundries which remained active well into the 20th century. Because they needed charcoal as fuel, immense tracts of forest land were cut down in the heart of Minas Gerais, and this damage has not been made good to the present day. Several large steel firms have their headquarters in or near Belo Horizonte, and heavy industry is showing the largest growth rates of any industrial activity. Other cities have become industrialised too, for example, Ouro Preto-Saramenha with its aluminium works, or Pedro Leopoldo which has a cement factory. At the end of the last century Belo Horizonte was expressly planned as the new capital of Minas Gerais to replace Ouro Preto which was poorly located, and offered little scope for expansion. The new capital rapidly expanded over the foreseen area of 50 km^2 and today greater Belo Horizonte occupies a space of 3800 km^2. The dynamic growth of the city can be attributed to its well-chosen site in the middle of the mining region. In the 1970s growth of the gross national product in Minas Gerais reached a maximum of over 10% per annum, about twice the national average at the time. Industrial progress is impressive: thanks to the one-sided development of heavy industry, Minas Gerais today produces almost half of Brazil's steel, over 60% of the cast iron, a third of all the cement, and every tenth car. In coming years emphasis will be laid on the electronic industry. This however has not only signified progress for Belo Horizonte, it has also brought problems, above all concerning the infrastructure which has not maintained pace with the rapid growth. And the capital of Minas Gerais also has its slum areas spreading out on the outskirts, air pollution from industry and motor vehicles has mounted alarmingly, and the formerly light and clean city has more and more become a second São Paulo, that is an agglomeration threatening to choke on its own size. Belo Horizonte's centre, with its right-angled and diagonally running streets still reminds us of its earliest days. The large suburbs such as Lagoa Santa, Santa Luzia, Betim, and Contagem, together with their industrial enterprises and apartment blocks are representative of the standardised ferro-concrete and glass construction complexes of our time. Belo Horizonte is today, as already mentioned, not only the city of heavy industry, but also of the motor car, since FIAT built a large factory in Betim.

Even outside the capital, Minas Gerais gives the picture of being an aspiring industrial state. This applies in particular to those mining regions where the ore is not only mined but also sometimes smelted. Itabira is a large iron ore town some 100 km east of Belo Horizonte. The Companhia Vale do Rio Doce (CVRD) is there engaged in the mining of high-grade iron ore (mostly 70% blood stone). A complete mountain overlooking the town is composed almost wholly of this stone, and despite 50 million tons being mined annually, there are enough reserves for decades yet. Open-cast mining is practised, and the excavation terraces surround the whole mountain. After blasting, the rock is taken by excavators to immense trucks which then bring it to the works where the ore is broken down in size, and the dead heaps removed. Afterwards the company-owned railway transports the ore the over 400 km to the coast and the port of Tubarão, north of Vitoria. From here, freighters, sometimes also company-owned take the ore to customers overseas, usually to Japan, but also to the United States and Europe. An increasing proportion of iron ore from other parts of Brazil is now being smelted within the country.

In the 1960s and 1970s several large hydroelectric power stations were built in Minas Gerais to assure electricity supplies. The major plants are at Três Marias on the upper reaches of the Rio São Francisco, and at Furnas on the Rio Grande. Thanks to the efforts put into road building, Minas Gerais now has a remarkable network of metalled roads whose main routes link Rio–Belo Horizonte–Brasília, São Paulo–Belo Horizonte, and Belo Horizonte–Vitória. But there is also a surfaced road into the agriculturally important West of the state, to Uberaba and Uberlândia in the so-called Triângulo Mineiro.

Although Minas Gerais is topographically mainly made up of barren mountain ranges, agriculture plays an important role in the economy of the state. The aforementioned zone in the Triângulo Mineiro is made up of fertile arable land where black beans, maize and cassava root, as well as sugar cane and citrus fruits are grown. Better known still are the milk

and dairy products, especially the cheese from the south of Minas Gerais, in particular from regions close to the markets of Rio de Janeiro and São Paulo.
But the success of industry and agriculture, plus the effort put into the infrastructure should not blind one to the fact that by no means all of the problems of Minas Gerais state have been solved. Besides the pulsating centre of Belo Horizonte and the prosperous mining areas, there are still remote and extremely underdeveloped regions such as for instance the valley of the Rio Jequitinhonha in the northeast. The old diamond prospecting town of Diamantina lies not far from the source of this river. This area is devoid of any development, and seems to have been forgotten. The inhabitants are engaged in a primitive hand to mouth existence, are utterly poverty stricken, sometimes undernourished, and have little alternative but to migrate. In Minas Gerais the neglect of agriculture in favour of intensive development of industry is almost a tradition, and setting this kind of priority in planning hits those zones particularly hard which are already underprivileged with regard to their distance from the towns and their lack of development.
The urban region of Rio de Janeiro lies among a steeply-sloping mountain chain, the Serra do Mar, whose 1500 m high peaks, or their foothills, in part reach as far as the coast. These coastal mountains, several large bays, as well as some offshore islands make the landscape livelier and more colourful than anywhere else along the Brazilian coastline. The whole coastal strip is in harmony here, with lagoons and long tongues of land formed by the north to south running Brazil Stream and several adjacent streams meeting the continental shelf. There is ample rainfall along all of the coast, with convection rain playing a major role. The luxuriant green vegetation on the slopes of the mountains contrasts vividly with the dark blue of the sky and ocean, the brown or black of the steep cliffs, and the white sand of the beaches. It is no coincidence that Rio de Janeiro which lies in the midst of this scenery has been named "Cidade maravilhosa".
Rio and its neighbouring town of Niterói both lie at the entrance to the Bay of Guanabara, Rio to the west, Niterói in the east. The waters of the bay widen again after the narrow entrance, the shoreline becomes flat, and is partly marshy. Further to the north, the land rises from the narrow foothills to the heights of the Serra do Mar. Rio itself lies at the foot of the Tijuca massif, a short mountain ridge between the sea and the Serra do Mar, to which it is in parrallel. Not the highest mountains, but certainly the best known are the 700 metre high Corcovado with its figure of Christ, hands spread in protection over the city, and the 390 metre Sugar Loaf, this distinctive peak occupying the entrance to the bay. Such peculiar conical forms can also be seen in other mountains along this stretch of coast; they are the result of weathering on crystalline schists.
The attraction of Rio de Janeiro as a city is to be found in the fact that it is not composed solely of one immense sea of houses, but that the individual quarters are spread in different "chambers" between the steep rock faces (Morros) and the water of the sea, the lagoons, and the bay. The striking landscape and the city mesh together naturally, with mountains, jungle, beaches, and water forming a harmonious unity with the houses, streets, squares and parks. With its population around the nine million mark, Rio is today just as much a port, trading, and tourist city as it is an industrial centre.
It has a broad spectrum of companies from a variety of sectors, from foodstuffs and textiles, to steelworks, petrochemicals, and shipbuilding. The elegant quarters of the city such as Copacabana, Ipanema, or Leblon, are all next to the sea where a fresh, cool breeze always blows, whereas the poorer classes live in a large circle around the flat bay and towards the hot hinterland, 30 and more kilometres distant from the city centre. In addition, countless numbers live in the Favelas or slums pitched on the steep hillsides, but also on flat ground in the north zone, on land which belongs to nobody, or from which the dwellers cannot be evicted when setting up their ramshackle huts there.
The problem behind the Favelas of Rio is the same as for all the slums in Brazilian cities (and indeed all Third World cities): in past years the city population has grown by one thousand per day, by migration alone, mostly from all parts of the interior (and in particular from the northeast as well as the poor regions of Minas Gerais and Espírito Santo). These

migrants all hope to build up a new and better existence in the city, but as the majority cannot read or write, and have no job training, they often remain unemployed, and end up in the slums, where they lead as miserable, and sometimes even more tragic lives as was the case in the countryside. They live in huts which are totally lacking hygiene. No urban authority has ever had the means to supply all these immigrants with employment and housing. And in Rio it has also not been possible to stem the tide of these Favelas. A well known symptom of such a development is the rapid increase in criminality, which has reached sometimes alarming proportions not only in individual suburbs, but in the city centre itself. In the past few years, Rio has tended to lose some of its ambiance and attractiveness through its phenomenonal growth, and the constantly increasing traffic problem. Here and there tree-lined avenues and whole streets have been demolished to make way for traffic or other developments. But there are also efforts to make the city pleasanter to live in. In 1970–1972 the whole beach in Copacabana bay was widened several times over, and in the Flamengo quarter a magnificent park was built along the shore of the bay.
What remains is the lovable nature and merriment of the Cariocas – the inhabitants of Rio, who despite all the tribulations of big-city life keep their cheerfulness and joie-de-vivre which reaches its peak in the annual carnival. The Rio carnival is principally the feast of the blacks and mulattos, but in fact it captures the hearts of rich and poor – of the suburban and slum dwellers as much as the inhabitants of the sophisticated quarters. Everyday worries and cares are forgotten for three days and the streets and clubs resound to Samba music and the sight of the population letting its hair down.
West of Rio de Janeiro is the Rio Paraíba valley, embedded between the Serra do Mar and the Serra da Mantiqueira. From early times on, this became the principal route between the two cities Rio de Janeiro, and São Paulo, and it retains this role to the present day. The Via Dutra, the four-lane highway linking the two cities passes through a landscape undergoing major change. In the first half of the 19th century it formed one of the richest coffee growing zones of the country, only to become an impoverished valley by the turn of the century, when coffee planters moved westwards to areas where more fertile and virgin soil was available. But thanks to its ideal location between the first two cities of Brazil, it came back into favour again in this century, above all as a communicating and transit region. From the 1950s onwards, more and more factories, above all the Volta Redonda steelworks, were established alongside this axis.
São Paulo, 900 m above sea level, is already to the west of the main watershed of the Serra do Mar in the catchment area of the Rio Paraná, and lies on a basin of the Rio Tietê. It is not only the major industrial centre of Brazil, but of all of South America. The city strikes one everytime anew with its imposing, gigantic, but sometimes fearsome dimensions. The population of the agglomeration, which includes the city itself, and 36 adjoining communities, is given as in excess of 9 million. The built-up area amounts to just under 8000 km^2. Within this area, there are some 100,000 registered industrial firms, and over 40% of the Brazilian national income is generated here. The development of the city is best mirrored by the population growth: while only 30,000 lived in São Paulo in 1880, this figure had jumped to 240,000 by the turn of the century. By 1920 the population had reached 580,000, by 1940 1.3 million, by 1960 3.8 million, 1980 7.5 million.This means that the population doubled and sometimes almost trebled every twenty years.
How can this phenomenal growth in the space of a 100 years be explained? The initial growth of the region was slow. The coastal zone around Santos was colonised by the Portuguese as early as the first half of the 16th century, and the Jesuits opened a monastery school on the present site of São Paulo in 1554, thereby laying the foundations for later developments. The big economic upturn came with the spread of coffee plantations in the state of São Paulo in the second half of the 19th century. The first plantations were in the Paraíba valley, and expanded gradually towards São Paulo, and then like a wave, spread out to the west. Planting coffee triggered off a veritable revolution, and led to far-reaching economic and demographic changes. The population of the state grew from 250,000 in 1830, 830,000 in 1870, to 2.3 million in 1900. Hand in

hand with the westward spread of coffee went the railway lines to open up the country. All these lines meet in São Paulo, and this not inconsiderably spurred on the later development of the city. Santos, whose harbour facilities were improved and extended in 1886 grew, thanks to the rail links with the interior, very rapidly into the most important coffee-exporting port in the world. In the 20th century factories were built along the railway lines, there being water power, and therefore electric energy in abundance.

São Paulo's growth is the result of the coffee boom of past decades. The transition from an all-dominating coffee economy to a prospering industrial region was not too troublesome, because even in those times, São Paulo more than any other Brazilian state, had a plentiful supply of skilled labour (many European immigrants) and significant capital reserves from the prospering coffee business. Industrialisation really began in São Paulo at the turn of the century, initially with textile factories. In the 1940s further businesses from various sectors were established, principally on the route between São Paulo and Santos. After 1950 came the iron and steel industry and the first automobile factories which today are among the most important companies in the agglomeration. Volkswagen do Brasil not only dominates the domestic car market, but is increasingly active on the export side. But São Paulo has since several years grown to such a size that the negative aspects are becoming more and more evident. Pollution, traffic chaos, housing problems for the poorer parts of the population, and ever growing criminality, are just some of the problems looking for an answer in this connection. In certain parts of the city, air pollution has reached such a level that whole groups of trees have withered, and newly planted ones refused to grow. Even in fine weather, a smoky haze covers the city, hardly letting through any sunshine. São Paulo holds the dubious record of being the most industrially air-polluted city in Latin America.

The rivers of the agglomeration hardly deserve the name anymore. They are, on the contrary, stinking sewers which have to take up waste water from all quarters. Just as hazardous is the fact that waste water is also partially fed into the large dammed-up lakes which serve as reservoirs for the city's drinking water supply. However, since some time now, and even if it is very late in the day, there has been an environmental law in São Paulo – incidentally the first in all of Brazil.

The second major problem is the permanent traffic chaos. Despite the many expressways and under-

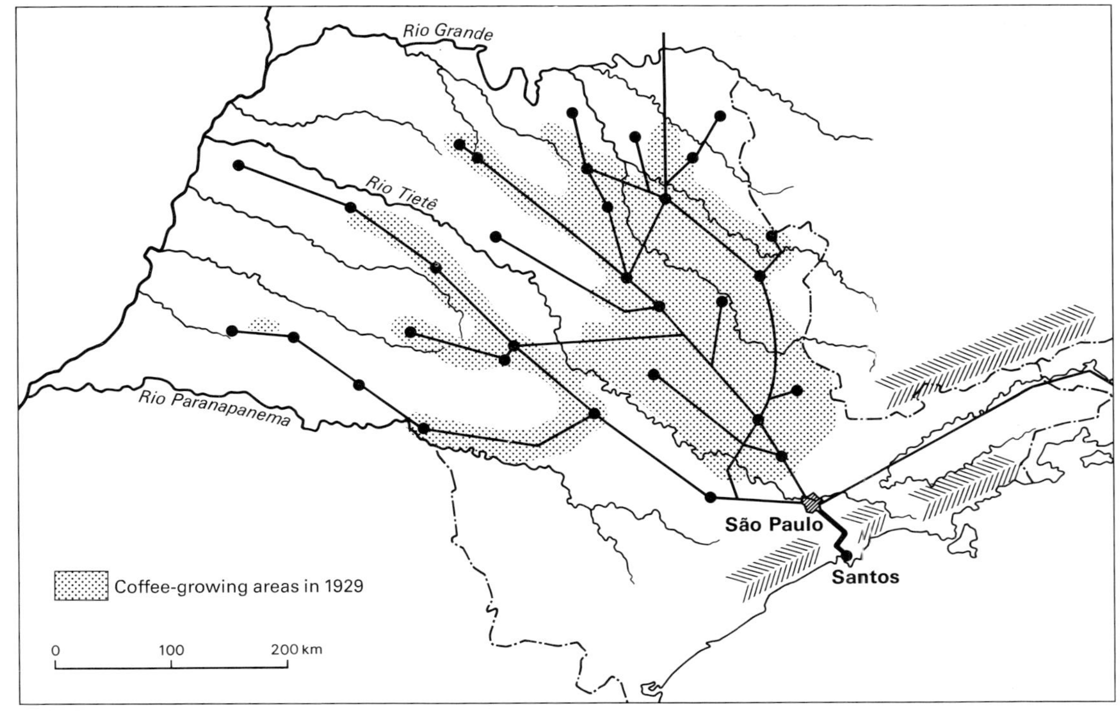

Railway network in São Paulo State in 1929

passes, traffic in some parts of the city stops more than it goes. In addition almost all public transport is by buses – which have to use the road.
An underground railway is under construction, and the first lines are in operation, but it will take many years yet before a comprehensive underground railway network can diminish the traffic jams.
No less a problem is the housing shortage, which is most acute for the lower income groups. Many of the migrants from the northeast settle in wood and corrugated iron hutments on the periphery of the city. Such slum areas are just as numerous in São Paulo as in other Brazilian cities. Even though the government undertakes the construction of social housing, the Favelas keep springing up practically overnight. Closely linked with the housing and employment situation is the marginal nature of some sectors of the population, amongst whom criminality is constantly rising. Not every migrant who comes from other parts of Brazil to São Paulo immediately finds suitable employment. Even though there are vacancies for unskilled workers in many places, they are often outweighed by the number looking for jobs. Many of the new arrivals cannot get used to the idea of regular working hours. They often leave their new job after only two or three weeks, as soon as they have been paid, or they are dismissed for absenteeism. Such conditions can be found in many Brazilian cities – they are a part of the general educational and training problem confronting the country. Solutions to it are being very energetically pursued.
As an agricultural entity, São Paulo state can be divided into three different zones: the first zone is formed by the land along the Atlantic coast. This is a narrow and more or less flat strip between the sea and the steeply rising Serra do Mar range. This was sugarcane land in colonial times, but now mainly citrus fruits and bananas are grown there. With the exception of the immediate vicinity of the port of Santos, the zone is sparsely populated, and the local inhabitants are engaged in simple farming for self-sufficiency, and fishing. The second zone is marked by intensive cultivation, supplying the capital with fresh fruit and vegetables. It forms a ring around the capital in a region marked by geological upheavals, and a landscape characterised by

22 *Negro slaves were "imported" into Brazil from Africa already in early colonial times, because experience had soon shown that the native Indians were not suitable as farmworkers on the big Fazendas, or plantations. The Indians, used to freedom, could not stand the hardships of forced labour, and either soon died, or fled from the harsh treatment of white plantation owners. Blacks from Africa were therefore required to replace the Indians, as the white masters were unwilling to do physical work. In the course of time, the slave trade brought hundreds of thousands of Africans to the colonial empire. The "Senzalas" or slave huts were grouped round the planter's mansion (Casa Grande). On weekdays the slaves had to labour for their masters, while on Sundays they tilled their own small plot of land to feed themselves and their families. Quite often, the plantation owner would seek out a black mistress for the slave. Children of slaves were also enslaved.*
Particularly the planting of coffee called for increasing numbers of farmworkers, and at the time of the Declaration of Independence (1822), 40,000 blacks were brought to Brazil annually. By 1850, this figure had risen to 50,000 annually. In the middle of the last century, Britain finally prohibited slave trafficking on the high seas, but slavery in Brazil continued. After serious internal disturbances, the "Golden Law" (Lei Aurea) was proclaimed on 13th May 1888: 1. It abolished slavery in Brazil. 2. All decisions to the contrary were revoked.
The illustration depicts "The Coffee Workers" by Brazilian painter Cândido Portinari (1903–1962).

23 *Ripe coffee berries are red in colour. They are stone-fruits containing two seeds – the coffee beans. They are usually plucked by hand and fall onto the sheet spread out under the coffee shrub.*

24 *Immediately after harvesting, the coffee berries are spread out in the sun to dry. Once they are brown, the seeds are extracted by crushing.*

25 *The coffee taster has an important job and – rather like wine tasters in Europe – he has to grade various qualities of coffee.*

26 *The coffee berries are picked up from the ground (red equals fully ripe, green not quite ripe) and "winnowed" on the spot in a special round sieve, whereby they are thrown up into the air by the plantation worker, who then steps back and catches them again. In this way, the relatively heavy coffee berries fall back into the sieve, and leaves, twiglets and dust fall to the ground beside the sieve.*

28

29

27 ◁ Coffee plantations or Fazendas are easiest to spot from the air. The centre is formed by the large square where the coffee is dried. Alongside, and partially covered by trees, are the living quarters and out-houses.

28 Seringueiro (rubber tapper) cutting a slit in the tree.

29 The latex is smoked over a fire.

30 In the Northeast of Brazil, the sugar cane harvest is still largely brought in by hand, involving a large labour force. Sugar cane is a sweet grass growing to a height of 2–4 m, with a high sugar content in its pulp.

31 Soy bean plantation in Paraná state. Brazil is, after the USA and before China, the second largest producer of soy beans in the world. They are mostly used as animal feed and for the production of oil.

30

31

NEUZA LEODORA
73

32 *After the downfall of the "sugar economy", which had permitted the colonisation of the Northeast, new agricultural products were called for. Cotton was another product which had a high commercial value. The demand for cotton had considerably increased with the coming of technical progress in Europe at the end of the 18th century. From this time on, until into the 19th century, many large Brazilian plantations took part in the cultivation of cotton. They were to be found all over the country, even towards the dry interior. Falling cotton prices led to a gradual reduction in cotton plantations. But today, more cotton is being cultivated again, and it is the number one agricultural product in several of the federal states. Our example of a naive painting of cotton workers is typical of the popular genre in Brazil, and pictures such as this can often be bought at markets.*

partly-wooded ridges, and basins. Agricultural smallholdings, together with their own sales organisation are a salient part of this zone, and a considerable role in its development was played by immigrants from Japan. The third zone, the real interior of São Paulo state, begins about 50–100 km west of the capital. Topographically it marks the transition from the already described small and hilly field cultivation zone into a broad, undulating land dominated by magnificent plantations and extending westwards to the Rio Paraná. This is the true agricultural zone of São Paulo with rich coffee plantations, sugarcane and cotton fields, but also plots of maize and potatoes, as well as vegetables and fruit, above all citrus fruits. São Paulo state produces about a quarter of Brazil's coffee (Paraná, the southern neighbour, produces 50%), a quarter of the country's cotton, a third of the sugarcane, and almost a sixth of the total maize harvest. Cattle raising is important too: a quarter of Brazil's beef coming from this state. Nearly all of its surface area is used for farming or forestry, although there are few forests left. The agriculture is diverse and efficient, and São Paulo state is well on the way to becoming one of the most modern agricultural areas in the world.

Contributing to this are several remarkable factors: the Agronomic Institute in Campinas has for years been engaged in fundamental research into tropical and subtropical farming, and today it is one of the world's leading centres on the subject. São Paulo state and its communities run an agricultural advisory service, with countless information offices in many cities and larger urban centres in the whole state. Many banks grant credits at reasonable interest rates for agricultural projects. The soil is in the main good, and the climate is good for cultivation, with relatively high temperatures all year, and sufficient humidity.

São Paulo's agriculture is the most mechanized in all of the country – with more than a third of Brazil's tractors registered in this state, but in comparison to Europe or the United States, still too few in number. A negative factor is that although there is a large supply of farm labour, most of the workers are without any education or even agricultural training, and they tend to change jobs very frequently.

The Southern Region It is composed of the states of Paraná, Santa Catarina, and Rio Grande do Sul, with a total population of 23 million, living in an area of 577,000 km^2. Economic development of the south, in comparison with the southeast of Brazil was much steadier, and today the south is above all a farming area, with the slowly growing industrial enterprises being confined mainly to factories processing the locally grown crops. The population of the southern states is made up of descendants of south and central European immigrants, with particularly the Italien and German groups being of importance. Even today many south Brazilians speak German or Italian because their parents, grandparents, or great-grandparents emigrated to Brazil from Germany or Italy decades ago, and they decided to maintain their mother tongues as well as the national language, Portuguese which is taught in all the schools. Many founded their own communities with appropriate names which still exist such as Blumenau, Novo Hamburgo, or Nova Itália. Blacks and half-castes make up a much smaller proportion of the population of the south than is the case in other parts of Brazil. What is also striking is that the average standard of living is higher than elsewhere, and that in the south there are more prospering medium and small farms than in the rest of Brazil. The property structure is well balanced, and not as extreme as in the north, largely as a result of Brazilian government policy in the last century which placed the emphasis on family-run farms in the south, following bad experiences with large agricultural units. Nevertheless the south is also witnessing a constantly increasing drift to the cities, often the result of inheritances splitting up farms into unworkably small holdings. Curitiba and Porto Alegre have especially grown in size in recent years, and regrettably there are now also slums on the outskirts of these cities. As well as the drift to the relatively nearby towns, there has for some time now been migration from agricultural areas in the south to other farmlands of Brazil, for instance to the Triangulo Mineiro, in the west as far as the Mato Grosso and Goiás, and to the north, right up to the Transamazônica. The migrants are usually young farmers who see no future in the south, or who possess little or no land. Land prices are much lower in the north and west, which makes a new start easier. As a result there are now justified demands in the south for more industrialisation in order to create employment and thus put a stop to emigration. Improvements to infrastructure are also needed (roads, energy and water supplies, waste water treatment, new schools and hospitals etc.). However, these difficulties in the south are far less pressing than further north to the Equator, even though there is a risk of the situation getting out of hand unless it is properly steered. Despite problems, the south remains a farming area sometimes European, and sometimes more North American in nature, where production not only covers local requirements but permits significant exports as well to other parts of Brazil as abroad. A dominating role is played by the livestock production with over 12 million head of cattle and 12 million sheep in Rio Grande do Sul alone. The most important field crops, often planted in rotation, are wheat and soybeans, the latter an important export item. Besides these, black beans, sorghum, maize, and like everywhere in Brazil, cassava root are grown here.

The Middle West The central-west region (Centro Oeste) of Brazil borders in the north on the Amazon, in the west on the neighbouring states of Paraguay and Bolivia, and in the east on the more densely populated states of the federation. The middle west like the north is sparsely populated (7.7 million inhabitants living on 1.9 million km^2 of territory) and nearly all of it is Cerrado country. Until right into the 1960s this land was hardly cultivated or in any other way used. At the most there was extensive livestock production here or there. But since the early 1970s this has fundamentally changed, with the middle west and its states of Mato Grosso do Sul, Mato Grosso, and Goiás coming more and more into the public eye thanks to increasing agricultural production. Marked growth areas were rice and soybean plantations. Nowadays a third of Brazil's rice production comes from the middle west, together with 10% of the cotton, 10% of the black beans, and all of the maize. Added to this are 30% of all head of cattle in Brazil, the middle west being the main breeding area. There is a promising future for mining too, the Urucum range, at Corumbá near the Bolivian border is rich in iron ore and manganese, and there are good prospects for further finds in other parts of this big territory. Although the middle west is thought by many to be the real region of the future, it also has its problems. In principle they are the same as those of the south, but in more accentuated form. In contrast to the south, agriculture is based on Latifúndio with the presence of agro-industrial mammoth farms, although this form of property is not so problematical here as in the northeast, because there are no small holdings, nor an unemployed poor farm workers' class. But in many of the newer large farms, agriculture is on a low level compared with the standards of São Paulo state.

Apart from mining, the middle west has hardly any industrial significance. Until recently there were merely several warehouses for agricultural produce, a few refrigerated storehouses for meat, a couple of mills, some woodworking, cement factories and a small metalworking trade. For the past few years though, a new development has got under way: large foodstuff companies have been transferring their factories from the southeast, where practically all Brazil's farm produce ends up, if not exported, and rebuilt them in the middle west, which is the main producing region. This has been done to save on transport costs, and it has benefited the middle west, whose largest cities, the state capitals, are in full growth. Goiânia, Campo Grande, and Cuiabá all have between 100,000–200,000 inhabitants, as has Corumbá, the frontier town to Bolivia on the Rio Paraguay.

Brasília This also belongs to the middle west region, even if it is on the eastern fringe. Brasília is a federal district, and has been the new capital of the country since 1960. In the roughly 30 years of its existence it has come of age. Coming in to land at the capital's airport one can see that the city centre's famous plan form is like an aeroplane's, with the government and administrative buildings forming the fuselage, and the wings being made up north and south by the residential quarters. In the east, the city is bordered by the half-moon artificial lake, the Lago do Paranoá. To the west the land rises slightly to the highest point of the city, 1200 m above sea level. Since the inauguration of Brasília much has happened; the number of streets and houses has grown, as have the number of trees, the city is no longer as bleak as it was a few years ago. Today it presents an attractive picture, generously laid out with broad streets, and without a doubt unique in terms of planning and architecture. But it was a long and stony path at first, and Brasília is still a highly controversial town planning experiment. Critics continue to maintain that it is impossible to take a city straight off the drawing board and so to speak, "breath life into it". To understand the differing opinions, one has to look at the background.

Plan of Brasília

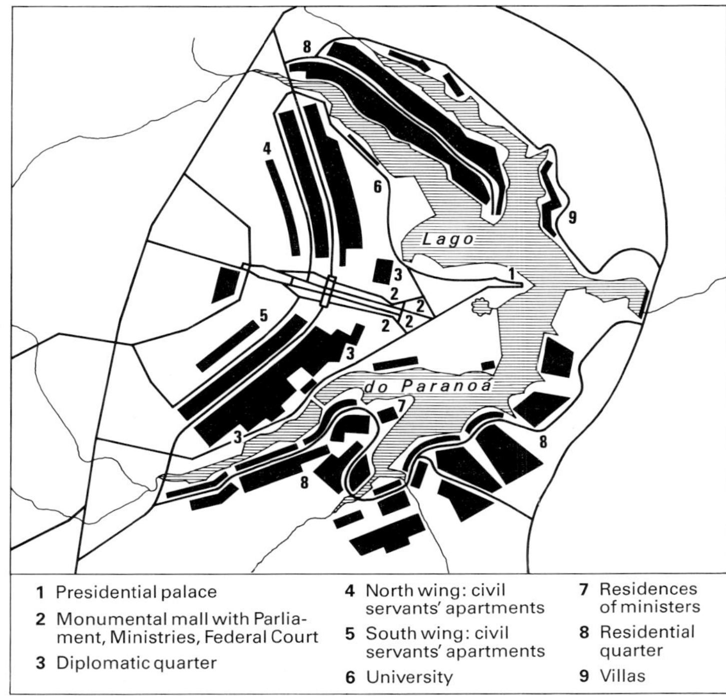

Brasília was first and foremost built in order to give an impulse to the development of the country's interior. Juscelino Kubitschek, President of Brazil from 1956 to 1960 wanted to open up the broad hinterland, not only the narrow coastal strip along the Atlantic, which represented civilised Brazil until the middle of this century. That is why he realised the old Brazilian dream of a capital not based on a colonial past: he built Brasília. The town is above all a political signal, and despite its fascination, only an urban experiment in second place.

Has Brasília proved successful? Did the political signal set things in motion? Is the urban experiment alive? Roughly 30 years after the inauguration of Brasília one can categorically state that the development away from the coast, into the interior of the country has overcome its thorny beginnings and has become a not to be ignored factor of contemporary Brazil. This is not only because the capital was moved 1000 km into the interior, there were other contributory factors. Today there is not merely a capital sitting on its own in the interior, on the contrary, it is linked with all parts of the country by usually good roads, and along these routes radiating in all directions, the wilderness has been cultivated. Smaller and larger settlements have sprung up along these highways in a previously unheard of fashion. Along the road between Belém and Brasília alone, some 4 million people have found a new life. From the point of view of providing an impetus for new development, Brasília can be termed a success.

Brasília as an urban experiment is a different matter. The new capital is made up of two domains: on the one hand the modern city or "plano piloto" built by town planner Lúcio Costa and architect Oscar Niemeyer where today some 400,000–500,000 middle class people live (civil servants of all grades, and diplomats), and on the other, half a dozen satellite towns, as far as 50 km from the centre, inhabited by workers (about 800,000) who hoped to find new employment in the capital. Many have succeeded, and form part of the workforce needed for the expansion of Brasília, which is by no means finished. But others are still without permanent jobs and form a sub-proletarian class which is to be found in all Brazilian cities. This fact, rather than the allegation that no one feels at home in the modern estates of the "Plano piloto" casts doubt on the success of Brasília as an urban experiment. Since the city has aged somewhat, there are more and more youngsters here who were born and bred, and went to school in Brasília – in short, it is their home. It is perhaps difficult for an outsider to imagine always living in such a modern city, but possibly that is because he himself has an optic cast in the traditional mould. If one asks where the quality of life is higher, especially for children and juveniles, in the canyon-like streets of Copacabana in Rio, or in parts of São Paulo where hardly a tree is to be seen, and where air pollution has reached a maximum, or in the six-storey apartment blocks of Brasília, which are well spaced with plenty of green zones, where there are trees and bushes, where the sky, clouds, and a lake can be seen, all by the wild Cerrado, then the answer should be plain. In this sense Brasília is an interesting contribution to urban development. Hardly anyone would today cast doubt on the architecturally appealing and attractive forms of Niemeyer's buildings, but there are many who see a danger in the fact that the original town plan by Costa is constantly being adapted to new requirements, and they fear that ultimately it will be changed beyond recognition. It is less likely to be a danger than a normal development in any living city, in fact it is proof that it is alive. Brasília has become a reality like any other city in the country even if initially it was difficult to coax the federal civil servants and politicians to move there.

The Amazon

Today's air traveller who can fly to Manaus in the heart of Amazon in just four hours from Rio de Janeiro cannot usually take in the vastness of the land he has flown over. His jet is all too quickly north of Brasília where the savanna-like Cerrado landscape gradually turns into increasingly thick tropical rain forest. The monotonous dark green jungle with its steamhouse climate swelters under towering white thunder clouds. The landscape is only interrupted by the odd river meandering without direction to a distant horizon. It is only very rarely that from this great height one can see signs of human activity in this seemingly unpopulated land. Here and there a column of smoke from a forest clearing made by burning, and very seldom, the arrow straight cutting in the red earth of a road through the forest, along the rivers one can perhaps see clearings with the fields and huts of settlers, but otherwise nothing. The countryside still looks as untouched as millions of years ago.

But the impression is false: the opening up of the Amazon has come into full swing in the last few years. Through gigantic roadbuilding projects, and utopian seeming schemes in the fields of agriculture, mining, and industry, Brazil's modern industrial society is on the way to mastering the north. These developments have gone so far ahead that ecologists in and outside Brazil are justifiably getting worried about the future of one of the last remaining regions of our planet which is still untouched nature. The Amazon, just as much, or perhaps even more than other Brazilian regions, is in a state of transition: the contrasts between old and new, large and small, extensive and intensive, are greater and more apparent than elsewhere. Until the 1960s this large region with an area of almost 3.6 million km^2 and encompassing the states of Amazonas, Pará, Acre, and Rondônia, as well as the territories of Roraima and Amapa lived a tranquil life on the broad rivers and verdant forests. The population of Indians and white settlers made ends meet with modest agriculture and forestry, by gathering wild fruit and nuts, and with hunting and fishing.

Today movement has come to this scene, and rapid changes are underway, which are being closely watched by experts and scientists all over the world. However, the 5 million people living in the region will experience these radical changes in differing ways. It is a revolution more economic and technological in nature, spurred on by specialists with vast technological facilities, financed by far-off firms, rather than a transformation affecting the broad mass of the population and its lifestyle directly. The majority of the people live in the few larger or smaller towns, or are small farmers, fishermen, or gatherers on the banks of the rivers. There are large differences in population density, ranging from the high density (for the Amazon!) of 20 per km^2 in the Bragantina east of Belém, to the Rio Negro, where there is roughly one inhabitant per 10 km^2. The towns, and not only Manaus and Belém are experiencing an unprecedented growth, only comparable with the rubber boom at the end of the last century, and due to the influx of more and more people from the environs. The country regions are stagnating, and threatening to subside economically. 60% of the total population of the Amazon area is less than twenty years old, and this produces almost insoluble problems in the realms of education, training, and employment, and even in food supply. Brazilian government circles see the fundamental problem less as one of sporadic overpopulation, and more a question of the continuing discrepancy between low population and a huge land area. This explains why Brasília repeatedly calls for more settlements in the Amazon region.

The River System The Rio Amazonas is some 6000 km in length (depending on measurements, or estimates, one also sees figures between 5800 and

Amazon Riverbed (Lúcio de Soares, 1975)

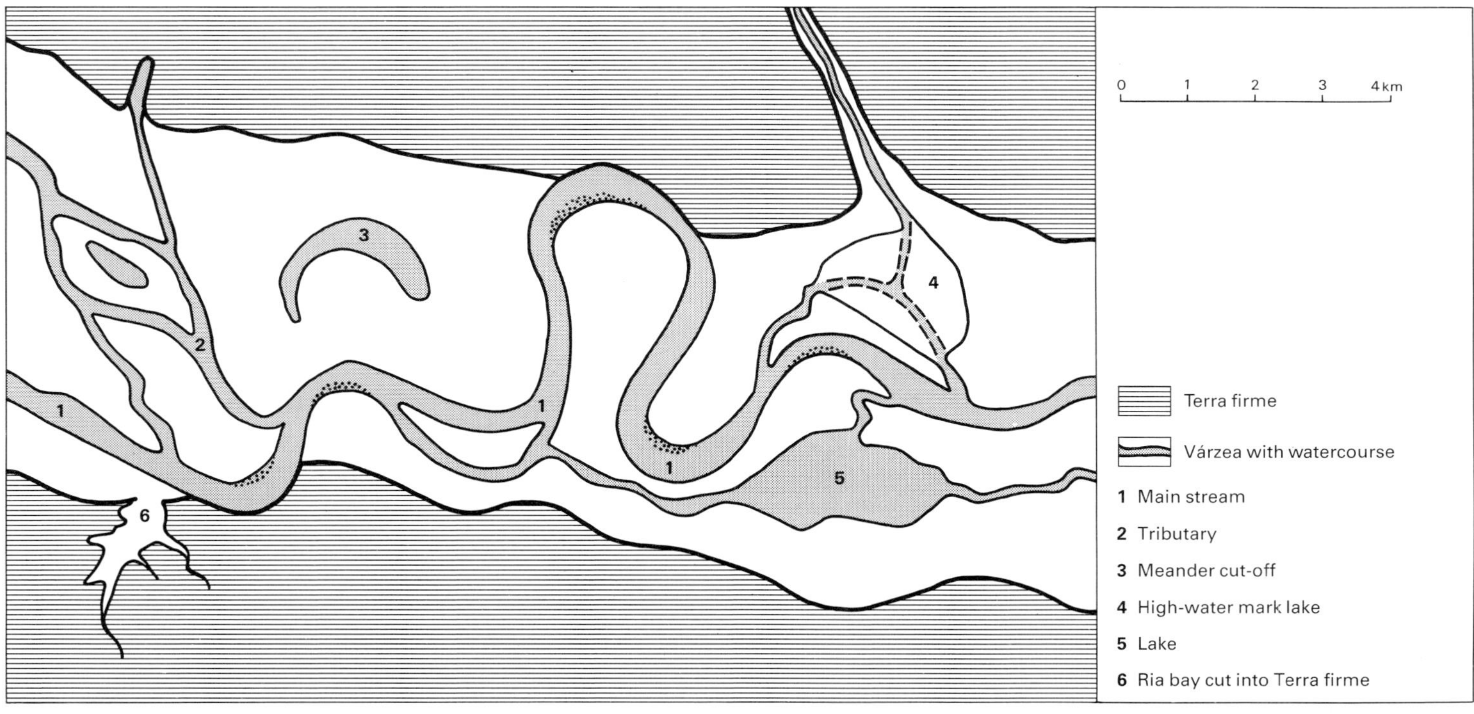

6600 km). The most important sources are the Marañón, the Huallaga and the Ucayali. The Marañón which drains large parts of central and north Peru, and with its tributaries also the southeast of Ecuador, in its upper reaches runs parallel to the Andes, and between these to the north, till Borja, where it flows into the actual Amazon basin. The Ucayali and the Huallaga drain the central and southern parts of the Peruvian Andes, the Ucayali resulting from the confluence of the Apurímac and the Urubamba, which both rise in the Peruvian highlands south of Cuzco. At Nauta, above Iquitos the Marañón/Huallaga joins the Ucayali and from there the river Amazon flows 5000 km eastwards to the Atlantic ocean. At Iquitos, still in Peru, the river is already 1800 m wide and 30–50 m deep. In the western part of the Brazilian Amazon region the river is referred to as the Rio Solimões, and only after the Rio Negro has joined it below Manaus, where it is already several kilometres wide, is it again called the Amazon. Its bed is deep enough to permit medium-sized oceangoing vessels to reach Manaus without problems, and ships of less than 3000 tons displacement can even go as far as Iquitos. The Amazon cannot be compared with a European or North American river, because downstream from Iquitos there is not one single riverbed, but several parallel running canals, separated by long, opposite-facing islands. In addition it is sometimes difficult to distinguish the actual shoreline, because this depends on the seasonal changes in the water level. In Manaus at the confluence of the Rio Negro and the Rio Solimões the water level varies by 8 to 12 m. Low water is in November, high water in June and July. This rhythm, which is displaced in time along the river's course, is reflected by the life of the river dwellers, above all with regard to the planting of the various crops, and especially when the fields are situated on the fertile Várzea soil, that is in zones which are regularly flooded at high water. The rivers ensure natural fertilisation of the soil by depositing a new layer of sludge every year. This is particularly true of the Rio Solimões and the other so-called yellow water rivers that come from the eastern foothills of the Andes and which transport much silt in their loamy-coloured water. This contrasts with the so-called black water rivers, which rise in the highlands of Guyana to the north, or in the predominantly crystalline rock of the Brazilian highlands in the south, which are rather poor in minerals, as evidenced by the dark water colour.

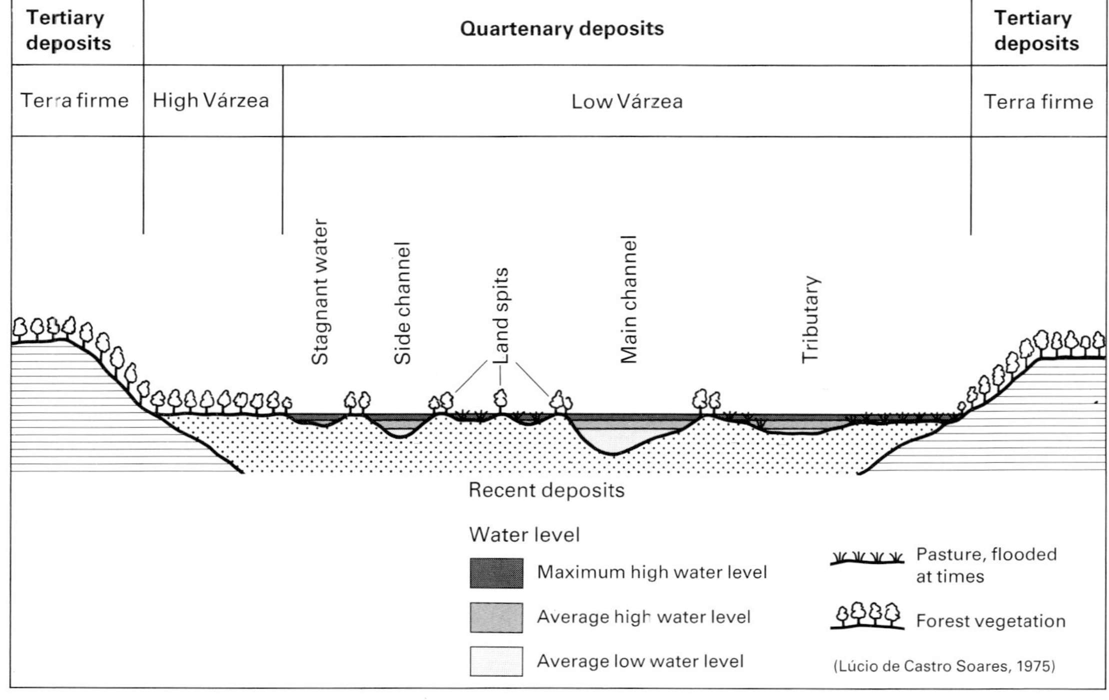

Cross-section of yellow-water river in Amazon region

Traditional Economic Patterns Most of the Amazon settlers (the Indians will be mentioned separately) live directly on the banks of the river, or not far away. The Caboclos, predominantly half-castes of white and Indian stock, build their huts and houses on parts of the riverbank not normally flooded at high water. Despite this, the huts often stand on 2–3 m high pilings to give protection against the sporadic extreme high water levels. The people are poor and have only the bare necessities of life, and sometimes not even that. Many suffer from intestinal worms and malária, many are latently undernourished. They all have boats as a means of communication, otherwise they would be lost in this region of water and jungle. Only a minority of these small farmers live in villages, the majority chosing to live with their families in unending solitude along the banks of all the large and small rivers. Downstream from Manaus, many river areas can be regarded as populated, albeit very lightly.

Traditional Amazon agriculture is based on three legs: food production for own consumption (subsistence agriculture), planting for the market (pepper, jute, some fruit) and collective plantations. In opposition to an earlier held view, there are indeed many factors which speak against widespread development of agriculture in the Amazon. A main obstacle in the "terra firme" (land outside the flood plain) is that harvests rapidly decrease because of the infertile soil (see p.23). A further difficulty is the absence of warehouses, a lack of primary processing facilities for agricultural produce, as well as an incredibly thin and inefficient route network.

Subsistence agriculture: the small farmers on the banks of the rivers, or on the edges of the big towns practise rather the same form of primitive land clearance by fire as the Indians inasmuch as these latter till any fields. The main difference is that today's settlers do not move their dwellings, instead, over the years they rotate the land they use, leaving some of it fallow (shifting cultivation). If land is to be made arable, the forest first has to be burnt down, and between the incompletely burnt stumps, the first seeds are planted. The first seeding usually results in satisfactory to good harvests. Such a field can usually be used for another one or two years before the return drops off, and a new field has to be chosen. There is hardly a settler who would know how to improve his soil. Fertiliser is unknown to most of them. This form of field rotation, with the farmers living in one place contrasts with the Indians' system, where the farmers relocate as they change their fields. In both cases the land, after lying fallow for 12 to 20 years, can be recultivated, although by that time it is usually covered by forest again.

According to the present state of knowledge about the ecology of tropical rain forests, this is the only possible agricultural use for tropical forests in equatorial zones. It consists of making very small clearings at just a number of places in the forest, rather like pinpricks. The wounds are therefore small enough for the forest to recover with ease, and to regenerate itself.

Such a form of economy is only possible in very large forests, with correspondingly low population density. These preconditions were in fact met in earlier times practically all over the Amazon area, and they are still true for some parts in the north. The limits of this economic pattern are discernible – the big question is at what percentage of cleared land to total forest area does one draw the line. In other words, at what point is nature endangered? Opinions on this point diverge quite widely, especially between ecologists and politicians.

Crop plantations for the market, both in Brazil and abroad, take up only a small area. Rubber plantations were set up here in the 20th century at various places, but most of them are in a neglected state today. There has been more success with pepper growing, the best known plantation being the Japanese colony in Tomé-Açu, south of Belém. It was the Japanese who introduced the pepper plant to the Amazon in the 1930s, and who later brought more suitable species from southeast Asia. Pepper in Brazil only flourishes in the Amazon region, and two thirds of it is exported, to the USA, Europe, and Argentina.

The agricultural area supplying the city of Belém is of interest for several reasons. It lies to the east of the city and originally extended along the 200 km of railway line between Belém and Bragança, a line which was originally built around the turn of the century with the intention of continuing it to São Luís. The rain forest between Belém and Bragança, the

Bragantina, has largely been cleared in this century, and parts of it have been turned into arable land. The Bragantina soon became a distinctly market-orientated production zone for cocoa, tobacco, and sugarcane, which however are grown over the whole flood plain of the Amazon. Besides these crops, of importance also are jute and kenaf (Java jute), introduced by the Japanese, both fibre plants which are mainly used to make coffee sacks. The Bragantina is one of the most densely populated parts of the Amazon, and this is largely due to the immigration of Nordestinos (people from the north-east) in the first half of this century. This dense population resulted in many places to intensive, or over intensive, and sometimes even exhaustive use of the land. Unfortunately the major consequence of this, that is decreasing harvests, was recognised far too late. Today it is virtually impossible to reafforest the land, and agricultural returns over the smallest possible area are only kept up by maximum use of fertilisers, and this usually means growing pepper. Of the other plants grown in the Bragantina, cassava root and kenaf offer the most satisfactory returns, because both only call for small land resources. Erstwhile crops such as sugarcane, rice, and maize have almost disappeared from the Bragantina, and the whole area is in decline.
Today we know that this land could have offered a passable existence to a smaller population practising a more extensive form of agriculture, and that the present situation only came about because of tree clearances to supply Belém with wood and charcoal, and then the long drawn out cultivation of the fields. The Bragantina, after nine decades of cultivation, offers a good example for discussion today about the extent to which the tropical rain forest can be exploited. Leading ecologists maintain that the Bragantina could at the most have supported a population of 9 persons per square kilometre, practising subsistence agriculture. The present density is today already between 10 and 25 persons per square kilometre and near Belém this figure is increasing.
The gathering economy is probably the best adapted form for this landscape, and it is largely rubber and Brazil nuts which are grown in this manner, as well as many fruits, wild vegetables, and medicinal herbs. In money terms, a quarter of agricultural production in the Amazon is earned this way, a proportion which will no doubt decrease with continuing opening up of the Amazon region.
In comparison with the time at the turn of the century, rubber is today unimportant. The Pará rubber tree *(Hevea brasiliensis)* is one of the Euphorbiaceae family, and stands up to 30 m tall. Although found all over South America's tropical forests it is hardly ever frequent enough to dominate other tree species.
Latest estimates indicate that there are some 300 million of these rubber trees in the Brazilian Amazon region. They grow best in the flood plain or Várzea, but can also be found on the terra firme. About 70% of the north's rubber production comes from the states of Amazonas, Rondônia, and Acre. Total Brazilian production in past years has amounted to between 25,000 and 35,000 t annually. Compared with Malaysia's 1.6 million tons annually, this is a negligible figure.
The Seringueiro or rubber gatherer is usually the tenant of large forest tracts, but he is only interested in tapping the latex from the trees, and indeed this is all he is permitted to harvest from the forest. He regularly visits his trees, usually between 70 and 250 in number, makes two incisions at an angle, and where they intersect, he affixes a cup or bowl to the tree trunk. After a while, the liquid rubber or latex drips slowly into the bowl. The incisions are normally made in the morning, and the latex collected in the afternoon. The frequency of incisions is dependent on the speed with which the tree can regenerate its bark, this means on average one cut every one to three days. At home, in his palm thatched hut, the Seringueiro starts with the smoking process. He dips a stout stick into the white latex and then holds it over a smouldering fire, which slowly turns the latex brown, and makes it tough. Once the latex is clinging properly to the stick, it is once again dipped into the bowl, and the process is repeated till a ball of rubber weighing 25–50 kg is affixed to the stick. This raw rubber is brought to market by the Seringueiro, or sold to passing traders. Normally the Seringueiros are not exclusively rubber collectors, but also fish, and keep pigs and chicken, and sometimes cows for their own food supplies.

New Developments since the Mid-sixties In 1966 the Brazilian government founded the state planning and development body for the Amazon region (Superintendência do Desenvolvimento da Amazônia). Called Sudam for short, it is analogous to the Sudene body of the northeast which has already been described. It was to be responsible for the development of the Amazon region, by which one hoped to increase the gross national product. The Brazilian government supported all manner of state and private development schemes, in agricultural cultivation and animal husbandry, in mining, in industry as well as in the transport and energy sectors, to name but the most important. Initial state aid was needed to build an infrastructure, above all roads, along which small farmers were given settlement grants. In addition massive tax concessions were given in order to encourage private investment in agricultural, mining, and industrial projects. The road building programme was implemented partly by state appointed companies and consortiums, and by army engineers. The prototype for the construction of these roads was the link between Belém at the mouth of the Amazon and Brasília, which had been completed in 1960 within a space of only four years, and was inaugurated together with the new capital. This road has a length of 2100 km, two thirds of it runs through the Cerrado of central Brazil, and one third through the actual Amazon tropical rain forest. Initially designed as a gravel strip, increasing traffic led to its being asphalted throughout between 1972 and 1975. While construction activity was relatively simple in the Cerrado, the stretch of road in the Pará jungle posed countless difficulties. Surveying and forest clearance in this totally unknown terrain was unexpectedly troublesome, not least because the ground was considerably less flat than had been assumed. The difficulties however were surmounted, and now roughly 30 years after its opening, some 4 million people live in the vicinity of the road, nearly all of them settlers who came after the completion of the road.

Further roads were built in succeeding years, the best known and at the same time the most controversial being the Transamazônica. The heart of this stretch is from Estreito on the Belém–Brasília road, via Marabá, Altamira, Itaituba, Jacareacanga to Humaitá, north of Porto Velho, and on to Rio Branco and Cruzeiro do Sul in the far western state of Acre. This is now a round the year through route, although in places there are still difficulties in the rainy season, when heavy downpours can wash away the road bed. In addition to the two major, abovementioned, west–east, and north–south links, the Brazilians have also built further highways, namely from Cuiabá to Santarém, and from Porto Velho to Manaus and Boa Vista. The Cuiabá to Porto Velho road was built much earlier, but as an unsatisfactory gravel road which it has remained to the present day.

The Brazilian government's expectations that neighbouring Peru and Venezuela would continue the roads reaching up to the frontiers of their country from Brazil, have not been met. The dream of a huge transcontinental link from the Atlantic through the Brazilian and Peruvian Amazon basin and over the Andes to the Pacific is still a long way from fulfillment. For several years the so-called "Perimetral Norte" has existed as a blueprint. This envisages a road along the whole north and northwest frontier of the country. As there is little economic need for such a route, which would at most be of strategic significance to safeguard the norther frontier, it is unlikely to be built in the near future. Besides roadbuilding, the early sixties also saw much government support for the setting up of small farms along the Transamazônica highway. The Federal Institute for Colonisation and Agrarian Reform, INCRA (Instituto Nacional de Colonisação e Reforma Agrária), coordinated the settlement of farmers along certain stretches of highway, initially between Altamira and Itaituba. The aim was twofold, on the one hand to develop the empty spaces of the Amazon, and on the other, by donating land to settlers from principally the drought-stricken northeast one contrived to help solve the problems of that region. Right from the very beginning a government decree reserved a 100 km wide strip of land on each side of the road for small and medium sized farms, thus among other things barring the land for speculative activities. Inside these 100 km wide strips, the first 10 km on either side of the road were reserved for small farms of maximum 100 ha in area. This land was divided up into plots of 400 m by 2500 m. Medium sized farms were foreseen for a further distance from the highway. Every farmer with a family therefore received a 100 ha plot of land, with the obligation not to clear more than half of it of trees. In addition each farmer received a simple wooden house, the most important tools, and seeds, on credit. INCRA regarded 50 ha as the smallest viable size of arable plot in line with protection of resources. The other 50 ha had to remain untouched in order not to endanger the ecological system of the tropical forest. This is a regulation which applies in all of the Amazon region. At intervals along the road, central settlements, so-called "Agrovilas", housing 48–64 families were planned, each with a school, shop, administration, and social centre, plus entertainment and sports facilities. Between 1970 and 1975 it was hoped that some 100,000 families would settle in the Amazon region, but in fact a mere 7000 made use of INCRA's offer. Of these, one third came from the northeast, 28% from Pará (mainly from the Bragantina), 13% from Maranhão, and 19% from southern Brazil. In addition many had little success in their new home, many gave up quite soon because they received little or no assistance from the state authorities. There were problems of organisation, such as badly functioning co-operatives, people had too little experience in tropical agriculture, there were no guaranteed markets for agricultural produce, there were no highgrade seeds, parasites and plant diseases affected crops, and there was not enough professional advice for the settlers. This list is not exhaustive. Not only did the pioneers have to cope with general difficult living conditions, but they also first had to gain experience with the poor soils. Some Agrovilas were closed down almost as soon as they opened, because the farmers did not want to commute between village and field. They preferred living on their own land. Because of this, most of the planned Agrovilas were never built. The settlers from the dry northeast had particular difficulties with the humid and hot climate, and were also prone to diseases (including malaria) which they had not experienced before. Soon there were more emigrants than new settlers, so that in retrospect this effort to settle small farmers in the damp Amazon forest must be judged a clear failure.

Apart from the state's efforts, there are also private schemes to bring agricultural development to the Amazon, but these also benefit from massive tax relief. Since the 1970s countless cattle grazing establishments have been founded on the southern border of the Amazon forest with the Cerrado. These cattle farms all occupy between 10,000 and several hundred thousand hectares of land. Here too, only half of the available land may be cleared of trees, although of course it is very difficult to check if these regulations are being complied with. The herds are largely made up of Indian bulls, as well as crossbreds from European breeds, and they have adapted well to the tropical climate, giving satisfactory beef in quality and quantity. The investors are partly big farmers from other regions of Brazil, but more usually trading companies, banks, insurance companies, and industrial concerns which have no links with agriculture, and are just looking for a safe investment. They employ experienced cattle breeders to implement their projects. There are differing estimates as to the extent of these cattle pastures. In 1977 this figure was put at 80,000 km^2, two thirds of it in the northern Mato Grosso, providing grazing for 3 million head of cattle. An averagely good pasture can support one to one point five animals per hectare, but here too there is a risk of overusing the land in time.

Most of the mining and industrial undertakings in operation or planned in the Amazon are privately or semi-privately financed. One of the biggest is a semi-private project in the eastern Amazon based on the iron ore deposits in the Serra dos Carajás near Marabá on the Rio Tocantins. After an estimated 18 thousand million tons of iron ore were discovered there, and the CVRD (Companhia Vale do Rio Doce) showed an interest in exploiting this ore, further valuable minerals such as copper, gold, nickel, and manganese were found not far away in the triangle formed by Belém–São Luís–Marabá. In addition one of the western hemisphere's largest manganese ore quarries is being exploited north of the Amazon river mouth in Amapá territory. Further to the west on the Rio Trombetas enormous bauxite reserves have been found. In order to ensure the necessary electricity supplies, various hydroelectric works have been planned or are already under construction, so that aluminium can be produced locally, and the Serra dos Carajás to São Luís railway line in Maranhão, opened in 1985, can be electrified. This all exceeds the investment potential of a single company like the CVRD by a large margin, and it has therefore demanded the formation of a state development authority for the region, along the lines of the Tennessee Valley Authority in the USA. At the moment much of this is only in the planning stage, but thanks to earlier learning experiences in the opening up of the Amazon, it is likely that a good proportion of these plans will be realised.

Development of Amazon area

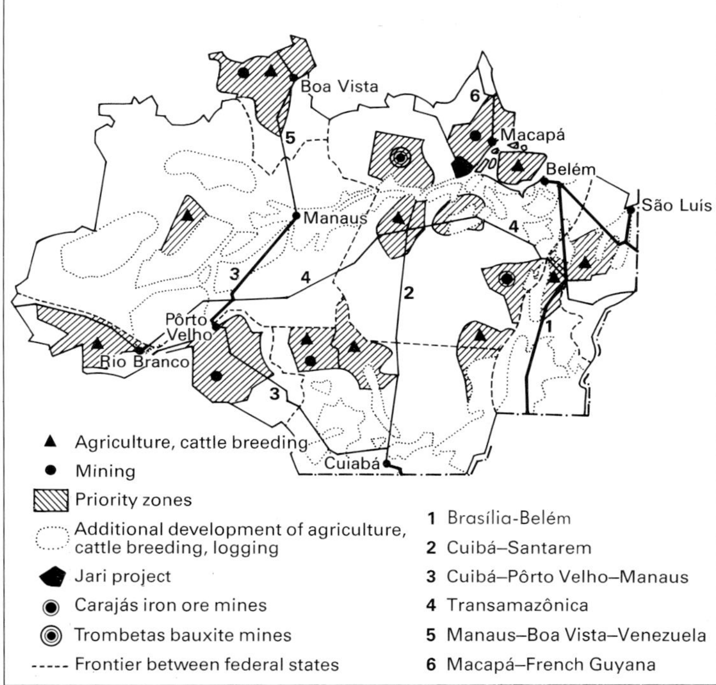

There are mineral resources in other parts of the Amazon: the manganese quarries in Serra do Navio in Amapá Territory have already been mentioned. They are linked to the port of Santana near Macapa by an ore railway 200 km in length. A modern mining town has grown up over the past three decades in the Serra do Navio. It has 3000 inhabitants, mostly miners and employees together with their families, benefiting from all facilities and modern amenities, including a well-equipped hospital, which is also open to patients not connected with the quarries. The future of this town, also called Serra do Navio, is uncertain, because it is expected that the manganese deposits will be exhausted within the foreseeable future. Finally, there are also significant tin deposits in Rondônia Territory. This rounds up this survey of the major mineral resources known so far – but more discoveries can be expected, because the Amazon region is, geologically speaking, still partly unknown country.

As well as promoting the mining of raw materials, Sudam also backs industrialisation in all its forms, although so far it is mainly the cities of Belém and Manaus which have profited. But this support is now to be extended to further towns such as Boa Vista on the frontier with Venezuela and Guyana, Rio Branco in Acre state, and Porto Velho in Rondônia state. Emphasis will be put on the use of local plant and mineral resources and products. At the forefront will be foodstuffs and textiles. Manaus, the former rubber capital, is an exception: with the creation of its free trade zone in 1967 it attracted both firms from the south of Brazil and from abroad, and they all set up subsidiaries in Manaus. Semi-finished goods and some raw materials were imported duty-free, and combined with local materials, and above all the cheap labour, were made into finished articles. Since 1967, 40,000 jobs have been directly created thus in Manaus, and an equal number, if not more, resulted indirectly. The most representative industries of Manaus are electronics, watches, clothing, motors, and plastics.

In consequence of the exploitation of further raw material sources, paper manufacturing, wood and cellulose factories are planned, also meat processing plants, and nearer the coast, fish processing is foreseen. The largest projects are a steel mill near São Luís (using ore from the Serra dos Carajás) and an aluminium smelter (using bauxite from Rio Trombetas) in Belém.

A remarkable experiment is being carried out on the Rio Jari, 500 km west of Belém. It is probably the largest private undertaking ever carried out in the Amazon: it is the attempt, by using all the latest available modern technology to manufacture cellulose on a large scale. The initiator of the project was a very rich over eighty year-old American called Daniel K. Ludwig who in 1965 bought up 20,000 km^2 of land on the Rio Jari and began clearing part of the forests there, in order to thereafter plant especially fast-growing tree species suitable for cellulose manufacture. They are cut down after eight to ten years, and processed in the factory. The firm does not only export wood pulp, but also considerable quantities of rice, which originally had only been planted to feed the employees. Another export product is kaolin, which was discovered by chance on the site. Yet another recent coincidental find has been rich bauxite reserves which will shortly be exploited. Several thousand relatively well-paid workers are at present employed on the Jari. The project is fascinating because account is taken as much as possible of the forest ecology. This means that the shallow jungle soil has to be very carefully handled, that the waste water is treated, and so on. But the project is still surrounded by many an uncertainty: for instance the tree monoculture practised calls for enormous use of pesticides.

All in all though, the Jari project is a highly instructive attempt at introducing an industrial economy into the tropical rain forest, unless of course one takes the view that no economic use at all should be made of this area. However, for some time now the Jari project has been in increasing financial difficulties. The main reason for this was the continual increase in oil prices, but also the fact that Ludwig did not receive the hoped for permission to build a hydro power station. In addition there were more and more doubts in government and military circles about such potential concentration of power in the Amazon in the hands of a foreigner. As a result Ludwig severely curtailed his activities, and ultimately in January 1982 he sold his company to a group of Brazilian entrepreneurs, who in addition received financial aid from the state.

In conclusion, to sum up the development impulse that has resulted in the Amazon from the already described activities, one can cite some of the points made in a survey by Sudam in 1977: of the just under 600 requests to set up a business of any kind in the three economic sectors, no less than 63% relate to cattle husbandry (steer grazing). Industry and mining account for a little more (39%) than agriculture (38%), with the tertiary sector in the shape of inland shipping, energy supply, and tourism accounting for 23%.

The number of new jobs created is very small when compared with the enormous investment activity. This is probably because the industries that have been planned are very efficient and not labour intensive, and the same goes for cattle grazing which needs very little staff, on average only one worker per 235 ha. Although the total for industry is proportionately higher, it still does not amount to more than a drop in the ocean. It would probably be much cheaper to create employment in areas where there is already an infrastructure and where conditions are not so unbearably hard as in the Amazon. New priorities were set from 1975 onwards with the naming of new development and economic target areas, 15 of which have been pinpointed in the Amazon region.

The Potential in Natural Resources

In order to assess this one first has to analyse in brief the sectors agriculture, mining, and energy supply, seeing as these will largely determine the future development of the country.

Agriculture For centuries Brazil was exclusively a farming country, and lived from its exports of agricultural produce. Even today 40% of Brazil's exports still stem from agriculture, and this percentage will have to increase somewhat in the future. 1980 was a record harvest for Brazilian food products, totalling 240 million tons, of which 50 million tons were basic supplies such as rice, black beans, maize, soybeans, and wheat. It is a paradox, but even this record harvest did not suffice to cover the food and foreign currency requirements of the country. Agriculture is expected to experience the same boom in the 1980s as industry had in the previous decade, because as well as the already mentioned functions, a third has been added to the list, namely the production of alcohol as an alternative fuel for motor vehicles. In order to achieve all these targets, agricultural production would have to increase annually by between 7 and 10%. In principle this would appear possible, but in fact would be very difficult to realise. Although in the past few years it has been recognised that the soils of equatorial forests are extremely ill-suited for field cultivation, there remain in other regions of Brazil many wide open spaces which climatically and pedologically

33 *The well-known Brazilian tobaccos are planted around the Baía de Todos os Santos (All Saints' Bay) near Salvador. Most of the tobacco is used to make cigars for export, but it is also used in cigarettes for the domestic market, while pipe tobacco is less popular than in Europe. The tobacco leaves are dried in the towns and villages of the interior, but cigar-making is mostly confined to the large centres.*

34 ▷ *The north coast of Brazil in Ceará is frequently marked by the abrupt termination of the old strata of the Brazilian shield, combined with a not very high, but nevertheless marked escarpment giving on to the beach below. The rock has been deeply weathered by rain, wind, sun, and the beating of the waves has also modelled the coast. On the beach one can see several Jangadas, the almost legendary fishing boats of the Northeast, which used to be a common sight on all the beaches from Bahia to Ceará. They are made of five parallel balsawood trunks which form the hull. They are some 7 m long, and 2 m in the beam. They are more rafts than boats, with every wave breaking over the boat. The three-man crew has to be on its guard so that nothing is swept overboard. The catch is immediately placed in a covered basket affixed to the mast. The fishermen usually set sail in these simple boats early in the morning, returning as a rule in the afternoon, although sometimes they remain at sea for several days. Unfortunately these boats have become a more and more seldom sight in recent years, as they are being replaced by the new and large ships of a professional fishing industry.*

35

36

37

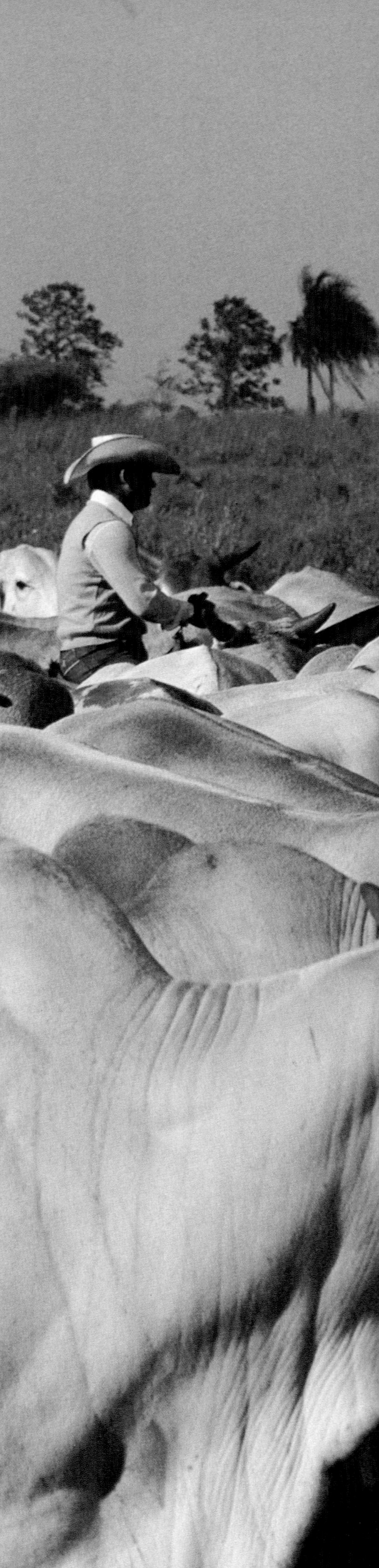

35 *A "Boiada" is a wandering herd of cattle on its way from the extensive pastures of the distant Mato Grosso or Goiás to the fattening areas of São Paulo state. The cowboys, here having a rest in the Cerrado, are called "boiadeiros".*

36 *The "gaúcho" is the cattle-drover of the Pampas of Rio Grande do Sul.*

37 *Branding a steer in the Mato Grosso.*

38 *Zebu herd in the Mato Grosso.*

38

39 *There are various sorts of bananas in all tropical countries: for cooking or frying, to be eaten raw, or as food for domestic animals. Four different sorts can be seen in the picture, to the left and right of the door.*

40 *The sailing barges from all around the bay still ply their wares in the old harbour of Salvador. The white tapioca flour in the large sacks is sold in small quantities to individual customers.*

41 *Fruit and vegetables make up a large part of the market in Caruaru, in the interior of Pernambuco state.*

39

40

41

FANTA
Coca-Cola
Betãnia
ANTARCTICA

42 *A motley crowd in the port of Manaus, where ships from all over the Amazon basin dock and merchants from the river banks congregate, but where "consumer goods" are also sold, and where cargo is transshipped from one vessel to another: this is the meeting place of the people from the vast forests.*

would be highly suitable. Particularly fertile are the volcanic soil in part of southern Brazil, and the Várzea flood plains which are widespread throughout the country. Many of these areas have already been ploughed, but others are still awaiting cultivation. As well as finding new arable land, agricultural experts also point to the potential for increased productivity on existing soils, that is more return per hectare. In this respect Brazil is quite backward in relation to other countries. There would be many possibilities to intensify agriculture, the obstacles being less technical than financial, and above all political in nature (agrarian reform, better training of farmers).

Mining (without energy sources) Brazil is mining country albeit of a one-sided type. It has almost infinite iron ore resources (known deposits equalling 10,000 million tons) which have only been slightly exploited so far in Minas Gerais. The country also has large reserves of tin, nickel, and bauxite. The tin deposits are mainly to be found in the Amazon region, particularly in Rondônia, in other words very far away from the industrial centres of the country. The nickel deposits are more conveniently situated in Minas Gerais and Goiás. Especially the Goiás deposits which were fairly recently discovered appear very promising, so that supplies, even taking into account a certain proportion of exports, are assured for years to come. Bauxite used only to be mined in Ouro Preto, but now huge amounts have been discovered, as already mentioned, on the Rio Trombetas in the north. Preliminary figures speak of 3–4 thousand million tons. Many other minerals are exploited all over Brazil, but (for the time being?) they are not sufficient in quantity to meet increasing national demand. Among these minerals are above all metals such as lead, chrome, copper, manganese, tungsten, zinc, and zirconium, as well as gold and silver, plus minerals such as barite, fluorite, graphite, kaolin, magnesite, and talcum.

Energy potential Brazil's energy resources are even more interesting, but also more problematical. As far as is known, Brazil has very little crude oil. What there is, can be found in the states of Alagoas, Sergipe, Bahia, Espírito Santo and Rio de Janeiro, mostly near the coast, and often on the continental shelf. The main producing zone is the region around

All Saints Bay in Bahia. In 1978 Brazil produced 9.6 million cubic metres of crude, of which 2.5 million came from the shelf area. Brazil supplies about one-sixth of its oil needs from local production. By maintaining the present rate of production, known reserves will last for about another 20 years, so that in future too, Brazil will be very much dependent on oil imports. Because of the innate uncertainty surrounding oil imports, the foreign trade balance has been negative for years, and at the end of the 1970s the foreign debt rose to over 50 thousand million US Dollars. So the government decided as early as 1975 to produce vast quantities of alcohol as an alternative fuel. Most of this alcohol is to be distilled from sugarcane, but also from cassava root as well as other plants. This means that the sugarcane plantations have to be doubled in area (from 3 to 6 million hectares) by 1985, unless one were to merely transfer all existing sugarcane production into alcohol supply.

Although Brasília has given assurances that this mammoth project will not be allowed to interfere with food production for the people, there are misgivings that arable land will be used mainly for the production of motor spirit at the expense of land for increased basic food essentials. Such a development would be a major disadvantage for the poorer sections of the population. In any case, already today between 8 and 16% alcohol are added to gasoline in Brazil, and there are already quite a number of pure-alcohol driven cars on the roads. The local industry manufactures motors specifically

Economic Activity in the Regions (from P.G. Geiger, Atlas Nacional do Brasil)

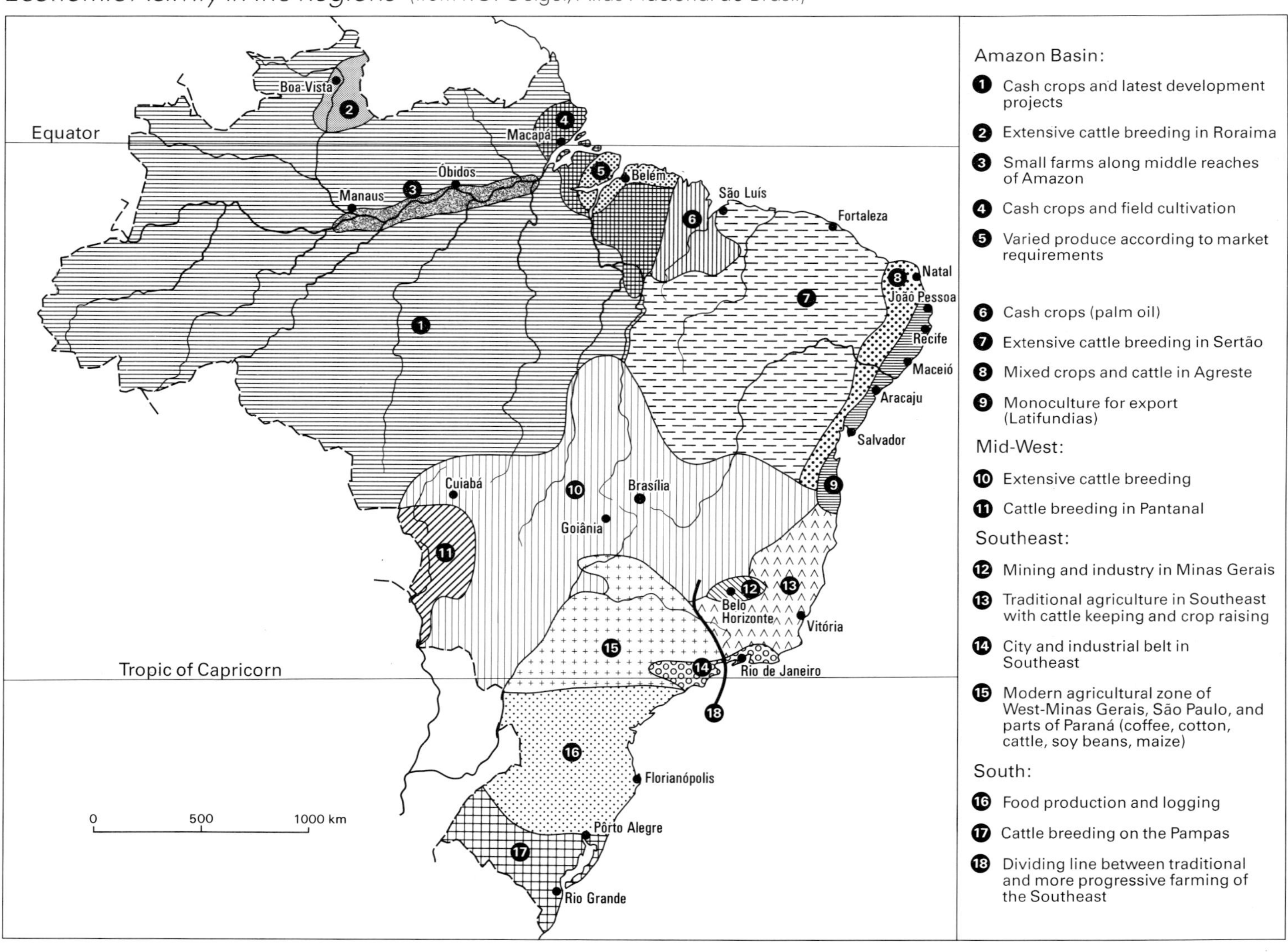

for alcohol fuel, and many cars have been converted. In theory the ultra-ambitious alcohol programme is fascinating, and in view of the climate of the country, it appears largely realistic.

But other ways of finding independence from expensive oil imports are being studied as well. In the southern states of Paraná, Santa Catarina, and Rio Grande do Sul oil shale has been found, some of it of very high oil content. Although commercial exploitation is too expensive for the time being, a research plant has been built in São Mateus near Curitiba, where studies into future uses of this oil shale have been under way for several years.

Brazil has considerable coal reserves. It is estimated that there are some 5000 million tons worthy of excavation. These deposits are for the most part in Santa Catarina, also in the south. New deposits have been found in Pará State in the Amazon. Mining has been rather moderate up to now (about 8 million tons annually) which can largely be attributed to the generally poor quality of this coal which needs much purification before it can be used. The main consumers are the steel industry and some coal-fired power stations.

Nuclear energy is also being pursued. An atomic power station is being built in Angra dos Reis on the coast between Rio de Janeiro and Santos. In its first stage it has to generate 625 MW. But there have also been increasingly critical voices in Brazil saying that in the light of the large water power reserves the country could forgo nuclear energy. Brazil has its own uranium, but its quantity is not said to be very large, and government sources indicate that it would only last into the 1990s.

Very promising is the already mentioned hydroelectric power potential of the country, which is under full development, but still far from being exhausted. In the past, right up to the present day there were always several large dams under construction simultaneously. Installed capacity has increased considerably every year. Brazil's official hydroelectric potential is put at a little over 100 million kW. This figure breaks down 35 million kW for the Amazon and its major tributaries, 12 for the Tocantins, 9 for the São Francisco, 28 for the Paraná, and 7 for the Uruguay river. While the rivers of the Amazon remain largely unused because of their distance from the main power users, the same is not true of the other rivers, which in part are already harnessed to capacity, or where the remaining possible power stations are under construction. Of the existing power stations one should mention the Rio Paraná with its Urubupungá works of 4.6 million kW installed capacity, and São Simão (2.6 million kW); at the Rio São Francisco, the Paulo Afonso and the Sobradinho stations, with together 4 million kW capacity, plus Três Marias (0.4 million kW). The Rio Parnaíba in the northeast has the Boa Esperança power station. In operation since 1984 are the Itaipu complex on the Rio Paraná, on the frontier with Uruguay (12.6 million kW), and the Tucuruí power station on the Rio Tocantins with 5 million kW installed capacity.

At the moment total installed capacity of all power stations, including countless small and medium sized hydroelectric plants amounts to just over 30 million kW. In coming years this figure will be drastically increased when power stations already under construction, but not mentioned here, come on stream. These efforts should ensure that Brazil can cover its power needs in the next ten years. Additionally, the reservoirs behind the dams often serve as irrigation systems, and one day when the whole network is built, it might be linked up as a large inland waterway system.

History of Brazil

There are many bizarre and unique elements in Brazil's history. In what other case have there been negotiations around a table over zones of influence and territories which had yet to be discovered. It was the Treaty of Tordesillas, signed by Spain and Portugal after arbitration by Pope Alexander VI in 1494, which set out the mutual spheres of influence along a certain line of Longitude, and thus gave the as yet undiscovered coastal strip of Brazil to Portugal. In April 1500 the Portuguese Admiral Pedro Cabral set foot, perhaps not just by chance, on the shores of South America. This marked the beginning of Portuguese hegemony in Brazil, although colonisation of this overseas territory was neglected for a long time. Because manpower and financial means were lacking, it was Portuguese policy from the very start to encourage intermarriage with the native Indian population. Only the hunger for gold and precious stones on the part of the colonials sealed the fate of the native population and led to the establishment of the slave trade involving Africans. The "Bandeiras" or expeditions of the combative inhabitants of São Paulo led to Indian hunts across large areas of the unknown interior, and brought the violent annexation of the vast country which is Brazil today. The native Indians died out or increasingly intermixed with the Portuguese and the growing number of imported negro slaves. This is the origin of the cosmopolitan race of which many Brazilians are so proud. The colonial and republican times brought economic booms due to the production of sugar, the discovery of gold, rising revenue from coffee, the rubber boom of last century, and again through coffee and industry. Brazil gained political independence from Portugal in 1821, but thanks to the continuation of the Bragança dynasty under Emperors Dom Pedro I and Dom Pedro II, the former colony remained politically united. This huge tropical country today boasts an area of 8,511,965 km^2. The question of slavery triggered off bitter fighting within the country in the second half of last century, and the abolition of slavery in 1888 led to the fall of the emperor one year later. Since then Brazil has been a republic. Industrialisation brought modernisation, but also resulted in social problems which grew more pressing, first in the urban areas and later also in rural regions. Getúlio Vargas attempted to solve these difficulties through state control. The construction of the new capital, Brasília, socialisation under Goulart and the military takeover are all steps on the path of progress of South America's largest country.

The Discovery of the Brazilian Coast and the First References to a Native Population

The landfall of a Portuguese fleet on the South American coast, on the "other side of the broad ocean", later hailed as the discovery of Brazil, took place on 22nd April, 1500. Admiral Pedro Cabral (1467–1526) had been on his way to the East Indies with 13 ships and 1500 crew. Two years before this event, his compatriot Vasco da Gama had discovered the sea-route to the East Indies around the Cape of Good Hope, and Pedro Cabral, sailing under the orders of the Portuguese crown was to reinforce the new possessions in the region of Calicut on the Malabar coast with more soldiers, administrators, artisans, and merchants. According to official accounts, a period in the doldrums before the African coast forced the fleet to set a marked westerly course, and led to the discovery of the Brazilian mainland. But there are also credible indications that Cabral's detour from the direct route to the Cape of Good Hope was no coincidence, and that the Portuguese admiral was carrying out secret orders from King Manuel I to set out for the western hemisphere and explore the New World. There had been rivalry between the two leading naval powers of the time, Portugal and Spain, over dominance of the Atlantic, ever since Spain's incursion into the Americas with Christopher Colombus's voyage of discovery in 1492. This rivalry was largely a question of who was to possess new-found territories. The Pope, as arbiter of Christianity, took it upon himself to apportion previously unknown "heathen areas" among seafaring nations. In 1493, the year of Columbus's return to Spain, Pope Alexander VI issued four bulls giving the House of Castile title to all discovered and yet to be discovered land in the areas explored by Columbus. Furthermore, the Pope, who was a descendant of the Spanish Borgia family, drew a demarcation line which was supposed to divide Spanish and Portuguese spheres of influence. This longitudinal line ran 100 miles west of the Azores and all territories to the east of it were to belong to Portugal, while all islands and mainlands to the west were given to the House of Castile. On his westbound voyage, Columbus had sailed the expanse of the Atlantic ocean without meeting land. The Papal Bulls therefore had no practical value for the Portuguese kings. Consequently the Portuguese monarch protested vehemently, going as far as threats of war, against the demarcation line. On the 7th June 1494 Spain and Portugal reached a compromise with the Treaty of Tordesillas. The Portuguese zone of influence was moved westwards, as far as 370 miles west of the Azores. Thus Portugal came into possession of the coast from the mouth of the Amazon and far down into the south, without any European at the time having even an inkling of the existence of the South American continent. Brazil was the result of this almost unbelievable coincidence.

After coming ashore on this unknown coast, the sailors ascertained that the newly discovered territory was within the zone that had been allotted to Portugal. They claimed the land in the name of the crown of Portugal by driving a stake, bearing the royal coat of arms, into the ground. This occurred in Porto Seguro, later known as Bahia. Having wrongly assumed that they had landed on an island, they called the new territory "Ilha de Vera Cruz", or Island of The True Cross. The sojourn of the Portuguese sailors lasted only a week. According to a custom prevalent at the time, Pedro Cabral left behind two pardoned prisoners and, in addition, two midshipmen fled on to land from one of the ships. A supply vessel was sent back to Portugal to bring the important news to King Manuel I.

A comprehensive account of this short visit to South America was given the king in a report written by his secretary, Pedro Vaz de Caminha. He wrote that the crew had seen a broad, high, round-topped mountain, and south of it, low hills and flat, forested land. The description of the natives is of particular interest: they came on to the beach in twos and threes, "so that there were already 18 or 20 of them when the boat came into the estuary ... they were brown, naked, made no attempt to cover their private parts and carried bows and arrows. They immediately approached the boat. Nicolan Coelho signalled them to throw down their weapons, which they immediately did. Coelho threw them a red beret, a fluffy cap and a black hat, whereupon one of the natives threw back a headdress made of long birds' feathers. The pilot of our ship took captive two native youngsters of good build who had been on a raft.

They are brown in colour, almost red, have pleasant facial features and well-formed noses. They walk around naked and are no more ashamed of showing their genitals than their faces. Both carry a stub of bone in their perforated lower lip. The bone is of hand's breadth, thick as a cotton spool and sharp as a drill. Their hair is thick, smooth and cut short above their ears. One of them wore a sort of wig made of birds' feathers; it was very thick and bushy and covered his head from temple to temple, as

well as the back of his head and his ears. Each feather was affixed to his hair by a waxy, soft mass, so that the wig was dense, round, and even ...
After a walk of a mile and a half, two Portuguese men came upon a village of nine or ten houses, each house as long as our leading ship. They were made of wood, with the sides boarded, and the roofs thatched, and quite high. The houses only had one large room, with no dividing walls, and very many posts. Attached high up on these posts were hammocks in which the natives slept. Underneath they kept a fire burning, presumably for warmth. Each hut had a low door on two opposite sides. There were thirty to forty people in each hut, eating edible roots."

Brazil's "birth certificate" and the first page of its history closes with the departure of the fleet on 1st May, 1500.

Brazil in Colonial Times

The Name "Brazil" – The First Settlement Further expeditions were sent to explore the most recent discoveries in the New World. The most important explorers were the brothers Martim Afonso and Pedro Lopes de Sousa. They sailed the extensive coastal waters and took possession for the Portuguese crown by driving in stakes with coats of arms. For many years the sailors of Portugal only used the Terra de Vera Cruz as a stop on their way to the Indies. The name Brazil appeared later, being taken from the main product of the region, Brazil timber or red dye-wood, which was much appreciated in Europe. Because of its purple colour it was called Pau brasil, and from this came the new name for the country. The name "Brazil" was recorded for the first time on Waldseemüller's famous world map of 1507.

The Portuguese monarchs had little appreciation for their new territory on the South American mainland, and the King omitted to insert the title of ruler of Brazil among the many he already used. Initially the new possession served as a kind of penal colony, and the first white settlers were prisoners or sailors who had deserted. Trading posts were established along the extensive coastline, but they were independent of each other, and had no common link. They served as market places for bartering with the natives, and as storage sites for timber. The first settlers lived very primitively in huts surrounded by palisades to ward of Indians from the stored barter goods. Hunting and fishing provided essential food and the local Indians had to provide the labour. Apart from the main product, red dye-wood, pelts, decorative feathers, and Indian weapons and implements were also traded. European contribution was a selection of inferior wares. After only a few decades, the coastal forests had been decimated, and the export of valuable timber declined rapidly.

From the very beginning the Portuguese crown encouraged intermarriage between Portuguese men and Indian girls. This was a question of policy forced on Portugal, which, with its small home population of 1,125,000 could not hope to rule its colonies in Africa, India and settle and Brazil simultaneously. Thus white colonials were urged to marry Indian wives, or at least live with them and to produce large families. The basic prerequisite for such marriages was that the Indian woman be baptised into the catholic faith. Thus the basis of Brazil's mixed population was formed during the first fifty years of colonisation.

The Portuguese Colonial Administration Portugal's South American possession was still only made up of a series of individual trading posts. After 1504 French vessels repeatedly approached the coastal region in order to secure supplies of the valuable dye-wood. Furthermore, the flanks of the Portuguese fleet sailing to the Indies were threatened by daring French freebooters who continually tried to set foot in Brazil.

But the Portuguese crown did not have the means to colonise the long coastline and, as a result, the King drew upon the resources of private entrepreneurs. The complete coastal strip from the Bay of Maranhão in the northwest to the Ilha de Santa Catarina in the South was divided into 15, some sources say 14, plots. Most of them extended 296 km from north to south, some only 178 km. The borderlines in the interior consisted of a series of parallel lines of latitude which reached up to the line set according to the Treaty of Tordesillas. These 15 plots were called Capitanias and were leased to 12 administrators, including the Sousa brothers, who as deserving sailors received respectively three and two Capitanias. Only a few of these territories came up to expectations in terms of development. Most successful were areas where sugar cane was planted. The leasing system was a failure, and as time went on the crown repossessed all the Capitanias. Brazil underwent a comprehensive administrative reform in 1549, with the setting up of a General Government Office (Governo geral) based in Bahia. The highest civil and military powers were now exercised by the Governor-General, the first one being Tomé de Sousa, who had several senior administrators at his side. With the hesitant progress in settling the coast – the establishment of individual supply bases and trading posts – the administration had difficulties in making asserting its authority and remained ineffectual right up to the end of the 16th century. Although the Governor-General was in name the representative of the crown and the highest authority in the land, he was hardly in a position to enforce obedience in this huge territory. Little Portugal, already engaged in Africa and Asia, could not indulge in real power politics in its Brazilian possession. The Portuguese rulers therefore left their South American colonies more or less to their own fate. Many of the measures taken seem more to be based on immediate and local conditions rather than to reflect a purposeful colonial policy. A system developed which was a mixture of local self-government and control by the royal authorities.

The Câmaras Municipais were of major importance as instruments of local self-government. These communal parliaments often passed laws which were enforced over a wide area. It was only the strengthening of the central power of the Governor General from the middle of the 17th century onwards which weakened this institution, and its powers were more and more curtailed by royal servants. After 1696 the elected local judges were replaced by justices appointed by the crown (juizes de fora). In 1714 the Governor General was given the title of viceroy, and in 1763 the seat of the central administration was moved from Bahia to Rio de Janeiro.

Portuguese Policy concerning the Indians The policy of the Portuguese crown with regard to the Indians changed according to prevailing interests. The dye-wood trade was totally dependent on the native labour for locating and felling the trees, not to mention transporting and loading the trunks. Until the middle of the 16th century, that is during the first fifty years of colonialism. The Portuguese treated the Indians as companheiros, as partners or employees. Once the settlers started enslaving the natives, however, the barter system was endangered. Increasing sugarcane plantations in the north called for more Indian labour, but as the Indians did not work voluntarily, the settlers saw forced labour as the only way to run their faziendas. To get slaves the Portuguese made use of Indian customs. During the constant tribal feuding prisoners were often taken with the aim of sacrificing them during tribal rites. The settlers called such prisoners "índios de corda", as they were normally led away on a rope. They traded such slaves for European goods and regarded them as well gotten gains – after all, they had saved their lives.

More slaves were taken in "just war". If natives resisted annexation of their territory they were taken by force. The question of the guerra justa started preying on the minds of the church and political authorities in Portugal. In principle only the king or his representative could declare war on the native population of the country. But once the Indians of the coastal region had been enslaved or driven off, the settlers started obtaining slaves by going on expeditions into the hinterland. These expeditions, known as entradas or bandeiras (from bandeira = flag), took on a military aspect from the 17th century onwards. Best known were the bandeirantes of São Paulo. The inhabitants of this town launched extensive raids far into the interior of the country. Some of them went as far as the Jesuit missions in Paraguay, from where in the years 1629–1632 they abducted tens of thousands of converted Indians. These expeditions showed the particular forest-marching prowess of the Mamelucos, half-castes of Portuguese and Indian blood.

In fact, the foundations of a moderate Indian policy had already been laid with the setting up of the Governor General's office in 1549. The aim of this policy was to convert the natives to Christianity, to protect converted Indians and to re-settle rural Indians in villages. These tasks fell to the Jesuits and, as a result, this missionary order was to be intimately concerned with the question in Brazil for the next two centuries.

The various royal decrees reflect the differing standpoints of the settlers and the Jesuits. In 1609 a protective law was passed which gave the Christian and non-baptised Indians and the settled and nomadic Indians the same legal rights, as well as making free men of them. From then on any enslavement would be illegal, but Indios captured during a "just war" would remain slaves. With further decrees putting more and more limitations on slavery, the settlers managed to impose other forms of forced labour on the natives, at the same time maintaining a semblance of legality.

The problem was solved in a different manner: Indian labour was replaced by African slaves, and except for a very small minority the population disappeared in the melting pot of the white and black races to form a major element of today's mixed-race population.

Political Independence

The Colonial Empire Although Portuguese Brazil remained in essence a coastal settlement, various undertakings had led to the major westward movement of the frontiers set by the Treaty of Tordesillas. Instead of an area of 2,875,000 km^2, which would have ensued if the agreement with Spain had been honoured, the Portuguese possession ultimately covered a surface of 8,500,000 km^2. The Portuguese had successfully excluded the French from their colony and an attempt at settlement by the Dutch West Indies company also failed. Although the capable Governor Johann Moritz of Nassau-Siegen conquered practically all of northern Brazil in 1637–1644, the profit-oriented merchants of the West Indies company were not willing to support such a risky adventure for long. Count Johann Moritz consequently resigned in 1644 and left Brazil. The size of New Holland shrank rapidly and the Portuguese captured the last stronghold in 1654. The bandeirante expeditions into the interior were largely responsible for the vast territorial expansion. During their expeditions, which often lasted years, they set up countless bases, whose agricultural production supplied provisions for the expedition members. Out of these little cells developed villages and towns.

An additional, highly significant factor in the settlement of central Brazil, however, was the discovery of rich gold deposits at the end of the 18th century. Hordes of gold hunters swarmed to the site of the first discovery, the location of the modern town of Ouro Preto (Black Gold). In the ensuing 75 years gold-mining became the most important economic activity (Minas Gerais, Mato Grosso, Goiás) in Brazil, surpassing even the booming sugar industry in the north. By the middle of the 19th century 600,000 people (a fifth of the total population at that time) had migrated to the gold mining areas. The gold hunters established small communities and towns, always well separated from one another. This marked a shift in economic importance from the old sugar cane areas of Pernambuco and Bahia to central and southern Brazil.

In the agricultural sector, livestock breeding was of considerable importance alongside sugar. But the less profitable cattle breeding industry had to resort to the dry regions of the north (Sertão). Cattle farms grew up along the rivers and by the middle of the 18th century covered an area of over a million km^2. Cattle breeding could not be intensively pursued, however, because of the negative effects of recurring droughts. Nevertheless the wilderness in the northeast was gradually opened up by peaceful means. The extensive plains of southern Brazil were also developed for the Portuguese empire by cattle breeders. A huge no man's land existed between the Rio de la Plata and its confluents and the Ilha Santa Catarina on the southern frontier. The region today called the Rio Grande do Sul with its grazing land, the pampas, offered ideal pasture land. The Portuguese landowners and their gaúchos, made up of Indians, half-castes and escaped slaves, formed the backbone of Portuguese power in the wars with Spain over this disputed territory. The cattle trails opened up the south too and, as in the north, this network of tracks from farm to farm was the prerequisite for the conquest and occupation of these regions.

Brazil gains Independence As was also the case in the Spanish colonies, the French Revolution had repercussions on the situation in Brazil. When Napoleon blockaded England, he demanded that its ally Portugal should give up its neutrality. But the Prince

Regent João, who was reigning in place of his mentally ill mother, refused to comply with the far-reaching demands of the French emperor, with the result that French troops invaded Portugal. Shortly before the occupation of Lisbon, the Prince Regent had decided to transfer the whole national administration including the royal court to its Brazilian colony. A large fleet with well over 10,000 men on board left Lisbon practically at the last minute and, under English escort, reached Brazil in January 1808.

Moving Portugal's authorities to Rio de Janeiro resulted in a fundamental change in the erstwhile viceregal status of Brazil, leading ultimately to economic separation of the colony from the homeland. Until then, Portuguese America had, from the economic point of vew, been totally dependent on Lisbon, but under English pressure, the Prince Regent decreed that the ports of the colony be opened to vessels of all friendly countries. In the circumstances, only English ships could take advantage of this freedom, and trade was taken up with them accordingly on a large scale. In the ten years between 1812 and 1822, the value of imports rose from 770,000 sterling in gold to 9,590,000. The transfer of the Portuguese administration to Brazil had a positive effect on all spheres of economic life. Foreigners streamed into the country, consumer demand increased, and Rio de Janeiro developed into a centre of economic importance on the Atlantic coast of Latin America.

The Regent, who became King João on the death of his mother in 1816, stayed in Brazil even after the peace treaties in Europe of 1815 which followed the downfall of Napoleon. This meant that the former colony achieved the same status as a kingdom as Portugal and the Algarve already enjoyed, and under the same Braganza dynasty. As a result Brazil also received favoured treatment in the shape of better roads, improved ports in various towns, new court buildings and university faculties, a national library, a military academy, and the opening of the Bank of Brazil. When the king was forced to return home by the Portuguese government in 1821, Brazil had reached a state of far-reaching autonomy. João took this into consideration by making his son, Dom Pedro, regent of Portugal's overseas territories. But the Lisbon government tried to regain control of Brazil and bring about a situation of dependence again. In the meantime the crown prince had become a symbol of Brazil's awakening national spirit, and his return to Portugal was demanded. This call only increased the antagonism between the powers in Brazil and Lisbon. The final breach came when the Cortes, the Portuguese parliament, threatened, in a manifest, to divest the prince of his right of succession if he failed to obey their orders. The Prince refused, and took over the leadership of the independence movement. His famous "call of Ipiranga" on 7th September, 1822 (independence or death!) was the last step in a process which had started with the relocation of the royal court to Rio de Janeiro. On 1st December, 1822 he was crowned Emperor Pedro I of Brazil. The imperial crown was a unifying factor because a member of the previous ruling dynasty, the Braganzas, was holding the vast empire together.

The Brazilian Empire

Emperor Pedro I Within a few years, the Great Powers had recognised the new state, even Portugal joined in after receiving an indemnity. On April 17th 1823 the Emperor called an assembly to draw up a new constitution, under the terms of which the ruling classes secured not only economic predominance for themselves, but also executive political power. But this assembly was ultimately dissolved by the Emperor in November 1823, after the various groups failed to reach agreement on the wording of the constitution. In its place, the Emperor appointed a council of state which in a very short time drew up a constitution that has gone down in Brazilian history as the Constituição outorgada, or imposed constitution. Local experience in legal matters was added to constitutional practice from Europe. The dissolution of the constitutional assembly brought Pedro I the enmity of liberal circles, who had been the mainstays of the independence movement. Several rebellions in the north had to be put down with force. The emperor became increasingly isolated from his people and was forced to abdicate in April 1831.

Emperor Pedro II The long reign of this sovereign (1831–1889) permitted the country to integrate its component parts and strengthened national consciousness, putting an end to any risk of the large state disintegrating. Initially a regent's council ruled the state in the name of the five-year old emperor. Revolts in Rio de Janeiro and other parts of the country were an indication of the instability of the new empire. The unity of the state was severely endangered by independence movements in Rio Grande do Sul and Santa Catarina. Only the personality of the young emperor seemed to be a guarantee, standing above party squabbles and regional strife. Thanks to a special law promulgated in 1840, Pedro II, who was then 14 ½ years of age, assumed the powers that by right belonged to the emperor of Brazil. After various amnesties he succeeded in putting an end to the civil wars. Pedro II had a talent for settlements and arrangements, and he was always able to mediate between feuding parties, between federalists and centrists and between government and parliament. Brazil underwent an internal health cure. As far as foreign policy was concerned Brazil was involved in a war, between 1865 and 1870, in alliance with Uruguay and Argentina against Paraguay, under its dictator Francisco Solano López. López was defeated thus ending the permanent threats to Brazil's frontiers.

Coffee Planting and Slavery The economic sector underwent a significant change which had started slowly in the first half of the 19th century and reached its climax in the last years of the same century. This restructuring was marked above all by a shifting of economic emphasis from the agricultural areas of the north to Rio de Janeiro and adjoining regions, such as Minas Gerais and São Paulo. This went hand in hand with a decline in production of established crops, such as sugar cane, cotton and tobacco in favour of more planting of coffee.

The coffee tree had been introduced to Brazil as early as 1727, during colonial times. But its cultivation remained insignificant for almost a century. It was only towards the end of the 18th century that coffee consumption reached an important level in Europe, and by the 19th century it had become the most important luxury beverage. Brazil offered highly favourable conditions for the coffee tree. The Terra roxa (red soil) is highly suitable for the plant, and central and south Brazil offered the same temperature and precipitation ranges found in tropical Africa where the coffee plant originates. "A green sea of coffee" was planted in these regions of Brazil – fazendas with hundreds of thousands of coffee trees. Coffee became the major economic factor in the country. In the 19th century the phrase was coined "O Brasil é o café" – Brazil is coffee!

Between 1821 and 1830 3.1 million sacks of coffee, each weighing 60 kg, were exported. By 1851–1860 this figure had risen to 27.3 million and by 1881–1890 to no less than 51.6 million sacks. These huge plantations called for ever greater numbers of workers. Until the French Revolution, English ships had supplied slaves from Africa. After the Congress of Vienna (1815) Britain changed its policy and tried to suppress the slave traffic on the high seas. After decades of struggle with the interested parties this policy succeeded. Brazil, together with Portugal and the United States, had put up the greatest resistance, because already during the time of the emperor's bid for independence, Brazil was importing 40,000 black slaves annually, and by 1840 this figure had increased to 50,000.

On 8th August, 1845 parliament in London passed the Aberdeen Bill, a law which declared that the whole slavery trade was piracy and that anyone breaking this law would be court-martialled. As a result, Brazilian ships were searched on the high seas and English warships threatened slave vessels in territorial waters and the ports of Brazil. An undeclared war existed between the two states. Brazil began to suffer as a result of the British measures and increasingly lost esteem abroad. In consequence of these pressures, the Brazilian government passed three laws in 1850 banning the slave trade, although slavery within the country itself remained largely unaffected. It took the pressure of changing public opinion and many an altercation between parties and organisations before slavery was finally abolished with the coming of the so-called "Golden Law" of 13th May, 1888.

The long drawn-out resistance of the coffee barons had prevented a gradual transition of black slaves to the status of free wage earner. Being very much overdue, the measures against slavery were taken in great haste, with the result that there were serious political and economic upheavals. During this unrest the monarchy was also abolished. On 15th

November, 1889 Marshal Fonseca proclaimed a republic. The new republic was accepted by the civil and military authorities without serious resistance following the abdication of Pedro II.

The Republic of Brazil

Political Conditions in the Old Republic For a long time the republic was the scene of internal political dissension and military risings. There were frequent financial difficulties; the time of the permanent republican crises had started. In February 1891 the new constitution of the United States of Brazil was proclaimed. The new laws were meant to lead the republican state into the modern era. Novelties included the admission of all religious cults, the separation of church and state and civil marriage. A significant change in the administrative sector was the granting of widespread autonomy to the individual states, of which there were twenty, making Brazil into a federal republic. The capital, Rio de Janeiro, was given the status of a federal district. According to the new constitution, legislative powers were vested in the Chamber of Deputies (Câmaro dos Deputados) with proportional representation, and a Senado Federal, comprising three senators from each federal state. The highest court was the Supremo Tribunal Federal – the federal high court. The President was given sweeping executive powers, and it was intended that he should be elected directly by the people for a single term of four years. The President had the right to appoint and dismiss his ministers.

This constitution, written in the spirit of the liberal epoch, and drawing on the US constitution, was based on the presidential system, on federalism and the granting of suffrage to certain categories of male citizens (women, clergymen and illiterates had no vote). Apart from a few minor changes, the 1891 constitution remained in force until 1930. Brazilian politicians and historians speak of this period as the "old republic" (República Velha), whereas the period after the 1930 "revolution" is referred to as the República Nova. This distinction is more than merely academic: in the first era the country experienced only power struggles between parties, politicians, and the military. After 1930 the power-wielders had to contend, in addition, with the political awareness of broad sections of the population, and increasing social problems.

The military leadership played the major role in the transition to a republican state. Logically the first President was Marshal Deodoro da Fonseca, who had led the military coup which toppled Emperor Pedro II in November 1889. But the Marshal's presidency, which started in 1891, only lasted nine months, after which he was forced to hand over power to the vice-president, Marshal Floriano Peixoto. He successfully suppressed several uprisings launched by the royalist navy, and defeated secessionist movements in the southern state of Rio Grande do Sul. His successor, Prudente de Morais, was the first civilian and directly-elected president. After many internal struggles he was able to bring peace to Brazil. The military action taken by the government against religious fanatics in the Guerra dos Canudos (1896/97) in Bahia was a burden. Antônio Conselheiro launched a mystical-religious war against the "Godless republic". Thousands followed him, and this uprising uncovered many unsolved social problems, especially with regard to the poor conditions of the people living in the undeveloped north of Brazil. The next head of state, Manuel Ferraz de Campos Salles introduced the "Politica dos Governadores". Under his policy, the state governors were given a decisive role in the selection of deputies and senators from their states. This resulted in the ruling-class of each state being very much favoured, with consequently no opposition to federal policies. Such a consensus led to the establishment of a governing class, and ultimately triggered off the revolution of 1930.

The political history of Brazil during the old republic was dominated by party quarrels and power struggles, as well as by presidential manipulation against opposition groups, which in turn were merely motivated by opportunism. Added to this were countless successful and unsuccessful coups by the military.

The rural population still made up the largest part of the electorate, so that political candidates had to seek their grass roots support there. As illiterates had no voting rights, voters were largely drawn from the ranks of landowners who, by and large, were the only ones who could read and write. This led to a preponderance of big landowners, and despite the liberal constitution there could no question of calling Brazil a democratic state. On the contrary, the freedom guaranteed by the constitution tended to ensure the privileges of the ruling classes.

Economic and Social Development up to 1930 The early years of the Brazilian republic were also fraught with economic troubles. The financial emergency had various origins. Not least among the causes was the abolition of slavery, which had been undertaken without any economic or social preparations whatsoever and thus led to a severe tightening of the money market. The wages of the slaves accounted for some 50,000 contos (the old currency) annually, out of a total money supply of 200,000 contos. The government thought it could counter increasing demand by printing huge amounts of paper money. This led to devaluation. The financial situation worsened further when, in 1896, coffee, the main export, dropped in price for the first time due to overproduction and a stagnating market. This is a difficulty which confronts Brazil right up to the present day. The Brazilian government, under political pressure, supported the coffee price and started storing the surplus, an economic policy which is still maintained today. More and more foreign capital was invested in the Brazilian coffee trade. Brazilians had to pay high interest rates and came under financial pressure from foreign creditors. In 1898 the Brazilian government was forced to declare a moratorium on its foreign debt repayments. This debt was not repaid till 1911.

New investment served to modernise port facilities and expand the railway network, which by 1920 had a route length of 28,553 km. Hydroelectric power schemes were begun. All technical development took place within an economy still based on agriculture, in particular monoculture of a few select export products of high trading value. More fazendas or plantations were a consequence of this situation.

From the 1870's onwards rubber had become a significant economic factor. The latex was won from para rubber trees *(Hevea brasiliensis)*, which grew only in the Amazon basin. Increasing European demand for latex brought a dramatic rise in price, which in turn led to an explosive upturn in rubber exports: in 1880, 7,000 tons were exported, between 1900 and 1910 34,500 tons annually, by 1912 42,000 tons. In succeeding years, however, the rubber market collapsed. Decades before, English merchants had smuggled seeds of the rubber tree out of Brazil (Henry Wikham in 1876) and planted them in suitable parts of the empire. The new rubber plantations in Ceylon and the Malay Peninsula practically eliminated Brazilian competition, which relied to a large extent on widely scattered, wild rubber trees. Manaus, the rapidly-growing capital of the Amazon state, with its luxury theatre and modern facilities, reverted to the status of an insignificant jungle town within a matter of years.

For a long time the lack of coal hampered the growth of heavy industry and secondary industries in Brazil, despite the abundant iron-ore deposits. But, thanks to the domestic cotton plantations, a textile industry grew up and further industrial activity followed. The naval blockade during the first world war cut off many imports and encouraged the production of consumer goods. In 1920 there were 13,300 companies employing a total of 275,500 persons.

The rise of national industry and the immigration of hundreds of thousands of foreigners into southern and central Brazil during the 1930's brought about a change in the traditional mentality. Parallel to this came an increase in the size of both the urban proletariat and the urban middle class. São Paulo, in particular, developed into a powerful centre of trade and industry. The ranks of the big landowners were joined by the new class of industrialists and bankers. While the rural regions stagnated and hardship drove many hungry land workers into the cities, the industrial workforce manifested its dissatisfaction with the economic crisis by agitating and going on strike. The Wall Street crash of 1929 also brought down the coffee-based economy of Brazil. Demand for coffee had dropped sharply, as had its price. In 1929 exports of coffee fell from 95 million to 66 million pounds, while the coffee price on the exchanges plummeted by two-thirds within a year.

43 *Many children of the wealthier Brazilian classes spend as much time in the arms of their "Babá" (usually a dark-skinned nanny) as with their mothers. This was already the case in colonial times, and in no small way helped to foster understanding between whites and blacks within Brazil. These nannies often spoil the children as if they were their own, and look after them with touching tenderness. Even if they do not want to show it, the children often retain memories of their fond "Babá", even for a whole lifetime.*

44 ▷ *Many Cariocas – as the inhabitants of Rio de Janeiro are called – spend Sunday on the beach. Once a week they leave the city to feel the fresh breeze and laze or swim in the sun. Or perhaps to sunbathe or take part in sports – in short, to meet friends and recuperate from their hectic, workaday life. Beach vendors offer Cafézinho, the small cups of black Brazilian coffee, chilled drinks, biscuits, or ice-cream, covering many kilometres of beach daily.*

MARINA
RIO

45

46

45 *Football fans can be found in all strata of Brazilian society, and thus the spectators in a football stadium represent a good cross-section of the country or region.*

46 *Three to four matches per week are played in the Maracanã stadium in Rio de Janeiro. A festive and at the same time combative atmosphere reigns not only among the players, but also the fans, who spur on their teams with flags, drums, firecrackers and cheers. There is almost a carnival atmosphere, with the supporters of the two teams sitting at opposite ends of the stadium. When a goal is scored there is an indescribable tumult on one side (foreground), and a deathly stillness on the other, punctuated at the most by whistling or booing. The stadium has a capacity of 180,000–200,000 spectators, but it is by no means sold out for every match.*

47 *These and similar larger or smaller welfare dwellings (this photo was taken in Natal, Rio Grande del Norte) built by the BNH-Banco Nacional de Habitação, can be seen on the outskirts of all larger Brazilian towns. The BNH, which is the federal bank for the development of housing, often builds up whole quarters of a town, thus permitting even simple labourers to purchase an apartment or house. Finance schemes ensure that the dwelling becomes the property of the tenant after ten or fifteen years.*

47

48

48 *Those who have enjoyed a good education, work in a sought after profession, and earn well, can live in luxury in Brazil, often in a large house with garden and swimming pool. The estate shown here, albeit a temporary one, was built near the frontier town of Foz do Iguaçu for the engineers working on the immense Itaipu hydroelectric scheme.*

49 *Favelas – slums in Rio de Janeiro, with the Corcovado in the background.*

50 *In the 1970s, the small settlers along the Trans-amazônica were given a 100 ha plot of land, and also a modest house by the government.*

51 *A poverty-stricken part of Salvador, called Alagados because the huts are built on piles in the water.*

50

49

51

52 *All over Brazil there are free evening classes for adults who wish to catch up with their primary or secondary education. Most of the pupils are illiterates who have later decided to learn at least how to read and write, as well as the basic principles of arithmetic. These schools and courses are staffed by state teachers, and run by MOBRAL (Movimento brasileiro de Alfabetisação) – the Brazilian movement for literacy. Although the courses take place in the evening, they are attended with much enthusiasm. Without a doubt, many of the pupils have the utmost difficulty in dealing with abstract problems after a hard day's work, which explains why the percentage of dropouts is high.*

Getúlio Vargas and the "New Republic"

Presidential elections took place in March 1930, in the midst of the severe economic crisis. The official candidate of the party of the previous incumbent won, as expected, but in nearly all the federal states a sizeable opposition party had formed. Calling themselves Aliança Liberal, the opposition rallied round the governor of Rio Grande do Sul, Getúlio Dorneles Vargas. The election result was challenged by the opposition, and with the support of part of the army, the Aliança Liberal rose up against the (real or imagined) ballot rigging, deposed the ruling President, Washington Luís, just a few weeks before his term ended, and put Getúlio Vargas into power. Congress was dissolved and political parties banned. The federal states were all given governors who toed the Vargas line. Vargas passed social legislation and introduced a new election law providing secret balloting and voting rights for women.

Coffee kept its dominating position in the economy, but the prerogatives of the coffee-growing rural aristocracy were to be cut back. This Vargas policy led to a major uprising in São Paulo in July 1932. But this attempt by the richest of the federal states to preserve its politically dominating role failed bloodily. The dictator had a new constitution drawn up which would give his government a legal base, and in 1934 he was elected president for four years by parliament. The constitution of 1934 contained corporate stipulations, and guaranteed corporations strong representation in parliament. The limitations on the autonomy of the federal states and the extension of presidential powers were to prove fatal for Brazilian politics.

Social questions were to be settled by the civil service, a move which cost Vargas the support of the initially sympathetic ultra left-wing factions. In 1935 the government was forced to suppress a communist revolt in Rio de Janeiro.

In November 1937 Getúlio Vargas, with the assent of the army, dissolved congress under the pretext that the forthcoming elections were endangering national security. Political parties were again banned. Under the constitution in force at the time, the incumbent president could not be re-elected for a further term, and so Getúlio Vargas ruled the country for the next 8 years as dictator. In 1943 he combined his comprehensive social legislation into a labour statute. This collection of legislation, the Consolidação das Leis do Trabalho, encompassed far-reaching regulations laying down working hours, minimum hygiene standards in factories, protection of female factory workers, social insurance, paid leave of absence, paid holidays, pension rights, and the so-called stability paragraph which stated that once an employee had completed ten years' work in the same job he could not be dismissed. Important for the future was the determination of a minimum wage (salário mínimo) for factory workers. This labour statute also regulated all trade union matters which were now completely under state control. Free trade unions were prohibited. This was a weakness of the syndicates, because they became instruments of the state and its control of the economy. Many of the laws and prescriptions in the social field could not be implemented; they were often a mere façade, or had negative ramifications for workers. Despite all the caveats one can make about Vargas' labour legislation, it must be admitted that it made an impact in a society where workers rights, demands or strikes had been immediately crushed by police action.

"Brazil for the Brazilians" was the slogan under which Vargas pursued a nationalistic economic policy which found widespread support among his compatriots in the time of the economic crisis and the second world war. The constitutions drawn up by Vargas in 1934 and 1937 included the principle of the economic emancipation of Brazil. Mineral resources, hydroelectric power and oil reserves were deemed to be national property. Their exploitation was restricted to Brazilian citizens.

A critical appraisal of Vargas' economic and social policies shows, however, that his measures one-sidedly favoured the industrial centres at the expense of agriculture. This explains why above all the industrial zones in central and southern Brazil profited from his period of rule, while the rural areas were sorely neglected from a technical and financial point of view. The difference in development levels between the various federal states, and indeed between urban and rural areas a whole, widened dangerously during Vargas' time.

After the second world war, and in the wake of worldwide "democratisation", the army forced Vargas to resign and make way for an elected president. The elections were won by General Dutra, who had been minister of defence under Vargas. The new president took office in 1946 and, the same year, a new constitution based on the 1891 model came into force. The federal states regained their autonomy and voting rights were extended to all Brazilians except illiterates. The president and vice-president were to be elected directly. Most of the social legislation of the Vargas period was included in the new constitution.

In the 1950 elections Getúlio Vargas, who had been forced to step down as dictator five years previously, was overwhelmingly voted in as president, well ahead of his two rivals. This charismatic politician had, with the help of a newly formed party, the Partido Trabalhista Brasileiro, again managed to mobilise much popular support. In contrast to previous terms of office, the now ageing Vargas was this time less successful; he failed to check rising inflation, nor did he tackle the problem of corruption among high-level colleagues, which erupted into a public scandal. The press, no longer fettered by censorship, mercilessly revealed the extreme moral weakness of the administration. A murder attempt on Carlos Lacerda, the editor of an opposition newspaper, resulted in the death of the editor's companion, who was an air force officer. The assailant proved to be a lieutenant of the presidential bodygard. The incensed army leadership called for the resignation of the president. Getúlio Vargas escaped threatening legal proceedings by committing suicide on 24th August, 1954.

Forced Industrialisation – The Construction of Brasília

President Vargas' legancy to his country included strained relations with the United States, an industrial workforce that was stormily demanding social justice which had been promised but not granted, nationalist leanings in politics and the economy, unfinished national economic experiments, a high national debt and inflation. Vice-president Café Vilho's interregnum could not solve these problems. The hopes of the people rested on a new president.

In the October 1956 elections there were three rival candidates: Juscelino Kubitschek, General Juarez Távora and Adhemar de Barros. Kubitschek won with some 3 million votes, Távora secured 2.6 million votes and Barros 2.2 million. With only 30% of the vote, Juscelino Kubitschek, former governor of the state of Minas Gerais, started his five-year term as president at the end of January 1956. He had announced an ambitious programme: "50 years' progress in 5 years". This was to be achieved chiefly by rapid industrialisation and the construction of a new national capital, Brasília. Hand in hand with this would come extensive road construction and improved power utilities. As a consequence it would be possible to open-up the Brazilian hinterland. Kubitschek had little time for social questions and took the view that industrial development would automatically solve the social problems. This was an underestimation of the extent to which the industrial triangle formed by São Paulo, Belo Horizonte and Rio de Janeiro would be profiting from his economic policies at the expense of the underdeveloped northeast and the interior. Nevertheless, as compensation, he founded the Sudene (see p. 39), which, although it boosted economic development, did not change the semi-feudal social structure of the northeast.

President Kubitschek's most obvious achievement was the building of Brasília, the new capital (replacing Rio de Janeiro), 1,000 km inland from the coast on the central Goías plateau. The new administrative centre was designed to give an impetus to the integration of the still undeveloped huge interior of the country into the economic life of the nation. It is hard to ascertain to what extent this aspiration or the personal ambition of the president were the motivating factors. The demanded speed of construction and the technical prerequisites exceeded by far the financial resources of the country. The freight costs of the building material were ten times higher than the value of the cargo itself!

The funds of the social security schemes as well as the city savings banks were used to cover the building costs. The cost of living increased critically. In 1955 the inflation rate stood at 13.1%, in 1959 37.7%. When, on 21st April, 1960, the architecturally beautiful city of Brasília took on the role of capital, in name at least, the country had already paid dearly for its ambitious dream in the form of many neglected social and economic problems.

The Institutional Crisis – The Administrations of Jânio Quadros and João Goulart

In October 1960 the electorate voted in the candidate of the opposition parties, Jânio Quadros, as their new president. He received 5.6 million votes, the highest any candidate had ever gained. Even João Goulart, the representative of the workers' party, scored a respectable figure of 4.5 million votes which secured him the office of vice-president. Jânio Quadros, former mayor of São Paulo, and governor of São Paulo state, could look back on uncorrupted and successful terms of office. His election symbol had been a broom, and the electors were expecting a clean sweep from him in the federal administration, a clean-up which, it was hoped, would prove exemplary for the rest of Brazil. The "forgotten" northeast especially was hoping for an incorruptible and independent president. During the election run-up many a wall and fence bore the slogan "Do not despair – Jânio is coming". Jânio Quadros started in severe "un-Brazilian" fashion. He fired many incompetent public servants and ordered long-overdue cuts in spending. In foreign policy he pursued a totally independent line. Diplomatic relations with the Soviet Union were re-established and diplomatic ties fostered with other members of the Communist bloc, such as Rumania, Bulgaria, Albania, and Hungary. Quadros defended the "right to self-determination of the Cuban people" and meant by this a Communist Cuba. The Brazilian delegation was ordered to vote in favour of Chinese membership of the United Nations. The president sent a special envoy to communist countries to arrange trade agreements. By taking the path of "neutralism" Jânio Quadros hoped to gain more room for manoeuvre in his relations with the United States. He wanted Brazil to act as the arbitrator of Latin America.

This policy earned Quadros countless opponents within the country, above all in church, industrial, and military circles. A factor adding to the increasingly negative atmosphere was the president's mer-

curial and brusque manner. Nevertheless, nobody was prepared for his sudden resignation after only seven months in office. "Dark forces", declared Jânio Quadros on August 25th 1961, "have made it impossible for me to remain at my post." Jânio Quadros' social, economic and political reform programmes had awakened much hope amongst the Brazilian people; his imprudent resignation was a severe disappointment to his supporters.
According to the constitution, vice-president João Goulart would have automatically been in line for the presidency, but as he was absent in the People's Republic of China on an official visit at the time of Quadro's resignation, Congress followed constitutional requirements and passed power, ad interim, to the president of the parliamentary assembly. Subsequently the three defence ministers (army, navy and air force) tried, by invoking "national security", to prevent the Socialist vice-president from becoming head-of-state.
There had been earlier clashes between the military leadership and Goulart. In 1954 Getúlio Vargas was forced to dismiss Goulart, who was then labour minister, because the army commanders had accused Goulart of trying to build up the state-run trade unions as a personal power base. Goulart, like Vargas, came from Rio Grande do Sul, and was a member of a prosperous landowning family. But he had turned to the trade unions and after the death of Vargas he took over the leadership of the latter's PTB, the Partido Trabalhista Brasileiro.
After the failure of the military to prevent Goulart's accession to the presidency, a compromise was finally agreed on: the presidential system was to be replaced by a parliamentary model based on Western European models. The head of state was vested more with representational duties than with real powers. This hastily drawn up compromise was passed by 233 votes to 55 in parliament and by 47 to 5 in the Senate. The threat of civil war was thus averted. João Goulart returned to Brazil and was sworn in as president on 7th September, 1961. From the very beginning the new president tried to cast off the fetters of the parliamentary system and to re-establish the old system with real power for the government. In January 1962, with the support of 80% of the votes in a referendum, he was able to rein-

53 *Diamond panners, called "garimpeiros", at work in Roraima territory in the far north of Brazil. Their work, which has hardly changed in a century, involves the use of basic tools such as a hoe, a shovel and a sieve. The washing is actually a sorting process whereby the heaviest particles in the sand, which include diamonds, remain at the bottom of the sieve. The sieve with its contents is then turned over, easily revealing any diamonds in the sand. The "garimpeiros" seldom strike it rich, and when they do find one or two more valuable pieces, it is usually the merchants purchasing them who make the big profit. In contrast to earlier times, the sand is no longer only sieved manually; nowadays strong jets of water are also used to turn it over. Brazilian diamond production in the 1970s reached 100,000 carats of industrial diamonds annually, and a similar quantity of gems. Most of the stones come from the mining state of Minas Gerais.*

54

55

56

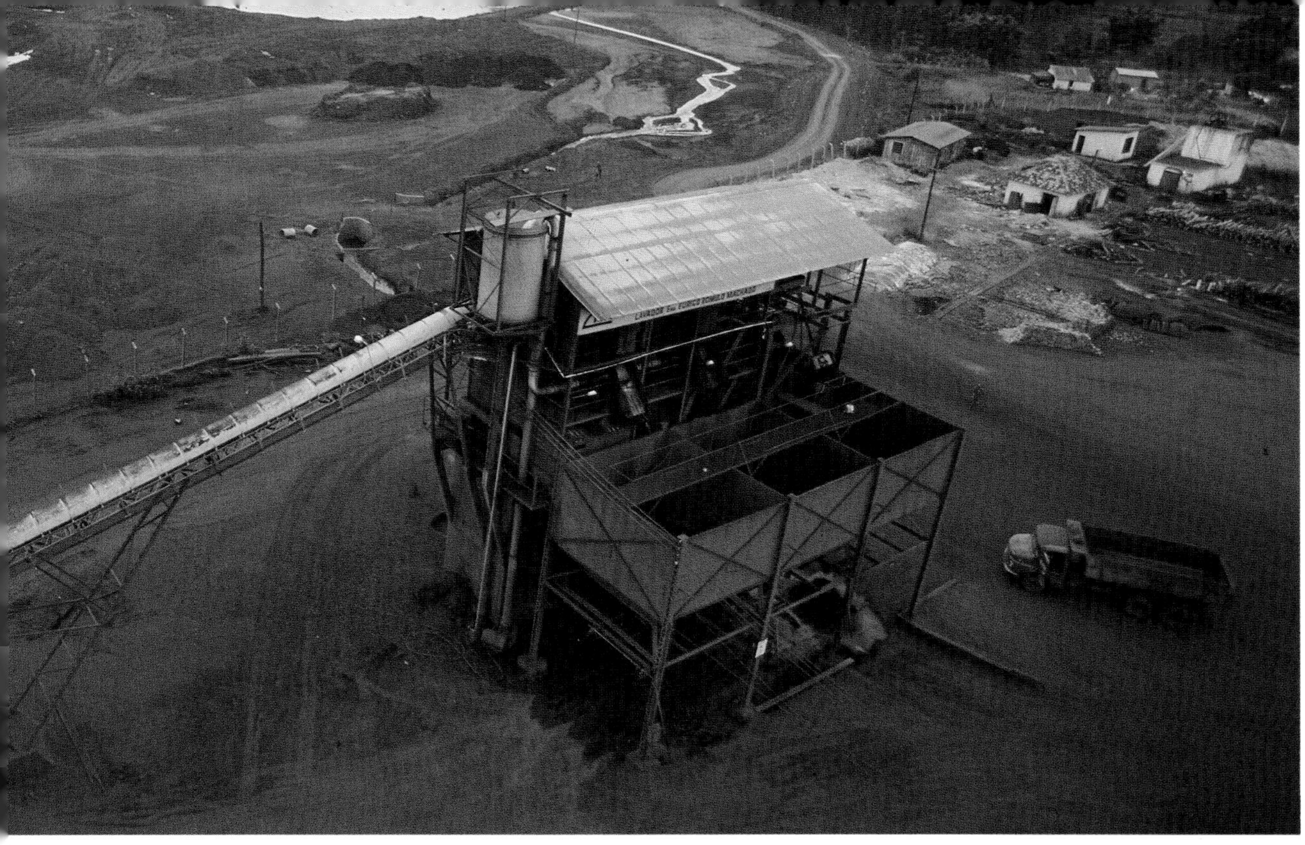

54 South Brazilian coal miner.

55 Butiá coal mine in Rio Grande do Sul supplied some 30,000 t of coal per month in the 1970s. Most of it was used as fuel for a nearby power station.

56 Surrounding the city of Belo Horizonte, high-quality iron ore deposits, mostly haematite, are mined in a belt of up to 100 km radius. Only a small part of this is smelted in Brazil itself, including in Minas Gerais. The greatest proportion is taken by train to the port of Tubarão north of Vitoria, and shipped overseas – mainly to Western Europe and Japan.

58

59

60

57 ◁◁ *Petrochemical complex at Camaçari, near Salvador da Bahia.*

58 ◁ *Fiat opened a modern car factory in Betim near Belo Horizonte in the mid-70s. A few years later it was already producing 270,000 cars and an additional 150,000 motors (for export to Europe) annually. The total workforce of the factory is around 12,600. Fiat produces not only for the Brazilian market, but also supplies other Latin American countries with finished cars.*

59 ◁ *"Embraer" aircraft assembly works in São José dos Campos near São Paulo. The picture shows the company's most successful product, the twin-engined turboprop "Bandeirante" for 18 passengers, designed according to the latest principles. The main customers are airlines in Brazil and abroad, which operate feeder flights and are dependent on a plane of this type.*

60 ◁ *The Hering company of Blumenau (Santa Catarina) is one of the major textile producers of Latin America. It supplies not only the domestic market, but also sells abroad, including to Europe, as far as permitted by European economic bloc import restrictions.*

61 *Ever since the discovery of Brazil, the search for metals and precious stones has repeatedly provided an impetus for the establishment of new settlements and exploration of the interior. Brazil is still one of the principal sources of precious minerals. The photograph shows: light blue = aquamarine, green = tourmaline, light-yellow = citrine quartz, violet = amethyst, dark-yellow = topaz Rio Grande, grey-brown = smoky quartz.*

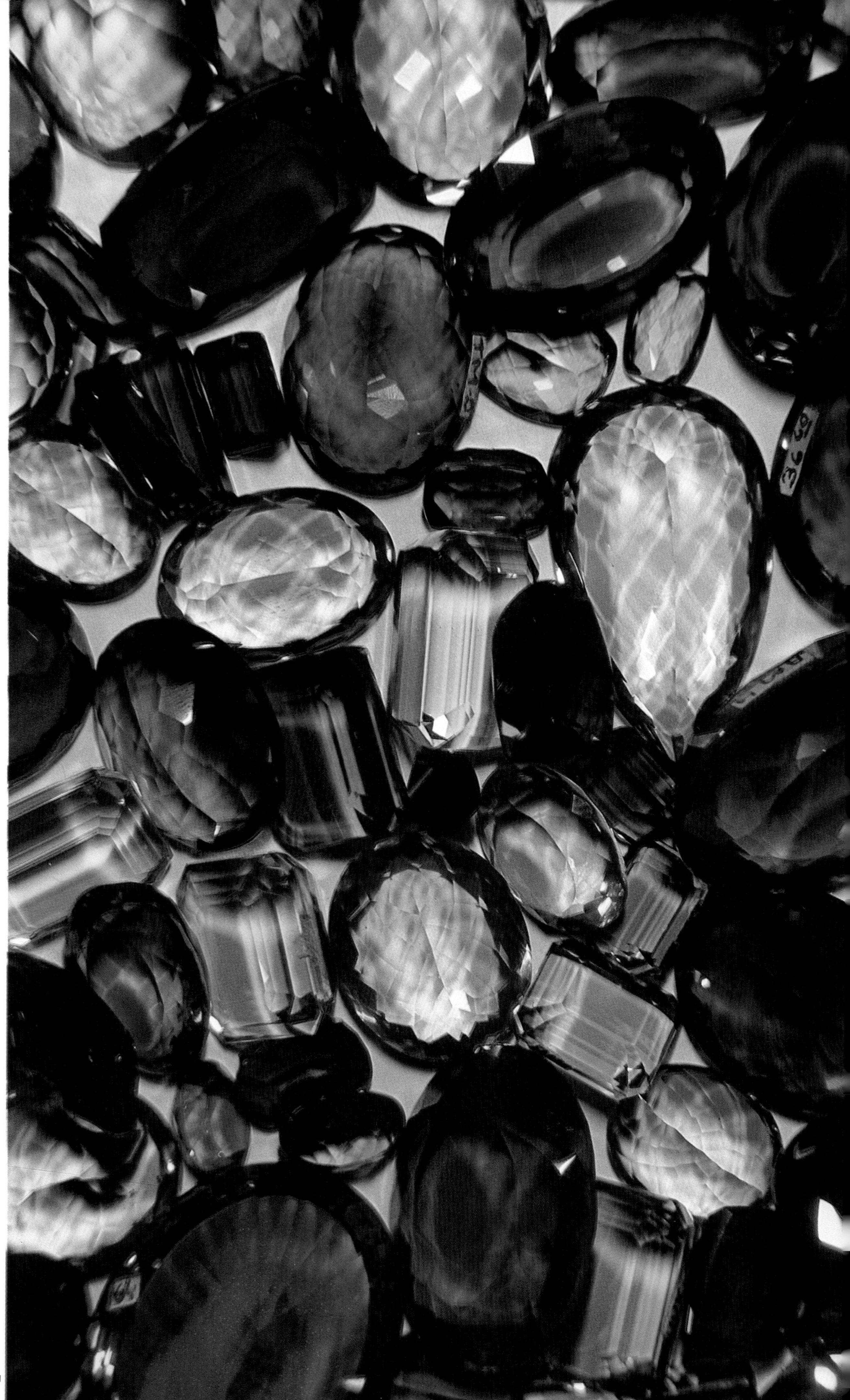

troduce the presidential system and to take over the reins of power. The economic and social situation was alarming, a fact which increased the political instability and discontent within the country. The balance of payments deficit, which had stood at 14 million US dollars in 1961, had climbed to the region of 360 millions a year later. Financial issues rose from 313.8 thousand million cruzeiros in 1961 to 508.7 thousand million in 1962. The cost of living, which had increased by 43.2% in 1961, rose by 52.7% in 1962, by 81% in 1963, and by no less than 42% in the first three months of the following year. There was hunger in many cities; strikes and lockouts paralysed economic life. The president often attended violent demonstrations and made progressive speeches. By expropriating foreign-owned oil refineries he sought to strengthen left-wing support for his administration.

Social questions in the interior of the country, still dominated by colonial structures, reached a burning level of actuality at the same time. In 1960 a survey showed that 81% of the arable land was split into properties of between 1,000 and 100,000 h. These Latifundia were owned by only 12.6% of the landowners; 80% of the land-workers were not owners, but tenants, day-labourers of farmhands. In 1963 Goulart passed a law which foresaw the founding of farmworkers' unions under state control. In retrospect, this law, as well as the land reform announced in 1964, appears as little more than demagogic machinations on the part of the president. Both measures offered no possible solution of the property distribution problem. The importance of this question is shown by the fighting that occurred in some of the federal states between landowners and unpropertied people.

The already present enmity for Goulart across a wide spectrum of the middle class, landowners, entrepreneurs, churchmen and officers grew rapidly. Many of these people were convinced that Goulart's behaviour, whether intentional or through ineptitude, would lead Brazil into anarchy. It was said that the head of state was increasingly dependent on the support of extreme left-wing elements. When Goulart tried to secure influence in the lower ranks of the army, particularly among NCOs, by founding trade unions, the army command, supported by the governors of the most important states (São Paulo, Minas Gerais and Guanabara, which is today part of Rio de Janeiro) rose up against the president. Large parts of the population supported the military intervention, which caused the fall of Goulart, with little opposition from his supporters. Goulart fled into exile.

Military Rule and its End

The victors of the 1964 "revolution" were in the first place the senior officers who had forced João Goulart out of office. To keep the existing institutions in formal terms at least it was decided not to dissolve Congress, and on 11th April, 1964 this body voted in General Humberto Castelo Branco as president. The General was the candidate designated by the army, and it is significant that the deputies cast 361 votes with 72 abstentions. Castelo Branco was a respected officer, distant in manner and regarded as incorruptible. Industrial leaders, landowners and the urban middle class, who had rejected Goulart, all felt that democratic institutions should be kept in being even in times of crisis. But the military had their own ideas about the path to be taken. Evidence of this was already shown by "Institutional Act No 1" of 14th April, 1964. This stated that, for a limited time, basic human rights would be abolished, political mandates of opposition party leaders could be set aside and judges and civil servants who incurred displeasure could be dismissed. There were differences within the military leadership between the compromise-minded wing and the "linha dura", the hardliners. The latter were openly pleading for a military dictatorship. Succeeding presidents, always put forward by the military and "confirmed" by Congress, favoured the one or other wing, depending on the prevailing situation.

The state of the country was perilous: the economy was in ruins, political strikes were rife, there was galloping inflation, anarchy in the transport system, radicalisation among the students, a loss of confidence amongst foreign creditors and insubordination in some army units.

The "Second Institutional Act" of 28th October, 1965 brought a change in domestic affairs. The thirteen old political parties were dissolved by decree. They were replaced by the "state" party ARENA

(Aliança Renovadora Nacional) and the "state approved" opposition party MDB (Movimento Democrático Brasileiro). Furthermore direct election of the president, vice-president and the state governors was repealed.

There was no more mention of the originally planned "redemocratisation" or re-establishment of a liberal but no longer "infiltrated" democratic system. Castelo Branco ruled under plenipotentiary powers and drew up for his successor a new authoritarian constitution. On 15th March, 1967 the former Minister of Defence, Arthur da Costa e Silva, became president after having been nominated by the army leadership and confirmed by Congress. The MDB opposition party did not take part in the election because they were fundamentally opposed to the new system of indirect election of president.

Two events marked Costa e Silva's administration. On the one hand the unsatisfactory nature of the new party line up became clear, resulting in the founding of the "Frente Ampla", and on the other, guerrillas appeared for the first time. The creation of a government party (ARENA) and an opposition party (MDB) was regarded from the very beginning by a large part of the politically interested population as an artificial construction only favouring the government. The Movimento Democrático Brasileiro was accused of being incapable of mounting true opposition policies, and merely serving as democratic window-dressing for the military regime. Carlos Lacerda, a politician who had previously been governor of the state of Guanabara and an opponent of Vargas, got together with former president Kubitschek and together they formed a people's party on the basis of the above-mentioned

Major Regions and Federal States

(T): Territories

"broad front". Kubitschek had lost his parliamentary seat after the military coup and the new leadership cancelled his political rights for ten years. Further proposed members of the Frente Ampla included João Goulart, with whom Lacerda had come to an agreement in September 1967, and Jânio Quadros, the "seven-month" president. But before this movement, which might have grown into a large popular party, could get really started, it was declared "an extraparliamentary movement" and thus illegal by President Costa e Silva.

In Minas Gerais, especially in the Serra de Caparáo and in Uberlândia guerrillas turned up who had been in contact with politicians who had lost their political offices and rights. The ensuing guerrilla war called for specialist troops and only ended after long fighting.

1968 was a year of worsening internal unrest. Street demonstrations and terrorist attacks multiplied. Open defiance by the prohibited student organisation, UNE, resulted in the arrest of hundreds of students. The opposition deputy, Marcio Moreira Alves, accused the police and some justice authorities of using torture, and published a book entitled "Torturas e Torturado" (Torture and Tortured).

President Costa e Silva answered by issuing Institutional Act No 5 13th December, 1968, by which the government were empowered to annul political mandates and rights of a citizen for up to ten years. It also permitted curtailment or abolition of constitutional rights. Congress was recessed for an undetermined period. From now on the federal government could directly interfere in the affairs of the individual states and local councils. A wave of arrests swept the country. Press, radio and television were censored, or put under threat of censorship for some time. At the end of August 1969, the president suffered a severe stroke in the midst of preparations for a new constitution which might have proved more liberal. Instead of the civilian vice-president the three defence ministers took over power. This was announced as being an "interim measure". Congress was called in again for the purpose of confirming the army's presidential candidate, General Emílio Garrastazu Médici, on 22nd October, 1969. On his appointment the new president declared his aim of re-establishing democracy in Brazil, but added that "it must be clear that the institutions which brought us the crisis of 1964 will not be allowed again".

General elections for Congress, the senate and political authorities in the federal states, held on 15th November, 1970, were the first step on the road back to democracy. However, every candidate was carefully screened to make sure that no "subversive element" were included. The military government was now ready for a democratic opening, but only for "democracy without risks". General Ernesto Geisel, who was president from 1974 onwards, initiated, within his personal limits, a further liberalisation. The MDB opposition chalked up a big increase in its share of the vote in the 1974 parliamentary elections.

João Baptista de Oliveira-Figureido became president on 15th March, 1979. The previous two-party system was replaced in March 1980 by a multi-party system. The first virtually free parliamentary elections in October 1982 confirmed the governing party (PDS – Partido Democrático Social, successor of the previously ruling ARENA) as the single largest grouping, but it was confronted by the PMDB (Partido do Movimento Democrático Brasileiro, the moderate wing of the former MDB) which, together with three permitted left-wing parties, had a majority in Congress. Meanwhile Brazil had become the largest debtor nation of the third world, with inflation running at an average annual level of 42.1% between 1970 and 1982.

On 15th January, 1985 an electoral college named Tancredo Neves president, but because of ill-health he never took office, and the first president to be elected since 1964 died on 22nd April. Vice-president José Sarney took office as head of state. In April parliament passed constitutional reforms with an overwhelming majority. The main changes include direct election of the president (from 1988 onwards), no restrictions on the formation of parties and the voting rights for the illiterate (some 20 million).

Chronology of Brazilian History since Colonial Times

1494 Treaty of Tordesillas between Spain and Portugal to define demarcation line between Portuguese sphere of influence and Spain's "discovery area". Pope Alexander VI initially sets point 100 miles west of the Azores, but a year later the Portuguese zone is moved to 370 miles west of the Azores. In consequence, Brazil's coast comes under the Portuguese crown.

1500 Landing by a Portuguese fleet on 22nd April on South American coast at Porto Seguro (later Bahia). Possession taken in name of King of Portugal (Manuel I). Initial name "Ilha de Vera Cruz" (Island of the True Cross) soon replaced by "Brasília", derived from the first merchandise to be traded the "pau brasil" or red dye-wood.

1532 First agricultural settlement founded in Piratinigua (São Vicente near Santos) by Martim Afonso de Sousa. This marks first attempt to colonise country following time of barter trade.

1534 Signing of first leasing contract by King João III, which gives Brazilian territory to tenant squires. The Donatários are supposed to administer and make prosper the 15 areas or "Capitanias" to their own advantage and in the name of the crown. Only a few Capitanias are successful, however, and finally the leaseholds are taken back by the king.

1549 Appointment of a Governador-General, Tomé de Sousa and further royal officials as colonial government of Portuguese-America with its seat in the newly-founded Salvador da Bahia.

1557–1572 Mem de Sa, the third Governador-General, succeeds in establishing stability in Brazil. He evicts the French who had settled on the coast and commences a purposeful Indian policy with the help of the Jesuits. Hostile tribes are suppressed. Conversion of the Indians to Christianity through the Jesuits is main aim of Portuguese policy.

1630 Occupation of northern Brazil by Dutch West Indies company.

62 *The Avenida Anhangebaú is so to speak the pulsating heart of São Paulo, the industrial and trade centre which as an agglomeration totals just under 10 million inhabitants. Despite the building of an underground railway, the streets are still full of buses, trucks, and private vehicles, so that on weekdays motoring conditions in the city are chaotic. Air pollution caused by these countless vehicles, together with industrial sources, has become an increasingly serious problem. São Paulo is a monumental city, impressive because of its size and vitality. The enormous growth from 30,000 inhabitants in 1880 to the present level was largely due to the prosperity of its agricultural hinterland, mostly coffee plantations, as well as to the fact that São Paulo is a nodal point for all road and rail lines from the interior, which then proceed over the Serra do Mar and down the coast to the port of Santos. More than a quarter of the Brazilian gross national product is earned in São Paulo, justifying its designation as "Brazil's dynamo".*

63 ▷ *Rio de Janeiro, the "cidade meravilhosa" (the wonderful city) of the Brazilians. It was the capital for nearly two hundred years, and it is still the pearl of the Brazilian cities. It lies on the large Bay of Guanabara, whose relatively narrow entrance can be seen in the picture. On the far right the Atlantic ocean can be seen. Rio's trade mark, the Sugar Loaf mountain, is passed by ships on their way into the bay, which widens out again towards the left (i.e. towards the north) and even includes some islands. In the foreground, adjacent to the bay, are the quarters of Urca, Botafogo, and Flamengo; in the background on the other side of the bay are the houses of the neighbouring town of Niterói. The other hallmark of Rio is the 700-m high Corcovado, with its statue of Christ spreading his arms protectively over the city.*

MENSAL
AVULSO
HITACHI
PRADA
GARAGEM
AUTOMATICA
SONY
SONY
BANCO REGIONAL
DIA 31, NOITE DOS CAMPEOES DO MUNDO ! ASSISTA NO PACAEMBU A CHEGADA DA
MONUMENTAL 55ª CORRIDA INTERNACIONAL DE SÃO SILVESTRE !
117 060
117 064
ANHEMBI

64

65

64 *The former gold-mining town of Ouro Preto flourished in the second half of the 18th century and is being rebuilt, after having virtually fallen into decay in the last century.*

65 *Landing at the Congonhas city airport of São Paulo is an impressive experience – with planes brushing past a sea of houses before setting down at the last minute on the single runway.*

66 *View from the historic town Olinda towards the modern port of Recife.*

67 *The "pelourinho" – the former slave market of Salvador – is regarded as one of the finest examples of colonial architecture in Brazil, and stands under protection. Today all buildings of the colonial era are being restored.*

66

67

68 *The Foreign Ministry (Itamaraty) is one of the most distinguished buildings in Brasília, surrounded by a large ornamental pond filled with water-roses and other plants. In the background, on the left, the Parliament with its imposing twin-skyscrapers, and the assemblies of the large and small chambers, symbolised by a dome and a shell respectively. All public buildings in Brasília are the work of Oscar Niemeyer, while town planner Lúcio Costa was responsible for city planning and layout. The construction of Brasília considerably stimulated the development of the hinterland.*

69 *Baptism in the modern cathedral of Brasília, designed by Oscar Niemeyer, in the shape of a crown composed of concrete arches stretching heavenwards, the individual arches being linked by a glass roof. The open sky over Brasília and the Planalto Central is always visible through the glass roof – a sight which never becomes boring thanks to the invariable presence of white cumulus clouds.*

68

69

70

71

70 *The influences of an advanced industrial world, emanating from the USA and Western Europe, leaves its mark even on smaller Brazilian towns: a shop-window blind in Curitiba (Paraná) proclaiming "fashion – youth – unisex" (moda – jovem – unissex).*

71 *Painted facades of demolished houses in Curitiba, depicting modern street scenes.*

1634 Count Johann Moritz of Nassau is successful governor in service of Dutch merchants. When hoped-for rapid profits do not materialise, Dutch West Indies company refuses further support. Moritz of Nassau leaves Brazil in 1644.

1654 Last outpost of "New Holland" abandoned.

1698 First discovery of gold in Ouro Preto area. This starts a 75-year "golden age" in Brazil with large-scale exploitation of gold resources. Most important consequence of gold-rush is the settlement of part of the interior.

1792 Inconfidência Mineira – plot by the Tiradentes, a small group of malcontents who tried to separate Portugal and its colony, Brazil. Joaquim José da Silva Xavier (called Tiradentes, or teeth-puller) is executed after his insurrection fails.

1808 Portuguese court and state administration flee to Rio de Janeiro to escape Napoleonic troops invading Portugal. The prince regent (later King João VI) issues decree in January opening Brazilian ports to friendly nations (primarily Britain).

1822 Return of João VI to Portugal. His son Dom Pedro is ruler of Brazil.

1822 Grito de Ipiranga (7th September) and coronation of Pedro I as emperor of Brazil (1st December).

1831 Abdication of Dom Pedro I in favour of his five-year old son after great opposition to him has grown up in Brazil. A crown council exercise power in the name of the young emperor. The former emperor becomes King João VII of Portugal.

1840 Pedro II accedes to the throne at age of 14 ½ following passing of special law. Long reign and prior period as regent (1831–1889) give various parts of large country chance to unify. Danger of fragmentation of Brazil averted once and for all.

1865–1870 War with Paraguay. Alliance with Uruguay and Argentina.

1888 Abolition of slavery after years of political squabbling within the country, and after England bans any slave trade with Africa in 1850.

1889 Abdication of Pedro II and dissolution of monarchy as result of political and economic unrest in wake of end of slavery. A republic is established.

1891 Marshal Deodoro da Fonseca, who toppled Pedro II, is first president. The first of countless internal and military disputes as well as financial crises.

1930 Getúlio Vargas comes to power in the midst of the economic crisis. With the aid of a new constitution and "state direction" he attempts to master the many problems connected with the onset of industrialisation.

1945 Resignation of dictatorial head of state Vargas as consequence of worldwide progress towards democracy.

1950 Vargas returns as "elected president". Increasing difficulties on the home front (high inflation, corruption scandals).

1954 Getúlio Vargas commits suicide to escape legal proceedings (because of conspiracy to murder opposition politician).

1956 Juscelino Kubitschek proclaimed president; motto: "50 years progress in 5 years". Rapid industrialisation, construction of Brasília.

1960 Inauguration of Brasília as new capital.

1961 Surprise resignation of Jânio Quadros after only seven months in office. Army leadership tries to prevent João Goulart from becoming President or at least to curtail his powers because of his "socialist leanings".

1962 João Goulart regains executive power following referendum. Increasing political dissent within country.

1964 Army leadership, with support of main state

governors, economic leaders and middle class, ousts Goulart. Marshal Humberto Castello Branco takes over presidency. "First Institutional Act" cuts out main constitutional rights and increases power of government.

1965 Two-party system introduced in "Second Institutional Act" of 28th October.

1967 Marshal Arthur da Costa e Silva is new president. New constitution.

1968 "Fifth Constitutional Act" of 13th December gives extraordinary powers to executive body.

1969 Emílio Garrastazu Médici succeeds ailing Costa e Silva, who dies in December.

1970 General elections symbolise return to a "democracy without risks".

1974 General Ernesto Geisel becomes president. Further steps towards liberalisation.

1979 General João Baptista de Oliveira-Figureido succeeds General Geisel as president.

1980 Abolition of two-party system – new parties formed.

1982 Opposition secures majority in elections. Military regime remains in power thanks to electoral system and gains in governors' elections.

1985 The civilian Tancredo Neves is elected president. A symbol of a new era in democracy he dies three months later, without ever having taken office. His successor, José Sarney, promises to implement Tancredo Neves' legacy. Approval is given to reform constitutional, including direct election of the president and free formation of political parties.

Slaves harvesting coffee in the middle of the last century.

The Culture of Brazil

Brazil's cultural adventure started together with its discovery in the 16th century. Pedro Vaz de Caminha's *Carta* was a letter to King Manuel I of Portugal (p. 89), in which he described the luxuriant landscape and the customs of the natives of this new land discovered on 22nd April, 1500 by Admiral Cabral's expedition. If we regard Caminha's *Carta*, which was certainly more than a simple bureaucratic report, as the first literary document from Brazil, then we can add to this list the later writings of the Portuguese Pedro Magalhães Gandavo, Gabriel Soares de Sousa and Pedro Lopez de Sousa, as well as those of foreign travellers and adventurers such as Jean Léry, André Thévet, Hans Staden, and Antony Knivet.

Brazilian fine arts, apart from pre-colonial work (rock paintings and Indian earthenware on Marajó Island in the Amazon region), are rooted in the functional art of the settlers: religious and profane buildings, artefacts of the Roman Catholic liturgy and furniture made by artisans who had come to Brazil with Jesuit, Benedictine, Franciscan, and Carmelite missionaries. Since it is impossible to show the whole spectrum of artistic activities in Brazil individually, we shall be giving a summary of developments since the discovery of the country up to contemporary times, while confining ourselves to language and literature, fine arts and Carnival, the biggest festivity among the Brazilian people.

Language

The official language in Brazil, from Oiapoque in the far north to Chui in the deep south, is Portuguese. But it is a Portuguese which differs as much from the language of Lusitania as American English does from British English. This goes as much for intonation as emphasis, as well as for the simplified style, not to mention the countless new words. Words adopted from other languages, above all from the Indian Tupi, but also from African languages such as Nagô, Yoruba and Quimbando as well as from French and English have served to enrich Brazilian Portuguese.

The adoption of countless Tupi expressions is understandable when one remembers that during the 18th century, when the colonisation of Brazil was fully under way, Tupi was more widespread than Portuguese, because the settlers, in particular the Jesuits, had to learn it to communicate with Indians all over the country. Tupi thus became the second language of other Indian tribes too. Many Brazilian place names come from Tupi, for example Andarai, Catumbi, Tijuca, Ipanema (part of Rio de Janeiro), Guanabara (the Bay of Rio) as well as the names of such states as Maranhão, Ceará, Sergipe, Pernambuco and Paraná. Frequent Christian names which also come from Tupi are Bartira, Iracema, Moema, Ubirajara, and Jaci. Animal and plant names, especially those of species, come from Tupi: Aratu (a type of snail), Jabuti (tortoise), Oiticica (a type of tree), Jacaré (an alligator species), Minhoca (earthworm). Particularly in the Amazon region many gastronomical expressions come from the Tupi language.

According to many experts, the African linguistic influence outweighs the Indian considerably, because the African languages have not only lent new

words, but also changed the structure of Brazilian Portuguese by simplifying inflexions and changing it phonetically. This is a continuous process, as can be verified by listening to everyday speech. The black slaves in the Bahia region spoke mainly Nagô and Yoruba, in other provinces, however, mostly Quimbando. African words are prevalent in gastronomy: they were introduced by black servants working in stately homes. The same is true for names of flora and fauna, not to mention terms in music, myth and religion. A few common examples in this connection are: Babalaô (black magic priest), Exu (daemonic god), Iansã (St. Barbara of the Jegê cult), Oxum (goddess of the Jegê-Yorubana cult).
In the field of the fine arts, in letters, science and fashion the French language has enormously enriched the Brazilian language. Many words have been adapted in their spelling: abajur (abat-jour), matiné (matinée), plissado (plissé), vitrina (vitrine), maquete (maquette), etc.
English has also made a contribution with words such as sanduiche, bar, clube, coquetel, futebol, time, basquete, etc. to give just a few examples.
Italian and Arab cultural influence can also be observed, emanating from the wave of immigration out of European and oriental countries, which started at the turn of the century and intensified during the Second World War.

Literature

If we disregard the travellers' tales mentioned above, the first works of Brazilian literature were the poems and religious plays of Father José de Anchieta which were concerned with the religious instruction of the Indians, as well as the epic *Prosopopéia* by Bento Teixeira which described how the state of Pernambuco was conquered.
The baroque style dominated the two cultural centres of Salvador da Bahia and Recife/Olinda in the 17th century. Three typical representatives of this style were Manuel Botelho de Oliveira, Brother Manuel de Santa Maria Itaparica (both sing the praises of nature and its gifts in native style) and Gregório de Matos Guerra, who wrote a satirical work with erotic if not pornographic tendencies, mercilessly depicting the social scene of his time in Bahia. The rapidly growing moneyed class, adorned with dubious titles, fortune hunters, mulattos and negros, the clergy and even life in Lisbon and Coimbra are all lampooned. Gregório de Matos Guerra, who was nicknamed Bôca de Inferno (gossip) and whose satirical strain brought him much unpleasantness, also left behind a religious and moral work devoted to metaphysical and sensual love.
The Traitors In the 18th century a group of authors called the "Inconfidentes" (traitors) became famous in the state of Minas Gerais. By then the capital had been moved from Salvador to Rio de Janeiro, which was nearer the gold resources discovered in Minas Gerais. Among these writers were Claúdio Manuel da Costa, Silva Alvarenga, Alvarenga Peixoto and Tomás Antônio Gonzaga.
Their name is derived from the fact that they had participated in the unsuccessful revolutionary independence movement (Incofidência Mineira). Their highly lyrical poetry combined European neo-classicism with Brazilian themes. Two works of the time, not influenced by this movement, are worth mentioning: *O Caramuru*, an epic influenced by Camoẽs, written by Brother José da Santa Rita Durão, and *O Uruguai*, a less traditional work from the pen of Basilío da Gama.
The second half of the 18th century is marked by pre-Romantic motives in the works of Antônio de Sousa Caldas, Eloi Ottoni, and Domingos Borges de Barros. The Romantic movement only left its mark on brazilian taste in the 19th century, in particular after the arrival of the Portuguese court in March 1808 which had fled in the face Napoleon's invasion of Portugal.
The Romantic Period Although imported by the royal court, romanticism only really established itself in the years 1850–1860, only to end in the following decade after flourishing briefly. The main themes of romanticism were a glorification of nationalism, nature, manners and customs, as well as extolling the myth of the noble (Indian) savage and personal emotions. The interest shown in history and the tendency to document and observe rather runs counter to what is normally understood by romanticism.
The romantic style which flourished after independence in 1822 was largely concerned with the liter-

ary development of Brazil's physical and social reality. No literary movement has ever been as Brazilian as that of Manuel Bandeira. Frédéric Mauro rightly pointed out that before 1845 there was little to distinguish Brazilian literature from that of the Portuguese homeland. For him the Romantic period led to a truly national literature, which did not totally depend on the Indian myths, but also had an eclectic and scholastic-philosophical dimension.

Antônio Gonçalves Dias *(Primeiros Contos, Suspiros Poéticos e Saudades)* was the real romantic author of the epoch. *A Moreninha* by Joaquim de Macedo is a superbly poetic novel dealing in intimate and humorous fashion with everyday life. In *O Guarani* and *Iracema*, two novels by José de Alencar, the author encouraged love across racial divisions and thus promoted the image of the Indians, while at the same time portraying the social problems of the young state.

Castro Alves *(Vozes d'Africa, Navio Negreiro*, both published posthumously in *Os Escravos* in 1883) wrote socially committed poems against slavery, as well as lyrical and sensual but never sentimental verse. In contrast, Alvares de Azevedo, who was influenced by among others Heine, Byron, Musset and Garret, wrote works which were halfway between sentiment and satire. Like Alves, he too died at the age of twenty of tuberculosis – the Romantic's disease. While Castro Alves supported the blacks, Gonçalves Dias took up literary cudgels for the Indians. These two authors were seen as exceptions by the young who fought against romanticism after 1870, because they had after all dealt with sociopolitical questions which were to become the main themes in the age of burgeoning realism.

Realism and Naturalism The historical and social upheavals in the second half of the last century fostered realism, naturalism and new philosophical trends such as positivism. The chief personalities in these two new chapters of Brazilian literature, which appeared after 1875, were Raul Pompéia, Aluísio de Azeveido (realists) and Joaquim Maria Machado de Assis, a naturalist writer and a mulatto born in the slums who founded the Academy of Literary Sciences in Rio in 1897 and who is regarded as Brazil's greatest classical author. The psychological aspect of realism dominates the works of Raul Pompéia, and in his most important novel, *O Ateneu*, he deals with ethical matters in a remarkably daring manner for the times. Aluísio de Azevedo, whose main work is *O Cortiço*, was strongly influenced by Zola and Eça de Queiróz, which explains his preoccupation with social conditions. Machado de Assis *(Memórias póstumas de Brás Cubas, Dom Casmurro* and *Quincas Borba)* became the Brazilian Flaubert, thanks to his acute powers of analysis, his pessimistic humour and realism, as well as the linguistic renaissance that he embodied.

Parnassianism and Symbolism The Brazilian Parnasianismo hailed from the French "Parnassiens" and tried to introduce an objective literary art based on formalistic and sometimes quite artificial efforts. Dominating criteria were metrical and grammatical accuracy, and clarity and precision of vocabulary. Among the most important writers of this school were the poets Alberto de Oliveira, Raimundo Correia and Olavo Bilac, whose strong lyrical talent always triumphed over the formal barriers.

Symbolism, in contrast to the severity of Parnassianism, brought free verse, a nebulous and diffuse vocabulary full of tautology, sweeping musical rhythms and a strong leaning to the morbid and esoteric. This movement, which reflected the strong French intellectual influence that was rampant in the 19th and early 20th century, had many followers in Brazil, Cruz e Sousa and Alphonsus de Guimarães being the two key names. The movement also bore the seeds of modernism.

The Modern Period A so-called week of Modern Art was held in São Paulo from 11th–17th February 1922, exactly a century after Brazil's independence. The aim was to achieve a radical break with the past by encouraging new aesthetic views, at the same time rejecting literary colonialism by creating a distinctive Brazilian modernism. This abrupt change, practically from one day to the next, had had the way prepared for it by the work of several transitional authors, including José Pereira de Graça Aranha, Lima Barreto and, above all, by Euclides da Cunha, whose *Os Sertoẽs* depicted life in the Caatinga while at the same time outlining a solution by means of rational analysis in the spirit of Marx and Taine.

Writers, painters, and sculptors – among them

Mário de Andrade, Oswald de Andrade, Manuel Bandeira, Ronald de Carvalho, Di Cavalcanti, Sérgio Milliet, Ribeiro Couto and Menotti del Piccha, all artists and authors from Rio and São Paulo – organised the Semana de Arte in the City Theatre of São Paulo. The ideas brought forth by this revolutionary generation soon led to fundamental social and political changes, culminating in the 1930 revolution.

The most important event of the week was the exhibition of paintings by Di Cavalcanti, Vicente do Rêgo Monteiro, Oswald Goeldi, Ferrignac, Joh Graz, Zita Aita, Martins Ribeiro and Anita Malfatti. Poets read their works before the largely shocked audiences of the still provincial São Paulo. Heitor Vila-Lobos played some of his compositions which had been inspired by Brazil's folklore, and the works of other musicians such as Guiomar Novaês, Ernani Braga, Licila Vila-Lobos and Alfredo Gomes were also performed.

At the end of the week of modern art Rio became the meeting place for writers from all the federal states and who wanted to belong to the best in the land. They included Carlos Drummond de Andrade, Mário Quintana, Augusto Meyer and the so-called 1930s generation of authors from the northeast; Jorge de Lima, José Lins do Rêgo, Ascenço Ferreira, Rachel de Queiróz, Jorge Amado and Graciliano Ramos. The common factor in all their novels is the social reality of the northeast with its traditional concepts of honour and strict moral code. A few words about Jorge Amado and Graciliano Ramos are representative of all these illustrious "nordestinos". Jorge Amado comes from Bahia and is probably the best known Brazilian author abroad. His novels have been translated into over thirty languages and adapted for radio, television and the cinema. His first novel, *O País do Carnaval*, was published in 1932. A lyrical touch and humour go side-by-side in all his writings. In an unconcerned style drawn from the language of the streets he describes the typical difficulties to be encountered in a society transforming from an agricultural to an industrial economy. Among his published works are: *Jubiabá* (1935), *Gabriela, cravo e canela* (1959), *Dona Flor e seus dois maridos, história moral e de amor* (1966) and *Tenda dos Milagres* (1969). Amado always expressed his great love for his people and his home city of Bahia. This colonial town and "melting pot of races and culture" is celebrated in *Bahia de Todos os Santos: Guia das ruas e dos mistérios da cidade do Salvador* (1945). He recently wrote in an article that appeared in *Le Monde* in Paris about Salvador da Bahia, which is the setting of nearly all his novels "...Bahia is steeped in secrets, in a burdening secrecy that everyone can feel... One can follow every road in the world but never will one find a town so rich in history, so picturesque and so profoundly poetic... This describes the town where people like to speak, where time has not taken on the crazy pace of the southern cities. No-one can speak like a Bahian, in that quiet prose with its rounded phrases, the long pauses and meaningful gestures, the gentle smile and loud laughter. Fat lovable mulattos, pretty women with golden skin – all shades of gold – attractive, bewitching... people of endless goodness, people who like bright colours, noisy, tender, soft, easily amazed, hospitable, unprejudiced and against all repression. It is impossible to explain away this city; its secret is like one of the clouds that sweeps in from the sea and totally envelops us: body, soul and heart."

Graciliano Ramos, who died in 1953, celebrated his literary debut at the age of 40 with the novel *Caetés*. In disciplined, almost tortured prose he uncovers the spectrum between the spiritual lives and the physical surroundings of his protagonists in works such as *Angústia* (1936) and *Vidas Secas* (1938). Graciliano Ramos' powerful literary output has been translated in Argentina and Cuba as well as in Europe (France, West Germany, Italy, Poland, Hungary, Soviet Union) and also in the United States. As a member of the Brazilian Communist Party he travelled to Czechoslovakia and the Soviet Union in 1952. His impressions were published in *Viagem* in 1954. Apart from this specifically Brazilian generation the thirties also saw works by authors influenced by European neo-symbolism, including Cecília Meirelles, Vinicius de Maraes, Augusto Frederico Schmidt and Henriqueta Lisboa, as well such novelists as Octavio de Faria, Cornelia Pena, Lúcio Cardoso and Érico Veríssimo, who invest their writings with an urbane subjectivity.

Post-modern Period The authors of the so-called

1945 generation were once again more concerned with form. Among these João Cabral de Melo Neto takes a place of honour because of his verbal inventiveness and social commitment. João Guimaraẽs Rosa creatively makes use of the vernacular of his home state, Minas, in epic novels such as *Grande de Sertão: Veredas, Sagarana, Corpo de Baile.* As Celso Pedro Luft has correctly pointed out, he "combines the archaic with the modern, the academic with the folkloric, the commonplace with the scientific, the pure language with slang, and should the native language not suffice, he makes use of Latin, Greek or some other foreign language".
Concretism was introduced in Brazil by the brothers Augusto and Haraldo de Campos, and by Décio Pignatari. Affection for the regional and traditional together with the development of a literary style are combined with social commitment in the works of the movement led by Ferreira Gullar, Mário Chamie, Mário Faustino and the contributors to the periodical *Violão de Rua.* Exemplary cases of experimentation with the language are to be found in the work of Osman Lins and Clarice Lispector.
Clarice Lispector *(Perto do Coração Selvagem, O Lustre, A Paixão Segundo G.H., Laços de Família)*, who died in 1978, has bequeathed us some of the most important works of Brazilian literature. Using very personal and basically subjective language she expresses perceptions, impressions and nuances of everyday life. Her realism, rich in flights of fancy but at the same time strange, anxiety-ridden and absurd, combines the fear of life and the absence of God. Her characters are existential somnambulists. Careful analysis of her writing shows her attraction to the word and literary art, without it's ever becoming an end in itself.
Existential questioning of the basic conflict between the individual and society is also a theme handled by authors such as Aníbal Machado, Adonias Filho, Antônio Callado and Dalton Trevisan.
The Present Day The 1970's were characterised by nostalgia, as evidenced by the publication of countless volumes of memoirs. What can explain this phenomenon which has gripped both veteran and young authors alike? Perhaps this hankering for the past can be seen as a reaction to the changes in the Brazilian reality caused by rapid industrialisation. The nostalgic cult of the small "I" is no doubt designed to give a higher value to the individual just at a time when technical progress is making more and more of a robot of him. This withdrawal into an inner world is thus by no means a sign of bourgeois decadence nor a betrayal of social conscience, but more a grasping for help to save the soul and a means to give it significance.
Pedro Nava, whom many critics have compared to Proust because of his painstakingly accurate qualities of observation, has published his childhood memoirs; Afonso Arinos has written political memoirs; Rachel Jardim has brought out an autobiography of her early years; Antônio Carlos Vilaça has published fragmentary excerpts of his life as a monk and later as writer. Gilberto Freyre has written about his youth (1915–1930) as has Érico Veríssimo, to name but a few.
Even if the memoirs were at the peak of their popularity, there was always other contemporary literature, represented by the lyrical and sensual works of Fernando Mendes Viana, by Telmo Padilha, whose vision of a bird and its painful flight can be put into

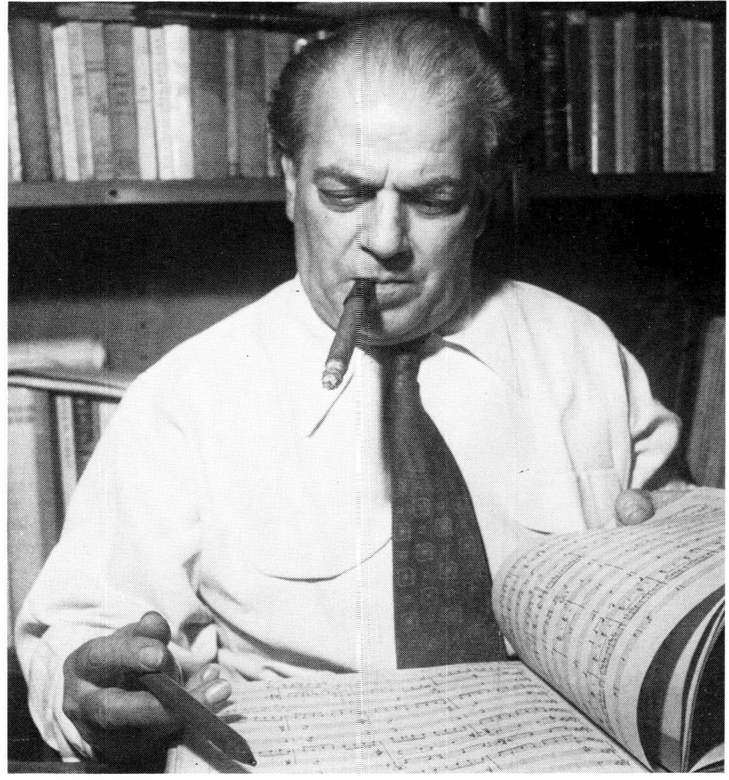

Heitor Vila-Lobos, a modern composer strongly influenced by traditional rhythms.

a cosmic, absolute perspective, by Alberto da Costa e Silva who portrays his childhood memories through ascetic and formal poems, by Carlos Nejars, whose lyrical epics are dominated by the Pampas and love, by Walmir Ayala's lyrical and metaphysical writing, or by J.P.M. da Fonseca who gives a Catholic view of the world with formal pithiness.

Among the novelists one can mention Nelida Piñon who uses a highly subjective and artistic style to plumb the depths of existential experiences, Judith Grossmann whose texts analyse the psyche, Moacyr Scliar and Josué Guimarães, who deal with the social situation in their home state of Rio Grande do Sul, the science-fiction books of Fausto Cunha and the fanciful tales of Victor Guidices.

The Visual Arts

Prehistoric Cave Paintings It is difficult to put a date on the Indian cave paintings, which were executed both before and after the arrival of the Portuguese and are remarkably modern in appearance. Such cave paintings have been found so far in 15 federal states and the results of a Franco-Brazilian archaeological mission (RCP 394 co-operative scientific group) from the CNRS in Paris who have investigated all of Brazil, are eagerly awaited. In 1978 life-sized colour photographs were displayed in Paris of cave paintings from the Lapa do Dragão, one of the most impressive sites in the Montalvania area in the north of Minas Gerais state. The thematic variety of the paintings which depict, sometimes realistically, sometimes schematically, human figures with exaggerated sexual features or animals such as birds, fish, armadillos, lizards, monkeys, and jaguars, at times approaches abstract art and takes into account the characteristics of the surface of the stone.

The rock paintings in the Lapa Vermelha are reckoned to be some 4,000 years old. Shades of yellow and ochre, as well as light to dark brown are the most frequently applied colours. Shades of grey are to be seen here, as well as the white and black often used in the region of Montalvania. In yet other places a pale pink has been used. Pierre Colombel says "the presence of coloured materials in the vicinity of the painted caves has determined which hues are used". Apart from that, the surroundings do not appear to have played a very great role in the distribution of these cave paintings, which can be found not only along the coast, but also inland, in the Caatinga, the Cerrado as well as in tropical and equatorial forests. The suitability of the surface to be painted was a bigger worry for these nomadic artists, who were productive from 2,000 to 3,000 BC up to contemporary times, than the bioclimatic environment. In other words, could the rock walls be used for the purpose of painting or engraving?

The first evidence of this magical and beautiful art form was discovered in 1834 by Jean-Baptiste Débret in his book *Picturesque and Historical Journey through Brazil*, which contained two plates of drawings and engravings which he made after visiting Brazil with the French cultural mission at the invitation of the King of Portugal. The pictures show Indian cave paintings from the Amazon region.

Apart from paintings and engravings which have chiefly been found in caves and shelters, mention must also be made of the remarkable Indian pottery as an example of prehistoric art. Examples include pots, small figures, urns, masks, which are probably in part also ritual objects, some of them stemming from the time prior to the Portuguese landing. They prove the natives' distinct preference for geometrical shapes in black, red and white. These ceramic articles were first found in Pacoval cemetery, and on the plain of Santa Isabel on Marajó island in the Amazon delta. This pottery is termed "precabralian" in honour of the discoverer of Brazil.

The Beginning of Historic Art After the arrival of the Portuguese artistic activity was confined to religious and profane buildings such as churches, monasteries, schools and houses, and liturgical articles and furniture. Many of the artists and artisans accompanying the missionaries were not Portuguese, but came from other European countries, like Brother Ricardo do Pilar who came from Cologne. He was responsible for the four remarkable ceiling panels of the magnificent church of São Bento in Rio de Janeiro, where he worked for thirty years. From the 17th century onwards we see the first examples of profane portraits as an artistic style alongside religious paintings, reaching their peak in the 18th century with the very popular portraits of viceroys and governors. This worldly form of art, unlike sacral art which dominated throughout the 16th and 17th centuries, served as a counterpart to the Azulejos (enamelled earthenware tiles with blue designs on white background), which were imported from Portugal to decorate the aisles of the monasteries. The realistic or imagined landscapes depicted on the tiles are combined with flowers or hunting scenes.

The Dutch View Most of northeastern Brazil (from Maranhão to the southern part of the present state of Alagoas) was held by the Dutch in the 17th century. The Dutch governor-general, Count Moritz of Nassau, was resident in Recife from 1624 to 1654 and, inspired as he was by the Brazilian northeast, he tried to set up a powerful and flourishing empire there. In the eight-year rule of this cultured man (1636–1644) Recife grew to be the cultural centre of the eastern seaboard of South America and attracted many a scientist, architect and artist from the old world. Frans Post, who lived in Brazil from 1637 to 1644, continued to paint Brazilian scenes even after his return to Haarlem. The vividness and meticulous accuracy of his pictures have led many critics to see in Post a forerunner of Henri "douanier" Rousseau. Albert Eckhout painted flora, fauna and the people of the country, but both painters were not satisfied with the edifying or illustrative aspect of painting "but rather created works that respected the rules of perspective, taste and the pictorial conceptions of the epoch" (Jeannine Verdier). And even if the documents brought back to the Old World by Post and Eckhout were not the first in Europe to deal with American themes, they at least had the "incomparable advantage as painters to have lived in the reality that they portrayed" ... because "until the advent of the Dutch paintings, such works had often been carried out by artists who had never even crossed the Atlantic and whose illustrations needed a firm supporting text to set the scene".

The paintings done by the two artists after their return to Holland are a valuable reflection of Brazil at the time. Post's and Eckhout's paintings (in the Rijksmuseum in Amsterdam, in the Mauritshuis in The Hague, and in the National Museum in Copenhagen) are of the Dutch school in style, and according to Mário Barata, illustrated "a foreign episode in Dutch history and an attempt towards a better understanding of the world by embracing a certain exoticism".

The Baroque of the Northeast and the Baroque of Minas Gerais The northeast, the cradle of Brazil, is steeped in history. Roger Bastide wrote, "If São Paulo has similarities with Chicago, then Bahia resembles a European city. Its stones sing of the past, and this goes not only for Bahia, but also some quarters of Recife and São Luís de Maranhão." This is thanks to the numerous churches and cloisters from the 17th century – Jesuit churches in baroque and rococo style, remnants of the sugar-cane civilisation that Gilberto Freyre studies in depth in his book *Casa Grande e Senzala* (Masters and slaves). The exteriors of these churches, which can be found all along the coconut-palm fringed coastline, are extremely simple. They normally have one or two square or round towers, a triangular pediment sometimes sitting on or rounded off with a spiral, and a row of five windows over the portal (an exception is the monastery church of the Third Order of St. Francis of Assisi, in Bahia, whose decorated stonemasonry façade is probably the work of a Spanish architect). The unpretentious exterior makes the rich inside of the church all the more surprising. Hardly have we entered through one of the three or five doors than we are assailed by an orgy of gold, a delirium, the beginning of a dream or, as Bastide so fittingly puts it, "An excess of treasures, of glittering extravagance of colours, a boundless symphony of light and shade which intermingle, chase each other, draw apart, come together again, and force the faithful who have been touched by these golden flashes and caressed by the soothing shadows to flee into ecstasy, to sink into prayer."

The baroque churches in Minas Gerais state (Ouro Prêto, Sabará, Mariana, São João del Rei), on the other hand, have curved gables and are often octagonal, round or oval in shape, sometimes with concave or convex fronts, and only one portal instead of three or five; instead of the five windows in the façade there are only two, separated by a bullseye or a cartouche. According to Bastide these stylistic differences can be explained by the varying economic factors underlying the two cultures: sugar in the northeast (17th century), gold in Minas Gerais (18th century), the one a rural and feudal society, controlled by the church, the other urban and bourgeois, ruled by middle class secular-legal authority.

Ataíde and O Aleijadinho In the 18th century Minas Gerais became a centre of literature and the visual arts, thanks to the economic upswing that followed the discovery of gold and precious stones in rivers and rocks in this state. Perspective motives, stimulated by the architectural illumination of Italian baroque, dominate the paintings. Although one can find examples of baroque chiaroscuro painting elsewhere in Brazil, it is mainly characteristic of Minas Gerais.

Manuel da Costa Ataíde, the most remarkable painter of the time, created the ceiling of the church of St. Francis of Assis in Ouro Preto, the high altars of the churches of Santo Antônio in Itaverava, Nossa Senhora do Rosário in Mariana, Matriz de Santo Antônio in Ribeirão de Santa Bárbara, as well as numerous individual paintings in Mariana. Ataíde's imaginative and inventive painting, with its fine multicolour technique, already tends towards the rococo style. His perfect craftsmanship makes use of the whole range of baroque elements: pillars, scrolls and flourishes, flowers and vases, vignettes, and stylised seashells. The perfectly controlled use of light and shade inevitably captivates the spectator. The sculptor and architect Antônio Francisco Lisboa has left us many masterpieces, including the *Prophets* and the *Stations of the Cross* (Congonhas do Campo), both worked in his favourite material, soapstone, which is abundant in this region.

This half-caste, nicknamed O Aleijadinho – cripple – because of his leprosy-stunted limbs, designed churches which showed Portuguese influence, but were also full of Brazilian sensuality and mildness. If they lack majesty, as Saint-Hilaire declared, it was only because "majesty does not belong to the Brazilian, even if it is innate in the scenery" (Mário de Andrade). And if the word "beautiful" is perfectly applicable to European churches such as Reims Cathedral or St. Peter's in Rome, it is not suitable for the Aleijadinho's churches, for they are "of such modest eminence, of such well ordered and quiet purity, that they exist to be loved and even caressed".

Apart from that, his complete work can be divided into two very different periods. The one, when he was healthy, can be illustrated by his constructions in Ouro Prêto and São João del Rei, which are of a harmonious lightness. The best examples of the irregular and unsteady, but at the same time dramatic combination of baroque and rococo are the *Prophets* and *Stations of the Cross* mentioned above, which were done when he was already ill. Changes in style which already appeared before his illness are described by Mário de Andrade as being first plastic and then expressionist in character.

Andrade, who devoted a study to the creative genius of Aleijadinho, writes that "he recalls the Italian primitives, moves away from the Renaissance, sinks into the Gothic, thereby becoming almost French, and yet again very German or Spanish in his mystical realism". Andrade continues, "a very varied irregularity, which would be tantamount to dilettantism, were it not for the power that is present in the seriousness of his everlasting works... It is Brazil's casting off the colony. It is the mulatto and it is, logically, independence."

The French Artistic Mission After the Portuguese King and his court had fled from Lisbon in 1808, one of the many initiatives he undertook in Brazil was to found an art academy. In 1816, on the advice of his Minister, Count de la Barca, Dom João VI invited a French cultural mission from Paris to Rio de Janeiro in order to set up and run the academy. The group, headed by Joachim Lebreton, included the painters Jean-Baptiste Débret, Nicolas-Antoine Taunay, his son and pupil Félix Taunay, the sculptors Auguste Taunay, Marc and Zépherin Ferrez, the architect Grandjean de Montigny and the engraver Charles Pradier, as well as other artists, who were all French, apart from the Austrian organist Sigmund von Neukomm.

Despite the King's kindness and the warm welcome from Minister de la Barca, the group had to confront a whole host of difficulties soon after their arrival. For one thing, the French Consul-General, M. Maler, a fervent supporter of the Bourbons, hampered the work of the French artists because he feared that they might turn out to be Bonapartists. In addition, they were not accepted by the Brazilian and Portuguese artists who had been established in Brazil for many years. They were all worried about their future and were jealous of the protection given to the French group. Other factors were the snail's pace of the joint administration of the kingdom, the sudden death in 1817 of the patron, Count de la Barca, the return of Dom João and his court to Portugal, the independence struggle within the country, the death of Lebreton and the return to France of the demoralised Nicolas-Antoine Taunay.

These happenings all delayed the inauguration of the academy until 1820, when it was opened by royal decree under the name Real Academia de Desenho, Pintura, Escultura e Arquitetura Civil. During the empire the name was changed to the Imperial Academia de Belas-Artes, and with the coming of the Republic it got its present name, the Escola Nacional de Belas-Artes. The first pupils were accepted only in 1826, six years after the royal decree. The academy was housed in a building designed by Grandjean de Montigny (the middle section of this building was demolished in 1838 and rebuilt in the central palm avenue of the botanical gardens). The first director of the academy, José Henrique da Silva, objected to French staff, and this ban lasted until his death in 1834, when he was succeeded by Félix Taunay, who improved the school facilities and increased the number of classes.

The Rio Carnival, as seen by Jean-Baptiste Débret, whose major work "Picturesque and historical journey through Brazil" depicted scenes from Indian and everyday life in Brazil in 156 engravings at the beginning of the last century.

The Graphic Art of Débret and Rugendas Until his return to Paris in 1831, Jean-Baptiste Débret was in charge of courses in History of Art and Historicism. Under pressure from the academy's directors he followed a classical line with his students. This style was nothing new for the Brazilians and had been used since the beginning of the 19th century in the paintings and sculptures on the altars of the churches in Bahia and Rio. According to Mário Barata, classicism had been taught in the Aula Pública de Desenho e Figura (a public art school) since 1800 by the painter Manuel Dias de Oliveira, also called O Brasilense or O Romano. Dias de Oliveira had learnt his classical skills in Italy from the painter Battoni.

During his sojourn in Brazil, Débret had painted small, monochrome coloured pictures, overloaded with detail. They depict the royal court: the landing of Princess Leopoldina, the coronation of Dom Pedro I, and the wedding of Dom Pedro II. But his most important work is the book *Picturesque and Historical Travels in Brazil*, which was dedicated to the Institut de France of which he was a member. It is a folio in three volumes containing 156 prints and accompanying texts. The first volume from 1834 is about the Indians, their customs, weapons and tools. The volume published a year later is a detailed look at everyday life in Brazilian high society, and the final volume is concerned with Rio's society. There are portraits of the royal family and famous personalities, flowers, fruit and architectural plans. This historic work, whose quality and comprehensiveness give it great significance, can only be compared with the work of the Prussian Rugendas, who came to Brazil in 1821. He stayed until 1835 and, at the request of the King of Prussia, also compiled *Picturesque Travels Through Brazil*, in whose pictures he illustrates daily life in the interior of Minas Gerais, São Paulo and Baixada Flumenense (part of the state of Rio de Janeiro).

Academism The whole of the 19th century was influenced by the classical themes taught by the academy. Life-drawing, perspective and chiaroscuro were the criteria, the subjects depicted had to be noble and inspired by Europe or the classical ancient times of Greece or Rome, as well as historical, biblical, or military events. Sculpture was carried out in noble materials such as bronze and marble.

This epoch, which at the beginning was also affected by the Romantic movement and towards the end by the Impressionists, brought forth the decorative panels by José Zeferino da Costa, on the ceiling of the Candelária church in Rio de Janeiro. Also worthy of mention are the paintings by Rodolfo de Amoedo, who was influenced by the pre-romantic and lyrical work of Puvis de Chavannes, and the pre-impressionist landscapes of Antônio Parreiras, carried out in pale and melancholy colours. The German immigrant Grimm painted in the style of the plein-air artists, whose themes were landscapes and still life.

Victor Meirelles and Pedro Américo created monumental paintings with historical and nationalistic subjects, Almeida junior painted realistic pictures of life in the country. Eliseu Visconti was influenced by art nouveau, while Pedro Weingartner engaged in maritime painting and Batista da Costa in portrayals of the landscape around Petrópolis. Rodolfo Bernardelli, finally, sculpted in a severe classical style.

The Modern Period The first exhibition of modern art, which passed almost unnoticed, was organised by Lasar Segall in São Paulo in 1913. This Brazilian of Russian extraction painted in a style on the borderline between expressionism and cubism. Although he was actually the first, it was another artist, Anita Malfatti who opened the way for modernism. In 1917, and also in São Paulo, she held an exhibition with pictures by expressionists, cubists and fauvists. This event provoked violent reactions, from, among others, the author Monteiro Lobato with his article

72 *Hieroglyph on the Ingá stone in Northeast Brazil (ingá = tropical tree and town in Paraíba state). Like countless other engravings, this relief has resulted in countless interpretations up to the present day. Some say it comes from Atlantis, from the Phoenicians etc. In all likelihood, the artists were Kariri Indians, who still live in the region. The meaning of the signs is not known.*

73

74

75

73 *Fort Orange on Itamaraca Island is a relic of "New Holland", the Dutch colonial property of the 17th century.*

74 *Neither of the two Brazilian emperors were able to get to know their realm at all well. Travelling through the Empire with the means of transport available in those days could have taken years. A visit to the Northern region was once planned for Pedro II, and in São Luís, the capital of Maranhão state, two palaces were built to accommodate him. But the visit never came about, the palaces not completed, and only the ruins remind us of the Emperor's forsaken venture.*

75 *During the colonial era, there were often bloody clashes in the frontier areas dividing Spanish and Portuguese spheres of influence. Particularly disputed was the "no-man's-land" in the South, which was finally won for Brazil by the gaúchos. Today the area forms the state of Rio Grande do Sul. Ruins still testify to the battles as, for example, São Miguel das Missões near Santa Angelo in Rio Grande do Sul.*

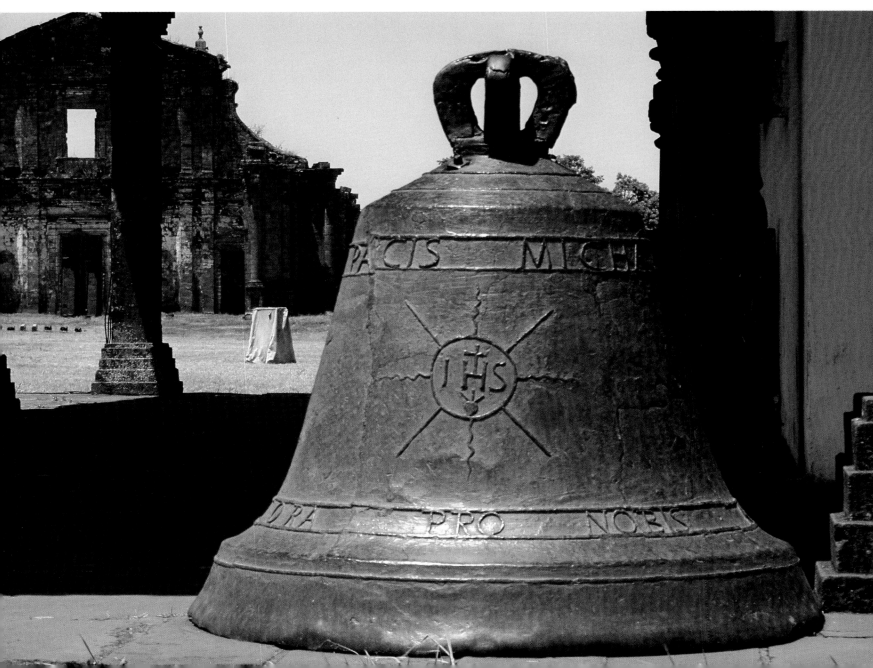

76 South America's greatest sculptor was Antônio Francisco Lisboa, who was born in Ouro Preto in 1738. He caught leprosy at an early age, and lost his feet and lower legs, so that he could only move about on his knees. In Congonhas do Campo, the stone figures of the "twelve Apostles" can be seen in front of the baroque church and on the church steps, a masterpiece by "the little cripple", as Lisboa was known by the people.

77 Apart from administrative buildings, many fine villas and palaces of the rich "coffee barons" were built during the time Pedro I and Pedro II resided in the prospering capital, Rio de Janeiro. The picture shows a patrician villa of the 19th century in Cosme Velho (Rio de Janeiro).

78 During the 19th century, countless Germans settled in the temperate zones of the Southern states (Santa Catarina, Rio Grande do Sul, and Paraná). As an example of German immigration the railway station of Joinville in Santa Catarina state is shown here.

79 A house in Salvador (Bahia).

80 Curitiba is the rapidly-growing capital of the equally fast-growing Paraná state in the South. Between 1950 and 1970, the population almost quadrupled. This was partly due to a strong immigration wave of: Germans (also German-speaking people from the Danube areas of Hungary, Rumania, and Yugoslavia), as well as Italians, Poles, and Dutch. This mixture of cultures is also reflected in the variety of styles to be seen (see our picture of a façade in Curitiba).

77

78

79

80

81 ◁ *The 17th and 18th centuries saw the development of a baroque style which incorporated local features. Countless churches, monasteries, mansions, and public buildings were constructed in this "colonial" style. Brazilian artists also created magnificent works, such as this carved figure from São Miguel das Missões.*

82 ◁ *Baroque art was very highly developed in the region of today's Bahia state. The capital, Salvador – referred to as the "Brazilian Rome" –, is steeped in Baroque art with its countless churches, chapels, monasteries, and museums. A fine example is the picture of the Holy Virgin "Nossa Senhora da Conceição", dating back to the 17th century (Museu de Arte Sacra in Salvador).*

83 *Besides the Cathedral, the most significant sacral work in Brasília is the "Blue Church", named after Dom Bosco (Don Bosco in Italian), the Italian priest and founder of the Salesian congregation. It is also said to have been Dom Bosco, who had a vision of a large city in the arable heart of Brazil as early as the nineteenth century. He is therefore credited with having predicted the building of Brasília.*

"Paranóia ou Mistificação?", which appeared in *O Estado de São Paulo* and became famous. Mário de Andrade, an unshakeable supporter of the modern movement, replied to the article and a mighty bout of polemical argument between the two writers ensued. But the Malfatti exhibition and the scandal surrounding it had prepared the way for the Semana de Arte moderna in 1922, which we have already mentioned under the section on Brazilian literature.

As a result, efforts to end the academic "empire" in which Brazilian art was imprisoned were no longer so moderate in tone. This was largely thanks to Mário and Oswald de Andrade, as well as sculptor Victor Brecheret, who was influenced by Bourdelle and Meštrović, and also to painters the Vicente do Rego Monteiro, who favoured the monumentalism of primitive sculpture, Tarsila do Amaral (Oswald de Andrade's girlfriend) and Di Cavalcanti. Tarsila do Amaral had studied in Paris, where she and Oswald had links with the avantgarde of the 1920s. In Paris she often visited the ateliers of Léger, Gleizes, Lhote, Delaunay and Brancusi with whom she had got in contact through the good offices of Blaise Cendrars, a friend of herself, and Oswald. This artist, influenced by Oswald de Andrade, started a style of painting called "Pau brasil", named after Andrade's volume of poetry dedicated to Blaise Cendrars and also called *Pau brasil* or red dyewood (Paris 1925). This painting style is a simplified, spontaneous, almost naive form of cubist aesthetics, using the colours pink, green, and light blue. Under the influence of Pablo Picasso, Tarsila also painted, in oils, Abaporu Antropofágico (1928), which portrays a huge revolting person with colossal feet.

This painting marked the start of the "Antropofágica" (cannibalism) period, whose aim was a "return to Indian life and the primitive earth". (In 1927 Oswald de Andrade had founded the *Revista de Antropofágia* in which he preached the necessity of swallowing and digesting the foreign culture in order to profit from its advantages, and then to build up one's own culture.)

Di Cavalcanti, who was also an author of consummate erudition, started under the sign of the impressionists. He loved French culture and Paris, which he visited countless times during his life, and, as a result, came under the influence of Pablo Picasso and became a cubist. The wavy, sensual lines of his paintings suggest the hot colours of the Tropics. The result is at the same time a baroque and romantic cubism. Adaptability is also typical for Di Cavalcanti, and for Brazil, because even if the influence of Europeans such as Braque, Picasso, or Léger is clearly in evidence in the work of contemporary Brazilian artists, there is no question, as Celso Kelly once said, of it's being "a transposition or consecutive effort, but rather a diffuse or accentuated presence in one or other picture".

Portinari The years from the end of the 20s to the close of the Second World War were dominated by the personality of Cândido Portinari, who, by means of the power with which he portrayed the working world and the tragic hunger and drought of the northeast, as well as the poetic-folkloristic scenes from his home town of Brodósqui in São Paulo, became the most important painter of this movement. The expressionist distortion, which together with violent colour and form contrasts are typical of his work, represents not only a cry of pain and the desperation of underprivileged Brazilians facing social injustice, but a general cry of anger for the suffering of the Third World. Before Portinari died in 1962, he created huge wall paintings in the style of Diego Rivera and Orozco, two Mexicans whom he admired, and thereby became the first Brazilian painter to realise the dream of placing the pictorial in natural surroundings. Among his most remarkable wall paintings are those to be seen at the UN headquarters in New York and in the old building of the Ministry of Education and Culture in Rio de Janeiro.

Across the Country Starting at the same time as Portinari were two other painters: Guignard, who was to be engaged mainly in painting delicate, poetic pictures of the small historic towns of Minas Gerais, and José Pancetti who became famous for his vivid seascapes.

The modernist movement did not travel beyond the Rio–São Paulo axis until much later. It only reached Belo Horizonte in 1944, with the construction of the Art High School and Pampulha church. At the same time Mário Cravo made his début in Bahia as a sculptor, as did cartoonist and carpet-weaver Genaro de Carvalho, who was influenced by Jean Lurçat. In Ceará the designer Aldemar Martins appeared, a graphic artist whose themes are always taken from the northeast: pets (cats, chicken), Mulher rendeira (lace-makers), Cangaceiros (bandits) and so on. Two other artists who appeared in Rio after the Second World War and who handle Brazilian motifs are Eméric Marcier and Djanira.

Abstract Art Increasing contact of Brazilian artists with Europe, the inauguration of the São Paulo art museum in 1948 and that of Rio in 1949, as well as the creation of the International Biennial Show of São Paulo in 1951 all favoured the introduction of abstract art into Brazil. The pathfinders were Cícero Dias (geometrical abstract art) and Antônio Bandeira (informal abstract art). At the beginning of the 1950's constructivist trends were given an impetus by the influence of artists such as Mondrian, Van Doesburg, Max Bill (shown at the first São Paulo Biennial), as well as the Bauhaus Manifesto, which had been seen as the precursor of industrial aesthetics.

Apart from the geometrical discipline of Tomie Otake, Ianelli, Samson Flexor and the two most important representatives, Lygia Clark and Ivan Serpa, the number of artists influenced by the informal, lyrical abstraction of Frenchman Georges Mathieu is much greater, especially following his stay in Brazil: Manabu Mabe, Fukushima, Yolanda Mohali, Lazlo Meitner, Di Preti, Wega Neri, Glauco Rodrigues.

Graphic Art Graphic art is one of the most popular forms of art practised in Brazil. But there was no breakthrough for a long time after the initial efforts of Darel Valença, Iara Tupinambá and Grassmann, in fact it did not come until 40 years after the advent of modernism. A decisive factor was the arrival of two big names in Brazil: Axel Leskoschek and Johnny Friedländer, who had fled from the Nazi regime in Germany. They left their mark on a whole generation of artists: including Fayga Ostrower, Edith Bering, Remina Katz, Ana Letícia, Isabel Pons, Roberto Delamonica, and Ana Bela Geiger. In Porto Alegre there is a group of artists who are casting off abstract art and turning to sources in folklore, while several young graphic artists have appeared in Rio, São Paulo and Bahia, who include Vilma Martins, Maria Bonomi and Emanoel Araújo.

Contemporary Art Since 1922, developments in art have been closely tied to economic progress. An interested audience has grown up since 1922, the variety of art forms has resulted in a corresponding guild of critics and numerous galleries have sprung up to cover the needs of the market. New centres of art have developed outside Rio and São Paulo: Porto Alegre, Belo Horizonte, Recife, Salvador and, only recently, Brasília and Curitiba. Since 1946 grants have been awarded for national and international trips, within the framework of the annual Salon of Modern Art. The impulses given by the International Biennial in São Paulo and the Museum of Modern Art in Rio, which was the site of the exhibition and of an experimental art laboratory, were vital for the birth of a Brazilian art scene.

In the 1960's the two big names of the avantgarde were Hélio Oiticica and Lygia Clark. (Oiticica spent the 1970's in New York, and died in Rio in 1980 shortly after his return from the US. Lygia Clark spent the 70's in France, where she gave a course at the University of Paris entitled "the collective body or the nostalgia of the body". Since returning to Rio she has been studying a therapy for psychotics, a pre-verbal relaxation form which she terms "self-structuring".) Both artists left the beaten path of art history to throw themselves into exemplary adventures. They were more concerned with expressions, gestures and behaviour than with art in the traditional sense, that is to say the concern for an aesthetic artefact. They therefore introduced the body into art. Oiticica organised happenings aimed at lifting the barriers between artist and audience, at demystifying art, in other words. Lygia Clark did this too, at first with her "bichos", metal sculptures one had to touch and let assume different forms, and then with her objects for the senses: labyrinths, masks, articles of clothing, which one had to try on to experience various sensations. Besides the activities of these two artists we should mention Frans Krajcberg who was also at work in the 1960's, using twigs, bark, petrified flowers and other natural objects from the Brazilian forests. His forays into the plant world have also resulted in topographical pictures of the earth's upheavals, as well as tracing-paper imprints of the weathered surfaces of rocks.

In the last ten years the number of artists has grown at an unprecedented rate. Among the new painters are: Wanda Pimentel, Pietrina Checcacci, Antônio Henrique do Amaral, Claúdio Tozzi and Glauco Rodrigues. Working outside the purely visual field are object and environmental artists such as Regina Vater, Waltercio Caldas, Cildo Meirelles, Antônio Manuel, Tunga, and others.

Architecture Until the middle of the 19th century Brazilian architecture was dominated by a style based on classical and renaissance origins.

Two fine examples of this neo-classical form are the Santa Isabel Theatre in Recife and the Museum of the Republic in Rio. The latter was formerly the palace of the baron of Nova Friburgo, built by the German architect Gustav Waldelnedt between 1860 and 1864 (in 1896 it was bought by the Federal government and named "do Catete" after the city quarter in which it stood. Until Brasília became the new capital, the palace was the official residence of the President. Since then it has become the Museum of the Republic, and the Edison Carneiro Folklore Museum has been accommodated in one of its wings more recently). From the beginning of this century until the advent of modern architecture there was a surfeit of foreign styles. This provoked a nationalistic reaction favouring buildings including elements of colonial and Marajoara style.

From 1931 to 1935 a small group of artists led by Lúcio Costa keenly scrutinised the plans and ideas of Le Corbusier. In 1936, Gustavo Capanema, the head of the Ministry of Education and Culture, called on Costa and the modernists to draw up a project for a new Ministry building. He organised a working group including Jorge Moreira, Carlos Leão, Afonso Eduardo Reidy (designer of the Modern Art Museum in Rio), Oscar Niemeyer and Eranani Vasconcelos. After the plans had been drawn up, Costa suggested to the Minister that Le Corbusier should be invited to Brazil. This well known architect drew up a plan before his young admirers which resulted in the Ministerial building in the centre of Rio. It was named Palácio da Cultura when the capital was moved to Brasília in 1961.

In 1938 Costa and Niemeyer's Brazilian pavilion at the world fair in New York received universal ap-

proval. Since then skyscrapers have started to appear in Brazilian cities. Niemeyer's style became more individuated, above all with the construction of the Pampulha complex in Belo Horizonte in 1944 (church: Niemeyer, gardens: Burle-Marx, oil paintings, wall-paintings, and tiles: Portinari). Niemeyer's style, exemplified by harmonious curves and through a certain scenic perspective, reached its zenith in the construction of Brasília, together with Costa who was responsible for the planning of the new capital.
Mestre Valentim, who considerably changed the physiognomy of Rio with his fountains and the Passeio Público is a good example of a 19th century landscape gardener. At the end of the 19th century a Frenchman, Auguste-Marie Glaziou, was responsible for the Aclimação gardens in São Paulo as well as for the renewal of the Quinto da Boa Vista (large gardens with royal palace, today housing the national museum. The Quinta da Boa Vista also houses the botanical museum and the zoo), the Praça da República and the Passeio Público. He gave them all a romantic air, mixing well with their luxuriant tropical vegetation and contorted ponds.
At the beginning of the present century the French gardens in the Praça Paris in Rio and at the Vila Penteado in São Paulo were laid out in art nouveau style. In the 1950's Roberto Burle-Marx designed the Ibirapuera park in São Paulo, the gardens of Botafogo beach in Rio, and in the 1960's the huge Flamengo park in Rio which covers an area of 1.2 km^2 of land reclaimed from the bay. Equally as famous as Niemeyer, Burle-Marx has designed many other gardens, both private and public, in Brazil and abroad, just one example being the gardens of UNESCO building in Paris.
Folk Art Brazilian folk art can be seen in multifarious variety all over the huge country. The artists behind these functional, but always aesthetic handicrafts are adults, youths and children who, thanks to their imagination, can make their mark felt at markets and fairs. Urban interest in folk art has increased ever since the government started giving subsidies, because sales of folk art to tourists bring in foreign exchange. Museums have been established in several cities, in order to protect folk handicraft from a wave of industrially manufactured "kitsch", and to further knowledge about it. Examples of native handicrafts include anthropomorphic pots and vases, decorated with "naive" drawings, lively coloured terracotta figures, or unpainted ones, representing the animals characteristic of a particular region; hats, baskets, straw fans, objects made out of the shield of a turtle and out of shells; figures or abstract compositions of coloured sand in bottles; all sorts of toys, including "bruxas", which are grotesque cloth puppets; masks, birdcages, miniature furniture, curtains, hammocks, crochet shawls, colourful patchwork bedspreads, lace, and embroidery.
The most important production centres are concentrated in the north and northeast, principally in Belém, on the island of Onças, in Cametá (Pará), Juazeiro do Norte (Ceará), Santo Antônio dos Barreiros, Caicó, Massoró (Rio Grande do Norte), Patos, São Mamede, Catolé da Rocha (Paraíba), Caruaru, Tracunhaém (Pernambuco), Penedo, Igreja Nova, Água Branca (Alagoas), Itabaianinha, Lagarto, Carrapicho (Sergipe), Maragogipinho, Amargosa, Rio das Contas and Serrinha (Bahia). In the south, production is concentrated in the Vale de Paraíba, in the towns of Taubaté, Pidamonhagaba, Tatui and Apiai (São Paulo), and not least in São José (Santa Catarina).
Folk artists who were unknown yesterday have become well known in the meantime. For instance, Mestre Vitalino from Caruaru, who, before he disappeared, founded a whole school of artists. His signed figures are highly sought after. In Tracunhaém, where ceramic figures with religious themes stand opposite common-or-garden glazed pottery, several artists have recently aroused attention: Antonia Leão, who specialises in making angels, Maria do Nuca, who designs dolls and lions, Zé do Carma, who models life-size holy figures. In Olinda, not far from Recife, Eudes Alves sculpts in natural-coloured terracotta with much success, while in Jaboatão, near Recife, Zézé decorates terracotta figures with Tace.
The votive figures seen in huge numbers in the vestries of small churches in the northeast are also a part of folk art. They are sculptures made of wood or even beeswax, representing that part of the body which is sick or injured, mostly the head, or arms,

legs, feet, hands, and very rarely the complete body. The votive pictures are often genuine works of art made in the hope of a miracle or as thanks for a wondrous healing.

Theatre and Film

The Brazilian Theatre The first performances go back to colonial times. Shortly after the arrival of the Portuguese, Father José de Anchieta started writing plays to be performed by the Indians with the aim of teaching these willing converts the Catechism. During the gold rush of the 18th century, there were regular performances in Vila Rica (now called Ouro Preto). In 18th century Rio two theatres had real success: Father Ventura's Casa da Opera and Manuel Luís' theatre. Shortly after his arrival in Brazil King João VI had the Real Teatro São João built in Rio for his court players. Today it is called the Teatro João Caetano in honour of the first Brazilian actor and playwright who used to frequent the court during the regency of Pedro I, as did Luís Carlos Martins Pena, the author of several moral comedies such as *O Juiz de Paz na Roça, O Noviço*, and others. From 1840 onwards several notable authors started writing for the theatre, including Joaquim Manuel Macedo *(O Fantasma Branco)*, José de Alencar *(O Demonio Familiar)*, Gonçalves Dias *(Leonor Mendonça)*, Machado de Assis *(Lição de Botânica)* and Joaquim José de França Júnior, who wrote critical comedies about life under the emperor *(Como se faz um Deputado, Um Carnaval no Rio)*.
At the beginning of the 20th century Leopoldo Froes founded the first Brazilian theatre company, with Viriato Correia (Sol do Sertão) and Oduvaldo Vianna (A Casa de Tio Pedro) as playwrights. This company also led to the founding of the following others, for example by Abigail Maia, Procópio Ferreira, Jaimes Costa and Dulcina de Morais. From 1940 onwards Eva Todor and Luís Iglesias popularised farces, and also staged plays by Shaw, Casona, Molnar etc.
During the Second World War several European artists settled in Brazil. The best known was Zbygniew Ziembinsky, who founded the "Os Comediantes" company, which played Pirandello and O'Neill and had their biggest success in 1945 with *Vestido de Noite* by Nelson Rodrigues. During the same period, at the suggestion of Paschoal C. Magno, the Teatro do Estudante staged the complete works of Shakespeare, while, in 1948, Lúcia Benedetti founded her children's theatre with her own production of *O Casaco Encantado*. Maria Clara Machado not only wrote for this theatre but also became one of the driving forces behind it.
New stage groups were formed in the 1950's by, among others, Maria della Costa, Procópio and Bibi Ferreira. The Serviçio Nacional de Teatro was founded with the aim of encouraging experimental groups and plays by Brazilian authors. One result was a play by Guilherme Figueiredo called *A Raposa e as uvas*, which was performed in Brazil and abroad. The splitting up of the TBC (Teatro Brasileiro de Comédia) led to the formation of new theatre companies by Tonia Carrero, Celli-Autran, Cacilda Becker, Walmor Chagas, Cleyde Yaconis, Sérgio Cardoso, and Nidia Lícia, as well as the Teatro dos Sete of Fernando Montenegro, Italo Rossi and Sérgio Brito.
In the sixties Jorge de Andrade made a name for himself as a dramatist in São Paulo with works such as *A Moratória, O Telescópio, Os Ossos do Barão*, while the "Oficina" troupe, led by José Celso Martins Correa, became famous with performances of plays by Gorki, Brecht, Frisch and other authors. The group rediscovered an old Brazilian text, *O Rei da Vela* by Oswald de Andrade.
Away from the Rio-São Paulo line, Ariano Suassuna made a name as the author and producer of two very successful plays: *O Auto da Compadecida* and *O Santo e a porca*, while the poet João Cabral de Mello Neto wrote *Morte e Vida Severina,* which was performed by the Teatro da Universidade Católica in São Paulo. This theatre gained first prize with this text at the International Theatre Festival in Nancy, France, in 1966.
From 1967 on Plinio Marcos, author of *Dois Perdidos numa noite suja, Navalha na carne* and other works, started to use the vernacular in his plays, a trend that was to dominate the works of young authors in the 1970's, including Antônio Bivar *(Cordélia Brasil)*, Leilah Assunção *(Fala baixo senão eu grito)*, Consuelo de Castro *(Caminho de Volta)* and José Vicente *(O Assalto)*. Today the theatre is almost as popular as the cinema, not least thanks to the slogan "Vamos ao Teatro" – let's go to the

theatre – which has made the theatre affordable for everyone. Both Brazilian contemporary plays and foreign works are performed in the many theatres.

The Brazilian Film The Brazilian film was born in 1898 with a short film by A. Segreto, featuring landscape scenes in Guanabara Bay near Rio, just two years after the very first film had been shown publicly in Brazil. Full-length productions began in 1934 with the founding of Brasil Vita Filmes, and later the Atlântida company in 1943, which produced several popular entertainments such as Canchadas, comedies, and musicals about the Carnival. One can also mention the Vera Cruz company, set up in 1949 and headed by Alberto Cavalcanti, who was already known in Europe. Neo-realism dominated the 1950's, with films such as *Rio, 40 graus*, by Nelson Pereira dos Santos.

The years 1959 to 1962 marked the appearance of the "cinema novo", with a series of 16 mm documentaries by young directors such as Linduarte Noronha *(Aruanda)*, and Paulo César Sarraceni *(Arraial do cabo)*. This cinematic movement, now known worldwide, was a breakthrough by film authors who managed to produce first-class low-budget films. The themes depicted were social conditions in Brazil. "Uma câmera na mão e uma idéa na cabeça" (a camera in the hand and an idea in the head) was the slogan of the "cinema novo". Among the works of this movement we can mention *Barravento, Deus e o diabo na terra del sol* (Gláuber Rocha), *Assalto ao trem pagador* (Roberto Farias), *Os Cafagestes* (Rui Guerra) and *Vidas secas* (Nelson Pereira dos Santos), based on the novel by Graciliano Ramos. In 1962 *O Pagador de promessas*, by Anselmo Duarte, received the major award of the Cannes Film Festival.

In the last fifteen years, and symptomatic of all times of crisis, the Porno-Chanchada films, i.e. commercially successful entertainment productions, have enjoyed a boom. But besides these there have always been committed works which have gained worldwide recognition and admiration, for example *São Bernardo* (Leon Hirsman), *O Predileto* (Roberto Palmari) and avantgarde documentary plays with historical themes, such as *Os Inconfidentes* (Joaquim Pedro) and *Como era gostoso o meu francês* (Nelson Pereira dos Santos). Among the latest productions are *Bye Bye Brazil* (Cacá Diegues) and *Gaijin* (Tizuka Yamazaki), which was shown at the Cannes Film Festival in 1980.

Music

Sacral, Classical and New Music The oldest known score from Brazil, discovered in 1967 by Father Jaime Dinis, is a Te Deum for four voices by Luís Alvares Pinto, who came from Pernambuco. Apart from religious music, there was no real musical life in Brazil's larger towns until the beginning of the 18th century. It started with operettas and operas by Italian masters and also works by the Portuguese-Brazilian composer Antônio José da Silva (O Judeu).

During the gold rush in Minas Gerais musical activity reached a first peak with Curt Lang's support and study of "Baroque Mineiro", an allusion to the prevailing style in the visual arts. It is something of a misnomer because many of the composers in Ouro Preto, Mariana and São João del Rei wrote works that were influenced by Pergolesi, Haydn or Mozart. Later products of Baroque Mineiro were Father José Maurício and Francisco Manuel da Silva. The former was a choirmaster under King João VI and left behind some 400 compositions, the most important of them being the *Missa de Requiem* and the *Missa Pastoril para a Noite de Natal*. The one is majestic, with surprising early undertones of Beethoven, the other is of a good-natured simplicity.

Francisco Manuel da Silva, a pupil of Father José Maurício and Sigmund von Neukomm, wrote the national anthem in 1831 and became the first director of the Academy of Music in Rio de Janeiro.

The Romantic style was in the forefront during the second half of the 19th century, its principal representative was Carlos Gomes, who composed mainly dramatic works. He had studied in Milan, thanks to a scholarship from King Pedro II, and in Italy he had come under the influence of Verdi and Ponchielli. A further important musician of the 19th century was Leopoldo Miguez, who composed the Hymn to the Proclamation of the Republic, as well as symphonic works in Wagnerian style.

Other names have enriched the musical panorama of these times: Brasílio Itiberê, who adapted folk themes into classical forms; Alexander Lévy, who combined Schumann's romanticism with Brazilian

sentimentality; Alberto Nepomuceno, who brought Brazilian themes and rhythms into his music after being trained in Germany. The major Brazilian composer of the first half of the 20th century was Heitor Vila-Lobos (1881–1959). In 1922 he went to Paris, where he was influenced by classicists and impressionists. His deeply Brazilian work drawing on native music, is made up particularly of programmatic compositions. He was one of the most prolific of all composers, with 1300 works to his name, including operas, eleven ballets, suites, symphonies, choral music including the nine monumental *Bachianas Brasileiras*, Lieder, oratorios, violin and piano concertos, chamber music for the guitar. Other brilliant composers of this period include Guarnieri, Mognone and Gnatelli, who have all composed works very Brazilian in character.
In 1939 the German conductor Koellreuter founded the Musica Viva group, which propogated Schönberg's twelve-tone theory and called for worldwide co-operation in the composition and furthering of avantgarde music, as laid down in a manifesto published in 1946.
Newer names are Claúdio Santoro, whose work includes very Brazilian compositions as well as investigations of radical avantgarde works. Guerra Peixe who after a serial period is again composing works with Brazilian themes; Edino Krieger with his compositions of simple musicality and joy, and Marcos Nobre, who, thanks to the influence of Messiaen, Ginastera, Malipiero and Dallapiccola, has found a new path to Brazilian avantgarde music.
In recent times a group orientated towards the works of the Swiss composer Ernst Widmer has been created by the former students of Salvador Music Academy, Lindembergue, Rocha Cardoso and Jamari Oliveira. They are engaged in post-dodecaphone combinations on an Afro-Brazilian basis. Of the contemporary composers one should also mention Gilberto Mendes, one of the pioneers of aleatory, audio-visual and electro-acoustic music, as well as Willy Correira de Araújo, Breno Blauth, Ilivier Toni, José Antônio de Almeida, all from São Paulo. Active in Rio are Esther Scliar, Ailton Escobar, and Mário Tavares, in Curitiba José Penalva, in Porto Alegre Bruno Kiefer, and in Recife the group around Professor Peter Johnson.

Folk Music The oldest expressions of post-colonial folk music are the Lundu, characteristic African dance and the Modinha, a passionate love song of Portuguese origin. At the turn of the century Ernesto Nazareth succeeded in blending the melodic and rhythmic elements of urban folklore with the harmonies of classical music, especially Chopin's.
With the first recording of the Samba *Pelo Telefone* by Ernesto dos Santos and Mauro de Almeida in 1917, this dance, together with the *Choro*, became the basic pattern of urban folk rhythms.
Sinhô, Donga, and Pixinguinha are three of the most important names of the first period of Choro and Samba. They were joined in the 1930's, upon the emergence of the Samba song, by names such as Noel Rosa, Ari Barroso and Lamartine Babo. The most popular singers of the 1930's and 1940's were Vicente Celestino with his songs of yearning, Carlos Galhardo, Orlando Silva, Ciro Monteiro, and Carmen Miranda, who also became famous in Hollywood. In the 1940's two composers became national figures: Dorival Caymi, composer of Toadas (simple, monotonous melodies), which re-interpreted Bahia's folklore, and Ataulfo Alves, a contributor to the development of the lyrical Samba.
Humberto Teixeira and Luís Gonzaga studied the exotic rhythms of the northeast and popularised the Baião and Xaxado, two characteristic dances or folk airs of the northeast.
Towards the end of the 1950's a "cool" style of singing grew up. Dick Farney, Lúcio Alves, Nora Ney, Doris Monteiro and especially Maysa pursued this style, which was the forerunner of the Bossa Nova. The first Bossa Nova record entitled *Canção do Amor Demais* was issued in 1958, and featured Elizete Cardoso with compositions by Tom Jobim and the recently deceased Vinicius de Moraes.
Bossa Nova has become a generic term for a light music style using clever melodic and harmonic distortion effects, and including a mixture of foreign influences and the best of Brazil's music tradition. Its international success has been fostered by composers, singers and guitarists such as Tom Jobim, Vinicius de Moraes, João Gilberto, Carlos Lyra, Astrud Gilberto (who has lived in the USA for years now), Baden Powell, Menescal, Boscoli, Nara Leão, Silvinha Teles, Rosinha de Valença, not forgetting the

Quarteto en Cy, the Tamba Trio and the Zimbo Trio. The folk and light music of the sixties is rich and at the same time contradictory. It can be characterised by the rediscovery of the old Samba composers, who have had a strong influence on the work of musicians such as Paulinho da Viola and Elton Medeiros. In Rio and São Paulo there have been many attempts to bring the old and the new together again, efforts which have brought fame to, among others, Martinho da Vila.
Television appearances have brought popularity to pop musicians such as Roberto Carlos, Erasmo Carlos and Vanderléia, as well as Elis Regina and Jair Rodrigues, these last two producing a more Brazilian sound than the others. Other personal styles can be seen in the performances of artists such as Milton Nascimento, Egberto Gismonti, João Bosco and groups such as the Quinteto Violado, Secos e Molhados and As Frenéticas.
Chico Buarque de Hollanda, whose music portrays the ups and downs of life, became famous in the 60's and is still at the top, among stars such as Maria Betânia and her brother Caetano Veloso, who perform tender love songs. Other idols of the student scene are Simone, Maria Alcina, Fafá de Belém, Maria Creusa, Alcione. The most popular disco star today is Rita Lee, whose songs are erotic. Dori Caymis' songs are less popular with the masses but mark out a path for the development of Brazil's folk music heritage.
Carnival Clearly, no description of Brazilian culture would be complete without a few words about Carnival. This tradition was introduced to Brazil by the Portuguese in 1641, and, together with "Entudo" and Zé Pereira, has grown into the biggest popular festivity of Brazil. (Entudo was an often violent mardi-gras custom where people were shot at with water pistols and similar weapons loaded with water, vinegar, wine or powder and chalk. The entudos continued long after they had been banned. Zé Pereira was a procession involving huge drums; it died out at the beginning of the 20th century.) The carnival has differing forms according to where it occurs in the country. Rio's carnival, whose major attraction is the procession of samba schools and balls of every kind, where prizes are given for the most beautiful creations, has become world fa-

84 *The traditional drink of the gaúchos in Rio Grande do Sul is "Chimarrão", the strong, hot maté tea, which is drunk out of a special beaker-like vessel, the "cuia", using the "bombilha", a sort of drinking-straw made of silver, and with a strainer at one end to filter out the tea leaves. The green tea-leaves float on top. The maté tree, a relative of the holly, is rare in Brazil. It is chiefly planted in Paraguay and Argentina.*

85

86

87

85 No public festival would be complete without food and drink. The "rodeio" (see pict. 86) calls for a "churrasco", the spit-roasted meat that is the traditional meal of the cattle drovers of the Pampas. Wine or beer is served, as are potatoes, rice, or grilled corn on the cob.

86 The counterpart of the vaquejada (see pict. 87) in the Northeast is the "rodeio" of the gaúchos in the South, especially in Rio Grande do Sul.

87 "Vaquejada", the rodeo of the Northeast in Pernambuco. Originally this meant the driving together of all the cattle on the farm (fazenda), which usually happened every winter for the purpose of headcounting, earmarking the cattle for slaughter, and branding of young animals. Every animal had to be brought to the farmyard, which was no mean feat, as the cattle were not used to any restrictions such as ropes or fences. That was why a "vaquejada" always put the cattle hands or "vaqueiros" to the test, in particular with regard to their riding abilities. Once the strenuous work was over, the festivities could begin, whereby the "vaqueiros" could show off their riding skills. Today any big riding contests are also called "vaquejadas", which then turn into a real public festival; however, the "vaqueiros" on their horses remain the main attraction.

88 ◁ Most of the typical folk dances of south Brazil can trace their origins back to the Iberian peninsula, and many of them were already danced in Brazil in the first half of the nineteenth century, as for example, the fandango besides minuets and waltzes, even at the royal court.

89 The clay figures ("bonecos de barro") at the Caruaru market in Pernambuco are representative of a form of art peculiar to that region, which is nevertheless also on sale in other parts of Brazil. The figures mostly depict all sorts of professions, from farmers via the artisan to academic professions such as the doctor or dentist. Originally the figures were neither painted nor heat-treated, but merely air-dried, later they were also partly enhanced with colours. Among the subjects to be seen are the farmer returning from the fields, laden with wood or fruit, the musician with his guitar, or the dentist with his patient sitting in front of him. A frequently recurring theme is "Lampião", with his mistress "Maria Bonita", both armed and wearing the typical Nordestino hat. Lampião is a legendary figure in the Northeast, as he was the leader of the "cangaceiros", a group of robber bandits who raided the Sertão in the 1920s and 1930s.

▽ 89 90

91

90 *Lacemaking in Santa Catarina was introduced to Brazil by immigrants from the Azores. In the second half of the 18th century, these immigrants settled in the coastal region between Ilha de Santa Catarina and the flatlands of the Rio Grande do Sul. They were mostly simple farmers or fishermen.*

91 *Young girl, an attentive and critical spectator at a "vaquejada" in the Northeast. Her T-shirt not only promotes the local folk festival, but also advertises the local sugar-cane brandy "Pitu".*

92 *"Bumba meu boi" (beat my ox) – a comical-dramatic folk dance from Northeast Brazil, of Portuguese origin, mixed with African and Indian elements. The dance portrays the death and resurrection of the ox (reminiscent of a bullfight). The street procession also includes other animals as well as the Devil, and human father-figures (picture).*

93 *Carnival celebrations in Salvador (Bahia). Everybody takes part, the dance is the "frevo" from Recife (Pernambuco).*

94 ▷ *The Carnival in Rio. Big prizes await not only the winner of the Samba schools contest (see pict. 98), but also the victors in the ball costume competition. Only the rich can afford the sort of "fantasias" likely to win.*

95 ▷ *Samba dancer in Carmen Miranda look and sweeping flowered dress.*

CORUJAS

94

96 *The Rio Carnival is increasingly becoming a parade and contest amongst the Samba schools. The more it is promoted as an official tourist attraction, the more it loses the character of a public festival.*

97 *This penetrating screeching instrument is onomatopoeically called a Quica.*

98 *Samba schools (escolas de samba) is the name given to carnival societies from the same outskirts of the city or the same suburb. "Portela" is one of these. The picture shows a member practising with the tambourine. Not only blacks and mulattos, but also whites take part as "sambistas" (dancers) or "bateristas" (percussionists).*

95

96

97

98

ACEB

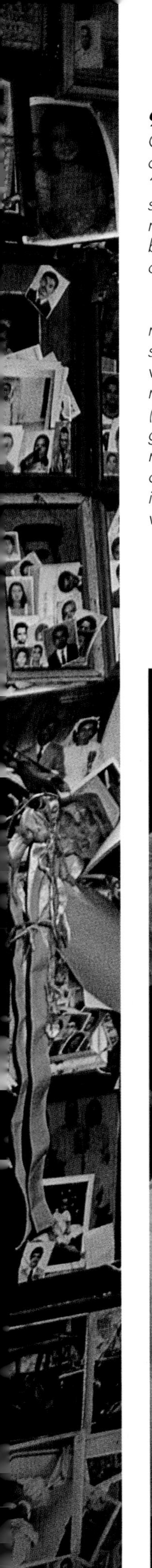

99 ◁ *Candomblé in Bahia. Candles are lit at the beginning of this Afro-Brazilian cult by "Daughters of God". Incense swirls around. They are the mediums that are later "ridden" by the ghosts or Gods (orixás) and fall into a trance.*

100 *There is still much devoutness, particularly among the simpler people. Countless votive donations have been made in the Bom-Fim Church (Salvador), as a sign of gratitude for healings, happy returns from travels, and good outcomes of difficult situations involving the individual or the whole family.*

101

102

100

101 ◁ *Baroque art in Brazil was to a large extent upheld by the Africans, who often portrayed characters in the Bible, or the priests of the church as people of their own skin colour. The work of art shown here, in the church of São Francisco, Salvador, features a black priest holding a white baby.*

102 ◁ *Macumba, near Rio de Janeiro, is a place of cult-worship at a waterfall deep in the forest. The initiated "sons" and "daughters" invite the Gods to the richly-laden table – flickering candles give support to prayers.*

103 *When President Juscelino Kubitschek inaugurated the new capital Brasília on 21st April 1960, he was fulfilling an old demand of earlier politicians and patriots. Construction had already been foreseen under the terms of a presidential decree of 1920. The Constitutions of 1934, 1937, and 1946 all contained plans for a new capital in the interior, in the region of Goiás. But the presidents kept postponing these ambitious plans – mainly because the costs seemed too high. Juscelino Kubitschek built Brasília in the space of just under four years, but the financial, economic, and political consequences of this gigantic project were not long in coming. Brasília has strengthened national resolve and enterprise. André Malraux described Brasília as the "Capital of Hope". Besides the fine buildings, there are also many works of art to be seen. "The Two Warriors" is a bronze sculpture by Bruno Giorgi, which is situated in front of the Parliament buildings (Praça dos Três Poderes).*

mous. Less known is the carnival in Salvador de Bahia with its Trios-elétricos, sambas and afôxes. The Trios-elétricos were originally developed by Adolfo Nascimento (Dodó) and Osmar Macedo. They are neon-lit trucks carrying an orchestra and driven around the streets during the carnival. Crowds follow the trucks, dancing to the rhythm of carnival hits. The best-known Trios-elétricos are the Tapajós and the Marajós. Afoxés are carnival processions of the blacks, who sing songs of the Candomblé cult in Nagô and Yoruba. The characteristic element of the Recife carnival is the Frevo, a dance mainly known in Pernambuco, which includes frenetic, self-improvised interludes, and the Maracutu, a procession which can trace its origins back to Afro-brazilian folklore of the northeast. Percussion instruments dominate the rhythm.

Throughout Brazil, the carnival lasts from the Saturday to the Tuesday before Ash Wednesday. But the pre-carnival celebrations already begin at New Year. People of every class of society and of every colour get involved in the merrymaking, because, as Gilberto Freyre has so succinctly said, "Brazil is more a democracy across racial demarcations than an ethnic democracy. Being a man or a woman is enough to qualify as Brazilian. There is no need to ascertain statistically how many people there are of each race and colour."

During the carnival, the decorated streets of Rio are rocked by much planned as well as spontaneous entertainment. This also goes for the beaches, clubs and dance halls. Caipirinhas, drinks made of sugar-cane spirit (cachaça), lemon juice, sugar and chunks of ice, Batidas, cocktails made of fruit juice (Maracujá, pear, coconut, mango, peach, etc.), mixed with cachaça, sugar and ice, as well as beer are consumed in quantity by carnival-goers thirsty after dancing in the summer heat. On Sunday evening the huge samba procession is held. It is divided into three parts. The first is made up of 14 schools, including the most important ones, which since 1952 have been judged by a jury from the Ministry of Tourism of Rio state. Salguiero is in red and white, Mangueira in green and pink, Portela in blue and white, Império Serrano in green and blue. These are the most famous schools not just because of their bright costumes, but because of the themes they choose, the choreography, the line-up of dancers: blacks, mulattos, coffee-coloureds, blonds, workers, society people and the world of the arts. Since 1952, when carnival juries were introduced, the samba schools have been registered societies with statutes and elected boards.

The Samba, characteristic of the Rio Carnival, as well as the Maracatu and Frevo of Recife, originated in Africa, more specifically from today's Angola and the Congo. They are based on an African round dance called the Batuque. So although the carnival was introduced by the whites, its spice comes from the blacks, a phenomenon on which Roger Bastide comments, "... there is perhaps no European folklore performance which has not, slowly or rapidly, been eclipsed by African versions, and the best example of this is the Brazilian carnivals". If this is true then, according to Bastide, "the Samba has lost its African roots, especially among Brazil's urban blacks, and become a part of the carnival". Until the beginning of this century, any music was good enough to play at the carnival – waltzes, tangos, charlestons, quadrilles. That had been the case since the first carnival ball of 1840 in Rio. The ball held in the "Municipal" (today the Canecão) was the high spot of the carnival for many years. From 1834 onwards, masks were worn, in line with French influence, and this custom of wearing simple or ostentatious masks continued until the 1930's, when increasing costs forced the abandonment of the practice. The same period also marked the ending of the "Corso", a tradition introduced in 1900 involving a procession of open automobiles covered in confetti and paper chains which would be driven along the Avenida Central (today called Avenida Rio Branco) from afternoon to dawn.

Let us, finally, turn back to the samba. The first school was founded in 1917 by Ismael Silva and Nilton Bastos, under the name Deixa Falar. Since that time the themes of the songs have become ever more romantic and increasingly concerned with conditions on the Morros, the hills surrounding Rio which are thickly sown with Favelas or slums. Since 1930, thanks to the Batucadas, the percussion instrument that dominates the music groups, the Samba has overtaken other rhythms and become the hallmark of the Brazilian carnival.

Brief Ethnology of Brazil

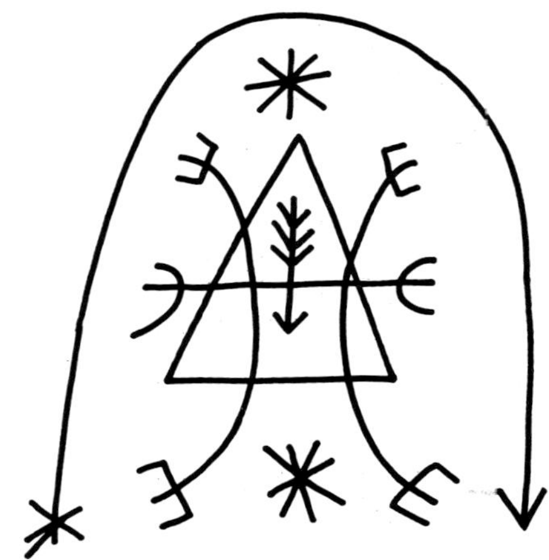

The ethnology of Brazil is as many-layered as the country itself, which both in land area and in its population of now nearly 130 million, makes up almost half of the South American continent. Although whites still dominate, the totals for blacks and mulattos almost add up to 50%, while the Indians at 1–2% are an infinitesimal part of the population.

The ethnic variety of Brazil can be explained historically: Indian native population, Portuguese colonialists, import of African slaves, and besides that immigration from non-Iberian European countries, Dutch settlers taking up a large part of the northeast in the 17th century, Swiss, German, and Italian immigrants who came to the south and southeast of Brazil in the course of the 19th century. In the present century Brazil experienced waves of immigrants from Japan and the Middle East. It is no surprise that ethnically Brazil is a microcosm of the whole world. So only a "brief" ethnology, selective in its themes can be offered within this framework, and with the white population taking a back seat, seeing as it largely came from Europe anyway.

Least known for the non-Brazilian are the Indians of the Amazon rain forests, and most of this chapter will be devoted to them and to their relatives from the savannas and steppes of the central highlands (and also from the coast).

Who are they, where do they come from, how many remain? How do they find food, how do they live, what faith do they have? These basic questions will not receive a scientifically accurate answer, almost an impossibility in any case, but a response based on experience and personal contacts, and designed to awake an understanding of this threatened minority. This same immediate and empirical method will be used to describe the African element to be found in Brazil, not taking the example of the Carnival, but rather the Black cult as the strongest expression of Afrobrazilian folklore. These cults are called Candomblé in Bahia, and Macumba in Rio. Similar in principle, they are collectively termed Umbanda, and also for many whites, they serve as a welcome bulwark to the existential banality that threatens life everywhere today.

The Indians

What do the Indians mean to us? Were one to pose this question in the street, the answer would probably be "nothing". Who cares about a distant, stone age race living in the jungle? At the most, the word Indian will trigger off memories of reading about palefaces and Indians in books such as Fenimore Cooper's "Last of the Mohicans". This may be true of the older generations, but the young have the even more dubious Hollywood image of the Indians. The following description has little or nothing to do either with the Hollywood Indians, nor with the nomadic prairie redskin of North America. For one thing, the surroundings of the Indians are totally different, being tropical or subtropical, and secondly the Brazilian Indians never had horses with which to gallop over the prairie, nor do they today have automobiles with which to drive to meetings. Present day North American Indians are almost totally civilised. The Brazilian Indian, in particular the Amazon Indian is very different from the North American Indian. He also differs from the Indians of Central America and the Andes, who are descendants of the advanced cultures of the Toltecs, Aztecs, the Mayas, the San Agustín civilisation, and the Incas. If one compares the sharply-sculpted features and frequent beak noses of the North American, Mexican, and Andes natives, as well as the mestizos, with the soft, harmonious faces of the Amazon Indians, then one begins to doubt if all Indians really are of the same race.

But the so-called man in the street would have to grant the Amazon Indian one significant role without quibble: namely that as one of the last representatives of an unspoilt lifestyle within our technological and automated world, he is of irreplaceable value to us, the civilised peoples. After all is it not remarkable that there are still people who go naked without shame, can make fire by rubbing two pieces of wood together, can shoot fish in the rivers with bow and arrow, and survive in the jungle, with its murderous climate and manifold dangers, and not go hungry into the bargain? Is it not a solace and easing of the mind for today's city dweller to know that the simple, natural life, ruled by providence, gods, and animal spirits still exists?

This outlines the purpose of this chapter: to create or strengthen understanding for the urgently needed protection of the primitive civilisation of the Amazon. Their survival is threatened by wholesale destruction of their tribal societies (ethnocide) or by the killing of their individual tribesmen (genocide). They are one and the same the consequence of the destruction of the environment, the forest, wildlife, fish shoals, the result of the onward march of civilisation, and of the greed and unbridled egoism of its agents.

Fostering understanding for the very different lifestyle of the Silvícolas (forest dwellers) is more than necessary, because only by doing so can one increase their chances of survival, only by pointing to the urgency of the matter can consciousness be raised. This is just as necessary amongst the Indians' white Brazilian neighbours, the half-caste Caboclos living on the river banks, and also the Europeans. Two stories may make this point:

While crossing the Rio Araguaia with a local farmer, he asked me if I knew why the United States had become so powerful. He answered his question himself, by saying that they had killed off all the Red Indians. Just a few moments previously this same man had lovingly looked at flowers and hummingbirds. But his love of life did not extend to Indians. The farmer's statement is tantamount to saying the only good Indian is a dead Indian, which is about the same as the popularly held view that the Indians are lazy and corrupt – hardly surprising when their land is taken away from them after they have been plied with alcohol (cachaça) and advantage is taken of their inexperience and gullibility in every way!

The other story: in Europe no one propagates the slaughter of Indians, but then they do not steal anyone's cattle here. A tremendous amount of interest and willingness to help is present in Europe when it is a question of protecting animals and saving species from extinction, but there is hardly a murmur when it is a case of saving African tribesmen, Australian Aborigines, or Indians, not even from ethnologists who should have a prime professional interest in saving the subjects of their studies. There is nothing wrong with saving animals – but protecting endangered native tribes should have priority.

If one asks what the Indians have achieved, then one can say the highland Indians discovered and developed maize and potato cultivation, from the Amazon region comes cassava, also known as tapioca or manioc, which comes from the Indian word "manihot". This product of the tropical rain forest is the staple vegetable food of all lowland Indians. It will be mentioned again under the heading of food supplies.

A popular drink in Brazil is guaraná, a non-alcoholic beverage with invigorating qualities thanks to the caffeine-content of a seed used in its preparation. This seed comes from a plant found in the Amazon region. The guaraná seed plays the same role in the life of the forest dwellers as the coca leaf of the Andean Indian. The seed is chewed or fermented in water. Guaraná powder is available in the shops, and before long, guaraná soft drinks will be competing with cola drinks in north America and Europe.

Drawing latex from rubber trees also stems from the Amazon Indians. "Kau-utchu" in the Tupi language means "weeping tree" and refers to the Pará rubber tree *(Hevea brasiliensis)*. Even today several tribes use latex to manufacture certain goods and cult objects. In the Serra dos Parecis (near the Bolivian border) I saw Indian boys playing with an inflated rubber latex ball.

The Amazon Indians have been masters in the domestication of animals and plants. Should the Indians survive, they would have a lot to teach the rest of the world in this respect. The expeditions of the white man reach the Indian settlements, look at their secrets, give them a few cheap articles such as knives, pans, soap, mirrors, glass beads, and then leave them to their fate without any further concern. Thanks to such expeditions, and their pharmaceutical harvest we have valuable medicines and supplements. The best example is the now indispensable curare, a type of strychnine which has many varieties, and which are prepared and used by Indian medicine men and hunters in different forms: as solids, liquid, paste, pure, or blended with other substances.

I would particularly like to mention paricá or epena, which is related to curare, and is used by many tribes, for instance by the Yanomami of northern Brazil and Venezuela who employ it not only as a poison for the tips of their arrows, but also as a sniffing drug. It is applied by one Indian blowing it up another's nose by means of a long tube. This paricá is a psychopharmaceutical consisting of several alkaloids, with hallucinogenic properties. It leads to changes of spatial perception. The Indian uses it to get in contact with the nature spirits, as Claude Lévi-Strauss has already surmised. After taking the drug, the Indian perceives himself, others, and the outside world as overpowering. Acts of physical violence ensue. The Indian is of course not conscious of the fact that by doing this he is venting his aggression, thus permitting himself to re-adjust better to his social order again. In the light of the possible carcinogenic properties attributed to the anti-baby pill it would be worth investigating the merits of a substance used by the Kayapó Indians for instance, for birth control (presumably from a Simaroubaceae species). The bark of this tree is also known as a medicine against dysentery. Birth control has been a dire necessity for the Indians for thousands of years – but cancer is not found among them.

Two hardly-known achievements of the Amazon Indians should be mentioned at this juncture; both concerning dyes. Decorative feathers are so to speak dyed-in-the-wool by the Indians, because they give birds certain liquids which result in the desired colour tone. As well as this, the Indians paint themselves with urucum, the red dye obtained from the annatto tree *(Bixa orellana)*, not only for religious reasons, but also as protection against the permanent annoyance of mosquito stings.

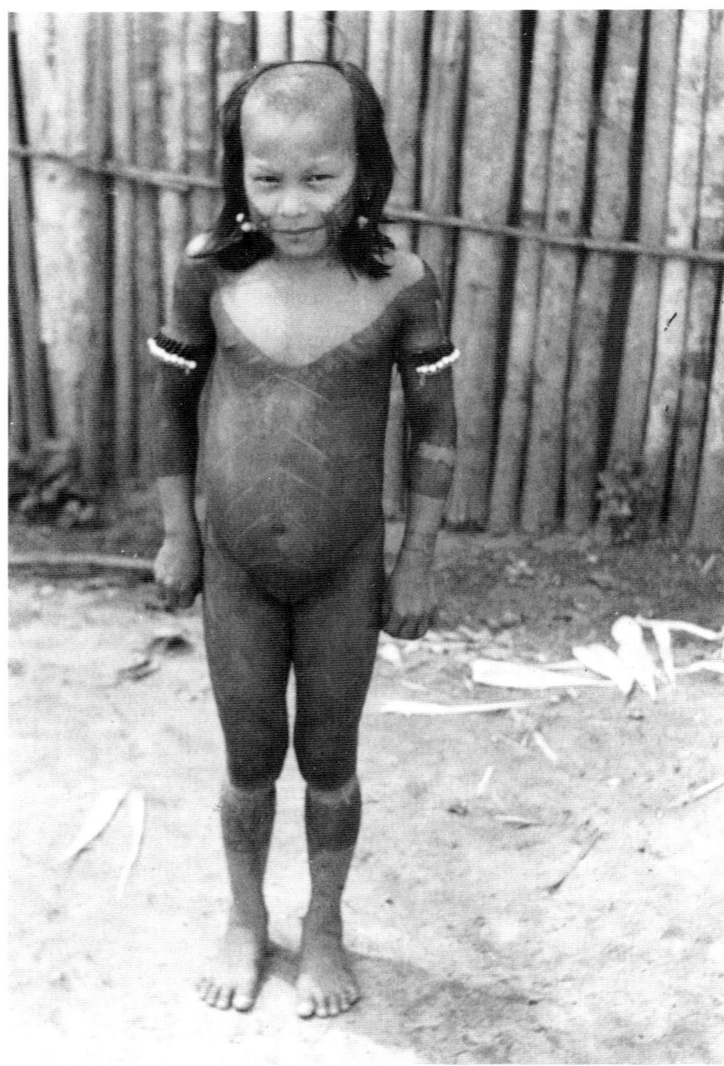

Txukarramãe child with ear and arm bangles, and cutout "neckline". The hair has been shorn above the forehead.

The Origins of the Indians

This raises the question of the first inhabitants of the Americas. Absurd theories that the Indians are descendants of the legendary continent of Atlantis, or even that the human race originated in what is today Argentina, have been given up, but without

giving a final answer to the uncertainty about whether the Indians were the first inhabitants of the continent, or if in fact they had been preceded by another civilisation. There are no indications that there was a pre-Indian population, so with the present state of knowledge one can say that the Indians must be regarded as the native population, although one that immigrated.
From where did they come? This question too awaits a conclusive answer from the anthropologists and archaeologists. It is certain that the Indians are of Asian origin. They have marked similarities with east Asian peoples such as the Mongols. The Indians are descendants of the greater Mongoloid race, indications of this are the yellow-brown skin colour, the smooth black hair, the frequent epicanthic fold, and the occasional blue spot (usually in the sacrum of children). According to recent research, the Indians crossed over the Bering Strait (an ice bridge at the time) from Asia to America, 30,000 to 40,000 years ago. Others put this figure as 12,000 years ago. In time they spread over all of North, Central, and South America. There are similarities of language between north and south. But it is also likely that east and southeast Asiatic peoples crossed the Pacific ocean. Amongst the now extinct people of Tierra del Fuego there seemed to be indications of Melanesian, Polynesian, and Australian antecedents.
The oldest human traces in Brazil today go back to 10,000–8000 BC (Lagoa Santa in Minas Gerais where paleolithic *Homo brasiliensis* was found, cave dwellings on Bolivian frontier). The Sambaquis, piles of mussel shells and other food remains found on the Brazilian east coast date back to 5500 BC, while the Marajoara culture started some 5000 years later. Marajó is an island about the size of Switzerland at the mouth of the Amazon, and on it were found dwellings with geometrically engraved earthenware urns, similar in style to Andean ceramics. The prehistoric pottery of Santarém reveals Caribbean influence, while the pottery of the Tupi-Guarani tribes in central and southern Brazil (1000 AD) probably came from the Rio Paraná region. Otherwise the pre-Columbian settlement of Brazil is shrouded in the mists of time. Known are the living spaces of the various groups, but not how they reached their new homes. The tropical and subtropical climate ensures that all organic remains of human existence are largely destroyed.
When Columbus discovered (central) America in 1492 he thought he had arrived at his destination, India, and thus named the natives Indians. This name has stuck to the aboriginals, even in Brazil which was first sighted and foot set upon in 1500, by the Portuguese Cabral, who afterwards really did get to India, but by way of the African south cape!

Indian Languages – Cultural Differences

The western world and science cannot conceive of such a complex phenomenon as "the Indians" in terms of a unity, a whole. They want to divide it up, distinguish, count, define, and therefore look for such factors to complete their picture. Thus ethnology orders Indians into categories, classes, and regions, without thereby doing justice to the nature of the person.
With regard to the abovementioned doubt about the distribution and links between the various Indian groups, one can say that language is a good indicator. Many of their idioms are to be found among the native population of Brazil. The discoverers came upon the Tupi language which through the centuries has become the daily language (língua geral) used in communications between Europeans and the natives. Although originally only spoken by tribes along the eastern coast, at the behest of christian missionaries it was raised to the status of official Indian language, and spread as far as the Rio Negro in the northwest of the Amazon region. The same happened in the south with the Brazilian-Paraguayan Guarani language. Together the two idioms became the grouping of the Tupi-Guarani language.
Other main tribal languages which continue to survive as well as Tupi, are Makro-Jé (mainly spoken in central and south Brazil), Carib (in the north), and Aruak (mainly at the foot of the Andes). These main tribal groupings are split into countless language families. In the same way that the Romance languages can trace their roots back to Latin, so the Indian language families and tribes can look back on

a common inheritance and therefore cultural relationship. But similarities and congruencies can also be attributable to the assimilatory effect of living in common settlements. Thus on the upper reaches of the Xingu river, and encouraged by the native reserve there, common rituals and practices have grown among peoples of differing languages. This applies to the death feast (kuarup), house building, the use of zoomorphous seats, and even the protection of women's pudenda. This is the cultural area of the Uluri.

The often posed question about the number of Indians is difficult to answer. Only estimates are possible, because how could one get hard and fast figures as to the numbers living under the huge spreading greenery of the Amazon forest? Censuses practically have to be carried out from the air, and in the past, before the advent of road communications with this 5 million square kilometres of territory, not even rough estimates could be made.

So how many million Indians were there when Brazil was discovered in 1500? That it was a question of millions is pretty certain – but was it 2 million or 10? Anthropologists think it was between 5 and 8, so most likely the true figure is 6 or 7 million Indians. The number of tribes would have reached or exceeded the one thousand mark, because even today one finds groups as large as 5000, or more. There are over 10,000 Tikuna in the western Amazon, and 8400 Yanomami, in Roraima in northern Brazil. And this is not counting the other members of the same tribes across the border in Venezuela and Colombia.

Darcy Ribeiro, Brazil's leading ethnologist says that around 1900 there were 230 tribes in the country, adding up to a total of perhaps one million people. In 1957, according to Ribeiro, there were 143 tribes left, with 87 groups having died out or been assimilated by civilisation. Extrapolating these 1957 figures up to 1980, one comes to a figure of about 100 remaining Indian communities in Brazil. As to the numbers of Indians, Ribeiro puts the 1957 figure at between 70,000–100,000, which appears too low, as present day figures of Brazilian Indians are put at between 80,000–100,000 (there is no figure for today, using Ribeiro's method). On the other hand, official statistics which place the number of Indians between 200,000–250,000 are certainly exaggerated. One therefore arrives at an average group size of 800,000–1,000,000 persons (with 100 groups), which is almost certainly over-optimistic.

Raoni (on right), cacique (headman) of the Txukarramãe, with a colleague, both sporting a botoque or lip disc.

The figures given above all stand and fall on the dividing line between Indian and non-Indian. Ribeiro and other ethnologists, such as Melatti, distinguish between isolated living communities, even if they occasionally have contact with the outside world, groups which have intermittent contacts with civilisation (contato intermitente), those with permanent contact (contato permanente) and finally those communities integrated into civilisation. These characteristics of contact with, or integration into, the national Brazilian world were carried over, in simplified form, into the Indian Statute (Law No. 6001, 19 December 1973). Article 4 of this law divides Indians into three categories – those living in isolation, those on their way to integration (with intermittent or permanent contacts), and those already integrated.

As a matter of fact it is of vital importance to make the distinction between these groups. Many a ream of paper and hours of discussion have been wasted because there was no clarity about the subject Indians being referred to. It goes without saying that isolated communities of Indians call for totally different treatment or viewpoints than for instance Indians who are clothed, who listen to the radio, know how to deal with machinery and money, in other words, who are integrated.

The main difficulty is to decide which of those groups who are integrated still belong to the Indian population. They are to be found mainly in areas where there has been much intermarriage with white (or black) Brazilians. In the major cities of the east, but also in the north, one hardly ever sees an Indian face, whereas in Manaus, Tefé or Tabatinga (in the west, on the mid reaches of the Amazon) one is constantly confronted by Indians or half-castes. Also of significance, apart from racial and language characteristics, is whether the Indian still lives in an Indian community. In Tabatinga there is a Tikuna village just past the airport, and its inhabitants go into the city to work and do their shopping. Another point is if cultural peculiarity is maintained, and above all, if the Indian still regards him- or herself as a member of a tribe. Science and the law (Indian Statute Article 3) thus regard self-identification as the determining factor.

It is of particular interest to know how many non-integrated "wild" tribes and members there were at the turn of the century, and today. Figures are available, at least for the years 1900, and 1957. They are taken from Ribeiro's calculations. If one ignores the integrated tribes and members, then there were approximately 200 "wild" tribes in 1900; by 1957 this had fallen to 100 tribes with just over 50,000 members, and would probably be about 50 tribes with 25,000 members for 1980 – considerably less for 1987!

Tribal groups	1900	1957	– decrease + increase	1900–1957
isolated	105	33	–72	
with intermittent contact	57	27	–30	
with permanent contact	39	45	+ 6	
integrated	29	38	+ 9	
total	230	143	–87	
*Tribal membership**	**	1957		
isolated		24 000		
with intermittent contact		10 000		
with permanent contact		18 000		
integrated		32 000		
total		84 000		

* rounded average between minimum and maximum

**Ribeiro gives no corresponding figures for 1900. A total figure of 1 million was assumed above.

Food Supply

Gathering This is culturally speaking the first step in the economy of human beings. In the garden of Eden fruit was only plucked, and not sown and planted. We do not know if hunting and fishing were already engaged in. In essence these activities are nothing more than an extended form of gathering, but a form with the need for talent and skill. Actually, gathering also calls for cleverness, that is precise knowledge about the plant and animal world.

This most primitive level of economy, marked by an absence of planed agricultural activity, corresponds to the nomadic and semi-nomadic existence of the Amazon Indians. Mark Münzel however is of the opinion that only a very tiny minority does not engage in cultivation, and that the majority of alleged nomads and semi-nomads is in fact made up of resident farmers. He himself mentions a whole host of nomadic tribes, but they include splinter groups which have been forced into a marginal existence by the advent of civilisation. These are undergoing a secondary primitivisation process, transforming them from farmers back to hunters and gatherers. Permanently fleeing from the white man, driven from hideaway to hideaway (usually on the upper reaches of rivers, above the rapids), these groups can never harvest their cultivations, because the intruders harvest or destroy their crops, so that in the end they give up tilling the soil completely. This is the case with the Avá-Canoeiros between the Rio Araguaia and Rio Tocantins, and also the Arara, south of the Transamazônica highway on the Rio Iriri, with whom contact was only established in February 1981. When they finally gave in to the blandishments of the official contact team under Sidney Possuelo, an elderly tribesman held a ninety minute speech addressed to the jungle, saying that now his people had nowhere else to flee... Of other groups contacted earlier on, or only in recent years it is assumed that they were nomads from the very beginning. In this category fall the Bororo and the Kreen-Akarore in the southern and western Mato Grosso respectively. Then as now semi-nomads are the Nhambiquara living in the Guaporé valley in Rondônia state. Claude Lévi-Strauss has described their living conditions in his famous book "Tristes Tropiques". When hunting and fishing are to no avail, they travel around, men, women, and children, in small groups, sometimes with a leader, and gather wild fruit, small animals, and other edibles. The leader, named captain (capitão) – there being some contact with Brazilian society – is the only man allowed to have several wives, a reward for the obligation he carries to find food for the group. He is helped in this task by his two, three or four wives. A consequence of this privilege is that there are often no women for the other men!

The Nhambiquara are among the most primitive communities, and were used by Lévi-Strauss to develop his socio-philosophical theories, in particular structuralism. These Indians, as I was able to ascertain myself, still live extremely simply. They sleep on the floors of their huts, without hammocks, but they produce skilfully-designed arrows and good basketware. Unfortunately this tribe has been very much threatened by several forced migrations, and most recently by road building projects.

One can only estimate the number of nomadic or semi-nomadic groups that remain. Based on Ribeiro's figures for the isolated tribes, there may still be 20 communities with a total of 10,000 members, perhaps even more, seeing as new tribes are uncovered every few months. Ribeiro has described groups as extinct, only for them to turn up again. This was the case with the Arara tribe.

Food that is gathered includes vegetable like such as pine-kernels and palm seeds, roots, and honey, and animal products such as turtle eggs, grasshoppers, grubs, ants, lizards, worms, and snakes. All these, as well as plant straws and fibres serve not only as nourishment, but also for the manufacture of tools – the extraordinarily sharp teeth of the dangerous piranha fish being used to cut, scratch or comb, the fibres of the *Mauritia* palm being used to make hammocks, bamboo canes for arrows and blowpipes, and so on. Wax from plants, and resins are welcome lubricating and glueing substances, kaolin is used to paint the body, and ghost masks. The Indians are masters of the clever use (and not over-use) of their surroundings. Plundering of natural resources is unknown to them. No one understands the jungle plants and their medicinal uses as well as the Indians. They also use nature for the purposes of their magical cults.

Hunting It has often been maintained that the Indians are lazy. This may be true of those who have been corrupted or spoilt by civilisation – in the former case by alcohol, which wears the Indians out physically and mentally, and in the latter case by their dependance on a government Indian post, or a mission station. After being fed and cared for by these mentors, the Indians see little reason to go back to hunting food for themselves or their relatives.

In his natural state, the Indian has a hard struggle to survive. His technology, in comparison to ours, is rudimentary, even if perfectly adapted to the surroundings. In addition he has to make all his own tools. Division of labour, apart from that between man and woman, does not exist. Every adult makes his own hunting equipment, his means of transport, is responsible for the storage and processing of food supplies, he makes his own bow and arrow, clubs, spears, boat, baskets, pots, et cetera – so there can be no question of being lazy.

For the Indians, hunting is not a pleasure or a pastime, but dire necessity, and something that goes without saying. It could not be called work, because that is a concept the Indian does not understand. Hunting is always man's work, practised alone or as a twosome, but mostly in groups. The prey is various kinds of deer (veado) as well as peccaris (porco-do-mato), tapirs, monkeys, and also the jaguar, which is hunted mainly for cult reasons, and for his fur, claws, and teeth. The fur trade, although prohibited has also found favour in Indian communities and is harming the ecological balance. Jaguar claws and teeth are used as a much-appreciated necklace. Birds of course, are also hunted, because of their feathers, although the largest bird, the nandu, a sort of ostrich, is also killed for food. There are food tabus which vary from tribe to tribe. In the Xingu Park for instance it is tabu for the Indians to eat monkey meat. The tough but very tasty monkey meat therefore remains the province of the white Brazilians.

Hunting methods, leaving aside the question of firearms, differ greatly. The Xavante lay a ring of fire around copses or undergrowth where animals are hiding, leaving just a small exit open. The animals are forced to flee through this and are consequently easy prey. Setting traps, digging pits, hunting stands or seats, on the ground or in trees, from which the hunters can shoot their prey at night – these are all methods with which the Indians are conversant. Hunting is easier in the rainy season because the animals in the flood zones tend to flee to higher ground, which forms islands surrounded by water. The Xokleng are said to chase the nandu, which calls for real sprinting abilities, as this long-legged animal can keep up with a bus on the road, as I have been able to confirm. Animals which live underground or in caves are smoked out of their nests.

Many tribes put poison on the tips of their arrows when using bow and arrow, and above all in the case of the blowpipe. Curare has already been mentioned in this connection. It is chiefly used in the north and western Amazon, on the high ground around the river basin, but not in the plain between Belém and Manaus. There are various kinds, composition and method of preparation varying from tribe to tribe. The poison results in rapid paralysis of the throat and neck muscles, then the limbs, followed finally by the respiratory organs. The victim dies by choking. The Indian can more or less just collect his prey, the traces of blood leading him to the animal, which half-paralysed tries to crawl into hiding. The meat of such animals can be eaten without danger, because curare is a poison which does not act through the human digestive tract.

To what extent these natural hunting methods are still in use is a subject for itself. The firearm, a gift of civilisation, has made hunting much easier for the Indian, but it has also brought him competition in the shape of whites and half-castes who would not know how to use bow and arrow. Efficient pursuit of wild animals by professional hunters and rifle carrying has resulted in drastic depletion of animal stocks, even in regions where wildlife has not had to withdraw from civilisation yet.

I shall never forget the disappointment, event desperation and hopelessness on the faces of Nhambiquara tribesmen returning to their families empty-handed from a hunting trip lasting several days. They couldn't hunt a single animal down, because any prey had been driven away by the ever-further encroachment of new farms. Hunting had become unprofitable. The men sank down tired on the floor of their huts, and tried to assuage their hunger with some cassava...

The Indians feel close in spirit to animals, and animals of prey in particular are often the subject of magical-religious ceremonies. The Krahó for instance rub their bodies with special herbs, or drink a herb tea, depending on the species of animal to be hunted. Other tribes hunt those animals which have appeared in their dreams, and the Yanomami name their children after the species which the father or uncle has bagged in a ceremonial hunt.

In the 1960s settlers along the Cuiabá–Porto Velho road were able to experience to what amazing degree even pets are susceptible to the will of the Indians. At that time members of the Cinta-larga tribe often visited the villages of the white settlers, and after they had seen and touched everything (including the women) they took anything they fancied, including the pet dogs. The domesticated dogs followed the Indians without demur, and no amount of calling brought them back. Pets seemed to have turned into wild animals again in less than a minute.

Fishing This is today more important as a source of food for the Amazon Indians than hunting, because the encroachment of civilisation has tended to deplete the forests more than the rivers. Fish is the number one source of protein for the Indians, and that is why most of their settlements are at the waterside, be it on the river itself, or on a so-called Igarapé or tributary, or on Lagos, lagoon-type bays in the river bank. The labyrinth of waterways formed by the Amazon can be seen from the air.

Fishing, like hunting, is undertaken singly or collectively. Certain methods call for team activity, this is the case when using poison. There are two kinds of fish poison. One type drugs the fish, that is it induces a paralysis which disappears if the fish is placed in clean water again for some time. These are saponins, called Timbó by the Indians, which change the surface tension of the water and thus prevent the fish taking in oxygen.

The other poison type lames and kills the fish. This is rotenone, called Tinguí by the Indians, and as with curare it still leaves the fish edible for human consumption, as it does not affect the intestinal tract.

The catch is organised as follows: lianas (called

cipó) or branches from poisonous plants (containing one or other poison type) are tied into bundles, placed in the water, after which the bundles are beaten by clubs in order to release the poison juices. The poisonous water drugs the fishes. Usually a sufficiently high concentration of poison can only be achieved by damming the river. Above the dam, children beat the water with sticks to force the fish downstream. At the dam, the fishermen wait in canoes to trap the shoals, and also to grab those trying to jump the barrier. Normally the fish are only half-stunned and still swim around slowly, but they are easy prey for arrows or clubs and can then be gathered by hand. According to a report from Harald Schultz, the Suiá and Krahó tribes use timbó, the poison that merely paralyses only in the dry season at low water, so that building a dam or weir is not necessary.

More typical for the solo fisherman is the use of the weir-basket, a kind of fish trap made in several versions: e.g. as a cylinder-shaped basket, closed at the downstream end, open at the top. The funnel-shaped opening, spikes, or a basketweave barrier operated by the current ensure that the fish cannot escape the trap. Fishbait is placed inside the basket.

I have myself seen how individual fishermen go to work with bow and arrow on the Culuene tributary in the Xingu native reserve. Sticks and twigs were placed from one bank to the other, a stone's throw away, thus slightly damming the fast-running current. On a tree and well-camouflaged was the hunter's position. Discretion is necessary because the fisheye can see what goes on on the banks. Jakaú, a member of the Iuaulapiti tribe took up his position, his eyes glued to the water. Three shoals appeared that morning, and each time Jakaú aimed for one particular fish: drawing the bow, taking aim, releasing the arrow. All this in just a second, the trained movements of the Indian's naked body making this a sports performance for the spectator. Jakaú scored twice, waded into the water up to his arrow, which at a range of 10–12 m had bored itself through the middle of the fish. The arrow was still quivering with the thrashing of the fish. Jakaú seized the arrow, withdrew it from the fish, and with one bite, severed its backbone. He then returned to his vantage point, and placed his bounty in the basket he had brought along. Joy, pride, even triumph radiated from the face of the Indian fisherman.

The fish is cooked by the women in the maloca or hut, by frying it in a pan or on a hot stone. It is eaten by children and adults together with beijú, or flat tapioca cakes. Part of the catch is smoked and stored, or processed into fishmeal, serving as food preserve for emergencies or on hunting trips – or even for village festivities.

Naturally the artefacts of civilisation have also reached the fishermen of the Amazon forests, namely in the shape of metal fish hooks, nylon nets, and even gelignite. But the traditional methods are still widely used, and this is to the benefit of the Indian culture.

Farming Tilling the soil is an advanced form of agricultural activity. This stage had already been reached by the natives before the arrival of the Europeans in the 16th century. This only applied to those with a settled existence, because clearly cultivation and settlement go hand in hand. Civilisation took over not only the products of the Indians, but also their planting methods. Maize, potatoes, and cassava are not only adapted to the surroundings, but their manner of planting, on terraces, is also ideal. Various crops are planted on the same ground, or above one another. At the top bananas and papaya, underneath maize on the cob, cabbages above the soil and in the soil cassava root, sweet potato and yams. The Caboclo or half-caste also makes use of this method of planting, so it is not visible at first glance if a plantation belongs to Indians or to a member of "civilisation".

Not all tribes base their food needs to the same extent on cultivation, and the crops they raise are also different from tribe to tribe, and language group to language group. There are characteristic differences, for instance the Tupi only have small plantations, mainly of maize and cassava. Tribes of the Jé group prefer sweet potatoes and yams in large plantations. The Xavante are said to have settled on mainly maize, pumpkins, and beans, but the missions (above all the Salesians) have transformed most of the Xavante villages into large farms, and the former acolytes are now emancipated enough to run the farms on their own, and they have already

asked the FUNAI (Fundação Nacional do Índio – the Indian agency) for trucks with which to take their produce to market.
The tropical rain forests of the Amazon are cleared by burning. In the dry season a piece of forest is earmarked and cut down, and then set on fire. Thicker trunks that have withstood the axe and fire are left standing, that is no attempt is even made to chop them down in the first place. This would prove too troublesome because many Indians still use their original stone axes. This means that even on decades old livestock farms one can see the odd dead tree trunk pointing to the sky. Trunks and branches which have not burnt to conders are collected and again ignited. The ground is covered with ash and roots, which hinders but does not prevent sowing and planting.
The conditions met in the jungle do not permit geometrically shaped and ploughed fields. The short period of use of such fields would not make this worthwhile anyway. Initially there is an overwhelmingly large crop, sometimes several times in the first year. But this diminishes radically in the second and third year, because the soil's fertility is quickly washed out by the tropical downpours. After a few years a new piece of virgin forest is cut down (shifting cultivation). This is not harmful in the light of the modest size of the Indian plantations, but if this method is practised in grand style by Brazilian farmers, it can lead to plundering and wholesale destruction of forests. Particularly negative is the destruction of all flora caused by the establishment of livestock farms, as has been the case for some years now in the Amazon, sometimes on a huge scale. Climatic changes are a consequence, and this has already occurred in Paraná state. The same fate is threatening the Amazon because of the policy of forced settlement and development.
Domestic Animals One can only talk about livestock breeding by Indians in terms of groups who have come into contact with civilisation, more particularly those who have been demoralised and made marginal by contact with alcohol and money, and who are subsequently supposed to become resocialised by working on a livestock farm. Such official schemes have already proved a success, and there are cases where the Indians have learnt the management of a livestock farm and now run this themselves.
Without a doubt, the Indians used to capture wild animals and domesticate them even before the advent of Columbus. They still do so today, capturing monkeys and parrots in particular, including the multi-coloured ara and the small, mainly green-coloured Amazon parrots. This is done for simple amusement, or for the feathers or fur. The Indians did not have either dogs or fowl before the white man came. Both are now common. Pigs also go back to the first Europeans, as does cattle husbandry. But as we have seen, original Indian communities still do not keep cattle. In contrast with northeast and south Brazil, the horse has not established itself in the Amazon region.

Villages and their Organisation

Inasmuch as they are not nomads, the Indians of Brazil live in villages. The village is their political unit, and it is a self-sufficient and independent structure. As far as is known, there have been no political unions in the lowlands, with the possible exception of the long extinct native culture of the huge Marajó island at the mouth of the Amazon. If one wants to extend historical reality into the realm of legend and myth one could also mention those Amazons seen by the Spanish discoverers in the sixteenth century, and who also gave the river its name. The village is led by a headman (cacique, taxáua, capitão) but his authority is sometimes challenged by a counterchief. An Indian village is usually a series of houses or huts (malocas) arranged in a circle, as can be seen in the Tukano tribe on the Rio Negro, the Borôro in the Mato Grosso, and the tribes of the Xingu region. The Xavante arrange their dwellings in horseshoe form. The Yanomami settlements in Roraima consist only of one large community house accommodating on average 12 families with 60–100 members. But the malocas (huts) of the other tribes are by no means detached houses, rather the families live in sectors of houses, attaching their hammocks to the centre mast or masts, and the outer wall. The shape and size of houses vary greatly not only from tribe to tribe but also among groups of the same tribe. The community hut of the Yanomami, 20–25 m in diameter, and up to 10 m high has an open roof in some clans, and is closed in others. The malocas on the Xingu are oval and arched, whereas those of the Xavante are beehive-shaped. The Tukano and Tikuna (on the Solimões) have gabled houses with two sloping flat roofs, a style which could perhaps be attributed to the influence of civilisation.

The building materials used include wood, palm leaves, tightly woven straw. There are low entrances, usually one on each side granting comfort and relaxation: The interior of the huts is cool, dark, and free of mosquitos.

Normally in the middle of the circular villages is the men's house. Out of sight of the women, the cult pipes are stored here. The ground plan of the village is of primordial importance to the Borôro and other tribes. Vera-Dagny Stähle has this to say in summary: for the Borôro Indian, the village represents the world of the living and the dead. The village is split in two by an east-west line. 8 clans and 24 sub-clans have their assigned places. The two tribal halves are exogamous, that means they may only marry someone from the other village half. The newly-wed husband moves over to the wife's half (matrilocal marriage), and the children will belong to the same clan as the mother. This is a matrilinear relationship. Also split into two exogamous village halves were the members of the Tikuna tribe, except that they followed patrilinear relationship, with the wife and children belonging to the father's clan. The Terena in the state of Mato Grosso do Sul could only marry within their own half of the village; they followed the endogamic system. The Timbira tribe on the Tocantins river permitted marriage on any side of the boundary half. If we are now talking in the past tense, it is because the christian missionaries have thoroughly destroyed the Indians' settlement traditions. I was able to ascertain this myself in the Meruri village. The Borôro Indians were now living in stone houses, each family on its own and clearly separated from the others. In the middle of the large square was the broken down shape of the cult house. Also crumbling were the spirits of the inhabitants, reflected in the sullen looks on their faces. A similar situation has arisen of the Rio Negro. The suggestion of the Salesians to rebuild the villages in their original form has come too late, the culture has been irrevocably lost. "The loss of the settlement pattern signified for most of the Indians not only an external and physical loss, but the forfeiture of an inner, mental order too. And so the coming generation has no roots either in the Old or the New World, and thus vacillates dangerously between the two" (Vera-Dagny Stähle).

Rituals, Cults, and Myths of the Indians

A rite is a ceremonial act, a ritual a festive custom, with usually, but not always, religious significance. In the latter case it can also be termed a cult. Among the non-religious customs are the transition and initiation rites with which the change from one existence to a higher form is celebrated, or rather executed. Thus practically all societies have birth, puberty, marriage, and death rituals.

In the case of the Brazilian Indians one should make particular mention of the initiation ceremonies for both sexes on reaching adolescence. It is normal for the initiation candidate to be separated from the community for weeks or months before the ceremony, and to be prepared, in isolation, for life as a full member of the community.

As in the case of living and working conditions, little can be made in the way of universally applicable statements regarding initiation rites. They differ from tribe to tribe. The long ago extinct Tupinambá had a practise whereby an initiation candidate had to kill a captive, who was then ritually eaten. This was a fate which until recent times could befall the candidate himself in the Xavante tribe. These Indians were regarded as the Sioux of South America, as the wildest natives of the Amazon basin. The young men 15–17 years of age first had to sustain trial by water. They had to stand in the river for days on end, constantly pouring water over themselves. After that they had to run for several hours, guarded, chased, and frightened by adult warriors in tribal masks. Anyone who collapsed was killed, and subsequently cannibalised.

The Kreen-Akarore, who were pacified in the 1970s have herringbone patterned cult scars all over their bodies, similar to the Suiá, their relatives on the Xingu river. Other tribes are satisfied by merely piercing ears, lips, or noses, or by having a special haircut, or by tattooing or painting their bodies. Indian cult ceremonies (rituals of a religious nature) are usually based on the depiction of a myth, that is a symbolic repetition of the deeds of tribal spirits and heroes. These so-called cultural heroes created man and the world and taught them to use the gifts of nature. Thus, according to Xingu legends collected by the Villas-Bôas brothers, in particular Kamaiurá legends, Mavutsinin created the first woman out of a shell. This woman had her children by a jaguar (onça). The heavy wooden blocks (toras) with which the Suiá and other tribes run races are meant to represent wild animals and plants, or their transformation into cultural values. This reminds the birth of Aphrodite from the sea according to ancient greek mythology, or also the grain given to Triptolemos, the king's son, by Demeter, the goddess of Earth.

The Indian does not have an abstract, universal god, nor a punishing or rewarding one. He lives happily, and also brutally in complete harmony with nature, with his ghostly forefathers, with tribal fathers and mothers, without morals and without sin in the western sense, in his magic world.

The Future of the Indians

The dramatic drop in the number of tribes and their members in Brazil and other countries since the colonisation of South America has already been pointed out. Everything that has happened in the past 450 years has occurred without any regard for the natives. This includes the hunt for slaves, the cultivation of the soil for sugar, coffee, and pasture, the combing of forests for rubber and gold, furthermore mining activities, shipping on the rivers, and road building, not to mention the unplanned, unbridled taking of land by small farmers. Ever wider spaces were occupied and civilised, at first along the coast, then in the east Brazilian hinterland, up the Amazon, and finally the highlands and the central west.

Large parts of the native population were killed during the pacification campaigns (guerras justas) carried out by the authorities against insubordinate Indian groups right into the 19th century, others died at the hands of murderous land speculators, and still others fell, and continue to fall, victim to infectious diseases to which they have no resistance. Laws and official protective measures have largely been crowned with failure to this day. The Roman Catholic and Protestant missions have almost across the board caused the dissolution of the structural and cultural frameworks of the societies they are tending, without being able to offer a real replacement for the natives. In the light of these ominous perspectives, how can one judge the future of the lowland Indians? There are a few tribes able to adjust to the modern world, without giving up their tribal traditions. Among these are the Xavante. With regard to the non-integrated ethnic groups, only a system of protected areas along the lines of the Xingu park created by the Villas-Bôas brothers offers any chance of survival. A number of such reservations have been decreed, but they require frontier

Liana fibres are used to secure the framework and roof of the new community house of the Yanomami (in Roraimi, North Brazil).

markings, and army or police forces to repel or expel intruders. Suitable measures have been taken by the FUNAI, the Indian development agency, but their actions are stalled for lack of money and because of the pressure mounted against the government by powerful interest groups.

So, for example, the privately proposed Yanomami reserve has been given the green light by the Ministry of the Interior, but its completion has time and time again been delayed. This reserve will determine the fate of over 8000 Indians living on the northern frontier of Brazil, the largest, still isolated tribe living in Brazil. Their fate could prove exemplary for the other Indian groups in the country.

Kreen-Akarore boys with pagoda-style haircut. Kreen means hair, Akarore means knife, thus Kreen-Akarore = cut hair.

Afrobrazilian Folklore

Candomblé

A "ghost ground" (terreiro) in São Caetano, a suburb of Bahia, the "black Rome". It is sunday evening, and the candles light up the altar of St. Anthony. An old man, the head of the congregation, is kneeling down before the altar. Men and women of every age, mainly blacks and mulattos are sitting around it in a circle. The "father" (pai do santo) reads texts from the Bible, prays, and leads the monotonous songs, which those present join in with thin and hesitant voices. Conversation carries on unabated in the adjoining room during the service.

Finally, and by now it is around nine in the evening, comes the amen. At the same moment a muffled drumming starts up in the house opposite. A hard, driving, even abrasive rhythm wakes up and frightens the still somnolent faithful and carries them suddenly and without a transition phase from the ranks of Christian piety to the shores of supernatural Africa. Everybody jumps and rushes out, as if electrified. The candles are snuffed out, and the barracão opposite from where the drumming is coming is soon tightly crammed. It is a sort of festive hut, with an earthen floor and a thatched roof held up by wooden pillars, open on three sides and only joining together to form a back wall. This is the big meeting place for celebrations in honour of the African spirits or gods (orixás).

In front of the rear wall, and facing the entrance are four pumpkin shaped drums, the largest and most muffled standing taller than a man. Behind them, and stepped-up are the drummers, who are muscular young blacks. Behind a low mud wall, to the right and left of the entrance the "Congregation" waits for the coming. On the right some fifty women, on the left the same number of men. Around the dance floor sit the initiated: the "sons" and "daughters" of the Saint (filhos et filhas de santo). They are the carriers, the actors, of the cult which is led by their spiritual father, the "pai de santo".

This same man who previously led the service in honour of St. Anthony now steps in and the Candomblé begins. At the entrance, on the side, and at the front, the "father" draws a ghost symbol with chalk on the floor. It consists of a triangle, arrow, semicircles, strokes, and stars. In the meantime the

"daughters" light up candles, and an assistant (ogão) of the "father" swirls smoke from holy vessels over the "sons", "daughters", and the whole congregation.
Now the drums start up again, accompanied by singing which is considerably louder than during the previous litany. The drummers strike the beat strongly with just the in- and outsides of their hands. Despite frequent changes of beat and accentuation, a continuous network of the most difficult tempi results, always adapted to the singers. The "daughters" wearing their long, loose-fitting flowered Bahia dresses start to dance, barefoot, and turning to the left, one behind the other. It is a simple samba-like step, with the body leaning forward, and the upper arms pressed to the sides, while the lower arms carry out sideward swinging motions. The first dance is for Ogún, the god of war and handicrafts. Iron and the colour blue are holy to him, iron tools are his insignia. In pictures he holds a sword in his hands. He is compared with St. George in the, for black religion and soul, so typical internal and external merging of both religious leanings.
The "father" now dances as well, in the same step, backwards and forwards, waving his arms. The rhythm changes frequently, but the dance steps remain essentially the same. The drums cease for a few seconds, and the assistant sings a verse in African idiom, with the congregation repeating it in a chorus. The drumming is resoundingly accompanied or even overpowered by the choir. Both drive each other on. Sudden changes of key and beat, in line with the drumming are accompanied by handclapping and thus prevent any relaxation, or dissipation of tension until, on the sign from the "father" the drums, and with them the dancing, singing, and clapping all break off. In a flash the till then racing hands of the drummers are placed flat on the skins. This accentuates the sudden silence which is almost oppressive and gives the impression of the room bursting.
There is a pause of a few breaths, one or two words are exchanged, drummers are relieved – and then everything starts up again, possibly even more violently. The choir stands up stormily, and the dance of the "daughters" has become quicker and more corrosive. Their bodies turn, lift, and sink, the fingers touch the ground. One of the dancers has a tin full of water in her hand, and with it she sprays the entrance. This is for Exu (pronounced Eshú) the Demon of the crossways, who is a sort of mediator between men and gods, and therefore deserving special attention. In order to guarantee an undisturbed festivity, he is "kept out on the road" by giving him holy water, and offerings of food and drink.
Exu has been tamed. The Candomblé can temporarily take a somewhat quieter course. Nevertheless the heightened tension of the congregation remains, and is even growing. Further dances and singing take place in honour of other spirits, but these are difficult for the casual visitor to tell apart from one another. They all involve the interweaving of beats, tones, and dances, which often crescendo into veritable tumults only to break off and resurge again. The climax is reached with the appearance of Xangô (shangó), the god of thunder and fisheries, who is identical with the holy Hieronymous or St. Peter. He is depicted by an assistant in a white-red robe, with a crown, and copper necklace and bracelets.
When this mime suddenly comes into the congregation from the entrance, he is enthusiastically greeted with loud cries of "aeoh, aeoh". He embraces the "father", sits down next to him, and receives the praises of the "sons" and "daughters", who as in the case of the "father", kneel down before him, kiss his hands, and touch the ground with their foreheads.
The coming of a ghost has had a stimulating effect, because not long after, the most peculiar thing of all, for the visitor at least, happens. One of the "sons" who has started to dance, a tall and thin man, suddenly tips forward, and then like a reed, bends backwards, sways, and is in danger to fall. His dancing has become a rhythmic clapping of body and limbs, dictated directly by the beat of the drum, and to the exclusion of his conscious self. This "son" has been overpowered by the rhythm, by his faith, and this together with the collective tension has taken him to the frontiers of madness, into ecstasy and trance. He has "fallen into his Saint" to whom he is consecrated. He is possessed by the god, is being used by him as a horse, as the popular phrases would have it. According to the conviction

of the congregation this is a manifestation of the presence of a god – which is after all the means and ends of the Candomblé.
As if infected, a "daughter" soon follows suit. She is a pretty girl with a light skin. She is followed later by two or three women, including a matronly negress. It is said that the "god-ridden" have the powers of soothsayers and faith healers, and can make wishes or maledictions come true. Sometimes they speak in a language they have never learnt.
A few of the possessed finally fell down to the ground with a cry. At the behest of the "father" they are covered with a sheet, and their cataleptic bodies are carried into an adjacent darkened room. One or other of them reappeared later and carried on dancing. One of the "sons", wearing Indian adornment, came as a "caboclo" which triggered off jubilation, wild drumming, and truly bacchanalian song.
The end of the celebration was fairly suddenly ordered by the ghost father around midnight. A few dancers were still in a trance. They were brought back to consciousness by various singing and chanting. One man, totally stiff, was carried before the altar, so that St. Anthony could wake him up...

This account of a personal experience shows better than any theoretical description what Afrobrazilian cults are all about. They are the expression of the religion brought over by negro slaves from Africa, like the Bantu from Angola and the Congo, the Yoruba from what is now Nigeria, Benin, and Togo. These people were rounded up from their homes in the most cunning and brutal way, and enslaved, with many of them already dying in transit. As if this were not enough, the Portuguese colonials proceeded to prevent these Africans from practising their cults in Brazil. The resistance to this ban was all the more stubborn, and this explains why African traditions have often survived better in the Americas than on the black continent. As a subterfuge, and a sign of their good nature, the black slaves embraced the Christian concept of heaven. But they were not willing, and their racially conscious descendants are even less inclined, to give up their traditional beliefs. If one talks of the concurrence of both religions, of their blending, or linking, one should not forget that

104 *Mekragnoti Indian. The Mekragnoti are a sub-group of the Jé-speaking Kayapó tribe which can be found all over the northern Mato Grosso and Pará region. Kayapó were, and are still sometimes feared by other tribes and the whites. Their facial paint is Urucum plant juice (bixin), the head decoration made of yellow japim and red arara feathers (see pict. 14).*

105 *The lowland Indians live in malocas, always several families together. It is a circular or elliptical building, cool and dark inside, and free of mosquitos. The hammock (made here of buriti palm fibres) serves as bed and chair, and is strung up from a central mast to the outside wall. The young mother is using a straw fan to keep the typical Indian fire going.*

106 *Jakaú, an Iaualapiti Indian, uses a bow and arrow to fish in a tributary of the Xingu (pronounced shingu, with accentuation on the second syllable). He has managed to hit the fish in somewhat slack water at a distance of 7 m from the border, and is now pulling out the arrow.*

105

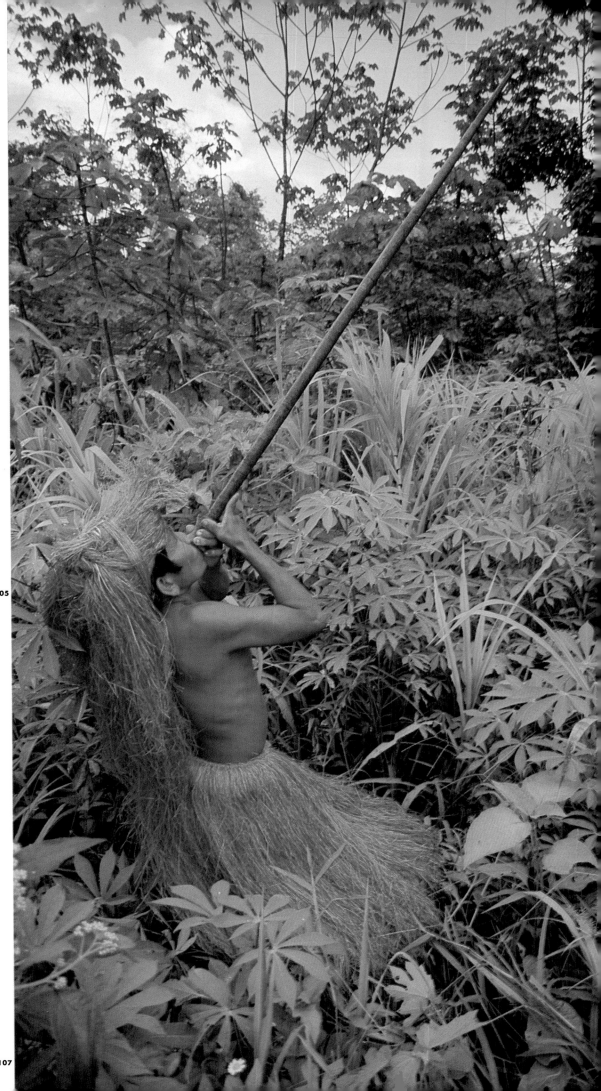

107 *A Yagua Indian (in the Brazilian-Colombian-Peruvian frontier area), hunting birds with a blowpipe. The zarabatana is the favourite hunting weapon in the higher regions round the Amazon basin. The arrows are usually coated with curare, whereby the prey is initially only paralysed and falls to the ground.*

106

107

108

109

110

111

112

113

114

108 *Fruit seller in Manaus in the Amazon.*

109 *Negro boy of a colonial family on the Transamazônica highway.*

110 *Cattle drover (vaqueiro) from the Sertão in the Northeast.*

111 *Xavante boy in beehive-shaped maloca (hut) of this tribe in the Mato Grosso. This picture can hardly indicate how wild and feared the Xavante (pronounced shavante) were, before they were driven by hardship to give themselves up to the Salesian missionaries in the 1950s.*

112 *Girl of German extraction from Blumenau, Santa Catarina.*

113 *Black girl from Salvador da Bahia.*

114 *Flower, vegetable and fruit seller of Japanese origin in São Paulo. He is reading one of the two Japanese-language newspapers published in Brazil.*

115 *Capoeira: traditional and almost ceremonial fighting contest of the Bantus from Angola. Although banned by the authorities until the beginning of this century, it remained, and starting out from Bahia, found wide popularity as an acrobatic sport. The aim is to topple the opponent with blows from outstretched arms and feet. Particularly appealing for the spectator is the two-footed kick, with the attacker supporting himself on the ground with his hands.*

116 *Five-hundred Cruzeiro note with symbolic representation of the various races to be found in Brazil.*

116

117 *This girl from Curitiba, the capital of Paraná state, came as a small girl with her parents from the northern part of Minas Gerais down to the South, where her father found employment as a factory worker. There are relatively few blacks and mulattos in the whole of the South, most of them only having migrated there in recent years.*

equating Catholic saints with African gods is only a matter of external appearance. Deep in his soul, the black Brazilians, as far as conscious of their origins, and along with them, many mulattos and whites, worship the African god. The negro religion has an all-encompassing god of creation: Olodum, but he is not a part of the cult celebrations. His son Oxalá rules the world as the "lord of the happy end" (Senhor do Bonfim). He is equated with Jesus Christ, in the same way that Yemanjá is compared to the Virgin Mary. She rules the rivers and oceans, and increasingly offerings are made to her on New Year's Eve along the beaches.
Exu has an ambiguous position among the African gods. He cannot just be dismissed as Lucifer, as the devil, because he is a demon capable of both evil and good, depending on what one commands him to do. He is a kind of messenger carrying out assignments of an occult nature, and he is also a crafty assistant, rather like the Greek Hermes, of whom he is perhaps the descendant (Greek mythology radiated as far as Africa). Exu is the key figure of black magic above all, of the Quimbanda cult, and is used to wipe out personal enemies, or at least to make them suffer, and generally to settle scores. On the other hand this multiform personality carries out good works in the white magic of the Umbanda cult. He cures illnesses, brings back unfaithful spouses, and can engender success in business dealings...
It is this shallow and popular aspect which has led to accusations that the Afrobrazilian religion is inferior and underdeveloped in an animist way. It should however not be overlooked that every faith has its excesses, and that everyone casting judgement on another religion has the tendency to see it as banal and primitive, in the negative sense of the word. More justified are allegations about mysticism and occultism in these cults. In fact Macumba, as the Umbanda cult form around Rio de Janeiro is known, operates with the spirits of the dead. But then which religion does not share this phenomenon? One could ask if irrationality is not the very essence, the counterweight that is necessary in our increasingly profane lives. This is the main reason for the popularity of the African, spiritualistic sects of Brazil today.

The proportion of pure blacks in Brazil's population has decreased sharply in the last decades as a result of intermarriage (from 11% down to 6%). The percentage of mulattos has increased from 34% to 42%. The black traits of vitality, musicality, and artistry rather than intellectual-technical leanings, can also be seen in fields other than religion. For example in the Carnival, which follows on from the activities of the Rococo court of Portugal, in sport – soccer star Pelé, whose real name is Nascimento da Silva, is a mulatto – and in the language, which has adopted many African expressions.

More and more blacks are conquering posts in the academic world, and in official life. The word "conquer" is used advisedly, because despite the racial equality that is anchored in Brazilian law, the mentality of white predominance is still widespread. But the favourable physical and mental attributes of dark skinned people, their loyalty and sociable nature, can only enrich the Brazilian national character.

Geographical Index

Numbers alone indicate page numbers in the text; P = colour photo number. Names of rivers are listed under "Rio", except where the name also applies to a state (e.g. Paraná).